Praise for

PANORAMA

"[Adler] produced a quantity and a diversity of writings about the Holocaust that seem to have been equalled by no other survivor. . . . *The Journey* and *Panorama* are very different works, each with its own distinctive style, but both are modernist masterpieces worthy of comparison to those of Kafka or Musil."　　　　　　　　　　　　　　　　　*—The New Yorker*

"Adler [uses] distinctly literary techniques to recreate the experience of having a civilization self-destruct. . . . One of the feats of the novel is to remain intensely, cinematically, in the narrative present, where the pressures of daily life eclipse the machinations of history. . . . *Panorama* should have been the brilliant debut of a major German writer, rather than the afterthought to a scholar's career. . . . That American and British readers have had such limited access to Adler's writing and thought for so long is, as the eminent scholar of modern German literature Peter Demetz has written, 'one of the great intellectual scandals of our time.'"

　　　　　　　　—The New York Times Book Review (Editor's Choice)

"A haunting narrative . . . [*Panorama*] is as remarkable for its literary experimentation as for its historical testimony. . . . [Adler] provides an artful and brutal description . . . that nearly guarantees *Panorama* a place in the canon of Holocaust literature."　　　　　　　　*—San Francisco Chronicle*

"An important literary and historical contribution to a lost age . . . much in the tradition of, say, James Joyce. . . . Through the sheer richness and volume of detail, it achieves an unimpeachable veracity of character and tone. . . . The reader owes Adler's translator a debt for introducing his work to the English-reading world."　　　　　　　　　*—The Jerusalem Post*

"Noteworthy . . . [offers] indelible glimpses of a world the Nazis systematically destroyed."　　　　　　　　　　　　　　　　*—The Wall Street Journal*

"Stunning. . . . Adler's stream-of-consciousness style is adeptly translated by Peter Filkins, and the reader is easily swept into the flow of Josef's thoughts. *Panorama* is no Joycean maelstrom of words and not-words, but instead a beautiful, accessible story of a young man's life."

—*The Historical Novels Review* (Editors' Choice)

"[A] modernist classic . . . at once realistic and impressionistic, nightmarish and richly satirical . . . [*Panorama* is] Adler's masterpiece."

—*Jewish Book World*

Praise for

THE JOURNEY

"I've read a lot of books, but nothing quite like this one. . . . The novel's streaming consciousness and verbal play invite comparison with Joyce, the individual-dwarfing scale of law and prohibition brings Kafka to mind, and there is something in the hypnotic pulse of the prose that is reminiscent of Gertrude Stein." —*The New York Times Book Review*

"As important a find as Irene Nemirovsky's *Suite Française*, and as well translated into English, it is indeed as Veza Canetti wrote to the author in 1962, '*too beautiful* for words and too sad.'"

—SANDER L. GILMAN, author of *Jurek Becker: A Life in Five Worlds*

"A tribute to the survival of art and a poignant teaching in the art of survival." —HAROLD BLOOM

"A masterpiece of modern fiction." —*The Times Literary Supplement*

"After Auschwitz . . . critics believed that literature was no longer possible. Adler believed that it was not only possible, but necessary. Writing this astounding novel, Adler amply proved his point."

—*Historical Novel Society*

"[An] extraordinarily ambitious attempt to articulate the unspeakable."

—*Kirkus Reviews*

"The rediscovery of a rich and lyrical masterpiece . . . Filkins' sensitive translation mirrors the taut, rising suspense of this moving novel."

—PETER CONSTANTINE, recipient of the PEN Translation Prize

ALSO BY H. G. ADLER

The Journey

H. G. ADLER

Born in Prague in 1910, H. G. ADLER spent two and a half years
in Theresienstadt before being deported to Auschwitz, Buchenwald, and Langenstein, where he was liberated in April 1945.
Leaving Prague for London in 1947, Adler worked as a free-
lance teacher and writer until his death in 1988. The author of
twenty-six books of fiction, stories, poems, history, philosophy,
and religion, he is best known for his 1,000-page monograph,
Theresienstadt 1941–1945, for which he received the Leo Baeck
Prize in 1958. *Panorama*, written in 1948, but not published
until 1968, is the first of six novels written by him following his
arrival in London. It was awarded the Charles Veillon Prize in
1969.

PANORAMA

PANORAMA

A Novel

H. G. ADLER

*Translated from the German
by Peter Filkins*

THE MODERN LIBRARY/ NEW YORK

2012 Modern Library Paperback Edition

Translation and introduction copyright © 2011 by Peter Filkins

Published in the United States by Modern Library, an imprint of The Random House Publishing Group, a division of Random House, Inc., New York.

MODERN LIBRARY and the TORCHBEARER Design are registered trademarks of Random House, Inc.

Originally published in hardcover in the United States by Random House, an imprint of The Random House Publishing Group, a division of Random House, Inc., New York.

This work, excluding the afterword, was originally published in Germany as *Panorama* by Walter-Verlag in 1968 and by Paul Zsolnay Verlag in 2010. Copyright © 2010 by Paul Zsolnay Verlag, Vienna. This edition published by arrangement with Paul Zsolnay Verlag.

Grateful acknowledgment is made to Zephyr Press for permission to reprint an excerpt from "Bohemia Lies by the Sea" from *Darkness Spoken: The Collected Poems of Ingeborg Bachmann*, copyright © 2000 by Piper Verlag GmbH, Munchen. English translation copyright © 2006 by Peter Filkins. Reprinted by permission of Zephyr Press, www.zephyrpress.org.

The afterword by Peter Demetz was originally published, in the German language, in *Panorama* by H. G. Adler by Piper Verlag in 1988 and is reprinted here, in translation, by permission of the author. Copyright © 1988 by Peter Demetz.

LIBRARY OF CONGRESS CATALOGING-IN-PUBLICATION DATA
Adler, H. G.
[Panorama. English]
Panorama : a novel / H.G. Adler ; translated from German by Peter Filkins.
p.   cm.
ISBN 978-0-8129-8060-8
1. Jews—Czech Republic—Fiction.   2. Prague (Czech Republic)—Fiction.
3. Bohemia (Czech Republic)—Fiction.   4. Holocaust, Jewish (1939–1945)—Czech Republic—Fiction.   I. Filkins, Peter.   II. Title.
PT2601.D614P313   2010
833'.914—dc22   2010015079

Printed in the United States of America

www.modernlibrary.com

2 4 6 8 9 7 5 3 1

Book design by Susan Turner

CONTENTS

TRANSLATOR'S NOTE

THE GERMAN TEXT FOR THE NOVEL IS TAKEN FROM THE 1968 FIRST EDI-tion of *Panorama* published by Walter-Verlag, which was awarded the Charles Veillon Prize the following year.

I am deeply grateful to the American Academy in Berlin for a Berlin Prize Fellowship, which was key to my initial work on Adler while translating his second novel, *The Journey*, *Panorama* being his first. Particular thanks goes to my colleague Chris Callanan for his immensely resourceful knowledge of German, and for his willingness to respond to and debate numerous questions on the text. I am also grateful to Jeremy Adler for his many patient replies to questions, to Philip Bohlman for his support and friendship, and to Peter Demetz for granting permission to reprint his excellent afterword. As ever, Susan Roeper has been there throughout, helping me to think through so many choices, while my editor at Random House, Paul Taunton, remains a guiding intelligence to this day.

INTRODUCTION

I still border on a word and on another land,
I border, like little else, on everything more and more,

A Bohemian, a wandering minstrel, who has nothing, who
Is held by nothing, gifted only at seeing, by a doubtful sea, the
    land of my choice.

INGEBORG BACHMANN
"Bohemia Lies by the Sea"

WHEN H. G. ADLER RETURNED TO PRAGUE IN JUNE OF 1945, HE CARRIED within him the remains of a time and place that was no more, and that would never exist again. Exhausted, nearly dead from the two months' trek back from the Langenstein camp outside Buchenwald, where he had been liberated by American troops in April, Adler returned to Prague by way of Theresienstadt, retrieving from Leo Baeck the voluminous notes he had taken during his two and a half years there. A decade later, these would become his monumental study *Theresienstadt 1941–1945*, his first significant publication, earning him the Leo Baeck Prize and early, yet fleeting acclaim. In that same ten-year period, however, Adler also wrote five novels, the first of which, *Panorama*, was produced in 1948, in the white heat of a survivor's fervor, Adler having moved to London and permanent exile the year before.

Panorama is Adler's elegy to a world that was no more. Pastoral, even comic in its rendering of the Prague and the Bohemia in which Adler grew up after World War I, it harks back to the past not out of mere nostalgia but, rather, to show how even amid the innocence of childhood and a world steeped in a history and a tradition that could be traced to the Romans, the seeds of its own destruction were planted, resting invisible and unknown beneath the surface but destined to blossom in the full terror and violence that would wipe out not only a people but also a language and a culture that had produced the likes of Franz Kafka and so much more.

For what is perhaps most important to appreciate about Adler and *Panorama* is that in many ways it is the culminating product of what is known as the Prague Circle of German letters, a distinct milieu whose writers and audience were primarily German-speaking Jews of the Hapsburg Empire, and who considered themselves citizens of that empire until its dissolution in 1918, their primary identification resting with the ancient kingdom of Bohemia throughout. After that came the formulation of Czechoslovakia, though even then Bohemia remained its largest and most populated region. Hitler's annexation of the Sudetenland in 1938 marked the first time that Bohemia's territory had been divided in nearly a thousand years. As we know, this annexation also set off the cataclysm that extinguished not only the writers of the Prague Circle but also their readers, not to mention every trace of the German language from the streets of Kafka's Prague. Born there in 1910, Adler was at the tail end of the generation that could count Kafka as its immediate ancestor and whose literary style had been shaped by him and by the distinct sentence structure and diction that were native to the Prague Circle.

It requires no great leap, then, to see that Josef Kramer, whose life is depicted in *Panorama*, and whose biography mirrors Adler's, is a clear manifestation of that other Josef K. of certain renown. Indeed, whereas Kafka's object is largely to illuminate the nightmarish unreality of the everyday world that Josef K. finds himself trapped within, Adler's is to create a mirror image of that world, in which he explores the everyday nature of the nightmare that he himself came to experience and to survive. At the start of the novel, the reader has no idea that Josef will end up in the Langenstein camp, or that, like Adler, he will end the book as an exile in England who cannot look forward without looking back. But the unknowable nature of such events is very much to the point, for neither could the young Adler, or the culture that bore him, see it coming. From the first page of *The Trial*, we know that Josef K. has woken to a world that will probably not allow him to survive. At the start of *Panorama*, however, we are immersed in the everyday charms of a milieu that, from the point of view of Josef Kramer, looking back through the panorama of his experience and memory, is all the more poignant for its unanticipated, yet inescapable, demise.

The consciousness at work formulating this past is also a key reason that *Panorama* is neither an autobiographical novel nor a bildungsroman meant to trace a certain kind of development and upbringing. For, indeed, the very conceit of formulating the novel as a panorama by structuring it as ten separate and distinct "scenes" from Josef Kramer's life with no plot development between them is itself an augmentation of the autobiographical mode. Yes, all the principle moments of Josef's life stem from Adler's own, and yes, Adler saw his life as emblematic of the experience of an entire generation. And yet it is *how* he writes that life which distinguishes the true nature and intent of the book as a novel bent more on capturing a consciousness as it reflects on experience than on depicting that experience in any sort of pedestrian or naturalistic way.

Consider, for instance, the book's style—the way its long, streaming sentences build clause upon clause in order to render the consciousness at work narrating the novel as much as the events themselves. Here, for instance, is Josef at around the age of eleven, living as a foster child on a farm in Umlowitz, a region and an experience that he loves through and through:

> Now Josef is also a herder for Herr Neumann, who owns some pastureland, though most of the cattle graze in Purtscher's fields on a side slope of the Haselberg. The cattle in the shed are tied up, and normally Poldi helps Josef release them, since he can't do it alone, it going all right with the goats and with Cappi, but not as well with the other cows, the worst being Liesel, who is a restless animal that requires more patience. Josef holds a big stick that he made himself, though Otto's is much nicer, even if it's shorter and not as strong, Fritz being much more gifted at wood carving, for he can carve decorations and letters into the stick, such that it almost looks like something out of a picture from a book about Indians. Josef isn't as good, having cut his finger once while he was carving in the open fields, the finger bleeding for so long that Josef had to wrap his handkerchief

around it, while that night Herma made a proper bandage, carefully washing the finger at first and rubbing it with alcohol so that it wouldn't get infected, though it burned like hell, Herma saying that was just what had to be, because there had once been a farm boy in Umlowitz who also cut himself, and no one did anything about the wound, such that the poor boy got a terrible illness called tetanus, and the next day he was dead, since there was nothing that could be done for him. And so Josef held his finger still, not wanting to get any tetanus, and two days later the finger was fine again and hadn't gotten infected.

Two things stand out here. The first is the way in which Adler's prose surreptitiously elicits how Josef's thinking meanders from thoughts about getting the cattle out of the shed, to the stick that he uses, to Fritz's talent for carving such sticks, to the dangers of cutting himself while carving, and, finally, to the importance of tending to such a wound in order to avoid infection and death. In a single stream of thought, then, we move from the child's excitement over his bucolic adventures to the ultimate undermining of such euphoria, with the threat of death at rest within it. On the one hand, this is a powerful rendering of Josef's own thought process, its motion and plummet, and the inner world that is quietly demarcated through it. However, the second, perhaps later impression that the reader will take away is the manner in which the arc of Josef's thought and Adler's narration anticipates the unknowable arc of Josef's own future demise. Herma's apocryphal warning about the farm boy who dies from tetanus because of medical neglect will one day culminate in the sufferings of the inmates at Langenstein, where "the smallest wounds fester straightaway, and everyone has such wounds from his slave labor, the limbs soon swelling, the body becoming discolored, nothing done in the infirmary, for there is no disinfectant, salve, or bandages." Hence, what is a rural tragedy of ignorance and neglect for the farm boy eventually becomes the calculated abandonment of the inmates once their utility as slave labor expires, Adler's evocation of the inmates' suffering only compounding its poignancy when we realize that the conditions that gave rise to it have in some ways been there all along.

Yet, despite the extremity of the suffering that the novel eventually evokes, Adler's style shares as much with what we think of as the stream-of-consciousness techniques of Joyce and Woolf as it does with the nightmarish atmosphere of Kafka. To the extent that it is an extension of the Bildungsroman tradition, it is essentially in the sense that *A Portrait of the Artist as a Young Man* is also seen in that light. Here Stephen Dedalus's journey from boyhood to committed young artist is granted a mirror image in Josef Kramer's journey toward eventual exile and conflicted freedom. In addition, the detached manner in which the events of *Panorama* are reported (Josef rarely speaks directly but, instead, spends most of his time listening to others) is reminiscent of the way Woolf's Mrs. Ramsay or Mrs. Dalloway report on the life they observe around them, while what we note is the shape and motion of each woman's consciousness as she observes. The result is a kind of engaged detachment, one that asks us as readers to read *with* each of these narrators as much as we read about them.

In Adler, this detachment has even deeper philosophical and moral implications. From the outset, the conceit of the panorama itself gives rise to the tensions that exist between the viewer and the viewed, between subject and object, and, finally, between present and past. To Josef as a small child, the trip on a streetcar to watch "various pictures from all over the world" pass by him, in the wooden cabinet for which his grandmother has bought two tickets, is a thrilling experience. Once again, though, and as so often occurs throughout the novel, the journey by train silently and menacingly foreshadows later travels by train that Josef cannot foresee. Similarly, the excitement of pressing his nose to a glass pane in trying to enter the world of "Vesuvius, Niagara Falls, the Great Pyramid," or even the marvelous unfolding of language itself, as Josef spells out the title of the week's program, "Li-ma, the Cap-i-tal of Pe-ru"—all of this is eventually turned on its head when, at the end of the novel, Josef considers returning to his homeland and the past but realizes that "he does not believe in the possibility of such a return, even though he knows that he can't abandon it, but a gulf remains between him and the images of the panorama" that now lie in his memory.

All ten chapters of *Panorama* mention travel by train or streetcar, thus developing the motif introduced in the brief *Vorbild*, which describes little Josef's trip to the panorama. Similarly, the Landstein Castle, which Josef so innocently visits as a fifteen-year-old member of a ragtag hiking club, will eventually be echoed by the Langenstein camp, and finally by Launceston Castle in England, erected by William the Conqueror, whose title further resonates with that other notorious "Conqueror" of Bohemia and of Josef's life. Add to this the way that the "true path" that Josef distrustfully and briefly explores with the New Age guru Johannes Tvrdil (who is modeled on the avant-garde photographer František Drtikol) also returns as the path that he walks along as a forced laborer, or how Tvrdil's mystical playing of a gong returns as "a gong, not a bell, a piece of iron rail that hangs from a rack that looks like a gallows" in Langenstein, and we begin to see that *Panorama* is an intricate web of themes and motifs that continually circle back upon one another. Be it apples, soap, bells, *William Tell*, Goethe, Schiller, or mushrooms, Adler threads a variety of repeated motifs throughout the novel, so that eventually Josef's life seems more intricately constructed than even he realizes. Such correspondence can be exhilarating for us as readers, once we see the linkages embedded in Josef's life and experience, but often linkages arise as moments of dark foreboding easily passed over, as when a pupil of Josef's describes an outing to the countryside and mentions "a glance back at the railroad tracks providing a view of a little town with a church tower and a couple of factory chimneys, smoke rising from them." But for Josef such repetition and return are constricting, if not chilling, especially when "the web of relations" he finds himself "ensnared in" threatens him with an existence whereby he must live for and with "memories that one can no longer enter."

Adler, however, is more a stoic than a tragedian. Just as Stephen Dedalus's heroism involves the arrival at a plane of regard that allows him to "pare his fingernails" before his own artistic creation, Josef's real battle is to maintain his own humanity in the face of the dehumanizing forces that continue to mount against him. His own "irrepressible vitality" is the best weapon against this, for "even in the grip of seeming doom, his ability to contemplate what he observe[s] spread[s] beyond the searing pain of the sharpest despair." Although this realization occurs to Josef more after the fact than within the camp itself, his determination not to give in to despair is also what allows him, at thirteen, to survive the grim atmosphere of the pseudo-military school that he attends, where he is slapped down by The Bull, the stern headmaster, for calling another student a "German pig," but only because he has been called a "Czech pig," which is of no concern to The Bull at all. As a distraction from this lonely, repressive existence, Josef, ironically, likes to secretly draw maps of railroads running between cities—Adler's dark foreshadowing once again flowering in the mention of how the "web of railroads grows ever more thick" upon Josef's hidden paper. Later, this secret will to map and describe drives both Josef and Adler to take notes on the horrors that surround them, the fodder of suffering turned into the fecund resilience of the imaginative act as it is shaped by sign and symbol alike.

When, some fifteen years later, Josef actually finds himself working as a forced laborer on the railroad that in all likelihood will soon carry him to the hell of Langenstein, this resilience is what allows him to acknowledge what a fellow laborer maintains; namely, that one "may indeed be a victim, but he is also a witness, and through that each can—whether through his own disposition or caprice—find a certain freedom, namely the freedom of knowledge or the ability to know." Soon afterward, when Josef is asked by a friend if he indeed has any hope, Josef is quick to reply, "No, not hope, that's not what he'd call it, but instead a readiness to accept whatever might happen, it's probably life itself that we should accept at any moment without fear. Nothing is more destructive than fear, for, senselessly, it leads to the death of meaning and is itself meaningless, fear able to enslave and murder before a death sentence is even lowered upon a man."

This combination of stoicism laced with a tinge of slightly rapt naïveté lies at the heart of both Josef's and Adler's worldview. At times it can be somewhat hard to take, with even Josef realizing that "his thinking is approaching the limits of what is permissible." For while the "freedom of knowledge or the ability to know" may on the surface seem a noble thing to embrace in the face of despair, it hardly seems capable of standing up to the mechanized annihilation inherent in the camps. On the other hand, a "readiness to accept whatever might happen," and to do so without fear, is a crucial last thread in the fabric of human dignity that no one would wish to let go of. In the end, in order to appreciate Adler's moral response to the cataclysm that he survived, one has to understand his arrival at a position midway between naïve idealism and stony fatalism, which Josef perhaps best describes as "a liberation from despair, from hopelessness, arrived at through resignation." This resignation, however, is not a capitulation but an "acceptance" of the way things are, such that once "all anxieties . . . have been overcome there is much grace that can befall one, because simply to *be* is grace in itself."

To ask whether this seems true or plausible in the face of the Holocaust is perhaps to miss the point of Josef's or Adler's arriving at such a perspective. Indeed, Josef makes very clear that he "wants nothing to do with empty equivocation leading to lame optimism or self-deception," and that he also wishes "to avoid any kind of blindness." Instead, amid the panorama of his experience and his memories, what Josef ultimately realizes is that "he cannot stand aloof."

> The viewer is also the participant, there being nothing arbitrary, everything is tightly intertwined, thus forming Josef's garments. Neither to extricate oneself nor to unite oneself is the first task, but rather to take something from it, no matter the cost. Sometimes it seems easier to judge the run of affairs than to take part in them, but nothing happens if one does, and sometimes that means entering the fray. It may be tempting to flee to one's tower, but to do so is to sleep as the world goes by, and we sleep enough as it is, and thus we are compelled to be awake and to function, the piety of the solitary person shattered by the functioning of the world.

Accordingly, Josef's mission and calling involves the implicit need to "bear witness to the existence of the lost ones." This is very much what Adler felt his own mission to be, one that in many ways bespeaks a kind of religious devotion in his determination to capture not only what happened to those who had died but also the dignity with which so many still lived up to the moment of their miserable end.

To do this, Adler chose two paths: that of a thinker and that of a writer. In a television interview in 1986, he remembered feeling, upon his arrival at Theresienstadt, that "when I was deported I said to myself, I won't survive this. But if I survive, then I will describe it, and I will do so in two key ways. I want to do it by setting down the facts of my individual experience, as well as to somehow describe it artistically. I have indeed done both, and the fact that I have done so is not that important but is at least some justification for my having survived those years." Hence, key to Adler's work is the dovetailing of fact and fiction in trying to both scientifically and imaginatively encompass his experience. *Theresienstadt 1941–1945* would be the means of examining his past through the exacting lens of a scholar and a social historian. However, during the same decade in which he concluded his thousand-page study, he also wrote twenty-five hundred pages of fiction, completing five novels, of which *Panorama* was the first. Given this bifurcated strategy—one unique to almost any writer we know—Josef's declaration that "the viewer is also the participant" also functions as a silent imperative behind the need for Adler's artistic and moral approach. Indeed, it was one thing for Adler to "judge the run of affairs" in keeping the copious notes that would lead to the Theresienstadt book; it was yet another thing for him to "enjoin" his imagination with what had happened through the writing of fiction.

Of late, W. G. Sebald, who features Adler and his Theresienstadt study in the closing pages of his novel *Austerlitz*, in many ways blends Adler's twin approach by presenting texts that seem to be carefully researched factual studies of the author's own experience, replete with their own panorama of photographs, but which are also highly manipulated forays into the fictional sublime. Sebald has been accused of bordering on a kind of preciousness in bringing such a highly aesthetic approach to the Holocaust, and it is a criticism that Adler, too, faced in his dispute with Theodor Adorno on the question of whether it was even possible to write fiction or poetry after the camps. At the time, this sentiment was felt so deeply in German letters that Adler was not able to publish *Panorama* until 1968, twenty years after its completion, while his second novel, *The Journey*, did not appear until 1962, eleven years after it was completed. Worse yet, two novels from the same period have never seen the light of day, and the last of the five, *The Invisible Wall*, which was completed in 1956, didn't appear until 1989, a year after Adler's death. Against such daunting opposition from publishers and critics alike, Adler's effort to render the truth through fiction must, indeed, have felt like a kind of "calling" in order for him to continue with it at all. Like Josef, he had to maintain "a positive attitude toward reality, or the seemingly real . . . for what we can know is a present—namely, *the* present." Indeed, the fact that so much of *Panorama* makes use of the present tense to elicit the immediacy of remembering the past also corresponds with Adler's urge to avoid "sleeping as the world goes by," a charge made all the more crucial by the fact that the novel is forced to describe a world that has vanished forever.

Unlike historical scholarship, whose job is to help us understand what was, what happened, and, perhaps, the consequences that we live with now, the object of fiction on its most basic level is to remind us of what it means "simply to *be*." For all its horror, for all the death and annihilation it unleashed, what we talk about under the vexed rubric of "the Holocaust" is also about those who struggled for the chance "simply to *be*." To forget this amid our supposed awareness of the suffering and violence that would not allow them to do so is to risk forgetting the very humanity whose loss is at the core of the tragedy of which Adler attempts to speak. In this sense, *Panorama* is not a Holocaust novel per se. It is one man's attempt to show us what it meant "simply to *be*" a boy in Bohemia in the early twentieth century, a young man in Prague in the Depression years, a forced laborer and an inmate during the great cataclysm, and, finally, a survivor and an exile in the postwar years bent on trying to understand where he had been, where he was, and where he was going amid the "panoramic view which allows the eyes to take account."

And so Josef awakens, just as, at the end of Joyce's novel, Stephen Dedalus finds that "his soul was waking slowly, fearing to awake wholly." The Frau Director, whose children Josef tutors, maintains, "The story of man is about the transition from sleep to waking," and this is very much Josef's story, too. Every scene of *Panorama* ends with Josef drifting back into sleep—except the very last one, in which, finally, Josef is wholly awake to who he is and what he embodies in having survived. No doubt Adler felt much the same, and, clearly, the writing of *Panorama* was vital to the process of waking from his own nightmare. From here, he would go on to the heightened modernism of *The Journey*, constructing "a ballade" of voices whose score explores the dark phantasm of the journey to Theresienstadt and Auschwitz and back. His last published novel, *The Invisible Wall*, completes the trilogy by coming out on the other side to render the nightmare of the survivor's guilt, memory having become as much burden as substance. If

Panorama plays off Stephen Dedalus's awakening, the ability to sustain consciousness through the sheer propulsion of language itself eventually lands Adler in the kind of linguistic brinkmanship found in Beckett—an ironic turn in itself, given Adorno's embrace of the latter at the former's expense.

However, there is no writer quite like Adler, despite all his modernist echoes; nor do we have a more substantive fictional rendering of the Shoah by another German-speaking Jew who survived it. Given Adler's special attention to wordplay in both German and Czech, this alone makes his work an essential engagement with the period and its history. Add to this his penchant for writing scholarly studies with the eye of a writer, and for writing fiction through the mind of a philosopher and a historian, and we end up with a voice that is unique not only for what it has to say but, principally, for how it says it.

What would it mean to be able to live one's life backward and to see how each crucial juncture is connected to, if not presaged by, every prior yet seemingly unrelated juncture? What would it mean if one were forced to? Jonathan Lear says of Oedipus that his main problem is that "he makes more meaning than [he] grasps." Far be it from Adler to embrace a Freudian paradigm, for he was always highly suspicious of psychology as a discipline, seeing in it the false control of the clinical mentality, as opposed to the interpretive freedom inherent in the mythic sensibility. However, as pure analogy the comparison holds. Josef's dilemma is that he has more meaning in his life than he knows what to do with—or, at least, to easily prevent it from gaining more control over his life than he has over it. *Panorama* is about the wresting of that control away from Josef's experience and into his hands as a thinker and an observer, just as Adler's writing of the novel is a means toward shaping that which all too menacingly sought to destroy him. Stephen Dedalus arrives at the aim of expressing "myself in some mode of life or art as freely as I can and as wholly as I can, using for my defence the only arms I allow myself to use—silence, exile, and cunning." Adler chose the same, the crucial difference being that his hand was more forced than he would have preferred, his exile more bitter and haunting, since he was unable to return to his homeland even if he had wished to.

In the first and last stanzas of his villanelle "The Waking," Theodore Roethke writes:

I wake to sleep, and take my waking slow.
I feel my fate in what I cannot fear.
I learn by going where I have to go.

This shaking keeps me steady, I should know.
What falls away is always. And is near.
I wake to sleep, and take my waking slow.
I learn by going where I have to go.

That Josef Kramer survives to take his waking slow, unlike his hereditary namesake, Josef K., is a blessing. That H. G. Adler lived to trace that waking, along with an entire world that "fell away" forever, is the triumph amid the darkness illuminating his *Panorama*.

Peter Filkins
October 25, 2010

for Grete Fischer

PANORAMA

THE VISIT TO THE PANORAMA

"THERE'S A NEW PROGRAM TODAY. WE'RE GOING TO THE PANORAMA." JOSEF hears the voice of his grandmother and looks up from his toy. Panorama. Various pictures from all over the world. "Really, are we going?" The toy is abandoned, the dominoes, the building set, the train. It's a long way, yet Josef and his grandmother love the panorama. They sit in the streetcar, the motor rattles and sings. Josef often plays streetcar. He runs along the long curbstones of the sidewalk, which is the track. Josef hums with his mouth closed and imitates the streetcar. First he calls out, "Ding! Dong Dong!," then comes the humming and sighing of the motor. Streetcar conductor is the best job of all, for you get to sell tickets, punch the tickets, and call out the stops.

"We have to get off, Josef, come!" They draw past the embankment and see many people all dressed up. "Give me your hand! It's so crowded here." Already they have turned in to the quiet little lane where the panorama is located. Now they stand before the door. It's a simple storefront with a small display window, and there Josef peers at the beautiful pictures, whether it be

Vesuvius, Niagara Falls, the Great Pyramid, or other wonders of the world. There's also an announcement for that day's program. Josef sounds it out: "Li-ma, the Cap-i-tal of Pe-ru."—"Come, come, there's more to see inside." They next enter a little lobby that is separated from the actual panorama by a heavy curtain. Behind a table on which stands a sign that says TICKETS sits a powdered woman. Grandmother gives her a silver coin and takes from the powdery lady two little red tickets, as well as a nickel and some copper change. Josef is allowed to pocket the nickel. "Save it! Don't spend it on sweets!"

The grandmother weaves her way with Josef through the curtain and enters an almost completely darkened room. Around a polyhedral wooden cabinet high stools are arranged. In front of each one there are two round openings, which are dark peepholes located beneath a metal shield. You hold your eyes up or press them to the shield and the program appears. An attendant receives the guests and takes them to two free spots. The grandmother sits down, but the attendant lifts Josef up and presses him close to the peepholes. The two peepholes are there so that you see everything just the way it really looks, and everything is enlarged so that it seems completely alive. Everything appears lit by brilliant golden light, as if dipped in tropical sunlight. Each picture stands there for a minute, maybe less. To Josef it feels like a good long time. He's pleased that it lasts so long, for he can't get enough of the splendid sights. But it's a shame that the people, animals, and wagons in the pictures don't move. Though the fact they don't move doesn't make the life depicted in the beautiful pictures any less marvelous, it does make them seem like something outside of time. Before the pictures change, the delicate strike of a little bell warns: "Attention, time's up! Get ready for the next wonder!" Then the picture moves away, another draws near, the next stands before Josef at last. If he doesn't turn his gaze away from the peepholes and presses his face hard against the shield, he feels completely alone with the pictures. The daily world disappears and is gone. The viewer and the picture become one on the inside, no one can get in. Josef himself, however, cannot wander off into the pictures, for he remains sitting on his stool, his upper body bent forward slightly. Because of this he cannot sit comfortably, nor is there any chair back, so there's no resting at all. In the panorama, however, that doesn't matter. Josef is content.

One can be comfortable anywhere else, it's only in the panorama that this isn't possible. Everything here is hard and fixed and tense. That's why it's not necessary for the grandmother to say, "Pay attention, in order that you get something out of this and learn from it!" Only when the pictures change does the tension ease for just a moment. Josef scoots forward on his stool in order to see better still. Beneath the peepholes a piece of tin is attached against which he breathes. The tin gathers moisture and sometimes Josef likes to run his fingers over its smooth flatness so that his fingertips feel damp. The grandmother pays no attention to Josef, for she knows how the panorama captivates him, so much so that he is better behaved than usual. That's why the little naughtiness with wiping his fingers remains ignored. Normally there is no opportunity here to misbehave. The otherwise familiar world has disappeared. Here is another world, which one can only gaze at, there being no other way to enter but to gaze. Only these little holes are there for the eyes. Josef can see so for himself, simply by touching the glass, that there is no other way in. All the people and the distant lands that you encounter in these pictures remain untouchable behind the glass walls that are only large enough for the eyes.

It's fairly quiet in the panorama. Except for the little bell that announces the change in pictures, you only hear the guests coming and going, or a stool scraping, now and then a couple of words someone might whisper to his neighbor. You hardly ever hear the attendant. Thus the world you normally live in is turned off, and has in fact passed away. Another world is risen, which neither reading nor studying nor even dreams can manifest. Nonetheless, Josef can step only a little way into the other world, though he cannot take part in it. If he shoves his knee forward he immediately bumps up against the wooden cabinet. Soon it's clear how little is allowed. Everywhere there are barriers, nowhere can you immerse yourself entirely. Josef sees the other world, but it doesn't care about him. It consists only of parts that are put together. The only way for it to be different would be for the pictures to move, to continue on and flow into one another, yet each is presented on its own and is clearly separated from the next. The other world is a program that is immensely beautiful, but nothing more. Next week the program changes, and so on week after week. There is no whole, only individual pieces without end. Even today's program has no proper end but just repeats itself over and over. There are perhaps sixty, maybe eighty pictures, though there certainly are not a hundred. Eventually a picture comes along that has been there already. Josef doubts this at first, but after the next chiming of the little bell another picture appears that is also familiar. The grandmother still looks on. She starts to get restless on her chair. After the little bell strikes again and a third picture arrives that most certainly has been there already, the grandmother turns to Josef. "It's over, my dear. We've seen that one already. We have to go."

The grandmother stands. The attendant is already there and lifts Josef down; the grandmother helps and takes the boy by the hand. Then the attendant pulls back the curtain. In the lobby the daylight is so strong that the grandmother warns, "Child, close your eyes!" She doesn't have to say anything, for Josef squints and allows himself to be led out almost blind. The grandmother doesn't let on how much it all pleased her, but says, "Be careful, and watch where you're going." Josef doesn't know whether the warning is about the spectacle in the panorama or the way that leads home.

THE FAMILY

JOSEF HEARS HOW MISBEHAVED THE CHILDREN ARE, SINCE THAT'S ALL THEY seem to talk about, nothing but trouble for the parents and teachers of the world. "Josef, don't you hear?" Yes, he hears, and the voices run around and have long, dirty spider legs, and indeed bad things can sometimes happen. "Pay attention, Josef! Didn't you hear what I said?" He always hears it. "Now be quiet!" The nagging continues, but no child wants to behave. "If only you would understand! It's for your own good!" Then Aunt Gusti gets mad, but that does no good, and the children get dirty, and everything gets dirty, and yet they continue to talk back, a result of disobedience, the same old song with Josef, as Aunt Gusti yells, "Don't you talk back to me!" Don't do that, she says, don't be so smart, and don't tell lies, that's the worst of all. "You'll get a long nose if you tell lies!" That's what Josef has to listen to, nor can any child be left alone, and Josef reacts badly because he is so angry. On the way home from school he is bad and gets into scrapes with ruffians, which is unfortunate, but then how can he be expected to sit up straight and be ready to learn in school. "Yes, he is a gifted child," Fräulein Reimann says, but terribly scatterbrained and inattentive. Children pick up bad habits from others, but there's no excuse for that, and so the aunt watches him like a hawk, but it does no good, not even at home. There the father is always so high-strung at meals, and the father must be spared any disturbance, yet Josef wriggles in his chair and the mother says, "Can't you sit still for a single moment?" But Josef can't do that. He holds his knife wrong and his fork, and that makes the mother unhappy, because she has shown him so often, but he has no manners whatsoever at the table as he screws up his face and wrinkles his nose. The mushrooms are so delicious, as well as the carrots, even though the war is on, but the father doesn't like mushrooms, either, and the grandmother says, "One shouldn't make faces in front of children!" When she was young, everything was much more strict, you certainly weren't allowed to leave anything on your plate, and yet Josef is not allowed to say "I don't want any more!" because a child is in no position to do that, and yet he does, and there's nothing to be done about it.

Then Josef is among his toys and someone says, "Only street urchins drag their toys around like that!" All of them are ruined because he bangs around with them and he takes everything out of the chest. "This room is a complete mess!" Anna is not there to follow Josef around and pick up after him just because he's so lazy, and one can preach a thousand times about how much money the toys cost, the father having to work so hard for it, he doesn't just go out and steal it. Yet it never does any good, and then the parents are unhappy, but Josef is also unhappy, and he told Aunt Betti so, but she just laughed, saying that healthy children are always cheerful, and Josef is healthy, so he can't be unhappy. He should just come along, for he hasn't been out for a walk all day, but he doesn't want to go for a walk. "I don't want to, because I'm tired!" The aunt gets angry and says, "You always have an excuse! Now come along! Otherwise there will be trouble!" And so there's nothing he can do, Josef has to follow along, and yet outside in the park it feels better. There he runs around on his own, and Bubi and Ludwig and the other children are also there, but the grown-ups shout, "No horseplay!" But eventually they have to leave, even when it's finally nice out, as Josef pleads, "Please, just a while longer!" No, otherwise Father will be angry, the gruel will get cold, so come along and let's go, and then Josef is home and has to wash his hands after the mother yells at him to do so, after which comes supper, followed by the washing up, all of it done in a frightful hurry. Then Aunt Gusti observes, "It's about time for the children to finally be in bed!" But even though Josef gets into bed he doesn't want to, he wants a story. It's horrible when he's so alone, alone the entire night—oh, it's just awful, what he really needs is for the mother to hold his hand and give him a kiss. But then she leaves, and everything is dark and scary, Josef can't get to sleep for the longest time, and yet once again morning is there and Josef is woken up, and he's so tired that he doesn't want to get up, but the mother nonetheless yells, "Quick! Quick!" And once again it's a new day, and once again comes the yelling, but they do so only because of how much they love him, they really mean well, Aunt Gusti often says so. And then he's off on his way to school, as he remembers what Fräulein Reimann taught last year in first grade, the first song they had learned, five tones that ran up the scale and five that ran down: "Clean, bright, and polite / Suits all children right."

That's the way it always sounds to Josef, he hears that, and all the children in the park and in the school hear it as well, and perhaps spinning such yarns does indeed make for better children, something that worked for model children in years past. Supposedly they still exist, but it must be rare indeed, the aunts now and then pointing out a child to Josef who is much better behaved than he is. But they are only examples that don't really exist, and Josef believes in them a little only because he always hears about them, and therefore they must be true. Even Josef wants to be better, but he can see that it's not going to happen the way that he wants, and he has to keep pressing himself, though it does no good. He is surrounded by everything, he is always in the middle of it all, and everything stares at him, the grown-ups and everything else. But it doesn't help that he likes to be on his own, that's not allowed, even if he's allowed to go to school on his own and doesn't have to be picked up, that's not the same thing, or if he's allowed to play on his own, that's also not the same, because no one ever seriously believes that he can be completely free and on his own. It's obvious to him that he's not at all allowed to do what he wants, for someone is always watching and the day is totally arranged for him, and there's nothing Josef can do about it. He sees this for himself whenever he yells, "But I want to!," because soon that's the end of it, and someone says, "A child must obey!" Therefore Josef can't want anything himself, because if he misbehaves he'll be punished and get no reward. But being rewarded doesn't please him, and he ends up feeling sorry for having broken whatever reward is given him, having done so deliberately because he is so angry that his heart nearly bursts. Yet he doesn't let his anger show, which is why it hurts so, and then the toy is broken, and unhappiness returns because of what he has done, and he often thinks how bad he really is, though he is indeed unhappy and re-members how Aunt Betti said, "Children are often such a bother these days." And Josef always hears so much of what the grown-ups say, and it must surely be clever, for grown-ups know, they know everything, but a child is always in the wrong and in the way of grown-ups, except when he is also big. Then the child earns money and no longer brings home report cards, the parents waiting for the day when report cards no longer matter. The grown-ups, they have it easy and are not anxious, it's the children who are anxious, for there's only so much that can be done for them, the little chicks, who indeed are always anxious, but are all right, for they run to mother hen, though Josef can't hide under her feathers, but rather in the feathers of the bed, where he feels afraid, for that's where he's alone. But when he goes to the grown-ups because he feels so alone and wants to ask them something the first thing they say is "Ask more politely!" Then he says, "How do the fish do it? How can fish breathe in water through their gills?" And Aunt Betti says, "You're such a question box. Look it up in your natural-history book!"—"But what about the carp at Frau Robitschek's? She took a hammer and hit the carp on the head. The carp slipped out and landed on the ground. And he was still alive. Even though he wasn't in the water."

Aunt Betti gets upset over such stupid talk, but even if she knows exactly what the answer is she never says so, saying only that she collected picture-postcards as a child, like so many other children back then, and Josef should do the same. Aunt Betti often says, "If you had a lot of cards you'd be a rich man, Josef. When you grow up, you could open up a panorama. All of us will come and watch your program." Josef is deeply curious why his aunt has never opened up a panorama, for she always keeps her collection in thick albums, gladly showing them, though she never gives any photographs away, and no longer collects them. They are only memories of a golden childhood, she says, with which she was blessed, and as long as one is good paradise can be found on earth. "Maybe I should have opened a panorama, but then Uncle Paul came along and I married him. So nothing came of it, my child." She has to help his uncle, she says, and hold down the home front, for Uncle Paul has been away at war for so long, though brave women hold everything together, while bad children destroy it all, the grown-ups having to repair it, and there's a lot of complaining, for they end up not accomplishing much. "Your father has such skillful hands, golden hands, my child!" So says Aunt Gusti, who so admires the father, he being the finest man there is. "He is so nice to Grandmother. He's a lovely son." He scares Josef, who doesn't have golden hands, meaning that perhaps he's a bad child, his hands so often being black and his mother yelling "Dirty bird!" when she's unhappy, at which Josef has to wash his hands. But the mother is seldom satisfied and takes to him herself with the nail brush, scrubbing until his fingers turn red, though none of it does any good, because Josef is dirty again before she knows it.

The father's veins always stick out so. Whenever you look at his hands they appear blue and lavender, these veins, and there's no gold in them, but they are the father's hands, which earn for the family their daily bread. It's all so hard. He has to slave away and put up with so much in his business, because the customers are always complaining about the goods, nothing is cheap enough, and it all must be the very best, everything served up in a jiffy, each having to be the first, though it takes forever for everyone to place an order, customers remaining the cross he has to bear. There's also too much competition, none of whom can be trusted and all of them wanting to do the father in, the goods becoming ever more expensive, thus making it hard to get hold of them, he having to petition for them, the mother not wanting Josef to become a businessman, since it means nothing but trouble and results in only a bit of salt on dry bread. Every occupation today has it hard, because no one is satisfied, and each yanks the last morsel from the mouth of the other.

Perhaps one day better times will come which Josef will live to see. The children have to be brought up properly in preparation for them, for they must also engage in life's battle, which is so hard, or so Aunt Gusti always thinks. She is a language teacher and has many students with whom she is also always angry when they don't show up on time, which simply won't do, for she doesn't want to have to make up for lost time, there's no way to, and what's the point as soon as another child knocks when the hour is up and there's nothing she can do despite her best intentions. And she has to be notified in a timely fashion when a child is sick, otherwise she's sorry, she cannot make up the lesson, she is much too busy. Josef should also take English with Aunt Gusti, but she doesn't want to teach him because he's such an unruly child, and she doesn't want to be constantly bickering with the father and the mother. "Perhaps when he is older and can pay better attention." The mother is unhappy about it, but the father says, "I, too, never learned any language, and I still make an honest living." Then the mother is quiet, because she knows that the father will get angry if anyone says anything to him, and he has enough worries already. Otherwise Aunt Gusti is very fond of Josef. He is often there when she gives lessons, sitting at a little table, in front of him a book or a toy with which he can play only at Aunt Gusti's, she having bought it special so that he has something there, and then she gives him some other goody, such as gooseberries or hazelnuts or cookies, though he shouldn't leave any crumbs. Then Joseph is on his own, but he also hears how his aunt teaches, how beautifully she explains everything—"fazur" is "father," she says, "mazur" is "mother"—while most of the children are older than Josef, though they don't pay attention all that well. Thus the aunt is often angry, scolding and yelling at them, though the children are never fresh to her, she simply wouldn't stand for it, and Josef should see how she handles them. Yet the worst is when the students don't have their assignments, or when they are lazy, for then his aunt is really mad and says with disgust, "You should be ashamed that your father is paying so much money for you. It makes no difference to me, but I'm not pleased, for though I am sure that you wouldn't want to be called a thief, what you're doing is probably worse than stealing." Then the aunt asks what the words are in English, and it also makes her a bit upset when the children know only half of them. But sometimes when Josef knows the answer and the child does not he wants to say what it is, and he in fact says it, but Aunt Gusti doesn't like that, it's not right for Josef to speak up. "One shouldn't speak if one is not spoken to!" He had often thought a great deal about that, because people always talk when they want to, but not at first, if they are asked something.

Children used to exist because they pleased their parents, but it has not been that way for a long time, because they are such a burden, and Josef doesn't know why, in fact, children exist at all, nor does he want to have any, for he doesn't even want to be a child, he wants to be a grown-up, because then everything is better, which is why people like Aunt Betti shouldn't envy children, because grown-ups don't have to be afraid, they can do whatever they want. But Josef is afraid, he's afraid of animals, most of all of dogs, and he prefers to walk on the opposite side of the street, because dogs are mean. Josef is also afraid of thunderstorms and is amazed that grown-ups can stay so calm when it thunders, his mother even saying, "You silly, if you're afraid of lightning that's okay, because it can strike you. But thunder can't harm anyone." The mother says that Aunt Betti is also a little afraid, but she doesn't want to show it, and that's good, for you should never show that you are afraid if you are going to become a fine young man. But Josef is afraid nevertheless. He's afraid of water that is deeper than up to his knees, he's afraid of fire and won't have anything to do with matches, and the grand-mother says, "At least Josef won't burn the house down." More than any-thing, he is afraid of the night, the worst punishment being to lock him in the darkened bathroom, and it's awful to have to lie at night in the darkened bedroom, not even the slightest bit of light coming through the door's opaque glass pane, that being when all the terrible ghosts appear, and the ghosts make menacing threats and climb down into the room from the tiled stove, which has a beaked nib, and then the ghosts slowly cross the bureau and ever closer to the crib, lying down on the blanket and pressing upon it, and there's peace as they approach his head and crouch down on the pillow next to Josef, though he can't shoo them away, for they have no names. He also can't tell anyone about them, for everyone says there's no such thing as ghosts, though it's good when at night his mother plays the piano, because the ghosts can't do anything then.

It's always best when someone is there, but at school there are too many, three kids on each bench, and whoever sits in the middle, like Josef, can't get out unless a neighbor makes room. Josef sits way up front, because his vision is so bad, and in front of him is Fräulein Reimann, for when she teaches she likes to stand in front of the first row, her hand resting on the back of the bench. All the children like her, she is so nice, and she likes to lead them in songs, the children taking up the "Songbook of the Fatherland" in its red binding, the teacher announcing the page number so that the children can open to it, all of them standing up and singing as one in chorus. Fräulein Reimann also has a violin, which she likes to play, yet she is also unsatisfied and calls out a name. "You're droning along, you're not singing! You have to sing out, open your mouth just wide enough to fit two fingers in. But the fingers should be one next to the other!" And she shows how wide the mouth should be. They all stick their fingers into their mouths and she praises the children who do it right. Josef also likes to sing along, though he doesn't like the exam, for then there is no chorus and you have to sing on your own, and the violin is of no help, it lies on the lectern, the teacher liking to have only the bow in her hands.

At recess, all the children have to head to the courtyard, except when it rains, the mother having said that Josef should take his cap in order not to catch cold, but he doesn't like the cap, for on it there's a name written, VIRIBUS UNITIS, which he doesn't understand, though the mother said that it's a ship that belongs to the emperor in Vienna. Everything belongs to the emperor, but the cap belongs to Josef, even if he doesn't like it, which is why he was not unhappy when Hugo Treml ripped off its band and tore it badly. However, when Josef got home the mother was beside herself. "Your beautiful cap! The good emperor would be so upset." Nonetheless, Josef was not upset, and there are other clothes that he doesn't like, such as a white sailor suit that annoys him, yet the mother is especially fond of it, saying that it looks so cute on Josef, though he hates the tie more than anything, the bow is hideous. It's a shame that a boy should have to wear such a suit, the bib under the shirt, which is attached to the underwear, is terrible with all those buttons, for they take forever, the mother saying, "You're dawdling again! One needs the patience of heaven with you! The coffee will be completely cold, and you need to be off to school already!" And the tall laced boots take a lot of effort, the mother not helping at all, or allowing Anna to help, but when Anna checks to see if the laces have been properly done up the mother says with agitation, "Anna, I'm asking you again! Please don't indulge him. A child must learn to fend for himself."

Because the mother wants Josef to do everything on his own, the mornings take forever. The cold milk coffee has such a grotesque skin on top of it that Josef is disgusted and pulls it off with two fingers, even though the mother has forbidden it, saying that you should only shove it to the side with a spoon if you aren't going to just swallow it, but never touch your food with your fingers. What the mother really wants is for Josef to drink his milk, but he can't stand it, he is unreasonable and simply doesn't see how good it is for him, how it would make him much less anxious, the doctor having said that Josef needs to drink a lot of milk, because he is always pale and anemic. The doctor had then wanted to prick his finger in order to examine his blood to see how anemic he is, but he let loose such a scream that the doctor had to stop, the result being that everyone now says that Josef is a sniveler. But he can't stand the sight of blood, Frau Robitschek's carp also bloody, the poor fish unable to cry out but only flip itself off the table as she beat it with a hammer.

Because it involves so much blood, Josef has no idea why the mother wants him to become a doctor, and when children fall they scream, are bloody and covered with dirt, someone saying, "You got what you deserved, you rascals!" But the father says he doesn't care what Josef will become, only that he make a decent and honorable living, while Aunt Betti says, "One has no idea what children will be when they grow up." But Aunt Gusti says, "Nothing can be made of lazy and unremarkable children. So who says that Josef has to study. Working with your hands has its rewards." Then the mother is unhappy when everyone says such things, and she says, "He should study no matter what. I'm hoping that he'll be a doctor. It's the best profession, because you help others." But Josef doesn't know how you help others if you cause them pain, and wherever there is blood there is no help involved, only a lot of pain. Only cough medicine is okay, it tastes good and is so gooey when you take a big spoonful, as Josef holds it for a long while in his mouth and swishes it around, the way he does when he brushes his teeth, normally the mother wanting him to spit it out, though not so with the cough medicine, which he needs to just swallow.

Josef likes to be sick, but not too sick, though being a little sick is pleasant, because then the mother sits with him and doesn't punish him but tells wonderful stories and puts a cold compress on his throat. She takes a wet hand towel and a dry hand towel, securing the outer wrapping with a safety pin. Then a thermometer is placed under Josef's arm, which he likes to press, and slowly a silver thread begins to climb up it, ten minutes having passed before the mother takes the thermometer and looks and says, "Your temperature is still up. You have to stay in bed." The mother is almost a doctor, which saddens her, for she was not allowed to study medicine, though she knows a lot about it and has a thick book that she also shows to Josef, there being many pictures in it that he likes to look at, the book titled *The Housewife as Doctor.* Josef then asks why you call a doctor when you're sick, since everything is in the book, and the mother explains, "A proper doctor has more experience. He sees many patients every day."

For coughs and sniffles and sore throats the mother doesn't call the doctor, since she already knows what to do, but when it's something else the doctor comes, his lovely voice dark and deep, with his marvelous beard, as he comes to the bed and says, "Now, what have we gotten mixed up in this time? We'll soon find out." Then the shirt must come off, the doctor examining him and telling him to "breathe deep" and "hold your breath," demonstrating just how to do it, then he places his big warm ear against Josef's back while tapping with his fingers here and there, after which he looks into the child's throat as he says "Ah," always "Ah," the doctor also saying "Ah" along with him. It's just like in school when they sing "ah" or "la," though Fräulein Reimann had also taught them beautiful and strange words that they sang up and sang down, *doremifasolatido* and *dotilasofamiredo*, because she said that was the way to do it. The doctor never does that, he only has Josef say "Ah" as he presses on his tongue with a wooden stick or the handle of a spoon, which is unpleasant, the doctor feeling around the throat, as well, to see if the glands are swollen, and then he scribbles something on a notepad, which says what has to be picked up at the pharmacy, telling the mother what she should do, and whether he will come again tomorrow or later. Now and then the mother takes Josef to the doctor, who has a waiting room with several chairs and two tables, on which there are magazines with pictures, though the mother doesn't look at them or allow Josef to, because she believes they are filthy, most people not being careful enough, making it easy to pick up germs. Many people are waiting, but sometimes the doctor opens the door and calls out, "Next, please!" He then sticks his head in the waiting room and looks around at each of them until the person whose turn it is rises and goes in.

Sometimes Josef also goes to the dentist, where he sits on a strange chair, like the one at the barbershop, and has to open his mouth as the dentist looks inside with his mirror, sometimes saying "Good," and sometimes saying that a tooth needs to be filled, which is bad. Josef doesn't know why Aunt Gusti always says, "The dentist has such soft hands. His touch is wonderful. One hardly feels a thing." Josef doesn't believe her, because the dentist sticks a drill inside his mouth which makes such a noise, the only funny thing being how he has to work the pedal with his feet like on a spinning wheel, as he sits there and pushes with his feet, the dentist standing, his mother having shown him in a book how it's like pedaling a bicycle. But the dentist's spinning wheel is noisy and rattles and scrapes like a thunderstorm inside the mouth, though eventually he stops and soon it feels better after he places a thick silver drop of quicksilver, just like in a thermometer, on the tooth. Once, Josef broke a thermometer, a shiny little ball of quicksilver showing up in his bed, the mother beside herself as she said that quicksilver is very poisonous, and that you shouldn't put it into your mouth. Since the thermometer was broken, Josef had to get out of bed and move to the couch, as the little balls of quicksilver were gathered up, and he said, "Won't the dentist be pleased when we bring him the quicksilver." At first this made the mother angry, but then she laughed and said that it couldn't be used, even though the dentist used it for the tooth and then said, "Nothing to eat for two hours!"

The best is the eye doctor, where you sit for a long time in the waiting room, because everyone is in with the doctor for a long time, and there are many more waiting. This is why the mother always brings along something to read, as well as some needlework, though Josef is impatient and beats time with his legs, which his mother doesn't like at all. But finally they are called, and then it's wonderful as the doctor takes Josef into a dark chamber, no one else allowed to come along, not even the mother, as the doctor sits him on a stool just like at home in front of the piano, though here the doctor sits on the other side of a machine that he turns this way and that as he covers one of Josef's eyes and Josef looks in one direction and sees a red light and a green light. Then the doctor sits even closer to Josef in the darkness and holds a tiny glittering light that is like a star and which Josef has to look up at, but which then goes out as the doctor places a heavy set of glasses on him that have no lenses, then opens a chest with lots of lenses, as he takes out one and drops it into the frame, one after another, turning the lenses around in the frames. Josef is given an "E" made of metal and has to show where the same "E" appears on a board, one after another, and in rows above and below, right and left, the "E" getting ever smaller until it is so small that it can no longer be seen. When the doctor has finally found the best lenses, he is satisfied and says to the mother that the eyes are better, after which he marks down the prescription and says, "Well, then, let's see him in another six months!" Meanwhile everyone thinks the doctor is too expensive, the father saying, "I'd like to be able to pick people's pockets like that!" Once Aunt Gusti got angry at that and said, "Sight is our most precious gift. Better deaf than blind."

Josef doesn't want to become a doctor, but he pretends that he is Uncle Doctor with Bubi. That's his best friend, who is a brash kid with a little sister named Kitti. Whenever the house is being cleaned from top to bottom Josef spends almost the entire day with Bubi, though when the painter is there he stays overnight, Bubi also coming to him when something is going on at his house, though Josef prefers to go to Bubi's because his mother is not as strict. There is also a young aunt there named Tata, who tells wonderful stories and is very pretty, and Bubi's father always tells jokes, for he is much more at ease than Josef's father. Josef plays with Bubi for hours at a time, the two of them making up their own games that no one would understand, while before they know it Kitti is hauled out of her little chair because they need it for their game, since it works well for playing doctor, one of them sitting on it, the other acting as a dentist who takes care of teeth, the sewing machine serving as the operating table after Tata has loosened the belt so that the machine doesn't get broken as the patient is placed on the iron grate that serves as a pedal but now is where the operation is carried out. The mother never allows such a thing to happen at home, but one can do it at Bubi's, even though he tends to boss others around a lot, yet Josef doesn't mind, for though normally he wouldn't put up with it, he does take it from Bubi because he's so fond of him.

Josef also has another friend named Ludwig, whom he also really likes, though he isn't as rambunctious and playful, which is why they play different games. Ludwig is terribly shy and serious, but he seems to know everything, and he has many toys and loads of books, and he loves plants and little animals and stones, which he collects while always keeping a lookout for something new. He shows Josef how to press flowers, the best way to catch flies, and Josef never feels disgusted by the earthworms that he holds softly in his hands and carries around, capturing caterpillars as well, though he knows there are some that should not be picked up, having long hairs like stinging nettles, Ludwig finding a leaf on which to carry them home. Yet he's not afraid of stinging nettles, for Ludwig says that you just have to take them firmly in hand and then they won't sting, while you can sting others with them if you just tickle someone's leg with a leaf.

Bubi can't stand Ludwig, and they always get into a fight in the park, Josef upset, because he wants to be good friends with both, Bubi once having said to Josef in front of Ludwig, "I can't stand Ludwig. It's up to you, Josef. It's either Ludwig or me." This makes Josef very unhappy, Bubi should either get along with Ludwig or let Josef stay friends with him, but Bubi will have none of it and says, "Either Ludwig or me, you can't have both!" This makes Josef incredibly upset and he nearly cries, but he holds it back and says that he wants to be Bubi's friend. But Bubi is really mean and wants Josef to help beat up Ludwig, at which Bubi tackles Ludwig, who, though strong and agile, is quite small, nor does it matter that he's so small, and even though Josef helps by blocking Ludwig's way, he also sticks out a leg and trips Bubi, so that Ludwig scrambles loose and darts away and is gone. Bubi, meanwhile, can't catch him and is too late. The next day the mother goes to Ludwig's mother, though Josef says that he won't go with her. "Why?" asks the mother, but he won't give any reason, though the mother is like iron and will stand for no secrets. Josef has to say why, and then he has to go to Ludwig's, both mothers talking for a long while before the two boys reconcile and everything is all right once again. But the mother is not entirely satisfied, and she also talks to Bubi's mother, such that Bubi and Ludwig must make up, though they don't really do so and don't want to, Bubi looking away whenever he sees Ludwig.

Once Bubi was really bad and didn't want to do what his mother said and screamed, "I'll shoot myself if you keep bothering me!" Then he picked up a cork gun from among his toys and pointed it toward himself as his mother went pale and yelled, "Bubi, you can't die! My poor child, Bubi! Bubi!" But Bubi is stubborn and just looks away as his mother comforts him, which pleases Josef a great deal, and he thinks that he'd like to try the same rather than always just making someone angry. So when Josef once again doesn't want to wash his hands and the mother scolds him as always, he says to her, "I'm tired of you always getting angry with me. I don't want to live anymore, I'm going to poison myself!" At this the mother quietly walks away and returns with a spoon, then opens the little medicine cabinet full of many bottles, jars, tins, and little boxes, after which she grabs a bottle and slowly removes its cork and pours something from it into the spoon that looks like water and has no color, and then steps toward Josef, who at first is curious and looks on, but now is afraid as she calmly says, "Take the spoon, my child. This will poison you and then you'll be dead." And so she holds the spoon up to his mouth, which he doesn't open, and he realizes that he doesn't really want to die, but nonetheless he grows terribly afraid and thinks how lucky Bubi is that his mother was so afraid, while Josef's mother will just let him die quietly because she doesn't love him at all. "I'm not taking the spoon! I don't want to!"—"You said you wanted to poison yourself. This is poison, my child. You won't have to be bothered by your mother anymore."—"I'm not taking that spoon!" And then he begins to weep horribly and cannot stop, and he never thinks about poisoning himself again.

Josef wants to live and grow tall, and he's astounded at how easy it would be to die from just a spoonful of medicine, which is terrible, not even the mother being sad once you are dead. But Frau Diamant is deeply sad and still wears black and always has tears in her eyes when she sees Josef and his schoolmates. She had a son named Georg, who was in Josef's class, and Georg had always been such a quiet boy whom everyone liked. But one day he didn't come to school again, and then Fräulein Reimann sadly said a couple of days later, "Children, stand up. I have some bad news. Georg Diamant has died from brain fever. We will observe a moment of silence in order to think about him and his poor parents." And after a minute the teacher said, "Now sit. Tell your parents that you'd like to contribute a little something. Bring it in with you so that the class can lay a beautiful wreath on Georg's grave." Josef told his parents, and the mother was deeply upset and said right way, "The poor, poor parents! What a terrible blow!" But Aunt Betti said, "One can't watch over children closely enough. They are such a worry. All it takes is a little bite from some bug and there's nothing you or I can do to prevent the child dying." Then Josef asked, "Will I also die?"—"We all have to die someday, child. But before that we should all live to be old. When a child dies, it's the worst thing that can happen to a parent, and terribly hard." Josef wants to ask more questions, but he doesn't really know what about, and then he can only think how sad it must be to be dead and no longer there. The next morning his father gives him a silver coin for the wreath, all the children in the class bringing in a contribution as the teacher writes down the exact amount she receives from each and, once satisfied, says, "It will be a beautiful wreath. Tomorrow is the burial, and I will attend for all of you and give my condolences to the inconsolable parents on behalf of the entire class. Today, though, you should all pray a great deal for the soul of poor Georg, so that he gets to heaven and becomes a little angel."

Josef often dreams, losing himself in his dreams during the day as well, not knowing if he's asleep or if he's dreaming. He holds on tight to his mother when he leaves the house with her, sensing how warm it is next to her, when suddenly he senses nothing and feels as if he didn't exist. Perhaps that's what it's like, being dead, as if looking down at himself, entirely separate and other, and he feels sorry for this Josef, who is always walking around hanging on to someone, this Josef down there below him. A different Josef has to always do as he's told, go to school, wash his hands, a Josef who is always afraid and isn't brave like Bubi, who sits atop a real horse that slowly goes around in a circle as it pulls the carousel, Josef trusting the artificial horses of the carousel, those that are dead, while Bubi rides proudly on a living horse. The Josef above pities the Josef below, but the one above is not really there, he is nothing and thinks nothing, though he is alive and is much more magnificent than the real Josef and better than him and all the children in the class.

In class there is a poor refugee from Galicia named Chaim Eiberheit, whom all the kids dislike, Eiberheit being completely poor, though there's no reason for him to be so filthy, or so say all the mothers, as well as Fräulein Reimann, though he does live in the worst house in the neighborhood, a building where many poor people live whom no one wants anything to do with, Hugo Treml saying of the house, "It's full with broken windows." But the teacher says, "No, Treml, you mean 'full of,' not 'full with,' nor is 'full of' even right in this instance." Meanwhile Eiberheit sits on the last bench alone, because no child can stand to sit next to him, not because he's a refugee but because his mother never cleaned him up and he has dirty ears, once having had a genuine case of lice in his hair, even though it never bothered Eiberheit. One time Frau Eiberheit came to school, waiting until recess, when Fräulein Reimann was still in the classroom, to whom Frau Eiberheit handed a large slice of bread covered with lard, which she just wanted to pass on to Chaim, though the teacher was anxious to speak with her. "It's good that you're here, Frau Eiberheit. But you must know this is not allowed." Indeed, Frau Eiberheit begs her pardon, she doesn't want to be a bother, but the boy had simply forgotten his lunch and he shouldn't go hungry, and Frau Eiberheit makes a move to go, but the teacher yells, "Frau Eiberheit, listen to me! You must . . ." Frau Eiberheit doesn't let her get out another word, even though all she wants to say is that Frau Eiberheit has to bathe Chaim and comb his hair, but Frau Eiberheit has already left the classroom, and the teacher can only shrug her shoulders. And yet Eiberheit remains as filthy as ever, nor does it matter to him, for he's happy to sit alone on the last bench, making faces and laughing whenever anyone turns around to him, which the teacher has forbidden them to do. "No turning around. That's rude. How many times must I tell you?" But Eiberheit says to her, "Pieposberger and Flamminger are also refugees, and yet they never get into trouble. Why don't you make an example of them?"

At home the mother says, "It's this terrible war that does this to everyone. It would be good if it would just be over with. Then we could get a letter again from Aunt Valli in America." The mother often talks about this aunt who many years ago left for America, where she lives quite happily, especially because the war zone is so far away, and war is simply horrible. Bubi's father didn't have to enlist, but Ludwig's father had to, and also Hugo Treml's and the fathers of many other children who are now in Russia or on the Isonzo and seldom come home when they have leave, several others also having been wounded, and some still held as prisoners of war. Meanwhile the children don't know where their fathers are, and the mothers say nothing, which is awful for the poor women, as Aunt Gusti says the children will too easily become like wild animals because the mothers have no help and have to worry about everything for themselves. Uncle Paul also enlisted and has been wounded at Vilna, Aunt Betti sighing deeply and saying, "The fact that the people don't want to sue for peace is a cross to bear!" As for little Ernst, whose hair is as long as a little girl's and looks as beautiful as a doll his mother adores in a storefront window, his father fell in Serbia at the very start of the war, three years ago, though his mother still goes around in black and says to everyone, "I live only for Ernst, he's the apple of my eye." Indeed, Ernst continues to look just like an apple, fresh and pure, himself not allowed to play with the other children in the park, though Bubi's mother once said to Josef's mother, "That's too much. It's not good for the child." Josef's father, meanwhile, had been enlisted for a brief time, then he was discharged because he is somewhat frail. He once had a problem with his lungs and his eyes are weak, the eye doctor saying, "It's a hereditary condition, which Josef got from his father." But the father suffers a great deal during the war, because he must work twice as hard in the store, and he can find no help to hire, which is why he's so late getting home, which makes the mother angry, but when he has to go into the store on Sunday morning she can't say anything, for he says, "There's no other way to do what has to be done. Times are tough, Mella. Be reasonable!"

The mother also contributes a lot to the war effort, serving as a volunteer nurse and often working at the new high school that has been converted into a military hospital. The mother is good at massage, the wounded like her, and they often come to visit once they are better, many of them poor men who have lost an arm or a foot, often still covered in large bandages. Sometimes the mother takes Josef along to the hospital, the huge gymnasium having been turned into an orthopedic ward, where the mother usually does therapy with the wounded and helps them exercise, sometimes a little party happening in the ward as well, such as on the emperor's birthday or when there is a visit by the proconsul's wife, who is so nice, everyone running after her and calling her "Countess." The mother takes a white overcoat with a red cross on it, as well as another pin that says VOLUNTEER NURSE, the mother also wearing a white bonnet that is as stiff and bright as the father's collars. The mother does what she can, because it is her duty to the fatherland to do something for the war effort when she herself cannot fight, and the emperor is fighting for what is right. That's what the children learn in school, the principal exhorting them to buy war bonds, though Josef's father doesn't want to, and when Josef asks if he can he is told, "That's for rich people. I have to work hard in order that you grow up hale and hardy." Josef asks, "But is what you do also for the emperor?"—"For the emperor, and for you as well." Then the father explains how he is fulfilling his responsibilities by tutoring the war blind to make grocery bags, the war blind making wonderful bags out of paper leather, which they then sell in order to support themselves. The mother has also bought some of them, as have other women, including Bubi's mother and Ludwig's mother, though Aunt Gusti says that you can buy better ones in the store and for less, but you should still buy them from the war blind, since they are so poor, and you can never cherish your sight enough, Josef having the good fortune to wear glasses, whereas the blind live in an eternal night.

Sitting under the stairs with his eyes closed, Josef thinks that he knows what it's like to have your eyes shot out. That's why it's good that the father demonstrates how to cut paper leather, how one weaves it and glues it in order to make a bag. Everywhere, people help with the war effort, such as in school, where they gather lint twice a week, which Josef likes to do. They are given bright rags, which they unravel with their fingers, taking a little piece and with two fingers pulling out thread after thread until a little pile lies on the desk, after which it's all gathered up in a big bag, which the custodian takes away as the teacher says, "The lint is used for pillows and blankets for our wounded heroes in the hospital, since proper feathers are in such short supply." Lint is also gathered at home, Anna happy to help out, after which it's taken away, though Bubi doesn't like to and says, "Gathering lint is stupid, that's girls' work." But Tata says, "Bubi, you have no heart. Just imagine if you were wounded and had to lie on some awful straw mattress without ever having a pillow or a proper blanket." Nonetheless, Bubi still says it's for girls or little boys, it being ridiculous when he has to do it, at which Tata says, "Fine, Bubi, we can switch jobs. You can knit pulse warmers for the poor soldiers, and I'll gather lint." To this Bubi says nothing and leaves the room, Josef following him, the two of them ending up outside on the balcony, where Bubi has a large pickle jar full of tadpoles that someone gave him, and he takes one tadpole after another and lets it fall and smash on the street below, but only when no one is coming along who might be hit, for he's very careful, since one time when he threw down a pot that nearly killed someone a terrible ruckus followed, Bubi's mother having to calm down the strange man because he was so upset that he threatened to call the police, after which Bubi got a spanking and was sent to his room for the entire afternoon, where he screamed loudly and cried that he would never do it again. For a long while afterward, he was not allowed on the balcony alone, having done worse things than Josef ever had, though when Josef points that out, his mother says, "You shouldn't just focus on the bad side of Bubi, especially when there are so many good things about him."

Meanwhile Josef has a nanny, the mother unable to watch over him as much because of all the time she must spend at the hospital, and because Aunt Betti can barely get by on her war relief she has to help Josef's father in the store and thus has less time for Josef, though this makes it easier for the father to run around, busy as he is, everyone having to work hard, which causes a lot of stress. It's become so hard to get essentials that Anna has to stand in long lines, and Aunt Gusti, too, which one cannot expect of the mother, since she's on her feet the entire day, though the father has connections and brings home flour or potatoes, all of which is incredibly expensive and just burns through their money.

The nanny's name is Jedlitschka, and she's thin and scrawny, the grandmother saying, "She doesn't even have enough strength to properly knead dough." The nanny's neckline reveals how much the bones in her chest stick out. Bubi doesn't like this, and says, "If that were my nanny I would simply throw her out." When Josef tells this to the mother, she replies, "You are an ungrateful child. Bubi and Kitti have Tata. They don't need a nanny. Their mother can shop. Why do I have to explain it all to you? Things are one way for them and another way for us." Josef likes the nanny very much, because she lets him do what he wants and he doesn't have to watch out what he does in the park, for she hardly keeps an eye on him as she talks with others or darns stockings, and whenever the weather is bad she plays fleas or fish with Josef at home. Fleas involves colorful buttons divided into six different colors so that six can play, though everyone plays alone, each person taking three different colors totaling eighteen buttons in all. There is also a large button that you use to flip the smaller buttons, the game requiring that you shoot your button accurately enough to land it on the other player's button, which you then take away, while whoever ends up with some buttons left is the winner. The game of fish is different. On the table you place a box made of cardboard that has four sides and is painted with fish, and you throw a bunch of paper fish into it, though old shoes, drowned cats, and other things are also thrown in to annoy the fisherman, while written on each fish is how much it weighs, with a little metal ring attached. The players get a pole, which is a wooden bar with a thread attached that is the line, from which hangs a magnet, which is the hook, whereupon each player dips his line into the pond, only one being allowed to do so at a time. Swishing around in the water, but without looking within, whoever is lucky pulls out a fish or several fish, though the unfortunate get nothing or a shoe or something else, the players continuing until the pond is empty, while whoever has caught the heaviest fish wins.

Fräulein Jedlitschka is very good at it, she has a lot of patience, but the grandmother is not pleased and says to the mother, "Mella, in my day it was different. Then the nanny would do some knitting or sewing while the child played on his own, and she just kept an eye on him." The mother replies, "Mama, please, let me worry about it. If you have something to say to me, please don't say it in front of Josef!" Then Josef responds, "The nanny plays really well. She doesn't just let me win at fishing, because she likes to win herself." Then the mother and the grandmother are angry with each other, the mother looking hard at the grandmother and sending Josef away and into the kitchen. Outside is Anna, who speaks warmly of her previous position, where she had spent eight years, the people there having been very good to her, there being no son to take care of, but rather a little girl named Angela, who is already grown, Anna still having a picture of her when she was very little, with two thick braids. She didn't have short hair like Kitti, who always cried when someone pulled her hair. "I'm gonna tell Tata! Bubi, you're so mean!" But Angela had been so well behaved, Anna always says, even to the mother, and she still gets letters from her, as well as colorful postcards at Christmas and Easter that are even more beautiful than those in Aunt Betti's collection, the mother saying, "Nothing is so precious as gratitude. See, Josef, you should take after Angela." But then Anna says, "Josef is also a sweet child, madam. God willing, he will also be a fine man."

The father also has a garden plot, because there is always less and less to eat. It's a large garden located on the edge of the city next to a brickworks, the father hacking away at the earth, though it takes too much out of him, and so he takes along Wenzel, a helper from the store, who also stays there the whole day through, the father also bringing along Josef and Bubi. The two of them have a large bed to themselves. There they grow pumpkins and radishes, potatoes and kohlrabi, lettuce and tomatoes, as well as poppies and strawberries and pretty flowers, though just a few, both of them liking to be out in the garden, because they like Wenzel, who is nice and lets them do what pleases them. They water the beds with a little watering can, then they yank out weeds, then Wenzel brings them coffee and something to eat, though they don't have to wash their hands.

Lots of people come to the garden on Sundays, Aunt Gusti saying, "There's hardly anywhere to go anymore. It's a blessing to be in God's nature and breathe a bit of fresh air. Josef, your father is so handy. We have him to thank for such splendor." Only the mother rarely comes, because she has to work, after which she's tired and needs rest, and she's happy to be home alone, though everyone else is there, sometimes Bubi's family as well, Wenzel, too, even though he doesn't have to be on Sundays, but he's gotten so used to being there that he wants to, yet Aunt Gusti says, "He only comes because he gets something from it as well, but your father takes good care of his people." Aunt Betti adds, "Wenzel also does most of the work, he deserves at least a couple of potatoes." This upsets Aunt Gusti, who says, "You never think of the family's interests, Betti. You're so strange." And when Bubi's father hears this he says, "Now let's not fight on such a beautiful Sunday. We should just enjoy the lovely sun instead. Who knows what next year will bring?" Then the grandmother says, "I agree completely. One never knows what will happen. Times change. In 1866, war was everywhere, and yet it wasn't as bad as it is today. Back then the Prussians invaded, yet there were far fewer dead than now, when the battlefields are much farther off." Bubi's father replies, "Yes, yes, that was quite a little war back then. Yet everything came out all right." But Aunt Gusti adds, "No, there's no way it was that pleasant. War is war." But Bubi's father counters, "We mustn't fight. What I once heard in Vienna is true. Whenever we've had enough of peace, then it's war, and that's a horror."

Then the quarreling is over, and Bubi's mother and Tata propose, "Now let's go and see how the cauliflower is doing." They head off, and the usual crowd lies down on extra blankets that were brought along, Bubi and Josef running around, though the father follows after the two women and shows them the beds, how everything is growing, how many potatoes can be planted, after which he cuts a couple of heads of cabbage and cauliflower for Bubi's mother, then pulls a pair of carrots out of the earth because they are so healthy, yet Josef doesn't eat them, except when raw, while Bubi wants nothing to do with spinach, because he thinks it's as disgusting as chicken shit, no one can eat it, though he does like carrots, his mother cooking them like nobody else, and if Josef doesn't want any it's only because no one knows how to cook at his house. But Josef says that's not true, Anna is a very good cook, she worked for Angela's parents for eight years and cooked everything there, and everyone liked it so much that they still wrote her letters, but nonetheless carrots are really awful, they can only be eaten raw, and for that they need to be fresh and tender and young, otherwise they turn your stomach, Josef's father not liking them at all. Then Bubi gets mad and continues complaining about spinach, wanting to rip it all out of the ground and throw it away, but Josef says, "Throwing stuff away is a sin. You should make use of everything. During war nothing should be thrown away, for the poor people are glad to have whatever they can get. That's what my Aunt Gusti told me."—"Okay, don't throw it away, just give it to the chickens or the geese, but the carrots I eat myself." Josef and Bubi argue loudly, and when Aunt Gusti notices she comes over and yells, "You two should be ashamed, arguing about food when there's a war on! Our brave recruits in the field would be thrilled to have fresh vegetables to eat for lunch. They often have to be satisfied with just a tiny bite of goulash out of a can."

Then Bubi becomes quite serious and says that he will become an officer, for then you have a servant and a horse and can order soldiers around. Bubi also has a lot of toys befitting an officer, such as tin soldiers, a helmet, a sword and sword belt, and a warship to play with in the bath. Josef has none of this, because his mother wants to spare children from the war as much as possible, they grow wild enough as it is, and if you raise them in the shadow of the war nothing good can come of it. But Josef doesn't care if he has war toys or not, though he likes to play with Bubi's weapons, and when Bubi is the general Josef is the adjutant and Kitti is the princess who needs to be saved, and so Kitti has to stay in the bedroom as Bubi and Josef initially storm the dining room, where there are trenches and barbed wire, the large table serving as a fortress that they carefully creep around, and even though there is no enemy to be found hiding out there, Bubi whispers, "Stinking foreigners," and very slowly crawls on his belly to the bedroom door, opening it just a bit at first, then ripping it wide open, though the enemy doesn't notice the heroes as Kitti lies on the sofa before the courageous warriors and screams, "Help! Help!" Then the heroes attack with mighty war cries, the sofa a dungeon where the unfortunate princess languishes. Quickly she is freed, and she is so thankful that she decorates her rescuers with laurels made of paper, but before they know it Tata is before them and says, "You can't keep playing war forever. Too much hellish noise! Who can stand it?"

Fräulein Jedlitschka can stand only quiet games, for everything else gets on her nerves, frightening her and making her skittish, so that Aunt Gusti says, "The nanny is very good, but she's too squeamish. A child needs to romp around, so he doesn't turn into a dormouse." But Aunt Gusti herself is afraid of thunderstorms because they crackle so. She just doesn't show it, for one has to control oneself and serve as a good example for the young ones growing up, and she wants to break Josef of the habit of indulging himself in so many silly fears. It's especially ridiculous in regard to dogs, especially when Josef wanders off on his own, and yet ends up afraid of every dog he encounters, even if it's muzzled and on a leash, his aunt saying, "A dog is man's best friend, remaining at his side no matter the danger. There's no reason to be afraid, dogs don't like it when you are. That's when they'll bite you." But Josef doesn't believe his aunt, because dogs have evil eyes, they bark so loudly, and their howls cause fear, at which Aunt Gusti laughs, for it's all in his imagination. One day she goes for a walk with Josef, and on the street there's a little wagon with a dog harnessed to it, a large brown mutt, and the aunt goes up to him because she wants to demonstrate how good-natured he is, she rubbing his neck and saying to the animal, "You beastie, you, you precious, sweet beastie, isn't that so? You wouldn't hurt anyone, would you?" Then she looks at Josef and prods him, saying, "Don't you see how obedient he is? He loves to be petted. Try it!" He tries to get his courage up, he wants to try to pet it and stretches his hand toward the mutt, but the dog growls and snaps at him. "That's only because you're afraid. He senses it, and that's why he snaps."—"I didn't tell the dog I was afraid. He also wouldn't know if I'm lying, for I didn't say anything that would cause my nose to grow long." Then the aunt is upset and she says, "You are an incorrigible child. It's a nasty dog, but almost all dogs are good."

Otherwise Josef is interested in animals and has a natural-history book with many pictures, which he loves more than many of his other books, his mother having given it to him so that he wouldn't always be asking about the carp and the earthworms or whatever. Bubi, however, isn't really interested in animals, because they are dumb, only the horse being clever and the elephant, though it's a shame there are so few elephants here, but Tata says it's only because such large animals have to eat such incredible amounts, and it's nearly impossible to fill them up, and everything is so precarious, so many poor people who can hardly buy enough for themselves. The grandmother adds that there have always been poor people, her blessed father having to worry about nine children, all of them having grown up to be people of good standing, though they are now gone, but at least they never had to see how terrible the world has become. Hard work and honor used to mean something, but now there are war speculators everywhere who hoard everything and then sell it on the black market and get rich, while others keep on the straight and narrow and yet pay the price, not being long for this life.

That's why the mother likes Frau Machleidt, a dear widow with two boys, Egon and Helmut, who lives in a single room with a kitchen that is dark and in which you can't even turn around. But Aunt Betti says that it's a model of cleanliness and tidiness, everything laid out in perfect order, such that one can appreciate the saying "Cleanliness is next to godliness." Aunt Betti loves this saying so much that she has often embroidered it and given it to the mother and to Aunt Gusti, as well as to many others, it also adorning the wall of Frau Machleidt's kitchen. There one can just barely read it when there's enough light, there also being a towel that is embroidered with red letters, the script lovelier than either the father or Fräulein Reimann can do, as it says:

> To cover up the broom
> Use me in any room.

And behind it there really are brooms, right in the middle of the kitchen, though properly concealed, while Anna always sticks the brooms in the closet, because the mother says that brooms don't belong in the kitchen, where everything should be clean and bright, especially the oilcloth, white and ready for washing, there being no need for soap. And there are lovely porcelain canisters in the kitchen, the mother very fond of them, though Anna says that they create dust, while the contents are printed on each, be it rice, cornmeal, breadcrumbs, flour, coffee, beans, even though there is nothing in them, the canisters there only for decoration, while small amounts of spices are indeed inside them, and there's salt in the salt shaker. The nicest thing in the kitchen was the mortar, all shiny and glowing, Anna grinding away with the white pestle for an hour, filling little packets, the mortar spick and span and bright as gold, though now it is gone, anything made of copper or brass having been confiscated and taken away, the same being true of the entire building. All the fixtures in the hallway, as well as the red furnace in the bathroom, have been taken away for the benefit of the emperor and the war, because brass is needed for the cannons, and everything the soldiers need has to be there for them. As a result the family has to give up many things, now a mortar made of iron standing in the kitchen, all black and unable to be polished to a sheen, as the mother looks at it sadly, though Fräulein Reimann says that is their duty to the fatherland, and after the war is over and won everything will be right again.

Frau Machleidt comes for a day or two each month to do the sewing, and she also goes to Ludwig's mother and others, so that she has enough work in general, sewing shirts and underwear and repairing most anything, since one has to scrimp these days, and one rarely buys new clothes. Frau Machleidt doesn't go to Bubi's house, for Tata sews everything there, making clothes for Kitti and for Bubi's mother and herself that Frau Machleidt doesn't know how to make, though the latter sews faster than Tata, everyone ending up happy with the situation, for Frau Machleidt doesn't take breaks, Anna placing the midmorning snack and coffee on the sewing machine, where Frau Machleidt eats with one hand and sews with the other. Josef likes to go in and watch her, for Frau Machleidt likes to talk with him and explains how the sewing machine works, a thread running down from above and up from below in order to hold everything togther nice and tight.

Josef always wants to see what it looks like when the machine turns, because he likes to see the thread wind onto the shuttle since it's so wonderful to see, and Frau Machleidt does just that. Her life had once been happier, when her husband, who was as good as Josef's own father, was alive, everyone liking Herr Machleidt, but when Helmut was one his father became very sick, and several doctors were consulted, each of them shaking his head and saying, Dear Frau Machleidt, you must prepare yourself for the worst, though she continued to hope, because her husband had been so strong, and she loved him very much, and prayed to God above to make Herr Machleidt healthy again, but it did no good, as the sickness got worse and worse, and the doctors could do no more. Then Herr Machleidt died peacefully in his sleep, and she was alone with the children amid dire need, thus Josef should be thankful because he still had his dear parents, or so said Frau Machleidt, for you have only one set of parents, otherwise there are only stepparents, though Frau Machleidt never wanted to marry again, not wanting a stepfather for the children, because she didn't think it was good for them, at which Aunt Gusti grew annoyed and said, "Even complete strangers are sometimes better than your own parents. Frau Machleidt is unreasonable, and not everyone has such good parents as you do, Josef." Frau Machleidt didn't take it well when Josef told her what Aunt Gusti had said. "Child, that is mean of you. You shouldn't just spit out anything that you hear." Josef doesn't know why he shouldn't do that, because the mother always says that you shouldn't keep secrets, especially a child, nor does Josef want others to do so, because he wants to know everything.

Bubi and Ludwig have lots of secrets and often tell them to Josef, saying that he can't tell them to anyone else, though he doesn't agree, which is why he never swears to, refusing to commit to either his most earnest or even most casual word of honor, though he does say, "If you don't want to tell me, then I don't have to know." Then they tell him everything anyway, after which Bubi says, "If you tell anyone, you're a no-good creep, and I'll be mad at you." Josef doesn't want that and therefore he says nothing, even though he hasn't promised anything, and it wouldn't be a sin if he did say something, but he betrays nothing. Josef believes that real secrets are only those you keep to yourself, and they are only what you believe and would say to no one, because you wouldn't know what to say if you did, and such secrets will exist until you know everything, but even then you'll know how everything is and how it is not, and you'll be able to say just how it is so, but when you're young you still have to search for the truth and ask questions, and, when no one wants to tell you, you have to ask again and again until you have learned everything and know it all.

The mother knows almost everything, but Josef is uncertain whether the father does, because the father has so much to do, and when you are allowed to talk to him he is so tired that you can't ask him any kind of hard question, as he says, "Child, that's what books are for, or ask someone at school." Aunt Gusti knows a great deal, since she is a teacher, but she doesn't know enough, because she says, "You never stop learning. You have to keep applying yourself in order to learn from more gifted people." Aunt Betti doesn't believe that and says, "I don't need to know everything. Everyone knows enough for himself. That's enough for me." The grandmother knows a lot, for she remembers the father when he was little and much more that happened before then, but she doesn't like that Josef asks so many questions. "You'll soon see. We do the best we can for you." Fräulein Reimann also knows a good deal, but she has too little time and has to explain everything to the entire class, and because many of them don't understand she has to repeat herself ten times, and yet still the children don't know anything, thus making the teacher mad when she has to give them bad grades. Anna doesn't know much, but she says, "I don't need to know a lot. Whoever works doesn't have to have a lot in his head. But Angela was such a clever child that she astounded people with how gifted she was as a little girl."

Bubi always says that all girls are dumb, only Kitti is smart and will marry a prince who will carry her off in his carriage, but she's still a little girl, younger than Angela was, and she knows very little, though Tata is very proud of her, since Kitti can already count to ten, as Tata says, "What a little scamp! No one even taught her. She learned it all by herself." But Kitti certainly didn't learn it all by herself, for it was Bubi who showed her again and again, showing her on the adding machine in order to teach Kitti, for she couldn't do it on her own. Bubi also thinks that Tata is not too smart, otherwise she wouldn't work so much, though whoever is clever is paid a lot, like his father, who is a director, everyone having to call him Herr Director, though he's not the same as the director of a school. Bubi thinks that if he doesn't become a general he'll be a director, though general is much better, at which Bubi asks Josef what he wants to be. Josef, however, doesn't want to say that he'd really like to be a streetcar conductor, that it's the best job, because you ride through the city all day and see so many people, as he's embarrassed and worried that Bubi will laugh at him, so he says that he doesn't know.

Fräulein Jedlitschka knows hardly anything, and everyone agrees that she's so dumb that she can only play games and nothing more, for she is so bad at darning socks that the grandmother says she has to redo them herself, because the Fräulein mends the holes with thread in such a way that they all rip open again and are worse yet. Now the girl has to go away because she has taken something, and there's nothing worse than taking things without asking permission, though Josef doesn't know what the girl has taken, and Anna has not told him. "That's none of my business. That's your mother's business. I've never taken anything. I worked for eight years for Angela's parents." On Sunday the family sits together and talks about the nanny, and the mother says, "There's a saying in English that one should never take as much as a needle. Josef, there's nothing worse in the world than to take something that doesn't belong to you." The father then says, "The child doesn't understand at all, Mella. We shouldn't involve him in this business. Josef, run along and play." The mother replies, "You're right, Papa." And then the grandmother, "Get rid of her, I say, get rid of her! No one wants to be looking over your shoulder all the time." But Aunt Betti says, "That will cause bad blood. You should give the nanny a letter tomorrow morning in which you suggest that she should look for a new position, since, unfortunately, you have to dispense with her services." Yet Aunt Gusti says, "Excessive kindness is also wrong. You just have to say to her without insulting her, 'We're sorry, Fräulein Jedlitschka, but we've decided to let you go at the end of the month. Please make the necessary arrangements.' " The father, however, disagrees. "I like a clean slate. I will give the nanny her last pay tomorrow and say that she doesn't need to come back." And then everyone says, "That's much too good a deal. You'd have to say so yourself, Oskar!" The grandmother then says, "If you're going to pay her what she has coming, then she should work for it as well. Everything needs to come to a good end, and then nothing more will come of it." The mother agrees, and no one else is against it, all of them agreed, all of them saying that there will not be another nanny, for they are done with nannies.

Now Fräulein Jedlitschka has to play somewhere else, with another child, so Josef wants to make sure to hide his toys so that she doesn't take any away with her, but in reality he is sad, though he's also glad, because Bubi can't stand her and says a proper young man doesn't need any such thing, he'd rather have a butler to wait on him. But butlers don't exist anymore, because there are no more men available for work, and even in the streetcar there are now female conductors who wear uniforms exactly like male conductors, and have a proper badge and wear a gray jacket like men, though they don't wear pants, the grandmother saying, "It's a scandal that they run around like that. In my day one would never have let a woman be gawked at on the street." But Aunt Gusti says it's great for the women, there's no reason for them to be ashamed, and the mother also thinks that the women are just fine. She bemoans the fact of how proper her parents were, otherwise she would have studied medicine, and then Georg Diamant and Herr Machleidt would still be alive, and the mother would be of much greater use in the hospital, for she would then be an orthopedic doctor, but her good father had only allowed her to study to be a good nurse and a certified gymnastics teacher and masseuse, because those were female occupations, though Aunt Betti says, "A proper woman belongs at home. It's scandalous that women must do everything these days, for the man is the breadwinner of the family. A real woman belongs at the stove. The war is to blame. My Paul would never have allowed during normal times that I should slave away in a store, and do it all on my own, though I do it because Oskar means so much to me." Aunt Gusti then adds, "I have no problem with women entering any profession and not just remaining done-up dolls who don't know how to do anything. You can trudge through life like Frau Machleidt, but how much better it would go for her if someone had taught her how to properly cut cloth. Then she wouldn't have to go from house to house looking for any work she can find. . . . She could have her own dress salon." Aunt Betti replies, "You wouldn't talk so if you had married!" This really upsets Aunt Gusti, and the mother thinks it's all terrible talk and doesn't understand why Aunt Betti has to hurt Aunt Gusti so, but the father has had enough and laughs and says something in partial Czech, which no one understands: "zum Pukken prasken."

Then everyone plays tarot, including the father, the grandmother, and the aunts, but not the mother, she doesn't like cards that much, and the father also says that she plays so badly that she can't tell the king from the queen. Josef would indeed like to play as well, but that's not allowed when everyone is there, they want to play themselves, and so they say that tarot is not a game for children, who have only two card games they can play, Black Peter and Quartet. Josef doesn't have any Black Peter cards, and whenever Bubi and other children come over they play Black Peter with tarot cards, which means he uses The Fool for Black Peter, but he has only three quartets—a flower quartet, a composer's quartet, and then one that is really beautiful, which is called The Age of Greatness. On it are the emperors of Austria and Germany, as well as the king of Bulgaria and the sultan, this quartet being called The State Leaders of the Middle Countries, though there are also enemy leaders, namely the czar of Russia, the kings of England and Italy, and the president of France, in addition to all the heroes, lots of archdukes and princes, field marshals and generals, admirals, U-boat commanders and fighter pilots, all the friendly ones adorned with flags and oak leaves, while all the enemies have loads of weapons, Bubi liking the quartet so much that his mother gave him one as well for his birthday, which pleased him no end.

Fräulein Jedlitschka is now gone, and she didn't take anything of Josef's, but instead everything went smoothly as through thick tears she said good-bye to the mother, whom she said she would never forget, she was so grateful, it was the nicest time of her entire life, the mother also deeply moved as they shook hands for the longest time. "Thank you so much. I wish you much future happiness, and I hope you have a wonderful life." Then the girl kissed the mother's hand and was gone, even though she never looked at Josef again. But the mother doesn't like having her hand kissed and never allows Anna to do so, though Anna wants to very much, especially whenever she receives a nice gift, for the mother always says, "A genuine grown-up doesn't do that and doesn't need for it to be done. One should express one's gratitude through simple respect."

Now that Fräulein Jedlitschka is gone, Josef is alone more often, but he likes to be alone, for that gives him the chance to read many books, and the mother lets him take some from the bookshelves, though not just any and always just one at a time. Josef is now at Aunt Gusti's more frequently than before, since she suggested that she could help the mother more with taking care of him. The mother is so stressed of late, since she is often at the hospital for the entire day, there being ever more wounded soldiers who need a massage. Which means that Anna has to do everything at home, with only the grandmother to help her out now and then, though everyone is happy with Anna, she's a wonderful cook, and the mother has only to tell her what needs to be done and she does it as well as can be done in the midst of this war. Bubi's father is also now enlisted, a first lieutenant, though he doesn't, thank God, have to go to the battlefield itself, since he has a stiff leg, so instead he trains recruits on the exercise fields, Bubi only sorry that he can't be there, though his mother says, "Don't think, Bubi, that it's any great thrill trudging along with a bunch of farmer boys who don't know what right or left is!" However, Bubi demonstrates how well he can march, since he is the best at gymnastics in his class, and he understands all the commands and barks out orders loud enough to make the panes rattle in the windows.

The father's store is now closed, because he doesn't have enough goods to sell and it's not worth opening each day just for repairs, and since one makes so little off them they're nothing but a bother. Now the father spends a lot more time at the garden plot with Wenzel, who has built a wooden shack there, though most mornings the father goes to work with the war blind. He shows them how they can earn their daily bread, though of late it's been difficult to do even this, as paper leather cannot be found, for despite the father's running from one official to the next, he still comes back empty-handed. Meanwhile Ludwig's father is at last home, having been granted a long leave, and Ludwig's mother hopes that he never has to go back to the field, for he's so miserable, even though his wounds are light, just a bit of shrapnel, though they had ulcerated badly, someone calling them boils, for they hadn't been treated right. The mother says that it's a shame, as she scoffs at every diagnosis, knowing how unsanitary the field hospitals are, and how bad things happen to the wounded there that need not happen at all, some getting gangrene, for whom almost all hope is lost, thus causing many brave soldiers to die. But luckily Ludwig's father has no gangrene, only boils that cause a lot of pain. Josef knows just what it feels like, for he once had boils and had trouble sitting, and the doctor said that they were caused by undigested cornmeal, after which all kinds of things were mixed in with it and Josef had to eat rusk biscuits, as well as being prescribed extra milk, but since he didn't like to drink it the mother told Anna to make it into pudding, which he liked very much.

Breaks from school are frequent now, even if they are not vacations, mainly because so many children are sick that half the class is missing. At other times there's no school for other reasons, such as if there is no coal and the furnace cannot be lit, or there are fewer and fewer class hours, as well as another school being set up in Josef's school as several classrooms are turned over to the many wounded, since fewer and fewer students come to school. But Ludwig's father is not in any school, he's fine at home, even if he spends a lot of time lying down, and he just has a leave since it was only boils, though that is not the only thing that exists in the field hospital. Dysentery has also broken out, and it is a very bad sickness that weakens men entirely, such that they can hardly sleep or keep any food down, many of them dying. Everyone says that Ludwig's father is very lucky, for though he's a bit weak, he's getting stronger and is sitting up in bed and in an arm-chair, but no one is allowed to visit him and Josef doesn't go to see him, only the father having visited once with the mother after he said, "At least we should make an appearance in case they need anything that I can get for them." Then they visited and took along some real coffee and a little cocoa. Ludwig's mother was so happy that she sent Josef a lovely book the next day, Ludwig bringing it to him.

Josef is very fond of Ludwig of late, and Ludwig comes over a lot in order that his father has more quiet for himself, which means that Josef sees less of Bubi, who doesn't want to come over when Ludwig is there, it being awful that time when Bubi came by once and at the door asked Anna, "Is Ludwig in there?" Anna had replied, "Come on in, Bubi, Ludwig is already with Josef inside." Then Bubi made a terrible face and slammed the door so hard that Anna almost fainted, later telling the mother that she wasn't going to take that from some little squirt, she simply won't let him in the next time he comes around, and that will be easy to do, as there's a peephole in the door, just like at the panorama, though only one, Wenzel always being the one to install things in the apartment, and in this case he had made a little cover out of leather for the peephole which you had to push to the side when you wanted to look through and see who was outside, the parents having reminded Anna to be very careful and make sure the chain was engaged and that Anna should let in no one she didn't know, even if he said he was collecting on behalf of the wounded or for the emperor and held some kind of list in his hand, and also if he said he was from the Red Cross, not to mention never a complete stranger, for there were so many bad people running around and taking advantage of people's good intentions, and you hear terrible reports of attacks and of people being beaten because they were not careful enough. Josef should never open the door or even come to it, even if someone rings twice, for untrustworthy people also know how to make such a sign, and no one knows who is really standing on the steps outside. Anna has also become cautious, and she says that her life is much too precious to hand over to such a scoundrel, so she trusts no one as long as this war persists. But there's no reason for Anna not to allow Bubi in, says the mother, and she will speak with his mother in order to make sure that such rudeness doesn't happen again, and that Bubi apologizes to Anna for his misbehavior. To that Anna had said that she wasn't nobility, so no one had to apologize to her, but Bubi just had to not be so fresh in the future and she would let him in. Indeed, Ludwig was pleased that Bubi had been so fresh, but only because he hadn't been allowed in. "Bubi can be so snotty," Ludwig says. "He thinks that he's better than all the other kids because his father is now a first lieutenant. But he hides out by the goulash cannons, where there is no shrapnel. Bubi just marches around and won't talk to anyone, nor does anyone want anything to do with him. He struts like a peacock." But Josef is still very fond of Bubi, who yesterday gave him half a pomegranate, it being the first time he'd ever tasted one, at which Ludwig said, "If he had given me ten pomegranates, I would have tossed them right back. He can have them all to himself."

One time the father says that things are bad, he doesn't believe any longer that the emperor can win the war. "It's all rotten through and through." Josef then asks what will happen if the emperor loses the war. "I don't know, son. But I'd advise you not to say a word to anyone about what

I said. Otherwise they could lock you up for treason, as well as your mother and me." But no one at school says anything, they only collect more money for the war, and since victory is at hand and our glorious troops will soon return home in triumph we will want to welcome them in a grand fashion. The newspapers that arrive each morning also say everything is going well, all the articles talking about the victories that our brave troops have accomplished once again. Aunt Betti is thrilled that the war will soon come to an end, for then Uncle Paul will come home, as long as he is not taken prisoner at the last moment, which would of course be terrible, though she firmly believes that nothing will happen, because he writes so confidently that the outlook is good. Aunt Gusti has also taken on an extra responsibility assumed by all women of the fatherland, namely to visit the war widows, as she tries to comfort them by observing how miserable it is everywhere and how it would really be best for the war to finally be over, saying, "Better a bad end than no end at all!" Every day she runs around, and when she has no lessons she has a list of addresses to visit, and she does what she can for the widows, learning in the process how bad things really are everywhere.

At school Hugo Treml says that his father has been awarded the Signum Laudis, which is a great honor for the entire family, Josef's mother having said so as well, for which they have a small party and drink rose-hip wine that the mother made herself, Josef also getting a small glass, the wine itself so sweet and sparkling as they toast the uncle and the emperor, convinced that victory is near, everyone proud of the uncle, Fräulein Reimann saying, "Your uncle is really something, Treml. You and all the children should follow his example. But even if you don't have a Signum Laudis you can still be a good man and still aspire to be something. In these terrible times the children should above all be thankful and cause their parents no worry. Everyone has to use their last bit of strength and each do what he can!" Only Eiberheit laughs in response from the last bench, which makes the teacher very mad as she replies, "You should be ashamed to laugh so! If everyone was as lazy as you and did nothing, we'd have no men at all who could be decorated with the Signum Laudis. If we didn't have such heroes, your homeland would not still be free and we'd have the Russians here. And yet they've been cast out, and you can go back home with Pieposberger and Flamminger, who have already left." Eiberheit, however, is not ashamed, though he doesn't say another word and is completely quiet as the class looks around at him, while the next day he doesn't come back to school, nor does he ever again, the teacher announcing one time, "Eiberheit has gone away with his mother and all his siblings without saying where to. That's the way the Poles do it. But we don't have to regret his departure." Fräulein Reimann also says that the situation is serious enough that, even though Treml's uncle had been decorated, people were going to have to store up for winter in order to make it through, each needing to help the other, the children needing to pitch in as well and not just play with their toys, for they need to be serious, because the times are so serious.

Josef now has terrible stomachaches that come on quite suddenly, at which he lies down on the sofa and holds his stomach, no one able to help him, though Anna is nice and brings him a warm compress, which she has carefully rolled up in a brown rag, so that Josef always has a compress on his stomach, though it continues to hurt. Aunt Gusti can't believe that a stomach can hurt that much, for stomachaches are more of an annoyance than anything, but Josef doesn't get the kind of upset stomachs that Aunt Gusti gets, his hurt lower down, the pain coming in sharp bursts, causing him to feel quite hot, and it's no better if he closes his eyes, but he doesn't want to keep them open, so he closes them anyway. Once a week Aunt Gusti has a migraine, for which she takes some powder that then causes her to barf, though the mother can't stand that word and has forbidden Josef to use it, because she says it is foul and is used only by crass, vile people, even though Aunt Gusti has herself used it, and she's not vile, only the migraines are vile. When they occur Aunt Gusti can no longer visit the war widows, but she can give lessons from her sofa, where she lies with a damp cloth that she continually freshens and places on her forehead, next to her on the floor a bucket of water into which she dips the cloth every half hour, wringing it out and laying it on her brow once again, the cool water helping a bit, though the aunt's face remains entirely green and she looks like an old woman, her hair disheveled because she has so much hair and she has squashed it so while lying there, wearing a shabby yellow nightgown that's seen better days, spots and stains all over it, the father not at all pleased with how the aunt lets herself go, though the mother says, "Don't be so heartless, Oskar. One can't help pitying Gusti. She has a heart of gold. Which is why you just have to forgive her for not being as fussy about her appearance when she has a migraine." But the father replies, "She's always a slob, not just when she has a migraine." The mother doesn't like it at all when the father talks about his sister that way, though Aunt Betti also believes that Aunt Gusti doesn't take good enough care and often spills something on herself, or she always eats sour pickles, which don't sit well with her, and even though they remind her of this a hundred times over, she won't hear anything of it, there being no help for those who won't listen.

When Aunt Gusti is so bad off, the grandmother comes and cooks for her and helps out in the house, but even when the aunt is so ill she still gives lessons, though some children dread coming to her and want to get away as soon as they can, migraines being a terrible sickness, the aunt continuing to take medicine that helps only a little. Josef doesn't understand how doctors are worth anything, for they can't do anything to help most illnesses, and maybe Tata is right when she says, "Nature has its own healing ways." Josef asks the mother why there are doctors at all if they know so little about how to heal sickness, and if perhaps a book like *The Housewife as Doctor* isn't enough in itself, since everything is inside it, though the mother explains that medicine is actually the greatest science and art one can practice, there is not a more wonderful profession anywhere, for nowhere else can you help so many people, and without doctors things would be much worse, advances are continually being made. For example, when the mother was as old as Josef is now there was hardly any way of filling teeth, so they just had to be ripped out, which hurts a lot, and isn't it wonderful how today you can be X-rayed if you break a foot, which was once not possible, the bones often not healing properly as a result. "Many illnesses that cannot yet be healed today will perhaps be able to be healed when you grow up and are a doctor yourself."

But it will be a while before Josef has to decide about becoming a doctor, though this week his birthday will be on Thursday, and since there is school that afternoon the party is held off until Saturday, and for the most part is organized by Aunt Betti. Yet first thing on Thursday a birthday table is laid out with a proper birthday cake on it, a bean cake, which Anna says tastes almost like an almond cake, this one homemade and filled with real marmalade, which the father says tastes like soap, while on top of the cake is written "For Josef," Anna having written it with sugar, eight burning candles encircling it, since Josef is now eight, he only tasting a little bit of the cake in order that it doesn't give him a stomachache, though he gets lots of fancy presents, the aunts and the grandmother having sent over their gifts, both toys and practical things, some books, and lots of sweet things to eat. Josef is happy, and it's good that he doesn't have school until the afternoon, for that allows him to play with all his presents, after which he can tell the others in the class what he got, how good his parents are, he announcing to Fräulein Reinmann, "Today's my birthday!" The teacher laughs and says, "How wonderful. Happy birthday, and I hope that you always bring your loving parents great joy!"

All the relatives come to the children's birthday party, except the grandmother, because she says, "I can't stand so much ruckus. But to make up for it we'll go to the panorama." All the others arrive, and Aunt Betti is particularly excited, for she has arranged it all with Anna so that it will all come off well, for these days it's very hard to have a birthday party. They all have on their best clothes, Anna having put together a white frock with some lace the mother lent her.

Aunt Gusti wants to play something on the piano and the mother wants to sing along, but first Josef has to recite a poem that Aunt Betti has written herself, which is about a special pond full of presents, each child needing to fish one out, as the poem explains:

> Give it a try, and here's a plan:
> Reel in the best thing that you can.

Aunt Betti is proud of having written the poem, the father saying, as always when she writes a special birthday poem, that she has a poetic streak in her. For his grandmother's birthday Josef has to memorize a poem, upon which he goes to her, dressed in his best suit, holding a flower in his right hand, the grandmother completely surprised as she sits at a table covered with a white cloth. The grandmother looks Josef in the eye, and as the mother gives him a sign to begin, he recites the poem, after which he gives her the bouquet, the grandmother's face flooding with happiness as she kisses him and gives him a little something in appreciation.

But Josef must recite the poem about the magic pond because little gifts have been prepared for everyone, though they could be nicer than they actually are. Nonetheless, all the gifts are wrapped and a large loop is attached to each little packet, a fishing pole devised from a cane that is much larger than the one that Fräulein Jedlitschka used, and on the pole there is a line that doesn't have a magnet attached to it but rather a hook that is then used to hook the loops of the little packets when anyone fishes for them, the packets piled up in a corner of the dining room, which serves as the magic pond. Anna reminisces how Angela also used to have birthday parties, and she was so pretty and all dressed up, but those were better times, the children drinking real hot chocolate with whipped cream on top, which hasn't been available for years, since there is hardly any real milk, the father complaining that they are always thinning it with more water, such that it can't even develop a proper skin. Meanwhile the doorbell rings, again and again, more and more children arriving who are brought along by someone, though only the children can stay, the grown-ups heading off and asking when they should pick them up, as they remind the children to behave and always say thank you, and not to cause trouble no matter what, so that they'll be invited back again.

Anna and the mother are outside in the foyer, the chain no longer on, since so many keep arriving and the children able to be heard as they come up the steps, as Anna opens the door before they even ring, and the children are led into the living room, all of them dressed up in their good clothes. Bubi and Kitti are there, as well as Ludwig, and though they act as if they don't know each other, they don't make a fuss, many other children also there whom Josef has played with in the park, a number of them having a younger brother or sister who is very small and hardly talks at all, Ernst with the long hair also there, and classmates such as Hugo Treml, though there are also other children Josef doesn't know at all, or just barely, they being not from his school or from the park but belonging to friends of his aunts. These children are very well-mannered and don't speak to anyone unless a grown-up asks them something, Paul Wetzler being such a child, who belongs to a friend of Aunt Gusti's, though Josef had visited him once and still recalled the birthday party they had put on, the Wetzlers being very rich. They had a real magician, who stood on a table and did many tricks with a

watch and with cards and with a diabolo and with balls and with handker-
chiefs and with eggs, though they weren't real eggs but white stones, the
magician also pulling gifts for the children out of his hat, then calling up
each child and, strangely enough, presenting him with a gift, the smaller
children afraid of the magician, though he said that he wouldn't hurt them
and no one should be afraid.

Once the children are all gathered together in the living room, the
mother says that she hopes they will all get along and have a fine time today,
because Josef turned eight the day before yesterday, and everyone hopes
that he'll be a fine young man. The children listen quietly as the mother
speaks, though they don't pay attention much, many looking around and
making funny faces. Then Aunt Gusti tells everyone to pay attention, because she is going to play something on the piano by Robert Schumann,
who was a great composer who wrote lots of beautiful music, and because he
loved children so he had written music for them, even though he wrote
other music that was not especially for children, because it was too difficult
and was instead just about children, though that which he had written for
children is delightful, and from which the aunt would like to play, as she
proceeds to present three pieces, one of which is called "The Merry Peasant." A little girl about the same age as Kitti, but much dumber, immediately begins to cry and says that she wants to go home, Aunt Betti going to
her and telling her that she has to be quiet so that others can hear the music,
saying that she must behave, because afterward there will be many good
things to eat and lots of surprises, after which she is quiet and only sniffles.
Then Aunt Gusti is soon done at the piano, and as she finishes, all of the
children cheer and clap, pleasing the aunt deeply, after which she says that
she was happy to play, especially as it brought pleasure to others. And then
the mother begins to sing, Aunt Gusti accompanying her as they do a number of lovely songs, such as "The Mill Wheel Turns" and "Do You Know
How Many Stars There Are?" Josef loves these songs, and the children are
pleased as well, all of them singing with soft, sweet voices, though the
grown-ups like to sing, too, there being once a month a pleasant musical
evening put on by the soldiers at the hospital, Josef having been allowed to
go the last time, when a man in a tuxedo had played a piano and his mother
had sung and everyone applauded loudly, while those who could not clap

because they were missing a hand had loudly called out "Bravo! Bravo!" and the mother had to sing another song and yet another, as she grew more and more pleased and smiled, until finally she said so sweetly that she could do no more, for there was lots more to come on the program, though she hoped she would have the chance to sing again if it pleased others for her to do so.

The mother had sung only three songs for the children, ending with "Sweetheart Mine," after which it was time, Aunt Betti anxious to move things along, Anna having already quietly opened the door four times to place two pitchers on the table, which today is set and doesn't have any dish towels on it, but rather a real tablecloth, the pitchers sitting there full of cocoa, as well as a proper cake made of flour, which no one has anymore, as well as cookies and gingerbread stars, all of the children surprised as Aunt Betti exclaims, "So, children, you've listened so sweetly. But you don't have to keep listening forever. Now it's time to talk and eat!" Everyone helps out and leads the children to the long table, and for the smallest who are too little there are chairs with high pillows so that the little tots sit no lower than the bigger kids and they can all reach across the table with their hands. As they all sit there in front of their plates and stare at the cups full of cocoa, and as the mother and Aunt Gusti place cake on the plates and hand out sweets, the children look pleased and happy just to see the way the steam rises from the cups, the mother laughing with delight and saying, "All right, help yourselves and enjoy!" Then they all eat and drink, and soon there are stains on the white tablecloth, but no one scolds them, the grown-ups not even sitting down, as today they are the servants and the children are the masters, the adults serving them, though the father looks exhausted and sits in a corner, the mother bringing him a cup of cocoa that he holds in his hand, now and then taking a sip, though he eats nothing, nor do the other grown-ups, since they are too busy and Aunt Betti's face is bloodred.

Finally the children have eaten everything, Anna starts clearing the table, the others helping, and then the table is shoved aside so that there is more space in the living room, all of the chairs placed in a row, as they begin to play games, though someone announces that two children have to go out, which they do, after which the musical chairs continues, but then one chair is knocked over so hard that it breaks, which will give Wenzel something to fix, as Aunt Betti says, "Children, that's too wild! This won't do! We need to play some games that are a little less lively!" And then Bubi says that he and Kitti have a big surprise, which he had said nothing about because Tata had said that he shouldn't, but that now Kitti would like to dance and Bubi would accompany her on the harmonica, to which the mother says, "How wonderful of you both to play something for our party! Go ahead and begin!" And so Bubi begins to blow on his harmonica as loud as he can, though he's not that loud, since a harmonica is not as loud as an accordion, as Kitti begins to dance around so strangely, lowering her skirt and raising first one leg and then the other like a chicken in the yard, and then she lowers the skirt again and spreads her hands wide, the mother and the aunts saying how charming she is, some of the other children pleased as well, the father laughing, though some of the children don't pay attention and just sit there biting their fingernails. Josef doesn't like the dance and such dumb blowing on the harmonica, for he never thought of Bubi as being so childish, especially since he wanted to be a general, and Ludwig comes over to Josef and says, "This dancing is stupid. Now you see what an idiot Bubi is." Josef half believes so himself, but he won't admit it to Ludwig, who has upset him by saying that, so Josef doesn't say a word. But finally the dance is over, almost everyone delighted and amazed by Kitti as they praise her, saying oh, how graceful, what a surprise, and Aunt Betti kisses Kitti on the forehead, though Bubi says that Tata had known that it would be precious, which is why she had sewn this dress special from an old nightgown with lace in order that one be able to dance well within it, to which Kitti adds, "I danced real nice! I danced real nice! I danced real nice!" Then the mother says, "If I understand correctly, my dear, you danced very well!"

Then the doorbell rings again and Anna comes in saying that Frau Wetzler's nanny is there and Paul must head home already, as Aunt Betti says, "Yes indeed, it's getting late, but the nanny should wait a minute. We're almost through here." And then the aunt says that it's time for the biggest surprise of all, one that will certainly please everybody, with something the children will never forget. Then Josef recites the poem that Aunt Betti has written, as she also opens the door to the next room, right at the conclusion of the final line, "Reel in the best thing that you can!," while Josef makes an inviting gesture with his hand, pointing to the door, just as he and Aunt

Betti had rehearsed in order that it look really elegant, it having taken a long time to get right. Then everyone goes into the next room, each child getting a turn with the pole as he is blindfolded and has to fish for a packet, while outside the bell rings more and more often, the foyer grows full, as well as the entire apartment, more and more people arriving, all of the children needing to head home, such that they give up on the blindfold in order to wrap up the magic pond more quickly, though it still takes too long, and the father says, "Whoever doesn't have a present yet should just grab one, though please, one at a time!" Then all the children do indeed have a present, though there are some left over, since there had been so many, and more children had been invited than had come. Now the last guests finally leave, but the foyer is still full of people looking for the children's coats, until everything is sorted out and the last step down the stairs is heard.

And once all the guests have left, how tired everyone is, the entire apartment a shambles, the place hardly recognizable, several things having been broken, not just the chair that Wenzel will have to fix but also two glasses that Wenzel can do nothing with. Then the aunts also say goodbye, Aunt Gusti telling the mother, "Mella, you need to finally get that piano tuned." Then there is only the mother and the father, Anna off in the kitchen, washing lots of silverware, though the mother soon joins her, saying that she'll help, as she thanks Anna for being such a dear, for there couldn't have been any party without her. Anna says that she was happy to do it, she also had fun, but back when things were better, when Anna lived with Angela, one could hire an extra maid to help out, something that will happen only when there is finally peace once again, though Anna cannot believe that life will ever be as good as it was before the war. The father is simply dead tired and says, "If the only trouble is that one can't have a children's birthday party, then as far as I'm concerned the war can go on forever. Unfortunately, that's not the case." Josef is also very tired, but he looks to see what presents are left in the magic pond, since now they are his, then he sits down in the rocking chair, slowly rocking back and forth for a while, it feeling like when he rides along in a streetcar or on a train, and he rides along until his eyes close and he falls asleep.

IN UMLOWITZ

HERR NEUMANN IN UMLOWITZ IS NOT TOO TALL, SOMEWHAT FAT, AND has seven children whose names are Rudolf, Adolf, Arthur, Erwin, Fritz, Otto, and Herma, though now he also has a foster son named Josef. Rudolf is already an engineer, but he doesn't have a job and spends most of his time at home. Adolf is younger, yet already married, having married a maidservant, which angered Herr Neumann, because the girl had no money and was common, which is why Adolf did not stay in Umlowitz but instead left with his wife and opened his own business in Kaplitz, which apparently is doing well, for he handles flour and other farm products, traveling with his wagon throughout the district and knowing how to bargain with the farmers, who are happy to sell to him because he pays so quickly, while sometimes he even ends up competing with his father, though that doesn't bother Herr Neumann all that much. Herma, meanwhile, is very sweet and very busy, for she runs the entire household, Frau Neumann having died when Otto was just a baby, after which Herma had taken over all duties, including the cooking and the washing, as well as keeping an eye on what's going on with the business, making sure all the male and female servants were kept in line, everyone fond of her, the people of Umlowitz saying what a good person Herma is, while Josef thinks of her as a second mother, though she's quite young. Then there's Arthur, who has just completed business school and is living again at home in order to help Herr Neumann. Meanwhile Erwin visits only during school breaks from his high school, and Fritz also takes courses at the vocational school in Budweis, staying there the whole week when classes are on, and returning home on Saturdays only to head out again early Monday morning.

The smallest is Otto, who is much smaller than Josef, for even though he's three years older he's a sickly child who has to be dressed each morning and undressed each evening because he can't do it himself, Herma most often doing it for him, and when she doesn't have enough time Poldi does it, or one of the brothers. Everyone says of Otto that he's a little slow, a sweet child nonetheless, but because he wets the bed each night one has to place a diaper beneath his bedsheet, as if he were a baby, though he can't help it, and it's just something unfortunate you have to put up with. He also has a very high voice, like a little girl, and he talks through his nose, so you have to listen carefully in order to understand what he's saying, though he can say a lot and he talks a lot, and he understands what you say to him, in addition to being able to sing many songs without ever making a mistake, even if his voice isn't too lovely, because he sings through his nose as well. He has gone to school for many years, but he's still in the first grade, as he doesn't advance with the other children and can only say "one and one is two," while in the reader he knows little more than the difference between a printed "i" and a written "i," for though he can point to a printed "i" and a written "i" with his finger, among the other letters he knows only the "n" and sometimes the "e" and "m" as well, but he doesn't know any of the other letters, even if you continually show him, Herma or Fritz having spent half an hour with him each day in an effort to teach him something. But Otto can only write the "i," and when he has written one he's happy and shows it to everyone, and everyone says how wonderful it is that he has written such a beautiful "i." But Rudolf often says that it would be best for Otto to be placed in an institution, to which Herma says nothing or simply that he is Mother's youngest son, while Herr Neumann says that not even his worst enemy could accuse him of being a bad father who would kick his own flesh and blood out of the house just because he's a helpless creature forced to go through the world lost and alone, though he hopes that one day Otto will be better. But if that does not happen, then Herr Neumann believes there will always be enough left over for him, and that the other six children will be kind enough to take in Otto, to which all of them say they certainly will, even if he remains the child that he is now.

Josef is to stay an entire year with Herr Neumann in Umlowitz as part of an exchange whereby Erwin will stay with his parents in the city, for Josef has become too anxious, his parents not knowing what to do with him, though when they proposed this exchange Josef was happy to take it. He now goes to school in Umlowitz, and though he should be in the fifth grade, in this school with six grades in total they didn't want to start him in the fifth. Principal Bolek had made sure that he didn't, he wanted to show the coddled city child a thing or two, namely that the farm children know a lot more than the educated people of the city think, which is why Principal Bolek made Josef take an entrance exam, although none was required, and Josef had good grades from the fourth grade back home already, almost all of them A's. Principal Bolek had made Josef write something in ink on paper, and Josef had done a beautiful job, but Principal Bolek was not pleased with how he held his pen. Which is why he pointed to a large picture that hung on his office wall, nothing else on it but a hand that is writing and, beneath it, "The Proper Way to Hold a Pen."—"Look, Josef, that's the way to hold a pen when you write, just like you see in the picture!" But Josef can't write with outstretched fingers, only with fingers curled around, which is why he doesn't like to write all that much, for he still remembers how he once cried in first grade, many others crying as well, when the teacher wanted him to hold the pencil in the right hand and not the left, because you are supposed to write only with the right hand, not the left, though it was always hard for Josef, and that's why he'd grown used to writing with a strongly curled index finger. But Principal Bolek had said, "No, this way of writing is not encour- aged here in Umlowitz. You need to write the way the picture shows in order to write properly!" Yet as Josef tried to write with outstretched fingers all he could produce was an unreadable scrawl, Principal Bolek laughing that one couldn't be allowed to write that way in Umlowitz. "All the children here learn how to write properly. If you want to study with us here in Umlowitz, you'll have to learn it as well!" Then the principal had asked Josef some more questions that he didn't know the answers to, though the principal had constantly replied that all the children of Umlowitz knew the answer, since this was the best school in the district, while at the close he had asked, "Tell me, what color is water?" Josef thought for a while, and because he believed water had no color he answered, "Water doesn't have any color!" But the principal said, "Water does indeed have a color." Then Josef recalled that the sea is blue, so he said, "Water is blue." Yet the principal had immediately responded, "That's wrong. Water is not blue. Water is green. When you look at clear water on a mirror, you will observe that water has a green coloring." Since then Josef knows that water is green, Principal Bolek having declared, "If you want to go to school here in Umlowitz, you'll have to be in the fourth grade, where you'll learn what you need to learn. The children in the fifth grade know all of that already. You just wouldn't be able to keep up."

Therefore Josef starts again in the fourth grade, though Herr Neumann had said that in Umlowitz all the classes learn the same things, it doesn't matter if you're in the fourth or the fifth grade, while Josef thinks that it would be such a disgrace at home, though here it's not a disgrace, because the children of the village know so much, yet no one thinks it a disgrace that Otto is still in the first grade. In the fourth grade there are sixty boys from the surrounding area, Herr Lopatka in his first year of teaching here, a very nice teacher with a black mustache that dips and rises like a swallow's wings when he speaks, which looks funny. Class is held only five days a week, Wednesday being free so that the children can help their parents, though often there's no class on Saturday, either, and all the children go barefoot to school when it's not too cold, their feet always dirty, even Josef now going barefoot and it not even hurting when he walks on stones, though Otto and the little boys and girls go barefoot most of the time in order to save wear and tear on their shoes and socks. At night Poldi prepares a large tub of hot water in order to give Otto and Josef a good washing, though only once a day, for you aren't at all expected to wash up as much as in the city, even though you get much dirtier in Umlowitz.

Josef told Herma that no one learned anything in school, even if Herr

Lopatka was a very good teacher, for the children can't understand what he says, though Josef can, but when it comes time to practice writing no one knows what he is supposed to write. The teacher had said the children should write down what they see in the classroom, to which all the children made such puzzled faces, holding their pens as they looked around, though the paper remained empty, no one having written down anything except Josef, who had listed everything in the classroom, the teacher praising him and saying that the other children should still be writing something down, though all they put down was "Our Classroom," as they wrote "Writing Practice" in brackets underneath, the date also set down in the margin as the teacher had instructed at the start of the lesson. Now the lesson was over, the teacher saying, "Today we'll have to skip natural history and spend the next hour doing our writing practice." During the break the teacher stayed in the classroom and in chalk wrote out a writing exercise on the right side of the board, underlining some words twice, simply writing out others, then on the lefthand side of the board he wrote out another exercise that was not exactly like the one on the right but somewhat similar, as he underlined some words twice as well. When he finished, the break was already over, after which the teacher divided the class into four groups, not the way they were arranged on the benches but instead mixing them up, each boy counting off one, two, three, or four, so that each one knew which exercise he was meant to copy down. Once the teacher had finished dividing them up, he asked each student again which group he was in and, once the children finally knew, he told them they should begin copying down the exercise, but slowly and neatly, so that no one made any mistakes and wouldn't make the teacher upset at having to make corrections. But at the close of the class not all of them had finished, and the teacher said that his patience was wearing thin, he couldn't wait any longer, at which he gathered up all the exercises, the children glad that the whole thing was finally over. Later, when the teacher handed out the graded exercises, Josef got an A, most of the children receiving bad grades because their penmanship was so poor.

This is the way that you learn in Umlowitz, and not a single teacher cares whether you hold the pen right or not, so Josef continues to hold it the wrong way and never learns the way the principal believes he should, he soon becoming bored with school, Herma having spoken with Herr Neumann, who then asked Josef whether he'd like to help out in the fields and become a herder. Josef replied that he'd love to, and so Herr Neumann said that he could and came to an agreement with Herr Lopatka, who understood completely that it was not his fault, and that all that was needed was for Josef to show up once in a while in order to see what he knew, so that Principal Bolek didn't complain. Then Josef became almost a family member, he liking Herma the most, and then Otto, and then Herr Neumann, who has a large shop where you can buy almost anything. To get to it, you climb two steps to enter through a glass door, and as you open it a little bell rings first in the kitchen, which is behind the shop, and to which the bell is wired, making a *ting-a-ling-a-ling* so that Herr Neumann or Arthur or someone else can immediately be there to serve the customer, though usually someone from the family is in the shop, or at least Leopold the clerk, a tall, thin man. The store is long and narrow, with a wide aisle through the middle, the shelves rising to the right and left, the goods stored behind them and wherever there is space, though not where customers can reach directly for them, one being able to buy almost anything at Herr Neumann's, much more than is listed on the sign outside the door, where JAKOB NEUMANN is written in big letters, while in smaller letters below there appears VICTUALS, TEXTILES, HARDWARE. There is also candy, red and white peppermints and other sweet things, as well as sour pickles, which float in a big barrel from which you fish them out with a pair of wooden tongs, as well as spices, fennel the farmers' favorite, for they like it in their bread, there also being lots of other grocery items, barley and cornmeal, beans and lentils, as well as cans and pots, harnesses for the horses, and scythes, and sickles and spades and shovels and pliers and nails, as well as buttons and darning cotton, knitting needles and sewing needles, lots of fabric like the kind that the farmers' wives like, which is measured with a wooden yardstick, and scales, as well as soaps and powders and toothbrushes, lovely candles, brown soup powder, normal salt and red salt licks, writing paper and picture-postcards of Umlowitz, one of which shows a panoramic view of Umlowitz with the Thomasberg in the background, the central square, the church, the school, the power station, other items being pencils, pens, and notebooks, slippers and stockings, Herr Neumann having the biggest store in Umlowitz, not even Herr Iltis having as large a store, though there things are properly displayed as in the city, while Herr Neumann says the way things are displayed isn't everything, but rather what matters is good and prompt service, and that you understand your customers and have the right connections.

Herr Neumann's store smells of all his goods, a sweet, pungent smell that Josef likes very much. Up front the store is well lit, in back it's darker, so that an oil lamp is always kept burning there, because the electric light works mostly just at night, Rudolf saying that they had done a bad job in designing the power station, for it runs on an oil turbine, and one can never get enough oil, nor is it economical, for electricity is still much too expensive. Some people have no electric lights whatsoever, while others do indeed, though they rarely use them and prefer to buy oil for their lamps or candles, Herr Neumann not having a single electric light in his entire house, not even upstairs in the living quarters, for one hardly spends much time there except to sleep, everyone instead spending time in the kitchen, which is quite large. Rudolf says that the power station should have been designed much more practically to use waterpower, but no one thought of it, and now it's too late, and many years will pass before someone decides to build a power station that uses water. And so an oil lamp burns in the store, Leopold always having to fill it with oil, clean the wick, and keep the lamp in good working order. Each morning Leopold sweeps up in the store, fills a large bucket of water, then takes the funnel he uses to fill the oil or vinegar and plunges it deep into the water, holding his thumb over the hole, as he walks through the store and behind the shelves to spray water in arcing lines that look like lots of off-kilter bicycle wheels, after which he takes wood shavings and strews them around, the floor as clean as it gets, for it is always gray and greasy.

Whenever Herr Neumann doesn't have anything else to do, he's in the store, especially on Sunday mornings during church, almost the entire family there as well, and the store full of people, because the farmers and their wives otherwise have little time to shop. Arthur says you run yourself ragged trying to serve everyone at once, but otherwise evenings are the other time they come, when it often is full, Leopold having to lock the shop so that no one else comes in, opening up to let customers back out when they are ready, for Herr Neumann doesn't like to let anyone out through the kitchen, as then the people passing through look into the pots cooking on the stove, which Herr Neumann doesn't like, since it's none of their business, which is why they all need to be let out through the front, even Josef helping to do so when all the others have their hands full. Otto also sometimes comes into the store, though he doesn't open the door for customers, and actually Herr Neumann doesn't like having him there, saying that Otto should go into the kitchen, but because Otto likes it so much Herr Neumann doesn't outright forbid him and doesn't say another word if Otto doesn't disappear. During the day only a few people enter the shop, usually not staying for long, unless the weather is bad, when they all have to talk with the customers a great deal about this year's harvest and the cows, the times, what's going on in politics, how good the corpse looked, what the priest said at the cemetery, as well as the most recent wedding.

Normally Herma is not in the store, but some women ask for her right off and she has to come in, but when she has no time someone has to ask that she be excused or says that she's not home. The men, however, like best to talk with Herr Neumann, especially the older ones, while the younger are also happy to chat with Rudolf or Arthur, and many others just want something good to drink. Way in the back to the right Herr Neumann has some schnapps, be it caraway, anise, or black cherry, and eggs stewed in Cognac, which usually Rudolf and Arthur mix up, as well as rum also made by them both, and finally plum brandy, which the farmers and Herr Neumann like best of all, the customers always saying, "Another shot, Herr Neumann!" And so he pours another jiggerful, the farmers lifting the tiny glasses to their mouths and bending their heads back, as one-two, the shot glass is empty once again. Everyone is sad when the plum brandy is finished, for it tastes so good, and then they have to drink something else, a caraway schnapps or a black cherry, a lovely red schnapps that almost looks like glowing raspberry water, though the men say that black-cherry schnapps doesn't warm them up the same, that it's only sugar water, not real schnapps. The shot glasses rest on a bare metal tray that Leopold says is made of zinc, and when someone wants a drink he picks up the shot glass and holds it out to Herr Neumann or whomever in order to have it filled, but when he doesn't want any more he places the glass back down on the metal tray or simply on the counter, though Herr Neumann would rather he didn't, for inevitably someone doesn't see a shot glass resting there and it gets knocked onto the floor and is broken. The shot glasses are not washed, and everyone drinks from them, no one afraid of catching anything, as once a week Leopold rinses out the glasses in a bucket that holds the water he uses to clean the store, Josef having once said to Herr Neumann that it cannot be healthy, at which he laughed and said, "We've always done it that way in Umlowitz, and it's never harmed anyone yet."

Herr Neumann has a large fat stomach that presses against the counter when he stands behind it and bends over to show the farmers' wives something, which causes difficulties in his breathing, such that he sighs when he's finally done and doesn't have to bend over anymore. Sometimes there's no one in the store, so Leopold straightens up the goods that have become a bit disarranged, especially when there's no time to pick up after the customers right away. But the store is not the only source of Herr Neumann's living, for behind the kitchen there's a room where Otto and Poldi sleep, and sometimes someone else, there being a third bed there, as well as Herr Neumann's desk with many drawers, many papers stacked up on it, causing Josef to wonder how Herr Neumann can find anything at all, though Rudolf and Arthur have no trouble finding what they need, either. Sometimes Herr Neumann sits there with all his mail, lots of letters and cards arriving every day, as well as newspapers, catalogs and many advertisements. But it's not the mailman who brings them, for the mail in Umlowitz takes too long to arrive, so it's picked up at the post office instead, Josef often sent to get it, once a day somebody going after it, except on Sundays, since there is no mail then, but instead an old woman sits there, the postmistress, who always gets two shots of plum brandy on the house when she comes into the store, which is almost every day, everyone having to address her as Madam Postmistress, while only Herr Neumann calls her by her real name, Fräulein Schunko, no one else being allowed to do so, she having all the mail ready to be taken back home if you showed up at the right time, after which it is brought to Herr Neumann, though when he's away Arthur takes the mail or Rudolf. Herr Neumann almost always goes straight back to his desk, where he rips open the letters easily with his fingers, while many other items are chucked into the wastebasket, but first of all he rips off the stamps, which he puts into a little box, since Fritz collects stamps and says he already has around five thousand, many of them doubles, which he takes with him every Monday to Budweis in order to trade them at school. Meanwhile Herr Neumann leaves a pile of important letters on the desk for Rudolf or Arthur to answer, Herr Neumann having printed up letterhead and envelopes and cards for this purpose, there being two kinds, where on one it says:

JAKOB NEUMANN

VICTUALS, TEXTILES

Dry Goods of All Kinds

UMLOWITZ

Located on the Central Square

And the other kind reads:

JAKOB NEUMANN

Real Estate Agent

UMLOWITZ

This card, however, is used much less frequently, because real estate is a different kind of business than anything else.

Arthur has explained to Josef that real estate is a difficult business, you have to know a lot, for otherwise you can lose everything, it being more about serving as an intermediary than really selling something, and when a farmer wants to get rid of a little piece of field or woods or meadow, he writes to Herr Neumann or comes to him himself. They then sit in the back room, no one allowed in, Otto also sent out, while sometimes Poldi also has to wait forever before she's allowed in, even if she says she has to get into her cupboard, Herr Neumann only calling in Arthur and Rudolf now and then, though it can also happen that he asks for Herma as well. Then matters are discussed at length, Herr Neumann and the man having red faces when they emerge, after which they usually go into the store and drink a few glasses of plum brandy. And whenever Herr Neumann is particularly interested in a field or whatever, and if it's not too far, but not directly in Umlowitz, then on the day he wants to look at the field he tells Toni the coachman (who otherwise drives the freight wagon to the train station each day) that he has something he has to look at, and that Toni should hitch the horses to the barouche, which is a black wagon much like a hackney. And then Herr Neumann rides off with Toni, but when he comes back he has a list of addresses on his desk from people who want to buy something, who should come to him soon or write to him, though they need to hurry if they are really interested, as there are several others who want to buy that piece of property, because it's valuable and a good location, which is why Herr Neumann can't wait for long or hold anything, for no matter how sorry, he is not to be able to do so.

When someone is interested, there are long discussions, and Herr Neumann has to give them plenty of free plum brandy, while everyone who is there has to continue to remind people what a special opportunity it is, for the harvest is very good from that field. But often nothing comes of it, the farmers are wily and do not believe they're being told the truth, as they hold on to every bit of money they can and always want to pay less than Herr Neumann is asking, he not able to go any lower, which then causes them all to get into the barouche and ride out again, the people maintaining that they need to look at the property again if they are going to buy it, otherwise it's like buying a cat in a bag, the price still too high, and they don't really need to buy right now, for then they will only have more work to do to tend it, which is why it really has to be a good price. Selling property takes so much effort on Herr Neumann's part that Josef wonders why he does it at all, it seems only to cause him grief. Josef also doesn't understand how you sell something that never really belongs to you, for the people who want to sell a piece of property could just sell it directly to those who want to buy it, or just place an ad in the newspaper, and then Herr Neumann would have no more problems, though Arthur tells Josef that selling property is an important trade, for people tend not to come to agreement on their own, nor do they have as many addresses and contacts as Herr Neumann, who then gets some money from both the seller and the buyer, which is called the commission, a completely legitimate transaction that Herr Neumann then has to pay tax on. Whenever Herr Neumann finally closes a deal, he still has more expenses to cover, for sometimes the sellers show up, as well as the buyers, all of them sitting down together in the kitchen, Herma then having lots to do, along with Poldi and the others, in order to feed them, as they serve up many shot glasses that don't contain regular schnapps but rather a special kind that Rudolf or Fritz mixes up out of spirits and essences. Josef wouldn't want to have anything to do with such a business when he grows up, for he'd be happy with just the store, though he doesn't really think about what he wants to become, except that it won't be a doctor, as Herma says, "When you don't know what you want to become, then fate will find its own way. Perhaps you'll follow in the footsteps of your father."

But that's not all that Herr Neumann does, for since he owns a business there is a lot to do, fields and meadows and a little bit of woods are all located outside Umlowitz, but the center of it all is the kitchen, which you enter through a huge passageway not often used to access the street, this being where the barouche stands, though it's used only on Sundays or in the evenings when the shop is closed, while to enter you do so not through a large gate but through a little door that is built into the gate. From the entrance some steps lead up to the second floor, but below you continue on into the courtyard, where chickens, ducks, and geese run about, a large dung heap to the left and behind it the chicken coop, which is just across from the pigeon cote, while beyond is the pigsty and farther on the horses, though Josef doesn't like to go there, because the smell is so sharp in his nose. Josef is amazed that Toni can stand it for so long, though he smokes a strong-smelling pipe that he has filled with nasty tobacco, the pipe dangling from his mouth even when it's not lit, while Toni is almost always smoking. His pipe is made of porcelain, on which is printed the face of Emperor Franz Josef, who is already dead, there no longer being any emperor, as with the founding of the republic he's been done away with, but Toni says that it doesn't matter that there is no more emperor, for the pipe is old and he still likes it, and it's okay that the emperor is still on it. A long green tassel that is badly stained also hangs from the pipe, Josef never touching the pipe, especially the long mouthpiece, for when Toni quietly takes it apart dark brown juice flows from it that stinks and looks like the liquid manure from the dung heap, though the juice smells different and stays in his nose even more than the manure, Toni then putting the pipe back together, sticking it in his mouth and spitting. He also spits in the kitchen, where he has a large mug of coffee that is always waiting for him when he gets back from a trip. Toni also spits in the store, though everyone spits there, never once using the spittoon that sits in the corner, the floor covered with spit, Josef surprised that no one is disgusted by it, and that Herr Neumann never says anything about it. Sometimes he spits as well and smokes a pipe, but one not as bad as Toni's and not always the same one, since he has a stand full of pipes that are of different lengths, himself making a funny noise when he smokes, like when you say a soft "p," and because Otto loves that Herr Neumann does it over and over. Toni also makes a noise when he smokes, but it's not really a "p" but rather something different that's hard to describe. Herr Neumann's tobacco doesn't smell half as bad as Toni's, which sometimes one can hardly stand, especially when Toni blows smoke in Josef's face, Josef turning his head away, Herma reminding him that Toni doesn't do it on purpose, as it's what he's used to doing, and no one has ever told him that it's bothersome.

At first Josef thought that Toni smokes only because he also can't stand the smell of the horses, but Fritz had said that you get used to that, for it's not so bad, Josef unable to stand it only because he's from the city, where children often have never seen a horse stall, which makes it harder to get used to later on, though in reality the smell is good for you, for it contains ammonia. But Fritz couldn't say exactly what ammonia was, or why the smell is supposed to be so good for you, he simply said that it just was, and that ammonia smelled like what you smelled in the horse stall, which is why Josef asked Herma if she could tell him what ammonia was, to which she answered, "It's the same as salmiac." He couldn't understand why salmiac would be considered healthy, for it stinks so bad, and even as a little boy it bothered his nose so much that tears came to his eyes, he preferring that stains be cleaned away with gasoline or turpentine, for these are much better because they smell more pleasant, and Josef would much prefer it if the horse stall smelled like turpentine or gasoline. But the awful ammonia doesn't bother Toni, he is even able to sometimes sleep on a blanket in the stall, Herma explaining that his wife was a vixen, which means a bad woman, who likes to hit him and take away his wages, keeping it all for herself and leaving nothing for him, even though he never gets drunk and has no more than six glasses of beer and a couple of shots. The vixen also gives Toni very little to eat, and when he doesn't get enough from Herma he goes hungry, though at night she gives him a little kettle of potatoes and a jar of cream soup, Toni dipping each potato into the soup and eating it in one gulp, for he bites into them only when the potatoes are huge. In the stall Toni gives the horses something to eat and drink, grooming them as well until their coats shine, for when they are not shiny enough Arthur throws a fit, since he keeps his eyes peeled, everyone in the house afraid of him, for he wants everything done right and won't allow losses to accrue, as he says.

Though they complain about Arthur and give him a hard time, he is still good enough to help out with any kind of work, people saying that he works like a horse, only Herma herself as diligent or Herr Neumann, but in addition, because he tends to both everything and nothing at once, he has a lot on his mind, such as the farm, which is why Toni sometimes doesn't drive the wagon to the station but instead out to the fields, helping with the plowing or the harvesting, Arthur saying that old Toni is the best at the plow, and that maybe Fritz will someday be just as good, but not he. Because Toni doesn't know how to write and only barely reads, he never reads *The Farmer's Almanac*. That's the almanac that Poldi always reads so that she can pass on all the stories in it, she being able to write as well, though Toni can only write his name, which he does once a week when he gets his pay, writing out his entire name, Anton Pascher, on a receipt for Arthur, though it's not much more than a scrawl, despite his being able to count just fine.

Most everything is located to the left in the courtyard, but to the right is the warehouse that contains the goods for the store, it being full of crates and boxes and barrels, Leopold usually the one who enters it with Arthur, or sometimes it's Fritz, though rarely Rudolf, since he's not as strong. After the warehouse is the cowshed, where there are three cows, namely Schecki, who is older and doesn't give much milk, though still enough, followed by Campi, who is dark brown and has the nicest coat, she also giving the most milk and the mother of a calf called Gabbi that is also in the stall, while last is Liesel, the youngest of the three cows, who had her first calf but doesn't give as much milk, though Herma believes that Liesel will once again give lots of milk, because her mother is the cow owned by the butcher Sekora, and it gave a great deal of milk. Then there are also four goats whom Josef likes very much, because they are so funny, much more so than the cows, among whom Campi is his favorite, though the goats don't have names, they being just called the "Goaß" in the local dialect spoken in Umlowitz. Otto loves to visit the goats, bringing them leaves to eat and calling "Come here goatie!" as he extends a bunch to them, each not wanting the other to get it as they lock horns and the winner snaps up the bunch of leaves, Otto thrilled by it all. When the weather is good, the cattle are let out to pasture, though the cows are also often needed for the wagon if one travels across the fields.

During the day two young girls and a boy come to Herr Neumann's, themselves children of cottagers in Umlowitz who go home each night, staying at Herr Neumann's only when the harvest is on, or if they are needed special, while for the harvest others help out as well, including everyone in the house except Leopold, who stays behind to tend the store. Herma also goes out to the harvest only rarely, because she has to cook and take care of everything at home, while Poldi doesn't spend the entire day in the fields, either, since Herma can't do everything on her own, Otto accompanying Poldi when she does go to the fields for a few hours, though he's not much of a worker, but nonetheless can't be left on his own, Herr Neumann and Herma insisting that someone always watch over him so that nothing happens, since he can't take care of himself and has no more understanding than that of a child. Out in the pasture he chases after the goats, though it's easy for them to run away from him, which is why he can never be alone with the cattle in the pasture, for cattle will do what they want and are not afraid of Otto, even if he swings the stick that he likes so much and which Fritz had cut and trimmed for him.

When everyone is in the fields from morning until night, Herma sends out lunch to them at midday, just simple things like coffee or soup, big slices of bread at least two or three centimeters thick, each a slice from the whole loaf and not just cut in half, some of them as big as a roof shingle or even longer. Herma also sends out a large canister of sour cream that grows even more sour in the canister, until it tastes really sour, while at other times she sends along a thick hunk of butter that has to be kept cool in the shade or in the creek, otherwise it will melt and look almost like flowing gold, while there's also cheese, though not like that you get in the city but one that is very healthy and tastes strong, Herma making it herself. Then folks yank potatoes out of the earth, a large fire is lit, people quickly drag sticks from the woods, after which they shove the potatoes into the fire, then they stir the coals with a stick, later rolling the potatoes out of the cinders, the potatoes black as coal and so hot that they burn your fingers when you touch them. Toni is the best at grabbing hold of them, for his hands are as dark as tanned leather, such that he can grab hold of anything and never get burned, after which everyone takes a knife and scrapes off the charcoal skin and sprinkles the potatoes with salt as they cool, though you have to eat them carefully, otherwise you'll burn your tongue.

Now Josef is also a herder for Herr Neumann, who owns some pastureland, though most of the cattle graze in Purtscher's fields on a side slope of the Haselberg. The cattle in the shed are tied up, and normally Poldi helps Josef release them, since he can't do it alone, it going all right with the goats and with Cappi, but not as well with the other cows, the worst being Liesel, who is a restless animal who requires more patience. Josef holds a big stick that he made himself, though Otto's is much nicer, even if it's shorter and not as strong, Fritz being much more gifted at wood carving, for he can carve decorations and letters into the stick, such that it almost looks like something out of a picture from a book about Indians. Josef isn't as good, having cut his finger once while he was carving in the open fields, the finger bleeding for so long that Josef had to wrap his handkerchief around it, while that night Herma made a proper bandage, carefully washing the finger at first and rubbing it with alcohol so that it wouldn't get infected, though it burned like hell, Herma saying that was just what had to be, because there had once been a farm boy in Umlowitz who also cut himself, and no one did anything about the wound, such that the poor boy got a terrible illness called tetanus, and the next day he was dead, since there was nothing that could be done for him. And so Josef held his finger still, not wanting to get any tetanus, and two days later the finger was fine again and hadn't gotten infected.

Whenever the cattle are brought into the yard they are happy, the animals know they are headed to pasture, where they love to eat fresh grass, only Schecki shying away from it, Arthur believing it's because she's somewhat old, which is why it might be best for her to be sold to the butcher Sekora next year. Herr Neumann says, however, that he can't as yet bring himself to do so, for he likes Schecki, and she's been a good cow, nor does it matter if Schecki has a bit of diarrhea, that will soon go away once she's fed right. Only Gabbi stands there dumb, because he's a dumb calf who still doesn't know that they are headed to pasture, though he follows Campi, who knows the way, while the journey home is more difficult, because he scares so easily and has trouble finding his way back to the yard. Once, just as Josef was still learning about how to herd cows, it happened that Gabbi was frightened by a horse wagon that was headed toward him, and so he suddenly ran off, Josef chasing after him, it doing no good as he screamed at the top of his lungs, "Gabbi! Gabbi! You stupid Gabbi! Gabbi, come here!" Gabbi was long gone, and so Josef got scared about how mad Herr Neumann and the others would be, and how much they would scold him if he returned without Gabbi, such an animal being worth the kind of money that Josef had no way of paying back, and so he returned breathless to the yard with his head hanging and his heart pounding, Poldi seeing him and laughing as she asked, "Josef, Josef, whatever is the matter? Where have you been? The cattle are already in the shed, but what have you done with Gabbi?" Then Josef couldn't keep from sobbing, but Poldi only laughed again at the fact that Gabbi wasn't there, saying, "Now come along! Let's go looking for that Gabbi!" And so she headed out through the gate, Josef sadly walking behind her with his stick, the two of them moving along until they reached the sawmill, where someone had tied up Gabbi, he shaking his head as he saw the two of them coming along, as if to say, "That boy's been running around like a fool! And here he is right back again! He needs to learn how to herd calves!" And yet Josef had never been so happy, for Gabbi was not lost after all, the good man at the sawmill having captured him and saved him, Josef having continually cheered, "Gabbi is back! Gabbi is back! Someone found him and saved him!" Then they were back, Poldi having led Gabbi, Josef saying that he'd give him a good beating if he weren't just a stupid calf, which only made Poldi laugh again at how inept Josef is, for a real herder would never have let such a thing happen, but he would have learned from the start how to tend cattle so that they follow along and don't run off. And so they were back in the yard with the runaway, Gabbi's eyes full of fear as they led him to the stall, because he was so stupid. Nonetheless, everyone had learned how inept Josef was, and everyone had a good laugh at that, though they also said it wasn't at Josef they were laughing but rather only the calf, because it was so stupid and had run away.

This doesn't happen to Josef again, for he makes sure that the calf follows behind him, and when he takes the cattle to the fields he always goes behind the farmyard and by the bay, where the chaff is cut across from the horse stable, the hayloft above both the bay and the stable, which is where Kreibidi the cat always has her kittens. Then Josef moves through the gate with the cattle, while across the way sits Herr Neumann's barn, next to and behind the garden, inside of which there is a pool into which Herr Neumann's geese waddle. Josef doesn't like them, for he's a little afraid of them when they hiss, though he's never afraid as long as he has his stick, he waving it at them if they come too near, and indeed they turn cowardly and run off as soon as they see the stick, beating their wings back and forth and looking silly. Right and left of the road are barns, haystacks, and gardens, all of them looking just like Herr Neumann's, after which there is Herr Schwinghammer's farmyard, which is an inn, followed by a crossroads, the road to the left leading to the main square of Umlowitz, while to the right is the highway to Zartlesdorf, which Josef turns into with the cattle. Then there are a couple of houses as the road slowly begins to climb, and then on the right is the power station that some would like to convert to a grange once the new power station that runs on water is completed, at least according to Herma, which would mean the local amateur theater troupe could move into it and have its own stage, though until then the troupe will continue to perform in the large hall at Herr Schwinghammer's inn.

Then the road climbs farther up the mountain, soon reaching the heights of Haselberg, its peak sitting off to the left, a short while after which a cart path forks off to the left, which in some places is cut deep into the clay, so that it looks like a ravine. Something similar also can be seen onstage when *William Tell* is performed, a classic work by Schiller that the local theater does, it pleasing Josef very much, though most folks in Umlowitz didn't like it, saying that it involved too much talk and too little action, the play also damned hard to understand, such that nearly everyone had better things to say about *The Country Girl* or *The Rape of the Sabine Women* when they were put on. But Principal Bolek had insisted that a play by the prince of poets should be done in Umlowitz, in order to raise the standard of taste in Umlowitz, the principal saying that *William Tell* was just the ticket, for it is easy to understand, and because it's not too sad, and because it is a celebration of freedom, which is the highest good of all. Some members of the local troupe were inspired by his suggestion, especially Frau Bilina, the wife of the dentist, who said that she'd once seen *William Tell* in a large theater in Linz many years ago, and it had moved her deeply, after which everyone agreed that it had to be put on. The principal had also promised to help them study the play in order to properly learn the verse and not declaim it in dialect, since it really is a classic work that simply won't stand for any dialect. So they studied a good while and staged the play, but it pleased only a few, though the principal made sure that the entire sixth grade attended, the poor children having been granted free tickets, most of them not liking it at all, for they said it was much too long and hardly anybody sang in it, and there really ought to be singing when you go to the theater. From the Neumann family Herma went and took Josef along with her, but Rudolf said he wasn't going to go, for he didn't want to spoil all that good taste, while Arthur wasn't in Umlowitz at all, and Herr Neumann never went to the theater anyway, saying that it just wasn't for him, it being enough that he paid for his subscription, so that nothing else could be expected of him, though Fritz said he would go along, but when Herma called out that it was already late, Fritz, we have to go, he replied that he had thought about it and he wanted to stay home after all. Herma didn't think that was at all right, but she was pleased by the play, because it is so interesting and inspired once you genuinely understand it.

Once you are through the clay path, the view opens, after which the path forks twice more, once to the right, then again to the left, Josef having hardly ever gone this far, coming out in a cornfield that belongs to Herr Neumann, the upper half of the field a part of Purtscher's fields, while below thorns and scrub brush grow, as well as wild roses and hazelnut bushes, blackthorns and bushes whose name Josef doesn't know, and between the bushes large stones. Josef gathers some of them when he makes a fire, as well as small stones that he stuffs into his pocket, for he needs stones when the goats stray too far and run across the field or into the bushes, forcing him to shoo the goats, though they are only small stones and therefore no cruelty to animals is involved, it doesn't harm the goats, and there's no other way of handling them.

In the upper reaches of the field the forest already begins and rises up even higher, but in the pasture Josef is often alone the entire day, except when it begins to rain, though he had already learned a bit about observing the weather, and if the clouds were threatening he drew the herd together. Otherwise he remained up there and headed home only at the sound of the church bell, which told him it was six o'clock, the time when the cows needed to be led home, it going much faster than it did when taking them out to pasture. The first time Josef went to the pasture he herded the live-stock along too quickly, for though it didn't bother the goats it was not good for the cows, they becoming restless and therefore not digesting well. As Arthur happened to observe this from afar, he came over to Josef and said that he shouldn't be doing that, as it was bad for the cattle to run so much, for the animals are too heavy and sluggish, and you had to be careful in order that the cows give good milk and don't get sick. Which is why Josef now moves along slowly, though heading home still takes a lot less time than going out to pasture.

Out in the fields Josef has little to do, for it's easy to keep an eye on the animals, and all he has to do is glance over at them from time to time, the cattle hardly stirring because they are so content, everything fine with the goats as well. Normally Josef looks for a spot way up the hillside almost to the edge of the forest, where he can easily see the animals and has a wonder-ful view. Just below him are the fields and farther off in the valley lies Um-lowitz, looking like a picture-postcard of itself with a stamp in the corner and the words "Panorama of Umlowitz" printed at the bottom, though from above it looks much more glorious than on the colored postcard, everything is alive and so marvelous in the sunlight, the parish church and its tower in the middle, as well as the high roof of the church. From there you can figure out where Herr Neumann's house is, for it's directly across from the church, a little left of the tower, while beyond that it's hard to make out the other houses, though the power station can clearly be seen in the foreground and to the right, where the highway to Meinetschlag runs, while at the very edge of town are three villas, one belonging to the dental techni-cian Bilina, who serves the farmers from the area, the neighboring villas be-longing to Fräulein Leirer, one of which she rents to people from the city in summer. But not many people come here for the summer to relax and re-plenish themselves, since Umlowitz is so far off the beaten track that hardly anyone knows of it, the rail lines far enough away that no one can easily reach Umlowitz without a barouche like Herr Neumann's, since only once a morning does the mail wagon go to the train station, which is nearly fifteen kilometers away, it taking three hours to get there by foot, the dusty road easily giving rise to blisters, especially when it's hot, while the mail wagon doesn't return until the afternoon, itself just an open wagon, the back of which is full of mailbags and packages, there being enough room for only two people up front by the driver, though they can't be too fat, for only one person the size of Herr Neumann would find room to fit.

There is always a lot of fuss when the mail wagon gets ready to head off, for then the postmistress, Fräulein Schunko, has so much to do that no one is allowed to talk to her, nor will she sell anyone so much as a stamp, not to mention send a telegram, while it's even worse in the afternoon when the mail wagon returns, especially when there are a lot of packages, for everything has to quickly be sorted, the two mailmen whose routes are in Umlowitz and some carriers who serve the surrounding countryside helping the postmistress, the front desk clerk not helping with the letters but worrying about the packages instead, thus causing him to break out into a heavy sweat. At such a time there is no hope of getting any service at the post office, and anyone who needs something must be patient in order not to disturb the postmistress or make her nervous until she is finally finished and has a cup of coffee, after which she tells the people waiting that she's at their service once more. The mail is then carried off to be delivered, though the mailmen serving the rural routes do not go to their villages until the next morning, their routes often quite difficult to traverse, as they battle rain and snow in order to get the mail to isolated farms and hunting lodges wherever they happen to be.

Since everything is so difficult in Umlowitz, strangers rarely pass through town, visiting only when they absolutely must, or if they are relatives who are picked up by the barouche or with a hay wagon. Herma says that Principal Bolek has long desired that Umlowitz would become a tourist destination, since Umlowitz sits 676 meters above the Adriatic Sea and possesses all the amenities needed for a mountain spa, while if you tested all the water and springs from the area, who knows if there might not exist healing waters and wells, such as you see in Karlsbad, and to which people travel for their health, gathering there from all over the world and bringing along so much money that the natives become rich themselves. But unfortunately there is not enough money to test the water, Rudolf chuckling about it and saying that if the water had some special value it would have been discovered long ago, there being no need for the principal to be the first to lead them to it. Yet Herma believes that the principal means well, and he himself says that if the kind of water needed to open a world-class spa doesn't exist there is still a lot that can be done to increase the tourist trade in Umlowitz, if only the right entrepreneurial spirit existed, the principal not understanding why Herr Schwinghammer, who has plenty of money, doesn't build a hotel, though first one would need a rail line that traveled closer to Umlowitz. Plans for such a project had long existed, though they had never been realized, for Umlowitz is located in such a neglected area, and the politicians had never shown much appreciation for it, which is why the principal will not vote for Wackermann the next time around, he being the representative for the district, the principal determined instead to vote for an opposition candidate, though even he would have to first promise that he'll take better care of Umlowitz. At one time the rail-line project had gone so far that they began to survey the land, and everyone knew where it was supposed to be installed, just a quarter of an hour from the church, where old lady Praxel's little house stands, which can be seen from the fields, but then the war came, which caused so much suffering, the rail-line project also falling victim to it, while now no one knows what will happen to the republic.

The principal goes on and on with anyone about this, and Herr Neumann says that the principal likes to feel important, though he's done a great deal for the town, at which Rudolf protests and says that it's ridiculous, you need only take a look at the schoolchildren to see how good the principal really is. Indeed, he must know a great deal, Josef thinks to himself, even if the children don't know much themselves, and even if the reason for this is that there are too many children for the school, classes having to be divided into classes of boys and girls, adding up to twelve classes with a minimum of sixty in each, there being no way for Principal Bolek to teach each of them. A lot is said in Umlowitz about the principal's plans, Josef often hearing people talk about this in Herr Neumann's shop, saying how wonderful the principal's dreams and wishes are, such as building a park with benches and a music pavilion, where the Umlowitz orchestra could play, directed by Herr Kreissel, the singing teacher at the school who twice a year presents a concert in Herr Schwinghammer's banquet hall. The principal also wants to see proper paths installed, with fine gravel that won't hurt one's feet, nothing more being required in Umlowitz, people will indeed come, as word will start to get around about all the black currants to be had, as well as raspberries, strawberries, and blackberries, so many mushrooms to be found in the forests that many are left to rot because there are too many to gather, since one can pick only what he needs for himself, almost all of the boletus disappearing, for no one wants the others, everyone drying the sliced mushrooms in their kitchens at home. On top of this the air is so good in Umlowitz, mainly because of the mountains, as well as the lovely forests, there being no better air to be found anywhere, there also being no tuberculosis like in the cities.

All of this occurs to Josef when he is out in the pasture and the town lies peaceful before him, stretching from Fräulein Leirer's villa out to Praxel's little cabin, while across the way stands the Thomasberg, some 814 meters high, topped by a rounded dome of dense forest, Herma having twice taken Josef there, which made him very happy, while behind the Thomasberg there are still higher mountains, though they are a ways off, not all of them visible from the fields, especially when they are higher than a thousand meters, the country's border also nearby and running straight along the peaks. Josef had never been there, but Herr Neumann had already promised that some Sunday they would take the barouche, in which four people could travel, six really, though only four inside, one having to sit up front with Toni on the coach box, from which nevertheless the view is even better without the roof of the barouche in the way. Yet when Josef rides along he likes to do so inside, where it is much darker, though more refined, for you have to find a way to ride out the bumps, and everything there is elegantly upholstered, comfortably cushioned and so wonderfully bouncy, as Josef has often found out with Otto, the two of them climbing in and bouncing away, just as if the barouche were really moving, though Arthur had reacted by saying that Josef is already much too old for that sort of thing, and that the barouche is not a toy.

Because it's so hard for tourists to get to Umlowitz, it's always a great event when they do, one that always has some special reason behind it. This is why the children of Umlowitz have hardly ever seen an automobile, though the great landowner Dordogneux, whose name Josef doesn't exactly know how to spell for sure, this man was a count when there had still been an emperor, and Count Dordogneux lives in a castle in Gratzen and has an automobile. Once he drove through Umlowitz in it when classes were under way at the school, all the children yelling "An automobile!" the teacher, Herr Lopatka, saying that, indeed, it was an automobile, then all the children piled out of their benches and rushed to the windows in order to see it, though Herr Dordogneux had only driven through Umlowitz and had never stopped.

Now and then a salesman travels to Umlowitz in order to show the new wares in his many suitcases, and when he comes he rents a wagon that he picks up at the station before traveling on to Umlowitz, where he gets out at Herr Schwinghammer's inn, though he doesn't eat there, except for breakfast, since he sleeps there, for otherwise he is busy making his rounds. His name is Herr Lieblich, and in Umlowitz he visits only Herr Neumann and Herr Iltis, as well as Herr Kosteletz, who doesn't have as big a shop as Herr Neumann and Herr Iltis. At Herr Kosteletz's he makes only a quick visit, and doesn't bring in all of his suitcases, but when he visits Herr Neumann and Herr Iltis he stays for a long time and brings along all of his suitcases, which he cannot carry alone, which is why Herr Schwinghammer's farmhand and maid cart them along, Herr Lieblich carrying only one case. Herr Neumann is always pleased when Herr Lieblich visits, though Herr Lieblich always announces his visits by letter ahead of time, so that Herr Neumann will know when he will arrive, and when Herr Lieblich steps into the store Leopold calls out, "Good day, Herr Lieblich!" After which he yells more loudly, "Herr Lieblich is here!" And everyone comes rushing in, for they all have time when Herr Lieblich is there, greetings exchanged all around, Herr Neumann and Arthur and Rudolf and Herma, even Otto, hurrying along and exclaiming that Herr Lieblich has arrived, everyone shaking his hand, Leopold already knowing that he'll have some plum brandy right off, at which Herr Lieblich lifts his shot glass, looks around at everyone, stretches out the hand holding the shot glass as if it were a barbell he was about to lift, as he calls out "Cheers! Cheers!" to each of them and drinks down the plum brandy and says heartily, "That felt good!" Then everyone has lots to say, first about the weather, what kind of year it's been, how the harvest is looking, and what is most important to Herr Neumann, namely business and family, as well as what Herr Lieblich has done with himself since they last saw him, how business has been in the district, and whether Herr Iltis has bought less than usual.

So it goes for a while, until Leopold lifts a case and lays it on the counter so that Herr Lieblich can open it and show what he has for wares, though they are full of samples that are not for sale and are only for show. Herr Neumann and Rudolf and Arthur become interested and talk about whether they could use this or that, Herr Lieblich always pointing out which ones will sell very well, or how many he has sold of something already, what great business he has been doing, and if Herr Neumann wants some good advice, then he should order it, for he'll then see people rush through the doors, simply because they'll be wild about it, which is why it would be best for Herr Neumann to order now, otherwise it could happen that there might not be enough wares to fill subsequent orders, or it just might be too late. Some things are just rubbish, says Arthur, which is what something is called that is not as good as Herr Lieblich thinks it is, though Herr Lieblich immediately replies that it's not rubbish at all, because his firm has nothing to do with rubbish, to which Rudolf says that, indeed, it may not be rubbish but it's still no good to them in the store, for nobody will buy it. Then samples appear, which no one calls rubbish, while Herr Neumann says that they are very good articles but the kind of thing that sells only in the city and not in Umlowitz, because here the people like simple things that are cheap and not too expensive, because people save their money, especially since the war, for they don't have much money and some have lost everything after purchasing a lot of war bonds, and no one knows now what to do with war bonds. Meanwhile Herr Lieblich says to Herr Neumann that he certainly knows what is best, and he agrees that you can't order everything, but he does wish to point out that Herr Iltis has already placed his order, and in Strobnitz, a market town in the district, Herr Lieblich has had numerous orders for the time under discussion, so many, in fact, that he doesn't know if he'll be able to fill them all, for he also has to serve the other proprietors of the district who are his long-standing customers.

Whenever Herr Neumann orders something, Herr Lieblich's face lights up even more than before, he is so delighted as he takes out a little booklet with a soft brown cover on which it says "Orders," after which he then inserts two pieces of carbon paper and writes down the list of goods that Herr Neumann wants, it always being a good number. Once one case has been sorted through, there follows another, but whenever a customer comes in everything stops, otherwise everyone is happy to keep looking, though Leopold gets upset whenever Herr Lieblich visits, because he has to continue to work and doesn't get to see all the things that Herr Lieblich is there to show off. One case is full of women's goods and fabric samples, and that's when Herr Neumann asks for Herma's opinion, which she then gives, telling him what she likes, what he should order and what he should not, as Herr Lieblich says how clever she is, and how happy it makes him to see a woman involved in a business, because women understand some things much better. With this he flashes Herma a charming smile, to which she only laughs and says nothing further. Then Herr Lieblich reaches for a hand-dyed purse made of real silk and a piece of soap scented with lily of the valley and a lovely thimble, all of which he presents to Herma as a gift, while in another case Herr Lieblich has samples that you can play with, even if they aren't toys in their own right, and from these he always chooses something for Otto, which makes him happy and for which he waits in expectation, Josef getting something as well, while for Herr Neumann there's a leather tobacco pouch, even though he already has quite a few that he doesn't use, including one made from a pig's bladder that he carries in his pocket, while Arthur gets a fountain pen, about which he says that it won't work for long, Rudolf getting a notebook, Leopold a nail cleaner, anyone who happens to be in the store getting something as well.

Once Herr Lieblich has shown all of his wares, which can take a couple of hours, Herr Neumann says that Herr Lieblich should come along with him, for Herma has cooked something good and Herr Lieblich must surely be hungry, Herr Neumann having slaughtered a chicken earlier. He always goes through the yard and deftly grabs a chicken, pressing it between his legs and bending over to rip out some feathers just below the throat, at which he pulls out a long knife and cuts the chicken's throat so that the blood quickly flows out and the chicken is dead, its wings still flapping a bit and its legs still twitching away for quite a while, Josef having been upset the first time he saw it, though he calmed down once someone explained to him that the chicken was dead already, and only its nerves were causing it to still move. Then Herr Lieblich is led into the kitchen and served a bowl of soup, after which he has some chicken that has been cooked in a paprika sauce, there being also dumplings along with it which Herma is so good at making, Poldi able to make only simple things, while afterward there is coffee and cake, though to drink there is also beer from Herr Schwinghammer's. All during this Herr Lieblich is told many things, but once he has eaten his fill and there are no more stories to tell he thanks them for the friendly hospitality, kisses Herma's hand, and says a heartfelt goodbye to everyone, after which Herr Lieblich heads off and someone shows up from the inn to pick up his cases.

Otherwise there are few visitors, only Adolf arriving two or three times a year, he not able to visit more often because of his wife, while he stays for only an hour when he does come, no one doing anything special for him, as only Herma serves him a coffee and says that he should have a look at the yard, and that Otto should show him the way, at which Adolf takes off already, saying that he'll be back when he next has business in Umlowitz. The townsfolk of Umlowitz, however, never visit Herr Neumann when they don't have something they are looking for, and even if they do visit most of them stand at the front of the store, nor do people sit out on a Sunday or during the evening as they do in the city, because everyone has something to do all day, and everyone sees everyone else all the time, few people even taking the time to eat together, while some eat something later on, because they have too much to do, though that is also good, since there are not enough places at the table. For the most part, Josef and Otto eat together, Herma normally joining them at the table and sometimes Herr Neumann, Poldi always bringing the heaping plates, which are so hot that Josef is amazed at how steady she holds them without spilling anything or scalding herself. Whenever Herr Neumann or Rudolf and Arthur or Herma are at dinner, sometimes someone calls out, at which they have to rush out right away because something is going on in the store or in the yard, and so they let the food sit in the middle of the table. Often it gets cold, and if it all takes too long Poldi carries the plates away and scrapes the food, if there's enough left, into the pot, for Poldi says that it can still be eaten. Everyone eats a lot, so there is always something cooking and the pots are never empty, there is always someone who wants to eat, the large bake oven also never going out after it's lit early in the morning, until late at night when it's shut down, though the stovetop remains hot for a while. Poldi makes goose noodles, which are oats used to fatten a goose, laying the oats on the hearth so that they roast, but not too much. Meanwhile, when Poldi eats she doesn't sit at the table but rather on a stool in front of the oven, where she chews away and holds a plate on her lap as she bends over her food, Toni doing this as well and all the people who work in the yard.

Kreibidi the cat also sits next to the stove, lazy and fat and purring throughout the evening, while during the day she spends most of her time in the yard chasing the chickens and the pigeons, after which Kreibidi hides in the granary or in the hayloft, where there are lots of mice, though Arthur says she rarely catches a mouse, because she gets too much to eat already, but Poldi is very fond of Kreibidi and constantly gives her milk, Kreibidi becoming so used to it that she hardly even sniffs at the potato placed in front of her instead. Foxy is also around, though he is not a proper dog breed but rather a village mutt. Completely black, Foxy is always running around, but he's not allowed in the store, and whenever someone catches him there he's immediately chased off, for there's nothing for a dog in the store, Leopold the one who usually has to send him packing, as he's the one who is in the store the most, he opening the kitchen door and yelling at Foxy to get out, Leopold giving him a light kick as he goes through the door, not to hurt him but so that he knows that he shouldn't be in the store. Then Leopold quickly closes the door, for otherwise Foxy would come straight back in, since Foxy is not that afraid of Leopold and is completely tame, sniffing anyone who comes along, his tail wagging, never barking or biting.

Foxy's best friend is Otto, who often plays with him by the hour, the two of them rolling around the ground or on the sofa until Otto is completely filthy and someone has to give him a vigorous scrubbing. Foxy lets Otto do whatever he wants, even if he grabs him by the snout or lightly steps on his tail, only yelping when someone steps on his paw, after which Foxy needs to be petted and calmed down, everyone happy to do so, even Herr Neumann, despite having hardly enough time. Poldi gives Foxy his food, but in a different dish than Kreibidi, though neither pays attention to the other, nor does either take anything from the other's dish, since each has plenty to eat already. Everyone tosses Foxy the tastiest bits, though Rudolf doesn't, for he says that to overfeed a dog is the same as animal cruelty, and Foxy has too much to eat already, and if Rudolf had his own dog he'd make sure to properly train him so that he didn't always run around and bark, as well as make sure that he was a proper dog rather than a street dog like Foxy. Rudolf, in fact, is right about Foxy being badly raised, for he's only been given a name and taught to put out both paws when someone calls out, "Foxy, give us a paw! Foxy, give us the other paw!" Sometimes Foxy goes along with Josef out to the fields or into the meadow, sometimes running ahead, but only rarely, and even then he stays only a little while, instead running around for a while and he's gone before you know it, though there's no need to worry, for Foxy always finds his way home.

When there's a lot to do, sometimes Praxel comes to help. She is the woman who lives in a shed down by the train station. Praxel is a terribly nice woman, sweet as they come, but she is afraid because she lives alone and has no one in the world, her husband having died long ago, as well as two children, both of whom died from scarlet fever in the same week, Praxel's heart remaining empty ever since. She is poor and has only her little hut with a tiny yard and a patch of garden, as well as a goat that provides her with milk, and four chickens, these all the animals that she owns. But since Praxel is so afraid because she lives alone, it happened that one night around 10 P.M. there was a loud pounding at the door, such that everyone thought there was a fire in Umlowitz and that Arthur should come, since he is a member of the volunteer fire department, but there was no fire. Otto had already been put to bed, while Josef was reading an old book that Herma had lent him, which was called *The Adventures of Draga Maschin*, an exciting story of the Serbian queen, and Herr Neumann had just been reading the paper and smoking a pipe, while Rudolf was away, and Herma was writing a letter to Erwin, as well as a note to Josef's parents to let them know how he was doing, since he didn't want to write anything more than a brief hello. Meanwhile Fritz was also at home and sitting at the table with tubes of saccharin and a jar of confectioner's sugar, as he continually emptied a tube of saccharin onto a piece of paper and then mixed in some confectioner's sugar, after which he filled the tube again with the mixture, so that there was always some saccharin left over, which Fritz then set aside, the saccharin having come from over the border. Yet Poldi was also there, reading her *Farmer's Almanac* on her stool, Arthur having lain down on the couch because he was tired, and only looking on at what the others were doing, the pounding on the door so loud that everyone rushed about, Arthur jumping to his feet, while the others stopped what they were doing and Poldi called out that she would go see what was the matter, and no sooner had she left than Fritz and Arthur followed, only to hear Praxel yelling that it was she, Praxel, and could they open the door quickly, at which Poldi turned the heavy key, which Josef was never able to turn in the lock, then threw back the bolt and opened the door.

Praxel then ran straight into the kitchen, her hair undone and herself pale as a ghost, her whole body trembling. She also wasn't properly dressed and had on only a slip and a blouse that she always wore to bed, while because she hadn't been able to untie her head scarf, she had run out with it in her hand. And now Praxel was standing there in the kitchen unable to say a word because she was so upset, everyone immediately asking her what had happened, all of them circling round her, Poldi and Herma helping her to pull herself together, making sure that Praxel took a chair and sat down. Then Praxel yelled out that there were robbers, though she couldn't quite say it right, so that no one understood what kind of robbers she meant, or where, everyone asking at the same time as Arthur said that Praxel needed to calm down a bit, otherwise no one could understand what was going on. She replied by saying that she couldn't calm down, because it was a disaster, and then that they were poor people who had nothing, and that it was a disgrace, for she was an old widow who had never harmed a hair on anyone's head, and that everything had been taken from her, just as she was about to go to sleep and blow out the candle, that's when she heard noises, though she had thought it was nothing, after which she blew out the candle and got into bed, but then she heard something again, her heart starting to pound, since after the war there were so many bad characters about, God forgive them, and then she heard a plate break, at which she gathered her courage and ran out of the room and into the kitchen. Soon as the robbers heard her they were gone out the window, though Praxel couldn't run after them, they were young boys who were as quick as rabbits, carrying nothing on them but what they found in the dark, though she did start to run as fast she had ever run in her life, all the while calling out, "Robbers! Robbers!"

At this Praxel could say no more, for she was trembling so and couldn't catch her breath, Herr Neumann asking if she wanted a schnapps, though Herma said that Praxel didn't need any schnapps but rather strong coffee and something to eat, while Praxel herself said "coffee." Poldi then went straight to the oven, the fire almost having died out, only a few hot coals remaining, though Poldi said that she would use some kindling to get the fire going again, and that what had happened to Praxel was outrageous, Poldi already having placed some kindling in the oven, a large fire soon following, at which she put on water for coffee. Praxel said that she would die of fright, though Herma reassured her that there was nothing to be afraid of here, since all the men were there, Arthur and Fritz, who could handle anyone, she just needed to calm down and not get herself so worked up, for she needed to think of her heart. Tonight it would be best if Praxel slept here on the sofa, and if she was still afraid tomorrow they would set up a bed for her in the room where Otto and Poldi sleep, since there is a free bed there, though Praxel kept on about what a burden she would be. If she had been younger the robbers wouldn't have gotten away, she would have thrown a pot of hot water and her clogs at them, doing anything she could to chase off those bandits. But she hadn't been able to do anything, and there was nothing to stop them from coming back, which meant that Praxel could never feel at ease in her little hut, and that she was only glad that she could now stay with Herr Neumann.

Herr Neumann said that it was a terrible shame, but there was also no reason she couldn't stay as long as she felt nervous, after which he asked her if she had anything in the kitchen that the robbers might want to take, to which Praxel said that she didn't think there was anything there, because the little bit of money she had was hidden in her room, for she never left it out of her reach at night. Praxel kept her money in a yellow change purse that she always took with her to bed and placed under the pillow, sleeping tight against it so that no one could take it away, for she would surely wake up if they tried, though it was possible that the robbers had taken the goat and the hens. Meanwhile Herr Neumann said that Praxel shouldn't worry anymore about it, for if someone had taken anything from her he would replace it, there was no reason to worry at all. Tears then welled up in Praxel's eyes and she said that Herr Neumann had always been so good to her, as had the late Frau Neumann, God bless her, and that God in heaven would surely grant Herr Neumann entry into paradise someday. Then Fritz said that he wasn't afraid, and he grabbed a knife and an iron bar and was ready to head out for Praxel's cabin, much to Josef's surprise, though Fritz was always ready for any challenge, and he'd already told Arthur that he should come along, for they had to see what the robbers had taken, and for that they needed a storm lantern from the dairy. Arthur replied that he was ready to go, but that first they should alert the police in order that they know exactly what had happened to Praxel, Arthur suggesting they stop at police headquarters first and bring one of them along, though Fritz didn't want to bother and said that Arthur didn't have enough faith in him, at which Arthur laughed, and Herr Neumann said that Fritz was being dumb, Arthur was right, that's what the police are for, and Arthur should go straight to them.

Arthur then put on his jacket, but didn't take his cap, while Fritz stayed behind, for Arthur could go to the police on his own, and Praxel had already said how good it was of Arthur to do so, since the police should be the ones to catch the robbers. By then Poldi had finished making the coffee and Herr Neumann lit a pipe, pointing a finger at Fritz and motioning for him to sit down at the table, but in such a way that Praxel didn't notice, Fritz understanding immediately, at which he cleared the saccharin and the sugar from the table, for the business with the saccharin was a shortcut to trouble, as it wasn't legal to mix it with sugar. Nonetheless Poldi had pressed a large cup of coffee into Praxel's hands, followed by three heaping spoons of sugar, leaving the spoon in the cup so that Praxel could stir it well, although she was still so upset that she completely forgot to stir her coffee, her hand jiggling the cup so that she spilled a bit of coffee, though not that much. Herma then stirred it for her and said that Praxel should drink some while the coffee was still hot, it would do her good, after which Herma asked Praxel if she didn't want a little something to eat, Praxel answering that she didn't want anything, though Herma didn't believe her and gave Poldi the sign to bring something. Poldi understood straight off and cut a large slice of bread and spread it with goose lard, since they'd just had some goose lard themselves, Poldi handing the piece of bread to Praxel, who indeed ate it, taking a big bite of it, while whenever Praxel forgot to eat Herma was there to remind her, until Praxel had eaten enough, at which Poldi brought her a second cup of coffee.

By then Arthur was already back, along with two armed police officers, to whom he had explained everything, though they still asked Praxel about everything that had happened, she telling it all once again, just what had happened, after which the police asked if she could give them her key so that they wouldn't have to break in or climb through the window. Praxel began to look for it, and was immediately shocked to realize that she had left it in the door, such that she was completely beside herself. The police cautioned how unwise it was to do that, for Praxel should have locked the door and taken the key with her, but Praxel shouted that she ran off as fast as she could, which was why she had forgotten everything, at which she remembered that she had left her change purse under her pillow. Praxel then began to weep bitterly, for by now it was all gone for sure, the cup of coffee falling out of her hand, the coffee spilling onto the floor and the cup breaking. Everyone then comforted Praxel, laying her back down on the sofa, the police saying that usually robbers didn't immediately return to the scene of the crime once they had been scared off, because they would be afraid to, though the police were ready to head over to the cabin, Arthur and Fritz accompanying them, as everyone wished them luck as they left.

After this Praxel calmed down a bit, as everyone wished her well before heading off to bed, even Herr Neumann, though Josef wanted to stay up, but Herma said it was already midnight and Poldi should go to bed, Herma would sit up with Praxel so that she wouldn't be afraid, while the two of them would wait for Arthur and Fritz to return with the police, Herma promising Josef that she would tell him all about it in the morning, but now he had to go to bed. The next morning Herma did indeed fill him in, telling him that no trace of the robbers had been found, and that nothing had been stolen from Praxel, the key was still in the lock, the purse was under the pillow, even the goat and the chickens were there, and only two plates broken in the kitchen, which Herr Neumann would pay for in order that Praxel would not suffer any more than she already had. Praxel stayed with them for three nights, after which she said she felt it was safe to go home. Arthur brought her a padlock from the store, Leopold having searched for it, and it was arranged for Praxel to get a dog that would keep a lookout so that she wouldn't have to be afraid anymore, everything finally working out for Praxel, though she remained afraid and made sure to lock herself in at night.

Up in Purtscher's fields, Josef thinks about Praxel. He thinks about everything that goes on in Umlowitz, as one day runs into another, everything that he has seen and heard, though he doesn't know that many people, just those who come to Herr Neumann's house and yard, Josef knowing as well the people he is sent to on errands, and the folks in the neighborhood, such as Sekora the butcher, though many of them he doesn't know at all. Sometimes he sees how Poldi chats with one of Sekora's assistants, and sometimes he sees Toni and how he talks about horses with the elder Sekora, who no longer works. Josef also knows Herr Schwinghammer and Frau Schwinghammer, who run the inn where the local theater troupe plays, as well as the orchestra, and the Schwinghammers' huge dog, which is even bigger than Cappi, though the dog is a good-natured beast and suits the Schwinghammers well, for they are also huge. Herr Schwinghammer in fact resembles Rübezahl, the old man of the mountains, though he doesn't have a beard, and Frau Schwinghammer is tall and much heavier than Herr Neumann.

Josef knows Herr Dechant, the priest, by sight, he being the one who performs the service in the church, as well as funerals and weddings, which Josef can hear when the horn music plays that is normally played at Herr Schwinghammer's for people to dance to. When it's a funeral, Josef rushes out of the store, as well as Otto and whoever else wants to, as the funeral procession leaves the church, the altar boy in front in black and white, carrying a cross, followed by the musicians, who play only a chorale at funerals, sometimes Fritz singing a text that Josef doesn't understand very well, since it's all in dialect, he knowing only a part of it, understanding just the bit that goes:

It's happn'd again, it's happn'd again, someone's dii-ied again,
I swear 'tis so—
Knock 'im down, knock 'im down, and cu-urse,
the dirty rogue.

But Poldi says it's a great sin when Fritz sings this, nor does Herma like it, but Fritz sings it nonetheless, even if no one wants to hear it, yet Otto loves to hear it and sings along as well. The musicians are followed by the funeral wagon with the coffin, loads of flowers and wreaths upon it, after which there often follows the volunteer firemen, Herr Dechant bringing up the rear with a cross in his hand, followed by two more altar boys and the mourners and sometimes other groups, all of them marching from the church and past Herr Neumann's store to the cemetery, which is not very far away.

Josef also knows the family of Herr Bilina, the dental technician, who once worked on one of his teeth and took care of it quite easily and without all the fuss normal for a dentist. Herr Bilina is also a photographer, and though he does it mostly for his own pleasure, he is willing to do it for a fee. Once Herma went with Josef to Herr Bilina, for Josef really wanted a photograph taken of the two of them together so that he could give the picture to his mother for her birthday. Herr Bilina was quite happy to do so as Herma chatted away with Frau Bilina, the two of them talking about everything that was going on in Umlowitz, after which Herr Bilina came in and said that he had prepared the plates, and that Herma and Josef should come into the garden, since in such weather he could take a better picture outside than in the office, at which everyone moved out to the garden. There the dental technician had set up a backdrop that belonged to the theater troupe in which Frau Bilina acted, Herr Bilina having allowed the troupe to use a shed in the garden, Herr Bilina's younger brother, who worked as an assistant to the dental technician, also helping out by painting the backdrops in his free time, most of the time through his own inspiration, though mostly using models, Frau Bilina claiming that the younger Bilina was a great artist as she said, "My brother-in-law should really live in the city, where he could earn a great deal with his paintings. However, my husband thinks it better that he remain here and help him."

Everything was ready for the photograph, Josef stood with Herma in front of the backdrop that depicted Italy with the great volcano that was there, as well as the sea and the palm trees, ships appearing on the water, as Frau Bilina proudly said to Josef that his mother would be very pleased if the scenery also appeared in the photograph, for that is the panorama that one sees from Naples. But Josef already knew this backdrop, for it had been used as scenery in *William Tell*, although *William Tell* takes place in Switzerland and not in Italy. Herma said that such a thing could happen only in Umlowitz, but not in a regular theater, there one would be able to paint another backdrop if one thought of it in time, and that Principal Bolek had discovered it too late, just in time for the dress rehearsal, and though he complained a great deal that such a backdrop wasn't right for *William Tell*, and that another one should quickly be painted, on which there should appear the Alps, the younger Bilina didn't have time, because the elder Bilina had too much to do, at which the members of the troupe told Herr Bolek that it was already too late, there was nothing that could be done, and that Vesuvius is also a mountain like the Alps, and that it doesn't matter if it spews forth fire, for people won't notice, and not everyone knows that Vesuvius is in Italy, or even that this mountain was supposed to be Vesuvius, and hardly anyone knows that *William Tell* takes place in Switzerland, while Herr Bolek remained against using it, though there was nothing more he could do about it. That's how the backdrop ended up in *William Tell*, even though no one made anything of it, since people found the play much too serious anyway, yet now Josef was glad to have it as background.

Frau Bilina gave Herma and Josef plenty of good advice on how to arrange themselves and what kind of expressions they should make, as well as how to place their feet and hands so that they didn't look posed. Josef had wanted Herma to place a hand on his shoulder, and Frau Bilina showed her how to do that in a way that made for a nice effect. When Frau Bilina was finally done, Herr Bilina began to speak, for before he had been hidden under the black cloth at the back of the camera, but then Herr Bilina's maid ran down to the garden to say that Fräulein Leirer had arrived, while Frau Bilina said that her husband wasn't seeing any patients now, but instead was taking photographs. But the maid claimed that she had told Fräulein Leirer all of that already, but the Fräulein had nonetheless said that she had a toothache, otherwise she wouldn't have come, at which Frau Bilina yelled up to the maid that once Herr Bilina was done with the photograph he would come up and look at Fräulein Leirer's tooth. But Herr Bilina said nothing and simply remained under his black cloth, while Frau Bilina told Herma that Fräulein Leirer always did this when Herr Bilina wished to make a photograph, for in fact she had no toothache at all, there being nothing wrong with her teeth, she only had a touch of rheumatism in her teeth and all it took was an aspirin and for her to lie down for an hour, for there was nothing Herr Bilina could do for her, since one couldn't take out all of her teeth just because they were sensitive. All the while Herr Bilina said nothing, but Frau Bilina remarked that around Umlowitz it was said that Principal Bolek was courting Fräulein Leirer, and though Frau Bilina didn't want to say anything herself, it certainly could be. Then Herr Bilina announced that he was ready to take the photograph, at which he bent forward a little and shoved the camera closer and called out, "Please now, hold still, just for a moment!" Then at last Herr Bilina snapped the picture and it was finally done. He then said that he would develop it right away in order to see how it came out, and that Josef could pick it up on Saturday. Then Herr Bilina said a quick goodbye and was off to have a look at Fräulein Leirer's sore tooth, Frau Bilina saying goodbye as well, but only after accompanying Herma and Josef to the front gate. The photograph, meanwhile, was a great success and they ordered a bunch of copies to pass along as gifts, Herma keeping one on her nightstand, as did Josef.

These are the people that Josef really knows in Umlowitz, some of them only by sight, while in school he really knows only Principal Bolek, his teacher, Lopatka, and Kreissel, the leader of the chorus who does the concerts at Schwinghammer's. As for the other teachers, he barely knows their names, nor does he even know the children in his class, for he is rarely there, Lopatka noting as an excuse that Josef is always so pale, though whatever question the teacher asks him Josef knows the answer, and knows it much better than all the other children in Umlowitz. But whenever Josef needs something explained he always asks Rudolf, who is happy to help him, or even Arthur, though he has little time, Herma and Fritz and even Herr Neumann also helping out now and then, while Leopold is happy to explain how to handle the customers in a way that satisfies them. Thus Josef learns wherever he goes, asking anyone in the house or even Toni, who says he knows only about horses, coaches, hay carts, and the barouche, though Josef loves to listen to it all, while Poldi shows him how to milk a cow, even though she never lets him do it on his own, despite his pleading that at least he'd like to milk a goat. Praxel also knows a great deal, telling Josef old stories about what Umlowitz looked like a hundred years ago, fifty years ago, and before there were any oil lamps, or before there were any doctors in Umlowitz, when one had to travel to Krumau or farther, people preferring instead to simply let the Reverend come in order to administer final rites. When Praxel's children came down with scarlet fever there was already a doctor in Umlowitz, but there was nothing he could do, and so Praxel also had to call the Reverend in order to have her children receive their last rites before they died. Since then, Praxel had trusted no doctor and wouldn't think of calling one, even if she were a hundred years old, that time with the children being the only time she had done so. If it involved an everyday ailment, no one knew better than Praxel how to take care of it, she knew all the herbs, and if the good Lord could not help there was no help to be had from either a doctor or Praxel.

Up in Purtscher's fields, Josef is happy and thinks that, if he were ever rich he would build a house here and live like others in Umlowitz or, better yet, he would see that the railroad came to Umlowitz, that a new power station was built down near the river, and that his own house stood at the edge of Umlowitz so that he could avoid all the smells from the cow barns, as well as all the flies. He'd like to return to the fields, as well as find a woman as good as Praxel who would bring him bread and milk and cheese, and he would light a big fire that would smell so sweet, and allow children to pick blackberries and strawberries in the woods, himself going into the woods in order to admire the swarms of red fly agaric in all their splendor, there being nothing finer, while he would own a barouche and travel about the district, climbing the high mountains at the border in order to see across Bohemia and Austria.

Meanwhile, yesterday Herma told Josef that maybe Herr Neumann would marry again, for he had placed an ad in the newspaper saying that he was looking for a nice woman of the same age who doesn't have to have any money, since he needs none, though she must be hardworking, as there's so much to do, though all she needs is to be in good health, the ad in the newspaper thus providing Herr Neumann with a slew of opportunities to meet another woman, since he had no time to do so on his own. Herma had said it was a good thing, for Herr Neumann was also getting older, Rudolf would most likely soon go off on his own, for he'd been offered a good position in a sugar factory, while the store should be handed on to Fritz, Adolf having already opened his own business, and Erwin wants to study, Arthur has no plans, since he wants to maybe buy his own farmyard and store in Kalsching, for which his father would have to pass his inheritance on to him now. Josef then asked Herma what she would do, to which she replied that perhaps she would marry as well and take Otto along with her, Herma adding at the end that, indeed, the new Frau Neumann would be arriving with her brother tomorrow in order to have a look at the farmyard and Herr Neumann. The next day Toni hitched up the barouche at four in the morning in order to be on time for the first train into the station and pick up the new Frau Neumann and her brother. Herr Neumann didn't yet know the new Frau Neumann, but her letter had pleased him more than all the other letters he had received in response to his ad, which was why he had written her and sent a photograph of himself. The woman had then written him back and sent her own photo, after which the two had written each other again, and Herr Neumann had invited her to come visit, to which she responded that she would come with her brother.

Until now no one had known about Herr Neumann's plans, but now everyone knew, there being a lot to get ready, at first someone suggesting that they slaughter a pig, but someone else said that slaughtering a pig was too much work, and it was also better that the new Frau Neumann got to know how things usually are, though everything was cleaned, Leopold clearing out the store and washing all the counters, Toni grooming the horses, Poldi checking on all the livestock, choosing two hens to slaughter and roast, Herma having already made a cake. Someone suggested that dinner be served on the second floor, where no one spent any time except to sleep, Praxel arriving to help out and clean the large room above, the apples swept up from the floor and a table placed in the middle of the room. Meanwhile Herma had made new curtains, since the others had hung there for many years, all the bedrooms above also being cleaned, including Herma's room and the beautiful bedroom that was Herr Neumann's, another for Rudolf and Arthur, then that which belonged to Erwin and Fritz, and where Josef now slept. No one really lived in these rooms but instead only slept in them, while in winter they weren't even heated unless someone was sick and had to stay in bed, only Rudolf sometimes having spent time up there when he wanted to study, though now Herma covered each bed with a beautiful bedspread, everything spruced up for the visit. Even the hayloft and the granary were tidied up, as well as the barn in back, while the garden was raked clean where only some apple and plum trees grew, as well as an old wild apple tree, there being nothing else but jasmine, hydrangeas and lilacs, and grass. Herr Neumann even said that he had not even thought about flowers since the first Frau Neumann died, but Praxel said that she had plenty in her garden, and so she brought some along, Herma coming up with three vases, one for the kitchen table and two for the big table on the second floor. Herma set everything up the night before, Josef helping her, the good silver taken out, the plates and cups from the good china, as well as everything anyone could need, Josef very careful not to break anything, for Herma had said that some pieces had already been broken, the kitchen meanwhile filling with the smell of wonderful delicacies. That night everyone gathered, Herr Neumann had a few schnapps, the others drinking as well, even Josef and Otto, though Herma and Praxel, Poldi, and two maids had their hands full, Praxel even staying overnight to help.

In the morning Herr Neumann is up before sunrise. He dons a stiff collar and a proper tie, which he attaches to his shirt front with a tie pin. He then puts on a dark-brown suit that is too tight, such that it hardly covers his stomach, Arthur having ironed the suit for him the day before, since he was the best at ironing, while on his head Herr Neumann places an elegant and stiff black hat that he wears only to funerals or weddings, he looking much more elegant than Herr Iltis, who also has a hat like this. Herr Neumann then has a cup of coffee while standing up, as well as two pieces of cake, claiming that he has to try some for himself, after which he is done. Toni has already brought out the barouche and hitched up the horses, bringing the wagon out through the gate and past the Schwinghammers' yard and around to the front of the house. Then he opens the door as Herr Neumann walks out, after which Toni opens the little door on the barouche, Herr

Neumann climbs in, Toni closes the door again and climbs up to the coach box, and the barouche rattles over the cobblestones of the square and away from Umlowitz.

Otherwise everything proceeds as usual, for Herma says that nothing should be left undone, that Otto also needs to be dressed up, that the livestock have to be tended to, though no one heads out to the fields that day, the cattle are kept in the barn, and everyone dresses well, no one runs around barefoot, though the store is opened as usual, Leopold having to tend it on his own, himself very excited and wearing his best suit, a rose placed in his buttonhole, he not saying a word to anyone that Foxy is in the store, even Arthur letting it pass.

Then right before noon the barouche arrives, everyone in Umlowitz peers out their windows, some even stand in front of Herr Neumann's store in order to see the new Frau Neumann and her brother. As they arrive, Toni jumps down from the coach box and opens the carriage. Herr Neumann steps out and is sweating, because the suit is so horribly tight, after which he bends back into the carriage and gives his hand to the new Frau Neumann, as she steps out with a handbag made of alligator skin and is almost as fat as Herr Neumann, the new Frau Neumann's brother soon following, himself having a mustache like Herr Lopatka's, though no one reaches out a hand to help the brother with his little traveling case that is clearly no longer that new. Everyone has gathered in front of the open door to the store in order to greet the guests, bowing to the new Frau Neumann, who shakes everyone's hand, as does the brother, someone then suggesting that they head into the store, Leopold closing the door behind them. The guests head straight into the kitchen, where there is a lace tablecloth on the table, Herma right away serving a cup of coffee to the new Frau Neumann, who says that she is very happy to be here, for it looks like a pleasant place to live, everyone looking so healthy and happy that even Principal Bolek would be pleased. Then everyone sits down, though the men don't drink any coffee, beer having been brought along from Schwinghammer's, as well as schnapps, the brother saying that he prefers to drink caraway rather than plum schnapps, and so they brought him caraway, along with homemade rolls with cold cuts so that everyone is satisfied.

Once they are finished, someone informs the new Frau Neumann that they must now show her the house and the farmyard, and she says that she'd love to see them, the brother saying the same, the woman mentioning that she has already seen the store and that she was very pleased by it, the brother saying that he can clearly see what a fine store it is. Herr Neumann then informs them that there are no electric lights upstairs, though he will install some if she marries him, to which she replies that it doesn't matter if there aren't any lights, one needs only to lie down to sleep. Then she looks at the room where Herr Neumann has his desk, after which they return to the kitchen and move on through and up to the first floor in order to look at all the rooms where everyone sleeps, as well as the big room, where everything is set for lunch, Herr Neumann saying that they usually don't eat upstairs. The new Frau Neumann replies that it's all fine with her, at home in Prachatitz they also eat in the kitchen when there's nothing special going on, after which everyone heads downstairs and out into the farmyard as Herr Neumann explains everything to the new Frau Neumann, the brother commenting on how well everything is fitted out, before they then walk around the stalls and look at the cattle, the woman saying that they looked like nice cows as she pats Cappi on the back. This pleases Herr Neumann, for he says that Cappi gives the most milk, after which they head into the granary, though they only look at the hayloft from down below in order not to ruin their nice clothes, and then they walk out the backdoor, where there are geese, at which the new Frau Neumann says right off what magnificent down they must provide, everyone agreeing with her about the geese, after which they inspect the barn and look at the garden, as Herr Neumann says that some flowers could be planted here, to which Frau Neumann nods in agreement. Then they all turn around and return to the second floor, since it's already time to eat lunch, the guests sitting down, the new Frau Neumann sitting next to Herr Neumann, her brother beside her, while everyone else is busy carrying out the bowls, moving back and forth. The three talk among themselves, but then the soup is served, Herma having never made a better one, the brother unable to praise it enough and asking for the recipe for the dumplings, while as soon as the soup is finished Herr Neumann stands and says that the two of them have decided to marry, and the new Frau Neumann says that she would love to get married, though she hopes as well that soon Herr Neumann can visit Prachatitz, where the wedding will take place, she also wanting to show Herr Neumann her brother's farm, after which, once they are married, she will return to Umlowitz with all of her things.

Everyone is pleased, Praxel crying and blubbering that Herr Neumann had always been so good to her, Poldi crying as well, everyone going up to Herr Neumann and the new Frau Neumann to congratulate them on their engagement, after which there is a lot of eating and drinking, until Josef is entirely exhausted from it all. Then it's time for the new Frau Neumann and her brother to head off to the station, Toni having already gotten the barouche ready as the brother grabs a bag. Many bundles of food are packed into the barouche, as well as a full bottle of caraway schnapps for the brother, Poldi even going so far as to quickly grab all the flowers from the vases and tossing the bouquet to the new Frau Neumann in the barouche at the last minute, after which everyone continues to wave goodbye until the guests are finally driven off. By then everyone is really tired, Herr Neumann most of all, as he lies stretched out on the sofa in the kitchen and immediately starts to snore, Otto having already gone to bed, Foxy once again in the store as Leopold pets him and Josef falls asleep in his chair.

THE BOX

A T 21 WEIMARERSTRASSE STANDS THE BOX, A LARGE TWO-STORY BUILD-
ing that stretches from Rosenbühlstrasse to Pufendorfstrasse, the sides
of the central building, as well as those of the outbuildings, lying on each of
these two streets. The school is on Pufendorfstrasse, and on Rosenbühlstrasse there are two buildings where some of the professors and teachers live, as well as the inspectors and some of the support staff. In one of the
buildings there's also a walk-in clinic with a nurses' station, this building
being surrounded by gardens, some of them enclosed, though there are little doors along the length of The Box that allow you to enter the courtyard,
otherwise you can exit directly into Rosenbühlstrasse, which is the only entrance from the street into the courtyard of The Box. To enter The Box itself, however, you must approach from Weimarerstrasse, where you ring the
bell, after which Herr Lindenbaum, the castellan, looks out the window of
the porter's apartment, a buzzer sounds, you push open the front door, and
amble through the front garden, which is tended but not used, a set of steps
leading down the path to the gate, at which the heavy door opens and you

go up a set of steps to the next level, to the right of which Herr Lindenbaum stands in his window and asks each visitor the purpose of his visit. Right at the end of the steps there's a door through which you enter the vestibule. To the right is Herr Lindenbaum's apartment, while farther on is a door on which is written OFFICE, after which the vestibule narrows to a hallway that is closed off at the other end by another door. Once you pass through this you reach a well-lit passageway, to the right and left of which are large panes of glass, while on the left is a glass door at the top of a set of stairs that lead into the courtyard, though if you go farther along the hallway you reach yet another door, behind which is the school. Here, to the left, is the door for the conference room, while the school has two sets of stairs, hallways running off each that lead to the classrooms, the lecture halls and labs for physics, chemistry, zoology, and botany, as well as drawing, and the large music room, where Herr Scheck leads singing classes from a grand piano set on a high podium, though the large assembly hall is the most beautiful room of all, its ample splendor opened up only for special occasions.

If you head back to the vestibule you'll encounter a richly ornate stairway with a sumptuous metal railing, halfway up the steps there being a memorial tablet made of marble on which is engraved in gold all the names of the students who gave their lives for the sake of the fatherland in the world war, The Box remaining proud of them to this day. Just past the tablet, some steps lead to the apartment of Headmaster Schorfing, a lovely bearded old man who is the head of The Box, and who stands straight as an arrow and looks like an admiral. The pupils call him The Bull and all of them are afraid of him and bow to him deeply and sternly, for respect is important to The Bull, not only the pupils trembling before him but also all the subordinates in the school. He knows the names of each of the two hundred and fifty pupils, The Bull sees everything and hears everything, nothing remaining hidden from him. The Bull has an assistant who is referred to as the Director, whose name is Winkler, and whom no one is afraid of, he having little to say unless The Bull himself is out sick. Yet once you are no longer a pupil The Bull can be quite affable, his deep voice growling less and less, and the former pupils, especially, once they have set a number of years between themselves and The Box, act as if they are on the friendliest of terms with The Bull, which The Bull by then allows.

Below in the vestibule on the left side there is a door labeled VISITORS ROOM, which is an elegant salon, all the chairs sumptuously covered in scarlet plush, a cut-glass water pitcher standing on the table with some glasses, at which the fathers and mothers sit and listen to what The Bull has to say to them, themselves hardly daring to say a word in response, since they are all smaller than The Bull, and only appreciate what a blessing it is for their boys to be pupils here at The Box. The Bull speaks in measured tones and with condescending friendliness, the fathers and mothers hearing that only obedient boys can remain at The Box, as The Box is not a reform school, but rather is there to raise sound young men who will one day be grateful that they have enjoyed such an upbringing, which is why things here must be run with a firm and unflinching hand, for the youth must not be coddled just because the war was lost through cowardly betrayal. One has to rebuild, and that can be done only with valiant men. Then the pupil is called into the visitors room, The Bull and the parents looking at him gravely, the pupil indeed lowering his head the moment he sees The Bull standing there, as well as his parents, who sit and gaze at their son with both a strong and a pleading sense of despair. But the pupil has no idea what to say and has nothing to say, daring only to greet his parents, since everything is so serious, and only when The Bull says a firm goodbye with a stiff handshake, followed by the father bowing and the mother standing up, only when The Bull is finally gone does the ice begin to melt a little.

Just past the visitors room you reach another door that is sometimes closed, though if you go through it you end up in The Box itself, a long hallway stretching ahead, with a large window to the right that looks out onto the courtyard, while to the left are heavy wooden doors, each with a thick brown window installed in it with a pane that serves as a peephole through which one can look into the classroom if you have the key that opens this pane. At certain times these rooms are closed, each one labeled I through IX in Roman numerals, though Room V is always open, and usually you have to go through this room to get to the other rooms. Across from Room V is the main stairwell, which leads down to the courtyard and farther into the cellar, where the baths are located and the furnace room for the central heating, The Box being equipped with all the latest achievements of modern times, the coal bins also located below, as well as the pantry and other rooms unknown to the pupils. If you climb back up the stairs to the hallway you'll find toilets to the left and right, as well as on the second and third floors in the same location, these specially installed for The Box, with urinals like any other, though the stalls with the toilet bowls are white wooden cages that boast an open set of peepholes for both eyes, so that no one can hide in the stalls. Near the end of the passage, across from Classroom IX, a side stairwell leads to the laundry room, where each week you bring your dirty linens and pick up clean ones, while upstairs is the music room, where pupils practice while learning to play the violin or the piano. Down below, next to this set of stairs, is a little room where the pupils who are not doing well in school spend time each evening in order to study with The Paster, which is what they call Herr Pastor, The Paster looking over their assignments during study hall between three and five o'clock each day, except on Saturdays, The Paster walking back and forth across the classroom in order to keep an eye on his cadets, though each pupil can ask The Paster for help, which he receives straight off.

At the end of the hall is a door that opens into the dining hall, which is very big, all of the two hundred and fifty pupils wolfing down the main meal here together, before which a loud bell sounds, electronic bells that ring at every occasion being everywhere in The Box, the pupils knowing already what each one means, since here they are so well trained that everything runs like clockwork. Before the meal they all gather in a long hallway, each pupil having his own place that is labeled with a number from 1 to 250, the same number appearing on his clothes and everything else, Josef's number being 33. Then they all stand up, the lowest number near Classroom I and onward up to Classroom IX, the even numbers on the right and the uneven on the left, and once everything is in order the door to the dining hall is opened, at which the highest number enters, all of them taking a spot at the long tables on each side, a light-gray tablecloth spread out upon each table, and all the pupils having to remain standing until the hall is full, the door is closed, and a designated student from the highest class says the prayer:

> *Come, Lord Jesus, be our guest,*
> *Let thy gifts to us be blessed.*

Then the pupils shove back their chairs, causing a great scraping sound, as they all sit down, followed by the Sprites, which is what the servant girls at The Box are called who bring the grub, which is what the food is called, four pupils always forming a group around each bowl, the oldest of them designated as the commander of the bowl who orders the others around and takes the first helping for himself, the youngest taking the last, though all the portions are divided equally beforehand.

During the meal loud talking is forbidden, indeed anyone who jabbers away too loudly receives a smack on the head in order to get his attention, the pupils never allowed to be alone anywhere or at any time, even in the toilets, where one can see whatever they're doing because of the peepholes, while in the dining hall there is always an inspector standing by. There are four inspectors, who are called Herr Inspector, one having recently died, the living ones being Schuster, who is the best and whose group Josef belongs to, followed by Bemmchen, the one who in fact is dead, and whose pupils have been divided among the remaining inspectors, followed by Faber and, last, Löschhorn, all of them older men, Faber the oldest, Löschhorn not so old, and Schuster in between the two. Two of them are always on duty, but since the death of Bemmchen there is often only one, though sometimes all of them show up together. There are supposed to be two in the dining hall, but now there is often only one, who walks between the tables in order to keep an eye on things, while at least for lunch some teachers sit at the end of the tables, eating the same grub as the pupils, though they get more, the Sprites bringing them their own bowls and utensils. Once the grub is finished, everyone has to stand up, the prayer of thanks is said, after which everyone leaves the hall again together, beginning with the lowest, followed by the higher numbers, though after the meal the pupils can scatter as they wish without having to march back down the hallway.

If you climb the main staircase to the second floor, you arrive in another hallway, but one that is shorter and ends abruptly to the right, while across from the stairs is a room called The Chapel, though there is no longer any chapel here, because it was dismantled after the war, not because of the revolution but because the space was needed, the stained-glass windows still reminding you that this once was a chapel, candles most often needed for light, as otherwise it is too dark. There are wash tables in The Chapel, just like those in the real laundry, that are made out of long iron frames on which rest black marble tops with holes that drain into washbasins made of tin, each basin resting under its number, and each pupil having a basin and his own spot. After washing, you turn over your basin and set it on the tin grate beneath the wash table, while during the washing up each morning the odd-numbered pupils come first, followed by the even-numbered ones. In the corners of the room are little chests that are full of drawers, though they cannot be taken out but only opened up with a key that the pupils have to keep on a key chain in order not to lose it, though indeed it is often lost or even stolen, and should one be found you have to give it to the inspector, who collects objects in a little glass box near the main staircase. The key is to keep your things locked up, each pupil's drawer and cabinet having a lock that the key fits, but many other keys fit as well, which is a problem, for then things get stolen from the cabinets all the time, though if you lose your key you go to the office, where the secretary gives you a new one and writes it down on your account.

From the numbered drawer you take your toiletry box, which is also numbered, and go to your spot at the wash table and lay it down on the marble shelf that is above the marble countertop, each spot having its own faucet. You then take off your shirt and wash yourself just down to your belt, for you don't take off your pants, but instead brush your teeth and wet your hair so that you comb your hair into a coif, which is what the barber calls it, almost everyone having a coif and proud of it. If you're in the odd-numbered group you have to hurry, for soon the inspector whistles and calls out "Second group!" so that you have to finish fast. Otherwise the washroom is open only before the noon meal and the evening meal in order to wash your hands, though not everyone does that, and if it's found out they get a smack on the head and have to head to the washroom. When the first group is busy washing up, the second group has to shine their shoes, which is why next to The Chapel there is a room especially for this, the pupils placing one foot at a time on a low bench, the tools for polishing also contained in a box similar to that for toiletries, though this one can't be locked, since no one ever steals such things, each pupil having his designated spot in the shoeshine room as well. Once the first group is done washing up, they head off to shine their shoes, and it often happens that you get your hands dirty again with shoe polish, but by then there is no longer any more time to properly wash them, which is why you then quickly run into the toilet, where there are faucets attached to water lines. You can also get a drink of water there, otherwise water is available only in the dining hall in the evenings, the Sprites placing a bottle of water for each group on the table, though they place them along with the grub only for those eating, after which everything else must be set out.

Everything at The Box is handled very precisely, and that is done in order to get the pupils used to good breeding and order, there being many rules, and you have to obey all of them in order not to be scolded and get a smack on the head, which is also why the setup with the washing and the shoe shining was put in place. Because it can happen that during the day your shoes might need shining when the shoeshine room is closed, the little cabinets containing the polishing materials are located outside in the hall, though there are no comfortable benches on which to place your feet, and so you place your feet on the windowsill, where some also like to sit, though that is forbidden. If the washroom is open, then you can walk through it to the dressing room, which has an exit to the side stairwell, but for the most part you use this only on Saturday afternoons in order to get to the laundry. In the dressing room light-brown lockers stand in a row and are fastened to the floor and consist of two parts, their surface covered with holes like showerheads in order that good air circulation is maintained, they capable of being closed both above and below, the lower part wider and containing two compartments where the shoes are placed on top of the linens, while the top compartment is where you put your clothes on wooden hooks and those that need to be ironed on metal rods.

If on the second floor you head left to the end of the hallway, you come to a door that is open only during free periods and especially at night, this being the playroom, where there is a piano on which anyone can play, yet only the older pupils are allowed in, as they try to pick something out on the keys, mostly songs, usually popular ones, there always being a group of them standing around, singing the two most popular songs, the first beginning:

> *Come, let's have a drink, my dear,*
> *Before I whisper in your ear.*

The other begins:

> *My son's name is Forrest,*
> *Since we met in a forest.*

Others belt out patriotic songs, but that doesn't happen so often, while to the melody of "Watch on the Rhine" some sing vulgar lyrics when there's no grown-up around, which begin:

> *A fart blows out the oven door,*
> *Mother thinks the coffee's scorched.*

There are also four billiard tables in the playroom, one for children, two others that are somewhat better, while one is the right size for grown-ups, only the oldest of the pupils allowed to play on it, there also being two other tables with special games, around which the youngest pupils gather, since they're meant for children, and in addition there's a row of different game tables that are square and have four chairs around them with hooped backs.

The playroom has another small door through which at night The Bull sometimes enters, since this door leads directly to his apartment, and whenever The Bull arrives most everyone is afraid, as whoever is sitting stands up and bows to The Bull, who only says "Evening" and gives a sign for them to continue playing. At the tables the pupils play chess and checkers and Nine Men's Morris and a fun new game called Don't Lose Your Temper, though cards are not allowed, except for children's card games. The Bull looks on, the pupils having to pretend as if he weren't even there, but naturally they are uneasy, many of them nervous and turning red in the face. The Bull likes to be affable when he's in the playroom, and as he chats with the pupils some of them want to suck up to him as they talk and smile at him, and if they feel comfortable enough they ask him questions and pretend they really want to hear the answers, and as The Bull explains something to them he sits down at a table, a cluster of pupils gathering round him in order to listen to him like placid sheep, their mouths agape in their wonderment at everything he has to say. The Bull also knows who among the pupils are the best chess players, for the pupils have a chess club that is divided up like the classes, each with a master, as they play tournaments against one another, and so one knows exactly who is the best in The Box. The Bull asks who would like to play chess with him, but only the very best feel comfortable enough to do so, for they are proud when they can play a game or two with The Bull, one even having once beaten him. Years ago The Bull also played billiards with the pupils, but he no longer does so, for he has a heart condition, one of the pupils having heard from Inspector Schuster that The Bull is not at all healthy, which is why many worry about him, as it's dangerous for him to yell loudly, though he still quietly bellows and gets red with anger. No one has a voice as powerful as The Bull's, no inspector can yell as loud, only Faber coming close, Inspector Schuster also having told a pupil that The Bull would probably outlive them all, for he has a wife who works on him with magnetization, running her hands over his face when he has a spell with his heart, as he lies in bed and she says prayers until he recovers and is again healthy and can be seen throughout The Box.

If you take the main staircase to the third floor you'll find the dormitory, which contains beds for all two hundred and fifty pupils, the toilets to the right and left, while the beds stand in long rows, all of them bolted together in pairs, a piece of black iron standing between so that none can move into the adjoining bed, though there is a bit of access between them, as holes are cut into the iron that create a pattern that reminds one of a four-leaf clover. And between each pair of iron double bedframes there is an open aisle with a stool at each end on which each evening the pupil lays his clothes and then takes his nightshirt out of the bed, his shoes placed on the shelf that is on each stool, where during the day he puts his house shoes, which is what slippers are called, though house shoes are worn only when you have to go to the toilet.

Eight-thirty is bedtime, a bell ringing just prior to it throughout The Box and the courtyard, at which everyone must head in, though in no particular order, many choosing to head to the toilets, though you hear "Hurry up!" because of the time, while near the main staircase, where you find the glass box with the lost-and-found items, stands The Bull, gazing on at the pupils, and it's normal, not required, that everyone go up to The Bull and give him his hand, which leads to a lot of shuffling feet as heels are clicked together and bows are made, and The Bull says good night to the pupils. The Bull doesn't like it if someone passes by without saying good night, but since there are so many pupils it doesn't really matter if one ignores him, Josef going up to him only now and then, and not liking to at all. The inspectors are also often there, and you can say good night to them as well, but that matters a lot less, and so only a few pupils go over to them. Above in the dorm you're supposed to go straight to bed, and there it's the opposite of how it is in the classrooms, for here the lowest numbers are to the right, instead of to the left below, though the bed wetters are placed right next to the entrance, the night monitor waking them up on a regular basis so that they can head straight to the toilet, himself sitting there throughout the night, except for when he makes his rounds. But when waking the bed wetters doesn't work then their beds are lifted up onto two stakes at the base, so that they lie there on an incline and are ridiculed by everyone, though doing this doesn't work, either, after which they are left alone.

In the dorm you have to undress quickly, for the inspectors walk through the room and make sure that everyone is soon done. Two inspectors spend the night, but since there are only three sometimes only one stays the night. A platform made of wood has been set up to the left and the right for them, a carpet leading up to it like a pulpit, though the bed cannot be seen, since curtains surround the platform which the inspector can pull open when he wants to look out into the room, while from below all that can be seen is his head. After the lights are turned off it's not really dark, for throughout the night lights are left on that give off a weak, strange light, which causes many new pupils to be afraid, for it's green, Josef thinking that in such a color is where one finds water spirits and mermen, if indeed they are not just fables in themselves. Once the big light is turned off, the inspectors make one or two more rounds, then climb up onto their platform and turn on their night light, which shines softly through the curtain, the night attendant also making a couple of rounds before retiring. In the morning everyone is up at five-thirty, the bells ringing again and for a good while, so that everyone wakes up, anyone who is not out of bed immediately being helped out, it's all done military style, though not quite, since all of that is forbidden following the war, although not entirely, in order that the young are not coddled too much. Only on Sunday is the wake-up call later, coming just past seven, though many are already awake, since they're used to getting up early.

Whoever wants to get to the courtyard from The Box has to use the main staircase, because the side staircase is always closed, the courtyard a huge square full of dull yellow sandy gravel raked smooth every day, which is why there are no flowers or grass, but there are trees that stand in three rows with tall, doleful trunks, two of them located at right angles to the third on the courtyard side of the main building, benches running the length of them as in a park, though the fourth side has no trees at all. On that side is the gymnasium, which is closed during recess, as it is used only for instructional classes, and it is opened for special events, usually in fall, when on one Sunday a big festival is held. That's when all the pupils and many of their parents gather there, for it provides a comfortable space for everyone to be in together as the former pupils are celebrated, Inspector Faber proudly leading them in and quickly installing them from the tallest to the shortest in a single row, at which the inspector orders them to be seated in order that others can see how splendid they look, and especially so that the current pupils can see how the older men look when they march in parade formation with the inspector at the front. The former pupils have already formed a society that almost everyone belongs to who is still alive, for there are many who died in the war, since The Box is indeed quite old, even though the building itself is not, it having been built just a few years before the war to serve as a modern and practical facility for The Box. Back then the entire Box was moved from the inner city to the outskirts, which in those days was a great advancement, though there are those who still re-call the old Box, because they worked there, The Bull having been there by then, and supposedly he had a beard then as well, though each little hair was black.

Many members of the alumni society are today distinguished men of the world, some even older than The Bull, with wives and children and grandchildren of their own, some of their children also having become pupils at The Box, though it doesn't happen very often. Josef would never send his child to The Box, yet some members of the alumni society think the education at The Box is excellent, but they don't actually think much about it, even though across the yard in the school building there is a special boardroom for them, with high-backed leather chairs that surround a conference table with green felt, though rarely is a meeting ever held, or at least Josef has never heard of one. Many members fought in the war, and some pupils went directly from The Box to the front because they volunteered, although they did not have to, the oldest pupil usually no more than seventeen and the youngest just ten, while in the war many pupils and even more former pupils were wounded, some turned into cripples, while for those who died there is the memorial tablet made of marble.

These former pupils also come to the fall festival and gladly don the caps that are worn exclusively by the pupils of The Box, which are brown caps with black bills, the members of the alumni society often looking funny in these caps, for they no longer fit them, especially with their big stomachs and beards and bald heads, although the pupils are urged to lend the former pupils their caps, for they are as proud to wear them as little children. Years ago The Box was completely different from today, for now there are too many wimps, mainly because proper exercises were no longer allowed, whereas earlier everyone had his own proper uniform, but Inspector Faber says that later no one was allowed to wear military dress because of the unfair peace treaty that had been signed. The education back then was far better than it is today, it now being no better than a girls' finishing school, where everyone is a wimp because marching exercises are no longer allowed, the inspector wanting to live only to see the day when everything is like it used to be under the emperor, because how it is now is a scandal, though no one can ever say that it's a scandal, for the Communists will just lock you up, which is why he'd rather not say anything, but that's what he thinks, a proper youth being someone who achieves a certain poise and keeps his teeth tightly clamped. Inspector Faber complains further about how sad it is that Inspector Bemmchen will never have the chance to see it happen, because he's dead, for he had suffered the ignominy of it all like no other, which is why it pained him so, though Josef doesn't understand it all, for he doesn't know how Inspector Faber thinks it really ought to be.

For the fall festival Professor Worzfeld, who is called Ojt, prepares a gymnastic exhibition that doesn't involve any competition but includes the high jump and the long jump, the shot put and the javelin, and much more, as well as team sports, especially soccer, which all the guests watch. They're happy to see how hearty the youths are, and that they indeed aren't wimps, even if they no longer do military exercises as Inspector Faber longs for. For the festival a large tent is put up in the courtyard, much as a circus does for its menagerie, and garden chairs are brought in so that all the guests can flee to it should there be rain, or a snack bar can be set up under it, the Sprites bringing from the kitchen large pitchers of herb tea like the kind that is sometimes served at dinner, and barley-malt coffee like the kind served for breakfast at The Box, the guests also having to drink such swill, which some also call donkey piss, without any milk, since not much of that is available. The barley coffee and other drinks are sold by women who are married to the alumni, while from baskets they sell the snacks, which include buns with margarine and liverwurst, though there is also cake that is not from The Box, tidbits also having been purchased from elsewhere, all of it on sale for exorbitant prices, but all of the guests are happy to pay since it's all for The Box. In the tent there is also a raffle full of valuable items that the members of the alumni society have donated to The Box, each item carrying a number, and one can buy lots made of white paper strips that have been rolled onto a needle and look like little scrolls, which you unroll to see whether you have won anything. Most of the scrolls are blank, yet you can buy twenty scrolls or more and not win anything, but when there's a red piece of paper with a number on it inside the scrolls, then you win a prize, which can be worth a lot or be a complete joke as well.

When there is nothing special going on at The Box, the courtyard is empty, except during recess, when it can be quite dusty if it hasn't rained in a while, and when it gets quite bad the courtyard is watered with a long hose, which really helps in hot weather, for then it's easier to breathe. For the most part the courtyard is empty, but there is a soccer field with two proper goals, though without nets, such that the ball always flies beyond the goal itself, breaking windowpanes for which the guilty pupil must pay, the pupils having to pay for everything they smash, or their parents do, for it's written down and kept in the office where the bills are made out. During important matches, however, there are nets in the goals, but only then, and in the courtyard there is lots of room for other games to be played besides soccer, such as rounders and handball or any kind of ball game, and yes, even more soccer, while in the two little courtyards to the right and left of the main staircase there are two tennis courts, though only the older pupils are allowed to use them and must pay to do so, two other little courtyards containing wooden frames on which clothes are beaten, the pupils sometimes having to beat and brush the clothes, after which their work is inspected.

That's the way things are at The Box, and though it is quite big, it's not too big for two hundred and fifty pupils, but in fact a bit small, for there is no place that you can ever be alone, nor are you allowed to just wander anywhere in The Box, and even where you are allowed you can't always get to, as everything is closed off in between. Since Josef is not happy at The Box, he can't get used to being there, and he also knows that he never could. Meanwhile, when he goes to sleep and is lying in bed and can't sleep he breaks down and sobs out of sadness. He no longer thinks that it is hard at The Box just at the beginning, when no one is happy, while later most of them grow to like The Box, such that toward the end they are sad to reach the highest class level and must leave The Box for good. Josef has often been told this, and he has tried to believe it, but now he knows for sure that it's not true for him; he is only suffocating here, many pupils are brutes, and he doesn't like what they say or even play at, nor does he know how to try to make things better, Inspector Schuster having already said to him a couple of times, "My boy, my boy, you have to pull yourself together in order to become a man! You need to play with the others and make friends!" The inspector means well, but his advice is useless, and Josef must only make sure that he doesn't cry too loudly, so instead he weeps quietly now and then in the dorm, no one noticing, until at last he falls asleep.

Every pupil in The Box has a proctor, which is a pupil who has been at The Box for a minimum of one year and whose job is to help you know what to do and get used to things, but everything is so monotonous there's no getting used to it, even if you do know how things are supposed to go, such as when to get up, and that you have to get dressed quickly, though you don't need to make the bed, for that's what the Sprites are for. You then rush into the washroom and hang your jacket on a hook, open your cabinet, take the box of toiletries, and run to a washing-up spot, as your neighbor wastefully splashes water about, the water ice-cold, such that in winter it even hurts your teeth. If you don't bend your head down close enough to the washbasin, you are yelled at and your face is pushed into the water, the floor full of puddles as you grab the hand towel, because you have to dry off quickly, folding it over so that you can dry off your back, but since it's so easy to bump your neighbor you hear again the cry "Hey, watch what you're doing! Can't you see that you're hitting me?" And once again someone shoves you, and those who are not strong enough to defend themselves get a thrashing. That's a main rule at The Box: you have to be strong so that you are able to thrash the others without being thrashed yourself, for that's how you learn to be a real man who doesn't let anything bad happen to him in life, since at The Box whoever is not a tough guy is a shit. The pupils use many such vulgar words, as they cuss a lot and are proud of how hardened they are, nor is there any protection available if someone hits too hard or is mean, except if you have an older brother or friend, and even then that doesn't always help. The bigger kids look down on the younger ones and are proud that they are older, and they say a beating does no one any harm, because they were beaten as well, though few of them admit this and act as if they had never been small, for it's a mortal sin to be a young boy.

After washing up and shining your shoes you rush off to the classrooms, which are arranged so that almost thirty pupils fit into each, everyone having his own desk with a chair, five desks always lined up next to one another that can be shoved out of the way if needed, the oldest pupils sitting by the window, the youngest getting the worst spots, even if their eyesight isn't so good. If you have bad eyes you have to be very careful, for if you don't watch out someone will rip your glasses off your nose and smash them on the ground in order to break them, or the attacker doesn't wait for the full thrashing to begin but instead goes straight for the glasses, everything lost after that, as it is better perhaps always to have a spare pair of glasses, though actually any glasses are a handicap, and you are laughed at for having them. Meanwhile, when you get to the classroom each morning the desk stands open, the lid rising straight up, and inside are schoolbooks and notebooks, while in back of your seat, where the number is painted, there is actually a compartment that can be opened, in which books and games and whatever you want can be stored, be it care packages from home or other extra things to eat, such as the malted balls that are always sold by a wounded veteran at a table by the main staircase. And, because locking it with a standard-issue key does nothing to prevent things from being stolen, you can make arrangements to get a padlock, for which you have to pay, some even making use of a combination lock, which you have to know which way to turn in order to open.

Across from all the desks in the classroom stands another desk that belongs to a pupil from the highest class, and whenever no grown-up is present he can order the others in the room about, especially during study hall, though he never says anything to those in his own class, the pupils from the highest two classes acting like grown-ups, each wearing a tie, and it being an embarrassment should one not wear long pants. That's why the younger ones also like to wear long pants, or if they are short they should be breeches, for they look somewhat grown up, while even the youngest also wear a tie. In each classroom there's a saying on the wall that says something about a good education, and in Classroom I, where Josef sits, it says on the wall:

Hard work and diligence help form the wings
That will help you attain most anything

But in another room, painted on the wall is:

Ohn Fleiß kein Preiß[*]

Once a classmate of Josef's had written *Preiß* with a sharp "ß," but when Professor Felger returned the notebook *Preiß* was crossed out in red, since it was wrong, because it should be spelled *Preis*, with a round "s." The professor was very angry and said that one should also not spell the plural as *Preiße*, as in the local dialect that would be taken to mean a "Prussian," for

---

[*]This phrase translates to our contemporary phrase "no pain, no gain." However, as the passage that follows is about how it is misspelled in German, I have chosen not to translate it in order to allow the difference between the sharp "s" or "ß" of the spelling on the wall to play out against the round "s" that Professor Felger says it should be. It should also be noted that *Ohn* is a very old-fashioned way of spelling *Ohne*, or "without," in German.

Preise was right, but then a student said that he saw it spelled with a sharp "ß" in study hall, where *Preiß* was written on the wall. Professor Felger, however, didn't believe him, for that was totally wrong, at which others chimed in and said that it indeed was written on the wall, Professor Felger deeply surprised to hear this, as he said he still couldn't believe it was true, for most of the students hadn't written *Preiß* but, rather, *Preis*, the professor then asking the entire class who thought that it should be written as *Preis* and not *Preiß*. Most then answered that they believed it should be spelled the way it was in the spelling book, but still it was written with a sharp "ß" in the study hall, at which Professor Felger said he had to see for himself, though he couldn't do so during class.

In the next period, when the professor returned after the break, he had indeed looked at the saying on the wall and found that *Preiß* was written with a sharp "ß," and said that he couldn't believe it, that it was a mark against The Box, as there had earlier been other painters and varnishers who were still diligent and who were respectful of the mother tongue, but these days no one ever cared about spelling anything right, illiteracy being rampant and causing everything to go to pieces. His own son, who had suffered a hero's death in the war, would, even as a young boy, have been able to tell the person painting the saying on the wall how to spell the word correctly, and even Professor Felger himself had known the correct spelling as a young abecedarian, and he said that he had spoken with The Bull and asked him why none of the inspectors had noticed that the children were learning bad German, the corruption of the language outrageous, though he would let the office know that the shoddy spelling would have to be corrected. Then Professor Felger explained what kind of silly results can happen if you don't spell things correctly, it being ridiculous to write *Rolladen*, for that's actually wrong and sounds like something you'd eat, though it has nothing to do with that, but instead the word is *Rollladen*, being a combination of *rollen* and *Laden*, since it's a *Laden*, or "shutter," that you roll, which is why it's not right to leave off the third "l," for the third "l" is needed, and it's not true that it looks awful. Whoever is not pleased by it should only recall that one must never corrupt the mother tongue, for through such carelessness one ruins both style and so much more, Professor Felger soon providing more examples to prove his point. Thus one should write *Damp-*

schifffahrt always with three "f"s, even if you don't put a hyphen between *Dampschiff* and *Fahrt*, for it's easy to see once you hyphenate the word how silly it would be to use only two "f"s. If you simply want to corrupt the language, then you could just write *Kaffeersatz* instead of *Kaffeeersatz* with three "e"s, but then you might as well say that two "e"s is already too many, and then just write *Kafersatz* with only one "e." But when the entire class laughed Professor Felger said that there was nothing funny about it, but rather sad, for he was afraid that someday no one would know the mother tongue, and that it would be worse than in the time of Frederick the Great, under whom at least many things were better than they are today, since back then there were noblemen who had their hearts in the right place, and who would hang their heads in shame if they were alive today. But back then the language was terrible, since everyone preferred to speak French, the king himself setting a terrible example, bringing that idiot Voltaire to Potsdam, though today there was no longer any reason to corrupt the language so, there no longer being any Frederick the Great, and French is never used, since no one now knew how to do anything except play soccer and drive a car.

Early in the morning the pupils briefly visit the classroom, though they're not supposed to be there at all, for soon the call for inspection sounds, which is held in the courtyard in good weather, and in the hall outside the classrooms in winter, the pupils having to stand in rows divided by class in front of their inspectors, while those who actually belong to Bemmchen are divided among the three remaining inspectors. The inspection of the two highest classes doesn't take long, the inspector looking the pupils over just for a brief while before he has them turn around, after which he usually dismisses them, though with the other classes it takes longer and longer for each one, since the inspection is very thorough and arduous. You have to hold out your hands in order to show if they've been washed well or not, whether the fingernails are clean and not too long, turning your head so that the inspector can look at your ears, checking behind each one as well, shoes having to be presented in order to check if they are spick and span, while you also have to lift each foot, for the heels and soles are also checked, followed by your clothing in order to see if there's a spot anywhere, each row turning around and bending, as well as having to lift your jacket so that the inspector can see if a trouser button is missing. It all goes according to command, and there's always something to be reprimanded for, since each inspector is tough, though no one cries or complains at inspection as much as Faber, who also hands out blows to the head with each reprimand. Some students are sent back upstairs by their inspector, and sometimes an older pupil accompanies them, since there may be shoes that need cleaning again, or your coif needs to be smoothed out, the throat or the ears washed again, the worst being when an older pupil takes on this job, since he can do what he wants with the younger one, and so he takes a hard brush and scrubs until everything is red and hurts, teeth brushing also sometimes needing to be repeated or something with the fingernails, or clothes needing to be changed. Such sinners must return to the inspector in order that he can see that everything has been put back in order.

After the inspection the bells sound again, everyone reports for breakfast, the line of pupils presses into the dining hall like a slow-moving cylinder, the Sprites already setting out the white enamel pitchers full of donkey piss, the pitchers themselves somewhat chipped and battered, the swill containing skim milk or powdered milk, which is what gives the barley-malt coffee its dirty gray color. Each group of students gets a pitcher and a saucer on which there are four minuscule lumps of sugar, each pupil getting two or three small biscuits with a thin layer of margarine spread on each, which tastes terrible, as if it were made of soap, the bread tasting like straw, all of it so dry that you have to wash each bite down with a swig of donkey piss. Yet these are hard times, it's not even four years since the war, and one has to continually tighten one's belt, as supposedly before the war there was more to eat at The Box, the biscuits covered back then with real butter. Breakfast lasts until seven o'clock, and at seven the bell rings again, at which all the pupils must be in the classroom for study hall, which lasts until eight, no one allowed to leave his place at his desk without permission, everyone needing to stay quiet, though whoever wants something must quietly go to the room commandant and whisper to him what he wants, which the commandant can allow or forbid, depending on how he feels, or you can go to the inspector who walks back and forth through the classroom, though no one is allowed to gab with his neighbor, because it's a disturbance, while turning around on or scraping your chair is also forbidden. You simply take your school things out of the desk and pretend, without playing around or fooling around or giving any sign, though no homework is done, as that should all have been done the previous day, and you need instead to get ready for what's on tap for today.

Josef is still tired early in the morning, and so are other pupils but you can't loll around and lay your head on the desk, for you can't be a sleepyhead at The Box, because then you won't grow up to be a proper man. Indeed, one must be brave in order to soon overcome the war that has been lost so that everything can be well in the world once again. Up till now Josef has always believed that everything will turn out okay once you've grown up, but now he always hears how terrible the world really is, every country run by scoundrels, and in Germany there's nothing but traitors in charge, nowhere being as well run as The Box, which takes only good children from good families, it being a school that prepares you for life if you stay here the whole six years, for there are no bad influences, and anyone who doesn't obey must be taken away by his parents, who will have to figure out for themselves what to do with such a misbehaving son, although none of this explains why so often most of the older pupils are so mean and priggish. It's these who please the educators, who say that they are on the right path, and that one should follow in their footsteps in order to become as sharp as they are. Is it a crime that one is still young and not so dashing? And why pick on the younger ones so and give them such a thrashing, rather than help them and show them how to do things better, to become truly dashing and upstanding? Yet Josef tells no one what he thinks, for they would only make fun of him, and everyone thinks that he's a sniveler, Inspector Faber having even said that Josef is a spoiled mama's boy who still needs the proper upbringing to become a man.

One time a pupil, who was only one class higher than Josef, called him a "Czech pig," because he was from Bohemia. This made Josef so angry that he said to the rascal that he was a German pig, at which the other boy went to The Bull and The Bull became incredibly angry, more upset than Josef had ever seen him become. Just before the long break, The Bull called Josef in, the rascal also standing there when he arrived, a number of pupils standing around, as well as a couple of adults, as The Bull asked loudly whether it was true that Josef had called the other boy a "German pig," to which

Josef answered yes, it was true, but before that the rascal had called him a "Czech pig," which was why Josef had said it back. At that The Bull looked like a cooked lobster and quite strongly asked whether he was a German, since in fact he spoke German and had no trouble doing so, but Josef was so upset and sullen and intimidated that he said nothing. He no longer knew what he should say, it was all the same to him what he was, and so he kept silent and just hung his head, though The Bull asked him even more emphatically the same thing again, and Josef continued to cower and to remain silent, as The Bull said again that Josef had to answer, at which he whispered in a monotone that hardly anyone could hear, "I don't know." Then The Bull laughed angrily and said, "That's something when someone doesn't know what he is and to whom he belongs! That's the way it is with the Gypsies, who wander from place to place without a land of their own, surviving on whatever slips into their fingers!" Then The Bull wanted to know whether other foreigners could answer the same question, at which a young boy stood up who was from Haida in Bohemia, The Bull asking him, "Tell me again, what are you?" The young boy had proudly called out, "I am a German!" At this The Bull said nothing more, but instead thrashed Josef and ended up slapping him a couple of times, saying as he finished, "Just so that you know what you are! You got what you deserved!"

Josef couldn't see or hear anything. The Bull had disappeared, the pupils let him go, and so he slowly crept off and felt ashamed down to his very bones, and more miserable than ever, and yet he didn't understand really why he had been punished, or why the rascal who had started it all had not. The other could take pride in the fact that his attack had been allowed, whereas what Josef had said was not. Many days passed without Josef speaking to anyone, nor did anyone speak to him, which made him feel as if he didn't have a single friend in The Box, nor did he want one, rather he wanted only to get away from here because he was so unhappy, even writing home to ask if someone could come visit, though he is told that he is being selfish, there is no way they can pay to make a special visit to him, for it costs a lot to go to The Box, and one must make sacrifices if he is to remain there. Then they told his father a bit about what he had said, yet they said nothing about what had been said to him first, although Josef did not want them to say what had really happened, for he began to feel guilty, since everyone was mad at him and believed that he alone had done something bad.

There was no way Josef could write about what had really happened, for he didn't trust the mail since it was censored in order to make sure that the pupils didn't spread lies or report anything that could do harm to The Box's good name. In general, you're allowed to write a letter home only once a week, but nevertheless, you must do so, which happens on Sunday, there being always something to tell your parents about, except for those who live nearby. The gathered letters then go to the head of the family, all the pupils being grouped into families, Josef a part of Ojt's family, the head of the family having to read all the letters from his family in The Box, there being nothing more for him to worry about, since it's not really a family at all, and in fact he lets the oldest pupil take care of the pocket money that he is supposed to disburse each Saturday, the money amounting to no more than is enough to buy three little clumps of malt, the administration reimbursing the heads of the family for it, since ultimately it is the parents who must pay. If you really want to write home, you go to the head of your family, and if he consents, then you can write an extra letter, which the head of the family reads through, and if he has no problem with it he seals the letter and makes a small mark on the back so that the front office knows that everything is okay, whereupon the letter is stamped and mailed.

Ojt would never allow Josef to write about the pig incident, the nicest of the heads would forbid that, and Josef wants to forget about it anyway. After a couple of weeks nothing more is said about anything that happens in The Box, since by then there's always something new that's happened, and you can't keep up with every incident. Several times things have been stolen from Josef, yet the culprits remain unknown. Once his wallet disappeared from his jacket in the washroom, once his locker was broken into and a packet of food from home was taken, though when he reported it he was scolded, since he shouldn't have had any food in there. Another time Josef lost his key, and when he left his desk open he told someone about it whom he trusted, but the other said it didn't matter, to which Josef added that he kept his stash of emergency money there, which the other also said didn't matter. But the next morning the packet with the money was gone, and Josef didn't know who had snatched it, though the boy was shocked and said he was amazed how many thieves there were in The Box, and that something could just disappear overnight, after which Josef told Inspector Schuster about it all, but he only scolded Josef for having lost his key again, asking if Josef suspected anyone, to which Josef answered that he knew of no one, the packet never appearing again.

Josef grows ever more lonely, sticking to a corner of the courtyard on his own, though when the weather is nice and almost everyone is outside, he holes up in the classroom, where he reads a lot and feels best of all, dreaming of what the world outside looks like, all of it open and beautiful and unattainable, as in a panorama that you see before your eyes, but which you can't enter, though he wanted to enter and go even farther, leaving The Box behind, Josef no longer having to spend time in the dormitory or eat with the students, The Bull's screams no longer audible, and no one calling him a pig. But Josef can leave The Box only during the vacation, or in special instances, when a visitor from afar asks for him at The Box through Herr Lindenbaum in the visitors room, and if The Bull grants permission for Josef to receive a pass. As soon as Josef gets such a pass for an afternoon's leave, he runs to the inspector on duty, who gives him the key to the clothing room so that he can put on a good suit, as well as quickly wash his face and hands, Josef running to bring back the key, at which the inspector casts another glance at him to make sure all is in order, upon which he runs into the visitors room to the waiting guest and is freed from The Box for a number of hours, though this happens much too rarely.

Only the pupils from the city and the surrounding area have it better, since they can leave The Box every week, or almost every week, as long as there is nothing going on, only new students not being allowed to go home in the first weeks, nor are others encouraged to visit them, The Bull very clear about this, since it does nothing to help them adapt to the spirit of The Box. Whoever has good grades can leave after the two o'clock meal on Saturday in order to get themselves ready, after which they are inspected and then get their pass from the same inspector, while others leave later in the afternoon, some having a bath first, though those who have gotten into a bit of trouble have to wait until nine o'clock on Sunday morning to leave, or even until eleven, though anyone who has behaved really badly has to stay at The Box. Pupils from the two highest classes who don't visit their parents can leave on Sunday after the two o'clock meal if they are in good standing, something that's called a free pass, though they have to be back by six o'clock sharp. They head into the city, most of them together, going to the movies, walking around, sitting in the pastry shop and stuffing themselves, some even going for a beer or a liqueur, which is forbidden, yet no one asks them about it, while at The Box they brag about it, and no one tells on them, for you can't squeal on the older ones, it being a sign of disloyalty to everyone. Whoever doesn't respect this is swept into a corner or a closet without anyone seeing and promptly thrashed and beaten relentlessly, Josef knowing this to be the case and having seen it happen for himself, though he has never told on anyone, for he wouldn't want a beating, it all frightens him so, and he wants to remain free. Josef has discovered a way to get on Herr Lindenbaum's good side. Accidentally, he had heard that you only have to give Herr Lindenbaum a present and he'll be very friendly, so Josef had brought him a piece of real butter, causing Lindenbaum to wonder to himself and ask if Josef was regretting something he had done, but he said he was just happy to give him the butter. Herr Lindenbaum then took it and thanked him and said that Josef was a good boy and should make sure to come to him if he needed anything. This pleased Josef, for he already knows that Herr Lindenbaum lets a few pupils whom he likes out of The Box for a couple of minutes in order to buy some crumb, cheese, and pound cake over at the bakery, these being two of the nicest minutes you can have, except that they go by too fast, Herr Lindenbaum saying that The Bull was willing to look the other way because the grub in The Box really wasn't all that good.

Josef had also discovered that the lenses for his glasses were quite specialized, because after someone in The Box yanked them off his nose they broke, and the optician to whom you were allowed to go from The Box, if the inspector gave permission, said himself that he couldn't get these lenses for at least fourteen days, though it was easier to get them in the center of the city. Josef informed the inspector of all this, and he agreed that Josef had to get there, and for that he got a pass. After that he sometimes secretly smashed his glasses into the ground in order to get out of The Box for a few hours, except that it was too expensive to do so very often, although it wasn't too bad, but he didn't want anyone to discover what he was doing and it didn't help all that much anyway. Josef did it only when he could no longer stand to constantly look at the faces in The Box and the courtyard and the classroom, it being wonderful when Herr Lindenbaum presses the button and the door opens, and Josef slams it shut with a bang, the first free minutes consisting of incredible happiness. He runs as fast as he can and thinks about freedom only for a moment, but it's over before he knows it, for Josef cannot go any farther, as he would be caught immediately, which would only mean more trouble hounding him, and so instead he tries to enjoy every second, looking at his pocket watch, which others in The Box call an ugly old onion, because it's not made of silver. Josef sees how the second hand continually moves and, once it has made a complete circle, before another minute has passed he has to be back in The Box, where the bell will continue striking, there never being an end to it. Then Josef puts the watch back in his pocket and only wants to forget it, vowing to have a bit more fun while buying some sweets and snacks, as well as a little present for Herr Lindenbaum, before he finally arrives at the office of the optician, who already knows him and says, "So the glasses have broken in two again? My boy, my boy, Zeiß the lens maker of Jena couldn't keep up." Then the glasses are fitted out, and it's already time to return to The Box, Josef feeling numb, his head heavy, his heart almost standing still. And then The Box is there again and looks as peaceful as other buildings, it being larger and carrying a gold inscription with the school's full name, Professor Felger sometimes commenting, "The institution is golden on the outside and cruddy on the inside!" Josef guesses that he should already be back by now as he slowly lifts his hand toward the doorbell, but he waits a bit longer, pulls the watch out of his pocket, and sees that there actually are a couple of minutes to go, after which he feels that he's magnetized, as The Bull is by his wife when he has heart problems, though Josef eventually must yield as he pushes the button, Herr Lindenbaum looking out as it rings, and Josef is once again stuck in The Box.

Once when the older boys were down below for their bath, Josef went into a classroom just to be alone for a while, only to discover the boy to whom he had said that he was worried that his packet of money could be stolen because his desk was open, then the next morning it was really gone.

This time, however, he didn't pay any attention to the boy and just wanted to read a book, but the boy said that it was time to take a bath, so why wasn't Josef doing so, and that he was just about to go himself, in fact they could go together. Then Josef left and took his swim trunks, the hand towel, the soap, the nail brush, and the comb, rolling them all up together as everyone did at The Box, the boy coming along as well, when suddenly the latter said that he had to go back because he had forgotten something, and that Josef should go on ahead of him, the boy would soon follow. Josef didn't think any more about it and was already in the bath, but when he returned from the bath to the classroom a classmate was upset that he had just received a packet of food that day and had eaten hardly anything from it, everything having been locked in the cabinet of his desk, and now it had all been stolen, only a couple of biscuits and some paper still left, while everything else was gone, even though he had asked his classmates if they knew anything about it, for everything had been there just an hour ago when he went to take a bath. No one in the classroom knew anything, everyone had left the little room, and after Josef listened for a while it finally dawned on him what had happened to his own packet of money, and so he went to the one who was so upset and said to him, "I need to talk to you, for I have a suspicion as to who it is." Then he told him what he had observed on his way to the baths, that he couldn't be absolutely certain, but that he believed that the boy must have taken it, and that he should inquire about him.

Then they went to the inspector on duty, who happened to be Löschhorn, after which they looked for the boy throughout the entire Box, until they finally found him and said he had to open his desk and cabinet, although he said that he had taken nothing, nor had he ever taken anything, though they said to him, "Then open up! If you haven't taken anything there's no problem, and you can just close them up again!" Then he had to open up, but he smirked through it all, for he was insulted that anyone would think he could have stolen anything, while once he had opened up everything it all looked as if there really was nothing inside that didn't belong to him, though Inspector Löschhorn simply reached in and found everything from the package hidden behind other stuff, the middle schooler recognizing everything that belonged to him, the next development occurring when there appeared the name of a fine-goods store in Meerane, which was where the middle schooler was from, Inspector Löschhorn asking, "Now, my boy, where did you get these things?" But the young boy still kept saying that he had never stolen anything, he knew nothing about how those things got there, though the middle schooler said that all of it was from the package he'd gotten that day, the young boy continuing to maintain that he had stolen nothing until the middle schooler yelled, "I also have witnesses!" The inspector, however, said there was no need for witnesses, the middle schooler just needed to say if all of it was his, whether anything was missing, at which the latter looked carefully at everything and said, "It's all here. There are only two apples missing, which were already gone." To that Inspector Löschhorn replied that the middle schooler should take all of his things, and the young boy would soon see the consequences of what he'd done, as the inspector would speak to The Bull, for thieves weren't allowed at The Box, the inspector saying that he would have to lock the boy in the little room where The Paster teaches his cadets, while the middle schooler should give Josef something as a reward, since he was the one who had uncovered the thief. The middle schooler did indeed give Josef something, and was genuinely friendly to him from then on, but no real friendship developed from it.

The boy who had stolen the things got a couple of slaps from The Bull, who then ordered even stronger measures, the kind that came at the end of a dressing-down from The Bull as he ordered a circle to be formed around the sinner in the middle, from which a couple of older pupils stepped forward to beat him for real. The one convicted is defenseless, even if he tries to hold his hands up to his face or pushes back with his elbows or kicks with his feet, for the others are much too strong, and the stronger boys like to hit with all their might until The Bull says that it's enough. The Bull then leaves and everyone withdraws, and the guilty one is reduced to a lump covered in blue welts, but no one pays him any attention, since no one is allowed to do anything more to him. Yet as the stronger boy whisked the thief away from Josef's classroom he no longer felt bad for him, for indeed he would not be allowed to remain at The Box, which is why a couple of days later he disappeared and went back to his parents who lived near Wurzen, since thieves were not tolerated at The Box.

When the study hall early in the morning is over, the bell rings again, and the pupils pack their schoolbags, running across the courtyard into the school in good weather, otherwise the doors are opened and you can walk across without even a coat. School lasts until twelve, sometimes until one, a short pause occurring after each period, the one at ten lasting a bit longer, during which two half slices of bread stuck together with margarine and beetroot marmalade are distributed as a second breakfast from large baskets, the pupils lining up on the first floor in order to get a single serving each. During the longer break you can also go to Marta, the head nurse in the infirmary, if you feel you have something wrong with you, but on the other hand you shouldn't just go anytime you feel like it, for Head Nurse Marta gets very cross if you show up needlessly, it being only reasonable to go if you're bleeding or feel really sick. The head nurse believes in toughing it out, instead of going to her for any old scratch, for you can put up with a little headache or tummyache, the head nurse having little time to do anything if all two hundred and fifty pupils came to see her every day. If you show up, the head nurse asks what's the matter, and then dispenses some kind of powder or a spoon of medicine, or sprays something in your eyes, washes out any small wound, smears on a salve, puts on a Band-Aid, or unrolls a bandage, everything taken care of in a jiffy. Josef can't stand her, nor can many of the others, she being helped by two regular nurses as well as two dispensers, since more and more pupils end up having to stay in the infirmary. When Head Nurse Marta thinks that something is really wrong with a pupil, she orders him to go to the doctor, who then performs a thorough examination, though now there is a new doctor whom the head nurse doesn't like, because he believes that one should be quite sympathetic when it comes to illness, and is against the use of powders and much more in favor of using wet wraps that slowly bring a fever down, this causing the illness to last longer, resulting in much more work for the nurses, which angers Head Nurse Marta more than anything else.

If a pupil says that he is sick, the head nurse sits him down in a chair, dips a thermometer in alcohol, and sticks it under his arm, and if it's higher than 100 she says, "You have to stay in the infirmary." If you have only a small fever you can get the things you need in the infirmary from The Box, but if it's higher than 102 you have to stay and have someone get what you need, be it a nightshirt, slippers, toiletries, or whatever else you want, though not all that much is allowed. When the head nurse thinks it's infectious, she has isolation rooms where you are completely alone, Josef having always wanted to get such a room, while others are afraid of them, saying that's where you go when you have scarlet fever or diphtheria, though if you are sick with these you don't stay in the infirmary but instead an ambulance comes and takes you away. If the isolation rooms are empty, then sometimes Head Nurse Marta can stick someone in one of them as punishment for causing too much trouble or mischief elsewhere, though again what a pleasure Josef feels it would be to be punished so, if only the head nurse weren't so nasty. Sometimes she also suspects that someone has intentionally made himself sick in order to get out of The Box for a while, yet she says she is proud to keep the pupils healthy, and that her sickroom is not overfull, except when there's a rash of flu or a stomach virus, which can never be completely prevented, but that's when the head nurse is in a bad mood and is always very upset that the new doctor is so against the use of powders. Josef wonders why so many pupils say how nice it is to be sick now and then, claiming that you can at least get some extra rest and don't have to get up so early, many going back again and again, for he doesn't find the grub up above any better, since it's almost exactly the same as what's served in The Box, except with much more broth, and herb tea rather than barley coffee, though it's true that the doctor is very nice, always making a couple of jokes during his examination.

Whoever among the pupils wants to be sick simply has to eat some soap, for it causes a fever, but the head nurse knows this and simply takes away all your soap if she suspects someone in the infirmary is doing this, making sure that you have some only when it comes time to wash up. Some hide a second bar of soap and chew away on it when the head nurse is not looking. Once Josef also wanted to get sick in order to escape the torments of The Box, slicing off a piece of his soap that evening and swallowing it, so that the next morning he felt terrible and feverish, then on an empty stomach he swallowed another piece of soap, after which he didn't want any breakfast. After study hall he was so miserable that he could hardly stand it, at which Inspector Schuster came up to him and asked, "Are you feeling sick?" Josef answered, "Yes, I think I'm really sick!" The inspector replied, "Go straight to Head Nurse Marta! It also looks to me that you're not well. You're as pale as milk!" Yet because Josef could hardly walk the inspector sent along an older pupil, who had to almost carry him up the two sets of stairs to the infirmary, but, sick as he was, the head nurse was angry at being disturbed that early, though as soon as she looked at Josef she said right away that it looked to be the flu, and as she took his temperature it climbed above 104, so she kept him there, while the older pupil had to take Josef's key and go back downstairs to get his things. Josef felt so miserable that he never wanted to eat soap again, and when the doctor arrived he explained that it looked like a bad stomach flu. It took ten days for Josef to feel better, although he no longer wanted to be sick at all, for he was indeed very sick, dreaming the first night that he needed to march in the courtyard, but there the courtyard was endless, going on and on, The Bull then showing up and asking loudly whether Josef knew who he was, at which he yelled so loudly in his sleep that even Head Nurse Marta was kind to him and sat up with him for a while. He got better after that, but the fever lasted an entire week, Herr Lindenbaum having twice sent him up a piece of cake that had been baked by Frau Lindenbaum rather than coming from the bakery, Inspector Schuster also sending along a couple of apples with the hope that he would soon feel better. Then Josef was once again healthy, and he felt a bit chagrined for having deceived others, for the flu had certainly been caused by the soap, even if the head nurse and the doctor had not figured that out.

When school gets out at midday, you have to return to The Box, and Josef doesn't know if it's better to be in The Box or at school, but he likes Dr. Wagenseil's natural-history class, for he's an actual scientist, and he writes down good marks in his notebook if you raise your hand and say something worthwhile, and that counts toward the final grade. He had also once shown how cocoa, cocoa butter, and sugar could be combined to make chocolate, after which he asked the class if they wanted praline or bar chocolate, everyone shouting "Praline!," and so he formed clumps that were meant to be praline, each student getting a piece, though Josef was a little disappointed, for it was actually only chocolate that wasn't filled with anything. Nonetheless, Dr. Wagenseil's class is often wonderful. Sometimes you get to look into the microscope when he demonstrates how quickly pollen from the stamen grows in a sugar solution, or he shows them infusorian and other tiny creatures or algae. Sometimes he turns the lights off and projects films onto a screen, once even showing them live water fleas, such that you could see their hearts beating, as he explained that his dissertation had been on the auditory canal of the water flea, for he had been the first to discover it.

Josef does well in Dr. Wagenseil's class, and he is also one of the best students in his entire class, even though he is not that good at math, Scheck the head teacher having assured him that he would never be a success, though Scheck is not even a mathematician but teaches chorus for the most part, being short and fat and very strict, for he carries a stick that he smacks people with, yet he's not all that bad, Josef even enjoying chorus with him, for he's good at chorales and canons, and can play the piano surprisingly well. Toward the end of the school year Scheck always assigns a song that begins with the words "Now for the last time," it being a crucial piece that every class except the highest practices, since it is sung to those students as goodbye, which is why it must be sung especially well, no one allowed to sing along who doesn't have a good voice or whose voice has recently broken. Scheck practices it for weeks during class and even more during extra hours on the days when those in the highest class are taking their final exams. Whoever wants to sing comes to the chorus room and is put into one of several groups labeled sopranos, altos, tenors, and bass, though hardly any of the students can sing bass and even fewer can sing tenor, as Scheck beats time with the stick, gesticulating so wildly and criticizing and praising, working on it until it is finally perfect. Finally the graduation ceremony is there, everything in The Box astir, everyone donning his best suit, the pupils leaving The Box wearing dark-blue suits, happy that they will soon be allowed to smoke, since that is strictly forbidden in The Box and actually rarely occurs. Now the graduates are quite nervous and run around the entire Box, all the rooms open all the way up to the dormitory, since the graduates need to pack their bags before ten in the morning, when all the adults and all the pupils enter the assembly hall, strangers also attending, be it relatives of the graduates or members of the society of alumni, who immediately begin appealing to the new graduates to join by having them fill out applications. Soon everyone sits in the assembly hall, the graduates in the first three rows, the faculty on the platform at a long table, the inspectors there as well, The Bull sitting in the middle, while behind them stand the pupils who sing "Now for the Last Time."

Then The Bull gives a long speech, which is touching but also stern, as he tells the graduates that they must make The Box proud and not forget it, that they should be grateful because so many had worked so hard to give them a good education in order to turn them into brave men who will serve the fatherland whenever it calls upon them, at which everyone pulls out his handkerchief, for on this occasion no one is a wimp if he cries, the wildest ones often being the most moved and blubbering uncontrollably as a result. When The Bull is done, the president of the class begins to deliver a speech from memory, saying how wonderful The Box is, that no one will forget it, and how thankful they all are to everyone for having given them so much, which is why the graduates honor them by carrying the banner for The Box onward in their lives, and that it will be an honor to do so, the class president then thanking The Bull for working so assiduously on behalf of the pupils, and if now and then they had disappointed him it was only because they were young, though they still knew his inexhaustible goodness, the class president then thanking all the teachers and calling out their names, as well as the names of the inspectors and everyone else who had contributed their time and effort in making The Box such a wonderful place. After this talk the graduates move to the platform, and the speaker extends his hand to The Bull and loudly clicks his heels, then he goes to one teacher after another, to the inspectors and especially all those who have squeezed onto the platform, and clicks his heels to each of them, all of the graduates now on the platform, each of them clicking his heels in turn, after which they return to their seats. Then everyone sits, only Head Teacher Scheck doesn't sit, but instead goes to the back and blows the proper tone on a little pipe, followed by a sign that tells the pupils to begin singing "Now for the Last Time." Then everyone begins blubbering, even those who didn't howl earlier, some on the platform blubbering as well, only The Bull not crying, today looking doubly dignified, providing a powerful sight, as if sitting on a throne and looking like a rear admiral, holding up his massive head with its white hair like a candle as the song comes to an end. Then everything is finally over, everyone leaves the assembly hall, the graduates stop sobbing, most of them staying for the midday meal, gazing at everything in The Box as if they had never really appreciated it before, then one by one the group of students begins to dwindle, their empty desks standing open, everything else open and empty as well, the entire Box looking strange.

In the school not all teachers enjoy as much respect as Head Teacher Scheck or Dr. Wagenseil, who is the student adviser. There is also Professor Gelbke, who often cannot seem to prevent chaos from breaking out in his class, the pupils competing in odd races in which they use the benches that are not attached to the floor, each row scraping forward more and more, the first row reaching the podium the one that wins, at which Professor Gelbke notices for the first time, though he still doesn't understand what has just happened. Once they locked Professor Wolkraut out of his room by placing a bench against the door, so that he could barely open the door and couldn't move a step farther because he couldn't shove the bench away, he cursing and hissing as always, and then he ran off to get Director Winkler, who was standing in for The Bull, who was ill, but as soon as Winkler arrived with the sick Bull there was nothing blocking the door, Winkler puzzled as he threw a questioning look toward Wolkraut, who could do nothing but look dumbfounded. Meanwhile Lampe taught French, there always being lots of noise in his class, everyone saying whatever he wanted to, but even though he didn't get much respect he wasn't afraid to smack a few heads, for whoever didn't speak French got his ear pinched by Lampe, which could certainly hurt, even though he was quite old. Lampe complains that hardly anyone has a good French accent, he having explained a thousand times the difference between saying *ils ont* and *ils sont*, though it always gets mixed up nonetheless, even when he stamps his foot and says, "The 's' in *ils ont* is like that in 'soap,' and in *ils sont* it's like that in 'zephyr.' " Nonetheless it's said wrong again, and Lampe takes his grade book and slaps everyone on the ear who doesn't get it right.

The most remarkable of all is Professor Felger, the old man who teaches German and botany. He has beautiful white hair and yellow horn-rimmed glasses, which he constantly takes off and puts on again, often looking stern and yet sympathetic as he gazes out over them. In his class it's quiet as a mouse, no one daring to make a peep, nor had he ever had to give anyone a crack on the head, as during the period he hardly ever gets up from his seat, his skin white and delicate and full of wrinkles, his hands bony. Josef had been in his German class, where he talked about poems and demonstrated how they should be said in order to recognize their meter, Felger saying them slowly and clearly, drawing out each stressed syllable to its fullest, saying whoever *rides* through *night* and *wind*, his head nodding to the beat and beating time on his desk with a pencil, after which he lifts his head and looks out at the class. Professor Felger is not happy with the state of things these days, especially at The Box, he often saying that everything today is rotten, the old ways are gone, and thus the war had been lost, though he still remembers how it was in 1870, when there was unity under Bismarck, but now all governments are a mess, no one can just go about his business, for the neighboring countries never will allow it, and the miserable German language is full of nonsense, everyone having spoken flawlessly when Goethe and Schiller were around, as well as having made sure to protect the language from corruption, while whoever cannot speak or write the language correctly has allowed his soul to be corrupted.

When Professor Felger was young, about as old as those in Josef's class, Uhland died, he having, after Goethe and Schiller, composed the best German ballads, though now there are no longer any good poets who have the power to write a good ballad, perhaps the last being Baron von Strachwitz, who wrote "A Savage Song," though it's not really a ballad but rather a pronouncement on our times:

> Come, O roar of battle, screaming thunder,
> Wounds gaping amid death,
> The people's anger, the people's murder,
> Our dawn will come still yet!

Such verse can no longer be written today, for the language has been corrupted, it being good enough only for bad novels that one shouldn't read, since their style is ruinous, and no new book ever touches the heart. Professor Felger loves to talk about his villa outside the city, there he tolerates no new-fangled contraptions and no silly luxuries, instead wanting nothing but simple nourishment, for elderberry soup was healthy, while Uhland had written such a lovely poem about how the poet had stopped for a bite at a wonderful inn, that being The Apple Tree, the best inn of all, nothing tastes better than a fresh apple, from which you can press apple cider, no need for any nasty-smelling beer. In fact, when his mother wanted to buy something special for the children there had been pineapple or numerous sweets, which only rotted your teeth, but the mother had roasted apples that came sizzling out of the oven, after which she read fairy tales aloud, which Ludwig Richter had illustrated so beautifully, it being the kind of simple life that everyone needed to return to. Professor Felger hopes that it's not already too late, though he knows he's an old man, which is why he changes nothing in his house or garden, where there is also a pump that has long been out of service, it having a tin roof over it, under which singing birds build their nests. Yet the pump is falling apart, its brittle handiwork having collapsed during a late-winter storm, though Professor Felger couldn't bring himself to clear it all away and throw it out, the rest of the pump still standing there today, reminding him of the birds that had raised their broods there. What has happened to the pump is the same as what happens to people, they are brought down by a storm, which is why it's good for children to revere their parents and be grateful to them, after which Professor Felger says something about his fallen son, though not much, the students laughing after the class is over, since they didn't dare do so during it, for if one so much as cracks the slightest smile at the corner of his mouth the professor looks at him so earnestly over his glasses that all laughter disappears.

Professor Felger also talks about the blossoming of cars and soccer, as they were blossoms that really grew on their own. Cars have blossomed most of all, creating dust and an awful lot of noise that rattles the windowpanes, it also being a blossom that stinks and is nurtured with gasoline instead of water, its flower not the rose but a blaring horn that scares both people and animals and causes them to run, especially the poor dogs and geese and chickens, which don't notice the cars blossoming everywhere that run over them, as well as swallowing up children at play, though people love the blossoming cars, because they speed along, such that no one has to remain stuck on a farm or in a pasture, while *whoosh! whoosh!* everything races by, no one thinking about the sanctity of nature. The blossoming of soccer, however, is even worse, for it infects children as well and holds them in thrall, twenty-two men running after the soccer blossom in order to try to press it into the goal, but it is the people who press against one another and become brutal, because soccer is not an innocent game that encourages good manners or simply passes the time, instead it represents at its core the ruin of Germany, and in addition one has to inflate the soccer blossom just like the egos of those that run after it, though there is nothing worse than the countless idiots who show up to watch twenty-two clowns scramble around the soccer patch. Having finished, Profesor Felger looks earnestly at the class, for he knows that the pupils have their own soccer patch growing in the courtyard of The Box, though he doesn't say another word about it.

Those who finish school at twelve, that being the younger pupils for the most part, run across to The Box and for an hour can do what they want, followed by the washing of hands and the midday meal, after which they gather in front of Classroom V, where an inspector hands out the mail and reads from a card who has received a package, which you can then pick up in the front office from the bookkeeper, which he then must record. If no one answers right away to his name being called, the inspector calls it out again, but when a pupil at last answers the inspector yells "Sleepyhead!," followed by everyone yelling "Sleepyhead!," after which they get a smack or a shove, but when someone doesn't show up for mail call, he then receives his mail during study hall, though he has to wait until afterward to read it. After the mail is handed out nothing happens until three, and if it's not raining it's fun to run out to the courtyard, where you romp about and chase after the soccer ball, which most like to do, it being lucky for Professor Felger that, except for teaching, he never spends time at The Box, abstaining even from attending the fall festival, and so he doesn't see what couldn't help but sadden him even more, namely how no one cares what he preaches to the students, no one takes his teaching seriously, for no one wants to be a wimp who still pees in his pants. Inspector Faber has never joined in on the soccer, he says, because he is already too old, but he does like it, because he says it keeps the body limber, and sometimes he helps with inflating the soccer ball, for especially when one is busted he knows how to fix it, knowing how to use glue to patch a ball and working hard at it, as he says that when one can't do proper exercises soccer is a good substitute. Indeed, soccer is a war game, you have to overcome your opponent and beat him, though you also have to remain sportsmanlike and nobly extend your hand in conciliation, because the inspector also serves as the referee. If a shot is fired that's especially strong, it's called a bomb, and Inspector Faber loves to see such bombs fly halfway across the yard, the other inspectors also liking to watch for a while, The Bull rarely showing up in the courtyard, but when he does he also has a look at the soccer game, though most often he watches from a window in his apartment while smoking a cigar, taking in nothing much of what's happening below.

Recently the dead inspector has finally been replaced by someone new who has to be told by the three older ones how to do the job, himself watching how everything goes as he follows like a dog at the heels of the other inspectors, though he likes best to shadow Faber, since no one is as strapping as he is, for Kunze, who is the new inspector, is a former officer who is tall and thin, such that he looks straight as a ruler, and no doubt he will make for a good inspector, since Josef heard Inspector Faber tell Inspector Löschhorn that one can rely on Kunze, and that he will work out fine. Soon it gets around The Box that Kunze is a straight-as-an-arrow nationalist who has real marrow in his bones and a genuine sense of duty, the others soon turning over to Kunze the pupils who used to belong to Bemmchen, Kunze quick to take charge and handle things even better than Faber. A number of pupils like Kunze because he likes sports and enjoys soccer, even wanting to play along with the pupils, at which they discovered that perhaps Inspector Faber had not told the truth when he said why he couldn't play, for when The Bull happened to see the new inspector kicking the ball he called Kunze over and told him that as a grown-up he had to maintain his distance from the pupils. Yet no one had any problem if you independently went to Kunze and asked to do some gymnastics and exercises, there being no requirement that one does, for it's all voluntary, but many pupils appreciate the chance to do so, it not being a daily requirement or anything military, as some say it is, but rather something that has more to do with physical development, which now Kunze often leads in the courtyard.

At three the bell sounds for study hall, which lasts until five. It's the same as that which occurs in the morning, except now is when you do your written homework, everything needing to remain quiet as one of the teachers, who is the head of the family for a number of pupils, walks back and forth among the nine classrooms, along with an inspector and The Paster, checking whether everyone is really working, though no one sloughs off or secretly does something else. But Josef knows how easily you can be distracted if you have something in your desk that is not allowed. Josef loves to make little drawings that are imaginary maps of realms that don't exist, beginning with the borders, after which he fills in squares, circles, and points for the cities, all of it outlined with ink, then with a pencil he draws lines for the railroads that run between the cities. Very slowly he does it all, it taking almost a week to complete such a map, himself enjoying how the web of railroads grows ever more thick, no one discovering Josef's little hobby, for he has good ears and his seat is in a good location such that no one can sneak up on him from behind, which the monitors so like to do, suddenly popping up behind one's desk without notice in order to see what the pupils are really up to. Josef doesn't mind study hall, for no one bothers him there, he's never bored, and he likes the quiet, as he enjoys a good number of his studies, though nonetheless he makes only a show of studying by staring into an open book as he dreams of what's going on in the world outside The Box. At four o'clock there's a break when everyone runs out of the classroom and storms the toilets, the afternoon snack handed out in the hall outside, all of it proceeding exactly as it does during the second breakfast.

Then at the sound of the bell the second study hall begins, which is just like the first, after which the bell rings once more, everyone free and sending up a great noise, each wanting to go out and play, soccer starting up again, everyone doing something, some yelling, and so on until seven, when it's time to wash your hands for dinner, after which you head off to eat, shoving your way into the dining hall, sitting down with your school group, the meal soon over, and off you go again, the evening study hall run on a volunteer basis from seven-thirty until eight-thirty, complete quiet also having to be maintained during it, though there is not the same strenuous oversight as in the regular study hall. Whoever doesn't want to visit can do what he pleases, be it walk along the halls or stand around, or even head to the game room or go out into the courtyard lit up by the sharp cold light of streetlights one usually sees. There has to be good light everywhere in The Box, in order that the pupils don't get into trouble anywhere, and the evenings go by so fast that before long everyone is tired, the bell sounding for bedtime as everyone climbs the stairs to the dormitory, another day done, just like every other weekday at The Box, Saturday and Sunday providing the only diversion available.

On Saturday there is no regular study hall after breakfast, since many are not present because of having received a weekend pass, the main activity on Saturday being the bath, which is horrible. You go downstairs to the cellar, which is incredibly packed, because the baths are much too small, there being some tubs that usually are not used by the pupils if they have not been assigned extra tubs, and so all bathing takes place in the showers. Inspector Löschorn once said that the baths were the only thing terrible at The Box, since there were so few showers, two pupils always having to share each one, the bigger one bathing first, followed by the smaller one. Then there's a wild press as one shoves the other in, it getting louder as they do, some lashing out and hitting others and pushing, as well as defending themselves, though the weak suffer and are helpless. There is also an inspector below, but always just one, who does his duty and turns the handle for the shower, since there's not much else he can do, while out in the front room where the pupils undress everything goes to hell as they put down their things, though it's best not to bring along anything valuable, no watch and no money, it being better to lock all of that up in your desk beforehand so that it doesn't get stolen down below. When during undressing or dressing the others find something funny about someone because there's something odd, such as silly underpants or something else, then everyone laughs or makes fun, and because Josef has the kind of underwear that buttons, some continually razz him, since no one else in The Box wears such a thing, it being for a baby or someone who shits his pants, nothing that a boy would wear, and so Josef had to ask that he be sent different underwear. Everyone has to undress in such a way that no one sees anything, for in The Box that always causes immediate shame, as someone immediately points a finger at your forbidden parts and says something awful if you are inadvertently naked for a moment or show too much, which is why each boy has bathing trunks that he pulls on before he takes off his shirt, while when getting dressed he does the same thing, taking first the fresh shirt and then dropping the bathing trunks and drying off underneath, after which he finishes dressing, though he has to wash and wring out the bathing trunks, so that they don't drip all over his locker. When you want to take a shower, there have to be sixteen pupils in order to save water, the inspector turning it on, though he purposely makes it too hot or too cold, only Inspector Schuster taking some measure of care, the water turned off after two minutes, during which time you soap yourself and then go back under the shower in order to rinse off, and then bathing is over, for there's a shortage of coal, which is why the swimming pool in the baths is most often empty, now and then it being opened up for a little while, the cool water only ankle deep.

After bathing there's nothing else special on Saturday, except that the school groups are not maintained that evening or on Sunday, each pupil sitting down to eat wherever he wishes, ad hoc groups forming, though otherwise Sunday is the worst day in The Box, especially when there's a hike. This is required of all healthy pupils and lasts four hours, when the weather allows. On Sunday there is no schedule to keep, since there is no school, and so from breakfast until the midday meal there is nothing at all, only a couple of pious pupils attending Protestant and Catholic services with their parents, which during the war had been held in the chapel, though those who do go to church say that it's no big deal. Inside The Box the hours barely creep by, as you write your weekly letter home, or at best read a book. But how can Josef settle in to read if he's constantly wondering if the weather is bad enough to prevent a hike from taking place? Most of the pupils don't like the hike, though at lunch it's always said that there will be a hike, although if one cannot be entirely sure what the weather will be like at two o'clock, then most likely there will be a hike, and if the sun shines most are sad that the hike is on for sure.

Five minutes before two the bell rings, "Let's hike!" is yelled throughout The Box, everyone heads out to the courtyard, where you form two lines, though you can decide whom you want to have as a partner on the hike, but before you head off you have to quickly get your school cap from the clothes room if you don't have it in your desk, and if it's not warm enough or it's raining you also have to take your coat, for no one should catch cold. There are always a couple of pupils who have a reason not to go on the hike, be it the sniffles or some kind of leg wound, though the inspector decides if it's a good enough reason to miss the hike, he telling most that it will do them no harm to go along for the hike, and that it's best to be off. Then the only hope is that at the last moment the weather will turn bad, everyone looking up at the sky to see if it will finally rain, the inspectors also looking up and saying that these are only passing clouds that won't amount to anything, the hike can proceed, though a couple of pupils call out that they have felt a couple of drops, it being better not to go for a hike. Then the two inspectors confer with each other and finally decide whether or not the hike will happen, it being a rare good bit of luck if the hike is canceled at the last minute, after which everyone can head back into The Box and do what he likes, be it play in the yard or in the hallways, in the classrooms or in the game room, while it can also occur that around two-thirty someone yells that the hike is back on, that they need to leave quickly in order to have enough time for a hike. The upper classes form the head of the line, the lower ones following, and at the end the inspector places a couple of older boys, who make sure that no one stays behind, the two inspectors seeing to it that everyone has a partner in order that the spirit of The Box is honored as they leave it, after which they hand out the afternoon snack wrapped in paper.

Then the pupils finally march off, not through the vestibule exit but directly from the courtyard into Rosenbühlstrasse, after which they hike through the streets, it being deadly boring, standing still not allowed unless it's at a crosswalk, where one has to wait, "Stay in line" often heard so that no space opens up in the lines, most often their path taking them over the bridge known as the Blue Wonder, and then up the mountain through the settled suburbs where Professor Felger lives, though they don't pass his villa. Farther on they head into the forest, which is quite desolate, even when the forest is beautiful, for you have to keep pressing on and cannot stray from the path, it only being rarely allowed for the two rows to stop to rest, but only for a little while before they are formed again. During the hike Josef feels more unsure of himself than he does at The Box, for during a hike there's nothing to do but hike, until finally you reach the destination that the inspectors say is their goal, it always being a coffeehouse, where one can rest and sit in the garden along with a couple of day-trippers who gawk at the pupils in their brown caps, some of them even knowing that they are from The Box, as the inspectors go to the innkeeper and order coffee for everyone that is nearly as bad as that served in The Box, the pupils opening up their snacks, making sure to throw the paper in the waste can, the snack over before you know it. Then someone again yells "Line up!," the hike is about to move on, though at least it's now headed back to The Box and goes along a different route, since it's better to hike two different paths, but it doesn't really matter what path you hike on, since it's all so miserable. Then finally you cross the Blue Wonder once again and head back into the city, Rosenbühlstrasse soon approaching and The Box, the gate to the yard standing open, then once more closed, the inspectors satisfied since they enjoyed the hike, yet only they enjoyed it, the pupils running from the yard as fast as possible.

Many are tired from the hike, Josef as well, and sit down wherever they can, the evening meal soon following, after which all the pupils who had a pass return, as the evening passes quickly by, the bell rings, eight-thirty already, time for bed, as they head upstairs to the dormitory to lay their clothes on a stool, the pupils pulling the blankets over them, the big light turned off, the green light appearing once again. Now Josef feels alone, though it's not so bad, as he thinks about everything that goes on in The Box, and why it is the way it is. He sees The Bull as he stands below, next to the main staircase, people clicking their heels to him, followed by Inspector Faber, who always wants to parade, Josef seeing everything that goes on in The Box, his feet somewhat sore from the hike. Josef knows only that he wants to leave The Box, for he'd rather not grow up to be the kind of proper man who, above all, will do honor to The Box, nor does he want to join the society of alumni, for as soon as he can get away from The Box he never wants to see it again, he never wants to pass by the castellan Herr Lindenbaum again, even if he has never done anything to him, since he's not a bad man. Even if Josef should one day see this city again, he'll never visit anyone in The Box, nor does he ever want to set foot in Weimarerstrasse again, Professor Felger being the only one he'd like to see, if he is still alive, so that he can show him the garden with the destroyed pump, under whose roof songbirds had nested until the brittle pump fell apart and became just a memory. From far off Josef can hear the song "Now for the Last Time" in his ears, though already he has forgotten almost everything, he knowing nothing more of The Box and thinking no more about how much he has been yelled at here, his eyes closing instead so that he no longer sees the green light, or hears the night attendant who sits up on his chair in front of the toilet in the foyer, everything going out inside Josef, because it's quiet, as he falls into a dreamless sleep.

LANDSTEIN CASTLE

Exactly halfway between Adamsfreiheit and Leinbaum, a little building stands in the open countryside, this the train station for Adamsfreiheit, with its three tracks running between tufts of grass and weeds, two of the tracks lying free, while on the third stands a couple of freight cars in front of the loading dock to the warehouse. Each day three passenger trains and a freight train use this narrow-gauge track. The manager's office, which also sells tickets, is staffed by two men, though otherwise the station is completely empty if no train is scheduled to arrive, while even then only a couple of people get on or off, the journey a slow one since the area is mountainous, not much attention having been paid when the tracks were laid, for they had to conquer unnecessary and considerable rises in elevation. Reddish-brown cresses grow in hanging pots at the station, next to it a little garden with fruit trees, between which vegetables and flowers flourish, while chickens strut and peck at the ground, the manager's dog now and then roaming about.

Downhill from the station the road travels past fields and meadows to a small village, which is Leinbaum, a somewhat neglected though not really poor village that is nonetheless active, and yet in which strangers are rarely seen, the entire area quite remote, which is surprising, when you consider what a well-known realm it is that Ranger Brosch oversees, one where two thousand years ago this area covered by dense woods was home to dreamy, sparsely populated villages, the *legio decima* of the Romans roaming the countryside, though today since the area of Adamsfreiheit is not known to the world and has no mining, but instead farms and livestock provide a humble living, the villages have few inhabitants, possessing neither industry nor any specific trade, the next small town over ten kilometers away. Adams-freiheit is a tiny market town, its majority of single-story houses giving it the appearance of a village, its little church made of gypsum also looking coun-trified, the school homely, the post office and telegraph depot hidden away in a neglected shop, the two shop owners carrying only the most essential goods in order to cover the reduced demand, while if one wants something special the reply is always "We don't have it."

Behind Leinbaum the immense forest district begins, Ranger Brosch's realm stretching out far and wide, full of unknown reaches and covered in dense woods. If from Leinbaum you take a right, you avoid the forest and come to Sichelbach, behind which stretches Sichelbach Lake, whose length presses deep into the forest. To the left of the lake runs a cart path that later disappears into the forest and winds left and right, while on the other shore of the lake after half an hour you reach a high clearing where there is an-other lake and a settlement consisting of just a few farms, and just a little ways away, directly on the lake, stands a splendid Baroque church with a rounded onion-domed tower. The church is bright white, its large windows containing clear glass, the single entrance consisting of a massive portal and some open steps, the church facing the lake, in whose glassy surface the bright walls and the red tower are reflected, only the front of the church cannot be seen, since it happens to be encompassed by a cloister that con-tains a large fruit garden and a high wall, the settlement also called Cloister in return. The interior of the church is quite bright, possessing only a bar-rel roof that is nonetheless powerful and brighter than is often seen in these parts, the main altar and the side altars built from dark-black wood in the same style and decorated, the ornaments made of silver without a spot of gold anywhere, the frame of the strong altar painting helping to set off its radiance in contrast to the silver and black, as well as the sunlight pouring in, though the monks perhaps do not realize how beautiful their church is, for they think the catacombs are worth looking at much more than the building itself, even if there is nothing striking about them, though the monk on duty will quickly approach to ask whether you would like to visit the catacombs, to which you agree in order not to upset the monk. Then he lights a candle and leads the stranger down a narrow set of steps into a damp, murky hallway, the cold dampness clinging to your skin, the monk holding the light up to coffins piled one on top of another, though there's nothing else to see here, and so you thank the monk, hand him a bit of alms, and breathe again as soon as you reach daylight.

If you don't take the road to the Cloister, but head left, you enter a lovely grove of black spruce, between which there also grows some beeches, alders, and deciduous trees, the forest opening up a bit here and there in reverent forest glades, followed by more woods, until finally you reach a crossing at which a devotional image is covered in glass and nailed to a fir, a clearing opening up a little where this year the Wanderers have set up their summer camp. If at the crossing you head left, after about half an hour you will reach the forest ranger's house, but if you head right you will soon be surprised to come upon an open forest meadow in the basin of a gentle hollow, a little creek flowing along its edge which is fed by Sichelbach Lake. The water is cool and fresh and safe to drink, though the Wanderers use it only for cooking and washing, hauling their drinking water from one of the many surrounding springs. If you head straight across this forest meadow you enter diverse woods, after which you pass through a valley that is not very deep, but which is surrounded by steep cliffs, the valley opening up farther on, the forest retreating as you soon enter an ancient village. Any stranger who shows up here is such an unusual sight that not only the children but also the grown-ups come out into the street to stare silently at the visitor, especially if it should happen to be such a wild bunch as the Wanderers in their yellow smocks secured with a brown belt, all of them in short pants, though of no uniform cut, all of them bareheaded, even when it rains cats and dogs. To look at this village, which is called Altstadt, you would think that time has forgotten this place, for where can one find now the glory of the Roman *legio decima* or hear about Altstadt, which until the days of the Hussites—or was it as late as the Swedish invasion?—was supposedly a thriving city. That is long ago, nothing left now but a mighty Gothic church with a defiant, freestanding tower as a memorial to earlier times, though only the building remains, the church now desolate on the inside, no antiquities hidden away within it, but instead looking quaint and devoid of any special features, the church never even full during Sunday service. Even if everyone in the parish came to Mass, the church would still remain half empty.

If you head back to the crossing above, where the Wanderers are camped, the path continues to run along level and then begins to climb the mountain, winding back and forth as it rises, then descending more sharply, revealing to the left the view of a mighty hill that rises up, not that high, but crowned by an imposing castle, which are the ruins of Landstein Castle, though the path doesn't lead to it, bending right toward a hollow instead, where it comes out in the little village of Markl, with its sixty inhabitants. If you want to get to the castle, you must climb a steep path that leads to a forebuilding that houses a couple of people who hardly pay attention to the rare visitor, only a woman calling out a warning to be careful, since Landstein is in ruins, and no one should risk the crumbling steps and fragile walls. The lofty edifice is immense, but the cracks in the walls are deep and wide, debris from the collapsing walls having piled up, the round bulk of the detached tower well protected, nor would it even be possible to climb it, though in more astounding fashion a single wall still contains some austere windows from the early Renaissance. About the men of Landstein hardly anything is known, the castle having been abandoned and let fall into ruin since the Thirty Years War, if not earlier, no one doing anything to keep it up.

The view from Landstein Hill has shrunk and is also smaller than it used to be from the tower, since the surrounding trees don't allow a panoramic view, yet the Wanderers love the castle and would like to save it, though they don't know how they would go about doing so. During one of their sojourns they had discovered it, and they were so taken with the castle and Altstadt and Cloister and Sichelbach Lake and everything around them that they wanted to set up their summer camp here, thinking right away of the clearing up above at the crossing, though they wondered if they would have enough privacy and could stay hidden. In Markl someone pointed them out to Ranger Brosch, who smiled and explained that if ten people a day passed by the crossing it would be a surprise, so he thought it a good spot, it had good water, it was well situated, there were plenty of wild berries and mushrooms, so the Wanderers should come if they wanted to, there being plenty of fallen limbs for firewood in the forest, as well as a vast amount of brushwood that cannot be exhausted even after years of continual gathering. Indeed, the group of Wanderers made up of twenty-four voices decided to set up their summer camp here, calling it Camp Landstein.

On the first of July the Wanderers travel to Adamsfreiheit, though beforehand they discuss what they should bring along, because the Wanderers want to remain on their own once they move to their summer camp. In the city all the necessities are purchased, while tools and other artifacts needed in the camp, which takes the Wanderers a month to set up, are kept at their club and divided among them, each boy carrying something in his pack, which is what the Wanderers call a knapsack. The leader of the pack is Alfred, who is already over twenty and studies medicine, everyone respecting him because he understands the boys so well, even if he's strict and has a thick skull, making him difficult to stand up to, though no one can make a campfire as well as he can, no one knows better the best trails to take, how to set up camp and be in charge, and he is the best storyteller, tells the funniest jokes, and is deeply admired, his word always trusted, as everyone tries to do what they think Alfred will think is right, hoping that through a brief word or a glance he will acknowledge it, each one believing that Alfred is fond of him, though he treats everyone the same, as the leader of a pack of Wanderers must, there being no dissent allowed in his presence. None of the others are over eighteen, the youngest being thirteen, while Josef is fifteen, his friend Fritz Hans Fuchs, who is known only as FHF, is sixteen, he among the oldest in the pack.

Things are divided up to carry to camp, the older and stronger boys taking on the most, though the smallest are given the most important things possible that don't weigh too much, such as the kettles, so that everyone has something for which he is personally responsible. But what is hard to carry, such as food provisions, a crate containing unwieldy tools, another full of dressings, medicine, all kinds of utensils and, in order to use up any remaining space, a few books, these are shipped ahead of time by rail to Adamsfreiheit, the address reading "Summer Camp of the Wanderers at Landstein, Adamsfreiheit Station." Meanwhile the older boys look out for the younger ones to make sure that their packs are in order, though a real Wanderer doesn't allow himself to be helped by his mother, being proud to do it all himself, everyone certainly wanting to be free of grown-ups, such that what a young boy can't do himself is better explained by an older boy rather than someone from home, Alfred deciding who needs to help out this one or that. At a meeting of the pack each has been given a list of things that he must not forget, such as the proper clothes and underwear, eating utensils and toiletries, personal items and a lamp, a small storm lantern being essential, as well as the right amount of blankets, each bringing along a tent, with an additional tent brought along to hold supplies, the boys also told what food they need to bring along for the journey and the first two days in camp.

At the last meeting before leaving, the camp leaders are chosen by a vote, these boys having a special role, and therefore needing to have set up camp at least once already, while those who have never set up camp must first undergo an initiation in order to become full-fledged members, although the ceremony is not a solemn one, because the Wanderers like to participate, and for the most part it's done in fun. Next they choose the head of camp, who is responsible for everything, not least the life and death of the entire pack, he allowed to have the final say when necessary, otherwise decisions are made by the pack, each member having a voice in the matter, though Alfred, of course, is chosen unanimously for the role. Willi, who is eighteen, is elected as the assistant head, his role being to help Alfred and stand in for him when necessary. Fabian is put in charge of provisions, though everyone knows him as Fabi. Hans is made the treasurer, he being the only one allowed to handle money, everyone turning their money over to him as soon as they get on the train, there being a shared kitty in camp, since within the pack it's important that no one be richer or poorer than another, it also being discouraged that anyone has anything sent to him, such as money or packages, though when an anxious mother can't control herself everyone's happy in camp, for only the food that will last is put in the supply tent, whereas the usual sweets are handed out immediately, which is great. Next up is the head of entertainment, and this year FHF is sought for this job, since he always has fun ideas, he being in charge of games and entertainment, such as the campfire and special occasions, and the opening party at which the initiation of the new scouts takes place, followed by a wild party called the *bal paré*, though there is no dancing at it but just a load of fun, the third and biggest party coming on the night before they break camp, this being the most fun, for at it they really let go, everyone dressing up and getting carried away in antics as part of what they call the Knights' Roundtable of the Great Commander. In addition to all these leaders, a cook has to be elected, that being Gustl, though he is called Bambus, since his last name is Bamberger, though the job of cook is not all that important, for each day of the week a different one of the seven leaders serves as head cook and is supplied with two helpers, the role of the cook really being that of an overseer, the menu planned out previously with Alfred, Willi, and Fabi. Last, Josef is chosen as head counsel, he being the one to whom others can bring any complaint, but when the head counsel can't come up with a solution with the help of Alfred and Willi, then he brings the issue before the entire pack, which meets two times a week around a campfire, the last recourse being to send someone to the camp council, which consists of the seven elected leaders, though it rarely meets, and only when the head of camp or a minimum of two other leaders demands that it does.

The trip to Adamsfreiheit takes a long while because the connections are not good, requiring them to change trains twice, and they also need to make sure to arrive in Adamsfreiheit early in order to be able to temporarily pitch the tents the same day, which means a night journey, and in addition they need to save money, so they take the slow train, which rumbles endlessly across the countryside. Some of the Wanderers have poor parents who cannot or will not pay the modest fees for the camping trip, and so there needs to exist shared funds for all of them, which means they have to carefully calculate what to spend money on, Hans always afraid that there won't be enough, and so he is always conferring with the others about the best thing to do so that the money doesn't disappear, though Alfred finds ways and has ideas about how to spend the least amount necessary, such as if something is completely free or can be borrowed, so that by the end of the trip there are funds left over that allow them to buy extra equipment and better furnish the club. During the journey Hans makes sure that nothing is stolen from him when he's asleep, for although he wears his fastened wallet on a string around his neck so that it can rest safely underneath his smock, he still asks Alfred to put the money in his pocket, but as soon as they arrive in Adamsfreiheit Hans asks for it back, while in camp it is kept in an iron chest for which Hans and Alfred have a key.

An hour before the train departs, the pack is supposed to meet by a side entrance to the central station in the early evening, the air lovely and warm, almost all the boys showing up on time, their large packs on their backs, each one packed with all sorts of things above and below, left and right, all of it tied down, the smallest looking as if they can hardly stand, yet that appears so only if you look at a new arrival from behind, where he seems to disappear beneath the huge pack and his bags of provisions, but if the same boy suddenly turns around, then he looks quite happy and satisfied, if anything a little excited, and even if the weight is a bit too heavy for him, each one of them is ready to tough it out. Willi, who among the older boys is the first to arrive—his punctuality so well known that during any journey he always takes the lead if they want to know precisely when to meet up with another pack—doesn't fool around, and says, "Men, don't wear yourselves out. Set your packs down!" Everyone is happy to do so, and everyone can see how well the boys have packed, even the new ones, for everything looks shipshape, the many little straps a source of pride, though paper sacks and string are frowned upon, since these make them look like philistines, which the Wanderers call almost anyone, especially grown-ups. By "philistines" they mean antiquated men who have no real love of nature, most of the teachers at school being philistines, as along with the parents they hold down the youths by forbidding everything and ordering them around, the grown-ups know no better, nor could they do it better, for they fight constantly and smoke and drink beer, and if they ever go hiking they yell and holler, toss papers into the woods, and drag their little children along, after which the philistines head for an inn, usually right next to the station, buying colored beverages for their kids that no decent young man would drink or even put into his mouth, the elders getting drunk in the meantime. The Wanderers will have nothing to do with that, they are against all oppression, no one should influence them, for they want to start a new life, which they learn about during hikes and in their club, above all in their camp. No single pack wants to get too big, thirty being the limit for each, each new member having to serve a probationary period of six weeks in order to see if he really fits in. Similarly, not just anyone is encouraged to apply, but instead is considered for a while before being invited, and once he's selected he is expected to fully turn against his parents and teachers, though he shouldn't be nasty but simply aloof and independent. No grown-up and no stranger is allowed into the club, not even members of other packs or organizations are allowed unless invited, for with other packs they maintain only loose relations, there being an annual meeting of them during the Easter vacation, which many packs attend, though they hike separately and meet up with one another only at the final destination, at which for two or three days they share campfires, talk, sing, and play games, after which each pack heads back alone.

No one wants to know much about other organizations, on the one hand because they are too much like the military and practice battle charges, and on the other because they are too middle-class and seek out the approval of adults, some also being too nationalistic, others too internationalist, others belonging to some church, still others being appendages of political parties that are always yelling out some party slogan, real Wanderers meanwhile not wanting to have anything to do with politics, for Alfred always says that nothing but bad comes from politics, while whoever wishes to do good in the world cannot allow himself to be swept away by slogans, for they enslave people and turn them into philistines, there being hardly any difference between being progressive or conservative, since it all amounts to nothing and, even if it's true that an individual cannot defeat all the evil in the world, at least the individual can stand on his own and triumph over the evil within himself in order to lead an exemplary life. Nonetheless it sometimes happens that a boy who is initially pleased by Alfred's central tenets, or who doesn't really think about them and is only inspired by life among the other Wanderers, suddenly turns and says that none of what Alfred and the others say is true, after which the boy will not allow himself to be persuaded by anything, and so he states that he is leaving and disappears into another organization or simply takes part in nothing more with this one. Alfred then says that one has to realize that hiking doesn't hold a lot for many young boys, and yet it's good when one at least has had the chance to spend a little time doing it, as something from it might stay with him nonetheless.

Josef, FHF, and some others believe that anyone who is not a real Wanderer in these times must indeed be a philistine, but Alfred just smiles at that and says that he hopes there are no philistines among the Wanderers, and that none will become one, yet there have always been people who were not philistines, and fortunately even today there were men and women who knew nothing about hiking and yet were not philistines, there even being grown-ups who were fine people, even though the young felt their generation was better than the older one. Josef is still skeptical, and FHF complains that in his family most of them are awful and complete philistines, to which Hans adds, "I think the scouts will be the first sensible generation to exist once they grow up." The worst is when young boys who for the most part don't belong to any organization, or at best a phony one run by adults, are complete philistines who have no interest in good books, who don't want to go for a proper hike, who run out of the rain, long for vacations in a summer resort with a bad orchestra and snack bars, who are interested only in soccer and boxing matches, who read sentimental stories about Indians and bloodthirsty detective novels, who are happy to be led around on a leash like a dog, who like pop music and dancing, and who like the kind of school outings that Wanderers would never participate in, laughing as they do when they come upon one of them cooking his dinner on a spirit stove instead of making a real fire, even when it is raining and the brushwood is damp. A healthy Wanderer hikes every week, even in winter, for he has boots that no mud harms when they are laced up, nor does any Wanderer shrink from sleeping outside overnight, as long as it's not so cold that he can't pitch a tent, which is possible almost anywhere, and even when it's too cold all you have to do is wrap yourself up well in blankets, two boys assigned to tend the fire until morning so that you can always stay warm. Only for the winter camp does the pack rent a lodge in the mountains, where you can have a warm meal in the morning and at night, though for lunch the meal is cold, while it's hardly ever the case that they pass a night on the straw of some farmer's barn, this happening only when the weather is completely miserable.

The Wanderer is well outfitted and knows which canteen works best, sensibly utilizing aluminum canisters and watertight pouches, though no paper sacks or cardboard boxes, but instead he has a normal drinking cup, as opposed to a collapsible one, an eating tray with two compartments, no one using regular silverware but instead a large spoon that can be used to eat anything, a fork being a luxury, though everyone has a knife, which is all you really need. A real Wanderer wears a coat or raincoat neither during a hike nor in camp but instead has a waterproof windbreaker that is not thick at all, and which preferably is always faded and old, though in town you dress inconspicuously, because Alfred says, "I don't want any of you looking like some man from the wild!" Most of all, it's important to keep clean and to wear nice clothes, most of the younger boys refusing to wear long pants and shirts with ties because they feel foolish in them. The Wanderers have no special insignia, or at least Alfred's pack does not, since they have all decided that a real Wanderer should be recognizable on the inside and the outside, but not by insignia, which can easily be just superficial. The only shared piece of clothing is the smock, each member of the pack owning at least two, a good one and an everyday one, the difference being that one is new and the other old, the old one used mainly for hiking, as well as the trip to the camp, but for festive occasions and the campfire the new one is used, while for the most part you run around camp in shorts and bare feet when the weather allows.

The Wanderers nonetheless do share a common symbol and that is their flag, a three-cornered cloth, blue with a yellow sun sewn onto it. Attached to a pole, the flag accompanies them on each hike, one of the youngest boys carrying it for the most part, the flag also brought into camp and attached to a good-sized spruce tree whose branches and bark have been stripped away, a rope then attached to it so that the flag can be raised. Each morning before breakfast they all gather round the flagpole, as Alfred steps up and secures the flag and slowly raises it high, while all the others remain quiet, standing there motionless for a moment and looking up until Alfred steps back, bringing the ceremony to a close. At night before they go to bed, the flag is taken down in similar fashion, a couple of torches lit for this, the Wanderers making them out of spruce branches smeared with resin, though when it's too rainy, paper is also wrapped around them and dipped into oil just before they are lit in order that they keep burning. Older boys hold these torches whenever the flag is lowered and taken off, at which Alfred yells "Good night!" and everyone answers back the same, after which he takes the flag with him to his tent.

Josef and FHF don't like this ceremony, Josef being decidedly against the use of the flag, the two friends finding the raising and lowering of the flag way too demagogic, such that it's counter to the spirit of the Wanderers, Josef declaring, "If the Wanderers really want to be entirely natural, then they have to abstain from using any outward symbols." He believes that every symbol is extrinsic and leads to disingenuousness, and anyone who is disingenuous is probably also a philistine, though Josef's proposal to do away with the flag at the annual meeting of the pack is voted down by all the others, after which Alfred explains during a short speech that everything in the world is symbolic, and if you employ a symbol in a disingenuous manner, then it means nothing, for you have to distinguish between a symbol and an allegory, the latter being really false, such as the insignia of political parties or a piece of kitsch that pretends to pass itself off as something that a work of art can express through completely other and more genuine means, an allegory providing only an outline, while a symbol is true to life itself. And so, much to Josef's regret, the flag remains, while a similar appeal from him and FHF about doing away with raising and lowering the flag in camp was also voted down after fierce debate, during which Willi, Hans, and Fabi declared that the Wanderers needed such a symbolic beginning and ending to each day, Bambus wishing that the ceremony were embellished even more and were accompanied each morning by the recitation of a pledge that all could then ponder, while in the evening there could be a special song. Most were against that, Hans and Willi saying that what they already did was just fine, though FHF laughed at this and said that the pack might as well put up a totem pole like the Indians and beat a drum while yelling "Wahoo! Wahoo! Wahoo!," though Alfred asked that they not continue arguing and not make fun of what was done with the flag, it being a symbol of their bond with one another, and thus each can be free to think about it however he wished, but they needed to come to an agreement, and so except for FHF and Josef everyone was for things remaining as they were.

Everyone arrived on time at the train except for two little ones, who were late for some reason, one saying that he had a fight with his mother, who wanted him to take along a scarf, to which he replied that no Wanderer would bring that along, she replying, fine, then you will be the first Wanderer to bring along a scarf, at which he answered that he wouldn't, though the mother kept threatening, fine, then you won't be going to camp at all, and so the boy had fought with his mother on and on until finally he was allowed to march off without a scarf. As for the other boy who was also late, no one really got upset with him, for he had just recently joined the pack and wasn't good at telling time yet, so Bambus said to him, "You can go to Willi to get a lesson on how to tell time." Now everyone is happy to be together and is in a good mood when Alfred says that Willi and Hans should get the train tickets, at which everyone hands over his ID, since after the age of six there are discounts for boys under eighteen who have proper government identification, an additional person over eighteen also allowed to travel for the same price. Alfred also says that Landstein works out very well for them, for the journey there is so circuitous that they won't encounter any parents who wish to make a surprise visit, as had happened twice before years ago when their camp was located near Bärenloch. Yet Alfred handles such encounters deftly, taking hold of the visitors and quickly showing them around the camp, then taking them for a walk as he accompanies them to a place where they can stay for the night or, better yet, leads them with many thanks straight back to the station, where they head off without fanfare, leaving the Wanderers to return to their quiet, free of guests, and with no insult to anyone. If anyone in the troop has real trouble with his parents, Alfred counsels him as to how to conduct himself, and then it usually works out, but when it doesn't at all Alfred gets himself invited to meet with the parents, which almost always helps, for the parents quickly respect him, though he is never obsequious.

As soon as Hans and Willi are back, each one takes his knapsack and heads for the platform, where they ask the conductor to point the way to the three reserved compartments, the knapsacks stowed away, the little ones unable to swing their packs up into the storage netting, Willi and Alfred having their hands full, as lots are drawn for the window seats, since they are the best for sleeping, while if you hang up your food bag you can also use that as a headrest, though the food bag can also slip from the hook, causing you to waken with a jolt. Soon after everyone is aboard they feel hungry, and so they eat their evening snack, and FHF says that it's the last meal without a taste of the woods, namely dried spruce needles and little leaves and twigs that manage to secretly turn up in anything you eat, one always having to check to make sure and fish out any from the soup and anything that's laid out, though Alfred maintains, "Boys, that's good for you! That you can digest! It's only a taste of the forest!" Still, he also spits when a taste of the forest happens to land in his mouth, while the meal in the train contains no such ingredients and is a real potpourri, since each boy has brought something different from what he normally eats at home, such that some rather unusual combinations are served, because no one, except perhaps the newest members, who have not yet learned to raise enough fuss at home, brings anything that's pre-prepared, for that's stupid compared with hacking off a slice of bread from the loaf, everything better if it can be bitten off and not just consumed in little bits.

Josef and FHF are inseparable. Unfortunately Alfred doesn't sit with them, but with Hans and Willi instead, while Bambus and Fabi sit in the third compartment. Josef prepares the evening snack in his compartment, because FHF doesn't care much about it, preferring instead to hold forth with stories about last year, after which he says what he knows about Landstein. Because he's interested in geography and history, he knows a hell of a lot, having already researched how many inhabitants there are in Adamsfreiheit and the surrounding villages, arguing that the Bohemian forest in Schiller's *The Robbers* lies neither in the Erzgebirge nor in the Bohemian forests, but rather in the woods surrounding Landstein, though FHF wants to ask Ranger Brosch about it, and hopefully he'll also be able to tell him where he can find the best traces of the *legio decima*, while because FHF is so knowledgeable Alfred has recommended, "Write a history of Landstein, but it needs to be ready by the Festival of the Great Commander!" To this FHF replies that he can't promise anything, but he does already know how Sichelbach got its name. "This is how it happened. One of the knights from Landstein once boldly and briskly rode on his mare along the length of a creek in his golden armor. He then spied something shining in the creek. Undaunted, he climbed down from his noble steed. Curious, he reached into the water and, to his complete surprise what did he pull out? Yes, a sickle! At this the mighty knight made a solemn vow that here at this momentous spot he would found a village. That village was to be called Sichelbach. And, as promised, so it came to be." After this moving legend, FHF asked if they wanted to hear more stories about the ancient past of Landstein and its surroundings, but everyone thanked him and said not just right now but, rather, as soon as FHF could attach exact dates to them, at which FHF immediately promised to do just that, for he is never afraid of providing dates and he could already embellish any one of his stories with the proper dates, but now his humble calling involved making sure that everyone ate fast and got to sleep in order to get the proper rest before his next lecture.

The train is already almost an hour late before it finally departs, so that already some of the boys have grown impatient, one of them calling out, "We should be helping the engineer!" Willi hears this from the neighboring compartment and replies that such help will be needed on the narrow-gauge train to Adamsfreiheit, when it will be hard for a pedestrian to walk as slowly as the train as it climbs the mountain, and, should the train be completely full, the conductor will ask them to get out and help push it, the danger being that you have to make sure to quickly jump back on as soon as it starts heading down the mountain, for then the train begins to race madly along. Hans states that he has heard from the station manager about the kinds of mishaps that have happened on the railroad, and which required only the most courageous of engineers, a cow once having walked onto the tracks that refused to budge, the express train having to slam on its brakes, the whistle blowing for all its might, though the beast didn't stir from its spot, the engineer finally having to climb down with some valiant men, who talked soothingly to the cow for a long time, until the cow standing there with its long rope finally grasped that the express train desired free passage to Adamsfreiheit, at which the cow quite courteously moved away from the tracks, and the train steamed off to its final destination without further mishap.

The train was off as soon as Hans finished his thrilling story, the conductor then appearing to ask for their tickets, as Hans begins to look around but cannot find them, saying that Willi must have them, though Willi answers back, "No way that I have them! You're the one who paid for them and stashed them away!" Then Hans looks some more, Willi beginning to search as well, both of them finding nothing, and then Hans begins to think that it's not entirely impossible that he gave the tickets to Alfred when they came through the gate, therefore the tickets must be with the money, at which Alfred begins to rummage around, even though he also protests that this couldn't be true, as he confidently pulls out the wallet, there being no trace of the tickets inside it, the conductor growing impatient, which causes Alfred to explain to him in detail that they couldn't possibly be trying to get away with something, for the group would not have been let through the gate without any sign of having tickets. The conductor then says that he'd love to believe that but he still needs to see the tickets, and Alfred responds that he understands but certainly the three reserved compartments are evidence enough that they also had tickets, to which the conductor answers that he doesn't doubt anyone, he really doesn't, but he still needs to be able to say that he has punched their tickets, otherwise he will have difficulties if an inspector shows up, at which Willi, Alfred, and Hans rummage frantically through all their bags, pulling everything out, the others beginning to rummage as well, even the smallest, as Hans calls out in exasperation, "I don't have the tickets! Everyone keep looking!" Everyone searches now, all of them nervous but remaining calm, only Hans sweating, upset and angry as he is with FHF, as he declares, "What a fine beginning to the history of the Landstein summer camp this will make. And so the epic will start. A classic Homeric opening, the heroes search for a flea." FHF replies by saying that he doesn't need to search, he knows that he for sure doesn't have the tickets. Meanwhile the conductor's face begins to darken, as he says impatiently that he doesn't have all day to waste his time with the young gentlemen, the train is overfull, but by the time they get to Beneschau he has to make sure to get through the entire train, the rules are the rules and they have to be followed, and he can't be blamed for doing his job, it being the young gentlemen who are causing all the trouble. Alfred tries to appease the conductor, saying that the Wanderers certainly don't want him to neglect his duty to the railroad, they will find the tickets, Alfred asking the conductor if he could go through the rest of the train and then come back to them, by which time the tickets will surely have been found, at which the conductor asks where the young gentlemen are traveling to, and when Alfred tells him their destination he calculates with relief that it will be almost five hours before they change trains, which means there's plenty of time, at which Alfred hands him three cigarettes, which he always keeps with him for such moments, as the conductor thanks him with a smile and heads off in an amiable manner.

Now the real search begins, Alfred, Hans, and Willi trying to think what could have happened to the tickets, combing their memories for any possible clue, but it does no good, each asking the other's pardon, though the tickets don't turn up, and Hans complains how awful it all is, such a drain on their funds, meaning that the camping trip will have to be cut short by two or three days or they will have to eat less, though Alfred tries to calm him down, saying that Hans shouldn't worry his head about all that right now or about anything else for that matter, but instead just take out everything from his pack, everyone needing to look around as well under the seats, Bambus finally walking over from his compartment to stand in the passageway outside Hans's compartment, watching for a while before he asks, "Hans, where did you put your map case?" This is a case for the maps that belong to the pack, and Hans slaps his forehead as he says, "That could be it!" He reaches for the map case and, indeed, there are the tickets, everyone quickly relieved, a cascade of laughter and ribbing pouring over Hans, Willi giving him a second friendly slap on his forehead, as Alfred says, "In the end it didn't matter, but the Landstein Camp has survived its first great adventure even before opening up." FHF then adds somberly, "The historian, meanwhile, notes the loss of three cigarettes to the conductor."

After this tense incident, it's time to think about sleep, and since most of the scouts are tired there's no need to remind them, they just go to sleep, only FHF and Josef remaining outside in the corridor in order to talk as they exchange impressions, share with each other what they've been reading and what they thought of it. Finally they are also tired and want to go back to their seats, but the little ones are already sprawled across them, so the two friends sit down on the fold-down seats in the corridor and nod off. Josef then suddenly awakens to find the conductor back again with his lantern, and he tells him that the tickets have been found, the conductor replying that's good, for he would have had to charge them a higher price than at the station, though the snoring Hans is not easily awakened as, foggy with sleep, he hands over the tickets, and Alfred wakes up and sees FHF and Josef in the corridor, remarking, "Are you crazy? Why aren't you in your seats?" FHF is about to explain why they are hunkered down in the corridor when Alfred interrupts and says, "Of course, our camp philosophers! Get back to your compartment!" Quietly they take back their seats, and so the journey continues in sleep or in half sleep until the station where they change trains, the troop almost sleeping through it, the conductor showing up on time and announcing that it's time the young gentlemen got all their bags together, if indeed their destination is still the same, but Alfred thanks him and says, "No, my dear sir, we are still headed to Adamsfreiheit!" Alfred then wakes up anyone in the pack who is still asleep, all the boys gathering their things and stumbling onto the dark platform, as they look for the waiting room, though it's locked, someone from the railroad obliged to open it up for them, the Wanderers pulling out their flashlights, the sooty, smelly room not all that inviting, though the benches are long enough that they can stretch out on them. The railroad worker promises to wake them on time, it's a good four hours before the next train arrives, the worker wishing them a comfortable rest as he closes the door, everyone already asleep, since Wanderers are used to such things, even dozing through the night on small, hard wooden benches with uncomfortable slats, the philistines generally not being able to sit on them for even a little bit when awake.

As promised, the worker wakes the pack on time, each of the boys gathering together his several things and all of them shuffling sleepily through the morning mist across the empty platform to the train, the air fresh and damp, most of them soon perking up, the Wanderers having the entire car of an almost empty train to themselves, as it heads off through the dusky countryside, many of them stretching out again and dozing some more, the older ones sitting up or standing at the window to marvel at the dawning day, except for the always-sleepy Fabi, the area both stark and lush at the same time, long lakes branching out into reedy, undulating swamps, dreamy forests standing motionless in between, and everything quiet beneath the light of the rising sun. A half hour before the next change of trains the sleepers are awakened, because Alfred wants them all to eat something, since they have a long day ahead of them, though there is nothing hot to drink, all the Wanderers refusing to carry a thermos, most having some cold tea in their canteen which is still lukewarm, which to no one but a real Wanderer tastes any good. Then it's time to get off and endure another layover of about an hour, Alfred and Willi making sure that anyone who makes use of the water fountain makes sure to pay attention to the signs that say ONLY FOR DRINKING! and NOT FOR WASHING!, after which many faces and hands are cleansed of soot, all of them completely black from the journey, FHF comically announcing, "The heroes from Landstein at the Castalian Spring, but not on Parnassus!" Meanwhile Hans tells FHF that he'd do better to make sure not to splash any around, for it's not water for washing but precious drinking water. At last all the boys are refreshed and bright-eyed, it being good that they're done, for a rail official arrives and asks whether any of them can read, to which Alfred responds in an exceptionally polite and peaceful manner, "Yes, we can all read." At this the official laughs heartily, flashing Alfred a dark look, after which the official turns on his heels and disappears, the rest prowling around for a bit before getting onto the narrow-gauge train.

Everyone by now is in a good mood and joking around, as excitedly the Wanderers admire the surrounding countryside, those who already know Landstein telling the others, "Just wait till you see the camp for the first time, as well as the mountain and Sichelbach Lake!" In the train are a couple of people from Adamsfreiheit, Alfred asking them where the baker is located, who the best grocer is, and so on. The train rolls on like a snail for almost two hours, the manager of the station and his helpers surprised to see such a pack of young men get off, all of them happy that the journey is over. Alfred and Willi inquire immediately if the crates have arrived, and hear that, yes, they arrived just fine, a driver from Adamsfreiheit saying that he had to pick up something in Markl the next morning and that he could swing by with the empty wagon and pick up the crates if someone sent two strong boys to the station early, and that it would be an honor to do it without charging the Wanderers. This all arranged, the pack heads off laughing and singing, the little ones a bit tired, their knapsacks having to be carried by others, the older ones somewhat uncomfortable now with a knapsack hanging from each shoulder. Soon they reach Leinbaum, where a farmer asks if the boys want some milk, the Wanderers not hesitating for a moment as they stretch out on the edge of the road across from the farmer's yard to rest, drink some milk, and eat something as the farmer introduces himself as Herr Hunger. Hans is glad they can order milk from Herr Hunger each day, but Alfred says it's too far to walk to Leinbaum each morning, it being easier to get milk in Sichelbach or Markl.

Willi recommends that they get moving, there being still lots to do that day, the younger boys also now excited as they soon reach the cool forest, having decided to pay a quick visit to Ranger Brosch, the ranger's house lying in a clearing amid a large meadow, some plowed fields, and a duck pond, where they again take a short break as Alfred and Willi and Hans go up to the house, though Hans comes right back out to yell, "Boys, quick! Frau Brosch has made lunch for us!" No sooner are they all inside with their bags and packs than FHF wants to know how big the district really is that Ranger Brosch oversees, though Alfred doesn't give FHF much time with him, for he thinks it's more important to speak with the ranger himself. Frau Brosch apologizes that she doesn't have enough place settings for twenty-four people, for though there is enough room, there aren't enough plates, Alfred reassuring her that the Wanderers have their own camp plates and are used to using them, though Frau Brosch says all the same, "Still, it's bad hospitality!" Then they all say that she shouldn't worry about it, and as the ranger comments that when it comes to food the stomach matters a lot more than the plate, his wife still insists that at least the older boys should eat off her plates, at which the rest say as one, "Everyone is equal among us Wanderers!" Willi adds, "Please don't treat us any differently." She understands, yet she continues to insist that Alfred, as the oldest, should eat from her dinnerware, otherwise she will be insulted, to which he finally gives in. A huge bowl with thick potato soup is then brought in, it tasting wonderful as it is quickly served up to all, everyone thinking this is the entire meal, for it's so rich and satisfying, but then the main course arrives, dumplings with sauerkraut and bits of bacon and gravy soon filling their bellies, as they lick up every last bite, which satisfies the ranger's wife.

By now it's high time they were on their way, though Herr Brosch wants the troop to stay and sleep in the hayloft for a couple of days or at least a night, during which time they can set up the tents, but Alfred turns down the offer with such gratitude that the Brosches are much impressed and don't press the matter any further. Instead, the ranger only offers to accompany them to their campsite in order to show them a shortcut, which he points out on a map. The offer is accepted with pleasure, Josef already convinced that the ranger is no philistine. They then march off, the ranger wanting to carry the littlest one's pack, though this boy, known as Pony, is not at all weak and ever so proud, as he tells Herr Brosch that every Wanderer has to be able to make his own way and not take any help from others, at which the ranger laughs, as they all happily hike to the campsite, where they throw off their packs, and Herr Brosch shows Bambus the nearest flowing spring and makes him promise that the Wanderers will take good care of it, making sure to protect everything they encounter in such a natural setting, to which Bambus answers in a dignified manner, "If everyone took care of things the way the Wanderers do, then the world would be a much better place, nor would there be any reason to besmirch a forest with ugly notices warning what not to do." Herr Brosch then smiles and wishes them all a nice time and a pleasant stay, shakes Alfred's hand, and says a warm goodbye.

Now the Wanderers are at last alone, most of them stripping off their clothes down to their shorts, some checking out the surrounding area, others wanting to clean up and head down to the creek to figure out where to set up a dam so that they have a place to wash where the water will reach up to their knees, and where the pots can be cleaned, and though everything will take time, a real Wanderer never complains about anything, some of them resting as FHF comes down to announce, "The travelers have reached their land. The holy line of the knights of Landstein lives once again. A new page in the history of the heroes is opened." Josef says to Alfred, "We've never had a better site, have we?" Alfred agrees and replies that it's good that a line of trees separates the site from the meadow below, for that way they won't be bothered by gnats, while Willi, glancing at his watch, says, "We need to call the others, for it's high time to start pitching the tents, otherwise the little ones will be too tired."

Alfred whistles for everyone to gather round, then he indicates a spot in the woods somewhat off from the clearing for the short-term tents, for the more permanent tents will be pitched in the real campsite, the temporary ones better off in the woods should it rain, since there you don't need tent poles the way you do in the open, you can hang each tent between two trees, while first you have to check the ground to make sure there are no roots or stones, as well as ants, though any real Wanderer knows to do this. Setting up goes quickly, two tent canvases are attached together, the wooden buttons called olives, then you thread a cord through two eyelets, lift up the tent, and tie the cord with a seaman's knot, though now comes the part that requires some skill, for since the tent just hangs loose from the cord its four corners have to be stretched out such that they form a precise square, even the most adept tent pitcher needing a little while to get the corners right. Meanwhile someone else presents the pegs, which are pointed stakes that are then placed in the ties at the corners of the tent and pounded into the ground, though you have to make use of the two loops at each corner, using a stone as hammer, as you pound the pegs so deep into the ground that they cannot move, after which you do the same with the middle of the tent, which also has loops, each tent finally tight and secure, the small Egyptian pyramids done, though you still have to dig a ditch around each one so that you aren't swamped if there is a sudden downpour. During one hiking trip they had terrible weather, FHF comparing it to the Deluge and saying, "One of us must have done something really stupid that has made Neptune mad!" Indeed, FHF is never caught off guard, and always has examples from Homer or history at hand when the others howl and complain, but the Wanderers got so wet that it was lucky that the next day the sun broke through, for then they spread everything out on a steep meadow to dry, which meant they had to abandon their entire plans for the day, though they were proud that at the next pack meeting not a single one of them was missing, nor had anyone caught a cold.

Once the tent is done, the edges are packed with moss and loam for further protection and to guard against moisture, after which one side is opened and tied back as an entrance, two boys able to lie inside it comfortably, sometimes there even being a third, or four if it's just the smallest ones. This time they erect thirteen tents, twelve for sleeping, one for provisions. Each boy stores his things and binds them together with a blanket, after which the scouts cover themselves up at night right up to their heads, if it's not too warm, and if it's really cold they crawl in with a neighbor under the same blanket, using their knapsacks as pillows, everything that can be too easily crushed or is too hard needing to be taken out, the preparations completed once the storm lamp is hung. Meanwhile it's turned dark, but the older ones set up a temporary kitchen so that they can quickly cook some soup or boil tea in the morning. This first campfire is made from just a few stones and poles from which hang a couple of pots, Bambus soon at work stirring some soup, no one knowing just what he's put in it, be it barley, oats, a couple of quickly picked mushrooms, a sliced onion, bits of sausage, and a number of herbs that Bambus has managed to gather, as well as salt and a decent amount of the taste of the forest, such that the soup is hardly a sumptuous meal, though FHF doesn't make fun of it but speculates that it's the same soup the Spartans ate, the one that was offered to Leonidas, which certainly was also not a godly preparation made of nectar and ambrosia, meaning that Leonidas would have been thankful for a cook as good as Bambus. To the scouts the soup indeed tastes heavenly, as they let FHF talk on, some being too hungry and too tired to fish out the taste of the forest, after which they wish one another good night, Alfred not having to yell out "Quiet!" in forbidding anyone to talk, since most of the boys are asleep already.

The night passes quietly except for one incident, when suddenly a horrible screaming is heard, as if someone were calling for help, almost everyone waking up, only Fabi sleeping through it, since he sleeps like a groundhog and snores, sounding like a thunderstorm releasing hellish claps of thunder. Everyone else, however, hears the screaming, two new members in fact scared as Alfred jumps up and calls out, "What's going on?" Hesitantly comes the answer, "It's me, Pony! I can't find my way back!" Hans and Willi then head out with flashlights to look for Pony, who stumbles toward the light, the rescue mission over after two minutes. Pony had to go to take a pee and went off so sleepyheaded that he couldn't find the way back to his tent, Alfred later asking him, "You idiot, why did you go so far away without taking a flashlight along with you?" Then everything is quiet again, Josef thinking that he'd never let something like that happen to him, he would make marks on the trees, as any good Wanderer would, in order not to lose the way back, FHF whispering to Josef that the incident fit in wonderfully with the history of the Landstein camp, for it reminded him of an episode of *Sinbad the Sailor*, though FHF cannot remember the segment precisely and so falls silent, as everyone sleeps peacefully until morning.

To the call of "Wake up!" the day begins, the head of camp being the one who should announce it, though he had always been happy to turn this duty over to Willi, who saves everyone the trouble of having to bring along an alarm, for he has the ability to wake up whenever he wants to. After the sound of the call to wake up, everyone must get up, but it always takes a while before that actually happens, one tent opening after another, Willi standing outside momentarily, Josef and Pony also quick to rise, as Alfred stands like a pillar, lifting his elbows and then his long arms upward, as he makes such a contorted face that FHF says, "Alfred reminds one of Saint Sebastian. He should be named the patron saint of the Wanderers." Meanwhile, it's sometimes difficult to rouse FHF from his tent, as it doesn't disturb him if you drag him out by his feet or by his head and shoulders, for the guy is unfazed and says, "Serenity in the face of any kind of medieval torture is the most admirable trait any Wanderer can have." FHF is not really all that strong, he reminds you of a badger who at any moment might crawl into his den or disappear into a hole. If anyone disturbs him and asks him to do something he doesn't want to do, he yells at his opponent, in the middle of a battle that doesn't look as if it's going too well for him, "Will you surrender? Will you surrender?" Watching this, hardly anyone can keep from laughing, everyone lets his guard down and backs off, which FHF immediately takes advantage of, pulling himself together and running off like a bolt of lightning to hide so that he can't be found, even though he never goes that far. This is why FHF is so good at playing hide-and-seek, which involves his being sent off to hide, though it needs to be an area that's well suited to this, he getting ten minutes to hide where he wants, be it on the ground, in a cavern, in some bushes, or in a tree, after which the others head out to look for him, though they have to be quiet and take care not to be discovered by him, since the moment they are he whistles and the player is out, the rest of the players having to stand still if they are near enough to have heard the whistle, after which FHF gets another five minutes to hide again. If someone discovers him during this who in all honesty did not hear him whistle, then FHF is called out and loses, but if FHF sees the searcher first, then FHF calls him out. After the five minutes pass, the others begin to search for him again, and often it's the case that ten or more boys are out before FHF is ever found.

The hardest thing to do is get Fabi up early in the morning, for even if you scream "Wake up!" at him, he only opens his eyes a little bit and says, "I need to sleep, it's only midnight!" Then he just turns over and begins to snore. You can try five times and still have no success, until someone finally decides to go looking for a bucket of water, though only the strongest dare do this, for then Fabi jumps up and yells, "Who ever woke a sleeping lion so suddenly? Can't one be awakened more appropriately to the sound of harps? Do you have to dump Sichelbach Creek on me?" Then a vehement struggle begins, which Fabi usually wins. Once Fabi is finally up, the scouts do ten minutes of exercise, after which they have to spread out their sleeping bags in the open air and then go wash up in the creek, which everyone enjoys, followed by the raising of the flag, but not on the first morning, since it's not until the second morning that the pole is ready, it being Alfred's job to look for a thin, straight branch, which he then saws off, cleans up, and sets up without anyone's help. After the flag is raised, daily chores are assigned, two boys being put in charge of guarding the camp, one of them having to remain there throughout the day, while the other can go no farther than a hundred yards outside of it, another two assigned the shopping, one of them needing to be a camp head, as they carry knapsacks and food bags through Sichelbach to the grocer and the baker in Adamsfreiheit, Fabi and Bambus telling them what needs to be bought, Hans giving them money to pay for it. Then the head cook of the day is chosen, his two helpers, as well as two wood gatherers who are in charge of collecting firewood, everyone who is able helping to do the same for the campfire. In addition, two dish washers are assigned, they in charge of cleaning the cooking pots, but not the Wanderers' own plates, while two Wanderers are also assigned to go to Sichelbach one day and Markl the next in order to bring back twenty liters of milk, last but not least two boys also being assigned to haul water from Sichelbach Creek. Thus each day seventeen boys are kept busy with assignments, particularly in the morning, the others pitching in, because there is so much to do, such as peeling potatoes and gathering mushrooms, for which several expeditions are arranged, most of them led by Alfred or FHF.

Alfred is crazy about mushroom gathering, because when looking for them he almost always finds good ones, starting pinecone battles along the way as well, while FHF goes about things completely differently, hardly ever discovering a useful mushroom, although he knows the various species better and always has his mushroom-classification book at hand, his knapsack always stuffed with books, for whether it be in camp or on a hike, he has Plato, Schopenhauer, and Goethe, plus a volume of world history, always ready to pull one out during a rest stop as he reads with his nearsighted eyes, while no matter how much racket surrounds him, nothing disturbs his concentration, nor does he ever completely cut himself off, for even when everyone thinks he's completely buried in his book and doesn't hear a thing he suddenly will let loose a remark that shows that he knows exactly what is going on around him. While gathering mushrooms, everyone brings him the strangest ones, which he then names on his own or consults the various types with Latin names in his handbook, and he is especially happy when someone brings him a mushroom that is truly inedible but not poisonous, he demanding that they bring it along as well, for it's an unfair punishment to say that it is inedible, the main thing being that it is not poisonous, it only being a question of how to prepare it in order to eat it or not, and anyone who doesn't want to count himself a philistine should at least give it a try. Usually FHF is the worst cook, so he's only allowed to boil potatoes or noodles or such things that are hard to mess up, while on his cooking days no soup is made, for FHF loves to throw everything into it, saying that the best recipe delights the taste buds the most, though, above all, he's not allowed to cook anything with mushrooms, for he once cooked chanterelles so long that they ended up tasting like dried leather, even when a lot of fresh butter was used on them. Whenever FHF returns with his mushroom hunters, Alfred, Willi, and Bambus function as a three-member commission checking out the suspect crop, all of them soon laughing about whatever happens to be there on any given day, for well over half of the mushrooms are thrown out despite protests from FHF, even the lovely red fly agaric, which FHF assures them tastes wonderful and is quite digestible as long as you trim off the colorful skin. Meanwhile, wild berries are also gathered in droves, for there is hardly any fruit in the surrounding countryside, there being loads of blackberries and raspberries, though rarely are there enough strawberries to fill a cup, since they are hard to find, and the gatherers prefer eating them on the spot, the raspberries and blackberries serving as dessert later on, sugar and milk added to them when there is enough.

In the first days leading up to the dedication of the completed camp the pack has a lot to do, all hands required especially in the first days, the crates from the station needing to be unpacked, two Wanderers having to go to Adamsfreiheit to shop, as well as check out the bakery and the post office more closely, the milk run taking two more to Sichelbach and Markl for milk, butter, eggs, and cheese, inquiries also needing to be made about straw for the straw mattresses, the dam needing to be set up as a bathing area in the creek, the fireplace spruced up, and, above all, preparations completed for the opening of the camp. This year the pack is fortunate, for Ranger Brosch has supplied wooden planks, which they only have to pick up and return after they break camp, Alfred having declared that this year a long table would be set up in the woods, with a bench long enough on each side to hold eleven scouts, with single seats at each end, Alfred, the Great Commander, at one, and at the other the court jester, that being FHF, who has no problem playing the portly role of the fool at the *bal paré* and the Festival of the Great Commander, though he avidly tells the others that having such a table and benches is an unheard-of weakening of the manners and customs of the Wanderers, who now need only don top hats and beards in order to parade around like complete philistines. FHF didn't mean this all that seriously, which is why he couldn't help laughing when Fabi took it seriously, for he called out in anger, "Down with the scandalous monarchy!" Alfred then got involved and asked, "Don't you realize that I serve as monarch in my ancestral capacity as the honored head of the knights and servants of Landstein?," to which FHF added, "The Roundtable of King Artus is founded once again. He will retire to the *atrium silvestre*, the chamber of the German forest, to feast and carouse with his men." Then it dawns on Fabi how dumb he has been, and so he shuts up, so that nothing more is said about it all, though FHF later allows himself to say to Josef, "He's wise, but not very smart."

Once when Willi was head cook, he dug into the canned goods and made a wonderful cocoa for breakfast, though the color was a little off, and the smell that rose from it, while really very nice, was still somewhat strange, Pony immediately spitting it out when, in haste, he was the first to take a taste, his face twisting up with disgust, though Alfred, who had already had a suspicion, asked with feigned sternness, because he was barely able to swallow his laughter, "Hey, Pony, what's the matter? Are you crazy, why are you spitting out the cocoa?" Pony yells, "You should just try it!" Alfred replies, "I'll do just that. But, before I do, tell me what's wrong." Everyone looks at Pony and giggles, at which Pony says, "Yuck! That's no cocoa, that's pure cinnamon!" Indeed he was right, it was cinnamon, everyone hesitant, but nonetheless curious to taste a bit of the cinnamon cocoa, though most are disgusted by the concoction, only Willi knocking some back with morbid caution and maintaining that he was really sorry that all of the cinnamon had been wiped out, but at home he always drank milk and cinnamon, and it was only their own fixed tastes that prevented the Wanderers from trying something new. Apart from Willi, only Josef and FHF tried some of the cinnamon brew, but they didn't finish their servings, the only thing left to do being to condemn Willi's screw-up with strong curses and avoid the cocoa for the rest of the morning.

Setting up camp goes so well that by the fourth night they can hold the opening party, after which begins the day-to-day life of the camp, the Wanderers' custom being to remain together at the same spot and not wander off too far, the nearby countryside thoroughly explored, while now and then they head off to Sichelbach Creek to bathe, during which a guard remains back in camp. But first they have to set up camp, which means gathering what they need, such as branches that will be used for tent posts, followed by the crates from the station, whereby the tools are unpacked. Then for each tent a foundation is built that is half a meter high, four main pegs for the small tents and eight for the big ones hammered into the ground, while as part of the camp's layout gates are set up, and in the middle of the space between the tents the flagpole is raised, near it the spot for the campfire being laid, stones carried from the creek below and arranged in a circle in which the huge fire will blaze. Between the main pegs for the tents are smaller pegs, and when the foundation is strong enough, cut and stripped branches are nailed to the post as slats, they having been planed down a bit so that they are all good and flat, after which the foundation is finished. Then comes the main job, which requires a great deal of patience, as the framework is interlaced with bushy sticks to make the structure waterproof, bricks of sod stacked up in order to cover the outside of the foundation, turning it into a simple wall, around which one digs a trench for the rain to run off into. Then the beds are built, two single beds erected in the smaller tents, two doubles in the larger ones, stakes pounded into the ground for each of these, small stakes also laid across one another and held together by a crosspiece, it being good to make sure that everything is built up to the same height before the planks borrowed from the ranger are laid on top, each tent then getting its door. Before the tent canvases are stretched over the frames, poles are placed inside the tents, the larger ones requiring two, all of which must be done carefully, which is why Alfred and Willi always come around to make sure that everything is done right, as they measure the height of each precisely. Then the tent is stretched over, the canvases draped over the frames, the tent poles forming points, or gables in the double tents, the tents then carefully set on the foundations, one Wanderer holding the double loop as another pounds two nails through it into the foundation so that the loops don't pull out, the tent finally complete. Now all that's needed is the load of straw that was ordered from Sichelbach, everyone filling his straw mattress and pillow, and once each has been sewn shut with thick cords and laid on the frames, then everyone is finished making his own heavenly bed in the Landstein camp.

During all of this the permanent kitchen is also set up, an actual stove constructed out of stones, a camp stove, a stovepipe, and a couple of hot plates big enough to hold some kettles and pots that have been brought from the city. Alfred and Bambus then attempt to light the oven, lighting a well-laid fire in order that the same thing doesn't happen that did at Bären-loch, where the oven collapsed and the entire midday meal was buried under it, while, even worse, the stovepipe fell over and burned Hans a bit, though luckily nothing else happened to him, Alfred proud of the fact that hardly anyone ever gets sick at camp, there being very few colds, even when it's soaking wet, the worst being a bit of a sore throat, which only means staying inside your tent for a day when the weather is bad, though stomachaches also hardly ever happen, because the scouts eat well and don't snack much, the occasional serious wound being inevitable, Alfred making sure to wash it and dress it well so that by the next day it's almost healed. Meanwhile, this year the kitchen does well when tested, a canopy added so that even when it rains hard you can still cook, though the rain can't fall aslant too much, for otherwise the cooking staff won't remain dry without wind breakers. Everything else has been completed as well, a wonderful bathing area having been set up, the table and benches now standing in the woods, as everything is hauled out of the tent and crates that hold the provisions and is placed where it belongs, all that is left being the mounting excitement over the opening party.

From now on proper food is cooked rather than just noodles, barley, or grits, for most cooks take pride in what they prepare, seeking the approval of others as they work their magic on soups, canned vegetables, flour or cornmeal dumplings, or potato dumplings or latkes. Only during bad weather do they make it easy on themselves, most of all with the evening meal, where they hand out chocolate bars when there are no berries. Sometimes Alfred denies someone his chocolate as punishment, but that rarely happens, usually a warning from him enough to make anyone want to be a good Wanderer. In the morning and the afternoon, each boy gets a big slice of bread with a pat of butter or marmalade, and each can have as much bread as he can eat, though it depends on what meal it is, for Fabi and his helpers hand out real bread only for the meals, whereas only dried bread is free, the rest being measured out precisely, though nobody goes hungry, all the meals are sumptuous, and hardly anything spoils, because nothing is left over, for there is always someone who will gladly devour what someone else cannot, Alfred not wanting anything to go to waste.

There is only one day on which the food is spoiled, and that is the day when the camp's hierarchy is turned upside down, Alfred handing his whistle over to the youngest scout the night before, since for the next day he is head of camp in charge of everything and takes overall responsibility, Alfred even handing over the flag to Edgar, who as the youngest this year is named lord of the camp, he then naming all his head assistants and handing out the day's assignments, only Hans remaining as the bookkeeper, since everyone urged him to do so. Alfred and Willi are made dishwashers, FHF and Josef have to gather kindling, and so on, Edgar taking charge of the kitchen while Pony is put in charge of provisions. Problems arise first thing in the morning, for even though Willi has been up for a while and has bathed, no signal has been given for the others to wake up, Alfred and Hans also already up, and everyone wondering when the day will actually begin, until at last Pony wakes up and pokes Radau to make him tell Edgar to order the others to wake up. Edgar then finally blows his whistle and yells, "Wake up!," but nobody pays attention, Willi eventually complaining that his bones hurt and he needs to sleep, at which Edgar says he can't have any chocolate, while also lowering judgment on a number of others until finally, at around ten-thirty, the cocoa can be served, it being only a bit burned, Bambus saying, since it's so late, "Edgar, why don't you pay a bit more attention to cooking unless you want the whole troop to starve by lunchtime!"

Edgar protests strongly, but nonetheless thinks that it might be good advice, except that he has the unfortunate idea of making rice, for which he grates some chocolate, in order to make a chocolate rice pudding. Although mounds of kindling stand at the ready, the fire simply will not light, so Edgar orders Alfred to light the fire, but he says that he's too young, he doesn't know how to light a fire, and Edgar yells at him, "I'm the head of camp and you have to obey! No more idiotic jokes, Alfred!" So Alfred lights the fire, and as it crackles Edgar says to him, "You can now go play ball. I don't need you anymore." Alfred goes off to play ball, but soon the fire is smoking badly, the flames smoldering, everything in the kitchen swallowed up in acrid smoke, the rice boiling and boiling, though Edgar is firmly convinced that the rice is not done and ignores any recommendation that's given him. By now everyone has deep doubts when Edgar finally decides that the food is ready, it being only an hour late and already two o'clock, as Edgar's helpers carry two full pots of a grayish-brown stinking mass out to the serving area, Edgar wanting to be the one to serve it up, himself covered in sweat, for the ladle fails to scoop out any of it, since the whole thing can only be picked at, so he reaches for a large kitchen knife and with effort saws away clumps that he then dumps onto each plate, though as he finally finishes he sighs from exhaustion, the remainder left in the pot as a disgusting mess.

Although everyone has gathered around out of curiosity, Edgar whistles and calls out, "Time to eat!," confidently adding, "Boys, it's a little burned. But that doesn't matter. I hope it tastes good. Enjoy!" Next to Edgar stands a tub of butter, grated chocolate, and sugar, but in his excitement he forgets to serve it, while Hans is merciless and calls out, "Edgar you forgot the chocolate! I can't eat rice pudding without chocolate!" Edgar wants to make up for his oversight, but Bambus yells, "You're crazy, Hans, you're wasting the only thing that's edible!" Edgar is deeply hurt and just wants to sprinkle chocolate on as quickly as he can, but luckily someone prevents him and recommends that he first taste the dish, though Edgar says in a quiet voice that he doesn't know if the rice pudding has turned out well, maybe someone else should try it first, to which Alfred replies, "That's right, no cook should be made fun of before his food has been tasted." Bravely, he cuts off a piece from the lump with a spoon and puts it in his mouth, and although Fabi warns him not to break a tooth, Alfred announces, "Mmm, good!" The rest, however, quickly say that it's inedible, Edgar ordering that bread with sausage should be handed out and two ribs of chocolate afterward, which he thinks is reasonable, and so it occurs.

During the meal Edgar comes to Alfred and says that he would like to have a little word with him, to which Alfred agrees, yet it's not until the end of the meal, when he's full, that he is ready. Edgar is also quite hungry, but he's done with his meal much earlier than Alfred, who chews his food with the patience of a saint and says to Willi, "I think we have plenty enough to do for today. Hopefully we'll be able to finish washing the pots by the time we go to bed. Before that we need to fortify ourselves as best we can." After the meal Alfred gets up slowly and tells Willi that they need to start the washing up, but then Edgar yells, "I'm ordering you to speak with me in private!" Alfred does just that as he recalls Edgar's request from earlier and walks off with him, while after they return Alfred says, "I'm here to inform you that I am once more head of camp. The reversed order is now over. As part of his abdication Edgar has only requested that Willi and I finish washing up the pots. I have said I will only support this difficult promotion if Willi is willing to go along with it." Indeed, Willi declares with a grin that he's ready to, after which the kitchen fire is stoked in order to boil some water so that they can loosen the remains left in the pots, though even with baking soda and wire brushes it takes another hour to do the job.

The opening celebration is the first real party in camp, and therefore the first campfire, which also makes everyone happy. After the evening meal, large amounts of brushwood are gathered, some of the older boys getting everything ready, stacking up the brushwood in the way they know works best, then each puts on his smock and they all sit in a circle and are quiet, as Alfred steps up and lights the fire, others later taking over the job of tending it, the order of shifts having been arranged already, as Alfred says, "I hereby open the Landstein Castle Camp and welcome its first members." After that it's again quiet, then Alfred begins to sing a song, everyone singing along, after which he makes a speech that doesn't last long, for the Wanderers are never allowed to make long speeches, as Alfred wants everyone to be able to express himself quickly and clearly. Alfred explains what it means to be in camp, mostly for the new members, then he speaks about the purpose of the Wanderers, what he expects from each, how to find direction in one's life, whereby one can distinguish himself from other people, Alfred saying it all simply and directly so that everyone can understand. After him others are allowed to contribute, though no one has to ask permission, but simply begins to talk, as they let some time go by after anyone speaks.

Willi, Hans, and FHF always speak at such moments, as sometimes do others. Willi likes to talk about the difference between the Wanderers and other people, comparing the two and saying what the pack still needs to do in order to become real Wanderers who live up to their goals. Hans, meanwhile, easily gets sentimental and talks about a number of symbols, such as what the flag means and the fire, that they all need to work together, help one another, and remain friends forever. FHF explores central directions of history and the actions of important men down through the years, seeing connections to the ideals that belong to the Wanderers, everyone needing to envision how humanity can work steadfastly toward the highest goals, which alter only in their outer manifestation, but never change in spirit, those being expressed today most likely soon becoming outdated, our children coming up with something completely different from wandering, which is why we have to remain young in spirit, in order not to stand in the way of those who come after us, but instead support them in the ways that we wish others supported us, the most important thing for ourselves being to remember how easy it can be to fail, since for all we know when they were young, many of our parents and teachers held such ideals, which they later betrayed and finally forgot, but if we don't forget and don't betray ourselves we will be a generation that won't stand in the way, and then—and only then—will we be able to say that as Wanderers we did not fail our calling but instead have fulfilled it. Meanwhile, when Fabi speaks he always likes to follow FHF, though what he says never sounds that clever, because he tries to disagree with what FHF has said, because Fabi believes that wandering will exist forever, and that we only need to make sure our children become Wanderers and, no matter what we end up doing, there will always be the Wanderers, and if one day all there was in the world were Wanderers, then peace and unity would exist among all people, yet in our times and earlier not much progress has been made toward this, the Middle Ages in fact being a disgrace, the Thirty Years War terrible, and, of course, the World War a calamity, one able to see all of this just by looking at the world around us, the great works of the past having disappeared without renown, though what the Wanderers will accomplish will not and should not be destroyed.

Usually Alfred speaks once more in closing, but just briefly, saying that we should certainly be pleased that we have the chance to be Wanderers, but we must be careful in the face of others, for when they foster other views and ideals it's important to respond with simple human decency and not with big words, but rather actions, and we should allow each his own views and actions but meanwhile observe whether these are genuine and honorable. If we see them as deceitful we should avoid them, as well as speak up without fear and worry when we are asked to keep still. After this last speech, the Wanderers sing and sometimes tell stories or read out loud, especially if someone has something special he wishes to share with the entire pack, while toward the end the fire is allowed to burn lower, many of them staring at the barely flickering flames, as Alfred closes the evening with a few words and best wishes to all, then the flag is lowered, the last coals doused with water that stands at the ready nearby. This time the campfire comes to a surprising end, for suddenly there is the sound of a trumpet, as Alfred half jokingly says, "Sounds like the fire station in Sichelbach." In fact, it really is the fire station in Sichelbach, for there they observed the glow of the fire and believed that a forest fire needed to be put out. Alfred stands up immediately and takes Bambus with him in order to rush to meet the firemen, who are already heading toward them, the latter soon relieved to see the Wanderers, no one in Sichelbach understanding what was going on because they had forgotten about the Wanderers, the people up in arms, but then happy that nothing was burning, Alfred reassuring them that the Wanderers had never caused a forest fire, as he handed out cigarettes to all the firemen and they headed off satisfied, though one could hear their little trumpets still blowing for a while.

One day pleasantly follows another, there being always plenty of diversions, games organized down in the meadow, even competitions, the surrounding area explored, FHF above all on top of things, taking over evening patrols as well with Alfred's permission, though only four boys are allowed to take part. There they listen to the lightly rustling sound of the trees and try to distinguish which are in a minor key and which a major, younger boys sometimes taken along in order to get them used to the lonely feel of the night, this being a night that they spend on their own at a spot in the woods when they are allowed to do what they want, though they have to remain quiet, they can make a small fire, and they can sleep, or they can look for one of the masters who led them to this spot as part of their test and will pick them up the next morning, they needing to dress warmly and bring along a blanket, a large slice of bread having been given them as provisions. Whoever passes this test is then considered a full-fledged Wanderer and not a novice, anyone being allowed to take the test, while anyone who is fourteen or older doesn't have to do it. There are in fact no other tests, nor are there titles, the distinction of being named a master in itself nothing but a joke.

Alfred knows all of the gamekeepers and forest workers, and so he knows that tomorrow is Frau Brosch's birthday, for which he quickly calls a meeting of the camp, at which it's decided that in the evening when it's dark they will hike to the ranger's house and serenade her and her husband under torchlight. They quickly get the torches ready and practice a couple of songs, then all of them except the camp guards head off to the ranger's house, where no one has any idea that they're coming, such that everyone is hugely surprised and even more overjoyed, the sight of the scouts truly wonderful as they all light their torches and gather in the ranger's yard, the couple coming out to say thank you and to praise them. The next night Herr and Frau Brosch pay a return visit to the camp in order to invite them all the following Saturday evening for a piece of cake, Alfred thanking them deeply and explaining that unfortunately the Wanderers won't be able to come, for the Wanderers have a custom whereby they participate in all celebrations together, but all of them won't be able to, since they have to leave two Wanderers behind as camp guards. Then the ranger says that he'd already thought of that, and they have to accept the invitation anyway, for he had arranged for two gamekeepers to serve as guards for that evening, and they were happy to do it, this leaving nothing for Alfred to do but thank him on behalf of the pack and accept.

On Saturday the scouts don their clean, good smocks and head off cheerfully to the ranger's house, where they are led into the great room, which they know from the day of their arrival, the tables bowing under the weight of the mountains of blackberry cake, as well as dark blueberry wine, which some cast doubtful gazes at, though Herr Brosch assures them, "There's no alcohol in it, so anyone can have some." Indeed, it's fresh berry juice, which everyone likes, but it makes their limbs feel heavy, it being as avidly shoved at them as the cake, such that a sugar rush comes to their heads, but then some wonderful coffee is brought out, which helps wake up the Wanderers once again, as they sing and laugh, telling a couple of legends from their history, until it grows late and Alfred suggests that it's time to head home, all of them saying goodbye after one last song. Outside the night is dark and gloomy, and so they take the long way back and not the shortcut, for that would be too creepy, though Willi begins to tell ghost stories that he has made up on his own, such as the one about the old crone who lives in Landstein Castle and still wanders the countryside, suddenly appearing in the old city, then causing trouble in the catacombs of the cloister as she throws bones out of the coffins, though she prefers to stay in these woods on nights when there's no moon, wrapped in a long sheet, and when she walks nearby the woods rustle with a light wind, her eyes lit up with a sick green color like two swamp spirits, and whomever she meets she shocks with an electric charge, shrieking "Memento mori!" At the same time, Willi gives one of the novices a light hit in the chest, then he goes on with his story, until once again he lets out a ghastly "Memento mori!" and scares another with a shove, some of the novices getting really frightened, while most of them think of it as fun.

When Willi tells a story that everyone likes, Alfred reminds FHF that he shouldn't forget to mention these mortal tales in his history, and so FHF makes sure to take note of it all as he writes it down and embellishes it with archaic language, now and then reading from the history back at the meetinghouse. All important incidents are called the Acts of the Knights, but only at the camp can a Wanderer first rise to the level of knighthood. Alfred had founded the Order of the Knights three years ago, naming himself the Great Commander, all the boys in the camp at the time being made knights, though FHF was the only one to turn down this honor, for he wanted always to remain the court jester. FHF explained that because of this he could never be a part of the order, but he is prepared to remain loyal to the illustrious Great Commander and the august Order of the Knights and to serve them as court jester, which everyone agreed to, FHF always fulfilling his position as ably as possible. It was also then decided that membership in the pack did not automatically guarantee membership in the order, yet every novice could be recognized as a candidate for entry if he so wished, FHF the only one in the pack who had never wanted to join. Whoever applies is soon taken and accepted among the knights, each servant recommended by his knight to become a knave as early as the third hiking trip, as long as the Great Commander approves and no knight raises objections, though as a knave one still stands below his knight and must support him in all matters of question among the order, but at the same time one can in a joking manner pretend that he's not interested in being accepted, though you have to make sure that it's taken the right way.

The culmination of the process of being named a knight takes place at the *bal paré*, which one can dress up for, yet hardly anyone does, for most like to save their best efforts for the Festival of the Knights of the Great Commander. At the *bal paré* they show up at the large table in the woods, lamps having been placed upon it, and at each seat a plate full of sweet berries, the Great Commander presiding from above, the oldest two knights on each side of him, the younger knights and the knaves filling out the table to the other end, for none of them are servants, since at the camp everyone is considered at least a knave, the court jester sitting at the far end. The Great Commander opens the *bal paré* with words by saying loudly that the knights will soon get the festivities under way and that they should add to their old heroic ventures, in order that the Landstein Castle Camp do honor to its predecessors and set an illustrious example for the heroes to come in later generations, while in his capacity as Great Commander he also tenderly acknowledges the young but brave knaves, who most certainly should meet with no opposition in being accepted today into the circle of knights, though first the Great Commander has to make sure that the knaves have memorized the sacred rules and mores of the aforementioned circle of knights and taken them to heart, to which purpose he then passes the tankard round the circle. The tankard is a milk can that holds almost twelve liters and for the *bal paré* is not filled with the usual punch but with hot chocolate instead. The Great Commander lifts it to his lips in order to take a strong drink, all the other knights doing likewise and acknowledging him, though no knight who cares about his honor allows a single drop to fall, while hardly anyone succeeds at this, since throughout the ceremony there's a lot of joking around and laughter, causing almost everyone to spill a bit or to choke, especially the knaves, since even if it were quiet they would barely be able to handle drinking from the monstrous tankard. The court jester, who is the last to drink, outstrips all the other knights in terms of poise, because no matter how long he drinks from the tankard he doesn't spill a drop, for even if the others try to make him laugh the court jester still maintains his focus. Once everyone has drunk from it, the tankard is set back down on the table, which is brown by now with a fresh coat of chocolate, a cover set on the tankard so that the hot chocolate doesn't cool, since until the end of the *bal paré* they will drink from it until the tankard is emptied of its last drop.

Three times the Great Commander pounds hard on the table with his fist, which is what is always done if someone wants to speak, for that way you can be heard and the others will quiet down. The Great Commander then asks those knights who have a knave assigned to them to tell the high assembly of their virtues and heroic acts in order that the illustrious circle of knights can savor and be refreshed by their uplifting examples, and so that it will be clear whether the aspiring knaves will be worthy of being accorded the distinction and honor of becoming a knight. At this, one knight after another pounds three times on the table in order to praise his knave, whereby an extended adventure unfolds which the Great Commander of the circle of knights allows to proceed. Pony is the knave of Hans, who tells of what he thinks is the truly considerable achievement of his knave's wandering off and being rescued from the ancient forest on the first night after their arrival, which the entire circle of knights acknowledges is a truly heroic feat, all of them proposing (with only FHF abstaining, since as a sanctioned guest of the circle of knights he is not allowed to propose anything) that the new knight be known by the name of Pony the Night Wanderer, which is supported unanimously. Then Pony has to walk with Hans up to the Great Commander, as Pony kneels down with Hans standing behind him, the Great Commander standing up and placing a cookie in Pony's mouth and tapping him three times on the shoulder with the flat of his hand, at which the honor is bestowed.

Bambus bangs on the table and proceeds to depict in glowing color the life and accomplishments of his knave, Edgar, who more than anyone surely deserves to be promoted from the rank of knave to that of knight, for if other knights may have achieved unsurpassable accomplishments they pale in comparison with the heroic glow that surrounds the humble Edgar, since in the glorious history of our order surely there is no one who has provided the knights with such uplifting and stomach-filling exhilaration, because although all the cooks of Landstein Castle know how to swing a spoon in masterly fashion, next to Edgar they are mere hacks. This is received with loud applause, but the court jester pounds on the table and says, "Indeed, not even in the Sun King's court at Versailles was such scrumptious food served as that which Edgar magically coaxed from our meager kettles. Lucullus himself would have compared his fortune with Polycrates and Midas if he had been lucky enough to be a guest at Edgar's table. Nor should anyone laugh! It certainly is possible. Couldn't Lucullus indeed have visited the *legio decima* in the woods surrounding Landstein? The only catch lies in the slight time difference between the eras of Edgar and Lucullus which certainly exists. Thus Lucullus had to bite the dust without having tasted Edgar's rice pudding. However, because of the great service done to us by our cook I ask that this time difference not be seen as a hindrance. I also ask that the knights honor him with the name Edgar the Cook of Lucullus."

This request by the court jester is also agreed to unanimously, but the jester pounds on the table three times again and says that the only reason he has gone back in world history to the Romans is that there is a real connection between ancient and modern Landstein through the *legio decima*, though this also made him aware of Fabi's feelings, for he didn't want to upset Fabi, knowing how much he was against the damnable monarchy, though Fabi yelled straight back, "There's no need to bring that up here!" He, however, is immediately called to order as the Great Commander says, "No one is allowed to interrupt someone who has banged on the table three times!" Then the court jester asserts that he can say what he wants, for he is after all the court jester, and he has to confess that at first he wanted Edgar's name to be Head Cook to the Sun King. At this Fabi bangs three times on the table so hard that the tankards rattle, as he yells that it doesn't matter to him in the least, and that it's a joke whether Edgar is called Head Cook to the Sun King, nor is he among the knights necessarily against monarchy, but rather just the present monarchy, since it's so worthless, at which Josef pounds on the table and says, "In some youth organizations everything is voted upon. They even vote about friendships, asking who is for someone and who is against. But there's no sense in voting about something that can't be decided or that nothing can be done about. But if folks want to vote, then the knights can put to a vote whether they are for or against the monarchy." Everyone laughs at this, though Fabi adds in all seriousness, "Of course we can vote about it!" Willi then states, "We can take that up at the annual gathering, if everyone thinks it's important." Then Alfred pounds on the table and says, "My noble knights, courageous knaves, and my dear court jester! We should not ignore the important issue of the monarchy, but perhaps instead at the Festival of the Great Commander we could hold a debate between Knight Fabi and the court jester. There is not enough time now, we need to move ahead with our nominations for knighthood. The noble Knight Bambus has presented his knave, Edgar, before me so that I may commemorate the promotion of this knave to knighthood."

Bambus then steps forward with Edgar, Edgar kneels down, and then the same thing happens as with Pony, though as soon as a cookie is held out to Edgar and he takes a bite of it he begins to spit it out in disgust and yells, "Ugh, that's soap!" What his eyes couldn't see in this light, the tongue tasted immediately, for shortly before the evening began Alfred and Willi had cut a piece off a soft bar of soap and shaped it exactly like the cookie Pony was given, this being a bit of payback for the burned rice pudding and even more for the hard work of having to clean the kettles afterward, though graciousness is still the order of the day, for the legitimacy of Edgar's promotion is still recognized, even though he has decidedly refused to swallow his soap cookie. Meanwhile, more promotions follow, the tankard passing quickly around the circle a number of times, each new knight receiving two cookies as Pony did, Edgar indeed getting three, though he looks closely at each before he eats them. After this the berries are passed out, a rule of the *bal paré* forbidding the use of a spoon or one's hands, as instead you must either pick out the berries with your mouth or pour the berries from the bowl directly into your mouth. Most of the berries are blackberries, and soon all the knights' faces are as black as after a battle, most of them heading down to the creek in the dark in order to wash up, the next morning the stains still visible on their faces, and they have to wash up yet again in order to look like Wanderers and not philistines.

A couple of days later, Alfred learns at the ranger's house that on the evening of the *bal paré* a boy from Sichelbach, who had been visiting a girl in Markl, passed by the *bal paré* at about ten o'clock at night on his way home, the scene around the campfire frightening him a good deal, for he thought it was Gypsies, of whom this boy was deeply afraid, while probably as a result he thought that evil spirits and magicians had been let loose, which then caused him to run wild with fear back to Markl, from which he dared set foot on the path home again only at first light, the farmers from Markl and Sichelbach indeed laughing so much over the scaredy-cat, since everyone in the villages had long known about the pack, as did the boy, for he had walked repeatedly by the camp by day and by night. The Wanderers also all laughed, the younger ones proud that they had already passed the test of staying alone in the woods for a night, nor had they ever really trembled during Willi's ghost stories. FHF, however, makes a serious face and says that perhaps not everything is as it usually is once the Wanderers transform themselves into an order of knights, for that goes back to the Middle Ages, when the world was a strange place full of mystery and terror, leading to fear and uncertainty, FHF believing as well that this has not entirely disappeared, for each of them is still lost amid a sea of fear, able at best to watch out for himself as long as he knows how to swim, though the ability to swim like this is the true goal of the Wanderers, for the world—so says FHF—is only partially visible on its surface, there being behind it an endless darkness, the philistines living in the darkness and not realizing it, since they themselves are a part of the darkness, unable to distinguish black from black, while when a light appears in the darkness that's when spirits appear, which could just be a bunch of philistines, though also Wanderers, people learning the strangeness that exists as they sit as if looking through a peephole behind which there is light, though to the philistines the light is unbearable, and that is why they are afraid.

Whenever FHF talks this way no one takes him completely seriously, for what he says sounds almost like a joke, and he just throws it all in amid the fun he fosters as court jester, which they love, but when he's really serious they just shake their heads and say FHF is theorizing yet again, only Alfred saying to let him be. Josef marvels at him when he shares some thoughts at night while lying in the tent after the lamp is put out, the two of them talking for a while quietly so as not to disturb anyone, as Josef asks, "How should one conduct his life so that the light can be reconciled with the darkness?" FHF explains that this only happens slowly, you have to observe the world, there being everywhere beautiful and exalted things, next to which there are evil and lowly things, though the Wanderers' camp is a piece of good fortune, for from there you can hear the dogs howling in the villages, you can trace the history of the fall of Landstein Castle, you hear the steps of the *legio decima*, the wind stroking the treetops then as it does now, the beeches sounding a major key, the birches a minor, Altstadt founded later, and then disappearing until the church was built, the monks constructing their white church and cloister, the old Landstein Castle abandoned and continuing to go to ruin more and more, the Wanderers now guests, and even this a tiny piece of eternal history.

When FHF talks like this, the past and the present flow together for Josef as if in a dream, himself hearing again the songs sung around the campfire, the flames climbing high and smoking when green branches are placed upon them, life is beautiful and free, no need to languish in a prison, there being no barrier between what is serious and what is meant in jest, the flames of the campfire also part of the breath of the eternal light, before which one sits as in a panorama and stares inside, mankind always bracing himself before this light which will not really allow him to find a way in, something always remaining closed off, unreachable, man an onlooker, though if he wishes to be more than that he takes many risks, for who knows who can prevail without being destroyed? But it's good to sit by the light and let it warm you. Soon Josef hears nothing more of what FHF says, all of it now a dream, the sound of the forest treetops resonating day and night, a timeless journey that goes on and on and yet remains completely still. Adamsfreiheit is on the narrow-gauge railroad line, so there are few daily trains; perhaps Fritz Hans Fuchs is no longer talking and has already gone to sleep; the flag has been taken down and is at rest; and Alfred is asleep, everyone is asleep in their tents, the farm boy from Sichelbach asleep, the lake asleep, the fish tired in the dark current, as Josef also sleeps through to the new day that will soon dawn.

THE TOWER ROOM

Thomas often tells Josef what a wonderful person Johannes is, the great questions of mankind often debated by his circle, free of superficial chatter, devoid of political jargon, though it's not just about art, but rather what cannot be learned at any school or university, nor is it religion or philosophy in the usual sense, all of that being too extraneous; no, it's about life itself, the inner life that you penetrate only when you concentrate on your deepest interior and peel away everything external. Thomas is the youngest in the circle, which contains remarkable men and women, as well as artists, who would really be of interest to Josef, as Thomas also mentions the poet and art collector Spiridion von Flaschenberg, though the most important is Johannes, who lives in seclusion above in his tower room and hardly ever comes out, but instead others visit him, the circle coming together each Wednesday, Thomas having told Johannes a great deal about Josef, such that he'd be pleased to have him visit. Yet Josef doesn't allow himself to be enticed by this invitation, because he finds that already at eighteen he has gadded about with other people too much, having experienced more than other people his age and fancying himself older and more mature. Often he thinks of himself as a finished man, and looking ahead at life he perceives no clear path, and you have to be on your own in order to find yourself, everything else is a distraction, Josef having composed a philosophy that he thinks is original but which Thomas doesn't find so unique, though he firmly agrees that it is real and deep, the great truths not having changed throughout human history, because there is only one truth, the great masters having found it, and perhaps our era's challenge is to show that there is still only one truth that can be reached in the end, people just have not woken up to it, only the great masters have known it or at least sensed it, Johannes being one of those who had indeed achieved it, that's what is so amazing about him, that he has perceived it, he sees all things as if they stood in a panorama before him, and since he has turned the light inside himself to the highest brightness he can survey everything in the world with this very same light.

Josef is mistrustful and counters that each person must find his own way, and that only on your own is it possible to do so, therefore no one can tell anyone what to do, it will quickly lead to misunderstandings, and there is nothing more important than to maintain your independence. Thomas assures him that is exactly what Johannes teaches, that in fact he says nothing, he only listens to people and shows them where they have gone wrong, and that it's only a matter of discovering the truth in yourself and thus attaining the peace that allows you to remain within yourself. Josef replies that this all sounds well and good, yet he does not see what it is he should be seeking from Johannes if he is proclaiming only what Josef has long been convinced of already. Thomas at first has to agree, but soon he starts his campaign again and repeats that Josef has no idea what he's missing by declining, for it is certainly right to want to be independent, and Thomas wants that as well, but to gather together with like-minded people is a godsend and an opportunity to share your innermost thoughts. Thomas can only underscore how much he owes Johannes, yet Josef shouldn't believe that he is just not ready, one is always ready, it always being obvious that you stand at the start and look inside yourself, everything seeming confused, the path that leads to salvation is long, while upon it one constantly discovers new passions that are contrary to the truth, so how can one arrive at equilibrium? Whatever happens is nothing but a distraction from the truth, the individual finds himself perpetually at odds with it, nor can you ever in life be completely at one with the truth, that being possible only through the deliverance that comes at the entrance to your final rest.

Why does Josef hang around Thomas? If you know who you are, then you are unaffected and it doesn't bother you and nothing will bother you, but whoever is still looking for something finds himself constantly ill at ease and is very far from his goal, just as the great masters teach. Whoever is still looking for something should go where there is more light than in himself, and that is what is so marvelous about Johannes. Because he has attained so much, he knows what it is possible for humans to know, the next step leading from earthly reality into the true reality, where everything consists of pure spirit. Josef listens, but many months go by before he is willing to consider visiting Johannes just once with Thomas, but certainly not his circle, just him alone, because the more he learns from Thomas the more mistrustful he is of this circle, feeling that it could be some kind of sect or even a secret society, and therefore a cliquish confraternity from which he believes he would then have to extricate himself. The true person defines himself and should seek nothing from other people who bind themselves together in tight groups, for that forwards a herd mentality, as in a religious community, or in a youth group, a political party, in school or in the military, in a social club, and most of all among all those people who cannot stand to be alone because they are afraid of themselves, though Josef believes he is now empty of fear and understands his life as a singular battle against fear in his effort to attain unadulterated beauty, though the world disrupts the harmony in which such beauty can be found.

Josef recalls with disgust how once out of curiosity he took part in a demonstration against the government, the people rubbing up against one another in a dense crowd as they pressed on toward the Heumarkt, inflammatory signs swinging to and fro that also adorned a platform, while there up above they stood, fists waving and mouths wide open, hatred and condemnations yelled and spit out against the exploitative power of the ruling class, a furious clamor rising up in the background as black-clad and well-groomed mounted policemen pushed their way out of Jacobstrasse and told the crowd to disperse because the gathering had become unruly, but then those up on the platform incited the crowd, unleashing a wave of hatred against the police. "Criminals! Exploiters! Executioners! Bloodsuckers!" Then cobblestones were pried out of the pavement and tossed at the police, who by riding toward the demonstrators with unsheathed sabers only exacerbated the situation, after which some enraged men tried to grab the horses by the reins and drag the police down in order to stop the attack, but the police swung their sabers unmercifully, while here and there they engaged in hand-to-hand combat, the stubborn ones arrested, some of the police wounded, a blind salvo fired over the waves of people, after which slowly but surely the fearful, raging mob was split up into smaller bunches that hastily tried to flee. Josef didn't want to remain among their number and tried to find a door to slip through, but all the houses were locked, and so he had to move along with the running horde until he reached a side street where it was likely that he could disappear among uninvolved onlookers.

What was the sense of it all, what was all the fighting about? Many friends tried to convince Josef how necessary such battles were in order to attain a more just and better world, and that meant action. Dreams were of no help, nothing but bourgeois lies, whereas true ideals demanded that they be realized, because society cannot remain the same, and it was not enough that it slowly decay, it had to be shattered. Besides, that's all there was to history, endless wars, robbery, murder, and pestilence, barbarity bubbling up, while in between ideals were like flowers in a garden cut off from all events of the world, and that amounted to nothing. Josef mustn't remain an individualist, so he let himself take part in a revolutionary festival as part of a day for the people sponsored by the party in a small town, letting himself be lectured to as on the decorated market square a delegate spoke to the people, telling them that today everything was a mess, in his opinion, everything would be better tomorrow once the party was victorious, and that was what had to happen, which is why you had to help it along and make it happen, and tirelessly work to make it happen. Everything he said was right, the cheers and applause confirming it, after which the crowd marched the length of the town and finally emptied out into a beer garden full of workers and farmers, wives and children, the beer flowing in streams. Josef was disgusted to see that kids were given beer, yet someone said to him it was the fault of the ruling class that the underclass would always drink away the last of its money until it was freed of its chains, which was why one needed to become brothers with the masses and warn them of the dangers of alcohol, whose consumption led them to be only more tightly locked in the grip of their class enemies. Yet Josef was unconvinced and asked, Why is it that now for the first time one claims to have discovered and seized hold of the people's salvation?

Truth can be found only through a spiritual life like the one Josef now embraces. Certain voices said that he must withdraw from the world if he wanted to attain true understanding, as nothing is as it appears, for everything evolves amid the continual depths in the midst of life, one having to be very still, for then the onslaught occurs, colored beams pressing down upon humankind from the firmament to the sounds of sacred music, slowly progressing toward the body that will be bathed in pureness, the beams then pressing their blessing into the body until they strike the heart, at which thunderous sound is released, you experience a freedom never felt before, you feel light, and you are released from the world and know that you are accountable only to yourself, everything else is immaterial and leads only to painful confusion, the inner realm the only thing that continues, each having to go his own way, though he must not be forced by anyone, for that is not allowed. The evil of the world comes directly from the impure spirit, for anyone who does not have an inner life must suffer, because only then will he feel worry and deprivation, which is the root of all fear and every terror. The true and good person lives selflessly, but at first selflessness involves spiritual sacrifice, and only when a number of people have chosen to embrace this can the outward circumstances be altered.

Josef could gather a circle around himself and spread the true teaching, but he feels no pressure to do so, it would too easily lead to endless misunderstanding, too many people valuing only speeches and gestures, seeking advice as to how to achieve blessedness, but such recipes don't exist, and whoever issues the clearest rules soon notes that the words are understood and followed but they do no good, for the secret, the mystery, cannot be explained to the uninitiated, which is also what Josef had told Herr Koppelter, whom he first spoke with on a park bench. Herr Koppelter is a member of a society, which he calls a circle of people in search of the true spirit from all different countries, Herr Koppelter having spoken about them in a positive and impressive way, such that Josef accepted an invitation to a gathering of the local chapter, though he found that what was talked about there sounded stilted, seeming to him a preachy mixture of science, philosophy, religion, and mysticism, the hall having a strange smell, women with sentimental eyes sitting around, men wearing high, stiff collars with lavender or green ties, some having long hair done in strange styles, and almost all looking rapturous. Josef disapproved of it all, and told Herr Koppelter so, but he replied that you just had to get used to it all, the teachings are all-embracing, it requiring decades to penetrate the master's enlightenment, though books full of such mysteries must be studied each day, all wisdom and an incomparable beauty rising from them as your awareness grows within the master's circle of light, which has truly grasped everything and explained it, he being the man for our times; nor can he be ignored, for without the proclamations of his teachings nothing more can be understood, be it the constant misery of the world, the unjust social conditions, the decline of culture, or the lacerated world, the teachings of the master are all that allow such to be understood, changed, and avoided. Josef counters that he follows no master, much less a single one with whom one must first study and be handed what no one has been handed before, such that everything that has come before him is taken only as a harbinger of this master.

Herr Koppelter says this is a gross oversimplification, for the master in no way thinks of himself as being above the geniuses of earlier times, but the world runs according to a certain plan in which the master plays his role, he not wanting to found a new religion but rather a spiritual science that doesn't have to be believed but simply learned, thus allowing everyone to test its particulars and verify them, but not through the usual methods, one needs to follow the master's method, which can be assessed only within the confines of his own teaching, since whoever approaches from the outside cannot help but fall into error. Josef has his doubts and explains that he must believe in himself above all others, he cannot accept any teachings that say how one should live without knowing whether they are true or false. Then Herr Koppelter asks whether Josef believes he is infallible, or whether it wouldn't be more reasonable and productive to first adopt through intensive study teachings familiar to the best minds of our times, such teachings being what enabled them to find and follow the right path, all their previous efforts amounting to nothing more than groping in the dark. Indeed, there are great men who are devotees of the master, among them a famous poet and another poet who devotes most of his time to the society, such that he is hardly able to bring out his own marvelous work, only because he finds the master's society to be decidedly more important, this example speaking volumes, as do so many others. Josef remains dismissive, though he cannot prevent Herr Koppelter from continuing to make his case at length, even though Josef has already declared himself so unsympathetic to the master that Herr Koppelter responds, "Perhaps on the surface you are so against the master because on the inside his teachings have so much to say to you. But you will only feel this power while young. Later you will stand empty-handed, feeling lost." Josef remained unconvinced by this view, for though the master's teachings attracted him a great deal, they also repelled him even more, he finding them bogus, the society an embarrassment, Josef soon turning away from Herr Koppelter.

In general, Josef had certainly turned away from most things and stuck to his own, mistrust the only means of self-protection once you were no longer young, for then you are lured and enticed by all sides, no matter where you go, as here and only here is where you find the truth, there being no need to be a Doctor Faust who first pledged his soul to the spirits, they are quite willing to offer themselves cheap, such that one can hardly resist them, but should you grant them the slightest sympathy, then you are already lost, since they debase anything that comes into contact with them, there being within such enticements a pact between the wooer and the wooed, which is the root of hatred, conflict, intolerance, and envy, and this is why Josef will have none of it, but instead chooses to keep to himself. Thomas protests that this is not what Johannes means to him, for he is so chaste and simple, his soft smile enchanting, his tenderness spreading to all, such that you can't help but find him a good spiritual guardian who listens to the experiences related to him by his friends, whom he doesn't judge, not wanting that others confess to him but simply asking quietly the mildest of questions, and how he does so is wonderful and inimitable, much guidance existing in the questions themselves, for in formulating your answers you find yourself understanding more clearly what you have experienced but often have not understood, to which Johannes adds wonderful comments, these often being small suggestions, after which you feel much better. Spiritual assistance is the most important thing to Johannes, but you have to seek him out on your own initiative, he doesn't want to serve as any kind of master or authority, though he possesses a natural authority that hangs on every word spoken from his lips. Josef then asks whether these questions and answers are shared in the open, as he finds it shameless to talk about his experiences openly in front of others, for who can understand such things, and one should keep such matters to himself, not out of selfishness and shame but rather out of self-discipline and composure. Thomas assures him once again that especially with Johannes there is no need to hide anything, you only need to throw yourself into it and experience it for yourself, there being a palpable bliss that everyone senses in the tower room above, the effects of which Thomas says nothing more about, but which clearly have captivated Thomas and softened him almost entirely, such that Josef finally says he would like to meet Johannes, but only just him.

Thomas is roused by this and takes Josef at his word, telling him they will go together next week, Josef recommending that it be Saturday, though Thomas explains that you can visit Johannes Monday through Friday only, no one allowed in on Saturday or Sunday, the door is not even opened if someone rings, since Johannes wants to be alone and doesn't go out. Thus on the following Monday the friends visit Johannes, who lives in the middle of the city, six flights up on the top floor, the place looking like a tower from the outside, it being unlike any normal apartment and more like a studio. Johannes is a photographer, having won many prizes years ago at various exhibitions, though that's long past, his career no more now than a fading memory, while to the left and right as you enter the building there are display cases with a few photographs in them, little notices announcing the visiting hours, where the studio is located, and that there is an elevator. But hardly any customers come to the studio, it not mattering to Johannes, Thomas explaining that Johannes needs to make only a little bit of money, although he has no means, but he never complains, and it's unclear just how he manages to make ends meet, especially given the household that he runs. The customers have long since disappeared, because of how long they had to wait in the waiting room, even then being told that Herr Tvrdil, sorry to say, was tied up and could do no photography today, so would one be so kind as to come back another day? The customers would ask if they could set up an appointment by phone, but they received a friendly smile and were told that unfortunately there was no phone, at which people would head off angry and not come back again, it being the case that, even when the customers weren't put off, it wasn't Johannes who took their picture but instead the doors of the studio would open and his assistant, Frieda, who had just greeted the visitors and led them to the waiting room, called them in and took the photograph herself.

Josef and Thomas climb the stairs, neither having a coin in his pocket for the elevator, and so they walk up to the door, on which nothing stands except:

JOHANNES TVRDIL
CLOSED SATURDAY AFTERNOON AND SUNDAY

Thomas knocks three times quickly, this the signal that leads to the door being opened, otherwise even on weekdays, when customers might show up, the door is opened only after some minutes or perhaps not at all, though this time the three knocks don't seem to do any good, as Josef asks whether Thomas needs to give the signal again, the latter reassuring him that someone will soon be there, for he certainly won't knock again, and finally they hear footsteps, as before them stands a woman roughly thirty-five years of age, Frieda the assistant. Thomas has already explained to Josef that Frieda spends most of her time with Johannes, this having been so for many years, for Johannes is divorced and has a twelve-year-old daughter who lives with an aunt and visits Johannes only once a week, there being no deep relationship between father and daughter, Frau Tvrdil a remarkable person, exceptionally lovely, though the marriage was an unhappy one, Johannes always saying that no one should do as he did and fall in love with and marry a woman simply because she pleased him. Thomas knows nothing more than this, but it must indeed have been a somewhat difficult breakup, for the wife eventually took up with another man and asked Johannes for a divorce, he having insisted as part of the settlement that the daughter must not be raised by the mother, which they both agreed to, Johannes having never seen the woman again. Until the divorce he had been outwardly successful, but afterward none of it mattered to him, as he found himself changing on the inside, for he began to search for the meaning of life, eventually joining a group of people who called themselves mystics and founded a society called the Burning Thorn Bush, after which Johannes began to feel good again. There they tried to understand the meaning of life through meditative means and spoke of an eternal brotherhood that knows no borders, the brotherhood representing the true path for humankind, all other outward powers of earthly states being powerless in the face of it, they believing in the immense power of the Guardian of the Realm and other mystical revelations that can be experienced only on the inside, they mean nothing on the outside, though they are reflected in the soul through the face of the initiated, such that they know each other as brothers and sisters anywhere in the world through a simple glance or a single word exchanged between them.

Johannes met Frieda in this society of friends, she falling powerfully in love, though not encountering the same love in return, but Johannes needed help in the studio, and since Frieda wanted to change jobs, anyway, she soon became his assistant. That was fine with her, nor did she wish to stop there, for she wanted to fulfill his life, though he gently held back without dismissing her from her position. After the divorce Johannes had given up his apartment and moved into the studio, which in addition contained two rooms, a kitchen and an adjoining room. Then Frieda began to clean for Johannes, to do the shopping, take care of the kitchen, and eventually cook and wash the dishes, Johannes accepting it all, not approving, though also not protesting, such that when Frieda's mother died he silently agreed to her suggestion that she move in with him, she bringing her own things and setting up a bed in the kitchen, while Johannes slept in the tower room, since then the two of them running the business together and living one next to the other. Long ago Johannes had eased his ties with the society of friends and then quit, after which he withdrew from life, no longer wishing to be misled into whatever circumstances might lead him to, for soon he wanted nothing more to do with matters of business or money, and if anyone wished to talk about them he would simply smile and say that silver can be found to buy bread, but gold comes from the sun, though his real earnings grew ever less, a studio assistant having to be let go, and Frieda taking over these duties as well, though Thomas didn't think she had been paid in years, and that her savings had been used to keep the business going, Frieda having come to terms with it all and living quietly next to Johannes.

Thomas doesn't know how the loose circle around Johannes came together, but supposedly after his departure from the society of friends some of them would visit him now and then, eventually doing so on a regular basis, others also hearing about the group, such as Thomas, who one day showed up at the studio uninvited, Frieda greeting him when he announced in the waiting room that he wished to speak with Herr Tvrdil, though Frieda thought he was a customer as she observed curtly that Herr Tvrdil was not available, but was there something she could help him with, though Thomas countered that there was nothing he wanted other than to see Johannes, because he had the feeling that he should talk with Herr Tvrdil, though he didn't really know what it was he wanted to ask of him, it being hard to explain what had brought him there. Then Frieda said warmly that she would be happy to let Herr Tvrdil know, upon which he welcomed Thomas like an old friend. In such manner the circle was formed, some bringing along friends, though it grew to no more than twenty people. Frieda is happy to welcome male visitors, and she's friendly to women as well, though she keeps an eye on them with poorly concealed distrust, especially if they are young and pretty, though such worries are pointless, for Johannes treats men and women the same, speaking to all of them with natural ease, noting Frieda's mild jealousy, though he ignores her and says, in case it should appear that he is discriminating against anyone, he first and foremost values all people equally, and that whoever senses envy or jealousy is not on the true path and should look inward in order to see how badly he is handling himself.

Now Thomas and Josef stand before Frieda, who lets the guests enter and tells them to take off their coats, then she stretches out her hand to each and says that Johannes will be pleased, for she has heard a lot about Josef, Thomas having said many nice things about him. She leads the guests out of the foyer decorated with photos and into the waiting room, in which there stands a large round table, a cupboard, a desk, and many chairs, prizewinning photos hanging on the walls, Frieda already having opened the door to the studio, telling the friends to sit, she will get Johannes. This, then, is the renowned tower room, a grand room with a great bay full of windows, another window that is half draped to the side, bookshelves and cupboards appearing to line the walls, though it's hard to see, since the tower room contains several folding screens, though there are not the odd kinds of shelves that photographers so often use. Meanwhile the room is covered with a thick carpet, the middle of which is kept as an open space, a photographic apparatus shoved into the corner with a black cloth covering it, two floodlights standing there as well. The bay is cut off from the rest of the room by heavy curtains, though they are pulled open, such that one can see the semicircular bench tucked into it, covered with pillows, and before it a wooden frame with an unusually large gong with a black-and-gold finish hanging from it. In the studio there are two standing lamps, but they are not lit, the gentle light that suffuses the room coming from a covered fixture in the ceiling, as Josef looks at a long, broad divan covered with a dark glowing throw made of an Indian fabric, a small, low table running the length of the divan before which sits a row of chairs, many more chairs standing around the room, the divan reaching to a corner platform on which some books rest, while across from it there hangs from the ceiling an eternal light framed by a soft red glow, no pictures on the wall nearby, the quiet ceremonial flame setting the tone of the room and not seeming strange but quite the opposite, causing Josef to feel safe and at home.

The visitors wait for only a short while, then Johannes steps through a door as Josef observes him, greeting the guests quietly and simply. To Josef he says that he is pleased to meet him, Thomas had indeed said good things about him, and how nice it was that he has come, today is the right day to get to know someone. Josef knows through Thomas that Johannes is over fifty, yet he doesn't look that old at all, his manner not seeming at all like that of someone his age, Josef having the feeling that he was sitting across from someone his own age. Thomas had in fact never said anything about Johannes's outward appearance, and so Josef is surprised, observing a man of medium height with delicate features, his skin as pale as that of a woman, the eyes fiery and almost mischievous, the head somewhat small, with a large pointed nose, unusually long ears that are well shaped and almost or-namental, the hair just touching them and rather plain, it being hard to de-cide if it's dirty blond or silver gray, it nonetheless lending the face a certain glow. Johannes wears a dull red silk housecoat, long pants, and a soft smock, his bare feet covered by small, soft leather sandals. Josef had heard that Johannes rarely wears city clothes, but that he wears different silk coats according to his mood, choosing warmer ones for winter, but never wearing socks, not even when it's bitter cold.

Johannes notices how closely he is being observed, but it doesn't seem to disturb him, he perhaps revealing a slight smile as he turns from Josef and speaks with Thomas, the two of them talking quietly, making a constant chirping, though Josef doesn't try to listen in but simply sits there quietly, feeling at ease, if not somewhat sleepy, until soon he feels left out and suddenly and without invitation he erupts with a question for Johannes: "Tell me, Herr Tvrdil, what is it that you experience?" Josef is shocked by his own question and is embarrassed, but he doesn't want to make a fuss and adds in a forced, cheery manner with a steady tone, "You have a very nice place. I've never seen such a big gong before." Johannes replies with a smile that he also finds it a warm and welcoming place, he always wanting his surroundings to be subdued, though it doesn't take much to accomplish that, it's the tone of the atmosphere that suffuses the house which matters, the gong functioning as a large, above all wonderful disk that serves to pacify unruly hearts, he having at one time struck the gong quite often, though now usually only when Thomas and the other friends were there, Johannes hoping that Josef might also come again in the future. Josef then thanks him for the invitation and wants to know more about the gong, to which Johannes says he has another, smaller gong that has a more silvery tone, but he puts out the larger gong because the number and quality of its overtones make for a richer sound and acoustical color, it being possible to play symphonies on it, for it's as good as any orchestra and far better than any organ when you know how to handle it, as you need to avoid hitting it exactly in the middle, because that never sounds good, but if you strike it just to the side you'll experience the fullest sound. Johannes explains that each different spot on the disk has its own special sound, which you then have to take advantage of, there being totally different results coming from hitting it near the edge and right on the edge, while to muffle the sound you use your hand by placing it on the gong lightly or more heavily, for you can just barely touch it with your fingertips or increase the muffling by pressing it with your whole hand, how hard or soft you strike also determining a great deal, as well as the speed with which you hit it, all of it leading to the louder or softer tones. Johannes prefers to play it very quietly, though he knows that in Burma and Bali they do it differently, beating it wildly and thunderously, it also being done in the open or in a temple, whereas for him it is music for the house which is best played *con sordino*, a lot depending on the right drumsticks, Johannes preferring kettle drumsticks wrapped with soft cloth, normal drumsticks resulting in a raw sound, but not the music that he likes, everything else a matter of the heart which cannot be talked about, mechanical means so often distracting people and not leading them inward, the result being neither a major nor a minor tone but instead much finer gradations or flowing sequences of sound, the most genuine music being a single tone, such as from a gong, though within this single tone there exists the mystical array of overtones implicit within all sound, and as soon as this and those overtones appear they melt again into the central tone, whoever really knows the art of playing the gong knowing true music as well.

Josef wants to hear the gong, but he doesn't say anything, yet Johannes has sensed his desire, saying that he will play it, but only just a bit, "Perhaps a bit of evening chimes in order to help us finish the day." Josef has never heard such playing, the tower room awash with a soft music, Johannes sitting quietly across from him, the touch of his hands and the stroke of the drumstick creating a uniform work, a little stroke of the gong releasing something immensely stirring that was satisfying, faint reverberations also bouncing off the heavy curtains and the folding screens. Johannes does not in fact play very long, but unless you checked the clock it was hard to say how long it is, the gong slowly emptying of sound, after which Johannes stands up, cheerful, and says, "I know that it pleased you. It pleases everyone, and that's good." Josef thanks him, but Johannes says quietly that there's no cause for thanks, for as long as you are grateful inside it is not necessary. "True thanks is silence. Words are of no use. What one wants to and can say has already been said. One should perhaps say something only in order to teach others just that." Thomas states which old masters had in fact taught this, but Johannes interrupts him, saying, "It certainly has been taught quite often, but one should also do it oneself." Then he turns to Josef. "What do you think? And, may I ask, how does it speak to your own experience?" Josef answers, "I try to listen within myself. I believe that everything is inside of us already. Unfortunately, it's difficult for me to always hear what is there. The self is a tune composed of 'I' and 'thou,' of each person and the All."

This appears to please Johannes, as he says, "It's all quite simple. Only the person himself is the greatest hindrance. He falls into confusion. Each should know this, and not criticize others when it happens but rather work on himself. Man's path is a pilgrimage, but one that ends within himself. There are two ways of approaching the world. In the first, one looks at the world through a peephole. One yearns for the world all the more, until somehow you step into it. But then the ground is swept from under your feet, or in fact what really happens is you lose your way, as you cannot merge with the world by striving to enter what you want to get lost inside of. Only through the second approach can one unite with the world. In this, one closes his actual eyes and looks inside himself at the same time. The real world that then arises is the true world. The observer is stuck in the middle, and here he recovers the entire world once again, only more beautiful and complete. In this it is also possible to unite with the entire world. Much more wonderful than any gaze is not to look at all. This you learn when you first learn the second approach. Then you recognize how everything repeats itself and always remains the same: it is all one. It is what is also called emanation. Whoever recognizes this ceases to look outward, for he has unified the outer and the inner worlds within himself. What one really knows, that is what one has, this being our true estate. One no longer has to observe the world going by." Josef affirms that he also thinks the same, but to manifest it within oneself is hard, to which Johannes adds, "That is the mistake people make, namely to say it's hard. Thus people deny themselves the chance at paradise. It's not hard. It's easy. As easy as breathing." Josef is deeply moved and says in a hoarse voice that he is pleased and would like very much to come again sometime, if that would be all right with Johannes, who then stands up with a huge smile and says, "Come whenever you like, Josef. But please, just not on Saturday or Sunday!"

Josef and Thomas warmly say goodbye, Frieda stepping in as well to spiritedly suggest that Josef visit again, after which there is a lot of hand-shaking until they reach the stairway outside, where Johannes and Frieda say "Goodbye!" several times, the door hardly having closed behind them above when Thomas triumphantly and proudly declares, "Well? Didn't I tell you that Johannes was marvelous? You could have met him much sooner if it weren't for your stubbornness." Josef has to agree, yet how could he have imagined how wonderful Johannes would be, for who knows what the others are like, which is still a concern, to which Thomas responds, "What do you expect? There is no one like Johannes. But among his friends there are wonderful people whom you will certainly like." Curiosity is indeed stronger than resistance, which is why Josef is ready to visit again on Wednesday, though he doesn't want to do so among so many strange people, and so he arranges things with Thomas, wishes him good night, and heads home lost in thought. What an unusual building Johannes lives in, it looking like a huge, erect flat iron, the sound of drumbeats pressing out from the nightclub located down below, as well as squeaking saxophones playing awful pop hits so loudly they can be heard in the street, whose own noise mixes with the sounds of the dance clubs nearby, creating a hellish mixture that nonetheless doesn't reach as high as the tower room, where Johannes resides above the stony sea of this godforsaken city, which, in contrast to Thomas, Josef described as a lovely stone corpse because of its magnificent churches and splendid palaces. In the middle of this corpse is the pulse of the living dead, the dusty tumult of noisy streets, where cars race by in a continuous stream, where strangers forever rush about, and where last year scrawny little trees were planted in thin rows at the edge of the sidewalks, the smoke and soot having already killed them this year.

What would it be like if Johannes ruled this city from his tower above? But he has nothing to do with the lovely stone corpse, the city not a part of his truth, but rather something foreign to him, since it disturbs his peace, and yet the way of the world goes on in this city without ceasing, so who can escape it except through high-minded longing, such that the blessed peace that Josef dreams of can exist only within the tower, it not allowing itself to be found in the light of day. Yet the moment you say that, then you are already divided and at odds with yourself, the true path lost. In contrast, Thomas believes he has found the true path, and he is able to unite his thoughts and his senses as he sits there motionless, while all around him move demons and spirits with crude gestures, this underworld raging because it has no power over Thomas, simply fading when he turns away from it, though what kinds of demons can they be unless they are nothing but illusions? Then they are the powers of fate which afford no one any peace, but Josef knows nothing of such demons, for if he thinks about his childhood, things were different then, there was only fear and unspeakable anxiety, those also being demons in the way they interfered with everything, though they eventually withdrew without Josef's doing anything. Perhaps it is as Herr Koppelter says, namely that Josef already possesses some of the true teachings inside, but it's not certain if they are entirely true, though one has to believe in something in order to have something on which to stand, so that everything is once again easy and given, nothing to worry about, all you need is to meditate regularly, it helps you to get through life, it all being like music, where all you have to do is listen, there being a music in all things, an overall tone, of which the gong serves as an emblem, since everything consists of symbols, as do the true teachings, and all we need do is make sure that the symbols never deteriorate into allegories. Perhaps a man is also a symbol, such that all such questions are pointless, as they would contain the answers already, while what stands between a question and its answer is only a conclusion, but just a kind of short circuit, the question and the answer melt together into a single entity, and so one must not draw conclusions, for one can save oneself a tiresome detour only by forgoing all questions. This is what Johannes has in mind when he asserts that it's not hard but easy to discard both types of approach, or at least to be leery of them, as they prevent your arriving at an unquestioning state, yet what can you do when the meaning of life is riddled with doubt? Once you have discovered the truth, every day that follows is pointless, and everything is over. Yet this idea is erroneous, because it's blasphemous, for it presumes the ability of the creator to judge creation, whereas one is a part of creation, a piece of creation that cannot hold sway over creation, and thus the nature and point of existence remains unknown. Yet such a consideration cannot be a mere fantasy, we are also born into life's design, even if each of us is mortal, for life is limitless and is not just the appearance of a being that begins and then ends, but its essence is transformation, we having come from others and then passing on into others, however unknown to us they may be, but we know this feeling of having seen something or experienced something before and wish to understand what it is. This never works, for the capacity of our memory is too small, it cannot include either birth or death.

Man wants to experience a great deal, and yet at eighteen what has Josef not already encountered that only someone who is seventy or eighty has, for Josef is taken aback by the speed of life, sensing that the end is already near, since he feels full to the brim already. How then can he believe that he'll live a long life? He has decided to keep a diary, having thought of a motto and written it at the top of the first page: "Don't be afraid of words!" In light of this saying Josef writes down his experiences, but not just the day-to-day ones, no, just the important ones, those he perceives, for he cannot leave the world without having done something worthwhile, future men needing to know something of him, since meaningful thoughts flow through his head, he not having wasted his time but instead having tried to make the most of every minute. Perhaps the true consciousness requires that one's spirit remain awake at all times by not frittering away each day, or chasing skirts like a drunk, or forgetting yourself and allowing yourself to be numbed by any means at hand, whether it be through hanging around in bars, dealing cards, chasing after dance partners, obsessing about sports, rather than continuing to try to think, read books, listen to music, make good friends, and seek replenishment in nature. Above all, it's important to handle yourself independently in all matters, rather than echoing others, empty repeated words being nothing but hypocrisy.

Josef writes in his diary and looks forward to Wednesday with Johannes, where he will remain quiet and observe the others, how they talk and what they have to say, as well as Johannes's playing of the gong. The days rush by, and the evening has arrived, Thomas showing up right on time, the two not saying a word after they first greet each other, though usually their time together is full of talk, neither able to say enough about what he has been doing, each having always been so unsettled by all that's gone on since they last met, it being a flood of dreams and nightmares, puzzling incidents that they can't help but divulge. Both are full of passion and hardly let the other get in a single word, feeling an inexhaustible pouring forth from within that they can barely keep up with in speech, the two also having experienced many symbolic events that strain the normal definitions of words, though the friends understand each other through hints and suggestions for which they have developed their own style. They spend long evenings together, either at Thomas's or Josef's place, playing piano for each other, their own tunes, which sometimes sound a bit off, Josef striking a tone with different emphasis in a rhythmic chain, loud or soft, again and again, heightening the effect with the pedal and the dampening of various keys in order to arrive at effects that from the distance remind one of Johannes playing the gong. What, indeed, would he say about Josef's piano playing? After many hours in the room together the two friends walk around at night for some hours more, heading out through the city outskirts and onto paths that rise into the hills, where they hardly ever encounter anyone else, here and there a farm or brickyard standing on its own, as Thomas thinks that all brickyards look almost like a place where evil spirits gather, one reminding him of the legend of Rabbi Löw and the golem he made of clay, it still seeming possible here even today, though Josef loves the feel of brickyards, and both love the many lights that stretch out like chains through the streets and that shine from the clusters of houses on the outskirts, as well as the murky shimmer whose lofty cloud of light floods the distance where the middle of the city lies hidden, it being somewhat unreal what they love, if in fact they believe it to be unchanging and constant, since they value only the eternal, rather than the everyday life in which one must scrape along in order to survive. Their back-and-forth does not spring from frivolity, there is nothing superficial about them. Since he was a boy Thomas has had to work hard to get by, Josef having it a bit better, though he, too, must count his pennies, both having learned not even to think about spending money on unnecessary things, for what good is the eternally temporal versus the temporary eternal which they continually aspire to so diligently.

But tonight the friends walk along without saying a word, moving as fast as the tumultuous streets surrounding the tower building will allow, themselves almost at the door, as below the sound of a tango whispers as it snakes its way upward as they enter through the sliding door, neither again having the right coins for the elevator, as they slowly climb up six floors and Thomas knocks three times. This time they don't have to wait very long, Frieda already there to open the door, all the doors of the apartment standing open, lights turned on everywhere, some voices audible, the door to the left leading into the kitchen, something that Josef didn't notice last time, though today Thomas takes his somewhat wary friend by the hand and heads in, Johannes there with two men and two women as he greets him heartily and says a couple of friendly words, to which Josef responds, "I'm so happy, Herr Tvrdil, that I could come again." But Johannes laughs and says, "What? My friends never speak to me so formally. To you I am Johannes and to me you are Josef." Josef wants to protest, but Thomas grabs him hard by the arm so that Josef knows that he shouldn't say anything.

One of the men in the kitchen is Herr Haschke, who quickly asks Josef, "Are you also interested in the true path? If so, you have found the right place here with Johannes. You have no idea how much I owe to him!" Josef is somewhat embarrassed, but he is spared from having to reply, for Herr Haschke rushes on about the incredible experiences he has had, though one should not think that it's that easy to remain on the true path, you must be careful not to lose hold of it and concentrate every moment in order to make sure that you are not led astray by false thoughts, people being so easy to seduce, such that you have to resist, for afterward you are disburdened and can float like an angel above the thorny way of everyday life. As he speaks, Herr Haschke's face goes all misty, and then he asks Josef gravely, "How long have you been on the true path?" Josef doesn't understand right away, and looks questioningly at Herr Haschke. "I mean, how long have you concentrated on it?" Josef replies to the query with a vague answer, though it doesn't satisfy Herr Haschke, who announces, "You have to devote yourself to the path, and that indeed requires concentration. That's most important in the morning when you first wake up, and in the evening before going to sleep. For then it functions all through the night. You sink inside yourself and think of nothing but the highest self that slumbers inside you and that through concentration will awaken. When you wake up, your aimless wandering is over. Oh, how lost I have been, but now I am somewhat enlightened! Oh, it's wonderful, it's so wonderful, such that I cannot describe it to you. Worldly matters disappear, and only the pure spirit is there. You must search for it! But it is incredibly hard, for evil spirits wish to distract you at first. Try reading the mystical writings of Kerning and Eckartshausen in order to be inspired!" Herr Haschke closes his eyes blissfully, his mouth open with rapture, his tongue licking a corner of it.

Josef doesn't know whether to laugh or be appalled, but then an old woman named Yolanda turns to him and says, "You really should know that Herr Haschke is the biggest fanatic among us. For a long while he had lost his way, but now he lives in bliss. I've not experienced it like him, for I was always God-fearing, but in a more churchly sense. I believed in the holy sacraments and in the grace of God. Then I had an epiphany. It was a genuine vision in which a white hand appeared to me, around which there was a soft light. The hand touched my forehead in order to bless me, and a voice said to me, 'Yolanda, you must not sleep any longer! My daughter, wake up!' Then I knew it was God's voice. But belief is not enough, you must also act within the world and engage yourself. Thus I devoted myself to the path. I always keep at it, and then it simply occurs. I am at it when I do housework, when I make batter for a cake, when I shop in the market, when I cook, iron, even set the table and relax on the settee, even then I am still on the path and at it. Then all my thoughts are with God, who gives me the strength for my work and his blessing." Herr Haschke looks up and takes Yolanda's hands. "Yolanda, Yolanda, it's all so wonderful. Your life is like the sun. I envy your husband and your son, Schorschl, who get to live within the circle of your light. With you at home, everyone must be on the true path. What a blessing! But no one at my house is on the true path. I have tried to lead my parents and my brother to it. But my brother is a total extrovert and loves going to the movies most of all. And my father says he just wants to rest after work. I have often wanted to explain to him that real and true relaxation comes through concentration, which sparks godliness. But my father doesn't believe it and doesn't understand me. Eckartshausen's *Mystical Nights*, which I gave him, he didn't read. He only reads the newspaper, and Johannes says I should leave my father in peace. But I suffer as a result. My mother has said that she has nothing against my being on the true path, yet she has no path at all, and so, end of story. Oh, Yolanda, your family enjoys God's true blessing!"

Johannes is caught up in other conversations, but toward the end he also hears Haschke, and says, "You should not be envious of anyone or complain about their family. It's simple. Each is granted the circumstances that best suit him. It only matters to recognize them and to make something good out of them. On one's way one shouldn't melt into sentimentality."— "Oh, you're so right, Johannes, you are always right! Don't think that I am really envious of Yolanda and her family! I'm happy that she has it so good. I also have it good when my sins are so great. For then is the grace of God even greater. Martin Luther was right, even if I never was a Protestant, when he said that one should sin deeply, in order to truly experience grace." Johannes only says softly that one should watch out for one's tongue getting caught up in idle chatter and parroting, especially when repeating mistaken ideas. Meanwhile more and more people arrive, Frieda responding to the doorbell and opening the door, but then it rings once more, and because Frieda isn't there Haschke walks out to answer, as guests pour into the kitchen and then leave it, lively voices filling every room in the apartment, as Frieda appears with a woman named Greta, and they announce that it's almost eight o'clock, almost everyone is there whom they expected, so they should all gather in the tower room and begin, during which time Frieda and Greta will get tea ready in the kitchen, at which Johannes gets up and turns to all those around him with a soft smile and says, "Yes, indeed, let us devote ourselves to the path!" Everyone heads into the studio, in the foyer and waiting room the lights are turned off, while in the tower room only the two standing lights and the eternal light are lit, chairs having been brought in from the other rooms, everyone gathering around the table except two or three, Haschke being one of them.

Josef is introduced to the regular guests, among whom is Spiridion von Flaschenberg, who animatedly turns to him, "Josef? Josef is a wonderful name. From both the Old and the New Testament. Have you ever thought about your name before? I don't want to spoil it for you, but you should look into it. I hope you'll soon come to visit me. Sunday mornings everyone— and by that I mean everyone, people, gods, spirits, and demons—are welcome to visit. The entire cosmos gathers at my place. Take down the address: Flaschenbergianeum, Balbinggasse 6, Electrical Number 8 to the final stop, then right on the first street you come to, and then the next left, where you'll already see the address, Flaschenbergianeum 9-11, home of the cosmos." At this Herr von Flaschenberg abruptly turns away from Josef and talks with other guests, making elaborate sweeping gestures with his hands, as Josef meets another man, Herr Ringel, who with his red beard looks sort of like a professor of history, though he is in fact an academic painter, he also inviting Josef to visit him, saying, "I live a quite humble existence. Today no one values artists. Raphael's paintings were, in a word, met with triumph when they emerged from his studio. Back then people knew how to honor the great, but today the world is awash in mediocrity. Hardly anyone believes in me, though indeed future times will erect a memorial and place my paintings in the most honored and sanctified places. That will no longer be galleries and museums, which are to blame more than anything for why no one understands painting today. Everyone is caught up in naturalism. And whoever doesn't paint in a naturalist manner is considered an outrage, mad, or just a fool—that is to say, an *artiste*. People have gotten used to looking at even the work of the past as naturalistic. Above all, no one knows anything about color. If you want to understand painting, then please don't visit any gallery, but instead come to me. I live for the most part in squalor, but no one buys paintings these days. And instead of Master Ringel I'm called Herr Ringel, which is really an insult, for art is mastery, not the pedestrian. The path to art has three stages: apprentice, assistant, and master. Painting is also a craft, not a trade. Through its nature as a craft it differs from arts like poetry and music, where there are no masters in this sense. In music the nonsense about maestro usually signifies a decline, it being diametrically opposed to the ancient notion of music. Musicians use it, I agree, but to err is human. But certainly it would sound ridiculous to say 'Master Goethe,' yet painters are indeed called masters. The term 'Old Masters' is still commonly used even today."

Haschke then interrupts, saying, "Oh, Ringel's paintings are epiphanies. He paints only while lost in concentration. It's marvelous! Oh, what paintings they are!" Ringel adds, "I don't mean to praise my own work. But in all modesty I can say that since my days at the academy I have not done a single naturalistic painting. I have dissolved all forms, I work only with color. Color is light, and thus it is divine. Each single color is a mystery that God, as it were, manifests in the rainbow. God himself cannot be painted, the Jews and Muhammad being correct about this. One can't even paint the sun, the ultimate symbol of Him. But God's manifestations can be painted, which share the colors we see in the rainbow. This is, as it were, my mission. I paint the path to God, and in a truly modern way, through bright colors and not in the illuminated darkness of Rembrandt, who for all his greatness was no painter. The Old Masters were also not genuine painters, but rather illuminators or colorists, they used color only for coloration, as a surface element, without having experienced it as a spiritual essence. That's also true of Titian, who attained the most, but I have made a considerable step beyond, as it were." Haschke then interrupts again, saying, "Oh, it's marvelous! You have to see it! I have one of Ringel's paintings, naturally just a small one, but for me it is greater than all the other paintings in the modern gallery. It hangs above my bed between a reproduction from a Sistine Chapel Madonna and the *Mona Lisa*. Ringel's painting is not done in oils but rather pastels, like the dust of a butterfly on colored paper. I tell you, it's like a dream. I have it framed in a magenta frame, for Ringel says that magenta is the color of the future. The painting is titled *The Awakening of the Soul*. Oh, it's marvelous! One figure lifts another one high, both pointing upward to where light pours down. It's deeply symbolic. At night I dream about it and am in a good mood when I wake up, look at the painting, and begin to concentrate."

Ringel wants to continue to explain his marvelous painting to Josef with the help of Haschke, but things are about to get under way, as Yolanda declares soothingly that there will be plenty of time later on to talk about painting, and that Josef can indeed visit Ringel if he's interested in modern painting. Then everyone quiets down and gathers together, though Herr von Flaschenberg uses the time for an extended explanation of a very important poem that came to him, which just yesterday he wrote down while on the streetcar, a cosmic poem whose inspiration came to him as he rode home with Achter from the registry. Spiridion is a registrar at an insurance firm and often explains in reference to his position that, through his work, insurance is tied to the entire cosmos and to eternal justice, but just yesterday while on his way home, as he thought to himself, it occurred to him to compose a poem in much the same manner that the electrical winds its way through the chaos of the city and finds its way to the harmony of the spheres. Meanwhile the other members of the group grow impatient, they don't want to delay the evening any longer, some asking to hear the poem, which they know Herr von Flaschenberg has in his briefcase, since he always carries his new poems around with him until there are enough to fill a new book, which happens at least once a year, he urging everyone he knows to take a subscription, writing long dedications to them in their copies which end "with exceptional love" or "in burning brotherhood." Spiridion also wants to say something quite brief about his poem, but he has to shut up, because Johannes, who smiles continually, gives a sign for all to quiet down, he wants to read something, as someone hands him the writings of Meister Eckhart, whom even Ringel recognizes with the title "Meister." Johannes reads aloud an excerpt quietly in a graceful flowing voice and concludes, "And so one must penetrate to the truth, to the one and only, which is God himself, without seeking a manifest being, for thus one arrives at a unique state of wonder. One should remain immersed in this wonder, because human understanding doesn't have the ability to get to the heart of the matter. Whoever wants to truly understand the wonder of God, he easily attains such knowledge within himself." Johannes closes the book and smiles again, a smile seeming to continually rest upon his face, though it's not frozen there but rather is joyfully alive, as he shakes his head in mild surprise and says, "That's wonderful. Yes, it is all that simple. One doesn't need big words. In the end, we all arrive at the same place."

Some guests try to comment on the reading, Johannes listening silently to most of them, now and then nodding lightly in agreement or disagreement. Once he says that it's good to discuss such matters, but one should also just listen, it's the truth that speaks and not the person, it being the beauty of truth that it doesn't say anything, one can't interfere with it, or search for God, but only search within himself for the God that is there. Yolanda then tries to elaborate, saying, "If you search for the truth as part of your day's work, that is good. As a housewife I can't afford to neglect my duties. The saying is true: first God, then others. But if you want to genuinely serve God, then you must serve others, and the work of a housewife does just that by managing the household. Then I think of that part of God's will that wanted me to be a housewife. That is the wonder that keeps me going. It makes me happy and gives me hope when my dear husband and my Schorschl are happy." Both nod to her and say as one, "Through Mother we are able to concentrate all the better." The opaque, smiling Johannes appears to agree, but then Haschke lets out, "Through Meister Eckhart one sees precisely how wonderful it all is! We humans are always lost in a duality, for we cannot concentrate well enough and listen too much to people who end up confusing us. Because it simply is, one should not search for

Being, which is hard, for at the same time one does want to search for Being. But one should just act in the knowledge that the truth is inside us, and thus God as well, for God speaks to those who can speak the truth. Oh, it's wonderful, Johannes! How wondrous it is, just as your reading describes!" Johannes only replies that one should be careful not to just turn himself into a wonder as well.

Frieda and Greta arrive with the tea, Yolanda and two other women jumping up to help them, plates with store-bought baked goods handed out, it being meager fare, sweet and salty, as Yolanda says, "Goodness, I have a cake in my bag outside that I baked for you all! Schorschl, be so good as to bring me my bag!" Schorschl runs out, the tea is poured, and each person is asked how many sugars he would like, followed by slices of lemon, which are handed out in little bowls, and raspberry juice in dark-red bottles, which almost looks like schnapps, some taking lemon, though more dribble some of the rich raspberry juice into their tea, others taking some of each, Schorschl appearing again and calling out, "Mama, I'm really sorry, but I can't find either the cake or the bag. I looked everywhere, your coat is in the kitchen, and I found your hat on the floor in the foyer. Someone must have stepped on it, because it was smushed. I straightened it out right away, but one of the berries on it is cracked and can't be fixed. I cleaned off the hat, but the bag is nowhere to be found." Frieda asks if Yolanda remembers where she put the bag, or if perhaps she left it at home, but Yolanda's husband knows better, saying, "No, no, my precious, you certainly didn't leave it at home. I took some paper out of the drawer and helped you pack it. We wrapped the cake twice so that it wouldn't leak any butter. Schorschl, do you remember whether Mama had the bag on the electrical?"—"Papa, I'm not sure. But I think Mama had it with her." Frieda asks, "Do you think, Yolanda, that you left the bag lying somewhere?" Greta declares, "No, I know she brought the bag here. I remember that Yolanda had this beautiful big bag with her, and I even asked, 'What's in the bag, Yolanda?' And Yolanda said, 'It's a cake, Greta. It's a new recipe I tried, which my family thought tasted really good. I also made one for you all at the same time.' Don't you remember, Yolanda? I then asked you about the recipe, and you said you'd give it to me, but first I had to try the cake and guess what was in it." Yolanda recalls, "You're right, Greta, I did promise you the recipe." Spiridion declaims, "Yolanda, it's a victim of God's mysterious ways. The cake has disappeared into the cosmos. Accept the sacrifice selflessly!" Yolanda replies, "I'm happy to make a sacrifice. But that's ridiculous. I made the cake for you all. And I'm pained about the bag, for Schorschl gave it to me for Christmas." Schorschl says, "Don't worry about the bag, Mama. I'll get you another one. But the cake, the one you made for everyone, you were so pleased with it!" Frieda appeases her, saying, "We know that the good Yolanda always wants to surprise us. But it's the thought that counts!" August adds, "My dear Yolanda, you all know her well! How well she takes care of Schorschl and me, always putting the family first and loving us with God's love. Yolanda put a great deal of fresh butter into that cake which she got from her sister-in-law from the village by Wlaschim. However, one must take it all in stride, whatever happens is to the good." Haschke recommends, "Yolanda, make a good example of yourself and concentrate until you think of where the bag is!" Yolanda responds, "I'm trying already. But as long as you all keep talking I can't help being confused. The next time I bake a cake I won't let it out of my hands." Johannes has listened to it all with a smile and says, "We thank you, Yolanda, but we have enough to eat already. The bag will turn up, it most likely is out among the coats." Then Thomas says emphatically, "We should all search at once, that's the best thing to do!" Most everyone then begins to look around, but at this Yolanda claps her hands together and yells, "I think I know! I washed my hands in the bathroom!" She runs out, the bag is found in the bathroom, everyone gathers round as Yolanda gleefully swings the bag back and forth.

Spiridion praises her, saying, "That's a lovely bag, Yolanda. It's made of calf leather." But then Herr Herold, who until now has not said a word but only sat there with an earnest face, stands up, feels the bag, and declares, "That's a fine bag, it's premium goods, but Spiridion, it doesn't look like calf leather. That's cow leather. If you come with me, I'd like to show you some calf leather, in order that you can note the difference." Spiridion laughs, saying, "My dear friend, you very well may be right. But I am also right. What is a calf? It's a young cow. The calf grows up and becomes a powerful animal, like the sacred cows of Egypt or India. We should bow before the bag, for it is made of calf leather. And Yolanda's cake is also sacred, since it was in a sacred vessel. But everything is sacred, for it is man who thinks it so." Haschke agrees, exclaiming, "Oh, Spiridion, what heavenly words you have spoken! Everything is sacred—the cake, the bag. It only needs us to call it sacred!" Master Ringel warns, "We shouldn't commit idolatry." Greta asks, "What do you mean?" Ringel explains, "If I paint a picture, a higher power, as it were, works through me. But when I go about my daily affairs I am more reserved, in order not to turn everyday things into idols. Whoever does that commits idolatry." Spiridion is of another view and says, "Master Ringel, that's not right. The everyday is indeed august. One only needs the right perspective, and that is the cosmic perspective. We all honor your paintings, but you yourself should know that it is easy to depict the divine in that which is not in fact divine. The everyday must be made divine through it in order to elevate it and make it worthy of God. That's my charge as a poet, as I have often explained here. Isn't that true, Johannes, have I not?" Johannes says nothing and smiles, then Spiridion continues, "I don't want the tea to get cold on us. Johannes, have some already, then we'll argue some more. Let us eat and drink so that we can offer our tribute to the ephemeral! Afterward you will all hear what happened on the electrical, how I gave voice to my conception, and about the streetcar with its motor, its electrical current, the conductor selling tickets, the driver, and the passengers."

Some of them look at Spiridion astounded, but Yolanda continues to hold her cake, which she has unpacked, saying, "Frieda, there are no clean dishes available, and there's no knife. We need a plate and a knife." Greta is at the door and calls, "I'll get the plate right away. Frieda, you just sit down, you must be dead tired! I'll bring a knife as well." Greta has already left the room, but as soon as she returns Frieda says, "The plate is fine. Yolanda, you can put the cake on the plate. But the knife is the wrong one and won't work, for I used it to slice onions. If you had just let me go, Greta!" Then Frieda runs out for a knife, while the rest of the women praise the cake, saying how good it looks, wanting to know what Yolanda did to give it such a lovely golden color, and Yolanda explains how she brushed the cake with an egg before baking, then baked it slowly in an oven that was not too hot, patience being the most important thing of all, though whoever is on the true path knows patience. Finally Frieda is back with the correct knife and wants to slice the cake, but Yolanda announces that she will do it, as Johannes says,

206/ H. G. ADLER

"You must indeed let her if she is the one who brought the cake." Yolanda counts the number present and is not done doing so before her son jumps up and says, "Mama, I'll count for you!" He counts three times and says he did so because he thought it was fifteen, but that is wrong, it's really fourteen, and she needs to cut twenty-eight pieces so that everyone gets two, but while slicing she miscounts, even though she laid out the planned cuts lightly with the knife a number of times, she ending up with twenty-nine pieces, Spiridion commenting, "Good, Yolanda, good! First we thought the bag and the cake were lost, but everything turned up. Everyone has two pieces, and we can offer up the extra one to the unknown God, much like the ancient Romans." This doesn't sit well with Yolanda, she thinks it a sin to waste food like that, so she suggests that the extra piece should go to Johannes for breakfast, Frieda lifting it up, at which everyone agrees and praises the cake, Johannes however simply saying, "Yolanda always makes us something good." She is proud of this praise, August and Schorschl also looking content that someone has acknowledged dear little Mother, the women meanwhile discussing what is in the cake, none guessing exactly, until finally Yolanda dictates the recipe as all the women write it down.

Johannes says, "Well, I hope everyone feels invigorated. Now I'd like to play some music before it gets too late." Haschke's face is awash with bliss as he closes his eyes and says to Josef that he should also close his eyes, you can concentrate better that way, it's a great opportunity to learn, for all you have to do is empty your head of thoughts and the music will put you in the right mood, which will help you attain true concentration. Josef wants to get away from Haschke, but Thomas has already guessed this and recommends that Josef follow him as they head for the chamber between the tower room and the foyer, where there are two chairs available. Johannes is already sitting at his gong, and Frieda turns off all the lights except for the eternal light, as Johannes waits a bit longer for everyone to be quiet, which takes a little while. Then the gong is barely struck, and as if from far off comes the sound, it seeming especially far from inside the chamber where Josef and Thomas sit, as if the sound were passing through a veil-like wall, though slowly the sound begins to swell, the disk sways and vibrates, sounding like leaves falling and metallic rain, an agglomeration of notes rising, echo and reper-

cussion, melodic notes with pacifying counternotes, moaning and sighs accompanying the tapping of the gong. Johannes releases more and more
tones from the disk, cautiously expanding his marvel and yet surprising others as he does so, Josef thinking what a canny spirit Johannes really is, but
then to string together notes in unique, strongly struck rhythms, what kind
of man is it who gets caught up with quarter-wits, if not half-wits, which is
pretty much what they are, though such a consideration now seems inap-
propriate and is already fading away in the face of the music that continues
to swell powerfully, the full blossoming of its sound born from the strength
of its quietness, a softly droning vibration that sends out waves and builds up
walls of sound, creating a joyful fullness as before Josef's eyes there appears
a powerful cluster of bright lights that burn everything from his heart,
whatever still clings to triviality there in the tower room. What kind of a
magician is Johannes, and what does he really want? What powers are at
work within him and emanate from him? There is a power here that burns
everything away, extinguishing all things, though the soul is what is rapt, Johannes a lord, everything extrinsic peeled away by his sound, as Josef grasps
something, or thinks he does, it is what Johannes releases with the gong, the
disk that commands all their powerful feelings, which can be released only
by the gong's copper casting, and not by the artificially constructed and
elaborate mechanism of a violin or even a flute, a swaying disk being all it is,
worked by hand, but what hands they are! What heart moves it! It's a heart
through which riches unfurl and ancient landscapes appear, sunken forests
rise up in twilight, crystals floating as well that shimmer and sparkle with
glittering colors that unfold and collect, melding together into a single
glowing stream, the symbol or even augury of a mystical brotherhood. Thus
love's law makes itself known, it being powerful and virile and yet tender,
the conscious wedded to an unconscious essence that the listener takes in
with each breath, Josef sensing his own heartbeat in the striking of the disk,
the gong growing more quiet, its heavenly sound a simile for the peace
among daily matters as it releases a soft glow, which is its blessing, its
shadow full of a warmth that is the peace of the tower room above the joyless depths of the hopeless city. Johannes pauses more and more, each time
longer than before, then he makes three muffled blows and waits for the

sound to dissipate, repeating this again and again, though ever weaker, the final blow resulting in nothing more than a breath of sound seeping away, the disk swinging without being struck, and then it's quiet.

Josef fears this is the end, but he also hopes that it is, for he figures that it's not possible to listen to such music for too long, which is what Johannes has to consider as well, for he runs the risk of destroying the spell, and so he gives the gong two final strong, muffled blows. Josef is pleased by this finish, as Thomas whispers almost inaudibly, "Now you know what kind of man Johannes is." Josef responds just as quietly, "I know."

Johannes has already stood and left the bay, turning on lights and returning to his previous spot, Thomas and Josef also returning to the group, the light dazzling them as they sit spellbound and silent, Master Ringel stroking his beard, Herr von Flaschenberg quietly shifting in his chair, though the rest simply remain there with dreamy or serious faces, slowly relaxing as Haschke tips his head back in ecstasy and licks a corner of his mouth before he pulls himself together and is the first to break the silence. "Oh, this music was heavenly! I always say that is true love. It makes us brothers and sisters, almost angels. How often have I told my brother that he should come hear it and not spend all his time chasing girls!" At this Johannes smiles once again, looking away as the others remain lost in a moony silence during which they pay no attention to Haschke, Thomas also turning from Haschke, who then turns to Josef, who has carelessly not turned away fast enough, and sweetly purrs at him, saying how wonderful it must be to experience this heavenly treat for the first time, to which Josef reluctantly asks out of curiosity where Haschke is headed, Haschke answering that he sings in the church choir at Saint Portiunkula, which he does in order to help the faithful attain a bit of enlightenment, since it's possible to do that when one's voice speaks from the inside and makes such concentrated music as Johannes. He says to Johannes, "In fact, if you came to Saint Portiunkula with your gong I think everyone would be inspired, the priest most of all." Johannes smiles opaquely and says, "You rave too much, Haschke. You use too many words. One must live more simply."

Haschke is not satisfied with this, continuing to complain about his lot in life and about his family, though this time Johannes interrupts him, saying, "Once a person knows how to be alone, then he knows how to be at home anywhere. You accomplish nothing by being so self-indulgent." Then Haschke is quiet a moment, but since no one else says anything to break the silence he feels uneasy and must speak again, continuing his same grumbling as he tells about a visit to the theater, where he saw a group from India that danced to its own musical instruments, a kind of gamelan with a lovely gong that would have delighted Johannes, as well as everything else, since it was all so intuitive and not so formal like the players that the Europeans dance to, but instead concentrated, like the *Bhagavad Gita*, which Johannes loves so, the dancing in fact religious, a kind of yoga, everything having been explained in the program, which Haschke will bring with him next time so that Spiridion can have it for his collection. Haschke had also thought that he always wanted to dance, so after the theater he tried it at home in front of the mirror, using the Indian dancing as a model, though in his own way, for he believes, as Johannes says, that one should always follow one's own path, and because he wanted to properly study dance he wants to have a Greek costume made out of an old throw that his aunt has promised him and which now decorates her piano. Haschke is indeed waiting for the day when he can dance for Johannes and the other members of the group, the spotlight turning on him, the regular lights turned off, he already asking that Johannes play the gong as always, for Haschke will dance to each and every tone.

During this story the group has begun to relax and return to the normal run of things, at which Yolanda speaks up and says, "You're right, Haschke. That's a good idea about the dancing." But Johannes says, "The only proper dance is silence and stillness. Why do you always want movement and agitation? Learn for once to remain motionless." The painter adds, "Dance cannot achieve the spirituality of other arts, because it is, as it were, a bodily art. Every body must relieve itself and is full of nasty substances. Thus it's a mass in which nothing august can exist. That's why I'm no fan of dance. If I understand Meister Eckhart correctly, namely the passage that Johannes read to us, then I understand that the wonder that one should remain caught within lies in the works that we perform, such as, as it were, my paintings. Dance is also seductive, because it wishes to transcend this need. It is a science that too easily manifests itself." Spiridion agrees, saying, "You're right, Master Ringel. I think dance is the expression of unfulfilled desire."

Schorschl then interrupts to say, "When you really love a girl, I mean, when you are really dedicated to someone, then it doesn't matter if you dance with her. It's simply a comfortable diversion, and you can still remain on your path. My mother always says that you can dance if you are a respectable person. She herself danced with Papa, and nothing happened. Isn't that so, Mama?" Yolanda is somewhat embarrassed by Schorschl's really childish talk, he being at least two years older than Thomas and Josef, but she says good-naturedly, "Whatever makes a person respectable cannot be bad, just as long as you don't forsake your honor and remain respectable."

During this Herr von Flaschenberg has pulled out his poem and waited for a good while in order to have an audience to read it to without having to cut off the conversation about dance, and so he speaks up during the pause that occurs after Yolanda's explanation about respectability, saying that every work of art can be grasped much like dance, especially poetry, so he would like to read his about the electrical, it perhaps being a bit late, since for a good poem one can't be too tired, otherwise it's too hard to follow. He then begins to declaim elaborate dactyls with deep pathos so loud that Johannes gives several signs for Spiridion to rein himself in, though after a couple of verses his voice begins to swell again, until Johannes finally speaks up and says, "We'll disturb the neighbors!" Then the poet tries to quiet down, but there really is no stopping him. The poem begins with the creation of the world, the Lord separating light and dark and then expelling the first man and woman from the Garden of Eden, such that upon the earth all things great and small are emblems, only man being so crude as to think of them in materialistic terms, although he can find no base matter, as it is always ever more apportionable, until it disappears, leaving pure energy in its stead, which is a divine or cosmic stream, the sharpest of eyes seeing without the aid of physics that there is no matter, but only the appearance of matter, for everything is an image of the spirit, every machine being alive as well, even when it doesn't have a streetcar to run, the great mystery being electricity, now appearing powerful as a flash of lightning, and at other times mellow as polished amber as it attracts metal shavings or passes through a tortoiseshell comb that a girl uses to comb her hair until fine sparks are given off which one can see in the dark. Strong and weak currents point to the macro- and microcosmos, together which make a single All, in the middle of which stands man, who looks at both the larger and the smaller worlds, arming his eyes with ground lenses in order to penetrate the mysteries of both worlds, harnessing electricity in order to protect against its dangers, Prokop Diviš having protected us from lightning before Ben Franklin, Thomas Edison surpassing both when he enabled a carbon filament to glow so that people from the mightiest palaces to the poorest shacks could use lights, which then spread across all countries like a fraternal network, power stations churning it out, a society formed through electricity and, so that all people can find one another within it, Werner von Siemens and František Křižík developed the electric streetcar, a subtle current generating enough power for a heavy wagon to move as it hurries through the city clanking and whooshing along. There is no more august occupation than that of streetcar driver as he stands before his lever box with his hand on the lever by which he increases or lessens the current through small adjustments in order that the wagon travels slow or fast, though if the driver thinks of his occupation in a funny way, he is a conqueror of chaos who out of the city's cauldron conveys the workers, teachers, and mothers to their destinations, their eternal homes, the conductor being the driver's trusted sidekick who sells all the passengers their tickets and calls out the stops, in order that everyone knows how much of the journey has passed, while if one thinks of the driver as the father and the conductor as the mother of the streetcar, then the passengers are the children, who are taken care of reliably in any kind of weather, the wagon a safe refuge, the driver and conductor in charge, the rails indicating a secure pathway, the issuing of tickets an emblem of the daily sharing of bread. Still, man's creation is childish and unaware, and it remains unconscious and innocent of what the poet sees, and who fathoms the emblem's meaning, and so the passengers travel safely as at the beginning of Creation and before the Fall, driver and conductor representing the ancient original couple expelled by the Lord from the Garden of Eden, and which will remain on earth until the end of days, when the Lord once again unites light and dark amid a blessed cosmos.

The poem is not met with overwhelming applause, some seeming tired, it having lasted too long for everyone, some suppressing a tired yawn, though most indeed say that it pleased them, as Yolanda asks with great interest, "Spiridion, will the poem be in your next book?" To which he replies,

"Of course. I don't write poems that aren't publishable." Yolanda adds, "That's good, Spiridion. Your poem is quite lovely. But one needs to read it a few times in order to understand it all." Haschke disagrees, saying, "Oh, it's clear as day! It's heavenly! If only I could do the same! You have created poetry like a fire-breathing Prometheus!" Herr von Flaschenberg corrects him, "Fire-stealing Prometheus." He in fact wants to explain further to Haschke, but Ringel wants to weigh in with his thoughts, and says, "The poem certainly has an elaborate structure. Perhaps it's a bit overdone, if you allow me. But in truth it's very modern." Spiridion explains, "I thought about the content a great deal. I wanted to express the flow of the electricity and to make the roar of the streetcar palpable. I thought of Verlaine's violin poem, in which everything is built around the sound of 'O.' But Verlaine, and also Wildgans in his cello poem, made it easy on themselves, for they wanted only to elicit the sound of music. They succeeded, but it's too naturalistic and not really symbolic. One needs to show with such a theme that everything is spiritual." Thomas then raises a few objections, saying that for him the repeated images are somewhat strained, and that in his opinion the poem doesn't manage to capture actual reality, at which point the poet interrupts to say, "Thomas, my young friend, you just try to write such a poem yourself! You couldn't do so if you had a year, and I wrote it in a single evening! That's not easy. But for critics it is. Look around at poetry today and tell me where you know of a poem like it. Walt Whitman would have applauded me, but he is most likely the only poet who would be able to grasp my boldness." Spiridion turns from Thomas in a huff and says to Josef, "If you're his friend, tell him how hard it is. I hope you understand me better than he does." Then Herr von Flaschenberg turns to Johannes, saying, "So what do you think? Don't you want to say how much it pleased you?" Johannes replies, "I think poems should express inner simplicity. Quiet as a snowflake and deep as a raindrop." At this, Spiridion wants to hear no more.

Frieda and Greta have cleared away the plates and want to clean up in the kitchen, Yolanda hurrying after them, the collective meeting in the tower room beginning to break up and spread out into the apartment. Josef doesn't want to talk with anyone else, though he walks through the rooms and listens in here and there, noticing people whom he hasn't seen before, they having arrived inconspicuously much later than the rest, Johannes now sitting with two of them by his side, older men who quietly yet keenly speak with him, as Thomas thumbs through the writings of Meister Eckhart, Haschke reads Flaschenberg's poem again and appears to be explaining it to him, Schorschl chatting with his father, the words "bag," "hat," and "cake" able to be heard. Then Josef overhears a conversation in the chamber where he had sat listening to Johannes striking the gong. Master Ringel is with Herr Herold, who says that he would love to buy a painting, he needs something for a wedding gift for his niece in Pardubitz, and that he'll pay the full price, as well as buy Ringel a pair of shoes of his own choosing. "But you know, it must be a beautiful painting, as beautiful as any of yours, though not just beautiful but also sensible, for my niece is quite normal. She knows nothing about the true path or about concentration. But she has good taste, and was herself a good draftsman in school, though her taste is somewhat out of date, more naturalistic and not at all mystical. The painting will hang over the credenza in the dining room." Ringel appears to be pleased by the proposition, but he says that he hardly has such a painting, he makes only paintings that are epiphanies, so he wants to know just what Herold would like to see in such a painting. A still life is the answer he gets, nothing mystical, but still well done. Master Ringel appears to have nothing that will fit the bill and wants to know whether it could be a bunch of flowers, which in fact also have a mystical quality, even though they look like real flowers that are recognizable, such as crocuses, lilies, and roses. Then Herold asks if they are indeed flowers that anyone in Pardubitz would recognize, Ringel assuring him that the painting contains a whole bouquet, a really lovely painting that he did especially in oils, its title being *Flowers of Hope*, which would make for an excellent wedding gift. Herold agrees and says he would like to see the painting, and so they set up a time for him to visit.

At this same moment Herr von Flaschenberg steps up to Josef and tells him, "It's not very nice of your friend to say bad things about my poem. He's done that to me a couple of times. He used to just praise me and visit me almost every Sunday, where he wanted to hear my poetry. And now he's different. That's hard to take, my young friend. I hope you'll soon visit me, for then I will explain all the symbols to you. But what do you think of my poem?" Josef doesn't want to give any verdict. "But that's not right, my

young friend! Your name is Josef, which is a lovely name. I have already said
that I don't want to just rattle on to you, but if you come visit I'll read you
my poem 'Josef Enslaved.' You can also find it in my book *Biblical Legends*.
Have you already read some of my poems?" Josef is forced to say that he
hasn't. "That's too bad. Everyone here knows my poems. But you can buy a
copy and have a painting by Master Ringel on the cover as a bonus. We
brought out a fine edition—a few poems, a few illustrations, and the book
design by him. You should get a copy. When I was your age I knew all the
poetry that was contemporary to my time, such as the German poets
Dehmel, Bierbaum, and Caesar Flaischlen, as well as our own Hugo Salus.
I also translated a great deal. Have you ever translated a poem?" Once more
Josef has to say no. "It's hard to do, if you've never tried it. Your friend
Thomas has also not translated anything, and yet he's happy to criticize.
Only a creative person has the right to criticize, for only he knows how hard
it is."

The women are done cleaning up, and people begin to get ready to
leave as Yolanda announces, "We have to head home. Johannes, thank you!
And Frieda as well! It was so wonderful what you read today, and then the
music! Also Spiridion's poem! Everything was just lovely!" Johannes asks,
"Wouldn't you all like to stay a little longer?" But everyone is ready to leave,
it's already late, and they don't want to miss the last electrical. Then Johannes says, "Well, then, if you feel you have to go I won't stop you. I thank
you for coming, and you, Yolanda, I especially thank you for the cake." The
guests reach for their coats, which are all mixed together because of
Schorschl having searched for his mother's bag, after which people start to
say goodbye, the women always having something to talk about and whisper
to one another, Yolanda advising Frieda what she should cook for Johannes,
all of it coming to a pleasant end as Frieda insists that they not clog up the
hall in front of the apartment, at which handshakes quickly go round, as well
as thank-yous and goodbyes, the group already heading down the stairs.

Haschke says, "Oh, it was wonderful today! Everything was heavenly!
And now I have to head home. You know, Ringel, if I didn't have your painting there, or Spiridion's poetry, my notes about our evenings and my inner
memories, as well as a couple of books on mysticism, then nothing would
please me anymore, for there's no one at home who understands me." He

adds, "Yes, I'm on the true path. But that's a lot easier to say in the tower room than at home." Meanwhile, below a couple of high-pitched tones that have slipped out from the bar can be heard, the group encountering the damp night air on the street, as everyone quickly says goodbye, Herr von Flaschenberg reminding Josef again, "Well then, goodbye, and I'll see you on Sunday!" Already they all scatter in several different directions, Thomas having also left Josef, who wants to walk rather than take the streetcar, Herr Herold walking with him for part of the way and telling him about the price of shoes, which can ruin the prospects of any good salesman, but Josef interrupts to ask, "How long have you been interested in the questions that are so important for Johannes?" Herr Herold answers, "I'm only an outsider. As a salesman, I'm interested in other things. But Tvrdil is quite a guy. My older brother, who made gingerbread in Pardubitz, was a student of Tvrdil's. He adored him. But my brother is long dead. It was in Italy during the war, back in 1918, when he didn't come back from the collapse at Piave. That's why I visit Tvrdil. The doctor recommended it as a diversion. My heart is still broken, so I have to take care. But now I have to go, for I'm already almost home. Good night!"

Now Josef is alone and happy that he can pilgrimage through the somewhat foggy streets. He feels numb from these people and their snooty talk, and does not know if he did the right thing in following Thomas's suggestion, since he hardly heard anything among the group that seemed worthwhile, he in fact being surprised that Johannes can stand that loony Haschke, nor do hardly any of them have a good idea of what they mean by "inward" or "outward," they are all caught up in sentimental feelings and wallow in overblown talk. God, this Haschke, who presents himself as such a pitiful man, lying in bed and staring at Master Ringel's painting, this *Awakening of the Soul* done in, as it were, dabbed-on pastels, an outrageous travesty of symbolic art. It pains Josef to think this way, for perhaps they are better people than himself who, he has to admit, strive very hard. None of Johannes's guests whom he met today are free and have courage, nor even the desire for real freedom, but instead they are like spoiled children who play with their own chains, and because those sit lightly they end up fooling themselves into thinking they are flower chains worn upon the true path that the fools think they walk along. And how odd that Johannes puts up with these hangers-on and doesn't try to set himself apart from them as he reads forth from great books that he can hardly expect are understood, supplying his opaque smile and his brief talk, then striking his gong, which radiates out past the borders of all existence, after which he allows Haschke to say that he'd like to dance to such music, followed by the vain conversation about Ringel's paintings, and then Spiridion reciting his poem—surely it must be this way every week. Josef will think twice about looking up this cosmic poet, even if Thomas said a lot about him earlier and his marvelous collection of precious stones and crystals, rare plants, old coins, woodcuts and etchings, though Josef doubts the sense of such a collection if it's not founded on a higher principle. Somehow the group in the tower room reminds him of a political rally, not at all like the one in the small town—there they drank bad-smelling beer, here there was tea with raspberry juice, there they listened to demagoguery, here there was mysticism—yet there was something similar about it all, and it takes a lot of courage to give yourself over to other people, for though human beings had accomplished the greatest works, where could you find them today, they are either all long dead or unattainable, everything is a miserable ruin, against which there is no cure, the escape into the internal being the only salvation, which Johannes had indeed made palpable, but only he, though he did so easily and in a genuine manner, for he simply let it happen, his calling of no concern to him, as he lets Frieda take care of him without worrying about it, nothing but adoration surrounding him.

Johannes may be important, but Josef is unimportant, though he has no problem making such a confession. He wants, in fact, to be honest with himself and to test his every assumption as best he can in order not to err out of vanity. He has graduated from high school and has passed his exit exam, but what does that mean? It was all child's play, there being a slew of questions that were of no surprise at all, superficial questions that were answered with information he'd learned by rote. Josef doesn't see this as an end point or a turning point, for no kind of liberation is granted through it or even offered. The world offers nothing but a puzzle that one can hardly solve, such that you are soon swamped, as Thomas believes, unsolved and unsolvable questions hanging before you like veils, and hardly do you pull away and think that you're making progress than you discover again the unchangeable, the sculpture at Saïs nothing more than an empty frame. You can pull back the veil without any trouble, but there is nothing there at all, only what is behind it and what changes the view is fleeting and does not exist, it being only a revelation that says nothing is revealed, only the empty image of an endless expanse, and that which appears within the empty frame is finally nothing but impenetrable fog.

Josef turns inward, feeling an emerging pressure as he is gripped by an immense current, which is perhaps life, a transformation of his inner music that powerfully builds, a music with neither a major nor a minor chord, a fugue of graduated sounds, the sound of a gong expanding, a curtain gliding open as in the theater or in a viewing cabinet, as he hears "Come closer." Then you stand alone, facing the court, thunderous voices crashing down upon you, declaring that you've missed your chance, for you have done nothing but simply live one day after another, and the days remained empty, nothing but riding on the streetcar, but the journey led only from chaos into chaos, the great parables all of a sudden meaning nothing, though one still remains a creation that doesn't understand his creator, which is what Meister Eckhart said, and then colors appear, spiritual colors, but hardly any images, it having nothing to do with any art, it is an endless realm of light, an awakening of the soul that stands forever in the middle of thunderstorms, full of frightful thunder, and if one is not frightened the result is arrogance, a ridiculous pretension in the face of the laws under which one lives, there being lightning strikes that cannot be harnessed, and currents that cannot be channeled, since they flout the determination of the will, though, of course, will is everything, it being left up to us to want things to remain as we want them to, that being perhaps a kind of inwardness, though a feeble inwardness that without a living faith crumbles to nothing.

Josef quietly opens the front door and slips into his room, sitting down at his desk and taking his journal out of the drawer as if he wants to read something in it, though he doesn't read, the characters seeming meaningless, his thoughts are still there, wandering clumsily through his head, continuing for a while, yet when he wants to grab hold of them and put them into words in order to hold sway over them, they once again slip away, he not knowing how to grant them credence, as he thinks about Meister Eckhart's sentences. Josef wants to disappear, to retreat into his inmost self, as he thinks about spiritual rebirth, which is a resurrection from one's own ruins, a death within a living body, which is a mystical death, after which one is reborn and sees oneself anew, a small child, holding his mother's hand while wandering through the world, which is completely changed and new, since everything is heard and seen again for the first time, as his companion explains everything, a spiritual medicine extended to you, a miracle in a cup, and a voice tells you to drink it and you will be healthy. Without a good doctor, many die, but whoever finds a good doctor will be restored to eternal life, and behind the gate sounds a scintillating song.

Josef gathers himself together and writes in his journal, "Today I finally went with Thomas to visit Johannes and his circle in the tower room." That is in fact everything that Josef writes, as he feels there is nothing to write, it all being fantastical and unreal, Josef not knowing what to write if the next morning perhaps nothing more of it were to exist, it having passed and been nothing more than a mistake. Thus it is only a vain game of fragile words, there perhaps being others who would zealously hold on to them while on the true path in order to bring fulfillment to their lives, but Josef feels nothing of that, he wanting just to sleep and wake up and sleep again, and for it to last forever, an endless exchange of images, such that as soon as one image freezes for a moment it is ripped away, though another one replaces it, the previous image now unretrievable and unable to be extracted from memory to see the light of day, memory's riches remaining dubious, even when one memorializes them in a journal, for soon they seem strange, strange and unattainable. Who could possibly one day discover such a journal and wrest it from what is forgotten? Thus Josef's memory will die with him, no one recalling it, both the true and the false teachings meaningless, for Josef is meaningless, Herr Koppelter is meaningless, Thomas as well, even Johannes is meaningless, soon it will not be memory but rather just the sound of the gong reverberating among the shadows, spreading throughout the world from the tower room like wafts of smoke, as Johannes opens the window during the night and plays much louder until it is no longer just chamber music but now a blaring temple music, though this music has the quality of being heard by only a few, even though its incredible sound vibrates over all, spreading out in unearthly, trembling waves and pressing to the furthest reaches of space, and now tumbling into and setting the room aglow as an almost unbearably strong voice calls, "And so one must penetrate to the truth, to the one and only, which is God himself." Thus one should forsake duality, it splits everything that is not a single entity, as the sound waves press the skin, already reverberating through the body and at last reaching the heart's loneliness until it responds to the All. Johannes is now nothing more than a memory, he is already forgotten, the drumstick having fallen soundlessly to the floor, the gong swaying quietly back and forth, as if it were a beating heart that does not beat in any recognizable manner, the heart beating like a gong, and then there is peace, the empty night, oneness, sleep, and deep endless sleep.

THE TUTOR

§

MAY I CALL YOU BY YOUR FIRST NAME? YOU ARE A YOUNG MAN, HERR Josef, and it's always been our custom to call all tutors by their first name. This results in a much friendlier atmosphere, and the boys will trust you a great deal more without any lessening of their respect, but rather the opposite, for you should know that I am for modern ways, naturally in pedagogy as well. If you only knew, Herr Josef, I mean, Josef, how I was raised in my time, unhygienic clothing, children not allowed to say a peep at the table, everything so impractical, though it was a strong generation. I always say, all that is long gone. Also the struggle of life was different, Josef, not easier, but life itself was easier. My husband works very hard, you understand, for he has plenty to worry about as director of the Stock Exchange. Indeed, you should simply call me Frau Director, rather than Madame, I never let myself be called Madame by the servants, I find Frau Director to be much simpler, it making clear to all the world that I always stand by my husband. So you see, Josef, in regard to modern pedagogy I always say I am for the new principles. I think free schools almost ideal, but I would never do the same with my boys, for then parental rule would be grossly undermined. Children should live with the family so that they benefit from the positive influence of their parents, but the children should maintain their own sense of free will and not be watched over all the time, though they can't be allowed to do just anything. My husband won't stand for that, I always say, for given how much he has to worry about the market, the boys naturally have to keep quiet. He is a wonderful man, and you'll certainly have a chance to get to know him."

Josef took the position as tutor, Frau Director having definitely wanted a philosophy student, since she always says that she is interested in philosophy, one needing to be a philosopher these days if one wants to survive the struggle of life, as the crisis is great, making it hard to know what to teach the boys. Frau Director loves Spinoza more than anyone, as it's solid philosophical work, his *Ethics* remaining always next to her bed in a leather-bound edition, though in between Frau Director also reads English and French, since one always has to stay in practice. It's so important for one to learn languages, it being terrible that these days in the schools languages are not taught in any practical manner, but Madame Forbette from Lausanne is in the house, a really charming person who helps raise Robert, Frau Director having taken her oldest son on summer trips to France and England, to the Riviera and the Isle of Wight, so that the boy could learn the right accent. Josef is told that naturally Frau Director hopes that despite his high intelligence he will also be willing to come along with them this year to Brittany, from which she also wants to make a couple of side trips with Josef and the boys, at least to Rouen to see the marvelous cathedral, Frau Director having received for her birthday a fantastic guide to the cathedrals of northern France, which she wondered if Josef knew. She'd love to show it to him, it's on the bookshelf, it needing to always remain closed and put away, she always saying that the boys are always getting into things such as Fuchs's book of morals, and Magnus Hirschfeld and so on, which are really not for boys. They are in the middle of puberty, so they like to look at the pictures, though Frau Director is no prude, no, not at all, but sexual precociousness can harm one, which is why the boys also do gymnastics, they needing to do sports, riding, and fencing. One has to keep them occupied so that they don't get lost in sultry daydreams, which is another argument against free schools.

Since the rise of psychology, everyone knows that the tiniest thing can lead to trauma, which is what she always says, and then a perversion follows. Frau Director of course has nothing against sex education, she herself has explained everything to the boys, as well as invited Dr. Brendel, a doctor friend, to explain all the biology to them, but only the scientific approach devoid of anything erotic. Even the concerns of venereal disease were explained as a diversion, but it also had a negative effect. As Frau Director wants to protect her boys from going astray, the only answer is to marry young, since one needs to be pure to enter into marriage. She wouldn't have any problem if at twenty her boys were to meet a proper girl, who is not rich and beautiful but homely and uncomplicated, though some possibilities are out of the question, Frau Director making it clear to the boys that they should quietly and quickly get married if these occur, there being today working students who live on their own, though Frau Director is in the fortunate position to be able to provide the boys with modest means, and they could continue to live in the villa, which is large enough, even taking over Josef's room. There is of course a room for Josef, so that he can stay overnight at the house, thus making it easier to mix with the family, for family life is everything, though unfortunately a blessing that hardly exists anymore, which is why Frau Director on this point is against socialism, which has a lot to say for itself, but it breaks up the family, and that is the beginning of the end for humankind, though the boys will be able to live with their wives upstairs in the guest rooms and remain under inconspicuous supervision, the daughters-in-law also then becoming a part of the family and thereby conquering any conflict between the generations, which is the cancer on the soul of today's society.

Frau Director will make an ideal mother-in-law and will instruct her daughters-in-law in all the secrets of being a good wife, since a man needs a thousand little things that too many women don't know about, which leads to a lot of marriages breaking up. Frau Director herself had to lay out a lot of money for instruction, since her mother died young, her mother-in-law was so nasty, and the Director was such a distinguished son, but to such a degree that he was perhaps too good for her. Frau Director didn't want to say anything to his mother, but the latter stirred up bad blood and agitated her son, which meant that Frau Director needed the patience of a saint in accommodating and adjusting, while her husband said nothing about any of what his mother said, as her word was sacred. Frau Director wept bitter tears, for she had no one who could defend her against the old lady, and naturally she doesn't want to complain after having been married so long, he being the most wonderful husband, as she always says, full of tenderness and tact, though indeed he has no higher intellectual interests, he is always absorbed in his work and reads only newspapers or something about the economy, he always surrounded by stacks of papers to get through and thinking of himself as an expert on it all. Otherwise he wouldn't have been made director, for he paid nothing to get the title, extra money being better spent on charitable causes, such as a servant girl's trousseau, none ever leaving without being completely fitted out by Frau Director.

It's of course difficult to be director of the Stock Exchange, he having to calculate the rise and fall of stocks ahead of time, which requires a good nose, otherwise you can end up just wringing your hands, Frau Director meanwhile wanting to know if Josef understood anything about the market and the national economy. Of course he had no idea, how would he? But Josef should not think that just because he's a philosopher he knows everything, only a novice believes that, which is why it's good that he's here in this house, where the Director can explain it all to him precisely, as well as advise him what to do if he ever had the chance to buy a stock at a good price or dump it, all of their relatives approaching the Director for free tips, though he gets no thanks at all for it. Frau Director has often warned him that he's too good-natured, as she always says, but he gives them tips nonetheless, which in the end is an incredible responsibility, for it's easy to ruin oneself, never mind one's family, especially now during the worldwide economic crisis, international uncertainty, millions of unemployed, and the general panic. The first years after the war saw the market climb, especially once German inflation was brought under control, followed by a nice boom, but since 1929 everything has gone to the dogs, and the signs of improvement are comparable to the single bluebird that doesn't make for an entire summer. Now taxes eat up everything, and if Frau Director didn't slow her husband down a bit and keep him from throwing all his money away at charities it would be nearly impossible for her to hold this house together.

The Director has a wonderful temperament and makes sure that she never goes hungry, the dear Lord having always taken care of them, though it's hard to feed a family on such pious thoughts alone. Frau Director doesn't approve when someone says "Prayer and work are what sustains," since work is a fine thing, but prayer is archaic. Frau Director believes in the goodness of the world, and has nothing against it when someone uses the word "God," but to think of the dear Lord as some bearded grandpa in the way that religion always wants to teach, that is nothing more than a crude father complex, which doesn't fit well with our times. One should apply oneself to an atheistic or abstract ethic, and since Spinoza stands on the threshold of modern times, as far as Frau Director can see, Spinoza is indeed an atheist who made certain concessions to his superstitious times, in much the same way one must always make concessions, there being nothing absolute, as can be seen through Einstein. Frau Director would love it if Josef could explain to her sometime what Einstein is really saying, she having read two truly excellent articles about it, as well as having attended lectures, the one that showed a film being very instructive, she only regretting that her husband wasn't with her, though he is always so tired at night, going to bed at nine, then reading for another hour before turning off the light, since he has to be up early in order to be at work in the garden soon after six. It's all healthy, certainly, but nonetheless a little too simple for a director, though he has something of the biblical peasant about him, Frau Director indeed recalling what she had been saying about God, which can in fact be seen in Michelangelo's painting in the Sistine Chapel, an august image or ideal, though there is no one today who would call it God. Frau Director doesn't want to give her children any religious instruction, it's too easy to end up with conflicting morals, which she wants to prevent, and which cause the children to have conflicting ideas that they ask the parents about, such as how the world really was created, and if it was really created out of nothing, causing one to lie to the children in almost nihilistic fashion, since they learn completely different things in physics and biology. That's why Frau Director explains to her boys that all that about God is a fable, though she doesn't rail directly against religion in order to guard against the children coming into conflict with other children at school, for one must be tolerant and respect the superstitious, as long as it doesn't go too far, though the story of Adam and Eve is lovely, other stories from the Bible being certainly of good moral use, though too much is Middle Eastern, while certainly much is obsolete. For example, it's terrible to lecture children, as part of the Ten Commandments, that "thou shalt not commit adultery!" for no child can understand the idea of coveting someone else's wife, which only leads to confusion. Indeed, psychology has begun a much more healing process and will prevail against any hostility directed at it.

Frau Director can only recommend that Josef study the books of Freud and those of his students, especially when he has something to do with children and wants to become a teacher. She believes the story of man is one about the transition from sleep to waking, awakening being something that happens gradually, sleep and waking two powers that can be observed competing for the human spirit, since even when man is awake he still often slips into a dream state, and thus exists between the two. The challenge for man is to destroy all dreams and illusions in order that an awake and healthy generation arises, something that Frau Director would like to write a book about, if only she didn't have so many things demanding her attention, though perhaps Josef could someday put her thoughts into good form and publish it himself, for which she will need no thanks, there being no gratitude in the world anyway, although that was the one good thing that religion did when it came to power, and that was somehow to make men feel grateful, previously man having always been focused on eternal retribution and the triumph of justice, but with what success? It is easily seen if one studies the Middle Ages, for better conditions first arose then through education, and through classics such as Goethe and Schiller, though Spinoza was in many ways the earlier herald of the new age. Frau Director takes a breath and says that this has been at least a bit of an introduction and she'd love to keep talking with Josef, but she has way too much to do and must beg his pardon, though the pleasant chat had helped give her a better idea of Josef and she can see that he is a gifted man who will feel right at home here, for everyone who has lived here has always felt at home. Working with the boys is not really hard, one must only gain their love and attention, which is easy enough, Irwin will soon be seventeen, Lutz has just turned fourteen, the boys are very close to each other, and even if they fight now and then that's just the way it is with children, though one can intervene before it goes any further and with a bit of reasoning get them to make up.

Frau Director rings a bell and the maid arrives, she introducing him to Sophie and her to Josef, who is already almost a doctor, so the servants should call him Herr Doctor. Josef wants to protest, saying that he cannot allow himself to be called a doctor, but Frau Director explains that all he needs to do is pass a few more exams, and so the servants should address him as Herr Doctor, and she didn't want to hear anything more about it, because that's the way it's done here, as without the existence of a certain distance bad habits can be incurred, Madame Forbette being the exception, she can simply call him Josef, though with the regular servants that's not to be tolerated. Then Frau Director looks with warmth at the maid and says, this is our dear Sophie, who is excellent, and then Frau Director asks, you're always happy to be here, aren't you Sophie? Sophie blushes, and then she's asked to call Irwin and Lutz, the girl bowing slightly and heading off. After a while the boys arrive, gangly and ill-mannered, as they kiss their mother's hand. The boys need to introduce themselves and greet the doctor, Frau Director explains, saying this is Josef the tutor, though he is actually a philosopher, and though they don't have to bow to him they must shake hands each time they meet. Frau Director wants Irwin and Lutz to sit down, saying that she hopes the boys will make their parents proud in making such an ideal older friend, for Josef is the right choice out of a large number of applications. Irwin and Lutz sit there uncomfortably quiet, squirming with impatience in their chairs and feeling shy, looking brazenly at their mother and bashfully at the new tutor. Josef suggests that perhaps it would be a good idea for them to get to know one another a bit, and that perhaps he could come to their room. Frau Director agrees, she warning the boys to be nice, and that she didn't want to hear any fighting, though Josef says that surely won't happen, he hopes to make good friends of Irwin and Lutz. Then Frau Director sends the three of them off with the remark, "Of course, you can have your snack on your own, but I'll see you all at dinner."

Josef asks the boys to show him their room. Irwin corrects him, saying it's two rooms, they share a bedroom and a living room. Lutz opens a door to the bedroom, and the boys look at Josef inquisitively to see what he will say. He wants to know if they clean their own rooms. No, Sophie does all of that, it's her job to, and in the morning there's often not enough time to clean up, for Irwin especially likes to sleep in, though Lutz does get up earlier, but as soon as Irwin is up the Madame arrives, though they didn't know if Josef had seen her yet. That's the French woman who is there for Robert, but that's by now the end of a long story that begins with Sophie knocking at their door first and Irwin shouting "Come in!," yet Sophie doesn't open the door and says only, "Irwin, it's already late, time to get up!" That does no good, and then usually Mother arrives, saying that it's unhealthy to lie in bed so long, and Irwin should see what his father has already done today, at which Irwin begins to make motions toward getting up, breakfast already laid out in the small dining room, the father sitting there with a newspaper, he needing to know what's going on with the market, the mother sitting down as well after she has walked through the entire house and told the cook what she should prepare for that day, Madame also arriving in the room with her lips smeared in red, the mother doing her makeup a bit later, Father wanting to speak with Madame in French, but Mother says to him in English that Madame is there for Robert, who is sitting next to her, at which Lutz arrives wearing a hairnet if he feels like making his mother angry, for she cannot stand the hairnet and makes Lutz take it off. Then Anton, wearing white gloves, serves breakfast, there always being coffee, tea, and cocoa to choose from, Robert always having cocoa with an egg mixed in, since Robert is so frail and because the family doctor has said that he should eat a lot of eggs, but Robert doesn't like eggs, especially hard-boiled ones, or even soft ones, though Mother doesn't allow sunny-side eggs to be served in the morning, she says that they are too hard to make and Robert hardly eats any of them, though scrambled eggs are the worst of all, they disgust him and lead to a scene as Madame squeals, "Sweetheart, you have to eat everything," the father urging him on as well, though Robert howls that he won't, and Mother makes an unhappy face, Robert should just eat it, why indeed won't he eat? She harangues him, saying how sad it makes her when he won't eat, he is indeed a lovely child, but he will always be pale and weak, and never as big as Irwin and Lutz, if he doesn't eat. Nonetheless, Robert doesn't touch the scrambled eggs, and then the mother says to the father

228/ H. G. ADLER

that the boy must have a complex, which nothing can be done about, but the father replies that no one has ever gotten sick from scrambled eggs, she's only imagining things, and you shouldn't coddle the children, though the mother responds that indeed it is a question of the imagination, many have become quite sick simply through imagining things, these being part of the sick complexes that the mother has many books about, but the father says that he doesn't believe in complexes, he recommends a good spanking or the rod. The mother is not at all pleased by this and says, "Quiet, I ask you to be quiet in front of the children," which she indeed says in front of Robert, who then gets his eggs how he likes them, always just one mixed in with his cocoa, this all happening at the last minute, for Robert likes to see how it curdles, his mother saying to him, "Look, that's the same thing as a scrambled egg."

But only Robert gets cocoa with an egg and three lumps of sugar mixed in. The father drinks two cups of coffee, but in reality it's just a couple of drops, most of it is milk, no one else liking it that way, though the mother makes it for the father. The mother just drinks a cup of tea without milk or anything else, she doesn't want to get fat. Madame drinks coffee, but just the opposite of the father, meaning lots of coffee and hardly any milk, though she does take four lumps of sugar, but she drinks only one cup. Lutz drinks cocoa or coffee, he preferring that much more, for it forms no skin on the top as cocoa does, which disgusts him, though the mother says that the skin is the healthiest part, it's the fat from the milk, but he always fishes out the skin, liking best to do it with two fingers when the mother isn't looking, though sometimes she keeps an eye on him, and then he uses a spoon, some part of the skin remaining in the cocoa and swimming horribly around on its surface. Irwin, meanwhile, prefers tea, for he likes to drink it all down like the mother, she making sure that he takes some milk with it and enough sugar, which is two lumps, but instead of milk he asks for lemon, which the mother allows because at least there are some vitamins in tea, which is important and healthy.

When everyone has gathered and settled on a breakfast drink, the father having put away the paper and everyone ready to begin, quite often Irwin has still not arrived, which means Anton or sometimes Lutz has to go see if he's still in bed or in the toilet, for though Lutz calls out Irwin! Irwin!, most of the time he is still in bed, which can often lead to a huge fight, since Irwin doesn't like taking orders from Lutz, telling him, "To hell with you and shut your trap!" Lutz then cannot return to breakfast, Irwin won't allow it, he doesn't want Lutz to tell on him, as that would be a violation of brotherly love, and if he does Irwin will thrash him and not play Ping-Pong with him for a week, so all Lutz can do is wait and keep pestering his brother as to whether or not he's going to get up. Eventually the moment comes when the mother shows up with Madame, who has to be there in order for Irwin to finally stir, though at first the women yell in both German and French that he should get out of bed, to which Irwin answers that he won't get up in front of Madame, he never rises in a room with women in it except for his mother, so Madame must leave, as he slowly begins to lift himself, testing his mother's patience, though she nonetheless waits until he's in the bath, Anton keeping watch at the door to make sure that he doesn't disappear again, and when he finally appears at the breakfast table the father is almost pale with anger, and hardly says a word, which then upsets the mother, she maintaining that the father doesn't concern himself with anything and leaves everything to her.

Josef asks if Irwin then ends up late for school, but the latter says that hardly ever happens, as the father takes him in the car with him on the way to work, the chauffeur having to make only a brief detour. Josef then asks the boys to show him their other room, where they talk some more. They lead Josef into a large room, which is much too richly decorated, the floor covered with a thick carpet, paintings hung on the walls, as they sit down, and Lutz states when asked that he quite likes going to school, though he likes vacations even better, while Irwin cannot stand school, most of the boys are stupid, all the teachers are stupid, and he'll be happy when he can finally leave school for good. As for what Irwin wants to be when he grows up? A lawyer, of course, that's a fantastic profession, the mother wanting him to do it as well, while the father says that a good law firm is a gold mine, Irwin wanting to head one someday, he loves court cases, since they are exciting, and you can earn a lot and quickly, without having to slave from morning till night. Josef wants to know how Irwin knows all this. He has heard it from a number of people, all you need is a good head, and it's nowhere near as risky as the market, which would have caused the father to collapse more than once if he didn't have nerves of steel, though he always manages to succeed somehow, having invested in many different areas so that he always has something left when some other segment collapses.

And what does Lutz want to become? He doesn't yet know for sure, though his mother would love for him to become a doctor, since he's interested in nature. He wants to show Josef his butterfly collection, in which there are not only butterflies he has bought from a catalog, but also many he has caught himself, he having also raised caterpillars down in the conservatory, though once Anton wasn't paying attention and threw out an entire case of specimens. Lutz would like to become a natural scientist, for he wants to go on an expedition, like Sven Hedin to Tibet or Nansen aboard the *Fram*, where he could take part in such an adventure and collect animals. But Irwin says that Lutz is very childish—a natural scientist, that's a romantic occupation, you can't make much money at that, and Lutz will end up a stupid teacher like old Wentzel at school, whom they call Papa Wutzl, he talking very slowly as he says that he can't ever let himself get excited, he has a heart condition, and whenever someone gives him trouble he never yells, but says, just you wait boy, I'll deal with you when your parents come in for a conference, and then he makes the test as hard as possible. Lutz protests that Papa Wutzl gives the best lectures, if only you paid attention to them, everything is immediately understandable, and he is especially good at zoology, as when he talked about antelopes and giraffes, the class right now studying ruminants. Yet Irwin makes fun of Lutz for being impressed by stupid Papa Wutzl, as Irwin is bored to death by zoology, though luckily he doesn't have to study it this year, for as far as he was concerned all those critters could just as well disappear, especially if they're of no use at all, while Lutz with his dumb love of animals will let a mosquito sit on his hand so that he can observe how the beast drills and drills in order to drink his fill, or most likely bring home a bedbug in order to see how it bites, what nonsense! Lutz, however, says that mosquitoes don't bite, but rather they press a liquid out of their suction tube, and the liquid and blood mix together, and then the mosquito sucks that down, though only the female does so, the male nourishing itself on plants, all of it wonderfully arranged by nature, which is why no one should kill mosquitoes, but if they should bite all you need do is press out the poisonous liquid and then it won't itch as much.

Irwin says that now Josef can see what a foolish romantic Lutz is. Josef, however, doesn't find anything foolish at all, for if that's what interests Lutz, then it's fine. Irwin doesn't agree and finds it childish, though perhaps Darwin was a great natural scientist who once said a few smart things about man being descended from the apes, and if you looked at most people and how stupid they were, then it was easy to believe Darwin. Lutz replies spiritedly, no, that's only what dumb people say, Darwin said something completely different. Josef stands up for Lutz, reminding Irwin that it would be unfortunate if everyone wanted to become a lawyer. Irwin counters that he wasn't saying that Lutz should study the same thing as him, medicine is indeed a useful subject, or he could even become a veterinarian, even though he wouldn't necessarily like to have a veterinarian for a brother, but if Lutz can't keep his hands off those critters, then at least be a veterinarian, though what is that compared with a real doctor, or a specialist, such as an eye doctor or a neurologist? Mother says that through new research you can see that everything has to do with nerves, the only exceptions being contagious disease such as strep throat, measles, or venereal disease, where disease is carried from one to another if you are not careful enough. But Lutz responds that there is a slew of doctors, but good natural scientists are rare, and that's what he wants to be and nothing else.

Irwin says that it's obvious that Lutz is indeed childish, for first you need to have talent, and then you can do whatever you want, but Lutz responds in a wounded manner, saying, "Mother says that you're nothing but an egotist who thinks about nothing but money! Yet one shouldn't only think about money!" No, that's not all Irwin thinks about, but first you need to have some, then you can afford to do what you want, because how is Lutz going to study zoology if someone doesn't buy his books for him, it costs a lot more than what Irwin likes to do, which is go to the movies or the operetta, he having seen *Die Bajadere* three times, because it was such a terrific production. Josef then asks if Irwin also likes to go to concerts or the opera. No, that's too boring, you can just as easily hear it on the radio, Father had a fantastic vacuum tube set, though no one really listens to it, Father dialing in the news and the market report, or the weather forecast for the following day, while Madame sometimes listens to French programs, Lutz searching around as well, though Robert is not allowed to touch the set, for he once turned the knobs so hard that it could not be repaired. Mother, meanwhile, can't stand the radio, because she shrieks like a stuck pig at the slightest background noise, though she doesn't notice if someone deliberately opens up the cabinet in the next room and turns the radio on and off, setting off a series of cracks and pops in the set that sound like a thunderstorm or machine-gun fire, yet she can't stand to listen to jazz even if it doesn't contain such rattling, especially any band with American Negroes singing, for then the mother begins to rage like a madwoman until someone turns it off. Once more Josef tries to turn the conversation to serious music, but Irwin refuses, he finds most of it to be stupid, and even the audience is bored, pulling joyful faces and clapping like mad at the end, Mother loving it all and saying that Father should go with her, though he says he needs his rest, and so most often Madame goes alone, though the last tutor accompanied her, he being an idiot.

Lutz disagrees, saying that he was not an idiot, he was very clever and there was nothing really wrong with him, but Irwin explains that Lutz doesn't know what he's talking about, he was an awful guy who had at first talked so pompously that Mother didn't realize how stupid he was, and thus she was so taken with him that she said he could be the next Goethe, Anselm Liebrecht his name. The guy had lived here and was so poor that two of Father's suits had to be altered for him, a new coat was purchased for him, the seamstress had made him new pants, and Father had given him some ties that were still in good shape. At night the guy sat up in his room, Mother warning him that he would ruin his health if he studied and read all night long, though he really didn't study but wrote poetry, some of which a journal in Bruex had published, though Mother wanted him to bring out an entire book, to which Liebrecht said that he had often tried to in Germany, Austria, and Switzerland, but no publisher wanted to, poetry never sold, only one publisher from Bodensee having written to say that he would like to publish Liebrecht's poetry if he would pay for two hundred copies, but Liebrecht didn't have the money for that. Then Mother had the idea to set up a subscription, but that angered Father, who asked if he should trade such stock on the market, and that Mother should not make herself look so ridiculous, at which she was deeply hurt, since she already had transcriptions of all the poems, she wanting to publish the best of them at her own expense and surprise Liebrecht with them for New Year's, they being hyper-sensitive stuff about love and nature and dreams, while on the parents' an-niversary and other special occasions he had put together a bunch of childlike stuff that Robert could learn by heart and recite, turning to Irwin and Lutz with such poems as well. Lutz didn't say anything, but Irwin had spoken the truth, namely that such stuff didn't interest him at all, even if it was a detective novel or the kind of books you're not supposed to read be-cause they excite the nerves too much, which is why they are hidden behind the first row of books on the shelf, but no matter, for he naturally didn't read such books, though Lutz yells, "Don't lie! You read them. Mother herself once caught you at it!"

Irwin shouts, "Don't believe him! I don't read any forbidden books! I only read Edgar Wallace and other crime novels. Mother never forbids those." Josef asks what happened to the poet-tutor. Irwin had indeed told him that he was not at all interested in poetry, he had plenty enough in school, where he had to learn such garbage, but the guy could see that there was no way to make any money from it, after which Liebrecht left the house immediately, as what Irwin was saying was a deep insult, which because he is the son of Herr Director he could get away with in making fun of the poor poet, though the art of poetry rises above all such crudeness, and perhaps one day Irwin will remember all this once Liebrecht is at last famous, for he certainly will have a great following, every little note of his will be collected. None of this impressed Irwin, however, for poets were all starvelings, even Schiller was poor, despite writing his popular poem "The Bell" and *William Tell*, Goethe the only exception, he having come from a good family, and himself a lawyer and privy councillor and even a government minister. Hearing this, Liebrecht was deflated, howling like a fool that he had had enough, he couldn't take it anymore, he was sick of this house, and he would quit immediately if Irwin didn't apologize, but Irwin didn't apologize, then the guy had accosted Mother and said he couldn't spend another day in this house, to which Mother said she found that a bit ungrateful, she had treated him like her own son, so why quit on the spot? Then he yelled out, "Because of Irwin!," and Mother began to laugh, saying he was nothing but a young ruffian whom no one took seriously, and why wasn't it enough for Anselm that Mother appreciated him, though she would speak with Irwin, for some-

234/ H. G. ADLER

day he will discover the beauty of art, something that the tutor also needed to inspire in him, maybe showing him how to write a poem, and the power of the material as captured in the form of poetry. Mother had said all this, for she liked to talk about art and had heard it all before in lectures she had attended, sometimes inviting artists to visit, total starvelings, who make only paintings and sculptures, Josef can even see the stuff throughout the whole villa, she inviting as well one or two literary people or someone from the theater, in addition to critics and a couple of women who marveled at it all.

Liebrecht said to Mother there was no way to show the ruffian how to write a poem, he had no respect for intellectual matters, but Mother was angered by Liebrecht's freshness, saying good, if he was that ungrateful he could leave right now, and she wouldn't have his poems printed, but then she also told him that she wanted to print the stuff, that she already had, and she wanted to support him and introduce him to influential people. To that the tutor said that it was obvious what kind of high culture prevailed in Herr Director's house, to which Mother asked, "Anselm, what do you mean by that?" He then answered exactly as he had said and requested immediate release from his position. Mother had nothing against this, yet he had to wait until Father got home, to which Liebrecht said, good, he was going up to his room to pack his bags, whereupon Mother went to find Irwin and Lutz, explaining everything to them and then asking Irwin whether he wanted to indeed apologize, but Lutz immediately said that he had no problem with Anselm, he only didn't want to learn about poetry from him, but Mother said it wasn't about what Lutz wanted but rather Irwin, who explained that he had only spoken the truth to Anselm, and that she should get rid of him. When Father got home he went upstairs to Liebrecht and gave him a fair amount of money, because it had all happened so fast, though Liebrecht nonetheless asked if he could stay the night in his room, which Father agreed to, though the poet did not come down for the evening meal, Sophie bringing it up to him instead. Afterward Father had not said another word about it all, nor had Mother, the only thing said being that they would now have to find another tutor.

That, of course, is Josef, and he looks much more reasonable than the poet from Oberleutensdorf by Bruex, where the foxes say good night, which is why the twerp had such beady little eyes, but Irwin can already see that Josef is ready to be good friends. Josef says he also hopes to be friends, but he asks Irwin not to be so hard on Herr Liebrecht, as it runs the risk of making Josef feel that he could also be judged just as quickly, and he would at least like to look at Liebrecht's poems, and then see how he feels. Irwin thinks that if Josef reads the stupid stuff he will see what garbage it is, but Josef is in favor of suspending judgment, which prompts Irwin to ask whether perhaps Josef also writes poetry. No, but he likes good poems, Irwin countering that he finds them useless, unless they are funny like those of Wilhelm Busch, especially "Plisch und Plum," though Josef has to agree that poetry is not natural, Father often having said that to Mother when she swooned over it, and he is certainly bright. Josef replies that one can be very bright yet have no sense for poetry. Irwin maintains that what one cannot understand is nonsense, to which Josef asks whether Irwin, for example, understands anything of medicine. No, but for that we have doctors. Josef means, however, whether Irwin himself understands anything about it. No, there's no need to, but he could learn it if he wished. Then Josef asks whether you have to learn about anything before you understand it, to which Irwin has no answer.

For a moment it's quiet, then there's a knock at the door, Irwin calling out "Come in!" at which a man dressed in livery enters with a large tray, this being Anton. Josef stands up, introduces himself, and considers for a moment whether he should extend his hand to the servant, then quickly stretches it out, the surprised Anton grasping it and begging his pardon, he had brought only tea and didn't know if perhaps Herr Doctor might want coffee. No, thank you, tea will be just fine, yet Lutz says, "Josef, you can order what you want. Here you can order anything!" Josef says thank you but everything is fine, as Anton sets everything on the table—tea, milk, lemon, sugar, a small basket with rolls and croissants, butter, marmalade, honey, a bowl with sweet cookies—and then Anton is off, Josef criticizing the boys for not having said thank you. Lutz explains that Anton is always there and is not used to being thanked all the time, though Josef hopes that in the future they will thank him, this seeming to disturb Irwin, for Anton should only worry about his job, which is what he's paid to do, and he might start to think he was performing some courtesy when he brings tea or does his work, whereas in school you don't thank the teachers, they are paid money to teach, and no one expects that at the end of the period the class should stand and say thank you as one, especially if it seemed as if they were kissing up to some stupid teachers. Then Irwin comes back to the question of tea or coffee, saying that it was unforgivable that Anton had not come before the snack to ask what Josef wanted, but since Josef found none of this to be worthwhile talk Irwin wonders about such indifference, he would not want to let anyone think he was so inconsiderate.

Josef asks if Irwin is always considerate, but he replies that if he were a servant he would certainly practice consideration to one's master, yet in general people aren't as considerate as Josef seems to think, even at school the teachers and the students aren't considerate of one another, and that's the way it is everywhere. Lutz believes, however, that it would be nice to be a bit more considerate now and then, Mother also wanting others to be nice to her when she has a headache or her stupid neuralgia, while Mother herself is considerate when Lutz and Irwin are sick, she does anything she can for them. Irwin finds it bothersome that Mother is always there when you're sick, waking you up and asking you how you feel, why you ate so little, whether you want some soda, lemonade, or raspberry juice, Irwin sometimes getting mad and not answering, but pretending to be asleep until Mother is gone, though she's back again five minutes later, looking through the cracked open door to ask in a half whisper, are you asleep? Lutz meanwhile doesn't think it's very nice of Irwin to talk about their mother like a fool when she does so much to take care of them, but Irwin responds angrily that he doesn't think anyone is a fool, he just wants his peace and quiet, because when Father is sick Mother is not allowed in, for he locks himself in and will not stand for messing with his pillows or taking his temperature, there being no need for Mother to make a scene, all he wants is two aspirin and no doctor, Lutz adding, "You see, Josef, that's why I don't want to be a doctor. You can't help the sick. If it has to do with nerves, then most medicines don't work. And when it's something else . . ."—"Quiet!" yells Irwin, it's not at all considerate to interrupt your brother, and Josef can see for himself that Lutz is talking like that only because he doesn't want to be a doctor. Lutz is romantic, but that can change, for when he was fourteen Irwin hadn't yet thought of being a lawyer, but rather only about soccer, which he played a lot of back then, though he gave it up because it's more interesting to watch, and in order to make a living at it you'd have to play on a championship team, and that's possible only if you're incredibly good, there also always being a great risk in sports of your getting hurt, be it a stupid pulled tendon or whatever, and suddenly your whole career is over, after which you can become a beggar or a trainer or a gym teacher, but none of that interests Irwin, he wants to get rich fast in order to be independent, sport being something to watch and talk about, it's all fantastic, especially the league championships, which are really exciting, he going to matches often on Sundays, though Lutz doesn't want to, he is a limp noodle always bent over his books and his butterfly collections, or who wants to be going on outings, indeed, the nature buff wanting to be in nature.

Then Lutz asks whether Josef might want to come along on an outing with him, for Lutz isn't allowed to go alone, though he wanted to join the scouts, who often go hiking and have a lily as their insignia, but Mother wouldn't allow it, for among the scouts there could be disreputable people, but because Lutz was so deeply disappointed Mother promised him a microscope as compensation, though he had not yet received it, because Father had said that Lutz could strain his eyes in using it, and the eyes are irreplaceable and cannot be bought with money, Lutz still hopeful that this year he'll get a microscope for his birthday, it being wonderful when you can look at cells, one next to another, Lutz having already observed algae in his natural-history lab and cut microscopic samples with a scalpel that satisfied Papa Wutzl. Lutz talks passionately about the microscope, as it is much more beautiful than the theater and movies, only a telescope is as beautiful, the macrocosm and the microcosm, these the most wonderful things to study, though Lutz wants to devote himself to the microcosm, there are great mysteries there, and it's marvelous what you can see through a pair of polished lenses, even a strong magnifying glass is terrific, though it's nothing compared with a microscope, the difference much greater than between opera glasses and a telescope, which Lutz saw at the planetarium, everything magnified so that you see how different it is and what it's really like. In fact, it's hard to know what's more real, what you see with your own two eyes or in the microscope, but the microscope is more mysterious, the image round and more clear or less clear when you turn the knob, while you can also shove the object around, which is like going on a hiking trip. Lutz asks Josef to say something to his parents so that he will get a microscope for his birthday, and Josef promises that he'll speak with Frau Director.

Lutz replies, "How happy that will make me, Josef! It's a substitute for not being able to explore the world like the scouts do. But I also want to do real hiking. Josef, couldn't you come with me sometime? Maybe on Sunday?" Josef explains that he will be coming to the house only on weekdays, not on Sundays, though he'd still like to go on a hike sometime soon. Lutz is happy to hear this, saying that's great, you'll need to plead with Mother, and ask Father and especially Madame, for if you speak with her first she often asks Mother on Lutz's behalf and has sometimes had good results. Lutz then asks if Josef really knows about hiking, for he had once asked Anselm, who then went along with him, though all they did was take a train ride rather than go by car, and once they got off they had walked only about a half hour from the station before Anselm said that nearby was a lovely country inn where they could rest, for he couldn't go any farther, his feet couldn't stand it, and when Lutz complained that it wasn't a real outing at all the poet had answered that Lutz was ungrateful, here there was fresh air and it was lovely, there also being refreshments, he could even order an ice cream, though if he wanted to see more it would be better to go by car. So they sat for a couple of hours in the garden of the stupid inn, someone playing a gramophone now and then, Anselm saying that this place was good at inspiring a poetic mood, it having a view where nothing much happened, just a bit of forest, but nothing really special, a glance back at the railroad tracks providing a view of a little town with a church tower and a couple of factory chimneys, smoke rising from them, though Anselm said it was a beautiful panorama, the kind of thing he needed when he wanted to write poetry, and that Lutz should be quiet so that he could write down something about the lovely contrast between the town and the countryside, which he would then work into a poem later on at home, there not being enough quiet here to allow him to forge his craft. Anselm had promised to title the poem "An Outing with a Student," and would read it to Lutz and dedicate it to his mother, which would please everyone, but then Lutz left the poet alone and slipped off, for he saw some beetles, so-called longhorn beetles, which are rust brown and have long feelers, while at the end of the garden he came upon an ant trail, which he followed right up to the anthill, the little critters scrabbling about hastily on their six flexible legs, Lutz having placed a small impediment in the way of one and watching how it got around it. But then Anselm was there again and said they had to leave since it was time to catch the train, which meant they needed to head straight off, though Lutz wanted to show him what the ants were carrying, they having just begun to drag a pupa along with them. This didn't matter at all to the poet, he saying that the ants didn't matter, and they had to go in order to comfortably get to the train on time. And so the trip was over, Anselm telling Mother at home how exciting it had all been, and that he'd had some lovely inspirations, enough at least for a poem, maybe even two or three, at which Mother asked Lutz if he had had fun, and he answering, "Not at all!" Mother then asked him why and scolded him for being an ungrateful child, but Lutz still said to her that he didn't need to go on any trips like that again.

Josef asks Lutz whether he went on any other outings, but he complained that he wasn't allowed to at school, except once as a child in a steamer to Königsaal and straight back, otherwise only in the car, and then which everything you want to see just flies by, since Father always wants the chauffeur to drive fast, which is fun, though Lutz likes to make frequent stops, Father saying that one can do the same at home by just sitting in the garden, while once they reach their destination Father gets impatient and gives the order to head back, since the chauffeur also needs time off. At best Lutz can only gather a few flowers and catch a butterfly before it's all over with and they head home. Irwin laughs, for he is not interested in such car trips and usually doesn't go along, at which Josef asks whether Irwin would like to join them for a hike, and he says why not, as long as they do something sensible, like hold some kind of fantastic race, or a steeplechase, since he always wanted to sit on a horse, and you can win a lot by betting on horses, and did Josef know anything about them? No, he knew nothing about them, though he very much likes to watch the races. Lutz says in agitation that he doesn't want to do that, it's bad for the horses, animal cruelty, he having read about bullfights in Spain, about cockfighting in Portugal, also about greyhounds in England, all of it involving cruelty to animals, nor are the animals that are taunted and killed able to say what has happened, it being no way to love animals, they should be observed in the freedom of their own habitat. This irks Irwin, who says, look, Lutz is just a complete romantic, talking about the freedom of animals, and then he goes and gawks at them in the zoo, all of it romantic nonsense, Mother also excited by the dreck served up to children, be it to Robert or to women who are always romantic, though Irwin would never marry a romantic woman, for he wants something completely different. Josef wants to know what Irwin means by "romantic," and he explains, "Anything that's not real, thus loony or impractical. No real man is romantic." At this there is a knock at the door and Sophie steps in to say that the Frau Director is in the salon and is asking, if the Herr Doctor has time, would he try to stop in to see her. Josef asks her to convey that he will be right there and then asks the boys what they are planning to do next. Irwin still doesn't know, maybe go to the movies, while Lutz wants to read. Josef asks about their homework, which the boys promise to do first before they do anything else, then Josef heads to the salon.

"It's so nice, Josef, that you're here! Now, what do you think of my boys?" It's too soon to say, but perhaps he could wait until later. "That's splendid. Others have rushed to judgment in talking to me about my boys, but I believe things will go better for you if I give you some advice. At first I was an openly critical mother, though of course I love my brood, but you must believe me when I say that I am objective and recognize their flaws, for I keep a much better eye on my boys than they think, even when I grant them the freedoms that they need. I am like a manometer, I mean a barometer, I measure the air pressure, Josef, the mental atmosphere. It's in fact wonderful to watch a young boy's soul unfold. A person is the greatest work of art possible, I always say, trust an experienced woman when it comes to that. There are predispositions, Josef. Consider Irwin, for instance, he's like my husband through and through, a powerful type, somewhat robust but simple, more practical and without any artistic curiosity. That pains me so, but unfortunately the times are such that one can behave like a beast, even if you're not as blond as Nietzsche, because the tender, excessively thoughtful people are the real shrinking violets. That's why it pleases me that Irwin is cut from more solid skin, I mean stock. As long as he doesn't find women threatening, he will do fine. You should know—under the veil of total silence, of course—that my marriage is not as happy as it seems. My husband is indeed a model husband, he has a heart of gold and grants me anything I desire, though I have already shared with you that he was an even better son, just as Freud has shared with us about Oedipus. Therefore I always had to stand in the shadows. But that was not the only problem, my husband has always been very interested in other lovely women, I having to close my eyes and listen to what, of course, always gets back to me. You see, Josef, Irwin takes after his father, these days studying too closely any skirt that passes his way. Sophie has more than once complained of his being too forward. I'm not a prude, I always say, I find it all to be quite natural, but it's dangerous, and I have spoken to Irwin indirectly—not directly, you understand—about it, though he didn't wish to understand and maintained that he didn't know what I was talking about. Since I couldn't confront him with Sophie all that well, you can just imagine how painful it was, while in the mornings Irwin often doesn't want to get up. That can only lead to bad blood, you understand. So please keep a close eye on him and keep me posted as to what you observe! Thankfully, Sophie is honest to the bone and won't allow herself to lose her head, but if it continues we will have to call in a psychiatrist, because my husband's brother—but swear that this will remain a secret between us!—was almost convicted due to some misconduct on his part. Only psychiatric expertise saved him, he having been placed in an institution for a while."

Josef wants to calm Frau Director down, but she feels there is no need, Josef is just too inexperienced as yet, for she also wants to be patient with Irwin, but it will likely all pass, fomenting youth, as she always says, yet one can now do something about it through psychoanalysis, it all being normal as long as it's properly handled and the complexes are sublimated. Josef should think about the sound of the word, how it reminds one of "sublime," which sounds like a flower, indeed a bit of a stretch, but with a certain poetic quality. Today everything can be controlled, or it's simply abnormal, the border never precisely drawn. Certainly the Director would be less complicated if psychoanalysis had existed and had been so widely accepted twenty years ago, though doctors back then were very old-fashioned, while the advances made now are fantastic, people should make greater use of them rather than being taken up by material inventions, such as the airplane, the radio, the many advancements in medicine, most likely there soon being something one can take for cancer without needing an operation, just as they now have insulin for diabetes, Frau Director's own father having died miserably from diabetes. The advances these days are really enormous, if the League of Nations could achieve agreement on disarmament, then eternal peace could now begin, enlightenment having at last prevailed. But there are dark powers, powers that exist in sleep and in dreams, which cannot be controlled by psychoanalysis or education, even though everything evil could be avoided if Freud's teaching were followed, for analysis should be employed in the schools, children needing to be examined as early as the first grade, pedagogy really a branch of medicine, she always says, an enormous revolution in the philosophy about and solutions to social problems at the ready when one recognizes that everything can be attributed to complexes and repression. How Spinoza could philosophize today if he knew all this, for the good person is he who can see through all his complexes and master them.

Perhaps the world will be a little less romantic, but it's more important that it's healthy. If the world changed to such an extent, then Frau Director would send her boys to a free school, but that's still out of the question, the corrupting influences are too many, which is why Frau Director wants her boys to have little to do with their friends. Irwin does indeed take dance lessons in order to develop some social manners, he liking this kind of music, while Frau Director patiently accepts that Josef doesn't dance, otherwise she would ask him to go with Irwin. Good society, however, is unfortunately dying off, Frau Director needing to make an effort to maintain a small circle of prominent people, but in the arts there are many suspect imaginations, for though Frau Director has a feel for what's modern, and the house is full of bold experiments, they are abstract works devoid of any romanticism, though the feeling within them is indeed genuine. Yet Frau Director is in her heart of hearts still somewhat unmodern, and it's hard to go against your nature, though her husband is completely unmodern, it not mattering if you show him a nude photo or the Venus of Portici, but when it comes to modern portraits like those painted by Kokoschka, he immediately yells take it away, it's hideous, he has no idea about what art is, Frau Director having taken a course on modern art with Professor Bäumel, a brilliant mind, she having wanted to bring Irwin along, but he came once and never went again, the fine things of life closed off to him, realism the only style he can handle, just like the Director, though the latter used to have a feel, a wisp of poetry, as did everyone before 1914, while Irwin is ice-cold, killing any and all enthusiasm.

This is a concern for Frau Director, and she wants Josef to make sure to take Irwin to a museum now and then, perhaps marble statues something that will move him, the coldness of the stone and the graceful warmth of the body, the combination of the spiritual and the sensual worlds, and perhaps this would allow Irwin to work through his sexual desires toward something more noble, which would then help him to sublimate the flush of puberty within the aesthetic. Frau Director had already tried this with the last tutor, but he was an overrefined bundle of nerves who needed to go into analysis himself, Josef needing to hear a bit about him before the children say anything, for he was a poet, very gifted, a good writer who had soul and a fine sense for nature, able to be swept away by a beautiful panorama, he possessing a tender, erotic air about him, almost French, though poets surprisingly are often not very good teachers, they are too egocentric, and so the boys didn't like him, Irwin especially having real problems until things eventually fell apart, the tutor feeling that his poetic honor had been insulted, which was of course ridiculous, but then he was suddenly gone, the Director having to reach deep into his pocket, as you can't simply let such a little heap of unhappiness simply go *vis-à-vis de rien*.

Neither randy Irwin, who can be downright fresh, nor Robert, who is enough of a handful on his own, causes more worry for Frau Director than does Lutz, her real concern, for he is just like his mother, a tender blossom, sensitive and dreamy, but unprepared for raw reality, with no understanding of the workings of the everyday world, truly without a care, yet in the wrong way. If only he were a girl, then his romantic inclinations would be fine, for he takes in so much that would be really useful if he studied medicine, a psychiatrist being half a poet in some ways, yet Lutz's interests have nothing to do with poetry but instead are completely romantic and can easily go astray. He wants continual adventure, as if life, as it is, is not a big enough adventure, he able to observe a wasp for an hour, or a common housefly will send him into paroxysms about what tender wings it has, how sensibly such a tiny animal is constructed, which makes the Director think that Lutz could perhaps be an agriculturist, though as a mother I don't want to hear anything about it, for if it doesn't involve climbing a career ladder, at least it doesn't have to mean descending one in return. Farming is not for such an overly excitable boy, no matter how noble a large estate or even a normal farm can be, for Lutz is not cut out for it, and such a career would break him.

Josef begs to differ, saying there is still time for Lutz to decide what he wants to do, and what the boy really wants is a microscope, which would seem a worthwhile desire in regard to medicine. Frau Director remains un-moved in her stand against it, a good microscope is expensive, and because of the current economic crisis it's hardly affordable, and Josef should make no mistake, it's still a naïve childish wish, for today Lutz wants a microscope, while tomorrow he'll abandon it out of boredom, his head full with the idea of getting a telescope. No, the boys must be raised with a sense of conse-quence, and not just have their every whim catered to, that weakens charac-ter and is a continual mistake in the way children are raised these days. Yes, if Irwin also wanted a microscope she could imagine that he would know what he would need it for, it even perhaps doing him some good, while if only to put an end to it all she had asked him if he wanted a microscope, to which he just laughed and asked what he'd even do with such a contraption, though a motorbike, well, that would please Irwin indeed, he'd speed around like a devil and break every bone in his body, while one could indeed give a motorbike to Lutz when he is bigger, if only to loosen him up a bit, for in short, Lutz requires a strong hand, Irwin a more delicate touch. To this Josef tries to raise some doubt in the hope of changing her mind, but Frau Director is firm in her view, there being no way to change how she in-tends to raise her boys, for while she is grateful for suggestions the basic questions are already decided, she wishing to remind Josef of his own words about not being ready to judge the boys. He begs her pardon in response, he didn't mean to be so forward, and meanwhile he will think about how he can be of help to Lutz, but it will not be easy to do so. In the meantime, Frau Director says that she attributes Josef's critical remarks to his youthful tem-perament, though she values real fire and doesn't like a waffler, since, as she always says, Josef is indeed far removed from true philosophy by virtue of his age, Frau Director also considers the tutor's upbringing, Josef still being half a child even at twenty-two, and he should enjoy his youthful years, as the years go by quickly.

Josef knows enough to express deep gratitude for Frau Director's advice, and then asks if she would be good enough to consider a suggestion. "Yes, of course, my young friend, let's hear it!" Josef puts forth the question of whether she would support his taking the boys on a short hike sometime soon, it would provide a good opportunity to get to know them better, and he'd be happy to set aside this Sunday or next to spend with the two of them or separately with each alone. Frau Director asks if Josef will be wanting to use the car for this. No, we will hike on foot, maybe needing to start a little ways by train. Frau Director needs to think about it for a while and speak with her husband, there is no real rush, though it's an exciting idea, and maybe even Frau Director could tag along, she's a good hiker, or they could organize a larger group and invite others, though this makes Josef immediately want to raise some concerns. However, there's a knock at the door and Lutz enters, standing by the door and waiting until the mother asks, "Well, Lutz?"—"I just wanted to see if Josef is coming back to us. We've finished our homework."—"But Lutz, come here first. You may kiss my hand." He kisses his mother's hand. "Lutzi, do you love your mother?" Lutz nods as she says, "I've been speaking to Josef about you boys. He likes you very much. Do you like him as well?" Lutz nods again, and Frau Director dismisses them with a wave of her hand. "Thank you, Josef. Take care, my sweet child, goodbye!"

Josef feels a bit dazed and wants to be alone for a little while, but he senses that Lutz would be disappointed, so he follows him to his room, which is somewhat messy, Irwin not there, and he asking Lutz where he could be. Lutz doesn't know, Irwin was just here when Lutz went to get Josef. Josef speculates that Irwin wanted to go to the movies, though Lutz doesn't know anything about it, or maybe he just doesn't want to tell on him, Josef deciding not to press him any further, but rather just to ask if Irwin is allowed to leave when he wants and without saying anything. Lutz can't say exactly, sometimes Mother gets upset, while at other times she's pleased about how independent Irwin is, praising him in comparison with Lutz and asking why he can't be as independent, although he doesn't dare to, for Mother would go crazy if he ever went off on his own, though Irwin never asks and just leaves, and as long as he shows up on time for dinner everything is all right. Only once did he arrive late, no one knowing where he was, everyone in the house upset as they interrogated Lutz, though he knew nothing and said only that Irwin had simply left, at which Father asked again in anger, Lutz, where is Irwin? He must have said something when he left, but Irwin really hadn't said anything, Mother wanting Father to calm down as she observed that Lutz never knew anything when asked, since he only daydreams, though Father had said to Mother that he never commented on how to raise the children, but he did expect them to be at the table each evening, to which Mother answered that it is too bad that Father doesn't worry more, for they are his children just as much as they are hers, adding in English that this should not be talked about in front of the children or the servants, but Father said he wouldn't hold back. And then there was even greater concern, for Irwin was still not there, everyone having asked around for him, including the tutor, which was Anselm then, who said he wouldn't know, he had no control over Irwin whatsoever, though that didn't sit well with Mother, who said that it was part of the tutor's job to take care of his students, and Anselm wasn't helping anything by just letting Irwin wander off. But the tutor argued that he couldn't just tether Irwin. Then they asked Sophie and Anton, though they also knew nothing, after which they called the cook and the chauffeur, the cook saying that she was stuck in the kitchen and didn't know who left or entered the house, the chauffeur also saying there was no way for him to know if the young master left. Later they observed that they had forgotten to ask Madame or Robert, but they knew nothing at all, and now everyone was worried about Irwin and couldn't eat a thing, only Madame having fed Robert and put him to bed, Anselm also having had his evening meal, though just a small one before leaving the room. Mother, meanwhile, had complained that she was worried, there are so many bad men about, and Irwin was such a hothead, Father having telephoned the police, who told him he shouldn't get so upset, the boy will turn up, Father then screaming into the phone that he paid his taxes, but when he needed the help of the police they are useless, to which the police said that he needed to calm down, they would look for Irwin. The parents had still not eaten a thing, but Lutz was so hungry that he wanted something, at which Mother asked if he was so heartless as to think about dinner when his brother was perhaps lost forever, at which Lutz then left the room and headed into the kitchen, where the cook gave him something to eat, it already being almost nine o'clock. Then suddenly Irwin turned up happy as a lark and behaving as if everything was normal, though Father never once asked him where he had been and why he was so late, but instead grabbed him and hit him and then gave him a couple of hard slaps left and right that turned Irwin's face completely red, Father then dragging him into the boys' bedroom and yelling that he didn't want to see the sight of him again that night, and if the same thing should happen again he could expect even worse. Mother stood there frozen, Father had for once done something, she wanting to talk to Irwin, since he had not yet eaten, but Father held strong, at which Mother cried, because she's opposed to beating children, it leads to complexes and can destroy the nerves, but Irwin was never that late again and nothing more was said of it.

Josef asks whether Lutz would like to be able to wander off on his own. Sometimes he wants to, and Irwin should take him along now and then, but he never wants to and maybe has friends whom he meets up with. Lutz would sometime like to go into the city on his own, he knows of a big store there that sells natural-science supplies, there being stuffed birds on display, including the butterfly bird of Brazil, which is called the hummingbird, Lutz having a book in which he could show it to Josef, though much lovelier than any picture would be a preserved bird, with its soft colorful feathers and the long, pointed beak. Lutz also wants an aquarium with bright-colored fish that can be completely red or completely transparent, and which move through the water so gracefully, though the chance to own such treasures is denied him because it makes a mess in the house, which is not a museum and not a garden. If Josef happens to know the zoo, he'd love to visit it with him, it not being true that the animals suffer there, Irwin having lied about that. When Josef says he would be happy to go with him, Lutz wants to shout for joy, though Josef says it will have to be another day because of the late hour, while today they can look at a book together, and Lutz should get one that he likes. Lutz then hurries happily to get a book about butterflies and begins to initiate Josef into the mysteries of these insects, these being the larvae, these the cocoons, these the butterflies, Josef also having to look at Lutz's butterfly collection, it all taking an hour as they soon become friends.

Suddenly the door opens without anyone knocking, as a man walks in, the Director himself, Josef standing up, though the Director first greets his son and glances at the opened book and the many display boards where the butterflies are spread out, carefully pierced by thin needles, at which he then turns to Josef and says to him that he must be the new tutor. The two men appear to check each other out more than to actually greet each other, though the Director is affable and seems to be pleased, saying that Lutz can entertain himself for a while so that Josef and the Director can get to know each other. They head down to the conservatory, Josef told that he can sit down, which allows him to study the Director more closely, his face golden brown and his hands somewhat hairy, he having a broad fleshy nose, almost a snout, with some distance between the nostrils, a repulsive face, certainly. As they sit silently across from each other, Josef is ashamed of considering whether the Director looks more like an ape or a man, the two of them observing each other without a word, nothing occurring to either of them to say, the Director finally asking stiffly if Josef is pleased with the house, Josef saying that he thinks it is lovely and huge, though of course he didn't yet know it that well, after which there is another pause that has to be painfully overcome with a question about how much longer Josef plans to study, he hearing himself answer as if from a distance that he thought two or three more years.

After some mildly awkward movements, the Director makes another attempt by asking if he can speak with Josef quite confidentially, since people say that the culmination of philosophy is silence. Such conversations always make Josef uneasy, nor does he have any idea what the Director is leading up to, but he presses the matter, and so Josef agrees to a vow of silence, at which the Director begins to praise his wife as a wonderful person, a pure soul, and certainly receptive to anyone wanting to teach her philosophy, though one doesn't always learn everything from the best of men, for no one knows so much that he cannot be wrong, yet you would have to agree that this woman is a model of perfection, such that in her case one can hardly speak of any failing. The Director remarks that his sentences aren't always clear in their meaning, noting that he deals with stocks, and he gets mud-

dled, then tries again and finally breaks off sheepishly, looking helpless as he
beckons to the by now somewhat confused Josef, who can do nothing for
the Director except wait patiently until he finally pulls himself together and
with an energetic thrust states that he wishes to speak quite candidly. He
wants, of course, for his boys to be well raised, and he will do anything to
make that happen, though within reason, the Director above all a businessman, and though not as well educated and well read, he nonetheless has a
good understanding of people, nor can anyone try to convince him of X
when it's Y, for he knows how to calculate, and Josef can be certain of his
support, no, not with raising the boys, he doesn't get mixed up in that, but
when it comes to business Josef can have any tip he desires, free of charge,
though it needs to be understood that his wife can't know about it. Josef says
that he doesn't know what kind of business advice he could need. The Director meanwhile keeps talking, saying that Josef can tap his advice at any
time, perhaps in how to save some money, or if he wants to invest or has in-
herited a few stocks, no matter, Josef can come to him and he will help him
out, though the Director asks for a small favor in return, what one calls in
business a usance, which has to do with the boys, but not directly so, for he
can't ignore the role of his wife in raising them, since she has such a good
relationship with them, which he admits he envies, and as a result she enjoys
the love and respect of the boys in a measure that one could only hope for,
but unfortunately there is also a certain extravagance or high-strung quality
that also accompanies it. She perhaps has too much going on inside her head
and wants to raise the boys with completely new ideas, while the Director
was himself raised quite simply, his mother a frank woman for whom everything went according to plan, or if not according to plan, then a smack
would soon follow, which did the trick, and that was that, the father of the
Director having always handled matters quite abruptly, his approach being
to say to us children, you'll have to figure out what to do on your own, and
that was that. But his wife, for all her bottomless love, has no idea what to
do with the boys, she's always coming up with new ideas, then she reads
some more books, which is fine, though too much of it is confusing when it
comes to raising children, and then she runs to Dr. Brendel, who is the family doctor, though quite confidentially Josef should know that Dr. Brendel is
not really a general practitioner, he is a neuropsychologist, certainly a capa-

ble man in his field, having served for ten years as an assistant in a mental institution. Frau Director trusts him implicitly and continually consults him, but it certainly cannot be good to ask a psychiatrist about normal everyday issues, a neuropsychologist having no doubt already been infected by the insane and thus half a fool himself, though here Dr. Brendel is considered a saint.

Through the Director's wife, Dr. Brendel practically wears the trousers in the family, which is a problem, though it was even worse when the last tutor was still with them. Josef should know about him, and must have heard something about him already, he being a poet, some even praising his poems, though others not, and those the Director agreed with, though Josef can form his own view, there are a number of his works tucked away on the bookshelves here, even though no one understands the stuff. That tutor was a fool, in fact incredibly ugly, for though the Director doesn't mean to speak badly of him, you would have to see him to appreciate his little green eyes and a mouth like a beak, which he often left hanging open for a while when he said something, as if something were about to fly into it, but it was all just a mannerism that meant nothing. This poet upset everything at home, always trying to present his new poems to the Director each Sunday, who then tried to avoid him, but his wife had nagged for the poet to read until the Director surrendered and left the room. This created a bad mood, he having to indulge the poet for the sake of his wife in order to have some peace, but then something else happened, which was the trouble with Irwin, though it was all a pretext, it being hard to know what it was really all about, yet, luckily the poet was gone, it costing a bit, but at least a scandal was avoided. Indeed, Josef should know that psychoanalysis is a sham, though he doesn't mean to insult Josef if indeed he believes in it, but here it only caused damage, and was bad for his marriage, even worse for the boys, while no matter what Josef thinks of such teaching, he asks him to refrain from it here in this house, and especially with the boys.

The Director thinks his boys are just fine, none of the three having any problem with nerves if you just leave them to themselves, and Irwin will make his own way, he has sharp elbows, and he's a bit precocious, but that's his nature and quite normal, and soon he'll be wanting a girl, which doesn't trouble the Director at all, nor can one stop it with new-fangled approaches, nor does it hurt anyone wanting to become a real man to have a couple of harmless tales about chasing skirts, Irwin will be all right. When it comes to Lutz things are a little more fraught, for it would have been better if he were not a boy, he even half looking like a girl, the Director in fact having badly wanted a girl who would have taken after his mother, but Lutz looks like the Director's grandfather, though Lutz is much softer, too soft, like butter, the grandfather having been hard, wiry, and tough, which Lutz will never be, though the main point is that he is already straying from the idea of studying medicine, which must be because of his disgust with blood and pus, thus leading to the decision that his mother will turn him into a neuropsychologist, while the boy in all his tenderness will turn out even crazier than Dr. Brendel, whom she holds up as an example when she talks about Lutz going into medicine.

The worried father speaks with frustration, and when he falls silent for a moment Josef begins to talk about Lutz, hoping to convince the father of that which he feared he had already not convinced the mother. Josef begins with a couple of comments about Irwin, whom, unfortunately, he did not have that much chance to speak with today, though he had a long conversation with Lutz and can agree with the father that medicine would not be the right choice, he having no real interest in the subject, but rather a real talent for zoology, as well as biology, he not only demonstrating his love of them but also an impressive knowledge for his age, all of which should be supported by getting him a microscope, so that what he plays with will feed what will inspire him to something serious. To this the Director shakes his head, saying that one shouldn't just give in to the boys, even though he would do anything for them, but it has to be the right thing, for certainly Lutz had won over Josef, he persisting whenever he can, but it would be a mistake to support Lutz in this, his love of animals is so girlish, and all it can lead to is a career that pays nothing, though perhaps there is a different way to go about it, the Director having already thought of this interest of Lutz's, which is why he also doesn't agree with the mother that the boy should become a doctor, as well as the fact that he will never be cut out for a business career in either the narrow or the broader sense, what he should go into is agriculture. He could attend an agricultural school and immerse himself in his love of animals, but in a sensible manner, while once Lutz has completed his training and seen a bit of the world, then the Director can buy him some property. Josef decides to take a bit of a risk and slyly says that he understands how Lutz's current interests could lead to agriculture and other similar pursuits over the short or the long haul, and of course biology is essential for that, which is why the interest in the microscope would help to keep matters on track, it being a preparation for the future, where any discouragement could result in the opposite outcome, namely a resistance to any occupation suggested to him. The Director interrupts Josef's wave of words, saying that he doesn't need to be told that biology is a part of agricultural studies, but there is time for that in high school, a microscope only leading to trouble before then, Lutz's playfulness too much already, for though he indulges the boys' wishes as much as he can, he does so within certain limits. The Director asks only that Josef tutor the boys with the intentions of their father in mind, and not those of the mother, the boy needing to be steered away from a track that will only lead to his becoming another Professor Wentzel, who is Lutz's natural-science teacher and idol, and whose zoology hardly even provides enough for him to carve a roast chicken at Sunday lunch.

Josef realizes that his efforts with the Director on Lutz's behalf will get no further than they did with the wife. He feels embarrassed and bad about his clumsy attempts, and so collects himself in order to think of a better way to express how he wants to help the boy fulfill his highest hopes, wanting to at least do something for Lutz in order not to disappoint him so bitterly, and so he tries to get the Director to agree to letting Lutz go on a trip with him sometime soon, though the result of this attempt is somewhat meager, for indeed the Director has nothing against going on a trip if the boy wants it that badly and prefers to squeeze into the packed train and then to get blisters along some dusty trail, rather than to sit comfortably in the car and take in the view, all that is a matter of taste, but he never discusses such questions with his wife, he lets her worry about all the little stuff and only brings up the important things that will most affect the boys' future. With this the conversation is over, the Director pleased, for his wife doesn't care for such two-way conversations between men, but the Director knows that he can count on Josef to keep quiet about it all in order to continue to profit from his gratitude. The two then separate, Josef encountering Irwin while on his way to the boys as he asks him, "What did you think of the film?" Irwin throws him an angry glance, wondering who betrayed him and said that he was at the movies, or whether Josef had told on him or had interrogated everyone else. Josef says with a smile that he's no snitch, and not even nosy, it just having occurred to him that Irwin might have gone to the movies. Irwin doesn't believe this, someone must have told Josef, and even though Lutz may not have snitched he still blabs too much. Josef says there's nothing wrong with going to the movies, Irwin himself had said he wanted to go. Irwin agrees there is nothing wrong, it's his business, nor had he asked what Josef had done for the afternoon. Josef wonders if he's really interested and not just curious, though he doesn't press the matter, even though he's willing to talk about what he did for the afternoon. Irwin, however, doesn't want to know, but he relaxes somewhat and indicates that he's willing to talk about the movie and answer any questions Josef may have, admitting openly that he was at the movies, where he saw a cowboy film that was excellent, Tom Mix in the main role, and so exciting that right up to the last minute he was on the edge of his seat, Josef should go to see it if he hasn't already.

During this conversation the two reach a door that leads to the garden, as Irwin asks if Josef has seen the garden already. No, he says, but it would be nice if Irwin could show it to him. Irwin says that they could head out into it, but if Josef wants to be shown around the gardener can do that, though unfortunately he's not there right now, he comes only in the morning, yet Lutz gets on well with him and can say what each plant is called, often even knowing the Latin name, but Mother doesn't like it when he stands around with the gardener, he able to do so only on mornings when there is no school, while Mother can't know, for if she does she calls him away immediately. She has indeed forbidden the gardener more than once to let Lutz in, as it only feeds his romantic dreams, which Mother hopes to stamp out. Father is also firmly against romanticism, but not against this, as he sees Lutz's learning from the gardener as preparation for a possible career in agriculture, though Mother rises up like a fury, saying that no child of hers will become a farmer, at which Father draws his tail between his legs like a wet poodle. But even Lutz doesn't want to go into agriculture, saying he wants to do something different with nature than does a farmer, he wants to study it, just as Josef must have heard already, though Irwin thinks it's a load of nonsense. Their talk, however, is interrupted by the ugly sound of a gong, Josef knowing without Irwin's having to say anything that this is the sign for dinner, the two of them stepping back into the house as everyone gathers in the dining room.

Josef is introduced to Madame and little Robert, as everyone sits around the large oval table, Josef taking his spot between his two pupils. Left of Lutz sits the mother, Robert next to her, then Madame, the Director between her and Irwin. Anton serves the food in tails and white leather gloves, holding out a dish first to Frau Director, who then sets one in front of Robert, the rest served in order, beginning with the Director and followed by Madame, Josef, Irwin, and Lutz, such that Anton must move constantly back and forth. The meal begins once all have been served, Robert slapping his spoon into his soup such that it splashes, which Madame tries to stop, the Director looking amused as he asks Robert, "Do you think you can turn the soup into whipped cream by stirring it around like that?" Frau Director throws her husband a dirty look and worries what Josef must think, he sitting down to the table for the first time and probably thinking that Robert has no manners, which Madame regrets terribly, though she says, *"Oh non, mon cher Robert est quelquefois méchant, autrement il est très joli, il est doux."* This time Madame gets a dirty look from Frau Director as she turns to Robert and says, "I know, sweetheart, that you love to splash around in your soup like that. But it's very nasty. Now please stop!" She lectures Robert about the danger of maintaining such bad manners, for if someone invites him to dinner and he splashes around in his soup, then no one in the world will ever like him to visit or invite him again, and he'll always have to sit at home. But Robert says he doesn't need to be invited, nor does he even need to be liked, and he can just stay home, since everyone else is at home. Madame says, *"Mais Robert, fi donc,"* and continues to say the same, as well as, now and then, *"Mange ton potage proprement,"* at which Madame demonstrates how to eat the soup and the other courses. Several times the Director says that Robert will indeed learn with time, which Frau Director then questions, for Robert can see already how mannerly everyone eats, even the new tutor doing so splendidly, nor will anyone want to play with Robert if he doesn't eat right. But Robert doesn't want to play with anyone, not even today, he has played enough already, and so it goes for the next four courses until they get to the fruit and cheese, though Frau Director more and more turns over the care of Robert to Madame.

Frau Director turns to Josef and asks if he finds his food to be excellent, and when he agrees she explains that, despite the financial crisis, nothing was spared in terms of food in this house, that is the last thing to try to scrimp on, good and wholesome food never having been treated as a luxury, though there are many who would be happy to eat this well, a coolie, for example, having to get by on a handful of rice per day, as she always says, whenever the boys pick at their food and say they don't like this or they don't like that, the cook *comme il faut* in terms of high society, she having learned her art in the princely houses of the old monarchy, even once having cooked for Archduke Josef, indeed the namesake of their own Josef, and indeed, was that who he was named for? Josef didn't think he was named for someone from the old monarchy. Frau Director thought that made sense, today it would be ridiculous to name someone after Franz Josef, such men being branded for life, but what had she been talking about? Well, then, enough about cooking, one shouldn't talk about food, as she always says, though somehow she had gotten carried away, but enough of that, for Frau Director wants only to recall Cato's saying *"Cato Maior apud conviviis magis sermonibus quam cibibus se delectavit."* Irwin then blurts out that his mother always says it wrong, for she knows nothing about Latin, though she loves to say something in it, but *apud* takes the accusative and *cibus* follows the second declension. Frau Director finds it highly rude of Irwin to criticize her at the table, it could be done privately afterward. Josef should in fact know that she had attended a girls school, where only modern languages were taught and no Latin, which she knows a bit of now, having taught it to herself or at least picked it up, it not mattering if she makes mistakes or doesn't know a declension, for indeed, she sometimes gets the declensions mixed up, but what matters is the meaning of what is being expressed, and Irwin should never correct her as long as he is lucky enough to enjoy the comforts his parents provide, for how fortunate the children of the unemployed in the Erzgebirge would consider themselves if they knew only half as much Latin as does Frau Director.

Frau Director had not wanted to discuss any of this, Irwin having only interrupted her so rudely, she wanting to say instead that the conversation with guests at the table is vital, Eckermann having become world-famous as a result of his dinner conversations with Goethe, while without them the poet Eckermann would have ended up a complete unknown, and Irwin should make note of that, he always has such scorn for poets. Irwin states that he has nothing against Goethe, and that what Eckermann recorded weren't dinner conversations but simply discussions between them. Frau Director says, conversations or discussions, what's the difference, while even more important than poets are philosophers, though philosophy is only for a small circle of well-read intellectuals who examine the inner meaning of life. Frau Director orders Anton to skip over to the bedroom and bring her the copy of *Ethics*, he knows what she means, the Spinoza bound in leather, she wants to read aloud a fantastic sentence from this most modest of philosophers, because although she can recall a few of the words from memory, she doesn't want to make a mistake, so once Anton arrives with the leather volume Frau Director opens to a page designated by a silk bookmark and reads, "Awe involves the perception of an object in which the spirit remains captive because this particular perception has no connection with anything else." That is a brilliant sentence, she always says, for man should always admire something, otherwise he will become too pedestrian, and that could happen to Irwin, because he's too materialistic, though if Spinoza had been familiar with psychoanalysis he would never have written this sentence, which is clear, although still a bit romantic, for the spirit should not remain captive, that is a religious prejudice which in light of our current understanding must be set aside. Such captivation involves a complex, and Frau Director loves most to talk about an awe complex, which one has to solve or at a minimum sublimate in a good manner. One only needs to listen to the sound of the word "sublime," a lovely word, not without a poetic tinge, in much the same way that there's something poetic about psychoanalysis, for along with philosophy it is the genuine poetry of the future, because abstraction is what triumphs in art, namely that which is completely removed from life, as Professor Bäumel had explained in his course, which would have been a real help to Irwin, if only he wouldn't run away from life's great puzzles, for in the dream that we are always caught up in, awe plays a vital role, as it's a type of love, an enthusiasm for the beautiful and the good. When Lutz is bigger he should consider that beauty is not sensual, because if you understand Spinoza you realize that no microscope will unlock the great puzzles of the world that men can only stand awestruck before. The true artist of our time is really the doctor, that will become even more clear as time goes on, though today people don't realize it entirely, but eventually crude medicine will disappear, with the exception of treating wounds, broken bones, bad teeth, or bad eyesight, it doing more harm than good when they inject the body with innumerable shots of poison in trying to heal what actually cannot be healed, while one day all of man's ills, with the exception of accidents, will be treated by healing the soul. People will become aware, then awe will no longer remain a captive perception, as one only needs to understand that one can in this way also solve and master the solution to the social question, because also within a nation it all comes down to the condition of awe, there no longer being anything that is imagined, as the imagination is also a kind of illusion, and within there is still something of romanticism, but instead pure awe will arise, and then even awe will pass, though only later will that happen, the right conditions needing to be fulfilled first, for awe is a kind of amazement. The sage, however, is not amazed, since he knows either everything or nothing, and in the same way awe is still a fixation of the libido, a kind of avarice, which is also the end of ethics, while after awe comes fulfillment. Irwin and Lutz should pay attention and not make such dumb faces, for if the boys don't understand they should wait for the future, when they will see the light, while for now at least they should be respectful, though indeed what does Josef think of it all?

Everyone has gone silent, only Robert scraping his chair with his foot, Madame having admonished him now and then, the older boys hardly listening, the Director nodding now and again and beginning to pick his teeth, though Josef had tried to take it all in, but it became harder and harder, such that when Frau Director asks him for his opinion he feels shy and doesn't want to say anything, though the boys unintentionally help him out, the meal now over as Lutz and Irwin ask whether they can be excused from the table. The mother gives them permission, and Josef wishes to be excused as well so that he can spend some more time with the boys, thus pleasing Lutz, which he shows openly as he stands by the door, Irwin glancing back at him as he waits, but Frau Director has other ideas and says that the boys have been rude, that they secretly laughed during the discussion of Spinoza and thought their mother stupid, wanting to embarrass her in front of Josef, instead of showing her how proud they are of their mother, and for that they can head off alone, and they can talk with Madame when she puts Robert to bed, for it won't hurt them to speak a little French if they don't want to make total fools of themselves this summer in Brittany. After this Irwin and Lutz have to kiss their mother's hand, while she kisses them on the forehead and says tenderly that they are her darlings and they just need to be sensible, they are going to like Josef, and she's happy that they both like him, though she doesn't want it to be just a flash in the pan. Then the boys say good night to their father, who stretches out his hand to them and tells them not to fight or stay up too late, and that Irwin should be so kind as to get up on time tomorrow morning, so that they don't all go through the same song and dance again. Then they both say good night to Josef, who promises to often spend evenings with them, this is not the only night he will stay over at the house, and they can also meet him in the garden in the morning in order to go for a run. Robert's departure follows on the heels of Irwin and Lutz leaving, the child fussing, since he's overtired and screams, though Madame understands and says, *"Vite, vite, mon enfant, je te raconterai encore un conte très très réjouissant,"* as Robert finally leaves after several hugs from his parents.

Frau Director is not completely happy with Josef, for as a supposed philosopher he had not supported her interpretation of Spinoza's view, or perhaps he was unfamiliar with it, which Josef had to agree with, he didn't know it at all, and above all she was not his contemporary and it wouldn't be right to debate her. At this Frau Director explains firmly and yet forgivingly that the *Ethics* is as elementary to philosophy as one plus one, and if she were a university professor she would make students learn the entire text by heart, for in doing so, even though Spinoza can seem somewhat out of date, one gains through him an ethical foundation upon which the modern understanding of the soul rests, much like a young seedling on an old vine, pardon me, I mean stump. Frau Director pauses for a moment and sighs that unfortunately it's impossible for her always to attain the highest level of thought when one has to simultaneously muck about in the raw reality of the everyday world, the noble being like a fragrance that floats away, shallowness triumphing amid one's daily cares, and with a sidelong glance at the

Director she adds that one can indeed see how her husband sits by above it all, which only makes her want to stir him up a bit. Josef looks at him and asks himself against his will whether the Director doesn't indeed look more like an ape than a man, but meanwhile Frau Director jumps in and asks her husband if things are bad with the market, mainly because he's making such a sour face. He says it's really not so bad, though tomorrow the market will be somewhat soft, but it will soon pick up, a lot of numbers look good and are holding strong. Frau Director says that's so nice, my dear, you only need a boom and everything for you will be as it was for the snake before the fall of man. Such talk makes the Director nervous, though she pays no attention and says to Josef that he should appreciate what a melancholy man her husband is, it all stemming from a bit of depression, which is completely treatable, though he resists the help of his neuropsychologist and runs from the room if I ask Dr. Brendel to join us at the table. It would be quite easy to take care of it all, but if you do nothing then everything, of course, remains hopeless. She pays no attention to how her husband stares at her beseechingly and implores her to stop, Josef cannot possibly be interested in all this, and it will only embarrass him. Her husband's pleading words only prod her on as she declares that his stubbornness is horrible, my goodness, I only mean well, and until recently there had always been unity in the family, which indeed there still is, for in regard to all basic questions they had never had a major disagreement, the Director is simply too easily excited and then soon sad, Dr. Brendel calling it a cycle that remains continual, the basis for it being the strain of his work, there not being a moment's peace, which causes the nerves to suffer, and which unfortunately the children also note, even though there is a cure in place for it.

When Josef sees Dr. Brendel, he will certainly agree with Frau Director that he is a fabulous person and not just a doctor, she always says that he acts out of the purest love for others, the Director against him only because he worked for ten years as an assistant in a mental institution, though Dr. Brendel had done that only for noble-minded reasons. The mental ailments today are by far the most dangerous ailments, the source of them has to be discovered, observed, and treated, in most cases there being something that can be done, while in most families one can see that the onset of some form of dementia is everywhere, sometimes taking the form of megalomania, sometimes a persecution complex or some other type of mania, sometimes one being lucky enough to suffer only from hysteria or a neurosis, a word by the way that has a wonderful tie to "sublime" because of a similar poetic effect, though it can all be healed through goodwill and patience. Frau Director considers it a blessing that in this house a modern and informal spirit rules, she continually makes sure that everything develops naturally, much like the transformation of a cocoon into a butterfly or the ugly duckling into a beautiful frog, no, I mean swan. She has many ideas about pedagogy that Robert especially will benefit from, since she can capitalize on her experience with Irwin and Lutz, for when Irwin was as old as Lutz is now she had hardly any awareness of pedagogy or psychology as she does now, but since then she had learned a great deal and continued to learn, each day increasing her knowledge. During all this the ape has gotten more and more red in the face, and can no longer contain himself, pressing a hand to his mouth, but then blurting out that he doesn't wish to say anything against Mother, she certainly has had outstanding success in raising the boys, which one can only envy, but fifty years ago people also knew how to raise children, back then a good spanking and that was it, while what is thought and done today is no advancement. Frau Director wrings her hands as she listens to this antiquated talk, wondering what it has to do with an evolved Western perspective, those are nothing but medieval methods, and those are medieval ideas, one can see what spanking has led to, there being no free people, but rather nothing but numerous enslaved souls, thieves, ruffians, murderers, as well as the many hellish thugs and sex criminals, while in a more ignorant time or with a less reasonable mother Irwin would by now already have come home with a venereal disease, though here that has been prevented from happening, spanking children on the behind also leading to the dangers of anal eroticism, as one day's spanking is the next day's sadism.

The Director is beet-red, beads of sweat springing up on his ape nose, his veins swelling up blue, as he yells that he has had enough of this nonsense, if his wife wants to feed on the slop she finds in her books and courses, then she'll have to do it in the Devil's name, but he forbids that his boys be further corrupted with these methods. This "pissiatrist" Dr. Brendel is no longer allowed in this house, otherwise there will be consequences, the Director slapping the table with the flat of his hand the entire time, then he jumps up and wants to leave and slam the door behind him, though at the last minute he composes himself and turns in the door, puts on a sugary-sweet smile and says almost tenderly, "Good night, Mother!" Then the ape quietly closes the door behind him, his wife quickly recovers from her shock and says next with satisfaction, "Just look, Josef, that will serve as evidence how right I am in my principles. From this you can hardly imagine what a lovely man he is, an angel, as I always say. But everything brings him worry and an unreasonable way of life, which traps him in this cycle." Josef has to continue to listen to such talk until at last he is able to go. He confesses how tired he is, it all being a lot to take in, and he needs to mull it over on his own, so he'd like to now go up to his room. "Good night, Josef, I'm quite pleased with you. You have a lovely kind of seriousness, though unfortunately you also seem to have bad nerves. But just wait, as soon as Dr. Brendel appears I will speak to him about you. Perhaps you are just animalistic, I mean anemic. Well then, good night, Josef, good night!" Anton leads Josef up the stairs and shows him his room, in which his suitcase already stands. Anton then departs quickly with a slight nod of the head, during which he gives a condescending and sardonic smile.

Finally Josef is alone. The room is larger and nicer than he had expected, but the air is heavy and stale. Josef goes to the window, before which there is a step that he climbs to open the window, outside of which is the garden, the night air not cold but full of a soft ringing, a light rain falling, Josef turning from the window and suddenly feeling happy without knowing why. The furniture is quite dapper, the entire accommodations quite comfy, it all looking similar to the boys' living room, yet simpler, and there-fore more appealing to Josef, only the two unframed paintings on the wall being not to his taste, for they look like mirrors, which he never likes, he only realizing up close that they are blank aluminum plates in the middle of which appear bright flecks and dabs of oil paint. Josef thinks to himself that this must indeed be the kind of art that Professor Bäumel admires, abstract and empty of life, though to Josef they seem disguised nonsense, form without mass and figure, he wanting to remove the paintings, they bother him, but they are firmly attached to the wall, so he takes a cloth from the table and covers them up.

Josef is depressed, feeling that tomorrow he should leave this house for

good, he feeling dazed, not knowing how anyone could take Frau Director
seriously and wondering how a professor at the university not only could
have recommended that he work as a tutor for a year but he had specifically
recommended this position, congratulating Josef when he got it. The Director is of course a businessman above all else, even somewhat genial, but
she is an unusually charming and intellectual lady, perhaps a bit high-
strung, though that's not so surprising amid so much culture, impressive intellectual interests, and a surprisingly well-rounded education. Josef would
have imagined things to be much different in this house, and he is ashamed
that he didn't handle himself better, for he shouldn't have remained silent
about a number of things, he being cowardly or not brave enough, but he
had to keep silent, for it was in the interest of the children and he has to act
on their behalf, or at least for Lutz, for isn't he adorable? No, Josef can't just
run off, he has a job to do, and he can't give up hope just because things fell
apart earlier, for perhaps the wife is better than she appears, and the professor was right about her being a bit high-strung, if not in fact way too high-
strung. But can any good come of it? No matter his doubts, Lutz needs his
help, and it's touching how such a mistreated child talks about animals and
plants, while Irwin had not yet made any such endearing impression on
Josef, he being the ice-cold son of a cool, if not weak, father.

Everything in this house is marvelous, but Lutz needs to be taken away,
he needs to be saved from it and yanked away from his parents. When the
boy raves about a microscope, his eyes shine as he starts to talk, his delicate
hands looking like his mother's, though more refined, while he has nothing
of his father in him, nor does Irwin, who is a very handsome boy, despite his
eyes drilling into you, his gaze never faltering. Lutz meanwhile sits completely still, his breathing inaudible, his microscope in front of him, he having adjusted the viewer, one eye closed, the other peering at the object
through a little round peephole, the right hand shifting the slide back and
forth, the left hand turning the knob, the picture becoming more clear, then
less clear, the object beautiful, the preparation a success. It's a continual
learning process, Lutz doesn't know what's going on around him, he not
hearing how his mother talks, as she talks constantly, because she can't stop
herself, she piling up strong words, though in a faulty Latin, her marriage a
happy one, the psychiatrist standing nearby, he admiring her soul and cap-

tivated by it. The spirit no longer has any connection with any object. It is all a quick view that is continually swept away, the object unattainable, no amount of enthusiasm doing any good, the hand turning and turning, the image never sharp.

Josef opens the door to the hall, all lights having been turned off, and even though it's not late, everyone here goes to bed early, the Director certainly already asleep, his wife reading *Ethics* or a book that Dr. Brendel recommended to her, something about blossoming neuroses or sublime cathedrals in the north of France, though probably not, it being too weighty a tome. Josef closes the door, but he listens hard, a thin thread of dance music audible, most likely a gramophone from the neighboring villa, the tones suddenly becoming louder, then becoming scratchy and muted and dissolving into single notes that can barely be heard and which the listener can transform into lovelier music on his own and to which he can add additional melodies until it all exudes its own richness. Thus it becomes dreamlike, and maybe now Lutz is enjoying a good dream. One shouldn't listen in on everything. Lutz is on a hike, just as he wanted. Josef goes to bed, the sheets cool and comfortable. He wants to read something, so he turns on the light, but the light flashes and makes a crackling sound, a short circuit, and then the room is dark. Amid his torpor Josef thinks about everything he has seen in this house, and then he sleeps.

THE CULTURAL CENTER

Professor Rumpler of course can't hire anyone at this time, he has enough people, and though it's clear that anyone would want to work for him, and he of course is happy to support ambitious young talent, one must also consider the times, everyone knows that things are bad in Germany today, it's a horrible time for intellectual matters everywhere in the world. "We continue to maintain, of course, our high intellectual standards, but what do you want to do here? You're a newly minted young doctor who studied, what, philosophy, but who knows nothing of life, can't do stenography, doesn't know how to write a proper letter on a typewriter, and yet here you stand with a heap of recommendations in your hand! Dash it all, I had to take my knocks in life first, and because of that I had no recommendations, I had to recommend myself. How old are you? I see, twenty-five. Do you know that I gave Schnitzler all the best ideas for his books? He was a talented writer and became famous, that was at the turn of the century. Do you think someone wrote me a recommendation for that? It doesn't matter, I built a position for myself, but of course everyone begrudges me my position, how few worries I have. You have no idea of the kinds of people who have worked for me; I could plaster the walls with university professors."

Josef stands quietly in the office of Professor Rumpler, who sits at an elegant desk, though it's hard to tell if it's made of wood, as the surface is covered with a heap of papers and books, a telephone, and a bust of Goethe made of waxed plaster, Professor Rumpler constantly reaching out to grab it by the crown, while in between he holds his own head and complains how no one knows the immense pressure the head of a cultural center has upon him. "You're constantly pulled to and fro, everyone wanting to put his two cents in, because he knows everything about the matter, though of course no one knows anything. What you think doesn't mean a thing, nor is it a question of taste, but you have to take precautions in order to defend democracy and freedom when they're threatened. But freedom, what is that? Goethe knew the answer, that's clear, but he didn't have to live in our times and take social and political precautions that I have to keep an eye on. You see, you have to make compromises if you want to balance the swastika with the Socialists. You also have to know the government's plans exactly and what it wants, in order to be careful. If I speak to someone on the left, then they scream that Rumpler is a Red, and then if I briefly talk to someone on the right, then the lefties start screaming that Rumpler is a Nazi. My friend, people begrudge Rumpler, but it's easy for people to run off at the mouth. Who today appreciates humanity and democracy? They don't mean anything, you might say, but you have no idea of the difficulties. Let me just show you what goes on here so that you'll get rid of your desire for a position in a cultural center. You should thank God that you're young. When I was young I had my whole life in front of me, and there was still a structure, the feudal and the liberal, and the emperor still ruled the people in a monarchy. But don't go running around and saying that Rumpler said he's for the monarchy, that's ridiculous, I'm not so backward, and I consider there to be no choice but to be for a democratic republic. Nonetheless I still say that people, classes, and religions understood one another better before 1914, but advances, yes advances, bring disadvantages along with them. Listen, my young doctor, you should write down everything I say, though I can't pay you any money, but it's a job for a young man, namely to write everything down, I'm ready to take on Goethe! You should do it voluntarily.

Nonsense, you'll say, but the board funds nothing, the state subvention is ridiculous, and also the school minister and the foreign minister and the President's Office all want this and that, numerous interests all competing with one another and never working together. But you should write it all down, the gathering of democratic powers, Switzerland a good example, my good friend Thomas Mann, dash it all, even he has to fight for his freedom. He should do a talk here so that we can fill the great hall once again. But, you see, no one comes to talks these days, education, who needs education? Lectures are a load of crap, and schools don't support us enough, so we give away free tickets, wads and wads of them, while tonight we have a lecture about the Red Cross, highly humanitarian, but what do you know, no one will be crowing for that, and yet you want a position? Do you know what you're asking? Everything eats up the tax revenues—health care, pensions— so how am I supposed to bring anything in? I don't even have time to chat with you, a million little tasks await me. You see, there are already people waiting outside, each of them wanting to speak to me, and I have no help, though there are requests to give lectures, concerts, courses, and various programs, all of them wanting to be on the radio or to take part in something. I can hardly keep up! If you want to become my Eckermann, dash it all, then you could learn a great deal and bring out a book, *Conversations with Rumpler!* Indeed, that could do well, why don't you write things down as I dictate them? Get a pad from Fräulein Grenadier, and learn stenography, but first show me your recommendations again. Well now, we'll see, first you need to have a look around, but a quick one. I don't know where my head is. You'll have to roll your sleeves up and dig right in, all of my men and women need, of course, to be hardworking. You need a strong measure of idealism in order to work with others, and there is no shame in having to take tickets, even I do that. Quite the opposite, it never hurt me, and with my bad heart! All of us do it, which is democratic. Of course I can't pay you much, you understand, the salary is small, but you will learn a great deal here, that's for sure, and you won't regret it. When I lie down for my final rest, perhaps you'll recall and say to your children what a character Rumpler was, a man, an upstanding man who always held high the flag of humanity. If a reconciliation between the Bolsheviks and the Fascists should ever occur, people will say that Rumpler dedicated himself to it, dash it all, having worked and fought for it, the popular reconciliation of free intellectuals, the symbolic renewal of Lessing and Beethoven, Nathan and Die Neunte! Dash it all, it's a difficult business! You have to sacrifice all your time, not a one of us works an eight-hour day. It's not like at a bank or in a store, where you can throw in the towel and have a party. Saturdays are never free, and even on Sunday someone has to be here to keep an eye on people. Do you have any idea what would be stolen if there were no monitors? The regular hours are from ten until one and three until eight, but at eight the lectures and everything else start, so each monitor has to stay until eight-thirty. My colleagues never go home before nine, and often it's ten or eleven. Not to mention that once a week each has evening duties until all the events are over. For overtime there is a tiny allowance, which takes care of everyone's needs. Now I'll show you the office, and tomorrow you can start."

Josef hasn't said a word, although he has tried to more than once, but Rumpler had only continued to indicate that he shouldn't be interrupted, his time is valuable, so he can't stop to listen to what others want to say to him, everyone wanting to talk to him, and where would he be then? Rumpler opens the door to the neighboring office, a tiny little room with two desks facing each other, on top of each an immense flood of disorganized newspapers, prospectuses, letters, baskets for records and files, parts of it all covered in a thick layer of dust, a couple of chairs there, as well as a door leading to the main administration office and the foyer. Dr. Horn sits in the little room, Rumpler's secretary, to whom Rumpler introduces Josef, saying, "I'm pleased to present a newly minted little doctor. You know, my dear Horn, that I need to take precautions, and the little doctor is gifted, the best recommendations, important ones, and I've seldom seen such talent, although of course somewhat inexperienced and green. I'll be counting on you, my dear Horn, to whip him into shape. You'll no doubt know, even though I don't yet, how the little doctor can be of help to us. What's your name again? Ah yes, Kramer, that's a memorable name. And so, my dear Horn, why don't you see what you can do, you never seem to be able to finish all your work, and maybe he can be of help to you. And you, little doctor, you must gather your wits and never forget that everything depends on trust, everything that happens is between us. Culture is a secret treasure that must be well managed, indeed, but you, my dear Horn, shouldn't smoke so much! Your voice has gotten husky again. Well then, shake hands, gentlemen, quickly, quickly! I don't have time! Come along, Doctor. Horn, drop in a bit later, we have lots to talk about. Doctor, did you hear me? Everyone here has to pitch in."

Rumpler pushes open the door to the main office. "I can't introduce you to everyone. Dash it all, you'll have to do that yourself. Ladies and gentlemen, I have here some help for you, a doctor. Now tell me your name again, I can't remember them all, Kramer, so this is Dr. Kramer, who will start tomorrow. Make sure that there's a spot for him. Everything of course is taken, each new addition an extra wheel on the wagon. Each has to elbow his way in and stake out his spot in the sun." The office is large, yet overfull, writing desks, other tables, some typewriters, a duplication machine, an area for the municipal and the house telephones, shelves on the walls with letter files, countless folders, forms, office supplies, and papers, all of it neglected and covered in dust, as if nothing had been put in order here for years, the tables so close together as to allow only small passageways in between, which you have to snake along in order to get to the workstations or the windows, pots, coffee cups, packets of food and leftovers lying all around. At least two men and three women seem to be busy working, but soon other employees appear, and Rumpler looks proud of the office. "Look, little doctor, this is my Reich. Everyone is diligent and loves their work. There isn't a single idle hand, everything runs like clockwork, each knowing his or her job and never wasting a free minute, this the center of the humanist spirit, and I am the father, I am the heart and soul!" Rumpler moves from workplace to workplace, his face serious as he asks each what he is doing. "Look, Doctor, it's a work collective. Dash it all, if only I didn't have to keep it all straight inside my head!"

Rumpler leads Josef into the next room, which is the business office, it looking similar to the main office, though a bit more tidy, there being a safe visible and some cabinets, the bookkeeper, the cashier, and an assistant working at three desks. Rumpler walks over to the cashier and wants to know what she is doing. Right now she is tallying the take from yesterday's lecture. "Fräulein Auer, that's taking much too long. Who reviews your numbers? Who tallies that? You don't seem to realize that it's not work meant for you. Who is there to correct any mistakes in your addition? It's just not right! Why should I just accept it as is?" Rumpler then turns to the bookkeeper. "Herr Krupka, you never do your job like you should. You are always behind on the books, what kind of accounting is that? Dash it all, if you don't know what Fräulein Auer is doing, Herr Krupka! You need to immediately review Fräulein Auer's receipts. There's no supervision involved if you review it side by side, because then you're all in it together. I will have to speak with Dr. Horn. Tomorrow I want to see a report for the current month, including tickets sold, the revenues, the classes of tickets, the courses, the cinema, the radio. Tell Dr. Horn, and please make a note of it, Herr Krupka. You never have a notepad at hand when I'm here. Fräulein Auer, take a note, a staff meeting for tomorrow, detailed reports for the current month, make sure to remind me about it! As you see, Doctor, I have to be everywhere. Fräulein, get a pad from Herr Krupka. What, you have no notepads, Herr Krupka? We got some new ones just last week, but they're all gone already? Well, Fräulein Grenadier has some, this I know. Talk to Fräulein Grenadier in order to get a notepad. Take pride, my good man, I can't always show up in accounting and help you, you have to take care of things yourself. If you'd like, after I get done with the radio at eleven we could tally up everything together. What's that, Fräulein Auer, unfortunately you're busy? No, don't tell me, you have a new admirer? Heh-heh, an admirer! Then I guess we'll soon have to look for a new cashier. What's that, Doctor, you'd very much like to be the cashier? It's a good job, full of responsibility, a great deal actually, but the work is not hard, no stenography, no typewriters, only the receipts need to add up, a little bit of adding is all that's needed. So you don't want to? What am I supposed to do with you? This is what is sent to me on recommendation! Well then, come along, come along!"

Rumpler suddenly dashes out of the business office, Josef following him into his office, where the Professor throws himself into his desk chair and motions for Josef to sit as well, as Rumpler holds his head in his hands and the telephone rings. "But Fräulein Grenadier, you can't just send anyone off the street in to see me, I'm not in, I'm wherever you want to say I am. Ridiculous! I'm not available for just any editor. What? It's something important? There's nothing important, I'm just overwhelmed. Tell him to call back at seven, or tomorrow. That's time enough. Dash it all, I already know how important it is and that I need to talk about it on the radio. Adieu, adieu!" Rumpler slams the phone down. "Now you see, Doctor, how much I am harassed. Everyone wants to use me! They climb the heights of humankind without impunity. I'm supposed to take care of everyone, and that's the way it goes each day, I have to bend over backward continually! Look, here I have some perfume, some herbal drops, which the doctor prescribed. I have a sore throat, I'm always hoarse, I'm too nervous, I really need a rest! Next month is the earliest I can go to Switzerland, on business, of course, for there's something I have to do in Switzerland, that blessed land still full of humanity and freedom like in *William Tell*, though Zurich exhausts me. Dash it all, how I have to run around there, and they also want me in Basel and Bern. At least I'll be able to get to Interlaken over the weekend in order relax a bit, but then I have to be back here, otherwise everyone will be pulling their hair out, and I have to handle everything and keep the peace. But off with you, little doctor, at least you've gotten a whiff of what goes on here, so goodbye, and give it your all! Yes, take it all down, you don't know anything yet! Well then, until tomorrow, when we'll see each other again, and you can start to write it all down."

Josef bows lightly and wants to head through the door into the foyer, but Rumpler takes a stack of papers and says, "Take these to Herr Krupka, he needs to have a look at them. No one knows what to make of them, but he'll know. He should be ready to report back at the staff meeting tomorrow. Note it, Doctor, note it, you'll never remember it all. You need to write it down! Where would we be if we never wrote things down? You just need to head over there, even if Herr Krupka is not there when he should be there, or he's settling accounts with someone, and before you know it the appointment with me is indeed forgotten. Or you tell someone else, who then forgets to arrange for it to happen. But then you have paper and a fountain pen, although it doesn't write because you've no ink at home, and you've forgotten your pencil as well. Then here, take a pencil. What's that, it doesn't write? Aha, no point, then get a pencil and a sharpener from Fräulein Grenadier! I want to help you, Doctor. Make sure to come to me if you need anything, or if you hear something, sense something, even if it's something small and particular, and make sure to write it all down! Well then, off with you now, go and tell Dr. Horn that I need to see him, he should stop in!"

Josef opens the door to the secretary's office as if entering a dream, weighted down with papers for Herr Krupka, stammering a goodbye as he leaves, though the Professor is no longer concerned with Josef, who simply wants to close the door, which slips from his hands and slams behind him. Josef sees Dr. Horn, who lights a cigarette with a still glowing butt. "Herr Doctor, the Professor would like to see you." Dr. Horn doesn't take his cigarette out of his mouth, casts a scornful look at Josef, and says through his teeth, "I'm still hard at work, young man!" Josef steps farther into the office and encounters glances that are part mistrustful and part ironic, as someone asks him where he's headed with the stack of papers. The Professor gave him these to bring to Herr Krupka. "That's fine. Just head on in, Herr Krupka will be pleased." Josef enters the business office, Fräulein Auer is still bent over her receipts, though she really isn't paying attention to them, but instead lights a cigarette that she then unconsciously lays on the table, which already has plenty of burn marks, as Fräulein Auer sits with a bottle of nail polish in front of her and paints her nails. "So you want to work with us? Great idea! Are you related to Rumpler?" Josef says no. "Well then, I didn't mean anything by it. It's nice here. You'll see. Do you need something from me? You can see that I'm busy. I can take down your information first thing tomorrow."—"No, Fräulein, the Professor asked me to bring these papers to Herr Krupka."—"Then bring them over!" Krupka, who has just taken a bite out of a sausage sandwich, calls to Josef, "What a lovely heap. What am I supposed to do with it? What did the old man say?"—"Herr Krupka, I'm afraid I don't know. Professor Rumpler said so much, I can't quite remember it all. Something to do with having a look at these and a staff meeting tomorrow."—"Well, thanks then. When are you gonna start?"—"Tomorrow."—"Already tom'w? You're in quite a hurry to join our cultural bordello! Well, I wish you a lot of luck. The old man seems to like you. He never took a new guy on a tour of the office before." Josef has nothing else to say, so he takes his leave of Krupka and Fräulein Auer, though she tells him that she has only one cigarette left and is wondering if she could borrow three from the Herr Doctor, she'll return them tomorrow, though Josef has none on him. Then Fräulein Auer complains that she won't be able to smoke anymore today, for she had lent some cigarettes to Dr. Horn, who either gives them back too late or not at all, and tonight she has evening

duty, so Josef should do her the pleasure of going to Frau Lawetzer and seeing if she can send over a couple. Josef doesn't know who Frau Lawetzer is.
That's the woman in the ticket office in the vestibule, and all Josef needs to
do is head over and say that Fräulein Auer sent him.

Josef goes down to the ticket office, but Frau Lawetzer is on the telephone taking a ticket order, two people also standing there waiting. Frau
Lawetzer has tickets for the cinema and other tasks in front of her, and she's
nervous, saying that she can't take an order by telephone right now, there's
a long line of people waiting and she has to take care of them. "What, you
want tickets for next Wednesday? There's plenty of time! Why are you ordering them already today? I don't even have the tickets for then yet, 'cause
the tickets for next week come on Friday." She cannot take an order that far
ahead, she's sorry, she has to hang up now, goodbye. Then she takes care of
a man who wants two tickets for the cinema that evening, but good seats in
the middle, he asking if the film is a good one, for he had heard it was miserable, though all he knows is this is where his wife wants him to take her
tonight. Frau Lawetzer says she has good tickets in the middle, but they are
the last, and the film is certainly not miserable, for Herr Klinger books only
good films. Then the man asks who Herr Klinger is, and she says that's the
man who orders the films for us. And is he not capable of making a bad
choice? Why would he book a bad movie when there are good ones, though
Frau Lawetzer has not seen the film herself, she hardly ever goes to the cinema, because she doesn't like how the movie flickers. The woman standing
behind the man then begins to ask about tickets, but Frau Lawetzer says, "I
get dizzy so easily." The woman says that she can't stand around forever,
they should get on with it, but then the man says that he doesn't want to buy
a bill of goods, so if he's going to go to the Bio the film must be reputable.
The woman says she has absolutely no more time, for her time has been
taken up already, she is due to play bridge at the Café Conti, she's needed as
a fourth. Then Frau Lawetzer declares that the man should decide, but he
has to think it over some more, so he lets the woman go first, he needs to
look at the seating plan more closely, he asking the cashier for the seat numbers as he stands to the side and buries himself in the seating plan, the
woman stepping up, but then the telephone rings again, Frau Lawetzer
making a face as she says, "You see, my dear madame, they are always after

me, and for this I'm hardly paid anything!" She has nothing but hassle, she should have quit long ago, except that she needs the work so badly, but the woman says that she should pick up the receiver, the ringing of the telephone is enough to do anyone in, so the cashier picks up the receiver and says, "Hello, Frau Lawetzer here." This time it's the in-house telephone, it soon becoming clear that Fräulein Auer is on the other end, as the cashier states that she can't be disturbed right now, her hands are completely full, well then, fine, the Fräulein should come down and help her if she believes that working the ticket booth is such a piece of cake, Frau Lawetzer would be just as pleased to loll around upstairs, reading newspapers and gabbing away. What? Cigarettes? A new employee? No, no one had spoken to her, there must be a mistake, but then Josef calls out that he's the new employee, and Frau Lawetzer says into the telephone, "Leave me be until I have time to speak with the new employee."

Frau Lawetzer sighs as she lays the receiver back in its cradle, but it rings again right away, and the cashier answers, "Hello, Frau Lawetzer here . . . ah, yes, my pleasure, Professor . . . yes, I always say 'Cultural Center, Ticket Sales' . . . Tickets for the Auchlicht lecture? . . . What's the name of the lecture again? . . . 'The Role of Hormones in Our Life' . . . I have no tickets for a lecture on hormones here . . . I can't, Professor, I have people waiting . . . Yes, later . . . also the Red Cross . . . I'll call you back . . . Yes, goodbye." Frau Lawetzer shakes her head doubtfully. "There you have it, my dear madame, the old man does that to me all the time! How am I supposed to sell tickets? Well then, what can I do for you?"—"I actually want tickets for the Auchlicht lecture."—"Auchlicht? Auchlicht? Oh, the one about hormones! Wait, let me have a look." Frau Lawetzer looks for the tickets but can't find them. "I don't have any tickets for it down here. They must still be up in the office. Now I remember. That's the block that still needs to be stamped, Fräulein Auer must have them upstairs. If you just wanted to head up to the office yourself."—"But for the last three days it said in the newspaper that advance sales are available. This is outrageous! That's always the way it goes at the Cultural Center!"—"Please, my dear madame, I just work here. You need to bring it up with the old man, tell it to Professor Rumpler!"—"I'm not going to your professor. I want the tickets, and right now! It says so in the newspaper!"—"But, please, don't get so upset. I can only sell what I have here in the booth. If you want, I can make a note. I'll reserve some for you. How many do you need?"—"Normally I wouldn't go to a lecture on hormones, but Dr. Auchlicht is a cousin of my sister-in-law's. So I have to. I don't want to cause you any trouble. But do you have any tickets or not?"—"I don't have any. I already said, I can make a note, or you have to go up to the office."—"Well then, for God's sake, make a note! Four tickets. Good seats. Will there be slides?"—"How am I supposed to know? Under what name, please?"—"Weislicht. Why don't you know if there will be slides or not? Do you know anything at all?"— "Weislicht. Please, with a round 's' or sharp 's'?"—"With a round one. But I want to know whether there will be slides."—"You'll have to ask about that upstairs."—"Well then, four tickets for Weislicht to see Auchlicht." The woman leaves in a huff, then Frau Lawetzer sticks her head a ways out the window. "So then, have you decided, my dear sir?" He has decided and wants the seats, the cashier ripping the desired tickets from the block, the man wishing to pay with a large banknote, though Frau Lawetzer hasn't enough change for it, and asks for a smaller bill. Unfortunately, the man doesn't have one. Then Frau Lawetzer calls to the new employee, but he can't change it either, so she asks how well he knows his way around the building. He knows only where the office is. To that Frau Lawetzer says that's all he needs to know, and would he be so kind as to pop up to Fräulein Auer and ask her for some change? Josef is ready to do so, but asks if he couldn't take along the cigarettes at the same time. No, that won't do, first she has to see if she has any, and Fräulein Auer should let her be, there are people at the ticket booth, business has to be taken care of first.

Josef runs upstairs, the door to the office is shut, so he has to knock, and while he waits he reads the announcement that's attached to the door:

VISITING HOURS
Secretary's Office open 5–6 P.M.
Daily except Saturday & Sunday
Director only by Appointment
Office Visits NOT Allowed

A young boy named Michel opens the door and Josef steps into the drab, murky foyer, where there is a table with a dirty green cloth and a couple of chairs, a few people sitting and waiting, as one of them says to Michel what a scandal it is, such miserable lighting, the kind a cultural center should be ashamed of, though Michel replies, "Please, it's not my fault. I'm not allowed to turn on any lights. The Professor gets upset if they are left burning while not used."—"Oh, give me a break, your professor can't just let the visitors sit here in the dark!" Michel responds that if there are visitors, then he can turn on the lights, but only then, and now at least a stronger lightbulb has been put in, one with twenty-five watts instead of fifteen. Meanwhile, there are three doors leading off the foyer, to the right the DIRECTOR, in the middle the SECRETARY, to the left the MAIN OFFICE, and in red below it ENTRY STRICTLY FORBIDDEN! Josef needs to enter in order to find Fräulein Auer, but Michel calls out that no one is allowed in, the Professor is in the building, which means that no one can enter the office, Michel has been instructed so, and that's what it also says on the door. Josef says that Michel must surely have seen him in there earlier, and now Frau Lawetzer has sent him to find Fräulein Auer in order to get some change. Unfortunately, Michel doesn't back down and says that it's not allowed, he can apply in writing to any of the gentlemen, but not to Fräulein Auer but rather to the Professor, though that is not possible today, as all the visiting hours have been taken, all of these people are waiting, the Professor never sees more than two or three per day, though Michel can try Dr. Horn, if Josef would be good enough to write down his name, the date, and the purpose of his visit. Josef tries to explain that tomorrow he will be working here himself, and that Michel should not hold him up, for he must see Fräulein Auer, because Frau Lawetzer really needs change, but Michel maintains that he knows nothing about that, and that others have tried saying this or that in order to get into the main office, though Michel is at least willing to tell Fräulein Auer that a man is looking to speak to her, but at that moment Dr. Horn opens the door of the secretary's office in order to greet a visitor, and so Josef quickly calls out, "Herr Doctor, I need to see Fräulein Auer, but this young man won't let me in." Horn laughs as much as the cigarette in his mouth will allow. "How dutiful, Dr. Kramer, I'm pleased to say. You want to see Auer? Then you can also tell her that she should give me a cigarette, which I guarantee she'll have back in the morning. Bring the cigarette to me in the office!" Michel makes a dumb face and wants to say something, yet Dr. Horn informs him, "It's okay. Dr. Kramer starts with us tomorrow."

Horn accompanies a visitor into the office, and finally Josef can head in as well, though Fräulein Grenadier stops him and wants to know where he's been, but Josef begs her pardon and says that he will tell her later, right now he has to pass on a request to Fräulein Auer from Frau Lawetzer, and as he explains all this the door of the office suddenly opens and Professor Rumpler appears, saying, "Dash it all, how nice, Fräulein Grenadier! Aren't you ashamed to already be trying to rope in the young doctor? You know how I value secrecy! And I expected more from you than gossip and spying! Didn't I say that everything here stays between us? No visitor's pass for you, Doctor!" Both want to counter the Professor's remarks, but he doesn't want to hear all the reasons for Josef's appearance in the office and begins to reprimand him, Rumpler regretting that he has already given Josef his word, otherwise there would be no position for someone who is not capable of doing honor to the persons who had recommended him, the Professor wishing to take this opportunity to rub his nose in this very fact. Then Josef pulls himself together and to the surprise of everyone is heard to say, "Excuse me, Herr Professor, but I have not broken your trust, nor have I done anything wrong."—"You're talking nonsense, Doctor! Trust? I don't even know you. No one in the world holds any trust. Dash it all, you have to earn that first, or do you think we all show up at the Cultural Center trusting one another already?"—"I want to earn your trust, Herr Professor. You sent me to Herr Krupka."—"And to do that you need to stand here gabbing for half an hour? Do you think my employees should be stealing away time to chat with you?"

Before Josef can answer, a man appears who wants to visit the business office, but Rumpler stops him and asks whether Herr Puttrich knows that he is the concierge and that he shouldn't be away from his station at this hour, because of course any number of people could come traipsing in, which would make for a fine mess, there being no way to monitor them, and so Puttrich should go back down to his station, though Puttrich shakes his head vigorously, saying he's sorry, but he has to see Fräulein Auer. Rumpler says that there is nothing Puttrich could possibly need from Auer. To this Puttrich responds, unperturbed, that Frau Lawetzer sent him and it's urgent. The Professor shouts that that is unheard of, but perhaps now Puttrich was taking orders from old Lawetzer, though there's no way of knowing what the old cow has in mind, for she's not in charge of anyone, though perhaps she had called him on the telephone, as her job is to sit in her spot and sell tickets, but then how is it that she approached Puttrich and sent him up here? Herr Puttrich explains that she didn't leave her booth and had only called, but Rumpler yells that she has no reason to call at all, so why did she, and even if she did there was no reason for Puttrich to leave his station, either. Undaunted, the concierge replies that Frau Lawetzer needs change and has sent him to get some, but at this the Professor loses all patience. "What, then, does she have a telephone for? Why didn't she call Auer?" He opens the door to the business office and calls Fräulein Auer, who sits there with her lipstick and smiles at the Professor, who yells, "What kind of plot is this? Why don't you give Lawetzer the change she needs?"

Then Michel comes up to him and says, "Excuse me, but there's a man here. I told him that he isn't allowed to go any farther. But he says he wants to burn down this den of thieves and wants his money back." Michel hardly finishes talking when the man storms in who wanted to pay for the cinema tickets with a large note, as the Professor approaches him and asks, "What do you want? You don't have an appointment! Not just any Tom, Dick, and Harry can show up here!" The man turns away from Rumpler. "Don't bother me! I don't want anything to do with you! Kindly let me through! This young man is supposed to be getting my money for me!" The man wants to get to Josef, but Rumpler positions himself proudly and angrily in the way. "Let me inform you that I'm the one you have to deal with, because I am Rumpler, Director Professor Dr. Kamill Rumpler, the Head of the Cultural Center!"—"As far as I'm concerned, you can be whoever you like, but this nasty business is going to appear in all the papers!" He pushes the Professor roughly to the side and is already standing in front of Josef, who gives back the man's bill with a stammering apology, an act that no one except Fräulein Auer and Fräulein Grenadier understand, as Fräulein Grenadier explains, "See, Herr Professor, you didn't want to listen to what I knew about the situation. The man wanted to buy some tickets, Frau

Lawetzer had no change, and so she sent Dr. Kramer to Fräulein Auer with
the bill that belonged to the man, in order to get it changed." Rumpler yells
in response, "Everything goes crazy, unless I take care of it myself."

Then suddenly Rumpler turns calmly toward the man, who doesn't
know what's happened, and sheepishly gives him his money back. "What
is your name, my dear sir?" The man stammers, "My . . . my name is
Krönert."—"Herr Krönert, indeed, how nice, for I always wanted to meet
you. We know each other, don't we? Dash it all, Krönert, Krönert, help me
now, Herr Krönert, help me! Perhaps if you told me your occupation . . ."—
"I work at the Central Agency for Agricultural Loans."—"Of course, Krönert from the Central Agency! My good friend Zenkl works there, isn't that
true?"—"Zenkl, yes Zenkl is the director."—"I'm very close with him, Herr
Krönert, please pass on my greetings, for he is my best friend, a splendid
man that Zenkl, so noble, cultivated! No surprise that he surrounds himself
with men like you, Herr Krönert! You look a lot like him. If you'll allow me,
I'll put in a good word with Zenkl for you, for of course you deserve a promotion, a good one. You're interested in agriculture, was your father perhaps an agrarian?"—"No, my father was a civil servant in the Justice
Department. My grandfather ran a small farm."—"Of course, your grandfather, that's right Herr Krönert, not your father, who of course had an important job working for the courts, indeed, an outstanding career! Are you
at all interested in the law?"—"Not really."—"It doesn't matter, my friend,
not all of us can be judges and lawyers! There have to be other professions
and hobbies. Certainly you have hobbies—reading, perhaps? Music? Com-
posing your own?"—"My hobby is raising canaries."—"Terrific, Herr
Krönert, it suits you well! Have you ever spoken on the radio about it? No,
really not? We really need something about raising canaries, interest in it
continues to rise, top prices paid, it'll draw! You should make a note, we
have an open spot next month that we could move you into, a talk about canaries!"—"I've never spoken on the radio."—"No backing down, my dear
sir! Rumpler won't stand for it! You have a wonderful voice for the micro-
phone! A terrific timbre! No, it's true indeed, very musical, much like the
canary, those little cheepers! Am I not right, Fräulein Grenadier? We'll do
up a contract in a jiffy? Make a note of it, Herr Schrimpl, a contract for Herr
Krönert, with the usual honorarium! Thank you, Herr Krönert, how nice of

you to do it! I'll make sure to listen in when you're on. I don't have any time, but I'll listen in!"—"Thank you, Herr Director. I don't know what I've done to deserve such kindness." Then the Professor embraces Herr Krönert and says, "My dear friend, dash it all, I'm the one who is in your debt! Canary-raising is something that needs to be supported! We've never had a lecture on that. I thank you deeply, it was a pleasure, it's all settled, and didn't you want tickets for the cinema?"—"Yes, Herr Director."—"A wonderful film, excellent, you'll laugh until your sides split."—"It's actually a tragic film, Herr Director."—"Doesn't matter, my dear sir, a wonderful film, gripping, I wept openly! Fräulein Auer, please give Herr Krönert free passes, loge seats, indeed as many as he wants, and so goodbye, it was a pleasure, it's all settled!"

After Rumpler says goodbye to Krönert, some of the employees want to speak to the Professor, but he insists that there be no more, for he can't keep track of his own head, no one helps him, he has to be off, an important call, the radio, a pressing meeting. "Puttrich, a taxi, but hurry! I'll be back soon, no one leave, we'll have a staff meeting, very important, the young doctor should also hang about! I had a call from the Education Minister about our subvention. Tomorrow the commission meets. Everything has to be prepared tonight, so we'll need every typewriter to be free, no writing radio plays for now, just reports, reports! There won't be any staff meeting tomorrow, since I have to be at the Ministry!" Rumpler wants his coat, hat, and cane from Michel, who says, "But there are still three men waiting and a woman. They all have appointments and have been waiting for a while. They've been here a couple of times before already. Please, they can't wait any longer."

"Be quiet, Michel, I have to go! Dash it all, I can't be in two places at once! I don't know anything, no one tells me anything, I also have to wait on the Ministry, but Professor Rumpler is always supposed to have time for everyone. Michel, tell those people to come back tomorrow, next week, but not today, I'm sorry, but let me see the list. Frau Butterwegh, Schrimpl, who is Frau Butterwegh? Do I know her? Can she do something for us? Does she need something? Has she been here before?" Schrimpl replies, "Herr Professor, that's the one who is always here. Once every three months she sings. On the recommendation of Deputy Assistant Under-Secretary

Kratochvil."—"Kratochvil, Kratochvil, somewhat important, that's good. Schrimpl, speak with Frau Butterwegh, give her something, ten minutes, fifteen minutes, that's too much, agreed. Next, Klebinder. Who is Klebinder? Don't I know a Klebinder, let me see, who is Klebinder?" No one knows. "Someone get Dr. Horn!" He's dragged in, having been busy with a visitor. "Why weren't you there when we called for you, Dr. Horn?"— "Herr Professor, I have someone inside, very important, a good lecture. It will draw well!"—"Nonsense, my little Horn, nothing will draw, it can wait, throw him out! Visiting hours are over. Report to the staff meeting, please make a note, Horn, this Klebinder, who is Klebinder? Who can he be?"— "Klebinder? Is that someone who once rented the hall? I believe we once had someone rent the hall who was named Klebinder. Krupka would know. Fräulein Auer, tell Krupka to come!" Fräulein Auer gets him, and the Profesor says, "Now, Krupka, I always have to check with you. Do you know this Klebinder? Klebinder?" Krupka asks in return, "Who is Klebinder?"— "Dash it all, Klebinder! Klebinder is Klebinder. Who can he be?"—"How should I know, Herr Professor?" Dr. Horn then says, "Herr Krupka, didn't we once have a Klebinder? A Klebinder rented the hall?"—"That could be. I'll have to check."—"Could be! Dash it all, Herr Krupka, if you could just keep something straight in your head for once! The new young doctor should help out in the business office. Look up Klebinder, report on Klebinder in the staff meeting, make a note of it, that's that! What else is there Michel?"—"Excuse me, but you have the list in your hand."—"Ah, I see, but why doesn't anyone help me. Here it says Kruczkewicz. You could break your teeth on that. Kruczkewicz?" Schrimpl chimes in, "He's a troublemaker, Herr Professor, he always wants to get on the radio. He's terrible and boring." But then Dr. Horn adds, "We have to take him. You know why already, Herr Professor." Horn whispers something into his ear, and Rumpler replies, "What a pain, arrange something with him, I can't even say the name. Let me know what happens, but not today, it can wait. What else? Kummerhackl, everything starts with 'K' today! Who is Kummerhackl? Oh yes, he has written a book. My dear Horn, I gave you a copy, you should report on it. Is it any good? Can he do something for us?"—"I gave you a report. You urged me to get it to you last week. It's on your desk in the topmost folder. Recommended by the Railway Ministry."—"My dear Horn, you shouldn't smoke so much. Dash it all, in the topmost folder! How often have I said to place it in my hands! Look for it, for I've not seen a thing, or do up a new report, and fast! Didn't I tell you that Kummerhackl was recommended by important people? You yourself said the railway. Talk to him, my dear Horn, I've got too much to handle, remind me what the book is about, I want to read it, but when, I don't know, I haven't any time! I'd very much like to have Kummerhackl. . . ."

The door opens and there stands a man with a red beard, clearly upset, as he yells without looking around, "I want nothing more to do with this stinking business! You can tell your Director Rumpler that Götz von Berlichingen is here! He cannot leave me waiting!" Rumpler turns around quick as a flash and says pleasantly, "With whom do I have the pleasure of speaking? I am Professor Rumpler."—"My name is Kummerhackl." Rumpler grabs his hand and doesn't let it go. "My dear Kummerhackl, it's indeed you! Indeed, what a joy it is to meet you!" Kummerhackl continues to talk loudly. "Three months ago I personally dropped off a copy of my book, *The Solution to the Social Question: A Practical Plan for the People of Europe.* I also followed up in writing. Then for the last three days I have shown up in person and each time waited at least two hours! Now I'm fed up!"—"My dear Kummerhackl, you must watch your nerves! Please, give me your hand, I see, a very fast pulse, you should not get so excited. My goodness, I'd hate to get so excited. You would not believe the beating that my nerves take, but one has to maintain self-control, please note, you have to take care of yourself! Your book is wonderful, full of new and clever ideas, reconciling people through their shared humanity. We all suffer from the problems of society. It's so important to solve them, you could even speak to the President, indeed, a practical plan, what an idea! Puttrich, quickly fetch two cups of mocha! Puttrich, the taxi! Fräulein Grenadier, call the radio and tell them I'm on my way! Dash it all, one has to control one's nerves. No, come along, my dear Kummerhackl, I've been wanting to talk to you about your book. My dear little Horn, you come along as well, of course with another cigarette already in your mouth, come along, before the taxi is here in two minutes' time." Rumpler then ushers Herr Kummerhackl into his office, and Horn follows.

Fräulein Auer asks Josef to take Herr Krönert, who meanwhile has been planning his radio talk with Schrimpl, to Frau Lawetzer and to give her the request for two free tickets, as Herr Krönert thanks her and bows to everyone there. Josef is also reminded to bring cigarettes for Fräulein Auer, she has no more to smoke, then the two men head downstairs, Herr Krönert wanting to know if the Cultural Center always seemed like a mental hospital, he having had little to do with it and yet now finding it incomprehensible, he'll have to tell Zenkl about it all. Then he asks Josef to tell him how one should go about preparing a radio talk, for Krönert has never done one before, Herr Schrimpl having recommended ten minutes on "Our Yellow-feathered Friend at Home," he needing to get the manuscript in within ten days, typed, and no more than 150 lines long, with no more than sixty characters per line, but Josef explains that he cannot be of help, today is his first day at the Cultural Center and he, too, is amazed by everything, to which Krönert says, "Indeed, it is amazing. You know, I don't know anything about culture. But if there is any culture here, it must be pretty lousy if such a man is in charge of it." Thus the two of them arrive at the ticket booth, where Frau Lawetzer is even busier as she hands out tickets to some people and is nervous, though Josef attempts to keep Herr Krönert from having to wait any longer by approaching the window from the other side, while those waiting complain about his bad manners and how everyone needs to wait in line, though Josef explains that he is there with instructions from the Director. Everyone then says, ah, the Director, well then why don't you do something to improve things around here, the dreck you put on for films lasts a minimum of two weeks before there's a new program, it's the worst cinema in the city, and it's only funded because it's a cultural center, but the films are a cultural scandal, the lectures get worse and worse, the members no longer have any privileges, and they're just treated like cattle, that's what you can tell Rumpler upstairs. Josef has to listen to this and much more, as he begs their pardon, for it's just a little matter that he has to take care of, and so he's allowed to step up to the booth, where he gives the order to the cashier, though she explains that she cannot do anything about this request, it has to be signed by the Herr Professor, or at the very least by Dr. Horn and Herr Klinger, Fräulein Auer's signature being no good, she has been chewed out by the old man whenever she accepts just any signature, so she can't do so now. Josef then asks what he should do, the man has been waiting so long already, and Professor Rumpler himself had given the order, but the cashier repeats that she can't do anything, the best thing would be for Josef to go up again and get the right signature. He'd be happy to do so, but he asks Frau Lawetzer whether she can give him any cigarettes for Fräulein Auer. The cashier gets angry and complains, it's not a time for cigarettes, you should appreciate that the customers are impatient and are complaining about the management, those waiting heartily joining in to support her, telling him that he should ask Rumpler to start keeping a better eye on things, otherwise he'll be mucking out his stall for good. Josef has to shyly back off, as he soothes Herr Krönert and asks him to be patient, none of this difficulty is his fault, but he will make sure to get the right signature or bring down Fräulein Auer herself. Herr Krönert doesn't seem as impatient as earlier and says, "The way things are run here seems really quite interesting."

So Josef runs upstairs and rings the bell, but after ringing twice neither Michel nor anyone else comes, though a different door suddenly opens, after which the door to the stairs is opened by Rumpler, who is with Herr Kummerhackl, the Professor wanting to know what the young doctor now wants, and why he still doesn't have a key to the office, he should get one from Herr Krupka, though Josef just asks for the Professor's signature on the note from Fräulein Auer for Herr Krönert, but Rumpler responds, "Krönert, who is Krönert? I don't know any Krönert. I'm not signing anything. You're not scheduled to start here for another day, Doctor, so if I sign anything now we'll have to pay you extra! Dash it all, I could spend all day signing things, everyone wants Rumpler's autograph. I'm sorry, Doctor, but no way, Doctor, no way!" Josef says, "The man with the canary birds!" Rumpler, however, isn't listening and wants to head downstairs, but that doesn't happen, as a man and a woman pounce on him and the woman yells, "An outrageous injustice, Herr Professor, only ten minutes for Butterwegh! Please give me the fifteen minutes that an artist of my stature demands! I cannot successfully sing three Schubert lieder in ten minutes!" Rumpler replies, "What do you mean, successfully sing Schubert? Sing Beethoven or Bach if you can't do Schubert in ten minutes, but fifteen minutes, that's out of the question, we are overbooked, goodbye, a pleasure, take a note, go see Herr Schrimpl. Go see whomever you like, but not me! Come see me when

284 / H. G. ADLER

I have time, it will be a pleasure, Frau Butterwegh!"—"But when will you ever find time for me? I need to speak to you right now!"—"I don't know, I don't know, ask Dr. Horn, he knows when I'm free. Please don't keep me any longer, I simply must go!"

Rumpler wants to leave, but the man stands in his way such that the Professor has to almost walk over him, the man not flinching as he holds Rumpler tight by his sleeve, saying, "Just a second, Herr Professor. My name is Klebinder. Last year I rented the little hall. It's a charitable function. Not political. We need three rehearsals and then the evening itself. But it has to be cheaper than last year. We have a very ambitious program. It involves conservation."—"That's not my concern, not my concern!" yells Rumpler. "Dash it all, we also could use some charity and conservation here at the Cultural Center! There you are, my dear Kummerhackl, just see how we are badgered. I can't manage it all! Meanwhile, social issues are the rub, and you want to talk about them on the radio and read from your book! Only politics matters these days. The only question you hear is, red or brown? Social issues no longer matter, for they've gone the way of human rights, for humanity is outmoded, and yet you still want to talk about it. It still existed for Goethe, indeed, but no one wants anything more to do with social issues!" Herr Klebinder returns to the issue of the rental cost with the Professor, who turns to him and says, "Yes, Herr Klebinder, what is it you really want from me? It's the same situation as with Herr Kummerhackl. Do you think the Cultural Center is in the business of handing out charity? You don't know today's audience. You sit at home and a write a book while sitting next to your stove and now want to turn it into a charity. Excellent, but who will buy it? Who wants it? It won't fly, my good man, the times for that are gone. Maybe before the war, but not today, for we can't even fill the room for the Red Cross, and you expect us to raise conservation to the level of culture! I can hear the chickens laughing all the way in southern Calabria! It's the same everywhere. Just ask Managing Editor Heinichen or the theater director Wenzig, none of it sells anymore! No one even puts on *William Tell* today. We did that with Wenzig for the schools, spectacular sets, a splendid production, reduced ticket prices, and a completely empty auditorium, which we had to fill with staff, just imagine! I'll have to think about it, my good man, but meanwhile take care. Now, then, Herr Kummerhackl, you must of course come along with me, but hurry, the taxi is waiting, Puttrich, I'm on my way!" Now Rumpler hurries off, Kummerhackl following him, but Michel suddenly appears, saying, "Please, Herr Professor! You're wanted urgently on the phone!" Rumpler shouts up the stairs that he's not available, and Michel yells into the office, "Sorry, Fräulein Grenadier, the Professor has already left!" It does no good for the Fräulein to run out, as the Professor is already gone, but someone opens a window in the office and yells down to him in the street that the general director of the radio wants to speak with him on the phone, and Rumpler replies, "I've already left!" He then climbs into a taxi, Kummerhackl following behind, and they're gone.

Everything quiets down after Rumpler's departure. Herr Schrimpl sits comfortably at his desk, unfolding a newspaper and casually unpacking items from a package, reading as simultaneously ten pieces of cake and torte from a bakery appear, at which Schrimpl tells Michel to bring a pitcher of water, but let the tap run so it's cold. Josef asks whether Dr. Horn is in, to which Schrimpl replies, yes indeed, but no one can enter right now, because he just had a visitor and needs a moment to himself, Josef asking for Herr Klinger, though he learns that he's been down in the cinema for a while. Josef then explains what he's there for, namely about Herr Krönert, at which Schrimpl laughs, knowing the man still doesn't have his loge seats and asking Josef to show him the note, at which he observes, aha, once again Lawetzer has refused to accept Auer's signature, adding, "Herr Dr. Kramer, every new employee at the Cultural Center has stumbled much like you. This mishap has occurred because Lawetzer used to give out free tickets for the most preposterous of reasons conjured up by everyone here, until Rumpler threw a huge fit. We'll just ring Lawetzer again." Herr Schrimpl chews his cake piece by piece and doesn't move from his spot, even though Josef says that Herr Krönert must indeed be growing impatient downstairs, Schrimpl chuckling, yes, one needs patience around here, you can't just lock horns with anyone, for even if you don't the Professor will badger you anyway, but first Schrimpl needs to eat, and then he will call Lawetzer, though Josef grows truly impatient, until at last Schrimpl says good-naturedly, "Hand the note here."

Schrimpl slowly turns in his seat in order to reach for the telephone, and then he slowly explains to the obviously upset cashier that she shouldn't make a fuss, everything is okay, he has a contract with Herr Professor Rumpler, the proper notice will soon follow, Schrimpl is initialing the note, she should just give the tickets to Krönert. After this Schrimpl turns back and scratches something onto the note. The order now has a grease stain as he continues to eat his cake, he advising Josef not to hurry, here such eagerness is uncalled for. Josef takes the note and thanks him as if Schrimpl had personally done him a special favor, and then heads off to Frau Lawetzer, who at the moment is free and issues the tickets while gabbing away, though Josef excuses himself, saying he's in a hurry, Frau Lawetzer calling after him, saying that he should stop by again, she'll be expecting him.

Josef wants to hand over the tickets, but Krönert is nowhere to be found in the vestibule, two attendants listening as he asks if they noticed a man who looks like such and such, but they know nothing, one of them saying there must be some mistake, the other saying that you can't keep track of everyone. Then Josef runs over to Puttrich, the concierge, but he has not seen Herr Krönert from inside his booth, and Josef shouldn't give himself any gray hair over it, for there have been many who have left the Cultural Center before they got their promised free tickets, in such situations it being best to give the tickets back to Lawetzer, because sometimes people come back to ask for them again. Josef thanks the concierge and decides to follow his advice, but Puttrich wants to ask Josef what he was really supposed to be doing, for he had already spent the whole afternoon running around. Josef explains that he will start the next day, and then he's asked what he wants to work on, lectures or courses, film or radio? Josef can't really say, he hasn't talked with the Professor about it, though it probably won't be the cinema, which Puttrich thinks is a big mistake, that's the only thing that does well, Herr Klinger being paid the most and able to do what he wants at the Cultural Center, everyone else having to follow orders, Rumpler chasing them this way and that, the salaries and wages miserable, everyone having to think of doing a little business on the side. Josef says he wants to work hard so that he can accomplish something, but the concierge laughs at this, for if Josef will take some advice he shouldn't strain himself very much, the best work is in the cinema as an usher, there you get tips, the students who help out now and then actually making a little money. Puttrich is convinced that Josef has taken a position at the Cultural Center only out of great need. "Stay with Klinger. It's a nice place to work."

Josef then goes to the cashier and gives her the tickets, she complaining what a pain it is, now she has to take the tickets back, the fool standing around for half an hour before he decided to buy the tickets, then she having to send Josef to get some change, and why had it all taken so long? Auer had given her the runaround on the phone, followed by Schrimpl, there being no way for Frau Lawetzer to keep the man from going upstairs, he was worried about his money. Josef tries to explain to the old woman that none of it was his fault, he was only trying to help out and wasn't meant to be starting work today, causing the cashier to then wonder, "If you are not yet on board, then take it from an old woman, don't be the first to jump on board!" Josef asks in reply, "What's all the fuss about here?"—"You'll soon see, Herr Doctor! What do you think? I'm not here for my own pleasure. I'm a widow, my husband fell at Przemsyl. I also have a crippled daughter. That's why I sit in this booth. Sometimes I have trouble figuring the take, since I have such bad eyes. So then I have to make up the difference. And almost everyone gets on me. Herr Klinger and Herr Krupka continually, as well as Herr Schrimpl. But Auer is an arrogant slut, her head full of nothing but men and always her difficulties with squaring the books. Horn seems extremely sweet, but he is a beast. He's run by the old man, who whistles his commands, but he does his bidding more than he should. Horn is always broke and borrows where he can. He's always after me, as well as the old man: How many tickets have you sold, Frau Lawetzer? How many do you still have? Everything is a mess. How should I know? They give me blocks of tickets that are stamped wrong or they change the prices. Then everything has to go back upstairs. Then there are events for which I get an almost empty block, because so many free tickets have been given away. It's often unbearable. And then when the old man . . . Herr Doctor, you won't squeal on me, will you? Not a word! Off with you, so that I don't talk so much."

The cashier is mortified that she has let her tongue run so freely, asking the now distant Josef to return as she praises Rumpler and Horn, saying they are lovely men who are only a bit high-strung. Then some people arrive at the booth, Frau Lawetzer quickly wrapping three cigarettes in tinfoil. "This is for Fräulein Auer. Tell her that's all I have for today." Josef once again returns to the office, where Fräulein Auer greets him in a huff. "Well, you seem a fine fool and quite the gossip! What did you get me into with this Krönert and his money? Getting into bed with the Professor is no way to build camaraderie, my friend." Josef bristles at the somewhat opaque accusations, he has no idea how business is done here, the incident with Krönert having nothing to do with him, Josef having helped out only out of goodwill and having come to the business office because the Professor had sent him to Herr Krupka, though it was Fräulein Auer who had sent Josef to the cashier. He is angry and wants to throw the cigarettes into the Fräulein's face, but instead he holds them out to her, saying, "A gift from Frau Lawetzer." The Fräulein is as if transformed, three cigarettes at once, and she is pleased as she says, "You are a little angel, Doctor! How did you manage that?"—"I stated your wish and this is what I got." Fräulein Auer lights up a cigarette right away, then gives another to Josef. "Bring this to Horn, but tell him it's only a loan! And you and I are friends. Whenever you need an advance, and the Professor won't approve one, then come see me. I'll get it out of him. Horn and Klinger live on advances. Klinger has two and Horn has taken part of his salary for the next four months."

Josef wants to take the cigarettes to Dr. Horn, but he's detained in the main office, where Fräulein Grenadier wants to introduce him to a delicate-boned person named Fräulein Maus, who greets him with a smile as she chirps, "I already know you!" Josef can't recall having met her. She explains that they took a couple of walks together near Wartensee am Roll, but Josef assures her, "I have never been in Wartensee am Roll." Fräulein Maus insists nonetheless, "We had a lovely time there. It was a couple of years ago. Don't you remember?" There's nothing to remember, as Josef learns that Fräulein Grenadier works with Fräulein Maus on preparing correspondence, the latter also working on the courses, meaning that she handles the entry fees for the courses that are scheduled for the afternoons and evenings at the Cultural Center, Fräulein Maus trilling in her jubilant voice, "Yes, I do the courses! That way there's the least hassle." Fräulein Grenadier then introduces Josef to a platinum-blond girl, Fräulein Weinstock, who mostly helps Herr Klinger, though she helps everyone, as Herr Klinger then shows up and looks sharply at Josef and says, "Good day, and welcome. Congratulations on your debut, given how you handled the Krönert case. Lawetzer is really impressed with you!" Then Herr Saybusch shows up, a tall young man who is an apprentice baker, which is why Herr Schrimpl usually sends him to buy cake, though that's not Saybusch's main duty, for he draws posters, signs, announcements, and also designs the flyers that the Cultural Center distributes. All of these are from the hand of Herr Saybusch, who normally draws upstairs in a classroom, he being deeply envied, for there he is out of eyeshot of Rumpler, though in the late afternoon, when all the classrooms are occupied, Saybusch has to work in the main office.

After a little while another man shows up, quite short, full of quick movements and with a good-natured demeanor, his name Ignaz, the factotum of the Cultural Center and somewhat hard of hearing. Fräulein Grenadier tells of how once Gerhart Hauptmann had given a talk, a good three years ago now, and for which they used the cinema, because the large auditorium was not large enough since they had to hand out a lot of free tickets, Ignaz helping out that evening as an usher, the Health Minister showing up, who is also hard of hearing, another usher having led him to the loge, where the Minister took his seat, though it wasn't long after that Ignaz believed someone had sneaked past him who didn't belong in the loge, and so he asked where the Minister's ticket was, the Minister understanding not a word, and Ignaz having to yell, until finally the powerful figure began looking in all of his pockets, but to no avail, such that Ignaz became angry about the alleged swindler and lost patience with his inability to produce a ticket, Ignaz calling from the aisle, what audacity, to sit in the loge without a ticket, the Minister standing there embarrassed, when luckily Herr Klinger arrived and led the Minister back into the loge, though Ignaz soon avidly observed such shamelessness and ran into the loge, asking what the man thought he was doing, this was not the place to be without a ticket, this was a prime seat, at which Ignaz grabbed the Minister by the arm and began to drag him out. The Minister then ceased taking it all in good humor and angrily wished to leave, himself already at the exit, but there stood the Professor and Dr. Horn in tails, looking like two excited head waiters ready to greet the illustrious guests, the Minister's punctuality having caught their attention, he now angrily wanting to leave, but the Professor stops him, saying Herr Minister this, Herr Minister that, what a terrible misunderstanding, that's unforgivable, who did this, Herr Minister? I will fire the scoundrel on the spot, dash it all, to think of throwing out my dear Minister, but of course the Herr Minister cannot be insulted so, who is it that has done this? Then the Minister begins to laugh, it all really doesn't matter, and the man should not be let go, but he really no longer has any interest in hearing Gerhart Hauptmann. At this the Professor expresses doubt, saying Gerhart, my Gerhart, you can't do this to my Gerhart, Herr Minister. That would be a shame, Herr Minister, it's such an honor to have two such well-read, humane intellectuals under the roof of the Cultural Center, the Herr Minister should indeed stay and after the lecture grace with his presence the modest reception that will take place in the apartment of the director of the Cultural Center, dash it all, destitute democracy needs it. So you see, a colossal debacle, and we nearly died laughing, and then the Minister said, good, he would stay because it was Hauptmann, but the servant at fault should not be punished, but the Professor explained, forgive me, Your Excellency, but a man who doesn't recognize a minister has to atone for what he's done, it's an abomination to throw out such a minister, a crime against humanity, and in a house of culture no less, but Gerhart will be pleased to make the acquaintance of the Minister. The Minister makes him promise that the guilty party will not be punished, at which Rumpler yells that the scoundrel belongs on the gallows, but Your Excellency is very magnanimous, that is the true spirit of humanity, not to hang either the mighty scoundrel or the meek, indeed, one can't help but note, a son of the followers of Comenius, much like Goethe and Herder wrapped together. The Professor then led the Minister back into the loge and said he hoped he enjoyed the lecture, after which he called Ignaz over and tried to make it clear to him what crime he had committed, to which Ignaz turned completely red and embarrassed as he stammered that he could do nothing about it, the man didn't have a ticket, Ignaz was only doing his job by checking tickets, though Herr Klinger and Herr Krupka's predecessor dragged Ignaz over to the loge, making him knock on the door, and, because the hard-of-hearing Minister didn't hear, Herr Klinger opened the door and shoved Ignaz into the loge, at which he bowed to the Minister, properly clicking his heels, and said, Herr Minister, my apologies, but it is difficult, I have to check the tickets, otherwise anyone can get in, and I don't take any bribes. The Minister laughed and wanted to give Ignaz a tip, but he just strongly waved his left arm as he always does when he doesn't want something, the Minister having to pocket his tip once again, though Ignaz returned proudly pleased, even if a bit upset.

Everyone listens to the story with pleasure, the telephone ringing often as it is told, normally Fräulein Maus picking up and having to talk with Frau Lawetzer. Ignaz draws closer and closer to Fräulein Grenadier in order to better hear, he getting upset, as if the story had happened just yesterday, as at the end he calls out, "Herr Klinger, wasn't I right? Anyone could have come along and said, sorry, I'm the Minister, and then taken the best seats! He certainly had no badge that said that he was the Minster. And he didn't have a ticket." Ignaz is red in the face and continues to wave his arm as he had at the Minister. Ignaz is not easily calmed down, Klinger and Schrimpl patting him on the shoulder again and again to appease him, while in the middle of this conversation and laughter Dr. Horn comes in from the Secretary's office and says that everyone is certainly having a lovely conversation, as if there were nothing more to do today, at which they all go to their desks or disappear, only Klinger not worrying about Horn, as Josef stands there embarrassed, but then gathers himself and asks whether he might speak with Dr. Horn, who agrees to do so. They head into his little room, where Josef hands him the cigarette from Fräulein Auer. "You have saved me, Dr. Kramer. Tell me, do you know how to work an epidiascope?" Josef doesn't even know what an epidiascope is, at which Horn shakes his head in exasperation and states that it appears that Josef doesn't know how to do anything, who knows what young people today are capable of at all. Horn has been thinking what he is supposed to do with Josef, for certainly one can't just stand around talking at the Cultural Center, Professor Rumpler having too many do-nothings in the building already, while the others at least get something done, but now the Professor has his doubts about Dr. Kramer, he can't afford to have any disruptive characters about, those with positive strengths, yes, but no nihilists, like those who seem to be stirring up things everywhere and who want to completely tear asunder the already vulnerable order of things. That's what one might call a doctor of philosophy who lets himself listen to stupid anecdotes about Ignaz in the office, taking in a bunch of chatter, as well as a bunch of gossip, not one word of which is true, or earlier lolling around with Fräulain Auer on his first day, for whom he got three cigarettes, it all calls for a second look. His love life or whatever it is should not be bandied about at the Cultural Center, there are other places for that, for here there is work to accomplish, not just adventures, no matter what kind, to which end Dr. Horn warmly recommends to the hopeful philosopher not to start gabbing with old Lawetzer, as well as with grumpy old Puttrich or with any of the employees, for the interests of the Cultural Center must be kept in mind above all, and not the people who visit it, whether they be paying guests or supplicants of all sorts, who indeed would like to pay something, including those wanting to emigrate from Germany, as they are certainly hard to put up with, but what can one do with them? Here there are only two alternatives, either to work for and with Professor Rumpler wholeheartedly or to disappear immediately.

Josef stammers that Herr Dr. Horn appears to have misunderstood him, he has not yet really started work, and he doesn't want to stand around talking, but rather work, though he still has not had a chance to do so, and besides, he was only trying to help, and he had spent no time talking to anyone, though he can't help it when he hears about the history of the center everywhere he goes. Josef is also not a nihilist, and doesn't understand these unjust assertions, for he doesn't pay attention to gossip, and certainly not to questionable stories, as he still believes in ideals, though he also knows that it's hard to do so these days, but nonetheless he is happy to start on the lowest rung and not shirk any work, but his goodwill should not be so relentlessly questioned on his first day, never mind the fact that it's actually the day before his first day, though to demonstrate his real attitude, Josef wants to know more about what the matter with the epidiascope involves. Dr. Horn explains that Herr Schuster, who usually runs the epidiascope, is sick today, which means that it has to do with a film projector, but had Josef never run one? Josef has to admit that he has also never run a projector, though he'd very much like to learn how, to which Dr. Horn replies, yes, to apply for a position, any dummy can do that, but before you get a job all you need is to get a doctorate, which any ass can do these days, though still you have to learn something even when it involves the most modest of knowledge, such as opening doors, ushering people to their seats, carrying chairs, working the lights, or to find your way around a projector. Otherwise there's a kind of thievery involved with letting yourself be hired by the Cultural Center by warmhearted Professor Rumpler as a result of the blackmail of recommendations, and then to ask, please, show me this, explain to me that. Indeed, Dr. Horn wants to know what the young philosopher thinks he *can* do here, for he should kindly consider that and show up tomorrow with precise suggestions, written out, for the Professor had asked Dr. Horn for a report, and it's not Dr. Horn's job to break his back over it. Josef suggests that someone still needs to orientate him, since he has no key, no desk, no writing pad, he hardly knows his way around the building, and he has no job description. Dr. Horn then turns the tables on him, saying that since Josef is the one who applied for the job he also has to have services to offer, otherwise he is of no use, nor will there be any instruction for just standing around and watching others work. Then there's a knock at the door, as Michel stands there and says, "Excuse me, Herr Dr. Horn, your wife is here." The Secretary dismisses Josef with the advice to search his thoughts and to heed his well-intentioned counsel to work hard at his humble duties or disappear.

Josef stands abashed for a while in the office, everyone else busy around him, then he gets up the courage to approach Fräulein Grenadier and asks whether he can be of help to her. She asks him with a smile in return why he wants to help, for he can of course help her with sorting the mail, but first she'd have to explain in what order to put the letters, and therefore she doesn't know how he can be of help. Then Josef offers to help Herr Schrimpl, but he says that he's right now working on matters for the staff meeting, and Josef should take his time and go easy, within two or three weeks of starting at the Cultural Center he'll be up to his neck in work, so he should just go down and watch the film that's on, if he hasn't seen it already. Josef then wants to see what work there might be in the office, but Fräulein Weinstock snaps, "Please don't bother me! If the Professor sees us, he'll throw us both out!" Josef should either follow Schrimpl around or, better yet, go away, but Dr. Horn's advice still eats at him, he has to make himself useful, so he enters the business office and offers to help Herr Krupka, who actually takes him up on the offer, as he opens a cupboard and gives Josef two blocks of tickets for the large auditorium and explains how to stamp them with the date and the different prices by pressing the stamp only so hard and not smear them, so that Frau Lawetzer can read every-thing, otherwise she'll constantly be calling up to ask what the real price of the tickets is.

As soon as Josef understands everything he is ready to start, but Krupka says that no strangers are allowed to sit in the business office, for if the old man finds out all hell will break loose, so Josef has to work in the main of-fice, but wherever he tries to sit down someone says not here, only Fräulein Maus is willing to make some room between her spot and Schrimpl's desk, but Schrimpl protests, "Fräulein Maus, that won't work. Dr. Kramer cannot sit here. I need room. He should sit at Klinger's desk if he's not here at the moment." So Josef sits at Klinger's desk, but hardly has he done so when Herr Klinger shows up and is perturbed by the uninvited guest, saying, "My desk is not a café table where anyone can take his favorite seat." Then they decide to send Josef into the foyer, where at the moment there are no lights on, since there are no visitors, only Michel, who sits at his desk in the dark and dozes, though Schrimpl turns on the dim lights and calls, "Hey, Michel! Wake up! Herr Dr. Kramer needs to sit here! You need to make room!" The boy stands up, drunk with sleep and wobbly, and makes room for Josef, who then begins to stamp the tickets. Michel looks on for a while and asks whether he will always be doing this and therefore sitting here, the latter answering somewhat uncertainly that he doesn't think so, after which Michel excuses himself, but he has to step out, he'll be right back, but Josef should open the door if someone rings, though he shouldn't let anyone into the office, there are no visiting hours now, but if it's urgent here is a form to fill out and a pencil.

Michel is not gone long before someone rings, as Josef opens the door and an old woman walks in, replying to his inquiry as to what she wants by saying, "I am Frau Michalik." When Josef repeats his question, she takes from her purse a small bag, from which she fishes out a colorful bonbon and lays it on the table. "I must see Professor Rapp, he is expecting me." Josef says she must mean Professor Rumpler, but he is unfortunately not in the building. Then Frau Michalik shoves the bonbon even more pointedly toward Josef, though she looks away at the same time in order to diminish the theatricality of her gesture. "I am here because of the radio. Professor Rapp promised me a spot last year, you know so, you were there." Josef explains that she must be mistaken, but she protests with a whine: "You're not being honest with me. Back then Professor Rapp called to you when I was with him. And he said to you, Frau Michalik is my friend, write it down, next month a talk for the radio as part of the series 'Classical Witnesses!' " Josef responds that he knows nothing about it, but she doesn't let up. "You know who I am. You often dealt with me. You promised me that my talk would soon happen." Frau Michalik shoves another bonbon toward Josef. "So don't make any excuses! My talk is wonderful. Professor Rapp was delighted. I read the talk to him. He thought it very concentrated, but ever since no one has let me in to see Professor Rapp. I have to speak with him now. I'm not budging an inch until I have spoken with him. I'll even stay here overnight." Josef suggests to Frau Michalik that she should fill out an application for Herr Dr. Horn, or perhaps for Herr Schrimpl, who probably has copies of radio talks, but Frau Michalik replies, "The Cultural Center is plotting against me. No one wants to speak with me. I'm a good and respectable woman, I don't take no for an answer, I won't stand for it. I was given a solemn promise about doing the talk. Two years ago I offered to read stories about animals. Such tales are good for young people, they prevent bad things happening. If you don't take care of animals, they become mean and nasty. The love of others can start when you first love animals, otherwise love only comes from your stomach. From that there also results many bad marriages. If there were more good marriages, people would be surprised how quickly hate would disappear and war, for then Czechs would marry Germans and Jews would marry Christians. I have suggested a statute through the Ministry of the Interior that establishes a society for mixed marriages between enemy nations, religions, and races. But they also never answered me. I have always believed that the Cultural Center is the right place for such a society. But politically one has to involve all the parties, which is what Parliament is for. But I sent you my animal stories so that I can read them on the radio. Now I finally want an answer, not to mention that I also insist on doing the talk for 'Classical Witnesses!' that I was solemnly promised. I have to do it. It would be best if it were on after the morning workout, then everyone will be fresh and alert. Everyone will listen in. Professor Rapp was impressed by the talk, I have taken beautiful passages from recent writers about innocent animals—*Maja's Bees* by Bonsel,

Salten's *Bambi* is also included." Josef tries in vain to fend off the woman's onslaught, saying that she should talk with Herr Schrimpl or Dr. Horn, but she shouts, "Dr. Horn is a criminal! I don't want to see him! He upset me and treated me like dirt!"

There is another ring, and as Josef opens the door he can't stop Frau Michalik from running into the main office. The new visitor is a heavy man, well dressed, wearing strong cologne, as he sits right down and says his name is Schebesta, and that he was here earlier today, around nine o'clock, no one was here, no one opened the door, nor did he wish to disturb anyone in the administration, but he had a meager request, but which is quite important, he having visited many editors already, though no one had time for him, the newspapers thinking only about politics, sports, and criminals, scientific sensations getting short shrift, even the academy not having the proper understanding, as there they continue to employ ancient methods, Schebesta pulling a bulky manuscript from his briefcase as he says, "Look here, this is my new method, I came up with it all by myself. As you know, none of the experts in the field have had any success, despite diligent effort, in raising fungi from seed. Only mushrooms can be grown. But with my method one can cultivate the spores of any fungus and let them thrive. One can also grow any of the poisonous sorts, which I am especially pleased with. After the seeds have been planted, you lay a piece of blotting paper over them that is soaked with salt and important nutrients. All of it is watersoluable. The chemical configuration is sound, and completely original, but it has to remain a secret. According to a schedule which I have calculated exactly, after two days the paper is watered with regular water so that all the nutrients in the paper dissolve. Then you take away the paper, and the fungi begin to sprout. The economic benefit of my invention is obvious, and I can explain it in greater detail if you wish. You can appreciate, however, that with this method you can grow fresh fungi in the middle of an industrial district. I believe the best thing would be for you to take my manuscript and give it to the proper individual to read. The Cultural Center could then spread the word about the advantages of growing fungi artificially and profit from it, my recommendation being that your share should be fifty percent."

Before Josef can say a word, the door to the main office opens, as Schrimpl vigorously pushes Frau Michalik out ahead of him and yells, "You can't just barge in here, Frau Michalik! Michel, you should . . . Where is Michel?" Frau Michalik is insulted, and says, "This is an outrage! I must speak with Professor Rapp!" Josef explains Michel's absence and the reason that the woman succeeded at pressing her way in, at which Schrimpl again yells, "There's nothing for you here! How often do you need to be told that it's forbidden to enter? You will get a written notice when it's time for your talk. Now just go!" More people enter the foyer, as Frau Michalik begins to rant that she wants her animal tales back, it's a den of thieves that has to be escaped. The noise upsets Schebesta, who calls out in the midst of it that he's not at fault, he only wanted to report about his discovery of how to raise fungi, even poisonous ones, though Frau Michalik doesn't understand, she doesn't know anything about fungi, she can't eat them, but Schebesta explains that fungi are healthy, the poisonous ones are only for display in gardens, one will no longer have to go into the woods in order to marvel at the fly agaric, for people used to place artificial reproductions of them in gardens, and now that will no longer be necessary once anyone can raise his own fly agaric. And when Fräulein Auer comes up, wearing a pendant that has a fly agaric mushroom on it, Schebesta points to it and says, "There, look! The woman is wearing a reproduction of a fly agaric! That's now outmoded, she can have fresh ones every day. She can have the real thing!"

Because of the ruckus, Dr. Horn steps in, Frau Michalik lunging toward him as she lets loose: "It's all your fault! You told them that I'm not quite right!" Horn wants to know what's wrong, it's like a madhouse in here, he can't even talk on the telephone in his own office, and the Professor will be back from the radio station soon, so no one should leave, everyone needs to get ready for the staff meeting, yet Frau Michalik bursts out, "To hell with your staff meeting! At last Professor Rapp is on his way, that's good! I have time, I'm not budging an inch from my spot!" Schrimpl tries to mildly push Michalik toward the stairs, but she stands her ground and screams, "Violence! You're hurting me! An innocent soul is being harmed!" The doors stand open, more and more people visible whom Josef doesn't know, a man saying he is supposed to be giving a talk today in the large auditorium, where should he put his coat? Michel, who finally is back, should show him where. An older woman wants to know, "How can that be? Today's paper says that a lecture on 'Chemistry in the Kitchen' is supposed to be given by

Marietta Stolz in Classroom 2. And why doesn't anyone know whether there's supposed to be a lecture, and where?"

Then Herr Rosensaft introduces himself, saying that he's supposed to speak about "Walking Tours of Naples," but he was just in the small auditorium and the epidiascope is not there, just a projector, but he needs an epidiascope, because he has photo transparencies, not slides, which he told them beforehand, yet Horn explains, "Certainly, Herr Rosensaft. But the man who runs the epidiascope is sick. I'm sorry, there's nothing that can be done." Herr Rosensaft yells, "This is a scandal! The entire gist of my lecture will be lost if I don't show my photos! You people have to make things right, or I'm not speaking!" Horn replies, "Calm down! It all depends on the lecture. Whoever talks about a landscape in a captivating manner does a far better job than any picture in rolling out a panorama before our eyes."—"This is the last lecture I'll ever do here! Twenty percent of the gross! No one pays as shabbily as does Rumpler! I must have the epidiascope! I need those pictures!" Saybusch then joins in to say, "Herr Dr. Horn, if you can pay me, I can run the epi." Horn is outraged, saying that if Saybusch can work it he simply needs to do so, but Saybusch responds that he doesn't have to, and no one can make him, for though he'd like to help, it would mean taking time from his time off, and that's not part of the usual overtime allowance, but Horn explains, "For talks on geography hardly anyone shows. There's no way that you can be paid for it, Saybusch. The lecture will take place without any pictures." Rosensaft gets excited, saying, "What do you mean that geography talks don't draw? In Graz the hall was packed. In Brno I had to deliver this talk three times, and twice in Reichenberg. If it doesn't draw, it's your fault, because you've handled things badly. I only saw four lines about it in the newspaper. You haven't done enough ads and haven't quoted any of my text." Horn counters that the Cultural Center could never support its program through the kind of advertising that Herr Rosensaft is demanding, not even Sven Hedin had been so prominently promoted, but Rosensaft complains that everything has already been bungled, now it's too late, and he needs the epidiascope, otherwise there will be no lecture, but Dr. Horn then threatens, "If you're talking about bailing out, then that means breaking your contract, and you are answerable and accountable for that. Be reasonable. Otherwise you will pay the price, that I guarantee you."—"You can't nail me with breaking the contract! What are you thinking? I can hold *you* accountable and show you in black and white where it says that you are to provide me with an epidiascope." Frau Michalik then jumps in, saying, "Just you wait, you swindler! Just you wait! Professor Rapp will be here any minute. We all have a bone to pick with him. It's simply unheard of how things are run around here!" Saybusch offers to set up the epidiascope for Rosensaft and to take over the running of it, but only for a fee. Rosensaft won't consider it, though, and stands on his rights, unwilling to pay any peon for what he is already due. Saybusch shrugs and repeats that he has to get something, either from the Cultural Center or from Herr Rosensaft, otherwise he doesn't want any part of it.

Professor Rumpler then arrives in the midst of this maelstrom. "Dash it all, what's going on now! I can't leave the building for a second! Why is everyone here, Horn? What's going on? There's no one downstairs at the cinema, where is Klinger? He's a joke, that Klinger, he doesn't belong in a cultural center. I have my hands full, is no one taking notes, who is taking notes? I've forgotten everything, what do you need? What's going on?" Some of the employees have left, though Horn, Schrimpl, Kramer, and Michel remain, as well as Frau Michalik, Rosensaft, and Schebesta. "I guess I have to take care of everything myself. Indeed, I can't count on anyone here to help! What do you want? What can I do? Who is that?" Frau Michalik wants to have at Rumpler, but Schrimpl holds her back, Schebesta meanwhile retreating into himself, as Josef returns to stamping the tickets, though Horn points to the angry Rosensaft and says, "Herr Professor, this is today's speaker scheduled for the small auditorium. The gentleman is supposed to talk about Italy, but he is making things difficult for us."—"What difficulty, sir. I'm afraid I don't know you, what seems to be the difficulty? Krupka should come in, how many tickets have been sold, what's wrong, why isn't anyone saying anything? What is Lawetzer doing? Fräulein Weinstock, Fräulein Maus?" Rosensaft then asks, "Are you the director?"—"Yes, I'm Professor Rumpler. But you, who are you to cause such difficulties?"—"My name is Rosensaft. I find that this man, who has not introduced himself, is impertinent. I arrive here and ask the concierge where my room is, then go up, only to find everything a mess, no epidiascope, and so I head to the main office in order to clear things up, and this man crudely throws himself at me in a way that no one has ever done before."—"Slow down, my dear Rosenblatt . . ."—"Rosen*saft*, please."—"Excuse me, Rosen*saft*, there's no need to get so riled. Have you ever given a talk that caused you to lose your nerve? Dash it all, then you should see Thomas Mann or Gerhart, I mean Hauptmann, before a talk, the way they sit completely at ease in my office and talk to me about the most sublime things, as if nothing were going on, each word a pearl, just think, Herr Rosensaft, indeed, it all comes from an excess of the most profound human intellect! Such giants don't get upset if something distracts me, it can happen that my telephone will ring, you have no idea what I have to tend to, but the great ones maintain their composure and thus help sustain me. No, take it from me, Herr Rosensaft, one doesn't create any kind of good impression with the public when you get so upset! Legions of people have spoken here and, not to insult you, some of them quite famous, genuine luminaries in front of full-capacity crowds, and yet the more important they were, you must believe me, the humbler they were as well. You should have seen the glorious impression made by Gerhart, he looking like the famous sunken bell, like *Hanneles' Ascension*, not the piece itself but it's author! You should have seen it, the wonderful head of Goethe, the gray Olympian—that's culture, the eternal values of mankind inside one brain. But Herr Rosensaft, you can still aspire to the same, you are still a young man. I mean you well, give me your hand. We need to be friends, we need to trust each other, we are all of us human, all of us human, as Schiller said."—"Herr Professor, that's all quite lovely, what you say. But this man insulted me. I don't compare myself to Hauptmann or to other celebrities, and all I want is to give my talk. For that I need an epidiascope and someone to run it. Italy without pictures, however, is not possible."—"But of course, my good sir, you should give your talk. What's it about? Ah yes, Italy! Also a wonderful theme of the master Goethe— Venetian nights, gondola rides, the moon rising with its lovely silhouette over the Grand Canal. I'd love to hear it myself, but unfortunately there's a staff meeting. Look at me, if you can see me at all, I haven't had a break since Monday, not even so much as for a cup of tea. But well then, Horn, what's with the epdiascope?"

"Herr Professor, Schuster is sick. I asked Dr. Kramer whether he knows how to run an epidiascope, but he doesn't appear to know how to do that and listen to insipid gossip at the same time. Then Saybusch said he was ready to, but only if he's paid extra, which is shameless." Rumpler yells, "That's unheard of! Get Saybusch! What's the meaning of this? Dash it all, do I have to run the epidiascope as well?" Saybusch then appears. "Why won't you do what you are told?" Saybusch doesn't allow himself to get rattled. "I do what I am told. But the epi is not part of my job. I won't do it for free."—"My dear Saybusch, you are still young, and therefore idealistic. The beautiful pictures, Italy, they will inspire your own drawing. Maybe you'll even take a trip there and will already have a taste of it. Do you know Herr Rosensaft's pictures? Dash it all, they are the finest pictures I know." Saybusch stands strong. "I'm prepared to do it. But not for free."—"My dear Saybusch, you are a materialist, which makes me sad, but come see me tomorrow, I want to talk with you in private. I'll give you a day off if you'll do it."—"Herr Professor, I already have three days off coming to me. I won't do it for free!"—"You scoundrel, then you'll have four days free, next week off from Sunday through Wednesday!" An usher arrives and asks when Herr Rosensaft will be ready, the audience is waiting for the man to talk about Italy, and they are impatient, it's already eight-thirty. Horn then asks how many there are. Fräulein Weinstock had sold sixty-three tickets at the door. Lawetzer had already sold four or five ahead of time. Then Rosensaft complains that it's a shame there are so few people, no one had circulated enough notices, as had been agreed to, too few advertisements, though Dr. Horn challenges him by saying, "Herr Rosensaft, we understand this business better than you. We know how much we tried to publicize it! Can't you see that Herr Professor Rumpler is completely exhausted? Please, just go up there and give your lecture!"—"And the epidiascope?" Then Rumpler says to Saybusch that he'll be compensated, he should head up with the epidiascope, but the latter writes out an invoice and hands it along with a pen to the Professor, who okays the extra fee.

Rumpler then wants to head to his office, and Horn should accompany him, but now there is no holding back Frau Michalik, as she wrests herself away from Schrimpl and throws herself at Rumpler, standing in his path and spitting at him, "Now it's my turn! Only over my dead body, Herr Professor Rapp!" Then the Professor turns completely soft and pats Frau Michalik on the cheek. "I'm so worried about you, my dear, you seem so upset! I'm not getting any younger, either. Dash it all, when people like us have to bend over backward!" Frau Michalik says, "If only I could speak with just you, then everything will be settled. You are still a human being, Herr Professor Rapp! No one will let me get in to see you! My love of animals is misunderstood, it's only a part of my love of people. You already know about my plans for a society for mixed marriage. I have to bring that up in Parliament, I have to get on the radio! To read the animal tales! But your people here are no good. Dr. Horn or Korn, whoever he is, is terrible to me!"—"My dear, he's not so bad! Our dear Horn is a bit nervous, indeed, but don't let him get to you, he just smokes too much and certainly didn't mean anything by what he said. Relax!"—"I am relaxed, but he can't say that I'm not quite right. I have to read my animal tales on the radio! Herr Professor Rapp, my talk, which you know and love, is supposed to be for the series 'Classical Witnesses!,' and it still has all those beautiful passages from new writers. That has to go on, early after the morning workout!"—"One moment, my dear friend! Take this down, Horn, remind me about this important woman, mixed marriages, Frau Michalik, a talk about classical animals, already on the program, after the morning workout, hand it on to Schrimpl, don't remember, I mean forget! Does that satisfy you? Of course we will write to you, tomorrow, take it down, everything is settled!" With grand gestures the Professor shakes her hand, and then quick as lightning he disappears into his office with Horn, though once more she opens the door to the central office and yells out, "I won! I will speak on the radio and read my stories, even if you all go to pieces! Give my best to Professor Rapp!" Then she heads off, slamming the door behind her.

Schebesta sits in the foyer, as well as Josef with his block of tickets, Schebesta asking him, since it's now quiet, whether he could again see the Fräulein who had the pendant with the fly agaric on it, but before Josef can reply they hear the voices of Rumpler and Horn calling, "Staff meeting! Staff meeting!" Josef says he cannot do anything for him right now, but he accepts a copy of Schebesta's manuscript as he renews his offer of fifty percent and says he'd like to have a response in the next week. Josef takes his two blocks of tickets, as well as the materials with which to stamp them, and the manuscript on fungi into the administrative offices, where Rumpler sits at his desk, his left hand on the crown of the bust of Goethe, Horn and

Schrimpl, as well as Grenadier, Maus, and Auer all there, the others not, which bothers Rumpler, who says, "How rude to keep me waiting. My young doctor, we'll see what this means. What did you get done today? Now show me what you've got there! Stamping tickets? Now, isn't it a shame that an academic should be reduced to doing that? I didn't even have to do that when I was in elementary school. Who gave them to you? It must have been Krupka. Indeed, I should have guessed, the blocks of tickets need to be monitored. What gave Krupka the idea to turn over the blocks to you? Did you know about this, Dr. Horn? I see, you knew nothing at all. Dash it all, Dr. Horn, I leave the building and everything goes to pieces. Where is everyone? Doctor, what else do you have there? Show it to me, that doesn't belong to you! Schrimpl, what is that? A radio talk, something important, make a note right away, someone should speak to Zenkl, something to do with agriculture, 'On the Growing of Fungi from Seeds or Spores, with Special Concern for Poisonous Fungi, by Lothar Schebesta,' a new discovery, Schrimpl, read it right away, Fräulein Grenadier, for the next staff meeting, Dr. Horn as well. Doctor, run around quick and fetch everyone and tell them they should come to the staff meeting!"

As Josef walks into the main office, the telephone rings and he reaches for the receiver, but he doesn't know how to work the system, so he sets the receiver down again and it stops ringing as he hurries off to the business office, where Krupka sits unconcerned. "Herr Krupka, here are your ticket blocks. I didn't stamp all of them. I will continue with it tomorrow, but today it was impossible to finish." Krupka looks at the tickets and notices that only half of one block has been stamped. "That took a little while, Herr Doctor. You should be able to finish two blocks inside an hour. But haste makes waste. Auer often doesn't do more than one block per day."—"Herr Krupka, you should come to the staff meeting!" The bookkeeper agrees, he'll be there shortly. At this Josef heads back to the administrative offices and is asked where everyone is hiding. Josef answers that there is no one in the main office, though in the business office Herr Krupka said that he'd be right there, but then Rumpler yells out, "Doctor, I already told you I have no work for you! Dash it all, don't you want to make yourself useful? What can you do? Nothing at all! Just saunter around the office and the entire building! I'm afraid I have to be candid with you, for at the Cultural Center we value candidness, and of course Herr Dr. Horn will forgive me, but he is very dissatisfied with your performance and capabilities thus far. I, of course, don't want to say anything, for you're just beginning, but you have been warned. Dash it all, you can't be my private secretary, for that I need a man, a lover of truth, discretion, honesty, true humanity, but no bloody beginner. There's nothing you know how to do, be it typing, stenography, the epidiascope, they are all Greek to you. Michel, the jackass outside, can stamp tickets. But where is everyone? Doctor, skip downstairs, Klinger should be there, I need Klinger right now!"

Josef leaves the office, but before he looks for Klinger he takes his hat and coat out of the main office, then he slowly and quietly walks down the steps, the entire building quiet, as he approaches the concierge's booth, Puttrich sitting there comfortably with a cigarette as he reads the evening paper. Josef wants to ask about Klinger, but Puttrich speaks up first, saying, "Had enough already for today or for good?" Josef replies that he wants to think about it, but it's enough for today, yet he still has an assignment, the Professor wanting to see Herr Klinger upstairs in the staff meeting, but at this Puttrich laughs heartily and says, "Didn't I tell you? Only the films are worth anything here, nothing else. Everything else is a waste of time. The old man can wait. Herr Klinger already said good night and is long gone." At this Josef also wishes him good night and heads out through the vestibule, the ticket booth dark and closed, Frau Lawetzer also having left, everything still, the quiet whir of the projector the only thing audible, Josef curious whether Herr Krönert had indeed picked up his loge seats. Then Josef looks over the notices in the vestibule, the lecture by Herr Rosensaft posted, other curious photos present there, as well as some photos of the lecturers next to a poster that says THE HISTORY AND MISSION OF THE RED CROSS, Josef also looking over the notice for the talk by Dr. Auchlicht on the role of hormones in human life, as he considers what Rumpler would say about it, whether it will draw or not draw. Then Josef thinks about the Minister of Health, who came too early to the lecture by Hauptmann and was thrown out by Ignaz from the loge, though Rumpler was there to save culture, he standing at the edge of the pool of humanity with his net as he snags the deaf fish, who is then thrown back into the watery film, though he sinks beneath the weight of the bell, ascension, dash it all, never taking place.

Josef is now on the street, standing under the blue neon lights that spell out CULTURAL CENTER in large letters, everything exuding the feel of culture, a place of Goethean calm and the pure human spirit, but all of it destroyed through stamped tickets, lectures churned out with accompanying photos, an epidiascope that is not run for free, radio talks trilled by canaries, it'll draw, all tickets sold out, a panorama of culture, people needing to be nourished by true intellect, though Josef is not a useful member of society, for he doesn't know how to properly stamp tickets, while others make epochal discoveries, Frau Michalik having selected beautiful passages from new writers about mixed marriages between red shirts and brown, and now everything on the street is still, the culture of the times concentrated inside this building, the conflicts between right and left resolved through the love of animals, Professor Rumpler raising poisonous mushrooms in the face of today's nihilism. Above, on the second floor, are the offices, lights on everywhere, even the drinking glasses and coffee cups of the employees visible on the windowsill, but not a single employee, while the curtains are closed at three of the windows, which must be the Director's office, everyone except the circus man Klinger gathered at the staff meeting, Rumpler and Goethe, Thomas Mann and Gerhart Hauptmann, Dr. Horn and Sven Hedin, Schrimpl and Krupka, as well as the four women, all of them deliberating, and Goethe speaking to them, patting Rumpler on the shoulder and saying, make a note, write a report, indeed, dash it all, of course, important, and everyone bearing up under it, nothing bad is meant by it at all. But Josef doesn't know what will proceed from what is going on up above, perhaps more ideas for Schnitzler, the subvention from the Ministry of Education, Kummerhackl's book, Klebinder's charity work, Eckermann or the President's office—Josef will never know, for he has decided not to return tomorrow, wanting to look elsewhere for someplace where he is needed, everything closed and silent, a thick mugginess hovering in the air above the pool.

Strong lights are turned on in the vestibule, the cinema letting out, a charming film, a brilliant film, a sad film, everyone moved to tears, the first guests now leaving, perhaps Herr Krönert and his wife among them, as Josef watches them leave, but only unknown people pour out, some criticizing the film, others chatting, Krönert nowhere to be seen, he most likely preferring to bow out and sit at home with his canaries. The lecture in the large auditorium also appears to be over, as well as perhaps the other one by Rosensaft, for also among the pictures had been one of the crater, with its triumphant cloud of smoke, no doubt it having pleased the audience, they are excited, which is no surprise, it only being too bad that not enough posters were made. Now the pond is drained, the last guests having dribbled out, the ushers leaving the building, the lights in the vestibule turned off, the neon light also shut off, culture attached to electric current, while the minute one turns it off culture disappears, not even Thomas Mann able to read in a darkened auditorium, but instead he is accompanied out and sits next to Professor Rumpler in order to listen to the staff meeting, take notes, and make a report about what fantastic ideas he has for his next book, Rumpler is indeed his friend. Thomas Mann is allowed to monitor the take, together with Hauptmann he'll forward true culture, both of them guests of Professor Rumpler, a humble invitation, to be sure, for Rumpler lives here in the building, the good man living on the top floor.

Puttrich has locked the front entrance, only the side entrance still open, the staff meeting still going on. Or is it over? The employees can now be seen. There is scraggy Fräulein Grenadier, the curtains now open in the Director's office, Fräulein Weinstock opening a window, then the lights in the Director's office are turned off, Rumpler now gone, he having wanted to pay a late visit to the radio station, but he doesn't come down, there being no taxi, which means he must be in his apartment up above. If he came down to the street now, Josef would say hello to him, but neither he nor any of the other employees show up, the work still going on up above, the quiet sound of typing still audible through the closed windows. Josef doesn't want to wait any longer, a policeman having looked sharply at him, no, Josef isn't breaking in, there's nothing to take here, everything is monitored.

Josef heads off from the Cultural Center, walking slowly through the streets, and avoiding those places where at this late hour the action is livelier and the streetcars clank along. He wants to forget the Cultural Center, it was nothing more than a dream, but he doesn't totally reject it, even if it casts shadows upon Goethe's bust, Professor Rumpler seeming almost like a bust himself, his head round, his gaze fixed and indeed silent, his mouth open, even when he isn't saying a thing, his voice cutting and strong, sometimes complaining and rushing, but his bald head remaining always the same, its layers of fat shining. Perhaps Rumpler is also now moving along the streets, sampling cultural works, looking for Fräulein Auer all done up, chatting with the street walkers and saying to them what they should make a note of, offering them discount tickets, though they must become members, carrying Saybusch's flyers listing the next week's events under his arm as he stands before the theater exit, pressing a flyer into everyone's hand, as he calls out Auchlicht! Auchlicht! for one has to start somewhere, nothing is for sure, one must earn his red cross, he wears it prominently clasped just above his stomach, the newspapers also need to earn the trust of the public, which is why the newspaper boys hawk their papers, culture offered everywhere, while Herr Schebesta is wrong, even scientific sensations are covered, not the actions of politicians, the results of sporting events or the horrors done by criminals. They should all just see how Rumpler does it, he the promoter of the intellect and the symbol of modern culture, himself the epitome of it, Rumpler's employees there to serve it, Michel opening the door, the most illustrious heads of the epoch taking their place in the foyer, Michel having them fill out an application, which he then brings to the Director, who decides about lectures and photos, the radio spreading the word out into the macrocosm, the world reconciled, the Cultural Center the microcosm in which all is arranged and decided, five minutes, ten minutes, or even if it's really important, fifteen minutes, one must make compromises indeed.

Josef walks on, having long ago lost any sense of where he lives, he not having chosen any direction but instead freedom, which still causes one to hunger, there being no way to prevent it, though it is its own salvation, there is no remedy that grants it. Rumpler can't sign for it, for he can't monitor it, nor does any subvention help, nor even the Office of the President. Midnight by now is long past, and it was four in the afternoon when Josef first showed at the Cultural Center, no, actually it was three, but it wasn't until four that Rumpler welcomed him, Josef climbing the stairs to the office, though Michel didn't have to open the door, the door to the foyer already stood open, at which someone spoke briefly with Josef, he doesn't recall who anymore, then he had to wait for an hour, Rumpler suddenly ripping open the door to the office and calling out, Quickly quickly, young man, I haven't stolen away any time just for you, why are you walking so slowly? What do you really want from me? Alas, everyone wants something from me, and when I was as young as you I wasn't allowed to do anything. Yes, you've already waited an hour, but that's nothing compared to a lifetime, we wait many hours before it's our turn. At your age I waited whole days, and no one paid any attention to me. What, then, do you want, my good man? Now quickly, quickly! Sit down, for I let no one stand within three meters of me when I was a newly made doctor. I always bowed deeply and didn't move from my spot, but I see that you have already taken on the ways of the new democracy whereby bad behavior is confused with freedom. Alas for the feudal grace of the monarchy, but nothing is forever, not even today, but what is it that you want? Make it snappy! Aha, a letter of recommendation, now let me see it, a good letter, no question, but only one letter! What, another letter? Impressive, I'll think it over, but of course I can't hire anyone in these times, I already have enough people, and indeed, everyone wants a job with me. . . .

Josef still feels that his adventures at the Cultural Center can't continue, it was madness, a nightmare, that cannot happen again, it's over, nothing more to consider, nothing to dream about, but Josef can't quite shake free of it, since he dearly wishes it could work out, himself holding on, helplessly clinging to it, though there is also release, the freedom of time, wounded freedom, the employees of the Cultural Center heading home at night, for it's late, they have all left and must head home to sleep, even Puttrich the concierge will sleep, even the restless Cultural Director is slumbering on the writings of Kummerhackl, the call to solve Europe's social question having frozen in its tracks, the social question now sleeping, as well as humanity, culture, the world's spirit, freedom, conscience frozen, too, everything asleep, as, exhausted on a park bench, Josef sleeps as well.

BUILDING THE RAILROAD

THE EIGHTY NEW WORKERS ASSIGNED TO BUILDING THE RAILROAD MARCH uphill along the dusty road until they get to the wooden huts, though at a good pace the trip takes no more than ten minutes before they reach the hut, with its black roof covered with tar paper, that is the builders' hut, which contains an office and a drafting room, next to which stands a couple of wooden huts, shacks full of building materials, tool bins, and two or three workshops. Everything is fitted out in meager fashion and hastily thrown together, nothing looks right. On the street side of the huts there is a canopy that protects against the rain, as well as two desks where the bookkeeper Podlaha and a secretary work, the new workers approaching the desks one after another. They have not come voluntarily, for the war is on, everyone must work, even the Jews need to do something for once, and even if building this railroad has no important relation to the war effort, each must still follow the orders of the state, which is fighting for Europe on all fronts. That's why the despised ones are ripped away from their families, the employment office having issued a summons, failure to appear resulting in each one writing his own sentence, the men arriving at the induction station, where long questionnaires are filled out that inquire about their various skills, after which they go to the infirmary, where they again fill out another long questionnaire, after which a doctor quickly examines them, the result being that each is declared ready for heavy physical labor. Soon they are informed of their duties and told they will work on the railroad in Wirschenowitz, and that they need to come to a meeting in order to learn all the details. There someone from the employment office tells the men that the times are serious, shirking work will be severely punished without mercy, but they are lucky, the work they will do is healthy and they will be outside in the fresh air, they will be paid, but they should fit themselves out with warm clothes, good shoes, two blankets, and eating utensils, while breakfast, lunch, and dinner will be available at reduced costs in the canteen. They will find out all the rest in Wirschenowitz, where the forced laborers have their own administration, the employment office having chosen a leader from among the roughly eighty men already at work there, as well as a doctor. Then a slip of paper with their issuing orders is shoved into their hands, it also stating the meeting point at the central train station at 8 A.M. on Sunday, tomorrow.

At the station the men stand ready, most of them between eighteen and twenty, though there are also some who are over forty. Two officials from the employment office travel with them, their job being to oversee the camp, though they are young, one always having a tobacco pipe in his mouth, the other simply a lout. The trip takes almost six hours, but everyone is in a good mood, as they all get to know one another and friendships are quickly formed, families talked about, the war, the days ahead, each debating and talking about whether the work will be good, whether it will be strenuous or bearable, some holding out hope that it will be fine, they will be in the country, almost all the people there being Czech and hopefully friendly, or at least not hostile, some of the group having already had some experience with such camps, all of them involving similar work, such as building roads, bridges, or canals, and while none have worked on a railroad, it's the same as building roads, for it involves leveling, digging, pickaxing, and shoveling. The youth with the pipe from the employment office also says a couple of things about Wirschenowitz, telling them that the little village is located in a mountainous area dense with forests, the inhabitants having hardly anything, since their houses are simple and for the most part covered with shingles or straw, ducks and geese waddling through the streets. The largest part of the town is in the valley, which is quite deep and surrounded by steep cliffs, from which a little river flows with cascading green water, three wooden bridges and a narrow footbridge crossing over it both in and outside the village. Until now the area has been reachable only by a narrow-gauge train that runs along the right bank of the little river, though the new stretch will run much more directly, meaning that the sharp change in elevation will have to be dealt with by digging and moving large sections of earth.

When they arrive in Wirschenowitz it's hot, the men are not allowed any water, but instead must immediately run from the station down into the village, where they soon reach the main street, the view offering three little shops, two of them inns serving food, followed by a post office, a hair dresser's, a tobacco shop, all of them except the inns looking as if they are shut. Then the group turns left and soon reaches the creek, where it crosses the footbridge and begins to climb uphill again, the strongest keeping up with the boys from the employment office, who hurry them along, while the weaker ones soon lag behind, each having to carry his things, whether they be knapsacks, suitcases, bags, or packages. Josef, meanwhile, stays in the middle. At the end of the village they approach the main road, which after another curve turns into the highway that leads the workers to the builders' huts and on toward Pechno. For a while the creek runs beside the street, which then turns away, after a few minutes landing them in the work camp, which consists of wooden huts surrounding an open space, the canteen to the left, which also serves as a gathering room where the mail is handed out in the evening, sometimes Otto, the leader of the group, speaking to the forced laborers, they also being able to eat dinner here, though since the canteen is so uncomfortable and dirty many choose to eat in the barracks. The canteen is leased by the fat, reasonable, and efficient Frau Miltschi, her two helpers not at all friendly, as together they prepare the meager fodder that they sell for chits—one can purchase a week's worth from Otto—during the same fixed hours each day, during which it's a good idea to keep a fork at the ready in order to scoop up some bit of potato or peas that would otherwise go into the garbage. The rest of the barracks are for housing, each containing four spacious rooms holding eight men each, the wooden pallets simple but functional, the straw mattresses stuffed full, a heavy table standing in the middle of the room, benches with no backs running along its long sides, there also being some shelves on the wall, the ample oven with a large cooker a welcome sight, next to it a wood box with beech logs used for heating. The accommodations are stripped down, but they serve their purpose and are welcoming, though there's no electric light, since oil lamps are used.

Nearby these barracks are others that house some thirty independent tradesmen who are part of a number of men from the surrounding villages who are involved with building the railroad. A bit farther on the overseers live with their families in two nicer barracks, they being called "Master" or "Herr Master," burly men in the prime of their lives whose names are Rubák, Vodil, Chudoba, and Sajdl. At the end of this settlement the highway leaves the creek and winds uphill to the left, then to the right and back alongside the creek bed until it turns into a cart path, two decorated block houses with little gardens standing at the beginning, which is where those in charge of the building project live with their wives and children. Head Engineer Čiperný is the leader of the section, at his side Technical Engineer Mozol, who has nothing against the forced laborers and, somewhat shy, does his best to chat with them, while the capable and somewhat intimidating bookkeeper, Podlaha, lends administrative help to the head engineer, who certainly is not a bad man, though he is tough on the forced laborers, there being hardly a day that passes when he doesn't reprimand Otto seriously, who raises issues with Čiperný, who then threatens that if ... And this "if" is so clear that he doesn't have to say another word, there's no messing around, for there are other means at the ready to deal with any troublemakers, and hinting at such unspoken means is enough to inspire fearful submission. Nothing, however, is known for sure, or hardly anything is known at all during this time, everything kept simmering behind a secret veil, though it must be something quite horrible, the men part of a regiment that is perhaps tougher than any ever experienced before by masters and servants. Therefore it's unlikely that the head engineer even knows the worst consequences of his own veiled threats, he having to remain fearsome and thus not free himself, freedom being for him a dubious concept that one must continually determine anew, and which according to current circumstances must be asserted or abandoned. The new arrivals are warned by Čiperný that what they do in their free time is not his concern, but no one had better be caught sloughing off at work, for at a minimum everyone has to keep on the go, not even the briefest of breaks allowed, and it should be noted that "eighteen" will be called out when there's a danger of falling behind pace, the workers calling it out the moment a monitor nears, at which they have to work twice as fast, though once the danger is over "twenty" is called out, a system they call "marking."

Otto gathers the new ones after they arrive out in the open air and says that things here work through camaraderie, everyone is in the same boat, Otto doesn't wish to command, but each must give his all so that there are no problems, the group leader expecting that they will understand his difficult position, and that they should make his unpleasant assignment easier, for he is caught in the middle between his comrades and the head builders, his job being to fend off trouble, Otto working to provide the best for the group as a whole, though he expects obedience from each, which the gathering vows openly, after which he warns that sick leave is to be avoided at all costs, the head builders having informed him that there are too many malingerers and deadbeats, which is what they call taking sick leave and slacking off. Then Otto explains the daily schedule, everyone rising early at the sound of the clock at five-thirty and needing to get ready to be at his workstation by seven, which can be as much as an hour away, lunch lasting only half an hour between one and one-thirty, which means only a few are able to eat in the canteen, so everyone needs to bring something along, though the head engineer lets one man from each section go to the canteen to get a pot of soup, lunch being picked up and distributed warm each evening, work lasting until five, everyone working ten hours a day, including the lunch break, Saturday afternoon being free, though sometimes you have to work voluntarily, for which there is special pay, the salary calculated on an hourly basis and paid out on Saturday every fourteen days at the end of work, while anyone who doesn't have any money can make a special request of the bookkeeper for an advance on the following Saturday, Sundays also free, travel home on the weekends forbidden, though you can shop in the village and get a haircut, although you should allow yourself to be seen in town as little as possible, but arranging for farmers to deliver milk by cart is allowed. Dealing on the black market, however, cannot occur under any circumstances, for any trespass of this rule will be harshly dealt with by the higher-ups with the strongest of measures, thus causing the entire group to suffer, so no one should allow himself to be caught. Visiting taverns is forbidden, and though walks are not expressly prohibited, it's not a good idea, nor should you move around town as a group, but instead use only side streets, no more than three men at a time and no farther than ten kilometers from the camp. Therefore you can't go to Sobolec, for it's eleven kilometers away, although there is a doctor there whom you need a pass from the bookkeeper to visit. Anyone who is sick should first see Otto and the group's own doctor, who is there to examine all deadbeats, while whoever is in fact sick should show up at 7 A.M. in the office of the builders' hut, where the bookkeeper will issue a note and the necessary pass that will allow the journey to Sobolec. With that you have to hurry to the station in order to catch the morning train, while in Sobolec you have to go straight to the doctor's office, since any detour, any dawdling, any shopping in any store is strictly forbidden, there being no way for Otto to emphasize enough how important it is to follow these restrictions to the letter, the police in Sobolec are not very pleasant to deal with, and Otto doesn't wish a visit from them here in the camp on anyone. The doctor has to make a very careful examination, as he's not allowed to declare more than five percent of the forced laborers sick at any one time, which is why Otto requests that they avoid asking for sick leave at all costs. The doctor in Sobolec will declare each one fit for work or grant a couple of days off from work, while some he will ask to see again as he hands out a prescription that can be filled at the pharmacy, after which you have to head straight to the station to wait two or three hours for the midday train, hanging around in the waiting room out of the question, so you have to wait on the platform, where you sit on the benches only when there's no one else to claim a spot, while after you return you have to inform Otto about the doctor's findings, which determines if you are allowed to go to your room or head back to join the afternoon shift. Otto then explains that on Sundays he collects food tickets for the canteen, each laborer having several in his pocket in order to buy bread, while anyone who doesn't want to eat Frau Miltschi's food can keep all of his tickets, though it's wiser to use the canteen, for it pleases the head engineer. Last, Otto commands the new arrivals to break up into groups so that he can lead them to their rooms.

The groups quickly form together according to where they were on the train, Josef finding his fellow travelers, young boys who are roughly ten years younger than himself. After a while Otto leads Josef's group into a freshly swept room, the head of the camp then proceeding to add to the instructions he had shared with them outside. Wood for heating will be provided twice a week, for which a small fee will be charged, the room needing to be kept clean, no one allowed to keep any forbidden or black-market goods, which in fact has never occurred at Wirschenowitz, though at a neighboring camp all the inhabitants of one room were arrested after a room search, all eight of them never heard from again. Meanwhile, as for the wood, since it's August there's no need for any heat, but it's a rough climate, and by September they will want some, the oven easy to maintain, cooking is allowed, with plenty of water available from two pumps outside, while washing can be done down below in the creek, though water can also be brought up, each room having a pitcher and two basins for this purpose. The room should be cleaned early each morning, ashes and garbage needing to be hauled out and taken to the cesspit, no paper left lying around, the beds made in an orderly manner so that Čiperný can see that he lives among civilized people. At night the lights need to be out by ten, eleven on Saturday, followed by complete quiet. Josef is then named head of the group and is made responsible for his comrades, all the group leaders needing to meet with Otto briefly each evening, after which at nine he holds open office hours, though he asks that he be bothered only for the most pressing reasons and that everything be worked out in a friendly manner, after which Otto makes final rounds, not in order to snoop but to know personally that everywhere there is peace and quiet.

The head of camp shakes each hand and leaves the room, Josef now alone with his boys, at which he discusses how they are going to split up the beds, he wanting to earn their trust, Otto returning once more, since he forgot to say that everyone has to be in his room by eight o'clock at night, for any violation of the rules that is caught by a patrol can lead to serious consequences, each needing to be in his room according to strict rules, and though Čiperný can say that nothing will happen to anyone who is inside the camp, it's still forbidden to be in the canteen past eight o'clock. At this Otto leaves the room and Josef can talk with his colleagues, telling them that he hopes everything will go well between them, saying that he believes everyone needs to make sure to stay healthy. The young boys are nice, and seem to have their heads on their shoulders as they settle in and get used to the camp and wander around to see the surroundings, all of them returning before it's time for the lockdown, Simon pleasing Josef the most, demonstrating cleverness and maturity, while others show signs of feeling demoralized, mild doubts having transformed into fecklessness, hostile resistance, and self-indulgence, two of them continuing to talk on salaciously after returning from their ramble, where they met a girl from the village who had no qualms about going for a roll in the bushes, and that she'll be there again tomorrow, and whoever wants to can have her, for she's pretty and totally wild for men. Josef doesn't want to preach manners, nor does he want to be a spoilsport, but he warns the two of them vigorously that they will be arrested if it gets around, and a problem with a girl can cost you your life, not to mention threaten everyone in the room, if not the entire camp, which Josef says is the main concern, any threat to which he will not tolerate, not to mention that the room is not the place for such filth, for though he has nothing against earthy humor, he has no time for base and lewd talk. Josef speaks firmly and politely to his young mates, they listening to him reluctantly at first, then approvingly, realizing the need to be clear and in agreement about the serious consequences that can result from any negligent action, to build a sense of community among themselves that involves the same rules and responsibilities for all, everyone wanting to live sensibly and orderly, no matter what circumstances arise. One day the times will change, whereupon each can live as he pleases, but in Wirschenowitz you can survive only by bowing to or following a number of repugnant regulations, not because you acknowledge them on the inside, since they are unjust and horrible, but because necessity and discretion demand giving in temporarily.

Josef soon sees that it will be difficult to keep the young men together, but he knows this is what he must do. That's why he tells all of them that evening to be ready to leave the room quickly in an orderly fashion the next morning. The canteen has no evening meal ready for them, and just some watery soup, for which an unreasonable price is charged, which is why the boys decide on Josef's recommendation to put together the provisions they've brought along in order to make a meal together, and so they gather together sandwiches and cakes, someone coming up with a pot and some wood in order to prepare tea, as they decide that if the food in the canteen is terrible and unnourishing, then they will cook together on their own. From others who have already been here longer, Josef learns that the work is hard and difficult, especially when it's unfamiliar work, though it is bearable. The incident with the canteen doesn't bode well and resolves Josef to get members of his group to feed themselves, but he's told that without buying food they will soon go hungry, the recommendation being to get used to Frau Miltschi's food, because she's nasty and dangerous, for she can sic the police on the forced laborers, which is reason enough not to bother to disturb the image of matronly care in the canteen and to keep silent in the face of the scandalous conditions. To his question about what the head of the camp does to try to change things, he's told that he does as much as he can, but there's not much he can do, the building company continues to issue a proper lease to Frau Miltschi, who perhaps has an in with someone in the administration, perhaps not even anyone high up, though if it has always been the case that nepotism stands in the way of justice, nowadays influence and power do not at all depend on the titular function of any position, now protection is tied to subaltern positions in government or to law-enforcement positions, nothing more need be said, insinuations being all that's needed, while now everything is insinuated, a wink being all it takes, the powerless individual hardly ever having been more powerless, because such dirty tricks, which earlier would have been kept hidden and at least had some kind of moral opposition, now are attached to an idea through which they stealthily achieve justification. Josef is well aware of this, and needs no lecture on the current regime, but he does want to have a good understanding of the way things work in Wirschenowitz so that he can adapt to them.

Throughout the camp Josef finds that morale is good, there are splendid men here who have already accomplished something in life but who, because of the necessity of the times, have been derailed and landed in onerous poverty, resulting in their often remaining strong in their moral conviction, though for some it may be the case that it results in a certain measure of nihilsm that does not speak to their true nature. Some have brought along serious books, making sure to keep up with their reading, gatherings taking place in some rooms where similar interests are discussed. Someone named Eugene draws Josef into a developing discussion about materialism and idealism, for he feels that the current times make irrefutable the danger of any kind of idealism and, aside from the fact of whether or not he's right, he knows he is right in terms of Fascist enslavement, Eugene protesting vehemently when Josef counters that this has nothing to do with either idealism or materialism, as the economic or social relations of the world would seem to indicate. Materialism conceals no less danger than does idealism, political movements latching onto this or that set of ideas, not because they developed them themselves, but rather to popularize them in watered-down fashion through ideology, though one should realize that one doesn't suffer because of one set of ideas or the other, but rather through the transgressions of the modern slave holders, one being as bad as the next, whether his ideology is drawn from idealistic or materialistic ideas. But Eugene can't appreciate this point of view, he finds it incomprehensible that one has to suffer a regime these days that openly taps irrational ideas—which he continually equates with idealism—to assert its power, nor can he accept such old-fashioned beliefs, which Eugene calls romantic and reactionary, he being certain that the times will leave dreamers like Josef behind. Josef then counters that his view is that no one has ever suffered from the protection of sound moral footing but rather through the public and private erosion of such footing, to which he adds, "It's not a question of metaphysics, but instead a matter of ethics. That's why it doesn't matter whether materialism or idealism dominates." Eugene cannot understand this and is irritated, though Josef tries to ease any antagonism between them.

In addition to the intellectuals in Wirschenowitz there are also rougher characters, many of them quite splendid in their own right, bowing to a kind of optimism that unfortunately knows no half measures, it involving much more an urge for dignity that will not give in, and that is fine, as long as one doesn't become unthinking and suffer from illusions, for the war will certainly not be over soon, as all the laborers and many inhabitants believe here, Germany having invaded too many countries for there to be a quick end, which for the laborer will most certainly lead to dire consequences, though hardly any of them are aware of this. Notwithstanding his skepti-

cism, Josef doesn't believe that Germany can win, because "The more enemies the greater the honor" may sound good, but not when it involves too
many enemies, for the entire world cannot be conquered, not even with
modern weapons, though how things will unfold is unclear to Josef, but he
knows eventually this monstrosity will collapse. Josef, therefore, is not that
different from the optimists, these children only hoping for the next day to
pass, believing in miracles as they conjure their possibility inside themselves. But it will take more patience than that.

Josef takes a breath, feeling more free here than in the city, everything
easier in Wirschenowitz, no matter how hard it may indeed be, but in the
city it's murky, every step contains potential danger, fear, and mistrust, people afraid of their neighbors and their neighbors afraid of them, while men
in strange uniforms stomp heavily through the streets and bellow repulsive
songs, Josef trembling when this wretched singing marches around the corner and pierces the walls like a machine, some fleeing ahead of them, while
in addition to this bellowing there is the Pied Piper music of the pipes and
drums, Prussian soldiers arriving to fight in the fields of Silesia in Bohemia,
this clanging and strife mixing hideously with the noise in the streets, while
even from a distance one hears the painful warbling of unmelodic tunes
from the fifes and the dry rustle of drums. Across from the building where
Josef had last lived in the city is the shop and apartment of a short tailor by
the name of Jaroslav Kverka, whose four-year-old boy marched along the
street in military step, mimicking with his innocent child's voice that awful
music, though the child's bawling was continually droned out by the loud-
speaker whipping the march into a frenzy with beastly distorted sounds, in
between which could be heard the buffeting of crackling announcements
telling those aghast at hearing it of the victory of indomitable weapons over
a subjugated people, the thumping little phrases hardly comprehensible,
Josef at least unable to understand them as meaningful examples of human
speech.

Wirschenowitz is free of such pain. Though indeed things here are
tough, and though Čiperný is mean and the work hard, the chaos of the city
is distant, as well as the innumerable pressing prohibitions that transform
every act and allowance into a conscious undertaking. Here each breath is
not stripped of its freedom, dense woods rise nearby and are enticing, Josef

wanting to flee to them on Sundays, where he will worship each moment and let himself get lost where no path leads, and where for hours there is not a human sound, the power of the Creator all around him. These are imaginings that Josef still conjures as he lays out his blankets for the night, after which he tells his roommates good night and promises not to let them oversleep, he able to make himself get up at whatever hour he wants to. And then the first morning light breaks across Wirschenowitz, everything beginning to stir, the brown water prepared that is supposed to be coffee, bitter stuff that is never quite warm. Afterward the new arrivals begin to gather, the two young men from the employment office offering up to each a somewhat dumb little talk that doesn't say anything that Otto hasn't told them in much more clever and sympathetic fashion. At the close of their lecture they accompany the new arrivals to the builders' hut in order to hand them over to the bookkeeper, after which the procedure takes some time, which the new arrivals are overjoyed at, because it means that their actual work will begin much later. Gradually things get under way, Herr Podlaha and his secretary asking each laborer patronizing questions, as if they concerned matters of the alphabet, though what they want to know is the boys' natural talents and special expertise, at which each must be satisfied to learn that there really is not that much interesting work available. Salesmen, clerks, tailors, musicians, lawyers, teachers, and students would seem ready for quite capable work, but luckily you don't need special training to build a railroad, as every man can be taught how to handle a pick and a shovel correctly. At last the long questionnaire is filled out, behind the counter eyes read through it all again, after which hands shove it once more across the counter so that it is signed, no, on the right line, even if you cannot see it, aren't you supposed to be an educated man, a doctor, indeed here in the little box, but legibly please. Josef writes his name somewhat obscurely, at which the bookkeeper hands the new arrival a little card with his name and birth date, and Rybák written in the corner, Josef looking questioningly at Herr Podlaha once he has it in his hand, whereby the former explains that there's no need to keep looking at it, for it says Rybák, and that means the workstation that he is supposed to report to.

Many new arrivals have gone off in the meantime, an older worker or guard standing by to help anyone who has a question, Josef going up to one and learning, "Rybák? For that you take a right outside and head straight on, the people on the road will show you where to go." So Josef heads along the new stretch that passes by the builders' hut to cross over the highway. Here there is work going on at the moment, the building having moved on, the earth stamped down firmly, the rails of a light railway traveling over it, it being easy to walk along, mountains rising to the right, while to the left the landscape descends steeply to the river. Soon you reach the forest, with only the passageway for the train roughly cut through it as Josef nears an odd-looking wooden structure and hears a low rumbling in the distance, more heaps of gravel resting here in various heights, a couple of men walking around or standing, a couple of laborers nearby, one of whom speaks to Josef and asks him what he wants, to which Josef says that he's new and is looking for the way to Rybák. "My friend, how unlucky! It's bad at Rybák's. If you just keep along this stretch, the first master you come to will be him. At least you don't have far to get back home." Josef, though, wants to know what is the structure from which all the noise is coming, and he's told that it's a gravel mill, there being only a few who work there, though the work isn't bad, especially when it's outdoors, for inside it's pretty dusty, but at least when it rains you can keep dry.

Josef then walks on farther and after a while reaches a deep cliff cut, everything looking smooth and almost done, just a few men working here and there, as Josef asks for Master Rybák. Yes, he's here, he's told, the question being whether the new arrival is supposed to work for him. Yes, he's supposed to work here, could they please point out the master. Josef is told to just go on straight ahead, he'll find the master either out back in his shack or somewhere along that stretch. Indeed, Rybák is in his shack and comes straight out as Josef greets him, which the master does not respond to in any kind of unfriendly manner but instead takes the card and looks at his new worker, after which Rybák gives Josef back the card and says that it seems that Josef has hardly ever worked in building. No, he had not. To this the overseer responds that it doesn't matter, for as long as his intentions are good it will work out, he having received five new arrivals of late, no doubt more will come, these being the gentlemen sent to build the railroad, hardly any of them having worked before as an unskilled laborer, though if they are willing and able, then none of them will have any trouble with Rybák, each only needing, of course, to do his work, no question about that, though at this site he needs no more new people, for everything will be done in four weeks, in fact just today they are starting a new section way at the end of the cliff cut, which is a good place to start in with easier work, Foreman Sláma ready to show them what to do, meaning that Josef should go to Sláma with his card, for he'll find him if he just continues along straight ahead.

Josef walks on again, the path getting tougher as he approaches a section where the work has not progressed very far, to the right the landscape falling off much more steeply than before, though the rush of the creek cannot be heard because it is drowned out by the thunderous noise that disturbs the peace of the wounded forest landscape, the cliffs shattered by jackhammers, the workers sweating and straining, having to pause again and again as the ringing and pounding steel hammer shakes them from head to toe. Josef is told by one of the many workers that Master Chudoba is in charge here. The route is uneven, it moves slowly forward, a light train moving toward Josef with full cars, a dumping site nearby where the rubble and earth are emptied out, after which it climbs to a position where most of Chudoba's workers are located, as they work at loosening stones with pickaxes, other men standing nearby who then shovel the rubble into the train cars. Josef goes on ahead, the forest stretching out from the rail bed, to the left fields and meadows opening up, to the right the glittering creek, while farther on is the village called Najdek, the rails of the light train suddenly coming to an end, the rail bed ending as well, which must be the end of the cliff cut, the terrain also sinking farther, though Rybák had indeed said that where Josef should head to is a new segment, which must mean the dump below, where there also appear to be workers who are working on a ditch that bores through deeply cut terrain that would be best bridged over, the workers perhaps preparing the first pylons. Josef heads down to them, though there is no path, just noticeable footsteps in the soil, it taking some effort to reach the ditch, which is traversed by two loose planks, someone telling him that the building of the bridge is led by Master Vodil, Josef told that wood is being gathered here when he asks what all the supplies are for, though he doesn't need to be told what the powerful concrete mixer is for, yet no one tells him what is really going on, and so he simply asks where he can find Herr Sláma, someone instructing him to follow the path down the incline as if he were heading to Najdek, but before he reaches it he must turn left and climb up the embankment that has no path, and there he'll find Sláma.

Josef walks on in the direction he was told and soon reaches the embankment, someone asking from above where he is heading and whether he is looking for Sláma. Yes, he's looking for Herr Sláma. That's good, says the voice, he should head up, for it's Sláma himself. Josef quickly climbs up to the spot where some have already gathered, having sat themselves down comfortably as if they were there to enjoy the view, it being quite beautiful from here, the edge of the village of Najdek lying to the left, a village much smaller than Wirschenowitz, the little village stretching out toward the creek, a hill rising directly from the other shore, while to the right the vale that will soon be bridged descends, with the hill behind and from which Josef just came, though he has no time to look around any further, for he has to greet Herr Sláma, who is already waiting, as Josef hands him the card, at which the foreman formally introduces himself as Florian Sláma, the name Florian resulting from his having been born at night, there having been a fire in Pechno and the mother thinking that one shouldn't spend too much time thinking about a name, the fire a sign of which patron saint to select for the child. Josef is surprised by Sláma's talk, and indeed the foreman quickly throws a glance at his worker's card and says that Josef is a common name in his family, his father was called Josef, which is why his oldest son is also named that, after which he says that Josef will enjoy working for him, Sláma thinking that for people like Josef things will get better with time, one can see that he is a studious man, perhaps a professor or a teacher, it not only being a shame but also an accursed waste of talent to send a doctor to work on a railroad. At this Josef says that he doesn't really think it's all that bad. Sláma insists that it's a shame, even a sin, that it can come to no good, each man needing to be allowed to work according to what God and his talent have readied him for. Josef doesn't press the matter, he doesn't want to insist on anything, though Sláma doesn't back off and bemoans the fact that a doctor should be put to work digging here, after which he asks him what kind of doctor he is, for Frau Sláma is not well, she has often gone to the doctor in Sobolec, though he can do nothing for her, she has such back pain, the doctor saying that it's rheumatism, as he writes a prescription, yet the

324 / H. G. ADLER

salve doesn't help, but maybe it will be better if Josef could have a look at her. Josef explains that he's not a medical doctor, even if he is a doctor. For Sláma a doctor is a doctor, an educated man understands health, and he has been awarded the title of doctor, at which Sláma says again what a shame it is how people are treated these days, just because they are Jews or doctors, things had been fine before, everyone living in peace, each having enough to eat and drink, even being able to save a bit, but now that's all over with, since *he* has taken over the country, Sláma not saying his name, though *he* has done nothing for Bohemia, the people have nothing, *he* gives the people no bread, but instead takes their bread away, injustice never leads to good, for now *he's* at war with the entire world, though *he* won't manage to get England, and then there's Russia, we'll see, Sláma being a simple man who doesn't understand as much about politics as the mighty masters, though he doesn't believe a word of what is written in the newspapers, for certainly *he* will never be able to handle the Americans.

Sláma interrupts his lecture, because on the path below he sees another new arrival, whom he calls to just as he did to Josef, asking just as quickly what he wants. Then Sláma says that they have to get to work soon, though there's still time, he's waiting until the entire party is gathered together, so Josef should sit down with the others. And so Josef sits down on the grass and observes Florian Sláma as he speaks with the broad accent of these parts and stands with his feet spread wide, it being funny how the little man is nonetheless wrapped in the great warmth of a much too large, thick dark suit, as if he were dressed for an important event, his hair still dark, though the goatee is silver-gray, the combination of his somewhat dour frown and roguish, twinkling eyes hard to reconcile, he seeming quite friendly one minute and quite different the next, as he continues to smoke a stubby pipe and spits often as he does. There is hardly a word spoken by Josef's colleagues on the grass, and he himself is quiet, soon stretching out comfortably and closing his eyes, the sun warming him pleasantly, he almost feeling as if he's on a comfy summer trip, Sláma now quiet as well, the wind blowing lightly, everything peaceful, himself ready for a good long sleep.

Suddenly Sláma calls out, "Boys, the party is gathered together! Now it's time we got to work! I'm not after anyone, but we have to do our duty. Everyone has to give all he can. Then better days will come, and our railroad will be done. Someday you'll bring your people here and tell them, 'This is where I worked, here with Sláma!' But before you can say that you have to accomplish something, otherwise it will all come to nothing. When Master Rybák shows up, make sure not to stand around like a pack of idiots. And when old man Čiperný shows up, then have at it, no looking right, no looking left, just straight ahead, and work, work, work! Meanwhile, come along with me so we can get some tools." Everyone jumps up, and Sláma goes with his people to the work site below, where the wooden storage shacks for the bridge builders are located, there also being a shed that Sláma opens and from whose stockpile of tools he takes a pickaxe, no shovels, for today they don't need them, Sláma looking over all the pickaxes and sometimes saying, "Not right, let's look for another," though finally Sláma is satisfied, he closes the shed, and they head back up the hill. There Sláma explains what you can see from there, it being a steep precipice, though it will soon be flattened, no doubt it will take a while, we'll just have to see how it goes, how it moves ahead, though no one really knows yet what kind of material they'll have to dig into, it starting with grass, then earth, hopefully a lot of earth and not so much sticky clay, after which there is always a lot of stone, followed by bedrock, which will have to be drilled into and explosives used, though by then all the new arrivals will be masters, today being when they will start in clearing away the turf. Sláma takes hold of one of the picks and shows how to use it, it only requiring the right approach, and by that Sláma means a certain knack, and once you get the hang of it and feel more sure, then it's easy, and it looks so when he does it, it being quite a sight as the stocky man deftly pierces the earth and with one tug releases a square of turf that he then tosses away.

Work begins, some having no trouble with it, some a bit more skilled and others less so, Sláma often taking the pick from someone's hand and showing how it's done. "See? *Shoop!* And I don't even have to strain at it. Out comes the hunk of turf!" But simply explaining and demonstrating is not enough, for some are still terrible at it, though Sláma doesn't grow impatient but instead talks to the boys, it being only the first day, they will all learn, you just have to find your rhythm, that's all. Some work too fast, the foremen shouting to them, "Boys, that's no way to go about it! You need to pace yourself and remain calm. Always the same motion. That way you won't be tired in the evening." Soon it grows hot, the workers throwing off their jackets, then their shirts, though some of the more sensible tell them that they should watch out for sunburn. Josef is neither particularly adept nor not adept, Sláma explaining how to do it a number of times and showing him as well, after which he doesn't seem to be too worried about Josef, who doesn't strain himself too terribly, though he gives his best, for Sláma needs it, and his intentions are good. The time passes frightfully slowly, each minute stretching out with a perpetual slowness, it having been about ten o'clock when each laborer pulled up his first hunk of turf, many of the boys tired already, their backs aching and their palms hurting, Sláma advising them to just spit into their hands, showing them how to, for then the shaft sits right in your hands, you need to draw back after each stroke and stand erect, and not hold the pick too tight, only one hand gripping it a bit more, the other relaxed and sliding back and forth, which makes it easy and helps it to feel good.

It's only eleven o'clock, but the boys take ever more frequent breaks, short ones at first, then longer and longer, Sláma reminding them that they have to do something, they can be seen from too far off, and all the masters have damned good eyes, so make sure to always work like a madman, especially if they're watching, rather than just dumbly slacking off and gawking or leaning on your shovel until you get swelling under your chin. Many of them understand what Sláma wants, though unfortunately others do not and believe he's a phony who pretends to be friendly and yet is a slave driver, but Sláma does what he can to take care of his men, he only reminding them of what is necessary, once yelling, "Boys, Rybák!" He has just seen the master as he starts to climb down the embankment, which takes about ten minutes, though it actually takes him about half an hour, because he stops to talk to Vodil. Everyone works vigorously, though Rybák is not fooled and knows that this hurry is not real, he telling the new arrivals that they should not strain themselves, no one expects anything superhuman from them, just honest work, as he goes from man to man and looks at each for a while, taking the pick from most and showing them what Sláma has shown them already, the master telling them that he also started as an unskilled laborer when he was very young and just out of school at fourteen, and now he's a master, meaning that everyone here can aspire to be an overseer, which is not bad, after which Rybák writes down all the names on a list, since Sláma has their work cards, on which he notes how many hours they work each day.

As soon as the overseer has disappeared behind the hill, the tempo eases a lot, everyone hot and wrung out, each wanting something to drink. Sláma asks if anyone brought a can for water, and indeed no one has thought to, at which it occurs to Sláma that there are some down by where they are building the bridge, so he sends a boy to ask Vodil for a can. Then someone says to Sláma that it's already twelve, he should let someone go to the canteen to get some soup, to which Sláma says he has no problem with that, except that unfortunately he isn't the one who can grant permission, it has to be arranged with the master, not with Sláma, who knows nothing about it and is just an everyday foreman who has to answer to Čiperný and, should he find out about it things could get sticky, which is why there won't be any soup today. The boy returns from Vodil with a can and asks Sláma where he can get some water, but the former has already picked Josef, telling him, "Go down toward Najdek, but not all the way to the path. Instead, head left until you get to a couple of houses. If no one is home, just go a bit farther until you come to a well." Josef is pleased by this unexpected reprieve, reaching the first house after five minutes, though no one is there, while at the next he sees an old woman who tells him to come as she asks what he wants. Josef says he wants to get some water, at which she tells him to come in and begins to ask what he's really doing, who are these people in Wirschenowitz, why have they been sent here, for there is no sense in building a railroad while there's a war on. It also doesn't sit well with the woman that the train will pass by her house, all that noise, and how easily a spark from the locomotive can land in your eye, that having once happened to her son, he having ridden on the train and stuck his head out the window, a spark having hit him in the eye and burning him terribly, such that he couldn't see for three days, nor does anyone in Najdek need a new railroad, but if indeed it is to be built, then it shouldn't be with forced laborers, whether Christians or Jews, she having already had a look at the people and concluding that they looked all right and not like criminals. For Josef the conversation takes too long, he needs to get the water so that his comrades are not kept waiting. The woman agrees, giving him an apple and saying that he should always feel free to come to her for water.

Josef heads back and wants to place the can in the middle of the site, but Sláma orders him to carry it from man to man so that each can have a drink, and as soon as he finishes his round some call out that he should come back, but Sláma declares that it's enough for now, you shouldn't drink too much, soon the lunch break will come and everyone will be thirsty, it being best for Josef to put the can in the shade so that the water doesn't get warm right away, and once the can is empty someone just needs to tell Sláma and he'll send someone to get more. The change of pace has done Josef good, the pick feels lighter in his hand, he pulling up one hunk of turf after another, as Sláma looks at his watch to see if it's not already time for the lunch break, saying perhaps it's not easy to hear the whistle from here, the locomotive of the light train is supposed to give the sign, though in a headwind they could have missed it, so Sláma holds strong, a bit more time passes, then it's one o'clock and still no whistle, then Sláma calls out, "Stop! Lunchtime!" Right away he lies down and pulls a sausage sandwich from his pocket, the other workers also sitting down and tearing into their snacks, though after a while a siren sounds. "Boys, they're late again! Lunchtime was supposed to start fifteen minutes ago!" Some have fallen asleep, others just stir and doze now and then. Josef squints at the sun and thinks about how best to fit in here, how things are with Sláma, it being indeed quite comfortable, though it can hardly remain so, one needing to be ready for much worse. A nice conversation with Sláma would be good, but Josef feels that it's better to keep his distance, for he doesn't want to become Sláma's pet. All too quickly the lunch break is over, although Sláma doesn't make them begin at one-thirty but instead waits for the siren, which means the break ends up lasting forty-five minutes, though the new arrivals are already tired, some of them with hands hurting.

The afternoon drags slowly on, Josef having three times looked at the clock, after which he vows not to do so again, it being better to work slowly and be surprised when quitting time finally arrives. He feels wrung out and empty, though he's not sleepy, not at all overtired, yet his life spirit is drained and dim, as if erased by a mantle of fog, his pick growing ever heavier in his hands, though it doesn't hurt, he believing nonetheless that he has gotten much more adept at using it, Sláma at least not having said anything to him, even though he corrected others, repeating the same words over and over in a monotone, Josef looking on as he stands behind and demonstrates once again the right way to hold one's hands, the pupil standing next to him with a somewhat strange expression, happy at least not to have to hold the pick for a moment. The fact that time rushes by concerns Sláma less and less, he only casting a furtive glance at people without saying anything, only once becoming more attentive when one of his group clearly isn't applying himself and keeps taking longer and longer pauses, Slama calling out, "Boy, what are you doing?" He's a smart guy who answers peacefully with the sheepish face of a schoolboy who's been caught, "Nothing!" Good-natured, yet unflinching, Sláma replies, "Then do something!"

Sláma appears to be measuring something, then three civil servants arrive, carrying a large crate, Sláma telling them where to put it, it having a hinged top with a lock on the front, which Sláma then proceeds to try to open. Then another civil servant arrives and announces that Rybák has sent along some stuff that is down below with Vodil, and since they need to haul the stuff up the boys stop digging up the turf and they all go down to Vodil, where they find a load of planks, boards, and battens that all have to be carried up, as well as a host of wheelbarrows that lie about with a wheel in the air, reminding Josef of beetles or bees. Most are happy for the change of pace, each grabbing a bundle of battens or boards, the long planks shouldered by two as they move them along the path below and then up the hill, they being too heavy otherwise, while the iron wheelbarrows take a lot of effort to push up the hill, Rybák, who shows up unannounced, ordering them to come up over by Vodil, where it's not so steep, for it's easier that way, and everything can be transported much better, even if it takes longer. Josef meanwhile looks out at the fields, potatoes and turnips still waiting to be harvested, the meadows taking on a late-summer look, everything encased in a golden hue, a cheerful sight, his eye sweeping along the edge of the forest, no one visible anywhere, the world's evil for once dissolving, the earth wanting to know nothing of what people do, it patiently withstanding everything that happens, though it is untouched by meaningless events, work carrying on, though the earth couldn't give a care. It means nothing to her when a cliff is detonated here and there, she just takes it in and feels nothing, and even when she does sense it she is wounded for only a short time and just as quickly forgets it, as only people suffer as a result of their work. Josef imagines all this, but he also knows how silly and sentimental his thoughts are, arising as they do from the constant trials of a sniveling powerlessness looking for comfort amid a hopeless situation, he having been condemned to loneliness in being separated from all his friends, no longer knowing whom he is close to in this world, while here there is no one whom he has known longer than since yesterday, and it weighs on him. Josef looks off into the distance, though there is no view here, everywhere there are impediments, woods cutting off the view, behind which there must be open land, town after town, on and on, there always being more sweeping views until you reach the nation's borders, though they no longer mean anything, for everything is up for grabs now, while farther on you can hear the whirl of snarling commotion, men also holding shovels and picks in their hands there, war being fought, Josef having learned as a school child the word "weaponry," something that spreads mounting noise, clashing and rattling, war on the loose, no one knowing what it's about, a mad grin lacing the battle, a dreamlike ambiguity covering it over with a green mold, puddles of blood, dung, stench, the earth there as well, perhaps frightened for a moment before ragged, smoking heaps, all of it too much to take, though the earth really isn't afraid, these being only childish thoughts.

Then it's finally over, Sláma calling out that work is finished, soon the evening will begin, only make sure to turn over the wheelbarrows so that they don't fill with rain, as well as clean the picks. "Boys, make sure the tools are clean! As we start to dig deeper, always clean the tools, so that nothing sticks to them! Otherwise the shovels will be too heavy. And make sure to leave none lying around! Never give your pick and shovel to someone else to take care of!" Sláma watches as they put the picks back in the shed, after which he locks it up, though no one is allowed to head home yet, but finally the siren sounds, everyone wishing Sláma good night as he waves in return. Josef is tired, but his legs feel fine and he heads toward home in a good mood, curious to learn how things went for his roommates as he quickens his pace, someone telling him that he shouldn't hurry so, for he'll get gravel in his shoes, and you can get blisters on your soles and heels, Josef thanking

the person for the warning, though he hardly pays attention to it, he knowing how to walk just fine. He sees that he doesn't have to follow the rail bed
all the way back to the builders' hut, for a good ways before the gravel mill
a shortcut branches off, running steeply down through roots and sharp
stones, but soon improving, though it's quite damp despite the dry weather,
the earth black, the air cool, the creek finally reached, the woods now behind him, to the right meadows ranging out toward the embankment on
which the new railroad will run, the last stretch passing by the engineers'
cinder-block houses. Josef looks at his watch, noting that even though he
hurried, it had taken him nearly an hour to get back.

Josef comes into the room, the others already having gathered there, all
of them much more tired than himself, he having handled it much better,
one of them working under Chudoba, while the rest are with Sajdl. The
youths lie about casually with their dirty boots on and mess up their bedding, though Josef tells them to take their boots off and pull themselves together, which they do as they begin to tell about how hard it is to work for
Sajdl, who is in charge of the area to the left of the builders' hut, the tempo
murderous, Sajdl a dog without the slightest bit of care for the new arrivals,
he instead having scoffed that they were young, fresh boys, so they should
pick and shovel faster, the light train bringing along huge cars that four men
were supposed to fill in half an hour, and then the train would pull away, but
not a single new arrival had succeeded, the older workers needing a minimum of thirty-five minutes. The master had screamed that they were idiots,
lazy vermin, for he can do it in twenty, you just need to throw your ass into
it, but still it did no good. Then Čiperný showed up, and even he said that
Sajdl shouldn't be so hard on his people. By afternoon things had slowed
down somewhat, but by then everyone was exhausted and needed forty minutes or even longer to load the cars, the master threatening that he should
make them work overtime if this continued to happen, but today he will be
lenient because it's the first day. There is only one advantage to working for
Sajdl, and that is that at noon you can run over to the canteen, toss down the
slop they serve, and quickly run back up to the work site, arriving breathless,
though soon the whistle blows and straight off you're shoveling away like
mad without having had any time to rest.

Josef advises the boys to stay at the work site in future in order to lie down and rest, meaning that they should take something along to eat and forget the canteen food. This idea is met with approval, the boys saying it was too miserable in the canteen, where last year's rotten potatoes are served, along with a disgusting broth, the soup tasting like dishwater. Josef then recommends that they cook for themselves each night, but the boys say that they don't know how to and they are too tired, though Josef says that's not a problem, for he's willing to cook for them, he only needs one helper to do so, and that they can simply buy food and make simple meals, while each week only four of them pick up food in the canteen, although this week they'll wait and see if the food is still so miserable and if they will have enough money to buy groceries. Josef will head straight off into town with a knapsack in order to see where he can get some proper milk, and maybe he'll bring back a few other things as well, though someone will need to go with him. Simon volunteers to do so, and also gets a knapsack.

Already the first farm they come to is ready to sell them some milk for ration tickets. Eight people. Let's see, that's no more than a liter a day, but we'll have to see what we can do, for it can be arranged, and if no one tells anyone, then there will be three liters a day available. Josef and Simon are satisfied with this plan, but before they head back they want to go into the village in order to purchase a milk can, but where is the best place to do so? Kopřiva is the best, and sometimes he won't even ask for a ration ticket. Go to Kopřiva, he's just past the bridge, the first shop, a tiny place, but chock-full of goods, where they find both people from the village and forced laborers, Kopřiva and his wife having their hands full with trying to serve all the customers, though finally it's Josef and Simon's turn as they buy a couple of pots, a pan, a five-liter can, two cooking spoons, and a good kitchen knife, after which they also take a couple of loaves of bread, happy that they are not forced to take only a part of each. They then promise always to shop there, if they can, and Kopřiva promises that, yes, they will always be well served, as long as possible, but ration tickets will indeed have to be used. But we can sell you what others are willing to do without, so they buy potatoes, barley, grits, and oatmeal as well. This is fine with Kopřiva, for no one in Wirschenowitz wants oatmeal, nor does anyone want the cornmeal that has been stripped of its oil, so they get cornmeal, as well as some proper flour. But only for ration tickets. Sugar must also go for tickets, as well as marmalade, salt, and some spices, and could they have some vegetables? Ah, I'm afraid there are none, just some leeks, vegetables are rare here in general, but you can have some dried onions, yes, and there's pudding powder as well, though hardly anyone wants it, for nobody buys it. Yes, we'd be happy to have some. Then Frau Kopřiva says that there are some sour pickles. This pleases Simon, who wants to take some—eight men, two for each, so sixteen in all. No, you can't have that many, only eight, no customer is supposed to get more than five, but since it's eight men we can make an exception. Simon can't wait and eats his pickle on the spot, Josef doing so as well, which satisfies each, after which the bill must be tallied, please could you write it down, what exactly does that refer to? Ah yes, the caraway seeds, and that's the barley, that's the grits, it all makes sense, here's your change, that's right, after which the two say goodbye with both knapsacks full, as well as their hands, and Kopřiva calls out, "Please do us the honor again sometime soon, we have good schnapps available!" But already they are on their way back, the milk ready at the farm, the only question being whether they want fresh farmer's cheese as well. Yes, let's have some, a kilo of cheese, here's the money, and the two turn away satisfied.

The boys in the room have been resting for a bit, and when they see all the groceries their eyes brim with joy, after which the stove is quickly lit, Josef begins to make a hearty soup, and when he discovers that he didn't get any margarine Simon gives him a little chunk of fat, though tomorrow they'll have to make sure not to forget margarine when they go to Kopřiva, while in the meantime sweet corn pudding is prepared. The wood provides a steady fire, the stove is excellent, and so the food is soon done, there being a lot of it, though no one worries that any will be left over, for everything is divided up and consumed. How quickly and easily they have arranged their own accommodations here, some saying how fantastic it all is, and that they want to keep doing the same. None of Josef's colleagues think about sneaking out the way they did yesterday, and although they are all very tired, each also feels very content, his bond with the others strengthening, his depression waning. Josef thinks his comrades will get used to it all, nor will Sajdl eat them up, they just need to be strong and keep their heads and not dwell upon their cares too much. Josef doesn't need to tell them to get some rest, for they are happy to do so on their own.

Simon still wants to talk to Josef and says, "My hands are clearly going to be ruined here. I play the violin. My hands will get too stiff from working. Already my fingers feel like clumps. I couldn't play a scale even if I tried." Josef wants to comfort him, for certainly you can't play the violin after such work, but in two or three years Germany will have lost the war, you have to be patient until then, while in the meantime it makes no sense to keep dwelling on the future. Simon agrees, though he cannot believe that the war will last only another two years, Germany is much too strong, and if it goes well it could last four years, and by then with or without forced labor the Jews will be finished, they won't be allowed to live in such half-free manner as they do here in Wirschenowitz for long, because it's only a transitional period. Simon has a cousin who has it on good intelligence that bad things are being planned for the Jews, and that they will be shut up in large camps and supposedly all sent to Poland, and whoever doesn't die in the process will be threatened with pogroms and hunger, the families ripped apart and destroyed, sick and old and weak people certainly having no chance of survival. Simon's greatest fear is that his father was taken as a hostage in Pilsen at the start of the war and was never let go, and that he is sitting in a German camp called Buchenwald, his mother continually afraid, for now that Simon is no longer with her she is alone with her aging mother, the father having run a busy practice as a skin doctor, the best specialist far and wide, he being a wonderful man, somewhat quiet but full of good humor. He made the most wonderful toys for Simon, none of the ones for sale half so beautiful, he once having built a medieval castle out of wood, complete with towers and battlements, and painted splendidly, while he had also taken such joy in Simon's progress with the violin, such that he came to pressure the boy a bit, saying that he must become a violinist, because he had what it takes, while the father loved to comment on Simon's playing, even though he wasn't a trained musician himself, he not understanding the expressive aspects of the violin, but rather the technical problems, such that Simon learned as much from him as from all his teachers. It's almost a year since he was arrested, yes, in fourteen days it will be a year, and he's only rarely allowed to write and very little, though they are valiant letters, he knowing marvelously how to conceal what he means to say, though the mother and son know exactly what he means to say, he telling the mother to be brave, for Simon to study hard and play his violin in order to improve, though it's been months since he's been able to, since he had to work in a factory during the day, and at night he had to help his mother, he being able to practice only on the weekends.

"I'm afraid that I'm finished with the violin for good. I don't even have it with me here. It would be ridiculous. I wouldn't risk taking my good violin along, and the bad one . . . No, it's just better that I don't have one at all." Josef reminds Simon that he's still very young, and he has a long time to decide whether or not he will become a violinist, so he shouldn't burden himself now, for these days it's easy to get lost in plans for the future, but he should still live for his music, and think about beautiful, uplifting works inside. It's especially in times like these that you question whether art is worth anything and, should you not want to make it, that doesn't mean that life comes to a standstill, for life is what the living value most, it can be willingly sacrificed out of dignity, but no price can ever be placed upon it, and even amid forced labor you don't sacrifice your dignity, for it's what allows you to endure. This helps Simon to think about how his father would handle matters, he no doubt suffering much worse conditions than anyone in Wirschenowitz. Josef reminds him of the hard work ahead of them tomorrow, that he needs to get some sleep, and that they will remain friends and will spend many hours togther on Sundays, after which they say good night.

The week marches on, the digging up of the area of turf nears an end, after which the heavier work begins, though it's not too strenuous, especially when the weather is good. Josef gets better and better at his work, it showing in the fact that Rybák is not constantly angry, Josef is not yelled at the way many of his colleagues are, while Sláma also remains friendly, and he is beginning to know everyone in his group by name. Josef has had a salve for rheumatism sent to him, one that's tried-and-true, and he gives it to Sláma for his wife, the former thanking him very much, saying that he knew Josef was a doctor, and if the salve helps Josef will get a hefty slab of bacon. Soon a bed is laid for the light train, as they dig up the ground with their picks and wheel the wheelbarrows, the extra clumps of earth are broken up with picks in order to shovel them into the train barrows, Sláma demonstrating how to handle the iron barrows, they needing to be filled properly and guided along planks, otherwise if they slide off the wheel presses straight into the soft earth and is hard to pull out, though no need to worry, it will all work with a bit of care and attention. Guiding the wheelbarrow up a narrow, wobbly plank and adroitly tipping it over above is harder, Josef often losing control of the barrow and spilling his load, it then taking a few minutes to fill the barrow again, though Josef is hardly annoyed but instead finds it funny, for he can't take the building of the railroad seriously, the track a ridiculous project that has no purpose whatsoever, the progress of the building even more ridiculous yet, for there is hardly any coordination of the work at hand, which could be utilized for quite different purposes if the Conqueror weren't so maddeningly fixated on shoving around the people he oppressed.

Josef notices a boy who is clever and dreamy and exceptionally handsome, who works quickly and easily, even though he is delicate and fragile, he remaining noticeably clean, Josef not having seen anyone among Sláma's crew who got neither his clothes nor his hands dirty, even his boots are not as dusty as the others, Karl Peters his name, his daintiness and his graceful movements causing him to be laughed at in the beginning, though now hardly anyone even pays attention. Once during the lunch break Josef seeks out Karl and begins to have a conversation with him, which is not easy to do, for Karl is quite shy and keeps somewhat to himself, although he's indeed friendly to everyone and very agreeable to work with. Karl explains that he is treating his stay in the work camp like an extended school vacation of uncertain length. "That's how I've come to think of it. I don't let myself be affected by what goes on around me."—"But you are nothing more than a forced laborer."—"Of course, but I don't let myself be conscious of it. I don't want to go crazy. Everyone is crazy these days. I don't like to get caught up in psychological problems. I want to stay normal."—"But you can't separate yourself from your surroundings."—"Unfortunately, not completely, though to some extent. Many things I simply choose not to see, they don't exist for me."—"Do you think that you'll be able to survive that way?"—"I don't know whether I'll survive. None of us knows that. But I won't let up so long as I'm alive." Karl works with his eyes half shut, he being quite sure of himself, even when he's moonily lost in a dream. Josef has never come across him on the path from work and learns from him that he doesn't follow the path the whole way, for it only reminds him more than necessary of the labor he's forced to do, which he shies away from wherever it occurs, instead having discovered a wonderful path that leads toward Wirschenowitz through dense woods, all you have to do is cross a bridge in Najdek and then head right, it taking a couple of minutes longer, though you hardly ever encounter another person and don't have to stumble along over the railroad ties. It pleases Josef as well and he also begins to use this path, but not every day.

Josef's roommates have long since settled in, one of them named Kurt having benefited from being too weak for the work done under Sajdl. There Čiperný had observed how Kurt strained himself so and yet couldn't do what was asked of him, and Sajdl called him over one day and had him come help in the supply shed, where boards, handles for shovels and picks, clamps, nails, oil, soft soap, and other items were issued, Kurt having it good there, though with a lot to do sometimes, especially when he has to help a strong civil servant saw some wood, whereby Kurt loses his breath, though luckily the sawing doesn't last that long. Jindra works under Chudoba at the dumping site, there being a foreman there who reminds one of Sláma and who is called Kalda and is a cottager from Wirschenowitz who maintains that the railroad will never be finished, at least not as long as the Conqueror rules Bohemia. The engine pulls the freight cars up the hill as they hurry to dump their loads, but it's not that easy, because the stuff in the cars often sticks, so they have to beat the sides with shovels, though that doesn't always work, and then someone has to stand on the coupling between two cars and tirelessly shovel out the earth and scrape it so that the load sits loosely in the car again, especially if it's full of stones, then everything rushes down the embankment with a great *whoosh*, Kalda wildly shouting, "Careful! The train will tip over as well!" That has actually never happened, but once it derailed, a freight car having rolled loose and clambered down the embankment almost all the way to the creek, Kalda at first having laughed, but then he became quite serious, Chudoba arriving in a state and yelling, "Sabotage! That was done on purpose!," he wanting to arrest everyone working at the dump site, but Kalda calmed him down and said that these people did a good job, it just happened because this freight car is in such bad shape and many of the railcars are worn out. Then Čiperný showed up as well, he yelling even louder about why they weren't more careful, the entire workday wasted, and then Chudoba had to quiet Čiperný down. Kalda was ordered to go down the embankment with four men in order to drag the railcar back up, they having neither ropes nor chains, so that they had to get those first from the supply hut, but even then it didn't work, for they needed another eight men, until finally the railcar was brought back up, on this day four fewer trains able to dump their loads, and Chudoba's men ended up taking a rest. Otherwise it's very quiet at the dumping site, "twenty" whispered when there is no train to unload, and only the rails needing to be extended when the dumping causes the embankment to extend farther, they needing to be always close to the edge, otherwise there's no way to dump, though the rails also cannot be too close to the edge so that the subsurface is strong enough to hold the weight of the train and it doesn't slide. In order to extend the tracks, a simple tool is used, namely the "dog," which is a rod that holds the spike in place when you pry the spreading rails back together on top of the anchored ties, after which you need to place stones under the ties so that the tracks run evenly.

Five of Josef's boys still work under Sajdl, and everything there goes according to plan. Sajdl gets after everyone as before, even doling out cuffs on the ears, though the roommates themselves have never been hit, but it's a grind, it taking thirty minutes or more to fill a railcar, and if only one among the crew doesn't pull his weight all the rest suffer, and because Sajdl never eases up on the daily quota they often have to work overtime. Simon finds it tolerable to work for Sajdl, and he no longer complains about what will happen to his hands because of this work. The communal group continues to fend for itself, Josef having to report at the gathering of group leaders just how they manage to do so, as Josef tells them about the shared funds, which are used to buy the groceries and the cooking utensils, and how it makes life easier, though you have to keep an eye on all your boys in order to make sure that no one takes advantage of the system for his own needs. Josef had to really get after Zdenko, who more than once had secretly taken some sugar, Josef explaining to him that such precious staples have to be shared equally, while bread is something each can have as much of as he wants, Josef offering potatoes as well. Lately communal arrangements have been springing up in a number of barracks, and sometimes they work out, other times things go wrong, there being no communal spirit that comes together, and the effort has to be abandoned.

One morning one of the new arrivals disappeared and didn't come back again. Otto was deeply worried whether the escape would lead to things going badly for the rest. People conjectured that the escapee must have stolen a good bit of money from his comrades, though no one knew just when he escaped, for the boy had been there in the evening, his roommates even confirming that he had gotten undressed to go to bed, though in the morning there was not a trace of him to be found. Otto couldn't keep the escape secret from the head engineer, who immediately wanted to inform the police in Sobolec, but with a good deal of begging the group leader was able to convince him that it would serve as a sign of the poor work ethic of his comrades, who in fact worked as well as they did because of the freedom and mobility granted them, all of which would disappear in a single stroke, it not being fair to let a hundred and sixty men pay the price for one boy's thoughtless, stupid action. Čiperný said that he was sorry, but it was his responsibility, and if it was discovered he would be arrested and punished, so he had to report it, if only to protect himself. With some effort Otto tried to convince him to simply report it to the employment office, since the escapee was clearly mentally ill and the comrades had noted from the very first day his strange ways. Luckily, Chudoba showed up in the midst of the altercation and explained that the escapee was a screwy bird, he having showed up to work in a huntsman's cap and leather gloves, looking around him as only a crazy person does. At this Otto could convincingly suggest that the escapee really was an idiot, and the question of whether Čiperný was going to endanger the entire group of forced laborers by reporting the incident to the employment office became moot, though he did wish to advise that the next time someone left the immediate surroundings of the barracks outside of work time, he would hold the group leader accountable for every escaped laborer. Then Otto said that he couldn't simply lock up his people like jailbirds, they had to go into the village in order to buy bread and other things. After a long exchange, Čiperný and Otto agreed that each evening at eight o'clock the presence of all laborers would be accounted for and the group leader would have to send the written roll to the head engineer in his apartment, the same form due each morning to Herr Podlaha. At this Otto appealed to the conscience of each room leader and the cooperation of all his comrades, each room leader having to send a written list to Otto accounting for all his colleagues each evening before eight o'clock, while in the morning he would personally visit each room in order to confirm the full presence of all the inhabitants himself.

Long awaited is the first free afternoon on Sunday, the boys in Josef's room sleeping like logs, though he himself is already up and feeling good, at which he decides to head into the village to see what he can find at Kopřiva's. The store is half empty, Kopřiva in a good mood as he tells Josef that this morning there was good news on the radio, namely that America will soon declare war against Germany, though Josef is not quite sure where Kopřiva stands on all this, which is why it's smarter to say nothing, ask nothing, and never once show any interest. Kopřiva is not satisfied with this and wants to know from Josef what he thinks of the war and the entire situation, and how he thinks it will all go. Josef replies that he hopes that the right side wins. Kopřiva says that the right side is like the truth, which always wins out, as Master Jan Hus teaches us, but who knows what the right side is. Josef agrees straight off that this is always hard to tell. At this the shopkeeper doesn't try to probe Josef's views any further, but then the door of the taproom opens and a drunken man stumbles into the shop, pointing with an outstretched arm at Josef and asking, "Hey, Jaroslav, who's that, who's that man there?" The shopkeeper declares that it's clear that he's one of those who are working on the railroad. "I say no one should be building any railroad here! That'll make our taxes go up, and we'll have to pay for it all! Jaroslav, no one should be building any railroad, that's no good, no, none at all!" Kopřiva replies that he doesn't know what's good or bad about such a railroad, for those in charge know, but Kopřiva knows that Šumpetr should keep his mouth shut, for he can clearly see that here there is someone who is building something, and that's indeed good, because it's good when these people get money that they can then spend in Wirschenowitz, which is good for everyone. "Jaroslav, you talk a load of crap! The tax office has done me in already, so I say no one should be building any railroad! And you from the railroad, what do you have to say about it all? Do you like working there?" Josef replies that he's quite pleased with it all, for the work is not that bad, though Šumpetr is not satisfied, everything these days having gone to hell, you can't so much as slaughter a pig when you want to, everything has to be delivered, and soon there won't be anything more you can do, and who's going to do anything about it, Šumpetr will hang himself if it comes to that, which is why Jaroslav should pour him another schnapps, but a proper Sliwowitz, not this damned woman's water that smells of perfumed sugar, and the man there from the railroad, he should also pour him a Sliwowitz, for today Šumpetr has money, he'll pay for it all, even Jaroslav should have a drink, and the man from the railroad should come along into the taproom. Jews, however, are barred from entering all inns, this being enforced with laborers all the more acutely, so Josef declines, but he doesn't use too many words to do so, but just says, "I'm not allowed to."—"What's that? Well, to hell with that, you're not allowed. You're allowed if I say you're allowed! Jaroslav, did you hear that, he's not allowed? Why isn't he allowed? Come here, Mr. Railroad Man, I want to have a drink with you!" The drunken man puts his arm around Josef and tries to drag him off to the taproom, but the proprietor says that Šumpetr shouldn't do anything stupid, Kopřiva could lose his license, they can toss anyone working on that railroad into jail, and Šumpetr could be thrown out of the bar and locked up for drinking with a laborer, though Šumpetr won't have any of it, saying, "No one is ever hauled off in Wirschenowitz, so I'm still in the bar! If I say something is all right, then it is! And I say we're all brothers! And whoever doesn't believe that I'll crack his skull!" Josef doesn't let himself be dragged into the taproom, but he does have to clink glasses with Šumpetr and drink a Sliwowitz, followed by a second one right away, but then Josef thanks him and says he has to go, for he still has other errands in the village, at which Kopřiva pushes Šumpetr on uncertain legs back toward the taproom, the latter yelling to Josef, "I'm going to drink to your railroad in the hope that it is never finished! They're robbing us all, I say!" Josef then disappears as Jaroslav Kopřiva pulls an unhappy face.

Since arriving in Wirschenowitz Josef has not had a shave, and since there is time he goes to the barber, who is a real character, and who also starts right in talking about the railroad. It's fine with him that they want to build it here, for it's good for him, namely because all the laborers do him the honor of bringing their business to him, and so they should always build, for then the area does better, and if they put in a main line here, then large factories will follow, and one day when there is peace, but not the Conqueror, then he will have left something useful behind, for that's the way things go, the thugs establish order, then they are done in, the poor people suffering a bit as a result, though they also learn something and get back on their feet again. Josef suggests that the people might also wish for something a bit better than that and not just to remain poor. But the barber thinks the people never learn any better, they always have to be pushed around somewhat, they need that, and thus the Conqueror is a pike in the fishpond which the slower fish let swim around and snap at them so that they work harder, then someone fishes out the pike with a hook and lays him out on dry land so that he dies, he having fulfilled his purpose. Josef cautiously disagrees with this, since he's not certain whom the barber is friends with, though it doesn't seem to be dangerous, for next the barber says that he wishes the Devil would haul off the pike, no one would despair at that, since he's so wild, though people shouldn't complain so much but instead train him like a beast in a circus in order that he does something worthwhile before the Americans arrive to fish him out. Such talk makes Josef uncomfortable, but he smiles and says it's certainly not that easy to train a pike, because when you let a beast free you never know what can happen. But the barber replies that the people go about it all wrong, for the fish don't complain about the pike because he is better than them, instead they complain because he can bite and keeps them on the move, all of them afraid of him and having to ward him off, but to get him to do what his prey wants him to do they who must flee should all treat him as their redeemer, though the barber admits that the Conqueror would have to no longer be a pike in a pond but rather a washtub, and best of all would be to see him cooked in a pan and served up with a little dill sauce.

Josef is happy when he finishes with the barber and heads back to camp, where Simon tells him what a wonderful man he met, a Dr. Siegler from the barracks straight across, and since he told him about Josef they should both go over and meet the doctor. Simon is so excited that he asks if they can't go straightaway, there being at least an hour before they have to think about dinner, and so Josef agrees. Dr. Siegler is friendly, and is one of the oldest men in the camp, certainly over forty-five, and a doctor who had a good practice in Saaz, though the events of 1938 forced him from the home where his father and grandfather had been doctors, he having lost both his house and his practice, his possessions seized, while for some months he has worked here in Wirschenowitz, which he's happy about, as he had no idea how he was going to be able to take care of his sick wife. In Dr. Siegler's eyes the world is going to pieces, such that the only thing that can be sensibly described is what we each experience alone, all people today becoming more and more enslaved because there is nothing to prevent it from happening. Josef wants to know what could prevent it, and Siegler says it's the strength of the unmediated life, which is a strength that develops within, much as ancient mystics taught, but this strength can unfold only when technological capability is not turned into an instrument of power by the politicians, which indeed is the case today, technology seeing to it that the life force is reduced and eventually annihilated, as it drains away life, replacing it and transforming it into a mechanical process, in the course of which humanity is subjected to slavery. Siegler doesn't believe this process can be stopped, not even through revolution, only a complete cataclysm could do so, though that would also mean the destruction of all achievements of culture and civilization, and should this fate come to pass all that a human being is currently capable of is to produce the courage and tragic desire for his own demise, in order that at least a heroic end is achieved. This also means that whoever pursues truth will at least be gratified when he sees with open eyes where he stands and that he is falling into an abyss that he can no longer avoid, but this plunge at least grants him at the very last moment of time the sense of something eternal.

Simon says that you might as well commit suicide then, but Siegler smiles at this, saying that's too easy, for as Grabbe says at the end of a tragedy, we do not fall out of the world once we are already in it, and so life in a certain sense is an eternal process from whose clutches not even suicide frees us, which Grabbe's hero knew. The views of philosophers from Heraclitus to Nietzsche aside, we indeed learn from fate, if only in the sense that we learn that life continues on despite its dissolution, and that in truth man cannot cut himself off from it, but instead must immerse himself, meaning that he may indeed be a victim, but he is also a witness, and through that each can—whether through his own disposition or caprice—find a certain

344 / H. G. ADLER

freedom, namely the freedom of knowledge or the ability to know. The difference between men may very well lie only in the degree to which someone takes hold of this freedom, versus those who deny it, despite whatever reasons there may be for seizing hold of it. At this Josef wonders whether it's because there is not an obvious cause to rise to, no clear act or even a way to prepare for it, whereby one's inner tendency remains independent of any possible or actual dissolution, meaning an act that one could accomplish and can accomplish in order to devote oneself to it and thus arrive at an overall sense of purpose that potentially leads one through any catastrophe, though Josef wants to again point out that it must require a *genuine* readiness. He is well aware that he is not expressing himself clearly enough, but what he is talking about is the need to maintain an unwavering intent that is not entirely tied to the general course of daily events but instead keeps its eye on an ideal that helps one become independent, no matter what goes on in the world, as well as remaining independent of the web of relations we find ourselves ensnared in. In short, Josef doesn't believe that all such supposed or actual ascension or demise is the final authority on how human beings should live their lives.

Siegler doesn't agree, it not being possible through reason to account for what really happens, it being necessary that a person breathe the air of the world as it happens in order to appreciate this formulation, for sometimes it rises and sometimes it falls, just as sometimes one is lifted up and at other times cast down, the only response available being the ability to grasp this and know it in the way that Siegler has already explained. Josef is not convinced, but no more is said about the issue, Siegler turning to a discussion of memory and saying that memory is solace, and man should not close himself off to such solace. Simon here is a good example, for he has music, and he can recollect powerfully what he has played or heard, all of which gives rise to images, perhaps images within tones, but images with foregrounds and backgrounds and, even more so, moving images that continually change, as in a panorama, which perhaps Simon knows as a precursor to the cinema, it being obvious that one can't just jump into such images but instead you stand before them, and where Simon stands there is a new railroad, then there is his work detail, then the pick and the shovel that he clutches, then there is the continual noise surrounding him, and his thoughts about his father and mother, then there is worry and fear, all of this part of an unbroken moment, the railcar needing to be filled in thirty minutes, always such hurry and trepidation about whether you will be finished in time, Sajdl a rather unpleasant colleague as he stands behind your work and pushes Simon on, your every movement watched, while you have to slog away twice as hard if your neighbor is lazy or can't go on anymore, all of this so immediate, so much the outward run of things which Simon can't escape. But for him there is something unattainable that no one can seize hold of, otherwise it could be gotten to, but through memory you can still access a part of it, and for Simon that means music, though Siegler admits that he has no such thing himself, he being not very musical, nor does he even have any kind of relation to art, yet perhaps his knowledge of literature is enough, novels and dramas coming most to mind, they being able to display life as an intricate amalgamation of social webs, though Siegler prefers to remain removed from literature, for his relation to it is intellectual, and memory is not part of the notional world, but rather it lives in the world of feeling, for he doesn't mean any kind of sloppy sentiment but instead a continuous stream, he thinking of his trip to Italy, though he has to correct himself, for it's not a thought but a memory, namely that of the view of the Umbrian landscape from Erementani near Assisi, the view from Orvieto down across the land, the view from the Neopolitan garden down to the sea full of ships, Vesuvius in the background, all of them such powerful memory images. For Simon it's music, for Josef it might be something else, something that stands outside of time, where time itself exists and is frozen solid, this world of images lending the viewer something to hold fast to. Whoever does not hold such a world within himself, whoever can't save it, he is today lost before he is even killed, for all will be killed, but Siegler hopes for the strength to be able to maintain such solace right up until that last horrible moment, he also wanting to advise Simon and Josef to maintain this world of images right up until the threshold of their own dissolution, for then it is bearable, you hold tight to your most secret feelings and aspirations, which perhaps are indestructible, even if they cannot be entirely reached.

There is a lot that Josef wants to say in response, he having experienced incidents of what Siegler calls memory intertwined with the present, it also being—as Josef believes—actually intertwined, but he senses that he

346 / H. G. ADLER

shouldn't say anything now, instead choosing to observe Siegler closely, he certainly being one of the oldest of the laborers, while with his noticeably heavy face full of sorrow, perhaps he is sick, Josef then asking him if the work is too hard. Yes, it's very hard, but he doesn't want to fall behind the young boys, for you can't show how hard it is for you, and he works under Sajdl, where it is certainly harder than anywhere else. Siegler smiles when Josef tells him that he works with Sláma. For Sláma is a summer camp in comparison, he being quite a character who loves to slough off while in Najdek, where Rybák rarely goes, he unfairly having a bad reputation because the young ones are so dumb . . . well, anyway it must feel like paradise with Sláma, for Sajdl is indeed ambitious, being wild for money and having, in addition to the regular take from the work, entered into a contract with the firm that pays per quota achieved, which is why he always gets after his people so much, for he's paid according to the number of cars that are filled, while in the evening he sits in the bar with Kopřiva and drinks nearly a full bottle of schnapps, his wife drinking nearly as much as he, though he's not really that awful, all you have to do is convince him that you're willing and not just sloughing off and you will be allowed to talk now and then, he even having a sense of humor.

Simon says that Siegler gets along well with Sajdl because he has been impressed by him, but for the young people it's hard, for nothing they do impresses him, and they all have to do whatever he tells them to. Siegler thinks the youths go about it all wrong, telling Sajdl always that they can't do as much as he wants, and then he gets angry, which is why you shouldn't cross people like him but instead work quietly and steadily without any breaks and without straining yourself too much, the result being that you can aim to accomplish an immense amount in a reasonable manner, which results in his noticing and appreciating such effort, though if you neglect to do so, then he thinks you are a troublemaker, causing him to of course note that everyone works much too fast when observed, while afterward they stand around with empty shovels and gaze off into the distance. Simon thanks him, saying that he had never thought of this and didn't know that even with forced labor on the railroad there was a certain psychology involved. Siegler confirms that a great deal or at least much requires a pragmatic psychology, for you always need to properly size up your comrades and your superiors, almost everyone, for example, being afraid of the book-keeper Podlaha and surmising that he is a slave driver who has no patience with anyone who is sick, for he swears like a sailor whenever anyone requests a sick day, but if Siegler happens not to feel well he quietly goes to him and says that of course you need to work, they need to finish the railroad, but unfortunately he's not feeling well and needs to see the doctor in order to get better and be back to work soon, he not wanting to be sent to the sick bay by the doctor but instead given some medicine so that he can get back to work by the afternoon, or the next morning at the latest. At this Podlaha turns completely soft and asserts that he's not a monster, for of course anyone can get sick, he himself having had pleurisy last year, which he wouldn't wish on his worst enemy, and so Siegler should hurry to Sobolec, nothing being more important than one's health, as is the case. This is how to handle such people, you just have to know their weaknesses and bring out the best in them.

Now Josef and Simon are ready to go, they have to get back to their room, it being time to worry about the evening meal. Siegler says that he finds this kind of communal arrangement a splendid solution, because it is so easy to do and yet not so obvious to all, though in his room no such arrangement seems possible, there being two roommates who are a problem, for they receive ample packages containing butter, eggs, bacon, and anything you might wish for, but they want to scarf down these goodies by themselves or trade them for cigarettes, he finding such behavior reprehensible when people are thrown together in dire circumstances, and although they are not starving, they end up trading precious foods, which most have to do without, for nothing more than expendable goods. Siegler's voice rises more than it has before, even revealing some bitterness, while Simon asks whether Siegler ever receives any packages from his wife. No, for where should she bring them, while, on the contrary, it's he who sends something to her, two months ago he having had some chance contact with a family of millers from Wirschenowitz, whereby he learned that they had a child who suddenly took ill, and because they had no way of getting a doctor a messenger had been sent to the camp, since supposedly every kind of profession was represented among the laborers, and there are even people in the village who envy the laborers and maintain that they have it too good, all of them nothing more than parasites, a little bit of hard work good for their lazy bones, even though that applied to only a few, though nonetheless it was true. In any case, they sent someone for Siegler, he protesting that it was forbidden to have anything to do with the villages, but then the miller began to protest that this was serious, the child was bright red with fever, the doctor had to come for God and the angels' sake. Then Otto said that he had no problem with it, for such a pressing matter demanded that he go, but he should make it quick, as it was still dangerous. Siegler was able to help, and the child, contrary to all expectations, quickly recovered, and since then Siegler goes to the miller once a week and is given flour and other groceries that he then sends to his wife. At this it's high time for Simon and Josef to be off, as they thank Siegler and leave.

The two friends consider how they might help Siegler without undermining the needs of their own roommates, but they are unable to come up with any satisfactory answer. They propose going for a walk after lunch on Sunday, the day lovely, sunny and warm, as they bring along a bag with a snack in it, since they plan to be away for a good while, six hours in all, maybe seven. After leaving the camp they walk along paths through the fields and after some minutes they come to the embankment for the new railroad near the gravel mill, it being somewhat hard to scrabble over the loose gravel for the embankment, the rail bed stretching out peaceful and empty and desolate, no guards anywhere, the gravel mill silent, the railcars standing idle, two locomotives from the light train resting quietly, producing no steam, everything asleep. Then the friends cross over the embankment and find a path that climbs uphill through the woods, tall powerful trees all around them with thickets in between, raspberries ripe for picking, a bird hiding within, two squirrels skittering deftly across the branches, though everything else is still, time having forgotten itself, quiet clearings that lie there small and appealing between the mild and clearly demarcated copses, followed by the new-growth forest, which has grown up thick, fungi having shot up within it, a bounty of edible mushrooms quickly stashed in their pockets, along with fly agaric, a logged clearing opening up its silent expanse, tree stumps everywhere, some trunks lying piled up, their branches cut off, the stripped bark a reddish brown next to the logs slowly sinking into the loam, tall wild flowers growing up in their array of colors. The path leads farther on, a peak likely nearby, no doubt the crest that Sláma had called Peperka, Josef translating it somewhat loosely as Pfefferberg, part of a memorable landscape, since it's a landscape the friends have seen before, Simon having often gone hiking before the war. And at last they reach the peak, a granite cliff looming high and covered with gray-green flecks.

For the purposes of trigonometric navigation a wooden tower has been erected on top of the peak, which is not very high, though it rises above all the treetops surrounding it, a narrow ladder the only means by which to climb up it, where a warning states: "Climbing the tower is not recommended and is dangerous!" Yet right now it doesn't look that dangerous, the friends not so bothered about being forbidden to climb it, since almost everything is forbidden these days, and so when it's possible to do something no one really worries about its being forbidden, thus they climb up, the view no doubt worth it, the friends reaching a platform made of planks, a second ladder leading from here to the top, though Simon doesn't want to go along, since he still feels dizzy, meaning that Josef should go up alone and report from above what he sees. So Josef heads up alone and happily looks around and calls down to say how beautiful it is, only Sajdl's work site visible, and the barracks as well, Wirschenowitz lying down in the valley to the left, the main road from there toward Pechno completely recognizable, behind it the wide fields stretching out, where there is a group of five slender poplars standing, the peaks and mounds of the mountains following one after another and looking lovely, fields and meadows decorating their slopes, though the peaks have bigger or smaller clusters of trees, a chain of mountains stretching out toward the horizon, their shimmering blue-green contours awash in a soft mist whose breath extinguishes all that is recognizable. Farther off to the left, beyond the creek that runs behind Wirschenowitz, the railroad can be made out, a sulfur-yellow fleck on top of which runs a red line, pastures stretching out behind it, single farms dotting the landscape here and there, and farther on the forest, nothing but endless dark coniferous forest, forest in every direction. Peperka is clearly the highest peak in the area, but far off in the forest landscape Josef notes another peak that is just as high, and which also has a wooden tower atop it, it most likely being Raventop, Sláma having mentioned this as well, the most beautiful forests in the area supposedly existing there.

Josef finishes taking in the panorama and climbs down after a while, Simon having twice asked that he come down. Josef then becomes very talkative, saying it's an enchanted landscape, foreigners hardly knowing it at all, most of their comrades having hardly any eye for such a landscape, and therefore they shouldn't go wandering about, the Conqueror doesn't want them to, his life being completely joyless, and therefore the lives of the oppressed should be even more joyless, the last vestiges of free movement perhaps about to be forbidden any day now, the laborers turned into prisoners in their huts. Certainly there are lovers of nature among their comrades, but worries and fears weigh upon their senses too heavily to allow them to take pleasure in the forest around them, Karl Peters himself having said that he preferred to read and study on his free days, others lounging about the room and playing cards, some playing football behind the barracks, some lying in the sun and chatting, there also being fervent letter writers, others simply tired or listless and dozing. Siegler had said that it had never occurred to him to go for a walk here, for he's always so exhausted from working that he has to take a breather on the weekend. Simon suggests that they cut up the mushrooms they found that evening in order to dry them and give them to Siegler so that he can send them to his wife. Josef thinks that's a great idea and says perhaps Siegler is thinking now of his beloved Italy, he being a deeply rooted man, the separation from his homeland too much for him, and possibly he'll never get over it, for he sees nothing but relentless destruction ahead and lives only for memories that one can no longer enter, as he said in comparing it to the panorama.

Simon wants to know whether Josef is not just as pessimistic. No, he's not pessimistic, yet optimism and pessimism are words he prefers to avoid, for they are questionable words, Josef preferring to think about his relationship to life in realistic terms, not clinical, because life is not clinical, though it is natural, but clinical is not the same as natural, Josef thinking of nothing less and nothing more than a positive attitude toward reality, or the seemingly real, but he doesn't feel comfortable spinning out any grand theory, for what we can know is a present, namely *the* present. The dangers are not to be underestimated, but as long as it exists a person should not doubt that the present is a continual source of renewal. In this sense memory is of no use, no matter how good and helpful it can be, but the present is something else, it being full of surprise and the unforeseeable, such that one should even dispense with any notion of free will, the desire for a view of the future that reveals all being unacceptable, Josef searching for the right words and finding that, yes, this desire is in fact impure, unclean, it is sinful, although he cannot deny that the horrible present circumstances prod each of us day in, day out, to conjure such a wish, at which Simon asks, "Do you have any hope, Josef?" No, not hope, that's not what he'd call it, but instead a readiness to accept whatever might happen, it's probably life itself that we should accept at any moment without fear. Nothing is more destructive than fear, for, senselessly, it leads to the death of meaning and is itself meaningless, fear able to enslave and murder before a death sentence is even lowered upon a man.

Simon says that, at thirty, Josef has already seen so much and lived so much, but he himself is still young, he having wandered through only a narrow portion, in which he has experienced an unforgettable family, the parents and the son, and not one of the three ever feeling alone for a single moment, and yet each was always there for himself without fail every time, each connecting happily with his surroundings, though that was never the main thing, for everything led back to the family, which after the father's arrest was horribly destroyed. Josef then asks Simon not to forget his music, for more important than the memory itself is to allow music in its essence to come alive within him, even without a violin or making a sound, for thus you live entirely through your spirit, since that you are sure of, and that you have within you. Simon is ready to believe that, but he is always ripped away from it and destroyed. Whenever Sajdl stands behind him there is no music, and all he can do is think how he can empty his shovel into the railcar with the least amount of effort, though Simon will try to do what Sajdl wants him to while he works, and perhaps he can also sink into his music, perhaps it's possible. By now the friends are tired from talking and stray from the path to find a bed of moss, resting there and eating their snack, it being warm and still, and immensely peaceful, Simon stretching out and going to sleep, Josef watching him and thinking, before the rustling of the leaves also causes him to fall into a reverie about the past and he sleeps.

LANGENSTEIN CAMP

I<small>T'S A GONG, NOT A BELL, A PIECE OF TRAIN RAIL THAT HANGS FROM A RACK</small> that looks like a gallows, someone having struck it hard three times with a truncheon, followed by many quick blows and one last hard blow! *Bong-Bong-Bong-zingzingzingzingzingzingzingzingzing-Bong!* It's awful music that sounds from the darkness, a miserable sound, gloomy, there in the night, the hut dark, the room murky and cold, full of a horrible smell. The gallows music dies away and again there is silence, no, not complete silence, there is heavy breathing, a whistling throaty gurgle, forty bodies stretched out dead to the world, neither asleep nor awake, simply lying there, time having abandoned them, neither living nor dead, though one can also say that many are alive and some are indeed dead, it being hard to make out in the darkness who is dead and who is alive. Nothing else is here, only bodies, and the room is made of wood, above, below, all four walls made out of wood, the wood is planed bare, it looks reddish brown in the light, clearly new wood that not so long ago was still in the forest, there where the trees had been felled, soft, thin boards cut from their trunks. There is also a door that cannot be shut, it has no latch and no handle, a door that is never open and never closed, instead moving with each gust of air, hanging on rusty hinges as it squeaks with the weaker and squeals with the stronger gusts of air. There is also a window, a simple frame with six small panes, for indeed the panes are set in the frame and are not broken, there also being a light, a bulb hanging from a wire, while above the socket that holds it there is even a tin shade.

Nothing else is here, no nails on the walls, no stools, no table, no bench, nothing, nothing at all, no beds, no straw mattresses, nothing but the bodies of the lost, clothed in rags of many colors, a few blankets scattered about, under which are bodies, as well as caps, ragged pieces of cloth without shape, a couple of tin bowls, some spoons, perhaps some other possessions gathered from the rubble and rubbish, otherwise nothing else, except fear, layer upon layer thickly packed together, living fear manifest within dried-up and evaporated bodies consumed by hatred and despair, though most of all fear, which will not die, even when they are whipped, as a sneer transforms itself into sleeplessness, and hope arises amid the decay, though perhaps hope cannot eradicate decay but instead struggles against fear. From outside there is a glimmer of light, while in a wide circle around the huts a network of barbed wire stretches through which electricity flows, cement pillars holding up the wire as it quietly runs along, separating fear from fear, since everywhere there is fear. There is no longer any difference between inside and out, fear cannot be checked by the wire, fear is on this side and that, as well as in the wire itself, powerful lamps attached to the concrete pillars that light up the night and stand there in the stillness of their own light, a light that shines on no one, nor does anyone think it real. But this light has a protective quality that cannot be destroyed by fear. It conquers fear as the light shines on the armed young men who crouch in the watchtower without rest. Yet there is no fear of attack, no one wants to defeat the fear inside, that which is well hidden away, no one wants to diminish it. The weapons in the tower are not aimed outward in order to protect fear from external threat, but instead peer inward so that the fear here remains constantly the same fear, the light illuminates fear, and those saddled with fear remain the enemies enclosed by the Conqueror with barbed wire in order that none flee, as they might be all that he has left to save him, since the Conqueror stands afraid and in dire straits. He has lost almost everything he has fought for on all fronts, everything now destroyed and laid to waste, and fear knows that the despot has gambled it all away, although he still has a hold of the fear he has robbed from almost every country, and since these countries are already freed of the Conqueror the fear hauled off from them waits behind the wire, hears the train rail struck, sees the wretched blood of life mixed with decay, feels the festering abscesses and the oozing streaks caused by the whip, tastes the bitter saliva and smells the corrosive dust of the stones, all of them knowing that it is the end, time long ago having dissolved, though now the end is near.

Now the sirens sound, from near and far they sound, an oscillating wail, slowly it gathers from below and climbs high, then sinks down once again and is muffled, then it swells once again and repeats again and again, then voices call out, "Douse the lights!" Then it's even darker in the room. As the lights on the concrete pillars go out there is even more night, everyone asleep and gurgling in his sleep, no one stirs inside the lockdown of the cold that holds sway over an endless weariness, nothing else but weariness. Josef, however, strains to listen, still under the blanket, only his head sticking out when the iron rail was struck, and now he is completely awake, never a heavy sleeper, only getting a few hours, lengthy sleep never possible here, though Josef himself doesn't completely utilize the shortened time that is reluctantly granted them, something drawing him awake while the others try to catch another couple of minutes, themselves insatiable and risking a beating as they sleep on into the day watch, which was long ago forbidden, long ago, that's what their couple of stolen minutes are, since every moment stretches out endlessly and no one knows what day or night means here.

Josef doesn't want to be woken if he can avoid it. He wants to wake up when he needs to, he wants to live, and nowhere is sleep more like death, when the bodies are packed as close as they are here, as they try to protect one another and not freeze, the nights bitterly cold, although it is already the end of March. Perhaps it's not always so cold, but here it is cold, here inside the wire, where fear lives, where three or four of the lost are lumped together, sharing two or three blankets between them, as long as they are not stolen, for when that happens a great hue and cry rises, as nowhere are human possessions guarded more jealously than in the lost ones' camp. But they are not possessions, they are loaned goods, and whoever thinks of property in the real world as anything other than loaned goods soon learns here that any possession is only borrowed, one cannot watch over it and guard it, it is simply surrendered, a thousand hands grabbing after every crumb and scrap, no scratched-in or painted-on name and no list making possessions safe from a neighbor's reach, for here it's a free-for-all, and there is no protection and no guards. Whatever serves the needs of the lost behind the wire functions as an act of grace, something that can lapse at any moment, for grace is not a possession to which any of the lost have a right, though the lost don't know that, they upon whom hangs the intense pain of the threat of it all going on forever and who only want it to end, which is why their misery is so intense.

To Josef's right lies Étienne, who was a cameraman in Paris and is a couple of years younger than Josef, while to the left lies Milan, the small dark-haired son of a murdered doctor from a small city in Banat who can't be any older than sixteen. The majority of the lost are Jews from many different countries, but divided among the huts are members of many different nationalities—Poles, Ukrainians, French, Belgians, Dutch, Germans, Czechs, and other Slavs, Balts, as well as Spaniards, Italians, Norwegians, and others. Most of the lost are young, often no more than children barely over fourteen, the majority between twenty and thirty, some between thirty and forty, Josef at thirty-five being one of the older ones, though some are indeed beyond fifty. But the lost are ageless, for certainly they are not young, though they are not old, either, as the lost are of no time or era that other people will discover in later centuries, while agreed-upon laws have lost their meaning, knowledge and culture have become pointless because everything they represent is different from what can be learned or demonstrated here. The lost remain outside legal designation and analysis, every attempt at understanding is pointless, because everything about life behind the wire is strange and ungraspable, language incapable of expressing the nature of the lost in a way that would be comprehensible to those on the outside. The lost themselves don't know this, for they have a language, many languages in fact, derived from languages that people out in the world would understand, though behind the wire these languages are diminished, expressing but little and shrunk to meager phrases in which hardly any of the artful structures from which they were derived can be felt, an abject language, the words hard, snarled and barked out, even when whispered, the language never forming chains of linked sentences, the conversations of the lost never flowing, either hinting at something or grasping at something, otherwise given over to screams, leaping flames, and spasms of pain.

Among the lost, normal forms of outward appearance have become meaningless, because decay is formless, and the lost have been condemned only to decay, all their hair cut off, scraped from their bodies with blunt instruments, the lost stripped in Birkenau, their shoes and clothes lying about like thick heaps of dung on the cold concrete floor. It's a huge hall in which the lost stand naked and freezing, two heavily armed conspirators rummage through the clothing, digging into pockets, looking for money, for watches and jewelry. A band of collaborators scurry about, themselves also a part of the lost, yet appearing nearly as powerful as the conspirators, nothing but rats disguised as humans, rummaging through the belongings of the living, and when the rats find what they're looking for they take it away, they surround the naked and scream at them with incomprehensible sounds, the sounds of greed and thievery, and whenever the rats spot a picture of a wife or mother or children in the hands of the lost they snatch it away and scoff, the lost allowed to keep only a belt that is bound about the naked like a penitent's cord, some having glasses that they are allowed to keep as well.

The rats swing truncheons with which they wale away at the naked, and the rats bellow out that this is no sanatorium, threatening to punish anyone who has hidden anything, for everything will be found, and punished, anyone who has hidden something in his mouth or in the folds of his body, it will be punished, all of it a crime, it will be punished, every possession is a crime. Then the naked learn that among the lost there is no such thing as equality, because the collaborators are powerful, the other lost ones powerless, the Conqueror's conspirators distant and with an exalted air about them, though the lost are made aware of it only from time to time, otherwise the collaborators take care of things for the conspirators, making sure to herd together and control the endless waves of the nameless. The lost are scolded as they are driven into the next room, there they are stripped of their hair by four Greek Jews, themselves also among the lost, crouching on stools and shooting unintelligible words back and forth, the rats saying

"*Klepsi*" to them, which means to steal in Greek. The naked must kneel down in front of the Greeks, who scrape off the hair on their heads, the skull naked and bloody, then the naked have to raise the right arm, the left arm, as the Greeks shave the armpits, the naked standing as the Greeks shave the pubic hair and the buttocks. Then the naked are shooed onward, stumbling into the shower room, where they are pressed together in close bunches under the showers, warm water beneficently pouring down upon them, though there is no soap here to wash with, only water, which flows for a while, the naked driven farther on until they arrive at a threshold and they have to wade through the reeking grayish-brown lye, striding past a lost one who holds a sponge in one hand soaked with the same cold solution, running it over the raw privates of each naked one and then over the skull, irritating and burning the skin like liquid fire.

The naked now stand in a cold hall, the bodies still damp from the showers, but there are no towels, the naked having to form rows as, without a care for shape or size, ragged shirts are tossed to them, dirty trousers and jackets often damaged and ripped, trousers and jackets with blue patches and made of gray striped material. In clothes made of the same material, the collaborators run about in "zebra stripes," though for ages there have been none available to the naked, the Conqueror's weavers incapable of fulfilling the endless demand, though from the repositories of the death factories the worst rags have been selected from a limitless supply of clothes that once belonged to the hecatombs of nameless murdered people, miserable trash still able to be utilized for the Conqueror's marvelous deeds and relief work, as now the mottled zebras are fitted out with the plunder of the murdered victims, after which a brush is dipped in rust-red varnish and circles and crosses are smeared on the trousers and jackets. Foot rags cut from soft, warm wool of the prayer shawls of murdered Jews are also thrown to the naked. Then shabby caps made out of zebra cloth are tossed in an arc to the naked. The last element of the wardrobe is the shoes, the soles made of wood, the black uppers of rough material. The naked have to dress quickly as they try to make the stuff fit them, some of it too short and too tight, other parts too big and too long, though that is preferable, while best is to find someone sensible with whom to trade clothes in order to look respectable. The naked barely finish dressing before being driven out of the hall under the threat of blows, as they stand in the dreary October cold of the year 1944, realizing at last that they are lost, though there is no time to reflect on this as they are bellowed at by angry voices that want to bring order to the misshapen heap, though it is not done with screams but rather with clubs and whips. Finally around a hundred of the lost stand in rows of four, then are led away from this cursed place which is called a sauna, the Finnish word for bath.

An armed conspirator and some collaborators proudly decked out in their snazzy garb accompany the lost along the length of a sandy path, on the edge of which stand some withered pines followed by nothing but crunchy gravel, to the left an open field where some building is under way, to the right concrete pillars that loom and are bound together by electrified wire, in between the covered watchtowers lifting up, behind them a camp for the lost, immense and bleak, every now and then an entrance, a wooden hut standing nearby, the word OFFICE legible on it, yellow and black letters on a sign spelling out the odd words SHH — THE ENEMY IS LISTENING! The entrances lead to separate parts of the camp, "F" written above the first entrance, which is called the sick bay, on the next the letter "E," the Gypsy camp, now only a reminder of the former inmates, who in large part exited the camp through a chimney, as a collaborator explains. Here the surge of lost ones remains standing, a collaborator hurries over to the office window, where he stands stiff as a board, then marches them off through the open gate. They move across a courtyard, then they arrive at some larger huts, then move along a road that runs through about thirty huts painted green, stretching back from the camp road almost to the edge of Section E, the huts standing one next to the other, always one to the left and to the right, and behind them wire stretched from pillar to pillar, each part of the camp remaining separate from the rest. The lost are not led to these huts right off, but instead they must stand in the far field, a gathering place where they wait a long time, though in the camp of the lost there is no time, or nothing but time, since it's all the same, whatever happens, or time is a tight net thrown over the lost, and each strand of the net cuts into life. There Josef gathers his wits and decides that he must hang on, he can't let himself wither away, and yet he doesn't yet know what such a proposition entails, what he even means by it. Suddenly he is driven into a hut along with his fellow marchers, the number 13 labeled on it, first through an entryway, then he sees a small room to the left and right, but immediately he is pressed into a long room that takes up almost the entire hut, someone suggesting that in old Austria, and later in Poland, these were the horse stalls of an army garrison. A waist-high brick wall forms the middle axis of the room, right and left of it there runs a narrow passage in front of triple-decker wooden bunks, upon which a couple of red horse blankets lie, though there are no straw mattresses, paltry light pressing through small, glazed portholes in the roof, such that it is twilight within during the day, perhaps lighter at night when the two lightbulbs are turned on. At the end of the hut there is another entryway with an exit, the floor everywhere consisting of nothing but packed-down earth.

In this hut and for many days to come, existence is reduced to this warehouse for humans. To get away from here, that is Josef's only wish. Although he has managed to steer his little ship through fateful seas, a feeling still compels him to do everything he can to get away from here, and yet he knows for sure that this place of sickness can only lead to another place of sickness, while in the end Josef is still determined that it shouldn't happen here in this near-grave which they call quarantine, whose destruction still presses through the chimneys that run day and night, where the flames are not lit to celebrate the sacrificed lives of the murdered but which nonetheless eerily exalt them, despite the will of the murderers, such that Josef senses this destruction much more as an eternal repose that wipes away all urge to fight back, an uneasy prospect of that indolent state in which the thinking being is robbed not of the justification for his existence, but rather of the ability to possess and reflect upon it, even when the inquisitive spirit poses endless questions otherwise unfit for grown-ups, questions of youth, with which one seeks to strip a secret of its secret, because the questioner has no idea that the question itself—though empty of insight—contains the answer, since the deepest questions have no answers other than more questions. This insight is lost upon the inmates of the waiting station, for here there is only a life of relinquishment, where even life itself is relinquished in much the same way that the sum total of all possessions are relinquished, a life of nothing more than inner reserves, in many ways a pure life, though pure rather than virtuous, for it is not a life lived in accordance with human nature, which does not feed on memories alone, but rather one that lives for discoveries that cannot be replaced simply by hopes and dreams.

The lost in Barracks 13 are not left on their own for very long, for two collaborators appear and yell out a speech to initiate the lost into the secret workings of the place, forcing them to sup from the shrieks that will soon fill their future. They who have been robbed of everything are pressed to turn in any hidden goods, threats demanding gold and jewels, the cowed ones searching around among their rags as if there were something to find within them, though the poor souls have nothing, and therefore can give nothing. With bit-off words the lost are exhorted to embrace cleanliness, hard work, and obedience, then they are dragged out in front of the barracks and told to form two rows that run the length of a wall, one of the collaborators telling them that he used to be a Hungarian officer, but he means well and isn't holding anything with which to beat anyone. He says that things are hard here, which is why you shouldn't make them harder, you just have to learn to take care of yourself, but the will to do so must be flexible, for in- deed a hardheaded will here only leads to trouble, there being many ways to die, whether it's hunger, exhaustion, illness, cold, the only other way out of this camp being through the many methods of beatings and degradation, there also being the bullet and the gallows, while the chimney is always at the ready. All of this is a good reason to take care never to attract atten- tion, to learn how to take a hit, to trust in your luck, but never let yourself fall to the ground like a Muslim, for you'll end up passing through the chim- ney, the only hope left being to remain strong, though this path to possible rescue is seemingly narrow, but indeed there have been men who for years have clung to it after having decided to last it out, and even if they are the lucky ones that doesn't mean others are unlucky, for no one can afford to be- lieve that who doesn't quickly go up the chimney. At this one of the lost calls out to ask what all this is about the chimney, for he keeps hearing about the chimney and doesn't know what it means, someone else yelling out, "The gas chamber! The gas chamber!" The lost one looks on puzzled, and then the collaborator says to the rows, that's the marmalade factory, and no one can work there, the people who work there are special commandos and cleared out every three months, while whoever wants to stay on here has to find a way not to stand out. Then the Hungarian goes silent, perhaps worrying that he has said too much already.

A Polish collaborator arrives, clearly having drunk a good deal of schnapps, swaying and reeking, his face red and swollen, he yelling that it's not cold, it's a beautiful day, the sons of bitches are in luck, they should pull themselves together, they are just a lazy bunch of garbage that have never had to work, but now they must stand at attention. Everyone has to stand there without moving and look straight ahead, the Pole yelling that he'll teach them how to keep in line, and they'll thank him for it, for he'll explain what "Hats off!" and "Hats on!" means, for if your hat is on your head, then as soon as you hear the command you yank it off as fast as you can with your right hand, and the moment you hear "Hats off!" the hat should be yanked off and pressed flat against your pant leg, while on the other hand if you hear "Hats on!," then immediately you put your hat on your head, making sure to keep your hand up there in a salute, though when you hear "Hats off!," then it has to be pressed against your leg quick as lightning. The Pole explains all this in detail, which only confuses the lost, but he knows how hard it is, which is why he yells, "Attention!" And then "Hats—off!" And then "Hats—on!" He is proud of how well he does this, and now he practices "Hats off!" and "Hats on!" with the lost for an hour or more, anyone who doesn't do it well getting a slap and then having to do it by himself, sometimes having to step forward as well. The Pole also explains that whenever "Hats on!" is shouted the hat should in no way sit elegantly atop the head but instead should just sit there and not fall to the ground, but how it looks doesn't matter, and when you're no longer at attention is the time to fix your hat. As they practice, the Pole talks to them, making little jokes, yelling out "Hats—on!" to the lost, who already have their hats on their heads, and when almost all of them rip them off, he chuckles with satisfaction, though he's not happy to just laugh it off, for his pleasure soon leads to blows, he being just as amused when he yells out "Hats off!" to the men with their heads exposed and most of them put them on. The longer this goes on the more the lost become confused, getting more tired and longing for rest and feeling hungry, though they know already that they will get nothing to eat today, they're a bunch of bellyachers who don't know anything about the camp yet, for even if they do want to eat they haven't done any work and have to first learn how to put on and take off their hats right.

So the first day creeps by, the lost moving around in groups, the wind blowing, a collaborator showing up now and then to shout a command for the lost to come out of their huts and stand in the yard, all of them showing up. The new ones don't know what it's all about, nothing really happening, maybe one group having to take a step forward or backward now and then, then all having to turn around and head back in, later all of them having to stand there forever, some of them kneeling. Then suddenly before the group there appears a band of musicians, lost ones with instruments, well-fed boys who look like a military band in an operetta, with their black-and-white striped pants and their dull, heavy boots, over which they wear padded dark-blue jackets, on the backs of which a small white felt strip is sewn, Polish officer caps sitting on their heads. A conspirator arrives and asks the band to play, demanding waltzes and marches, a schmaltzy, merry mix of sounds as you might hear at a fair, though the conspirator can't stand listening to all that noise and demands, "Play something good, something really good!" He stands so close to the horn players that they have to blow straight into his ear, he almost pressing his head into the horns and trombones. As the lost ones freeze in the chilly wind and yet must not move a step, the musicians break into a sweat as they are relentlessly commanded to play a march until the conspirator yells, "Enough!" and this afternoon's concert in the Gypsy camp is brought to an end.

The lost ones march back to their huts, which the new ones are happy to do, first because it feels good to finally move, and second because they hope they'll be allowed to get some rest in their huts, but then they have to line up against the wall where they had earlier learned the art of what to do with their hats, someone saying that it was time for roll call, and if it comes out right, then they will be allowed to go to their huts. Thus they have to stand there some more, though they are allowed to move a bit where they stand, yet no one is allowed to step out of line, while leaving is out of the question, there being nothing to eat or drink, except for what one might have stashed in his pockets. Then throughout the Gypsy camp, as well as within each section, steadily stronger and yet monotone voices yell, "Every-one-out-roll-call!" Everywhere the lost ones gather before their huts, the collaborators coming out of their offices, both elders and clerks, the entire staff, all of them strong young men, some of them splendidly decked out, most of the collaborators here being Polish or German, most having been stuck here for years and feeling right at home, hardly having anything to do with the lost ones anymore, though their world has become familiar, they know of no other any longer, this being the way things are. One must understand that within this world they remain in command by spreading terror in order to live a life on the margins of life, the dangers here having evolved such that they are hardly more than the dangers that surround and threaten any existence anywhere. The lost ones have it even better, for the dangers are no longer unknown or hidden but instead openly here, moving among the huts, living atop the watchtowers, bullets being cheap, circulating through the electrified wire, just one step and it flows through you, one hanging in the barbed wire who is left there undisturbed, as cutting off the current will do nothing to help drag down the cramped body.

And here all around the camp are the death factories, choking down bodies and burning on unimpeded, because the Conqueror needs the sacrifice of degraded lives, telling them, go on, you lost ones, go on, let yourselves be selected by the tall handsome man who is a doctor, wait for him, strip the rags from your body, look, he's coming, he's a hardworking man, he comes after you in your barracks, he has good eyes, he's a good judge of the flesh, he assesses your worth and decides your fate in the name of the Conqueror and all of his conspirators, never doubting the everyday order of things, the Conqueror having released it from mere contingency, by which death or life is dispensed through the blind will of nature, whereas the Conqueror handed over the natural order of things to the control of his conspirators, he whom they call the Great Benefactor giving commands, while their loyalty is their glory, the handsome doctor before you here also being one of his loyal followers as he chooses you, selects you, and judges whether you are ready for the harvest of death. Eternal justice is embodied within him, made manifest in the immediate surround from out of the ungraspable beyond, you now being tested, not questioned, not heard, not touched, only silence and acceptance available to one, as all are told, nothing is going to happen to you, you are free, as you have never been before, for you stand before the judgment of the Conqueror in the stillness, you don't need to think of anything, though you indeed are afraid, but there's no reason to be afraid, you can give in, you can hope, you want to hold your head high, you still want to serve the Conqueror in your drudgery, you don't feel ready for your death and don't want to be separated from life, but patience, the handsome doctor is loyal, he will visit you again, and by then you will be tired, you won't want to live any longer or save yourself, you will stand naked, your flesh melting and hanging slackly upon you, your gaze cloudy, you no longer able to stand erect. Today, however, you have not yet let yourself go, you are still too proud, arrogantly you believe in your own worth, you think defiantly only of yourself, you don't think about the Conqueror's transport, to which you've been assigned, and which will be dispatched at his discretion when he makes known his resolution through his conspirators. You pull yourself together, you put on a peaceful face and stand up, you brace yourself, the eyes of the handsome doctor rest knowingly on your feeble appearance, he saying nothing, not even waving once, you already past him, it having taken hardly three seconds, the handsome doctor doesn't have time to busy his eyes with yours, he has to care for millions, and he knows how worthless you are, he has a pretty good idea, you alone still considering your existence worth something, but this means nothing to him, it being beneath him to encourage you in your vanity. It is prudently arranged that the doctor cannot spare any time for you, and, besides, he really wants to serve the Conqueror slavishly and selflessly, because the doctor is weak and can be human, but the wisdom of the Conqueror has already decided to do away with the love of one's neighbor and of humanity in general, which is why he gives his conspirators hardly any time to do their work but instead only that needed to get the work done. That's the way it is, and not a word about it!

But the handsome doctor has not bothered about you, never once having shifted his gaze, and you have been passed by, you once more are wearing your rags and wander back to the huts, where you stand among the lost ones, everyone quiet and appearing not to breathe, pressed to the cracks between the boards until everyone has passed by the doctor. Nothing else appears to have happened, he turning away and heading off to other huts in order to ordain the living as dead, who are then separated out and wait until enough are gathered together, no one wanting to waste the precious poisonous gas, the Conqueror's conspirators economizing in order to better serve his glory, though even up until the day of sacrifice the doomed are given very little earthly nourishment, for hail to the Conqueror, the loyal followers don't want to do him harm by wasting precious goods! Stripped and hardly sheltered from the elements, the doomed are loaded into trucks, their tired feet not having to walk much farther, the conspirators striking the doomed from the rolls, order always maintained, the doomed trucked once more through the camp toward one of the temples of murder made of concrete, the doomed unloaded between the flower beds of the front garden, then pushed or dragged down some steps into the dressing room with the reassuring sign announcing THIS WAY TO THE SHOWERS. See, here you will wash up, your soul has grown dirty, you need a good scrubbing, but now you will be clean, you will sanctify yourself in order to meet your salvation, while you can thank fate that you don't have to disrobe, because you have been brought here naked, just like from your mother, you not having to wait in the dressing room like those from the arriving trains, who are dressed for the city and are led in unwittingly, men and women, old folks and children, healthy and sick ones, none having a clue about their sacrifice and thus unable to ready themselves. You, however, can gather together, you have grown strong from the duress of the camp, even if you've only been here a few days, as you stand before the steel doors, look, how this is a shrine into which you are being led, you are precious, we want to keep you secure, you shouldn't run away, just go on in, go with the others, just as thousands and thousands have gone before you and will follow you, go, it's so easy, just go. You see indeed how easy it is, there is not a trace left here of those who have already entered, so go and wait until the shrine is full so that one can seal it for good. Then the lights will go out, then your mortal being will be consumed, it won't take long, soon salvation will follow, the shrine is opened, then a special command of lost ones who serve as the lowest peons of the Conqueror haul the mortals from the shrine who cover his earth with their bloody eyes and noses and mouths, filthy and piled up in clumps so thick that the bodies often cannot be separated, the special command having a hard job to do for the Conqueror, since carrying out the murdered isn't easy. They are then schlepped over to the roar of the furnaces, but first the gold is pried from their mouths, for the Conqueror needs the gold with which the sacrificed haughtily decorated their teeth, and when it's time the hair of the women is cut off, for the Conqueror needs the locks that bedecked the bodies of his victims, after which each body is quickly burned, though only that which the Conqueror no longer needs is burned, ashes, horrible ashes, these the Conqueror can use to bless the accursed earth of his thousand-year realm with the victims of his sins and the power of their salvation.

What has not been turned into ashes climbs the powerful flames rising from the chimneys, the flames flaring up strong and lambent, billowing up and wrapped in smoke, the camp filled with its stench as they burn without cease through the night, and since flame entangles with flame, and ashes are mixed with ashes, you are one with the others, you no longer feel the painful separation that all creation feels, you are released, the Conqueror has finished with you. Yet you still resist him, still you are crippled by fear, there being nothing but fear for the lost one who calls the Conqueror a fiend, condemning him, refusing to recognize him as humanity's greatest benefactor, as he has declared himself to be. No, he cannot be that, every living being must condemn him, but condemnation is useless as long as he exists and goes about his work, even if you turn your own land into a wasteland of burning and explosions, for that does not drive away chaos but only increases it. Yet all such thoughts are fruitless, they simply drift off when the lost ones stand amid the dung or dust while awaiting the roll call, they always having to be gathered, none allowed to escape from the conspirators, which is why one speaks of prisoners and not of the lost when Josef and some of the others express sympathy for them, though it's not appreciated. For they are minors, children of the world without a clue to what is happening to them, which is why they are brought together so that the section leader can count them, they themselves needing to do nothing and not needing to know that they are being counted, though they always have something to complain about and remain stuck there amid their unnameable fear, everything being unnameable to them, because they hunger for names. In the quarantine of the Gypsy camp no one has a number, there is no sign by which they are known, all they have to do here is wait until they are sent to the slave camp, which is where the Conqueror wants them, so that their powerless hands can hand him his power. In the slave camp the lost ones are granted numbers by which they are known, which they then sew into their shirts and pants, the numbers also written down in books, in which the prisoners' scribe writes down their names and other details that each lost one tells him, the scribe taking it down completely on trust, no one able to check what is there. In the Gypsy camp, however, the lost ones are no more than a part of a larger number, and whoever ends up remaining is tattooed with a blue number on the inside of his arm, though in the Gypsy camp the stay is usually brief, often just a matter of days or hours, and seldom longer than four to six weeks.

Thus the new arrivals can remain in Birkenau for only a short time, for soon some men will come to visit who do not wear black-and-white stripes, not the rags of the lost ones, or the dandified rags of the collaborators or the uniforms of the conspirators, no, most of these men wear a suit and hat and a raincoat. The lost ones line up, wanting to look strong and healthy in order to keep out of the chimney's clutches, while the one with the raincoat stands there somewhat awkwardly and controls his feeling of horror or has already grown hardened to it, whether it be because he has stood before other lost ones or because he has learned from the Conqueror what he thinks of Jews and criminals, the times being serious as they are, the dear fatherland threatened and grappling with an unrelenting battle for its very existence, while every prisoner here would fight against the fatherland or agitate if the Conqueror had not locked them up, they indeed remaining a danger, for shh, the enemy is listening and no one should speak with him. Only the most loyal of the conspirators are called to the task on behalf of the Conqueror to watch over the danger imprisoned in the camp, each weapon not sounding the whisper of the destroyer but instead a weapon is just and protects the loyal ones from straying, and the conspirators from betrayal, and so the weapon is the power of good in its avenging of evil, which the Conqueror has surrounded with electrified wire, thus securing himself against the internal enemy, who is tamed and made useful, for now he must work for the Conqueror, *Arbeit macht frei*, and honor his superiors, who transform his reluctance into readiness. This is why the man in the raincoat stands there, he oversees the unwilling in order to tease out their defiance and transform it into compliance with the Conqueror, who needs new weapons, because the Reich is surrounded by an external enemy, which is why the slaves must conquer the inner enemy.

Two conspirators and a collaborator, ready with pencils and lists, stand on either side of the man in the raincoat, who asks each lost one what he can do, whether it be working in the forgery, metalwork, lathe work, welding, carpentry, or bricklaying, a glance assessing the emaciated figure, the face, the legs, the hands. The lost ones can do anything that they are asked to do, for they lie, having hardened themselves against truth, since they want to escape the chimneys, the lost ones calling out, we can work in the forge and do metalwork and lathe work and welding and carpentry and bricklaying and anything you ask. The man with the raincoat stretches out his right index finger and says, him and him, they should step forward, he'll have them, they should send them to him. Then the prison scribe goes over to those selected, each of them coming up with a name, an age, an occupation, he wanting to be named thus, aged thus, and have this occupation, the collaborators writing it all down in their lists, one of them having a pad with blue ink and a stamp, which he presses onto the lost one as a sign of his having been selected, there on his naked chest, doing it as if he didn't know that the ink can be wiped away with one's fingers. Then the selected are brought to a special hut so that they are ready to be called and whisked away, which can happen by day or by night, tomorrow or four weeks from now, no one knows, free wagons being seldom available, and all wheels must roll toward victory. Soon more and more transport groups are brought together in one hut, several hundred pressed together in the tight quarters, where they are chased from the right-hand side to the left and then back again, this happening several times each day, as someone yells "Into your bunks!" and "Out of your bunks!" Then the lost ones must scramble past the barricade and out again, but they must always be at the ready, which is why they have been ordered to rest in such a disastrous manner, there never being any quiet to be had, while above all they must not walk along the streets of the camp, for this is exceptionally dangerous, there collaborators on patrol will beat them, but no one is safe in the huts, either, the section elder could be in a bad mood, ordering the lost ones to clean up the place and going after them with brooms, sticks, clubs, and horsewhips, while helping out with the task is the section elder's messenger, a fourteen-year-old darling who is fat and has rosy cheeks. He hardly reaches up to most of their shoulders, but he's a strong little bugger and can do whatever he pleases, a brutal creature eager to deal out blows, his being well aimed, himself able to beat the strongest men, while they are not allowed to defend themselves, because the tiger is protected by the section elder, who is ready to beat down anyone that his little darling complains about.

The huts are scrubbed the entire day, for they must be clean, buckets of water hauled in and dumped upon the floor, then the dirty brown water is swabbed about with a huge broom, whereupon they start in once again, and then it's quickly mopped so that the floor almost dries, after which no one can step on it, or you have to walk across it barefoot with your shoes in your hand, none daring to let them lie about, for they would be stolen straight off. Nothing is safe here, everything disappears, even what's worthless and worn out is coveted, whoever can put it to use always feels needier, though it's strictly forbidden to possess any goods in the Gypsy camp, yet things are constantly exchanged, a spoon handed down to someone else or a knife, a rag used as a handkerchief or shawl or a belt, a little piece of soap, cigarettes available as well, or perhaps a single slice of bread, or maybe two or three or even more, the camp soup also for sale, or a dab of margarine, sausage, or marmalade, a potato. Shaving is also important, it needing to happen once a week, otherwise one looks too old, though it's not done for free, a couple of lost ones having got hold of a single blade or a half-rusted razor with a dull blade, as well as a brush and some soap, this being good enough for the customers, though the barber growls that he needs to save his soap as he scrapes someone clean, even though it's not proper shaving soap and is so bad that it creates no foam at all, the soap and shave costing a slice of bread, the barber indicating how thick it needs to be.

Everyone in the Gypsy camp owns at least a spoon, the handle on Josef's having worn down to such a sharp edge that it can be used as a knife to cut bread, meaning that the spoon had not been an expensive one. But on the first day, when Josef was in the hut of the old Hungarian officer, there were no spoons, meaning that no one could eat in any kind of civil manner, the first camp soup available only on the second day, the work crew sending some new arrivals to the kitchen, they needing to run along in order to escape a beating, themselves standing before the kitchen, then the kitchen capo, one of the most important collaborators, appears with his entourage, the food fetchers from all the huts soon standing ready before them, at which time the numbers of all the huts are called out, followed by someone immediately coming up and taking a full barrel, though inevitably lashes land on their backs, for no one is so fast as to avoid the anger of the kitchen capo, as he yells, "Quick, now quick, get out of here! Get out!" But the fastest of the food fetchers lets the soup slop out and burns his fingers until finally the barrel stands on the porch of the front room. Next the section elder and his collaborators are given ample portions, then cups are handed out for eating, these being cracked bowls, cups, and pots of all sizes, even washbasins and a chamber pot, numerous beaten and dented lead vessels, though hardly more than thirty such vessels are available, and so only some of the lost ones can get anything, one of the barracks workers pouring a ladleful of reddish-brown soup into a cup, at which they all need to hurry so that the next group can use the lead bowls to feed themselves. The soup had always been terrible, yet better than what Josef and his colleagues have to slosh down now, for earlier there had been bits of potato, slices of red beets, some roux, and some kind of meat, but in this poisonous red borscht nasty onions float around, glass shards, sand, bits of rag, nails, wood chips, and other garbage, one needing to be careful in order to avoid cutting his tongue or gums. But how are you supposed to eat soup without a spoon, except to open up your mouth and slurp it down like a cow and make a mess, always surrounded by greedy colleagues and mean-spirited boys from the work crews who yell, "Quick! Quick!," and who are already snatching the bowl from your hands, while on each side fists are at the ready to prevent anyone from going back to the barrel for another helping, and should anyone be suspected of doing so he is beaten on the head with a ladle until his hide is bloodied.

Josef thinks about the Gypsy camp and sees it as both the darkest and the lightest time of his life, he having openly resisted such destruction, which is why he doesn't feel the kind of misery that he sees in others' eyes, but instead he feels defiant and strong before the final end, and he can bear the pangs of hunger and the incredible weariness, he having remained locked up within himself, as others have done as well. For instance, there is little Jossel from Lodz, almost a child in years, but one who feels that all is lost, though he faces it stoically and wants to learn a great deal from Josef, asking him about Spinoza's *Ethics*, after which Jossel recites some Yiddish poems, since he can't write them down, because there is no paper or pencil, but nonetheless he knows them by heart anyway:

> *No grain in the fields and no bread,*
> *Hard times can be found all over.*
> *The young flock in droves toward death,*
> *And the children learn nothing more.*

> *Men are cut down like harvest meadows.*
> *Who is left to mourn them now?*
> *Yet a generation rises, demanding to know*
> *Life will return to these fields somehow.*

Thus Jossel recites his poem, though he also brings a slice of bread, insisting that Josef take it. Almost ten years older than Josef is Mordechai, who knows that his wife is hidden away somewhere with Taubele, his young daughter, no chance of any henchman finding those so well hidden away, both of them having fake papers while living with reliable people, evil having no chance to hurt his loved ones while they are in such safe confines. As it is allowed to ponder such things here in the quarantine, Mordechai speaks about what is written in the *Sayings of the Fathers*, namely what Akavia ben Mahalalel said: "Observe three things, and you will not fall into sin: know from where did you come, where you are headed, and before whom you will lay yourself one day in order to give your account and be judged. And from just where did you come? From a miserable drop of nothing. Where are you headed? To a place full of dust, mold, and worms. Before whom will you lay down to account for yourself and be judged? Before the King of Kings, before the Holy One, may He be blessed!" Josef should consider well that, above all, such consummation is possible, above all, there is good counsel to keep, above all, and even if it is done silently, one can still lift oneself in prayer, Mordechai saying that indeed there is mercy in their being able to come to the huts and stand inside next to Josef in order to talk and exchange ideas, none of that is pointless, even if they don't survive this test. "Yet why shouldn't we survive it?" says Mordechai, receiving a smile in return. "That they give us slippers made from holy prayer shawls shows how foolish they are, for we end up walking at ease within them, for in such shawls we cannot be harmed as long as we pray!" There are other men in the huts who lose themselves in timeless questions, it being easy to think on the meaning of life here, there are no limits to the moment, time having been stripped away, the only thing to do is to wait, and when there is nothing to look forward to, then everything is easy. What still exists cannot be found in one's surroundings, they are of no help to the spirit, each having to depend on himself, one's perceptions seeming more true than ever before, as alone a person considers his true worth.

On a narrow planted strip between the huts, where otherwise there is nothing but sticky excrement that turns into a filthy sty when it rains, some flowers are growing, which Josef marvels at, it seeming a sign, as well as the chain of mountains to the south, namely the Beskydy Range, a minimum of two days of strenuous hiking away, gray-blue they stretch away, the foggy, damp air above the passage in between not allowing the mountains to appear any closer or lighter in color. The mountains are pure, and there it must be pleasant, closer to home, even a part of the homeland, and there you would have no idea of the Gypsy camp and the chimneys, those seeming part of an evil tale that cannot be true, no, none of that is true, simply invented by evil-minded vermin who smear the pure name of the Conqueror, oh no, those supposedly murdered are in fact alive, and the dead simply slumber and are not murdered, what strange ideas others have. Woe to those, however, who dare to violate the everyday with such mad visions of innocent children thrown into the fire whose leaping flames are oil-fired and fed by living bodies, no, those are all lies, the conspirators have never done that, and whoever did happen to do that did so against the will and without the knowledge of the Conqueror, no, nothing more about such horrors, for not even the most unforgiving enemies in Russia or America would believe it! It's understandable that a genuine opponent of the Conqueror would not see him as a benefactor, but instead they hate him, they who reside in the Beskydy Range, as well as in subjugated lands such as here in Birkenau, but the Conqueror also has his merits, he is not guilty and means well, he not having promised his own people that much, but giving them something, namely work, fuel for winter, Volkswagens for his autobahn, and the power of a thousand years of joy. Who wants to smear the

Conqueror by saying there are flaws in his Reich? He knows nothing of them, he is kind and gentle, he can't even kill an animal and eats only vegetables, he loves the silent glory of the untouched Alps, where he watches over the good of the people from his mountain retreat.

Josef imagines all of this and sees as well the chimneys smoking before him, hearing the screams of those choking on the gas, the screams of the departing intended for this world, other screams breaking into praise, as amid the moment of death they say the name of the One who is the only One. Josef's thoughts must wrap themselves around the death rattles, as he sees how the blood runs from the eyes, from the nose, from the mouth, he sees how body after body writhes and stretches and rears up and screams, screams, screams, as long as they can scream, and how their screams seethe, how they sink together, the Zyklon gas having already exterminated them. It's important to guard those crystals, they're expensive, use them sparingly! That's why the dusty purveyor of death is slowly transported in sealed and protected lead containers to the killing grounds in a car on whose sides and roof an insignia is painted that some still hold as holy, though through this misuse it is forever put to shame, the insignia being that of the Red Cross of the Geneva Convention. An accomplice takes the murderous cargo from the car with its red cross, and soon he is atop the roof with a mask on his face, opening the tin can and dumping its contents down into the narrow shaft. In this the cowardly hero has simply done his duty, the victims decimated, a single heap of lifeless bodies. Josef sees the lost ones who are part of the special command, themselves used to the goings-on inside the circle of murder, everything the same there, today the dead, tomorrow the living, and to it all music flutters and whistles and tweets, "Play something lovely, really lovely!" Each morning and evening this music can be heard at least once, as out of the neighboring D-Camp the lost ones march out to or back from work, marches pressing them on, pleasant marches, audible all the way out to the beetle grove and birch woods that are just beyond the plain where the lost ones' camp is located. This area used to be a hinterland that few people knew before the most loyal ones under the accomplices settled in where the borders of three kingdoms meet. Among the hecatombs, hardly anyone knows the name of the place, the accomplices having earmarked it as a place for extermination to which the victims were sent from many countries in endless trains. For three years it has gone on, and there is no end in sight.

First the victims are gathered together in each country, all of them not being able to come here at the same time, exhaustive plans needing to be worked out, for the most loyal of the conspirators have many worries, it all needing to go faster, always faster, there being so many obstacles to overcome in order to get the lost ones onto the trains, it requiring epic battles with the army, with the railroad administration, with the opposition of the church, with the hatred of the saboteurs, with the ignorance of the stubborn, with the recalcitrance of the Italians, with the mawkishness of the Germans. Not everyone knows about the Conqueror's plans for extermination, he cannot make it public and explain it such that every last dimwit is assured that murder isn't taking place here, and mercifully not in any mass manner, and so the Conqueror must hide it all, the people cannot know the truth, everything is secret and almost invisible, but not everything can remain hidden, and that's what leads to difficulties that make the most loyal of the conspirators groan. The victims have no idea where they are being brought, nor do many of the collaborators know as they help round up the lost ones and load them onto the trains, for while it's clear that the lost ones are being sent off to work, and thus have to be resettled, most don't know the name of the place to which they are being taken. In France it was called Pitchipoi,* the children robbed of their parents having coined the name, such that whenever a train left from there for the east, both large and small said it was headed to Pitchipoi as goodbyes were said, hope and sadness mixing together among those leaving as well as those remaining behind, everyone believing that the journey will be easier than staying, it won't last much longer, the Conqueror will be defeated, then they will return from Pitchipoi, everyone will celebrate and they will be celebrated, then the brotherhood of all mankind will arise, the Conqueror, however, having to appear before a court of the people, in which they will raise the brazen charge, "Why didn't you let us stay in our houses? Why did you drag us off to Pitchipoi?"

---

*Pitchipoi is the imaginary place to which displaced Jews in France believed they would be deported to while interned at the Drancy internment camp awaiting transport to Auschwitz.

That will certainly be the last trial that humankind will hold, for it will be followed by eternal peace, which can already be clearly seen as it expands, it being seen whenever the iron rails ring and clatter, *Pimmm-Pimmm-Pimmm-tititititititittititi-Pimmm!* Peace is at hand when one's gaze reaches out toward the Beskydy Range, whose gray-blue waits in the distance, ourselves already on the threshold of freedom, the furnaces that consume their victims today extinguished forever, no one yelling "Hats off!" and "Out of your bunks!," no roll call taken, no section elder reporting, "Section 23 present with 327!" Then all of this will be just a phantom, it never having existed, just the spawn of a disturbed mind, there never having been a Conqueror, not even a war, people were not chased into slaughterhouses but simply remained at home and went about their peaceful business, it having been a golden age then as it will be again. Josef does not despair completely, a confidence having been granted him, although reason would seem to rule out any positive expectation, yet his trust is not completely destroyed, it is still there and has even strengthened somewhat in the camp of the lost, though he's somewhat ashamed to admit it, but he still wants to maintain it and believe in it, it being a thick coat that protects his wounded nakedness, he not totally lost even when he is surrounded by filth and vermin when he lies with Milan and Étienne under a blanket, for perhaps it's even worse in Mordechai's quarters, where there is hardly anything to take one's mind off how things are in the Gypsy camp.

Josef's group waits for fourteen days under the smoke clouds of the chimneys, their imminent departure often postponed and rescheduled, but then it's announced that several groups will be transported together. Then the lost ones are shoved once again into the baths, though it's not a large sauna but instead a small one in the Gypsy camp, the lost ones having to stand outside for many hours in the rain, all of them freezing in their rags, until finally they are pressed into the rooms, commanded to take off everything in the front room, until they are left with only a pair of shoes that they carry in their hands, while everything they have accumulated in the camp, except that which they can always carry on their person, has to be abandoned, spoons and cigarette butts, all of it yanked away from them under the threat of blows. The naked are herded with heckling calls into the sauna, nothing visible except steam and murk, an ear-shattering noise ripping through the room, everyone wailing and thrashing about, Josef never having witnessed such bellowing in Birkenau, everyone senselessly lashing out at everyone else, senselessly shoving one another around, all without reason, even without intent, no one even wanting to blame the other. Finally the showerheads are turned on, the water is too hot and burns their naked skin, though most are happy, it's the first shower they've had in weeks, despite each hut being outfitted with a latrine that doubles as a washroom, though no one would think of using it as such, for you can only stand it there for a while and only on the rare occasion, there being hardly enough time to wash your hands and face, as in general there are too few washstands, the water pressure is poor, and there is no soap or towels. In the small sauna the lost ones can scrape the dirt off their skin with their fingernails, their backs and limbs turning red from this and from the hot water, though there's no way to dry off, so they all stand there barefoot on a cold stone floor with their shoes in their hands, the water dripping from their heads and shoulders. The lost ones continue to scream without ceasing, even though they still have no reason to, it perhaps being the horror of it all that is indeed abysmal and continually gives rise to new terrors, the room seeming ready to burst with the chain of screams that continue without end. To the collaborators it all seems so stupid, for they are just trying to do their job, and with horsewhips they flog the naked, who want to avoid the blows, thus causing each to trample on the other, the floor slippery and painful for anyone who falls, while if care isn't taken they can be trampled, the blows bringing no end to it all, but rather only worsening the puzzlement and confusion of this carnival, which takes on its first bit of orderliness the minute one of the conspirators appears and waves his pistol about. Then clothes are handed out, which goes about the same as it would in the big sauna, as plunder is taken from them with their having no choice in the matter, though the clothes they are given are not the same as what they had on before, because after bathing and disinfection in the Gypsy camp they don't get their stuff back, but instead the lost ones get something better, the working slaves destined soon to be transported receiving underwear and winter coats, which is more than what they had in quarantine, even though it's no better in quality. Josef is somewhat lucky to get a miserable pair of shoes made of torn linen, none of the stuff is made from the wool of a prayer shawl, instead a narrow pair of leggings and stained pants are made from thin cloth, which was once brown, though he does get a good green vest, the black jacket having no doubt been part of a good suit, while the hand-sewn winter coat was once quite fine, Josef reading on a sewn-on silk strip the name and address of a Jewish tailor in Lodz.

They are not allowed to dawdle while dressing, "Hurry! Hurry!" shouted at them continually, as if the train were already waiting for them above on the ramp, where each of them arrived sometime in recent weeks, but there appears to be no train waiting anxiously, for next the lost ones are forced to stand and wait for hours more in front of the sauna. Then they file into rows and the entire group marches to the yard, where the prison scribes appear with their lists and begin to count the number of lost ones in each group, counting them again and again, two groups missing a couple of men, Josef's group having one too many, which causes a lot of squabbling and complaint, though neither gentle talk nor threats seems to work, the numbers don't add up, and so each one has to be asked who he is and which group he belongs to, though in the chaos of the Gypsy camp it simply isn't possible to maintain such control, the names of the lost ones often falsely given or written down wrong, no one having any papers, for all their possessions were taken from them by force in the big sauna. Thus it takes over two hours before the count is right for each group, too many having snuck in, for they want to get out of the camp, some of them beaten as a result, but then sent on without further punishment, they even allowing some to be exchanged between different groups so that fathers and sons and brothers can stick together, until finally the groups are formed, everyone takes a breath, though once again it is announced that the journey has been postponed, everyone back in the huts.

It turns out this doesn't mean that Josef's group is to return to the same huts they were in before, instead they are led to the gate of the E-Camp, where they stand for a long while, threatened all the while with severe punishment if anyone dares to try to take anything out of the Gypsy camp but what they've been fitted out with already, though after the plundering that occurred in the small sauna hardly anyone has anything, nor do most of them want to risk a flogging for it, only here and there someone allowing a spoon or a knife to drop to the ground. Then the group is counted more than once by the helpers and the accomplices, and along with sections D, C, and B they are led off to A-Camp, where their marching ends at a barracks where the section elder appears and takes charge of the group. With his scribe he stands before the lost, playing with his riding whip as he sticks one cigarette after another into his clever and inscrutable face, introducing himself as Pinks, there no longer being anyone like him in the A-Camp, for the lost ones need not stand still while listening to him, as he is a good father and treats the men—which is what he calls the prisoners, as do others—with solidarity and compassion, there being no one who can force him to kill anyone in his barracks, which is part of his goodwill, though they should inscribe on the inside of their forehead that here they are not in the Gypsy camp, here different rules apply, here only good men live who also want to work, no riffraff, for here one has to keep everything and himself clean, for if you have a louse and are such a pig, then you will be tossed out of your lodgings and will get twenty-five lashes on your naked ass, thus no one should even dare to wear his boots inside, and the blankets must be cleanly folded and remain on the bunks, no one can take them, here they are to live like gentlemen, nothing will be stolen from anyone, but if someone pinches something, then Pinks will have nothing to do with him, only good people will be allowed to live under him, and the culprit will be relegated to the shit command that takes away all the shit they produce because they eat too much, Pinks ready to close his speech by saying that each should know that Pinks is fair, and if the new ones behave and he hears no complaints about them, then he is like a father and has a soft heart, but when anyone doesn't obey, then his heart is hard, while he will repeat again that this is the A-Camp and not the Gypsy camp, and so off with you, you all look tired, the men should be in their huts, and so the staffers show them to their places.

The setup of the hut is no different from those in the Gypsy camp, but it really is much cleaner, everything painted white, the bunks fitted out with tin plates on which numbers are written down. Josef's group stays only one night in the hut, but that's enough to get to know some of the inhabitants. Pinks comes by again with a cigarette in his mouth, and once more during the night, acting out his role as father as he speaks with each of them for a short while or even longer, though sometimes he has to reveal his hard heart and takes someone out to beat him with his belt. The regular inhabitants of

PANORAMA / 379

the hut are used to how things work in the camp, most of them experienced lads, hardened and tough, the uninitiated having a hard time understanding their talk, it being a thick accent full of cussing, though the boys are unbowed, most of them seeming strong and fresh, while what's going on around them doesn't seem to disturb them, though many are good-natured, tossing potatoes and slices of bread to the guests, obviously being well nourished themselves, having bacon and tinned foods in supply, chocolate, as well as good clothes and woolens, leather gloves, and their exquisite boots standing underneath their bunks. All of this is the booty from possessions of the newly arrived lost ones, this only a small part of the untold thievery that doesn't benefit the collaborators and the regular lost ones, but rather the conspirators, whose most loyal members need to be compensated a little for the great service they provide the Conqueror, though no matter how hard they try the most loyal ones couldn't possibly keep the measureless amount of stolen goods for themselves, and so they have to be a little honest and distribute on behalf of all conspirators a good amount to the general public for its own use. This is why huge storehouses have been built here, which are referred to as "Canada," they being full of gold and jewels, clothes and shoes, bedding and handbags, watches and perfumes, children's clothes and toys, all of which had been quickly and carefully packed by the clueless, they who had readied themselves for the journey to Pitchipoi, since for such a journey they took their very best things, often carrying their most expensive items in the hope of using them to trade for necessities or to save for future times, only to have everything taken away on the ramp or in the room where they disrobed before entering the gas chambers, or remaining behind in the big sauna, where after a while they end up in the storehouses, albeit not as items recorded as tremendous losses. Instead, announcements are made that say the wares have been confiscated as stolen or fenced goods, the will of the Conqueror having been fulfilled, for which many people are thankful, though often they have no idea what they should be thankful for, since the countless owners of all these goods have long since been consumed by the flames.

The next day Josef's group is transferred from the A-Camp to the D-Camp, which means that they will likely not be transported soon, though it could also mean that it will be today for sure, but many doubt it, no one knowing what to believe. This also gives rise to a shower of hope that Germany is no longer able to use trains to transport prisoners, the Russians already having reached Krakow and perhaps ready to break through any day, meaning that they are preparing to empty the camps. This news, which means so much to the lost ones, also makes them realize that the present situation in the camp is markedly improved since earlier times, they having already experienced the worst of what they'd seen, there having been hardly any transports from the west in more than six months, many of the conspirators having become nicer or at least more careful, supposedly having been warned against listening to German-language radio out of England and threatened with punishment if they did. In any case, the improved relations with the lost ones is a good sign of a quick end to the war, the Conqueror's days numbered, his enemies not even allowing him a chance to catch his breath, while also having overrun the fatherland's western border, a thousand planes crisscrossing by day and by night, as Germany is transformed into a single mound of rubble, the Resistance also beginning to hurt it, the lost ones needing to stay confident, for the hour of liberation is at hand. Nonetheless, many turn away from such far-reaching hope as they look at the charged barbed wire and upward at the weapons at the ready in the watchtowers.

The day moves on wearisomely, time seeming fragmented, they having to file in again and again, after which the lost ones are led back into the barracks, then back out again, so it goes, over and over, roll call occurring as evening descends, all of them then suddenly pressed into an overflowing hut and ordered to get into their bunks. One bunk is meant to hold six men, but now twenty-five to thirty have to squeeze in, no one allowed to disrobe, though that is a ridiculous order, for the lost ones have no room to rest, screams traveling through the cool, damp, muggy air, which are then smothered, at one time "Sleep!" ordered, then "Everyone get ready to march!" Then someone finally says, "Everyone go to sleep!" The light is put out, the air in the hut grows heavier, then suddenly there is light, capos and staffers and who knows who else barging into the room with long sticks and beginning to aimlessly lash out at the lost ones and the bunks, yelling as they go, "We've had enough of you bums! The sanatorium is closed! Time for the pigs to come out! Out with you. Out! Get up, you weary sheiks! You miserable idiots! Rotten pigs! Money-grubbers! Assholes!," the Polish and

Ukrainian curses following one upon another in a hellish uproar, and so on, and so on. That they finally leave is good, but first they have to pass through hell before they go, everyone has to leave the hut through the front door, no one allowed to stay behind, the collaborators lining up on the way out, such that everyone must pass between them, at which they hit the unprotected heads and bodies of the lost with their sticks. Finally everyone is gathered together outside and quickly counted once again, after which they begin to move on their own feet like a slow waltz toward the main camp road, picking up speed as they climb the ramps that serve as a narrow passage, garish arc lamps lighting their way, prison scribes hastily counting off the travelers shuffling through and calling out numbers, the count needing to be right, each lost one getting a loaf of bread, a hunk of margarine, and a slab of sausage, though many leave empty-handed.

Hurry! Hurry! Get in! Though no one really worries about whether the lost can reasonably fit into the cattle wagons, it being dark everywhere, the chaos churning the people into a teeming brew, sixty men to a car, there being no room to tuck away bodies and limbs, though slowly they push against one another, many wanting to remain comfortable and thus pressing at a neighbor, but finally all of the lost ones manage to gather together and the loading of the train cars is done. A long train has been put together, in each wagon a bench for the guards, and after they climb on the lost ones have to shove even more tightly together, the guards and their bayonets are from the army, two soldiers for each car, they also having machine guns at the ready. Finally the train pulls away, the journey lasting through the night and into a cool autumn morning, the countryside shimmering in the sunlight, the day beautiful, the journey passing through Silesia, where beets are harvested, fields tilled, on and on, the train stopping rarely, then traveling through the hills, soon after the mountains, it all looking much like Bohemia, home must be nearby, happy conjectures about where they are headed shared, Josef also beginning to feel hopeful, these appearing to be the flat lands, and indeed the train enters the plains and stops for a while. When the journey starts up again, hopes sink, Bohemia is not the final destination, though the landscape is beautiful, it being a pleasure to just look at the landscape, though only a few of the men have an eye for it, most of them having ceased to say anything, for they are hungry and tired and anxious, as

382 / H. G. ADLER

the train passes through Waldenburg, the high mountain with its snowy peak looming above, Josef pressing nearer to a crack in the siding in order to get a better view of the forest, pressing as if he might spring into the picture itself in order to escape into the countryside, though such thoughts are fleeting and bring no hope. They have already passed Hirschberg, Görlitz soon disappearing into the twilight. The long-silent soldiers in the car now talk in a friendly manner, asking for songs to be sung, Yiddish and Polish or Russian folk songs, doleful wise men mixing painfully with the knocking sounds of the train rolling into the distance, a second long night during which sleep is hardly possible. The unrest among the lost ones begins to climb, many showing no mercy toward their fellow travelers as they elbow them in the ribs, though finally this night passes and they find themselves in western Saxony, passing through Wurzen, Leipzig soon following, though the journey circumscribes the city limits, after which it stops, three wagons separated, this being Josef's group, which believes it has reached its final destination.

This, however, turns out not to be true, and the journey continues, the lost ones growing ever more hungry and tired and anxious. A Slovak Jew, a doctor, begins to talk in a confused manner, he having lost his bearings, as Josef and two others talk to him and try to calm him down, the journey crawling forward, the train stopping often, though later they reach Halle, then finally Eisleben, night falling again, a third night spent on the train, the lost ones feeling very down, as vainly some try to keep up the others' hopes, the disturbed doctor from Ružomberok now talking senselessly and continuously. The train has stopped again as he begins to thrash about and launches into a blaring tirade, even the German soldiers want to quiet him down, but nothing can control the madman as he screams about how the liberation has come, enough with the murder and oppression of innocent people, the revolution is here, the hour of reckoning and revenge, and whoever doesn't lift a hand to help is a coward and a traitor, the hangman needs to be hanged, victory is certain if everyone takes a stand. The mad doctor then lunges at a soldier and tries with his bare hands to strip him of his weapon, the other soldier shooting him, though he doesn't want to kill the disturbed man, and so he shoots him in the foot, the wounded man screaming all the louder, knowing that it's the end for him, but before he dies he curses Adolf Hitler, the destroyer of the people and the murderer of millions, cursing as well Josef Tiso, that dog of a priest who sold out Slovakia to Hitler and delivered the Jews to his slaughterhouses. Then some shots ring out from a machine gun in the car, the prisoners anxiously pressing against the walls, bright lights flash, the dying man is yanked away and put out of his misery with a single shot, after which the soldiers alert the transport commandant and are quite up front about it all, insisting over and over that, no, it was not a mutiny, the others were reasonable and quiet, only this one had gone crazy. Then the commandant begins issuing threats, the first being "We should kill them! The entire carload!" Some prisoners, meanwhile, have to take care of the dead man, which forces them to squeeze together even more, the corpse stretched out in the middle, which otherwise would have remained free, though if anyone were to say a word he would be killed without warning, the soldiers in the car standing, the journey pressing on in fits and starts throughout the night, the machine guns trained on the lost ones, who are silent and sit there motionless, from time to time a beam of light shining from a flashlight, until finally the train stops at a small station in Eichsfeld, the journey at last over.

The group doesn't have it so bad here, which is how one talks about a good camp in the language of the lost. There are two factories that have been stripped of their previous contents and converted into a small slave camp that is overseen by those who run Buchenwald, wings for the Conqueror's planes being fabricated here, many of the civil servants acting friendly toward the prisoners, while inhabitants of the village who work there are even kinder, yet many of the lost are weak, while others find no favor among the conspirator who runs the camp. Then one day a hundred and twenty men are needed for Langenstein, this also an outlying camp of Buchenwald, and so the weak ones are sent there, as well as those who are not liked, which includes Josef. It's now been six weeks since he first came here, Josef amazed each day that he is still alive, there are many and much younger colleagues who have died, and who came with him at the same time to Langenstein, even on the very first day one of them stretching out and dying, another of the lost finding that his feet had swollen up, two days later his face was bloated, each creeping step becoming more and more difficult, his gaze growing empty and unsteady, at which the lost one was capable neither of work nor of making a clear decision, though the slave drivers don't want to spare him, and so he is holed up in a corner of the underground factory, while during roll call at the end of the day there is often one missing, no one able to find him and everyone having to look, until finally he is found, sometimes barely conscious, while at other times the accomplices and henchmen kill him on the spot, this being the home of unhappiness, at which someone calls out, "You two Belgians, quick! Hurry! Hurry! Go carry your buddy home!" At which they have to carry the dying or the dead back to camp, though for two broken-down and half-starved prisoners there's hardly anything more difficult than to carry someone who is dying through the halls of the underground factory and then over the rubbish dump while being pressed by the henchmen to hurry as they schlep him back to camp.

Josef hears steps outside, these being the collaborators, the camp guards, and staffers, they soon bursting into the room with clubs and whips as they yell, "Everyone up!" Blindly they lash out at the lost ones, beating anyone who is not standing. Josef doesn't wait, but instead wakes Étienne and Milan, his warning for them to flee hardly an advantage, for there are no lights on, since the windows cannot be blacked out, thus making it hard for the lost ones to handle their attackers and to find their bearings as one stumbles over the other, none able to find their things, their shoes gone, it also impossible to find the miserable washroom, where even if you have light and self-discipline there's little you can do, each possessing a little piece of terrible soap, though hardly anyone has a hand towel or a toothbrush, eight washstands having to serve sixteen men at the same time, and which in turn are also meant to serve seven hundred to eight hundred men who are crammed into the small camp, where on some days there is not a drop of water to be had. No wonder, then, that everyone is full of lice, for lice scurry through the blankets and the rags that cover their bodies, there not having been a change of clothes available since Josef came to the camp, so everyone wears only what he has on his back.

Langenstein is a deep hole of horror, human brotherhood barely traceable here, it being better that it not show itself before the ever-lurking malevolence, most of the collaborators being hardened young men who wildly and maliciously run the place with complete abandon, their better spirits not allowing them to remain cool-headed, even the decent collaborators needing to appear to succumb to the inhumanity of the place, as no one is able to escape such corruption. The small camp is only for skilled workers, who were generally selected out at Birkenau, barbed wire separating the place from the larger camp, where there are no skilled workers, it being a penal camp, the lost ones not allowed to move from one to the other without special permission. A band of collaborators runs things in the small camp, the camp guard led by a nasty Ukrainian, followed by the section elders with their followers, who hold back a large chunk of the spare rations granted the prisoners. The kitchen is located in the big camp, where a lot of food disappears straight off, the most valuable items regularly going to the conspirators who hold sway over Langenstein, for they take for themselves a measly and insufficient amount for each of the watch posts under their command, after which all the collaborators take their cut at each post, the lost ones indeed getting a couple of sips of brown, lukewarm water first thing in the morning, which sometimes is called coffee and other times tea, the lost ones getting nothing as they slave away during the day. Up until now there have been only two days when Josef had to stay behind in the camp, each day lasting up to twelve hours, the journey out and back taking a minimum of another two hours, and the roll call in the yard each morning and at night using up another two hours, which means sixteen hours total for each day. Throughout all this time there is nothing to eat, four weeks ago the prisoners having been served a midday soup while working in the underground factory of the little camp, but this was taken away as punishment more often than not, especially the Jews in general getting nothing, but now the soup is gone for good, and no one needs to be worried about getting hit while trying to get his share, for now they hold it back, even the civil servants in the works receiving meager rations, though the lost ones have the hardest slave labor in having to dig down in the caverns and work outside the mountain the whole day long with nothing to eat. Only after the roll call in the evening is there soup, which is usually served around eight o'clock, by then the soup cold and almost always sour, consisting almost entirely of water and salt, a few slivers of carrots and potato peels swimming in it, a liter of the disgusting liquid all that one gets for the week, only once long ago having been replaced by a light, sweet, runny gruel. Bread is also handed out in the evening, up until two weeks ago it having been a large hunk, but since then it's only been a thick slice, three times a week a dollop of margarine, and every so often a spoonful of lean raw ground meat or a thin slice of watery sausage or beet marmalade.

Their hunger is so immense that most of them immediately wolf down whatever is handed out, this being the smartest thing to do, for whatever you might carefully stash away under your blanket is almost always gone in the morning, while no matter how much yelling there is, there's nothing to be done, and so the hungry one must wait until evening. More and more of the lost ones die because of hunger, there being no escape, as they lose their human appearance and shape, becoming unconscious and like animals, clawing away at unsuitable rubbish wherever they find it, at the hard ground in the camp, at the heaps of kitchen scraps, on the way to and at the work sites, everything and anything picked up and devoured as a dog would, even though it is strictly forbidden and they can be beaten for it, someone hanging signs on the lost ones that say:

I'M A VULTURE
WHO EATS RUBBISH

Raw potato peels and rotten beets are dangerous to eat, so the lost ones suffer severe diarrhea, unable to hold in their stool, thus soiling themselves and their rooms. The prison doctor can provide some relief by saying they don't have to work, but then they get less bread and still run the danger that they will be hounded out of the room and into slave labor. The miserable sick bay at the big camp is the only place where one is granted any special favors, and even then for only the most severe illness and wounds, while also having limited prospects of ever getting out alive. There is no bone char, nothing to stop the diarrhea, and therefore the patients suffer from monstrous hunger, they being pressed to get up and get to roll call, though often they can no longer stand on their legs, some of them even dying in the yard. But as long as one is alive two colleagues are sent to help the lost one, because he has to show up at roll call and stand there, even if he collapses into the dust, but the count must be correct, and it's too much to expect of the section leaders to also have to count the prisoners in the stinking rooms of the infirmary, for it could be simply that someone has run off, which happens regularly, as indeed there's no trust here, not even the helpers can be trusted, which is why the section leader is so narrow-minded, and the count is often not right, there being always groups that have been commandeered elsewhere or sent off in the middle of the night, or someone has wandered off to the latrine and fallen in, or someone has died without being noticed.

Much can be withstood by sheer will, because one cannot give in and succumb to each day's demands, but instead must remember what's needed to supersede such hardship, be it a friendly word or a bit of encouragement for a neighbor in the room, on the way to work, as both provide strength to the slave. For it's no longer just a rumor whispered in the latrine, but rather the truth, the Russians have crossed the Oder at Küstrin, the Americans have taken Frankfurt and are now marching on Bamberg, it will not last much longer. For many, this is of no help at all, because they are too broken, the smallest wounds fester straightaway, and everyone has such wounds from his slave labor, the limbs soon swelling, the body becoming discolored, nothing done in the infirmary, for there is no disinfectant, salve, or bandages. If one opens an infected wound, all that can be done is to wrap some paper around it, the pain soon following, blood poisoning soon whisking the lost one away.

Shrill whistles sound, as well as the air-raid alarm, but today it's already too late for the morning dispensation of something to drink, though the light is on and the plunder remaining in the room is quickly gathered together, as everyone assembles outside on the square in the small camp, all the helpers there as well, the camp elders, the hall capo, who helps the supervisor of the lost ones in the underground factory, the camp scribe, the hall scribe, the hall translator, Jacques, a pleasant Frenchman, the horde of overseers who don't work at all, the camp guards, and the section elders with their boys. Everyone is there and screaming at the mob of lost ones, all of you get into your groups, though since there are more attractive groups and less attractive groups, a wild tussle breaks out as each tries to get into a better one, the number of workers from the underground works changing daily, which results in a great deal of anxiety, for whoever is not able to slip into a position that will lead to good work has to join another group, which normally has to do heavy digging or carry heavy goods, these being commands from the big camp, where any lost one from the small camp is often treated badly, since the overseers there want to teach those who have received the preferred jobs what it really takes to work hard. Each wants to avoid such trouble, as it involves being shoved around, threatened, and hit, all hell breaking loose, the camp guards and the overseers ganging up with their clubs, sticks, and lead cables swinging to each side of everyone's head. Also, whoever is clever doesn't shy away from this battle, because if one hangs back in the background and doesn't fight for a spot in a better group he risks being put in the worst of groups, and that can be very bad, for tomorrow the blows will be worth it, as they only hurt for a while, but to slave away for an entire day in a bad group can mean death, even a miserably painful death.

Once all the groups from the little camp are divided up, they cross over to the big camp, where again they all report for roll call, the groups arranged in four rows, most of them carrying a flag with a number, the overseers swinging their batons, until finally the camp gate is opened. Milan, Étienne, and Josef stand in a row together, they having promised to stick together, though it doesn't always work out, they sometimes being separated because of a beating, as now an order is barked out: "Attention! All together—march! Hats off!" The rows stream out of the gate, two lost ones counting them off, while as soon as the long lines of lost ones are past the gate they are made to stop. Without seeing the lost ones, a stranger would have no idea what kind of camp exists only a few steps away, the work on the railroad having only been started a few years prior without any great effort applied to it, though the site was cleverly chosen, the camp lying in a small, steep wooded valley, only part of which had been cleared, the woods even today rising up with thick pines just at the edge of the large camp, some of the huts even situated among the trees. Across from the camp a hill rises that is also partially covered by trees, mass graves dug into it halfway up, for there is no crematorium here, the mortality rate continuing to rise over time, two weeks ago there having been hardly more than twenty or thirty, while now it's probably more like sixty, and soon it will be eighty or a hundred if the liberation doesn't occur soon. In any case it will be too late, even tomorrow is too late for many, which everyone knows even at the work site, because of the need to replace positions, though what good does it do to have to keep sending more and more over to Langenstein? The supply won't last that much longer, even if the conspirators tirelessly ship over men, for they have no idea that their hour has come, even though they chatter on continually about the final victory, meaning by that the Conqueror's victory. Recently Josef overheard a speech given to the sentries, someone wanting to cheer them up, telling them they should stay on their toes in front of the prisoners and not relax, the need for discipline needing to remain ever sharp. Nonetheless this doesn't always seem possible anymore, for it's rumored among the lost ones that more and more sentries have deserted their posts, while others steadfastly believe in the Conqueror and obey the conspirators above them, who order them to march the prisoners to their slavery while keeping their weapons trained on them, so that they can shoot if they need to, while when the lost ones are marching many sentries are sharp on their tails, making sure that whatever rubbish they pick up is ripped away from them, especially if it's a piece of wood, beating the unfortunate ones with rifle butts and sticks if they do.

The path leading to the camp looks nice enough, some cherry trees there having blossomed, the breeze blowing through the forest, though it is cold and damp, the path muddy and wet, as you sink in with miserable soaking shoes, the mud clinging to them, each step even more laborious for your tired feet. Finally the funeral procession takes shape, the overseers and sentries again count the rows, the weapons brought to the ready, a whistle at last blowing to start the march, the hill with its mass graves now behind the procession, the march easier for the next two hundred meters that run downhill, each one obeying when "Hurry! Hurry!" and "Keep together!" are yelled out, such that the rows march on without interruption. Then a highway is reached and crossed, after which it gets tougher, the lost ones having to cross a small embankment as they pass along the floor of the valley, this being a rail bed for the narrow-gauge railway, as the walking gets more difficult and they stumble along, tottering, the procession unable to stick together, the front man having been lost, nor does it help that they are beaten because of it, as well as being prodded forever to "Hurry! Hurry!" and "Keep together! Front man! Keep it straight!" Though many are able to keep their balance, many fall, others trampling them, the sentries impatient. Finally they press past this stretch, after which they climb a bank, a steep embankment on which the narrow-gauge trains travel day and night on several rails as they transport the white limestone and sandstone that thousands of slaves dynamited at Zwieberge before picking, shoveling, and loading it onto the small railcars.

Finally they reach an entrance to Zwieberge, though there are others, Josef knowing of at least three. They then pass by a dumping site, this being where the freight is loaded into the hoppers of the trucks, as well as into the larger cars of the narrow-gauge train, the ingress still small and not yet complete, it also being clogged with railcars to the right and left, leaving just enough room to pass by on foot on the uneven earth, someone having quickly shoved them back as continually they are pressed on, as it is better not to be at the back, for it's much better at the front of the ranks, the best position just behind the leaders. The ingress is much too poorly lit with bleary lighting, as slaves work here, lost ones lost amid the muck and dirt, Josef thinking of the sufferings of the children of Israel in Egypt, how in the Bible it says that a new pharaoh will arise who knew nothing of Josef, but who observed the quick demise of those who hurried the lost ones on. The path leading underground is at least a kilometer long, Josef having counted the steps that run from the entrance to the ingress to the gathering spot in the underground hall, but he has already forgotten the number, it being inconsistent, since sometimes you have to take detours through side chambers. It is bitter cold in the passages, a damp, penetrating cold that the lost ones can't protect themselves against, as it is strictly forbidden to wrap a blanket around yourself, though Josef does it nonetheless, there is no other way to stand it, this also the only way to prevent having your blanket stolen back in the camp. Josef keeps all of his necessities on him, as do others, no matter how forbidden it is to do so, but he's not afraid and thinks about how he arrived here from the camp in Eichsfeld with a number of small items, gifts from a couple of good-hearted Germans from the village and the remainders of a package from Bohemia, some food, a razor, a bar of soap, a hand towel, an anthology of poetry that contained Nietzsche's verse:

> *The crows cry*
> *And fly off towards the city:*
> *Soon it will snow,*
> *For the homeless, such pity!*

And this book of poetry is about all that Josef has had for so long, while here among so-called civilization there is almost no one to turn to, which is why he has to carry everything on his person, such as the little tin box made in Milan, a cigarette holder that Josef carved out of wood, a tiny piece of soap passed on by a Dutch civil servant, as well as a spoon, a pocketknife, a rag that serves as a scarf, but most important of all, Josef's own notes, which he has stowed away in the tin box, some of them from the last camp, some he has secretly written down below the earth in Zwieberge.

Josef has certainly been plenty afraid to have the notes about him, he once having been stopped in the underground factory as a conspirator and an overseer were frisking people in search of stolen goods. Thankfully Josef had nothing they were looking for, though he did have a blanket wrapped around him, which he respectfully removed, but then the notes appeared and that was bad. The conspirator flipped through the pages and began to make out what they said, saying it was sabotage, a conspiracy and an uprising against the camp leaders and the Conqueror, saying to Josef's face that all these words were intended against the Conqueror. Josef denied this, saying that it wasn't against the Conqueror, though he said openly that they had to do with what went on in different jobs at the camp, but that he wasn't scheming at anything, and he protested when the conspirator asserted things that were neither intended nor in fact there. At this the conspirator coldly threatened Josef, asking if he knew what the consequences were for all this. Yes, Josef knew, at which the conspirator said, "This will cost you your life!" Josef answered, "Yes, Herr Troop Leader, I know!" He took the notes and wrote down Josef's prison number, 95714, though he didn't do anything about the blanket, which the overseer was still concerned about, while even the pocketknife, which as a dangerous weapon Josef showed to those better armed, was returned to him. After that Josef figured his time had come, he not being surprised that when he returned to camp, number 95714 was called as they entered the gate, numbers always being called when any of the lost ones were seen as a threat of escape, or had stolen something, or committed some other transgression that needed to be pointed out. These prisoners always have to stand by the gate after the march back to camp before being ordered to see the section leader. Among those held back, Josef is the last and has to look on as his comrades are whipped, after which the section leader asks him, "Why are you here?" Josef clicks his heels and relays with a firm voice and precise words what he has done. For a while the section leader looks intently at Josef, who doesn't stir, and then finally says, "Aha, so you're the note taker!" He takes the notes that are lying on the table and hands them over to the obviously surprised Josef with the words, "There! Next time don't write such stupid stuff! But if you have to write, don't let yourself get caught! Now off with you!"

Josef escaped the expected punishment and since then has enjoyed the heightened attention of the most powerful collaborators who make plans for his transport. On that day he was doubly lucky, for in the yard the lost ones were subjected to an intense body search, they being forced to hand over their coats and everything they had or were not supposed to have. After that there were random beatings, the worst offenders being those who went around with a blanket wrapped around them. Just after Josef had been let off by the section leader the search took place, so he behaved as if none of it had anything to do with him as he passed beyond the group in a wide arc and entered his hut from the back entrance, where there was no one who cared what he did. He still carried his notes with him, for he wanted to save them, as he wasn't yet done with life, he wanted to survive, and now more than ever he wouldn't let himself die, he wanted to bear witness to the existence of the lost ones. At the same time he could not grasp *why* he, and especially why *he* should survive. He feared that afterward life would be bleak and empty, nor did he know where he would go after the war, and therefore perhaps anything he could say would be senseless and would find neither acceptance nor sympathy, and he would be alone, without a wife, without a family, without friends or anyone, homeless, Bohemia no longer his homeland, yet where would he find a homeland? The world will seem strange, Josef no longer able to immerse himself in day-to-day life, a table, a stool, a bed, none of it will be a comfort. Josef just wants to sleep peacefully for once, to sleep forever, and he wants to be alone, to not have to listen to the iron rails, not have to wait for the next blow, not have to wolf down the sour, watery soup. Everything has become rotten and disgusting, everything is destroyed, mankind having dragged itself into the muck and done itself in, Josef only able to mourn the fact that no day will ever be untroubled again, for the eyes can find nothing beautiful to look at, the ears no pure music to listen to any longer. Instead there will only be trains headed to Pitchipoi to the calls of "Faster! Away! Away! You greedy bastards, why don't you just pack it in, you miserable assholes!" Poisonous gas wipes out the masses of people, the flames spit out of the chimney of the Red Cross! And yet Josef wants to live on, he wants to survive the curses raining down in so many tongues, for on those evenings where you are not forced to stay too long in the underground factory and are able to crawl out of the cavernous works, then the sunset is still there, the rays of the sun spread their red over the lit-up hills, the woods stand quiet, Josef senses the breath of approaching spring, the view opens up, something that cannot simply be forbidden, he having said so to Étienne and Milan, even pointing it out with his finger in order that it be noticed, though a lost one never wants to be noticed, for that's too dangerous, any opinion, even the slightest word, allowing attentive guards to rush in, though fear no longer made any sense. If the oppressor wants to raise the cane, it no longer causes any fear, for there is now only everything to win and nothing to lose, though, indeed, one doesn't want to be arrogant or foolhardy, since razor-thin is the path on which the lost ones stand, the precipice steep below them, and whoever wants still to be standing tomorrow has to take care today.

Sometimes Josef would like to lie in the woods, to pick bright berries and look for fragrant mushrooms, these being the start of the Harz Mountains, it not being far to Goslar, and Wernigerode after that, followed by so many wonderful places, though they are still distant. Josef also longs for solitude, which he'd give anything for, as he is exhausted and drools at the idea of rest. Everything is a useless nightmare, no one able to think beyond the day itself, the panorama narrow and closed in, the panorama underground with its view of nothing more than the concrete hall that is now complete, where garish neon lights glow, everything at last ready, the masters imagining that they can make airplane parts here, a firm with the fable-like name of Malachite Works, Inc., Halberstadt installed here, the firm part of the Junkers airplane works, nothing more has been done as yet, for first the lost ones have to wearily install the machines under duress, as well as fill the hoppers with material made of aluminum.

After a difficult start in Langenstein, Josef is assigned to a typewriter, his fingers stiff and clumsy in the ice-cold chill of the underground hall, he not being allowed to wear a coat, though it's much better than having to slave away at backbreaking work on the transports, where one of the overseers even beats German civil servants, while even in front of the typewriter Josef is not freed from being ordered to schlep heavy goods, whereby he is exhausted after an hour. The man in charge of Josef and some of his comrades is named Kiesewetter, and demands high productivity, though he doesn't beat the lost ones who sit at the typewriters, and at the request of his prisoners he even makes sure that his people are excused for the most part from having to schlepp heavy goods. Josef has a view of the continuing armament of the Conqueror, despite being on his way to defeat, hundreds of letters from German firms passing through Josef's hands, he having to fill out orders for supplies and confirmation of their arrival, all of it in duplicate, though it's all quite chaotic, the whole war machine having run itself into the ground, the foolhardy game played out no longer winnable through the slave labor of the starving lost ones, their labor of no value even if they worked their best, the slave holders having miscalculated, as it doesn't matter if Herr Langer, a German who has a minor position here, and who, after wondering why Josef is "in this club," pompously claims that "German ways will save the day," and that once the war is over better days will dawn for Josef and all the Jews, and when Josef looks him in the eye and asks directly, he answers convincingly that of course Germany will win the war, the Conqueror has yet to realize his greatest triumphs, there are new secret weapons, and the Conqueror is a good person who will find for Josef and all the Jews a nice spot on earth where they can live well. No, such empty words no longer work, for chaos is already spreading its demoralizing effects among the Conqueror's own ranks, orders greeted by counter-orders, the civil servants no longer working full tilt, but instead continually going through the motions until exhaustion sets in, the belief they had at the start now lost, they having lost their wits as well, no longer seeming human, but instead continually ridiculous, for even if they remain a danger until the very last moment they can no longer be taken seriously.

Josef laughs at how they carry on, how they order equipment to be moved from one hall to another, then back again, no one knowing what the other is doing, a confusion of terms having set in, all of them speaking the same language but no longer understanding one another. This makes

Herr Weber want to scream, though it does no good to complain about the conspirators and the collaborators in charge, all of them are already confused, having been told only a couple of days ago that the malachite operation was to be moved from Zwieberge to Leopoldshall, and that prisoners from Langenstein were also to be sent there, but now that's not what's going to happen. Instead, it's too late, the fools have run out of time, though they themselves still don't realize it, and so the gears keep grinding, each day consuming more lost ones. Meanwhile, the tank works at Zittau are supposed to be moved to Zwieberge, railcars full of machines from Zittau standing on the supply lines that run from Halberstadt to Zwieberge, some already having been unloaded and schlepped into the hall and set up by the lost ones, who are continually tormented, though the civil engineers cannot get them to work since they have been damaged and won't work anymore, the efforts of millions of men wasted, the work of the Conqueror destroyed, it having done itself in, though don't the masters see at all that it's time to give up? No, they don't see it, and so death continues its harvest in Zwieberge, the conspirators continue to harass the lost ones, six men always assigned to the foul-smelling morgue of the Langenstein camp to carry rough-hewn wooden boxes, two skin-covered skeletons in each, those carrying them hounded out of the gate and toward the pits, despite almost buckling at the knees because of their own weakness, the skeletons tipped out there, some chlorinated lime spread over them, then the boxes are carried back to camp. This goes on for days, maybe even weeks, for here in the halls bad characters can still swing their heavy batons and yell, "Hurry! Hurry!" At this you schlepp pieces of airplanes out of the bins that are no longer fitted together, schlepping them to the waiting railcars, which will transport them to Leopoldshall, Zwieberge emptied out more and more, a frayed network of finished and unfinished passages, a maddening ant heap full of whining and whimpering, the lost ones as lost as ever, an idiot from the factory guards watching over the spigot that only uniformed men and civil servants are allowed to drink from, though the old man in black clothes fends off each lost one wanting to ease his thirst, as if he were death itself.

The atmosphere in the mine shafts, as well as outside them, is unreal, the air-raid alarm never stops, locals flood into the halls, these people having nothing to do with either the malachite works or the tank works, among them worried mothers with fearful children, everyone thrown together, only the tormenting of the lost remaining ceaseless, the sufferings of the others only mixing in with their own. The day passes very slowly for Josef at his boring typewriter, he feeling restless and wanting to walk about, some of the lost seeking the side shaft that serves as a latrine, though Josef stays away from the stinking mess, it also not being safe, as an overseer has been installed there, a professional thug who is called a shithead capo, he rushing everyone and sometimes knocking some of them to the ground from the toilet, his bad mood growing when the little Czech lost one whom the shithead capo has taken a shine to doesn't rub his arthritic back with both hands. And so Josef takes his chilly place in front of the typewriter called Olympia, an audaciously vain name for this place, he able to chat pleasantly with the Dutch civil servant who now and then sneaks him something and shares the news from the army, the translator Jacques another one he can talk to while keeping an eye on Milan, who still has a head wound as a consequence of being mishandled, Josef also looking over at Étienne, who understands only a few camp expressions and cuss words in German. Josef then buries himself in his work again, or at least appears to, as he secretly takes more notes.

Thus each day stretches on, things carrying on out in the hall, murderous events occurring as a result, more and more prisoners falling absent, almost all of the lost ones now devoid of their own humanity, nasty to one another and pushing one another around, any sort of restraint having fallen away like walls from the soul, they now no more than poor, frightened animals, robbed of their intelligence and their reason, blind and broken, wanting only to cower in their lousy rooms and wait and wait until these inhuman creatures are able to head back to the camp. They have to withstand what is pounded into them, the count taken over and over, it not being right, then not right again, and never right, then finally it's right, Hurry! Hurry! Then they rumble and pitch over the many obstacles, over the sand and the stones, past the railcars, bent over, sweating, wounds dripping. They are the lost ones, not people, for they know nothing, raw unbridled drive still moving them along, constant blows still pushing them to hurry, as they scramble down the slope to the rumbling sounds of the dumping sites. Then they have to gather together, four rows, fall in, line up, the one in front count off again, followed by "Hurry! Hurry! Keep together!" Then the tramping and slipping down the embankment, the small embankment. "Hurry! Hurry!" Finally, on a smoother path, "Everyone halt!" The open gate, "Hats off! March through the gate in step!" Count off, fall in, stand there, stand there, count off, some talking, then threats, blows, finally in their rooms, cold, sour watery soup, scuffles and screams, chills, bread, margarine, hunger, odors, no one full, everyone sinking down, the living dead, a pigsty, order, idiots, greedy bastards, dirt bags, this is no sanatorium, just a voice: "You were shipped from Auschwitz to escape death! What shit!" You should kick the bucket, you lice, lice crawling around, nothing to be done, one is crushed, rattles, is flattened, dead, too bad, the iron rails sing and hum, air-raid alarms, lights-out! It's over already, the camp guards barrel in: "Everyone asleep! Close your eyes!" Night, the lights are off, the lost ones have crawled under the blankets, Josef, Étienne, and Milan whisper to one another as comfort, as they press tight against one another to fight off the cold, everything done, finished, yet quiet, no, someone is moaning, on and on, otherwise it's almost quiet, cold comfort arriving with sleep.

LAUNCESTON CASTLE

IT IS VERY QUIET, HARDLY ANYONE CAN BE HEARD TALKING, AND ONLY A BIT of the ruins of the castle erected by William the Conqueror is visible. The tower is mostly what's left, crowning a small hill, surrounded by a park full of shade trees and bright flowers and dozens of benches. Parts of the gates also survive and serve today as entrances to the site now stripped of its walls, a plaque informing one about the castle dungeon where Oliver Cromwell kept George Fox, the Quaker elder, imprisoned for a long time. Yet now it is quiet, only some children playing, a couple of visitors looking at the tower without really taking it in, and then, as if fulfilling a duty, climbing its hard steps, which don't go all the way up, it only being possible to walk around outside or within its walls, there being no privacy amid these ruins, though where the bulwark is broken through from behind there opens a pleasant view of the Cornish countryside, with its lovely rolling hills and valleys, the small town of Launceston, which is named after the castle, situated directly on top of the hill. Josef is alone here, sitting quietly upon the grass, for he needs quiet, he having been initially forced (and then of his own free will) to live among others all too much in recent years, while the question of how to think about that time has remained unresolved for him, even though it has taken up almost all of his energy since the end of the war, during which time most of the people he knew did all they could to escape this same question once they had survived the immediate consequences of their imprisonment. Now for the first time Josef weighs whether or not he should set such deliberations behind him, even if leaving behind the source of such suffering seems both strange and almost overwhelming, but he believes that he has to arbitrarily turn away, realizing as well that the source of suffering is much older than even the experiences he himself has survived, and that he must crawl further and further toward a future of inconceivable length.

Josef is almost asleep, happy to stretch out his limbs, no one caring what he does, no one speaking to him. He was one of the lost ones, but today he is one of the forgotten, the times having forgotten him, such that he is alone. No, he doesn't really sleep, but within him is the remoteness of sleep, in which the clouds of lucid memory swim, called up perhaps by the view of the town from which occasional muffled sounds waft, perhaps by the sun-drenched view of the countryside, a peaceful view into the distance that at first manifests the sensible landscape but then behind it reveals incomprehensible landscapes, landscapes of the memory that contain unreachable distances, and yet they are near, they are within Josef and leave him never, saturating him and nourishing his thoughts, which indeed rest, but which amid the quiet never stop occupying him. Josef feels that he will never be free of his own preoccupations, though he also feels a continuity without purpose, nothing resulting from it, and nothing really there, it being actually a memory of the fact that nothing is there, even though everything seems to be there, a kind of accompaniment, much like what this site presents in and of itself, as one speaks of history, memory, something deeper than commemoration or what the plaques inform one about, the pride of the inhabitants of Launceston wanting to involve the visitor in the past. All the details of such experiences that are embedded in Launceston Castle are almost too precisely posted at the entrance to the park, such that the visitor is awestruck when he reads about the ungraspable past in catch words and dates in golden script, though the visitor thinks nothing of it, or he is briefly amazed and almost doesn't grasp that something happened here, here the Conqueror spent some time, here this count and that duke did this or that, here they locked up the Quaker elder with bread and water, because it satisfied a whim of Cromwell, who once again in history unintentionally demonstrated that from power, even when it doesn't shrink away from employing dungeons or murder, nothing comes, it only maintains the suffering of the world, acknowledging it openly, in order that people remain unsatisfied. For why should they be satisfied? It doesn't matter that they may wish to be, for most likely such wishes are sinful or, actually, not the wishes but the means to fulfill them are sinful and lead, in the long run, to a reality negated by perverse means.

What do the visitors think about when they look at the little bit of dungeon left? Slowly it dawns on them, yes, this is where it happened. The reckoning lasts for a moment, yet they don't dwell on it, it doesn't affect them and in fact it doesn't matter, Josef perhaps overly sensitive when he finds that it does affect him and causes him to sink into his old suffering again and believe that the strange and long-dead suffering here is his very own, even though it's unhealthy to think so, lunacy, if not presumptuous and out of line. Much better is the fact that someone has hung a wreath from an iron bolt, a nice demonstration of thoughtfulness that seems reverent and touching, rather than simply strange, even if somewhat inept and in any case helpless. Josef would like such commemorations to effect a deep transformation, for posterity cannot simply weave a wreath for such suffering, because even if it is not one's own one can surely empathize with past suffering, yet it no longer burns in your heart like a glowing thorn from having survived those times of extermination, though Josef feels the general suffering before him, which through someone else's memory results in the hanging of an ornament, thus turning the strange suffering into a comfort, whether it be far off or in the past. Also, the wreath hung in honor of the Quaker elder will soon decay, it already having dried out while hanging from its iron bolt, which indeed makes it touching, such commemoration now a responsibility, as the wreath needs to be replaced, someone showing up to do it and taking the old one down, which is not allowed, that being a desecration, but it's done nonetheless and the wreath is tossed away, which is completely improper, for at least he would sit there quietly after a new wreath is put up. Josef realizes how unreal it all is when one gets involved with past suffering, most pieties being disingenuous, since they mix the pure feeling of the honored ones with a certain strangeness that they can never penetrate, and which they never fulfill and know that they don't, veneration an odd game in which nothing is so sacred that it is spared.

Now the dungeon is empty, everything completely desolate, though no longer sunk in darkness, for it is half destroyed, the four walls still rising, though they are broken here and there, neither roof nor ceiling arching over the prison, daylight fading, night just beginning to encase the ruins in silent darkness and renew each evening the fleeting hours of the once continual darkness so fitting to imprisonment, though no visitor can witness it, because the town fathers close the site for the night, even though historically there's no real reason to do so, but historically this is what has been done, no one should see the darkness firsthand, the darkness that is history, all that is past, no need to think of it beyond what the visitor's imagination can conjure already. The town fathers are right to forbid the night, for night is dangerous, people here have no relationship with the night, as they want the day to be eternal, for it values anything that has been secret and brings it into the light so that it can be seen by anyone, and seeing is valued by human society, or so one generally thinks, which is why we have symbols, or so we are told. But it doesn't work, because sorrow is everlasting and is nestled away forever just out of the reach of day, no matter how much light shines on it, but sorrow is locked up and kept invisible, such that evil is not taken seriously, there being nothing that is evil. It's right that plants should grow amid the dungeon, no one having worked harder to make things thrive than the gardeners here, but it is fresh growth, a lush profusion of leaves that possesses its own time, it being protected, since no one can enter the dungeon, although entry is not forbidden, though the visitor sees that a bar prevents entry into the prison, it being unbelievable that such a peaceful place once hid a prison. Thus, outside in front of the prison one composes one's thoughts, for there is nothing for the viewer to see on the inside, and so what else can he do? It won't do any good to barge in, there is nothing there to see that can't already be seen from the outside, the plaques having already let everyone know what there is to know.

But how was it in the prison? There is nothing to be seen that provides

a clear picture, appearances show only that it must have been lonely and op-
pressive, the prisoner unable to enjoy the flowers, or the view of the Cornish countryside, the prison a chasm meant to punish, one that should have
caused a complete conversion, though that didn't happen, and so it became
a source of shame for the oppressor. It's a pity for his posthumous reputation that today it's so peaceful here, for that is not what he sought, but fleeting history has easily whisked away the sins of the powerful Conqueror and
precariously transferred them to the control of those he hunted down and
tormented. Does Josef indeed understand these ruins? No, he doesn't, he
values the present and doesn't linger amid the strange memories that mean
so much to the English, particularly the people of Launceston and the
Quakers, but which to Josef are foreign, he unable to know anything of it,
he not a part of it and just here to enjoy the quiet and the view. No one in
Launceston knows Josef except the hostess in The Red Bull who took down
his personal information in the thick guest book of the small hotel, where
peppered cabbage is served up morning, noon, and night, just as it appears
to have been served for centuries, the hotel quite old, the door originating
from the beginning of the fifteenth century, as a plaque informs one, though
who knows how things looked then when the stubborn Quaker was locked
up in the castle above and fed only bread and water by the prison warden,
while the prisoner would have been happy to have a bowl of cabbage from
The Red Bull served up to him each day, though that hardly happened,
George Fox perhaps never having heard of this inn that stands no more than
ten minutes away from his dungeon. Josef, however, can enter whenever he
likes, the door to The Red Bull always open to him, he having only to pay
in order to have the right as a guest to sit in the solarium, where he can have
a small snack and a drink, or read the paper or a book, no one there to
bother him with their views, for the people talk quietly and are discreet,
they being quite civilized, only the old worn clock dicing up the time with
resonant thrums, striking every quarter hour with four breaking chimes.
Josef finds their intrusive beats to be bothersome and hopes that the Quaker
elder was spared them, but perhaps he loved clocks and found their disturbing beats a comfort in the dungeon, yet Josef never liked loud clocks, he always wanting the one in the underground hall to remain quiet, he now able
at any time to escape the bongs of an English clock, as there are quieter

rooms for the guests, or Josef can go to his room, though it's not all that homey there, it being an affront to the customs of the land to spend the day there, the room only a place for sleep and unconsciousness, Josef avoiding The Red Bull except at night and during meals.

Josef feels like a stranger and knows he needs to remain so, for he needs for once to be at peace within himself. It's not his fault that he can't quite do so, for that is only because he is alive, he is here, and he is always here, which is not an illusion that stubbornly persists, no, it is indeed true and is also so in sleep, everything part of the sleeping state that fills Josef and surrounds him. That's why it's fine that the place has a foreign history that Josef hardly knows, and which is not necessary to know any more of beyond what he read on the plaque and considered, it calling out to every visitor to be read and appreciated. For certainly Josef is also free to ignore the plaque, but that would be ungrateful, since this indeed is all there is, there's nothing more to learn, there's nothing else to know, what the town fathers pass on to the general public is indeed the proper proportion of what has been left behind, namely matters of historical interest, for which there is also the town library or the Quakers themselves, who might have more information to share. Josef doesn't need particulars, he's willing to believe what's written here and trusts the town of Launceston's own valuation of the truth, they have made sure that all the dates are exactly right, after which the inscriber took the carefully prepared text and dutifully and reliably carried out his handiwork, someone making sure afterward to compare it with the original before it was installed, the pride and satisfaction in Launceston immense, everyone pleased at last to have the Quaker's broken past restored, the inhabitants of Launceston now able to quietly go about their daily business, the park with its tower and castle ruin turned over to the care of the gardeners and the attendants.

Josef is at peace with everything here and is even happier here than at the hotel, for he feels better in the park and more readily engaged, sensing a deep connection between the setting and himself, he feeling safer than he has ever felt before, on more solid ground, as if it were a home of his own, although he is only a guest, albeit a welcome stranger, welcomed with ample friendliness, which allows him to feel at home, he knowing for the first time that it is possible to feel at home anywhere once again, a feeling almost forgotten, as if there were a sunken golden city beneath the castle, with its cathedral and its famous stone bridge running between two towers above a stream. A home and the feel of home, something Josef has not been granted for some time, a painful expulsion that is now chosen, as Josef feels forever cut off from everything back there, where he cannot be, where he does not want to be, where he is supposedly answerable to many layers of public authorities, even after the Conqueror was incinerated, the authorities still feeling they have the power to debate where he should reside, and then he reached the island, passing more than a year of uncertain status here as well, but in the castle grounds of Launceston all such limitations fell away, no one asking him for his papers at the gate, for at last he was simply allowed in. Josef is not demanding anything, he expects nothing more than to be allowed to simply be here, which he appreciates in itself and feels grateful that he has been accepted as someone familiar to this site. He is pleased that no entrance fee is charged for this prison, that it is a free prison, unlike the Spielberg in Brno, or like torture chambers and towers and dungeons throughout the world which people ignobly and shamelessly charge to visit, though no one has a right to demand the merest of coins for the chance to see wretched sites of degradation. That it's different here likely has to do with the fact that initially Launceston was not a prison but rather a castle that William built and which belonged to several powerful kings, a dungeon also having modestly been incorporated into the castle in order to have a bit of pain contained within its walls and close by, an inconspicuous chamber to the wayside, while the arches and halls of the castle were decorated with the vain pleasures of guest artists, these remaining undisturbed, for, indeed, it is good when a castle has a dungeon, even if in our more fastidious times people complain that, be it the Tower of London or the Bastille, they were also dungeons, though recently such places experienced a sad transformation, helped on by the modern jails that take such torments out of the home of the oppressors that build them.

Josef sleeps, though it is not a normal sleep, he is still conscious. He looks inward and can almost see himself entire, though he doesn't know whether he can entirely penetrate within, it remains uncertain whether one can know oneself completely, because while it certainly seems impossible to know all else, even one's true self can seem distant and unknowable. Most likely nothing is what it is in and of itself, the past exists only within humans, yet in the outer world it is not manifest, which is why in the deepest sense it doesn't exist, all efforts to conjure it being devices, meditative attempts. It involves only groping in the dark amid uncertainty, nothing true any longer, though it should not be taken as untrue, that can be dangerous for the soul, as one needs to surround oneself with fictions, to look around oneself, which only means to look within oneself. There he will find images that one cannot say if they exist within or are projected without, though they indeed exist somewhere, even if they cannot be precisely placed, the images visible, though they cannot be approached, oneself simply a witness to these images, a witness to oneself, since it's in the nature of Time that one cannot exist at all, for Time controverts reality, and so Time is always in counterpoint to Being, which is hardly or only partially bound to Time, for even though physical reality doesn't altogether disappear, space is still devoured by Time. All times and Time itself encompass all spaces or any single space, both being conflated with each other within man's consciousness, since consciousness needs Time and has no space, while Being needs space and has no Time.

Josef is alarmed by the possibilities resulting from such wayward thoughts, but he can't keep himself from falling into such thoughts, while as soon as he immerses himself in a thought he wants to rebel against it, but that doesn't work, for it is always with him, a panorama he cannot escape, himself invited in, no entrance fee required, it taking no effort at all, he is already there, his spot ready and waiting, the only question being whether he wants to open his eyes, though the answer is easy for Josef, he not wanting to protect himself from himself, even when no one is looking. Who in Launceston cares that he has quietly and inconspicuously traveled across the sea? A stranger is allowed to show up unnoticed, he can travel by train or by car, he showing up one day, The Red Bull taking him in, everything in order, it being only for a few days, Josef needing no permission to visit, he knowing neither the town fathers nor their constituents, they knowing nothing of him, Josef nothing more than a chance visitor in Launceston, not a conqueror who wants to build a castle but someone who will leave quietly, carrying his little bag to the train and in the process passing the ruined castle once again. Then everything is over, the chance encounter dissolves in the end, the history of Launceston and Josef undisturbed by each other, the place not remembering the visitor, though Josef picks up a few postcards and maybe never looks at them again, he certainly throwing away the hotel bill before he climbs onto the train that stops briefly in Launceston proper, Josef then traveling on, leaving Launceston behind after a few minutes, other places appearing, places from the past, where certain acts were committed, where events unfolded, moving ever forward and back again. Which is why it's good that all of this takes place during sleep, for it's comforting, they being images that remain for a brief while, a little bell rings, attention, a new image is on the way, or an old one, it's hard to tell, the overview is lost, nothing but heightened momentary views that continually greet and confront one.

"Don't you recognize me? You once stopped here. Why won't you admit that it was really nice here with me? Three years ago you were here for a couple of months. Then you went away. Then the cherry trees in front of the gate blossomed, the countryside was ravaged by war, but spring returned. You wandered off to the nearby city, which was in ruins. Amid the rubble you found refuge. White and black soldiers tramped through the destruction, the inhabitants intimidated by them. You got sick and couldn't take care of yourself. Everything in you was also destroyed. Had enough? Then move on! Head this way and that, in order to find your way. These memories aren't good for anything, they're extrinsic and contain nothing of your experience. You are now too old. You know it when you look back. They never completed the railroad. The countryside is exhausted, the traces of its humble life erased, yet the hills are still there, the little village by the river, though you had forgotten it. Then they loaded you on the train. Why did you resist? You didn't resist at all, except to take care of yourself until you were transported, the train slowly rolling along, locked down so that you couldn't escape. At first the familiar landscape passed slowly by through the valley of the Moldau then the plains, over the Georgsberg, where the legendary Krok dispensed the land to the Bohemian princes. You should have had a chance to say goodbye to your homeland, for there was no way to know if you would outlast the Conqueror. You kept up your hopes, you had no idea of the threat. There was an unbelievable giddiness, as though someone had freed you of the idea that the journey and banishment spelled your annihilation. Go back further! You lived in your fatherland and re-signed your position at a cultural center. You left your home and traveled about the world. You believed victory would be yours, and that anything in between would easily be overcome. You also believed whoever strode on confidently would reach his goal. Did you never think that no one awaited you? That you were nothing but an intrusion? Anyone is in some ways su-perfluous. You always took yourself too seriously. You don't seem to be cured, your appetite remains insatiable. Do you still want to educate the young? You resigned as a tutor. Don't you see that no amount of will can overpower the world? Will can only destroy you. Whenever anything is too much for you, you fall asleep. The gong sounds, the window is opened. Below on the street you stand amid the whirling noise of the night, but the sounds of the struck gong above in the tower hurry you along. You act as if nothing has happened, because you are frivolous and want to enjoy yourself. But what did you once say about symbols? Sunbeams shimmer on the wind. You stand upon the fallen castle and gaze off into the woods. You don't let yourself think about how shallow you have always been. Why did you pass so sadly over the bridge? I won't go any further with you in order not to sad-den you any more. There is still much to say. You didn't want to become a doctor, for you didn't believe in helping others. You have settled in wherever you have been and taken each place as your own, but did you never consider yourself a stranger? Not even in the park? In the ruins? In the fields? Always you were a stranger. You didn't realize it for a long time. Now that you know it, you don't want to change it. And so it's done. You will have to take care of yourself or I'll demolish you. I have already given you many signs. You say that they haven't bothered you, but words fall easily from your lips."

Josef knows that he has been awash in delusions, that they are always about him, for everything that happens around him that he can follow with-draws from him whenever he wishes to seize hold of it, for though he had been given so much, it was only lent to him, though he didn't want to pos-sess it, instead his consciousness was only filled with more memories. Josef needs to rest, for though he never wanted to that badly, now everything is finally weighing him down, now being the time to rest, he cannot continu-ally just walk through life like an actor playing a part, no matter how appeal-ing it may be to dream one's own existence, or does such a disguise exist only in order to protect oneself from the world? Neither solitude nor the company of others can be fully realized, always there are threats to each which keep one from attaining the smallest of goals, even though one may want to pursue them, certainly yes, though one cannot pursue them, not in the least, for that which is attained is mirrored by that which is destroyed, making one seem ridiculous in the face of it.

It's good to rest in the park at Launceston, it being a place that does not reassure the self, but rather lightens the load upon it by reigniting the senses and returning one's thoughts to life itself. The sufferings of the world lie in the fresh and the dried-up wreaths that from time to time are replaced, all of it well arranged, the people of the town below knowing that they don't have to climb the hill to see for themselves that it's been taken care of, the fate of the inhabitants of Launceston the only thing that really matters in these parts, if only because Josef is allowed to remain a stranger, and because he doesn't really need to know anything about this place, because he senses the benefit involved in his being free of all the fortunes of the citizens of Launceston, because all that is required of him is that he not cause any trouble, as he is otherwise free of any ties and able to leave at a moment's notice. Josef doesn't need anything, finally, there's nothing that he wants, and yet he is still granted so much, for he is a stranger, and there's nothing better one can do for a stranger than to let him be. Indeed, a park with various inscriptions has opened for him and silently allows him to enter, the paths laid out beautifully, each grain of sand and every blade of grass maintaining the open access enjoyed by every visitor, he feeling his gratitude for the unwritten laws of this place, much care expected of everyone, almost to the point of curbing freedom, but that is not the intent, no, as there is a wonderful opportunity involved in allowing one to walk around freely in a prison.

When you quietly pass the time, you can empty your mind, the surroundings insignificant as you close your eyes and dream, although even with open eyes you don't have to take in anything. So much freedom suits you, and that's what makes you start to think how you want to live, what will best suit you. This is a powerful word that reveals its evanescent validity only in the panorama, but Josef will abandon it at closing time at the latest, when the guard comes along ringing his bell. Before then there is so much that causes Josef to drift away from the world. Nonetheless he must think of other things, namely the unattainable and therefore never the known, but such worries are idle as long as the present is still certain. Memories don't have to be sought after when experience is enough, and thoughts of the future are idle, the view easily giving rise to them, there being no thoughts of the beginning or end in the panorama, for what's certain is that it will unfold despite these, and in the end it cannot be controlled. Thus there develops a readiness for acceptance that is often condemned in human history, it being called passivity or fatalism, but Josef finds such characterizations almost comical, they have nothing to do with the truth, instead representing only a rebellion on the part of the uncertain, who because they are never at ease can never see eye to eye with others. Yet what can one really do? Only the gravity of a playful obsession engages with such alienation and is surprised only when the gates are closed which no hand will open again. While asleep Josef still knows that when he is awake he will not be much different from anyone who never plays to the audience, but he also cannot wait forever and just let everything happen, though he will not be like those who are only able to stew in their own sorrows, they being the ones who indeed never can stem the tide of things and are unable to lift themselves out of their narrow confines.

Josef experiences a deep confidence, for he feels a peace that he has never known, not even in those years when he thought himself versed in deep dark secrets, though they were only trumped-up vanities that he succumbed to and thought important. Now for the first time he has vanquished the charming errors of his early years, even though they are still so strong in his memory. Just as Josef has seen himself pass through many transformations, so, too, his gaze has passed over the world, noting how much it has changed, the great hopes that existed at the end of the war and which were tied up with the downfall have already and easily been trampled under, the war instigated by the Conqueror having lasted six years, the world at first unwillingly, then slowly mobilizing to repudiate his unbearable demands, the prison house of Europe broken open and laid to waste, the shouts of liberation and brotherhood stomped out, humans soon growing weak and now everything lost, the game not yet over, but one player has been closed out, only a little more than three years having slipped by and the misery that has hardly passed now reduced to a myth, for new pressing concerns always turn the too-weak heart full of its greedy demands away from the horror of yesterday's atrocities.

There are many lives that a person lives, thinks Josef and, even if almost everything in him prevents him from doing so, he can do nothing in this garden but submit to it, the only liberation lies in the power of forgetfulness, not loss, there being no liberation possible through weakness, since weakness merely buries the past. They have to learn that one day that which has been entombed will be dug up, and then there will be mourning and a sorrow without end, but the power of forgetfulness will stride through many changes and be continually conscious of its own moment, which will lead it into innumerable new realms. Then perhaps there will no longer be any more disruptions, then everything will be continually meaningful, and the heart won't grow weary as long as it keeps beating, a continual process that will be strengthened by the quiet, while suddenly one will be carried forward, everything seeming so much easier than it ever was before, a steady stream, and there will clearly arise an inexhaustible happiness, not just a easy happiness that tries to avoid sorrows, for it will be a happiness free of sorrow, a happiness of permanence, because it will never forsake itself, since it will be childlike and genuine, attaining an equilibrium. Perhaps this is only a dream, the musings of a never-satisfied demeanor; perhaps it's all idle thinking, but perhaps not, if only this sleep will last long enough.

It is remarkable to come to your senses, and here and there encounter something familiar in which you find a blessing. For how is it that one comes to survive his own destruction? What always succeeds doesn't do so on its own merits. It's arrogant to speak of one's own success, since it's merely allotted to one or another, while to do so is only an attempt to give shape to the inexplicable run of events because at some point they seem to make sense. All that's certain is that Josef is not satisfied with remaining just an observer, he wants to be an active observer, he seeing his life up to now as a kind of primary school that has led him from contemplation to action, he having devoted a great deal of time to it, or it was granted to him, he having been dealt with mercifully, as what happened to him was a lot less worse than he could have expected. As a result, Josef was split between the Josef who looked on and the Josef who spoke, these being two different natures that have formed within him and are not always in accord with each other, one trembling before the other, and both rarely able to agree with the other, such that one no longer knows much of the other, after which they separate, hardly able to understand each other any longer, out of touch, one making fun of the other, who then condemns the other in return. Josef thinks for a moment that he stands at the end of a process, but he quickly dismisses this notion, since he recalls how often he similarly thought that he had arrived at a certain conclusion, only to find himself once again on a path that seems to be approaching an end but which then turns off, often in the blink of an eye, which is enough to change his entire perspective, the path running on, and Josef having to accept that not once has an especially important stage of his life brought him any closer to the supposed end point. In his early years Josef not only had believed in decisive or transitional points in his life but his early death also seemed certain. Now however, after surviving the killing grounds of the hecatombs he smiles until he almost has to cry when he considers the childish dreams of consummation that seemed the crowning glory of his meager existence, he deeply moved by it all, though he did not die, for they were only warnings that this path certainly didn't lead to the eternal, but rather that one had to reckon with one's own death without impertinence, Josef hearing this memento mori and humbly accepting that all that was left to him was the vanity of thinking that one could make sense of one's future. The staggering, playful conclusions of his younger years were a natural consequence of youth, but the manifest events of more recent years pointed to a more probable end, though meanwhile Josef has come to value readiness more than sheer resignedness, and in this he has found solace and certitude in the will to persist.

What affects Josef today is not some great turning point in his life, for life doesn't change, and such a belief leads only to awkward expressions of an overreaching spirit that insatiably gathers all events together into a dubious sense that imparts a precarious arrangement to them, while in actuality they remain the inscrutable unfolding of reality that frays the tattered threads of thought. And so Josef no longer sees things in this manner, but certainly there is a part that remains a kind of expectation, and every expectation works as a preparation, each rung of life repeating the same set of experiences, however deeper or more rich, while what appears to change are thoughts and feelings that are seemingly unrepeatable, although they soon resurface as memories. But what Josef is experiencing now is indeed a turning point, no, a reversal, it perhaps being best to think of it as a convolution, earlier everything having come at him from the outside as a continuous stream of stimuli, a kind of visitation from the many that touched upon the one, while now it was the opposite, the one seeking the many, the observer marking his surroundings, whereas before appearances affected contemplation. That could not continue, you need to point to and attest what you want to make of experience, and this requires that you look into your surroundings, it no longer being good enough to simply look on, but instead you have to examine closely, the panorama now turned around, the right to impartial observance is now forfeited, the spotlight is on and there is nothing for it but to wait and see whether it suits others to come and observe as well, but nonetheless impartiality has been destroyed. Until now there was an appeal to being anonymous, and even if generally no one was willing to admit it, so it was indeed, you paid a little fee and enjoyed yourself as if it didn't really matter what you did. Now even the highest fee isn't enough to successfully enter the panorama, Launceston Castle the last image of what is the irrevocable end of the show, the role of the guest now over, it now being enough to point out what he has learned and accomplished for himself, he ready to give up his seat or open his own panorama. Josef doesn't yet know how he will begin, but he doesn't believe a simple reversal is possible. As good as it is to be alone and unknown, he still has to gather and also look at the images as they slowly pass by, but it's important to realize that there really are no new images, something that already reminds him of the past, when his grandmother put her arm around him and said, "It's over, my dear. We've seen that one already. We have to go."

Now it's late enough that Josef has to leave the show, needing to go to the gardener and his helpers in order to thank them, for he has to appear grateful, he unable to enjoy himself without passing on some kind of consideration, he needing to at least say how much he enjoyed himself, many thanks, the castle ruins are impressive, too bad the hill isn't a bit higher, for then the tower would allow you to see all of Cornwall, but oh, the prison, that really pleased me, I'll never forget it, it is only a shame that not everyone knows about it, perhaps an even bigger inscription about the sufferings of George Fox would be helpful. After that Josef would have to praise the view, many aspects of it being remarkable, but though it is sweeping, it doesn't go on forever, and in the end Josef doesn't approach the gardener.

Josef thinks back to Landstein Castle, where the past and the present were inextricably linked quite differently from here, history remaining unknown there, no inscription, no sense of duty demanding that people be provided with the residue of the past, no park full of flowers there, while here in Launceston there was nothing but the enclosed garden design, from which all sense of the wilderness had been stripped, which is why it was so upsetting and peaceful at one and the same time, Josef always wanting to rise up against it, but then it eased his senses, he immersing himself in the surroundings that no longer possessed any suffering, everything here having been tidied up and protected by certain measures, though the possibility of some kind of harm suddenly bursting forth was still an open one, as each guest still had to behave himself, otherwise he would not be allowed in and would have to leave this country so full of history. And yet Josef cannot quite accept that he has been swept up by a powerful force coursing through the park, for all around it no longer seems as peaceful, which is visible only to Josef, it being good that no one is nearby to notice his stupor, for he cannot control his mounting concern that many voices are calling out and disturbing his sleep, which once seemed so safe, he having to take care that he is not caught, it being easy to grab hold of him since he is so weak, the steps going down that lead from the tower to the lower rooms of the castle, where Josef could be locked up in one of the cellars, no one knowing that any such thing had occurred. But those are ghostly thoughts, ridiculous and childish, for the inhabitants of Launceston walk within shouting distance below in the street, no one wanting to threaten Josef, and all of this simply a result of his imagination getting caught up in confusion. He thinks how his childhood was a bundle of anxieties, and how easy it was for this never quite conquered sense of dire concerns to erupt again, since only by the thinnest of veils is a person separated from past experiences that were once his present, though he must resist their shadow and not give in to them by allowing his senses to be broken, he needing to distance them within his own soul if he wants them to cease. Only then can he gain his own sense of security, reassurance calming him down, and perspective restored once again such that the heart can know the real truth. The only question is whether that can last, for the everyday world demands its measure of backbreaking work as soon as the outer danger is no longer unquestionably apparent, the wonderful power of the imagination lasting exactly as long or as short as the threat itself. Josef realizes that during the years of terror it was easier to maintain a certain composure than in times that are not as rough, for when dissatisfaction creeps in one is caught up in demands and feels pulled in many directions at once, without really knowing why. A person ends up turning this way and that to fulfill all such demands, but soon he notices how few things actually work, the result being insecurity. Yet should Josef withdraw? Launceston is a quiet town, for centuries the inhabitants here having been spared any terror that has been stamped into the lives of others. When the world fell into its great cataclysm, this place was forgotten.

Apart from practical reasons that forbid it, Josef cannot live in Launceston, he is such a stranger that everything here that could protect him would quickly fall apart, and the allure of his anonymity would soon pass, thus causing him to have to share in the fortunes of this place and the various plights that only the stranger is spared, since he knows nothing of them. Only the stranger can stride through such a small town in the sound belief that everyone lives here in peace, avoiding enmity as well as nasty rumors, the community governed in exemplary fashion, everything clean and orderly, the houses well appointed, flowers and fruit growing in the gardens, as can happen only in a blessed locale, the population amiable, everyone talking in the musical tones of the local vernacular, the Celtic influence pressing through it all, the saturated weight of an ancient culture traceable right up to the present. Meanwhile, in the surrounding villages one is greeted by none other than genuine farmers, tall serious men in country clothes who quietly smoke their pipes in dignified fashion as they drive along the cattle they care for, the wide-open farmland dappled with many colors, filling the mountains with their lit pastures, the entire area a single garden. Josef doesn't wait long to do what he needs to do, for soon he will be locked out from it all once it's noticed that he's an intruder who should move on, extended hangers-on not being wanted here, especially people with Josef's past, it being better to head for London if he wants to settle in this country. There he can live inconspicuously in the city that is not a city, but instead a sea of settlements, a disorganized, endless string of settlements, such that this sea has an indistinct countenance, a sea of houses and yet no homes, everything there unrelated and indistinguishable, the only kind of person found being the stranger, about whom no one asks, he allowed to wander through the numberless streets and to ride in the public transport, while places like Launceston want to remain themselves and don't want gypsies like Josef.

It's curious that Launceston had indeed recently taken in strangers for a long while, though they were not there of their own free will, they were German prisoners of war who were placed here in a camp, where they walked around in British or more often German army uniforms, POW painted on the backs of the jackets, mostly in white letters, the outfits often spotted with color here and there and with patches of other material sewn on. Many of the prisoners of war were put to work in agriculture, Josef thinking about the men with curious interest and mild lament, and how they must have felt adrift here and sometimes bitter as they marched through the streets and byways of the old town, filing into the plazas in groups and astonished by the offerings in the shops, their dull gaze drifting across the unfamiliar surroundings. What kind of memories and what kind of hopes and what kind of apprehensions did the men who were allowed to freely walk around experience? They must certainly have thought their fortunes unjust, feeling conflicted about their lot, not knowing why they were granted all this and what for. Often they were practically homeless, just as Josef has been, or at least since then. Many prisoners were also displaced persons, having come from Romania and the Baltic countries, a good number also coming from Bohemia, and some of them had lost all of their loved ones or didn't know what had happened to them. This causes Josef to think quickly and longingly and sadly about where his relatives and friends are, his relatives having been crushed and killed, there being only a few friends left and all of them scattered, the others ground up and killed. The prisoners didn't know what was going on elsewhere, their heads were lowered out of shyness, rubbing their hands in embarrassment as they stood in front of the noble church dedicated to the penitent Mary Magdalene, a lovely Gothic building, rich with ornamentation from top to bottom and covered with figurative reliefs, the prisoners slipping through the heavy Gothic gates to the town, some also not too shy to make the easy climb to the castle park, where they lay down on the grass where Josef rests today. How comfortable the prisoners must have felt in the commissioned boots in which they had trod through the fighting fields of Europe and North Africa, while with such frightening glee the murderous places had once been called battlefields, these men having been on just such battlefields, traveling there in armored vehicles through the fields and sowing death and destruction in the country-side, the Conqueror having ordered it, they obeying, whether they wanted to or not. But they didn't know what they were doing, even when they thought they did, they really didn't know, nor did they know what to do in Launceston, why their fortunes had led them to this Cornish backwater and to such a remote land of plenty, as they forged plans for the future and thought about their families, gathering provisions that were sent back to their devastated homeland.

Then the prisoners of war disappeared from Launceston, they being re-leased, though Josef still sees them, having visited the barracks where their camp was, seeing them in the fields and in town, hearing the soldiers talk, their coarse language still in his ears, but now they are gone, having headed back home, even if in many places they had been hounded from house and home, somewhere still serving as a home for them, somewhere a place where they are taken care of. Josef knows the prisoners of war are no less strange to him than the people of Launceston, since for him all people are remote, he unable to approach them, even though he would like to talk to them and even exchange pleasantries, but he is not a part of them and re-mains distant, there being no tie between them, neither joy nor sorrow. For who really knows another, even if one suffers under him? Each person is be-yond the border of those closest to him. Any kind of closeness, brother-hood, or camaraderie lasts only up to a point in dreams, it being imagined as a wish or a demand, and yet it should come about. There should be some-thing that binds one person to another, something that requires no dictate to set it in place or force it to happen, for that would be bad, because the urge should come from inside, though it must also be something that is not simply asserted by one's ego but which instills something into this ego in order that it also exist in the other without killing itself. This, however, is in-conceivable, even in feeling, it being the human equivalent of the panorama that no amount of will can allow one to escape this situation, the panorama therefore a great danger in itself, perhaps just another name for the root of all evil, it perhaps being best not to let oneself look or let oneself be seen. For then the panorama is the defeat of one's humanity, it being inhuman, an addiction, a curiosity that can't be satisfied, but also a sacrifice of all sanctity, since each is unmasked within his neighbor's panorama as well.

In the history of humankind there has never been a time in which this circumstance was any different, even when one imagines some cultures or earlier times having had a different consciousness that was more collective and potent. Even then the individual was separate from all others. He felt it perhaps more easily, for though some conflicts were spared him, the basic conflict has existed ever since each person became self-conscious. How can one sink beneath oneself or climb above oneself in order to overcome the insularity of the observer and the observed? For this there were no sacred teachings, the lessons ignored this conflict, since no one yet dared ponder that which, when falsely pondered, led to madness, namely that which was self-evident, but which, when properly pondered, leads to the most solitary duress. Instead it was best left untouched, though perhaps this given was not consciously known, the self too powerful to acknowledge it, even when it realized its own powerlessness, yet the understanding of one's powerlessness related only to the transitoriness of the one who realized it, perhaps also to his own imperfection, but never to the irreconcilability of being one being among many others.

Despite this Josef presses on, wanting to guard against such thoughts and instead to dip into the satisfaction of not knowing, though this will never be allowed him. He smiles at his limited education and knowledge, for he can find nothing that will help him, he recognizing that he must resign himself to it all, scaring himself, as he knows he must wipe out his own nature in order to change it, he realizing that Johannes's tower mysticism has nothing to offer him. For Johannes never faced the kind of difficult question that plagues Josef in the midst of the panorama from which he cannot turn away, he drinking in with his gaze and his heart what the images offer up, though he cannot penetrate them, either, he being able only to take them in and complete the magic trick through which he heedlessly identifies reality with what happens, on which his own existence seems to depend, he projecting himself into the panorama and finding himself pleasantly surprised to see that he exists. Then some sort of oneness seems to have been attained, but it is a oneness founded on loneliness, there being no one else but Johannes at one time, and now the panorama. Thus this path offers no solution, so long as the conception itself doesn't provide a solution to this ancient dilemma.

There may be a timely advantage to being spared this conflict, because then everything is much easier and schematically simplified, which lends one a certain contentment, such a person hunkering down in his booth, the cabinet satisfactory for observing the panorama in front of him, as he remains inside and sees only a few things that he absorbs, such that a harmonious connection with the universe appears to be maintained. Much more frequently encountered than the followers of Johannes are the frenzied, such as the Frau Director or Professor Rumpler, who are constantly on the move, though they don't feel bothered by the fact that they are just observers in the panorama, even observers with closed eyes or eyes that shift away, fidgety guests sitting on their stools in the observation room full of restless visitors who cause so much trouble that they disrupt the attention of the other onlookers, for although the fools manage to keep all eyes on them, they have no more to say than do the others, though they hardly know that.

The situation for humankind is everywhere the same, particularly if one looks at the world for what it is, with all its surface illusions, which indeed have their own reality, since they are tied to the outer and inner conditions of humanity on many levels. Even if you look beyond such illusions and manage to avert them, the heart cannot ignore them and indeed knows, despite it not being to its advantage, that it must still take joy in and suffer these illusions, its despair and resignation growing ever deeper, there being no way out but to face matters as best you can. No one escapes the tragic, even when it's forgotten for a moment, which is what looking is for, consciousness emptying itself as one looks on, while in contrast that which is suffered, and which functions as an image to be taken in by other viewers, serves the purpose of letting you know that you don't experience pleasure and agony alone. This is a conception of man as observer and observed, as subject and object of the panorama, though it is only an illusion, for in fact what occurs to one and what one grasps, or at a minimum what one perceives, is that there is no longer any panorama, it appearing to have disappeared amid a series of alternating and penetrating movements and actions, it indeed having done just that. However, isn't it obvious that the individual remains cut off from his surroundings despite such a process, if in fact he has not been killed? If indeed a man survives and can look at himself the way others do, then Josef's idea of the panorama prevails, namely that one can see others but never reach them.

On these assumptions, even if they didn't know it, great thinkers have based their teachings, though they have never admitted it to themselves or to the world, or so Josef thinks, though he recognizes a great flaw in his thinking, as it is undeniable that human beings form relationships in which they do indeed come together with another, the panorama dissolved which was nothing but an illusion, though Josef still doubts that the borders between people can be dissolved, there always being something to prevent a seamless merger, there being no such thing as a complete union, for that would amount to a murder, the only exception being connections that are formed through media, and that is something imperfect, the media is the equipment, the machinery, the mechanism of the panorama. The panorama is the mediator that is inserted between human beings. That which cannot pass from one being into another is the body of life, the construction of the panorama. The world itself is a panorama and remains always in opposition to that which names itself, that which knows itself, that which wishes to assert itself and which also perhaps asserts what it is. Thus in life there is a dualism in which the panorama constitutes matter and essence constitutes spirit. Essence never entirely becomes matter, and matter is never essence, they being finally beyond each other's grasp, the one remaining estranged and distant from the other. Therefore it is the task of matter to hinder a complete union. Both principles transcend each other, alienating humankind, preventing each other from triumphing as long as life goes on. Yet this principle is not satisfied with just being true in itself. It plants as well an unshakable bitterness in one's essence, causing it to be consumed by fear and unable to know how to insert itself into the panorama. One realizes that every attempt by oneself or anyone else to gain a foothold in the construction of the panorama can only lead to pain. No kind of idealistic or materialist philosophy is of help here, for philosophy certainly cannot solve the puzzle and cannot point toward any way of avoiding the conflict or solving it. Neither type of system can escape some falsification of the facts, they having instead to proceed violently when they encounter insurmountable obstacles, namely that reality does not adapt itself to what the teachings want it to be.

Theoretically one could ponder the possibility of some kind of synthesis between both systems, but the moment reality refuses to bend, any such synthesis becomes moot. The nature of reality will only tolerate the existence of both principles next to each other. This is a not a solution but rather a resolution that allows the understanding of both principles, and yet it gives rise to the vital question of how both principles can be reconciled in order to resolve the conflict between them. Josef wonders whether both principles can be followed along parallel lines, perhaps each developing on its own, or whether there is an unknown principle, something not yet in existence, that would indeed allow for a synthesis or another solution, though such a third principle could not be squared with reality and the world as it is. Only the supposition of God and his intervention could support a belief in the possibility of conquering or changing the world as it is. By this Josef doesn't wish to feed the nonsense of commonly held beliefs about religion, for their conclusions give the lie to their assumptions. Such religion has produced no findings that cannot be found by other means. And such religiosity has mangled the genuine problem at the heart of religion, especially when it proffers a solution, but not a method of fulfillment that allows for a way to break through reality as it has always been conceived. This is why everyday religion ties its promises to death. It remains separate from life, insofar as it calls itself a religion, which then remains hidden behind each deeply mystical saying. Above all, religion has never addressed humanity seriously in itself but has always addressed the individual, which isn't enough, especially when so much is promised in this manner. That is why everyday religion is just another image in the panorama, and—how monotonously repetitive!—images remain out of reach, they being simply seen and experienced but never reached.

Who knows of any way out? The view presents itself, but it's better not to attend to it, it for once needing to be enough, perhaps being different outside, one forgetfulness able to exchange with another forgetfulness, everything immediately there when the view changes as it grants the feeling of life, there being no need to speak any more of difficulty. It is good not to be naïve, even though one holds the fool's cap at the ready nonetheless, Josef needing only to think back a bit when there was the emperor with his white beard, the last year of the war when Josef was still living at home, everything taken care of for him, he not knowing why he had to take part, no one having asked him, as he indeed was a part of a surround. That's the way things were thirty years ago, then came the tender lovely days in Umlowitz, intimate and peaceful relations followed by the time in The Box, the first difficult trials popping up, it soon becoming clear on what track history was traveling. Then for the first time Josef felt discord with what he experienced, but no one asked him what he felt, just as no one ever asked him about anything, for that is the way it was—the way it is—certainly a shallow, indeed a horrifying, irrefutable truth, nor does it help that he wanted it to be different in order to pursue a dreamed-of better world, one such as he enjoyed in hiking and camping with the Wanderers, for there he felt himself among others like him whom he thought he understood and felt a part of during that time of naïve pride, each day filled with cheerfulness. It had been a long time since he felt that, the happy gatherings having become meager affairs, most of the boys having quit the troop, the hiking club having disbanded, after which Josef found himself filled with a conscious pride, as he began to read and ponder matters continuously, the unattainable seeming near with the figure of Johannes, who meant something before Josef's rising distrust, while most of the members of Johannes's circle demonstrated how something marvelous could so easily dissolve into the shallow and the ridiculous, though once you left the tower you entered a hopelessly disturbed world, its chaos sweeping over you. Josef wanted to take on such a world on his own, but there was no escaping it, thus causing him to be consumed by the worst kind of self-deception, for even if it were possible to help himself through such deception it did not please him for long, because as soon as the years arrived that led the way to the Second World War oppression returned to the country, the handling of individual people often manifesting itself as crass and senseless, it not mattering what he did, fate had already begun to play with him, taking charge of him, he having been taken charge of. Now all that is over, though even this can be a deception, especially if Josef remains undisturbed by it all as he rests in the castle park at Launceston.

And so Josef sleeps, there being nothing at the moment to prod him to do anything special, he able to move around as he pleases, no neighbor fighting with him over space, or anyone approaching him to order, "Josef, get up, get a shovel and dig your own grave!" The brothers had not strangled him, so that they could say that an evil animal had eaten him, but instead they had sold him into slavery, though this is only a dream from a bad source of dreams, it is all over, there are no ignoble brothers here who want to throw him into a ditch in the middle of the desert, there being no one who comes, no voice raised, no glance that threatens, no nod of warning, no one in Launceston who wants to control him, just a few rules that are not at all burdensome to follow. Josef is completely alone, no one wants to cut his hair, no one creeps up from behind and hits him on the neck with a gnarled stick, it being wonderful and unbelievable how peacefully everything goes. That's why it's good that in front of the dungeon the wreath in honor of the Quaker elder hangs, it guarding against the unexpected outbreak of something awful, though indeed the Conqueror had also tossed wreaths to his dead accomplices without accomplishing anything good, though here it seems to help, since it's been so many years since Cromwell held his prisoner George Fox in Launceston, memory having accumulated a great deal of time that had come to fruition. For indeed the climate is mild, there being nowhere else that such a soft rain can fall, tiny silver drops descending from breathlike clouds, falling softly and soundlessly, not even bending a single blade of grass.

Now Josef is free, he can pass the time in the castle park in Launceston, though he doesn't need to invoke his right to do so, he knows that he has permission to enjoy the sweeping view, to rest here, to feel the blessing of sleep, the grace, the freedom, the grace and the freedom that appear to be two names for one thing. Maybe grace is the third principle that mediates between the principles of essence and matter, grace surpassing all else in the world, it being not an earthly but a godly principle, and no way to philosophize about it, since nothing can be known of grace and its freedom, they possessing neither time nor space, though grace and freedom transcend essence and matter, and are not the same as either of them. The nature of grace and freedom is a miracle, which is why there is less grace and freedom in the world than there are miracles. For, indeed, when is the third principle grace and when is it freedom? Josef considers two aspects of the answer, one that is neither human nor worldly, while the other is both human and worldly. That which is not worldly, and therefore beyond life's realm, conceives of the principle as absolute freedom, which then becomes grace in its resolve to flow forth into life. By the world and by humans this principle is experienced as grace, as it imparts a measure of freedom, though that is not absolute freedom, for it is never more than the measure of grace that has been dispensed. That's why freedom and the measure of freedom in the world are not definable, for the measure of grace cannot be calculated, though certainly there is no freedom without grace. In this sense life is never completely without or completely filled with grace, since even in such extreme cases life is presumably nothing more, indeed cannot be anything other than, what we conceive it to be. Josef believes that even a minimum amount of grace would be able to almost completely dissolve the contradiction between the two worldly principles of matter and essence. The possible connection of two individual essences would be something more difficult to bring about or would be virtually nullified, for essences could no longer connect with one another through matter, because the latter would likely drown the former, thus ending all confraternity.

The spiritual principle can give rise to grace in life when some kind of freedom exists between essences, though one cannot conjure grace but, at best, invoke it, and there is no guarantee that any prayer will be met with measurable success. Every attempt to control the principle of freedom in the world is an undertaking that attempts to attain the unattainable. That is, of course, impossible, for freedom cannot be demanded, nor is there anything that can give rise to grace, even if perhaps some kinds of behavior are better suited to grace, deigning to make more of an appearance in life than do other behaviors. But such talk is blasphemous and has more to do with merit and good deeds than makes sense, since grace hearkens only to its own freedom and relates only to a pure belief in the good deeds of human beings. Nevertheless, Josef thinks, the essence of the world can assume the existence of an array of fundamentals—or at least has to—as, indeed, it's not an illusion or a contradiction to think that laws were once formed that require humankind's adherence to certain customs. When fulfilled in the right spirit they lead to blessing, while violating them leads to nothing but trouble. People should know this, but they forget and don't want to know. In the history of humankind, hardly any trace of freedom has ever manifested itself without there also being some form of subjugation alongside it.

Josef feels that his thinking is approaching the limits of what is permissible, but he also believes that he is alive only because of an act of grace, and to him it seems that the grace experienced by an individual cannot exist without limitations. Since man is an individual, he cannot experience the grace of another. Therefore the freedom of the individual is always more limited than the grace afforded a community or a people, whereby the freedom that courses through all of its members in unknowable measures is made manifest, while the grace experienced by the individual can indeed have an effect on the world, though it remains undefined. The individual is created in the same way as all of his fellow beings, which is why each person and all people and presumably the entire world are accountable, he being an accessory to everything that happens in the world, in much the same way that he wants to be a part of any of the benefits accrued in the world. Josef thinks a dangerous temptation exists when a person presumes that he enjoys a personal grace or even believes that grace involves some kind of merit, for when this occurs grace immediately retreats from human beings. No one can possess grace, no one has a right to grace. To any claim a human being might raise, grace is always something ancillary, and no being would exist or have the right to exist if treated according to its merits, even if he thinks he has a right to it. Grace has no measure, since it cannot be measured in terms of the freedom that it grants, though it ebbs and flows at the discretion of freedom.

Freedom can dispense grace indiscriminately, it being just as available to the guilty, and is perhaps expended only on the guilty, since before grace there is no one who is not guilty. So there is no need for grace to be kept from anyone who adds a new sin to established sins, though it can withhold itself, as grace is the freedom that exists which no one can do anything about, and therefore cannot possess. Often a person assures that grace will not occur, although he has nothing against it, for he infers demands that have nothing to do with it. This gives rise to the paradox that grace can cause harm, but when it does it is no longer grace, for though grace is indeed salvation, when defined by humans it is no longer grace. But if grace is to give rise to freedom, then grace must remain free, as it can work only in freedom. Thus that which is unfree is part of the sinful, and the realization of the nature of that which is unfree places the world as well as the individual person in a state of sin or guilt, which are two words for the same thing.

The entire world is a world that is guilty before grace. Guilt and oppression counter salvation and freedom, though guilt cannot be reversed by any redemptive act, for guilt contradicts it. If one doesn't wish to believe this, he has only blinded himself and isolates himself within his guilt, even if he tries to remain free of personal sin. The burden of his own lack of freedom is already the punishment, which is also felt in the blindness and deafness brought on by his audacity. Thus collective guilt is the same as one's own guilt, even if one refuses to accept it, or if one doesn't want to acknowledge it and foolishly chooses to ignore his part in the guilt of the society in which he lives. But it is also guilt when one believes that he is graced and has nothing to do with collective guilt. For even if one can indeed believe that collective guilt cannot be shared, one still cannot separate oneself from the world, or lower the amount of guilt, but instead only point to it, while perhaps gaining a small reward through this action alone, though there is nonetheless no redemption and no forgiveness of the sins against the slaughtered Lamb of God. On the contrary, all beings must accept collective guilt, as well as their own guilt, and do what is possible so that guilt is dissipated and new guilt is avoided, whereby freedom will stand in opposition to human guilt, so that the grace of the undivided community can occur as a collective grace. In the preparation for such an occurrence in the world, Josef sees the possible start of a way to an undivided salvation.

It's good that Josef sleeps, it's good that he's alone, for now he wants to talk to someone else, but he should keep quiet, he should wait and know that his clever words are only the helpless attempts of one who has been abandoned and wishes to overcome his loneliness, as he doesn't always want to remain an onlooker, though he should indeed realize that he will always be only a viewer. He sits before the glass panes of the panorama, he being allowed to decide as he gazes deeply into the viewing booth whether what he sees will be just a view of the streets and houses of Launceston below or of the walls across the way where George Fox sat imprisoned, or a view of the entire ruins, or of the solitary visitors who come and go, or a view across the countryside that is bathed in soft light, or of the Church of the Penitent, the gates of the town, The Red Bull, or of the corrugated huts that have been abandoned since the prisoners of war and their bundles were sent back to Germany, or perhaps a view of nothing immediately here, but a view inward to see if it appears to be turning outward, views of the countries that Josef once saw, a view of his own family and of Bubi and also of Wenzel sitting in the garden, the view from the meadow above Umlowitz down onto Praxel's hut, or of Herr Neumann's property, or of the home of the dental technician Bilina, or of Thomasberg, or a view of the classrooms of The Box, or of the courtyard where The Bull screams and Inspector Faber stands in charge, or through the peepholes in the toilets, in the auditorium, where "Now for the Last Time" will be sung, or up at Professor Felger's garden, where the broken pump lies, or of the train station in Adamsfreiheit, in the catacombs of the cloister, or up at Landstein Castle, or of the ranger's house in torchlight, through the woods and on the ground, where cool berries and moist mushrooms grow, or the view of the night streets of the city, the rushing people and the police, or in the tower room of Johannes, or of the eternal light and the gong, or a view of the Frau Director's villa, or of Lutz's butterfly book, or out into the garden, or the view into the ticket booth and old Frau Lawetzer, into the main office and Professor Rumpler with his bust of Goethe, or the view of the railroad site, of the wooden barracks, of Sláma's work site, then of the tower on Pfefferberg, and across at the poplars and into the lush density of the woods, and many views of the camp of the lost ones, of the electrified wire, of the yard where the lost ones collapse in exhaustion, or the view of horrible red smoke as Mordechai speaks of the blessing of the prayer shawl, or the view of the singing rails and the underground halls everywhere where the Conqueror continues to forge his weapons.

All of them are temporal views, all of them limited, none of it enough for Josef anymore, for he's had enough of them and doesn't know where he should look, though he still sees them all, it not mattering if he closes his eyes, for he sees, and he can leave them open and he still sees, he hears the little bell, the view changes, it all repeats again, the order in which they do having been lost, no one watching any longer to make sure that the show runs smoothly, the views all mixing together, no, they are not views, for Josef is at peace, he controls the order and selection of views neither through his will nor through his fantasy, as they breed their own confusion, a continual interchange, everything mixing with everything else and shaken together in kaleidoscopic fashion. Josef is happy to be lying down, for if he were standing he would not be able to keep his feet still, as everything is dissolving together, he no longer knows which way is which, the times also spliced together, though it all gives rise to a feeling of happiness, the experiences of the past years appear to be compressed, Josef now able to preserve what he once experienced. Now he can look on and realize the tables have turned, he is the embodiment of all that has happened to him.

Most likely a person exists only by virtue of the world that is mirrored within him. Josef is an object of the world, so any hope of engaging with it is an idle thought. Yet this engagement happens nonetheless, for it is a chain of unconscious phenomena that are nonetheless expressed in people's actions. This does not amount to simple acceptance, or inaction, but is instead a chosen acquiescence so that the world can be, and no one resist that. Instead, one should simply fulfill it and be prepared to respond to any impetus in a vigorous manner. For it is also not an involuntary process, nor is it a soulless mechanism, nor fatalism, though indeed it does involve the destruction of the illusion of an independent and arbitrary agency. It involves immersion in the general run of things that appears to be brought about by the actions of all people in the world. The idea of a world soul that contains the individual soul makes sense. Thus conquering empty isolation is possible, the challenges faced by the individual demanding that he discover the link between all events and grace, and through that manifest his own approach to life. Through this Josef's childhood dreams should have been fulfilled, for he had always thought that all individuals shared some path together on which salvation could be found in their lives, but it had always been apparent how much selfish and rampant resistance stood against it, the existence of the common questioned by the individual or even denied, which then leads to the destruction of all order. As a result, those who have a vision and those who do not both suffer, nor is the recognition of a common path shared enough by individuals, since that does not cohere with the ways of the world. Also, when individuals wish to unite and become the many, it does not happen as long as the formulation of such a common path does not lead to a recognizable commonality. Such a formulation is hardly ever sought, so it can't help but fail. And thus those with no vision become the masters of the world, the conquerors arising from within their ranks as well as—often just as dangerous—the nattering fools who preach penance and meditation. Those without a vision lend the Conqueror and the fools an ear and a following, and soon evil grows, again and again resulting in destruction. So Josef thought, though now these thoughts dissolve inside him.

If one finds his Launceston amid his sleep, then he is free not to act, but instead to rest, to germinate, to multiply himself, he containing a world of seeds of consciousness that quietly and yet excitedly interact with one another, this being no wild, tattered delirium of fears and dangers in which force rules most any day. Josef reckons that he will no longer be threatened by this shadow, and he hopes for an end to the frightful and the abysmal, but already he has realized how idle it is to formulate his own future. He wants to get up and once again have a look at the withered wreath and the Quaker's prison, after which he would like to visit a bookstore in order to learn more about George Fox. No, he won't do that, for there is nothing to learn here, and Josef feels it is forbidden him, and he needs to conquer the past for good, to bury it, nor should there be any monuments set up to it, no memorials, instead a garden, a lawn, no painted plaques, but instead allow the site of suffering to sink into soothing, blessed forgetfulness, leaving only something felt in the heart, but no thoughts of any places through which one can just naïvely stroll. That is not an irreverent wish, it is the desire for life, as only then will forgetfulness be freed of the burdens that the afterworld presses upon it without indeed trying to maintain any kind of genuine reverence, for though everything meets its end, forgetfulness is new as it emerges, the voices of its unconscious experience remaining loud, as a new show begins, the public needing images to look at to set it at ease.

Josef takes stock, sensing a comfortable certainty, but he also worries, for he knows that the moment he gets up frightening faces will reveal themselves, faces full of tense expectation, empty faces, perhaps, that don't want to reveal anything, but Josef looks into them more deeply and sees through their fleetingness, their endlessly anxious apprehension. Then he sees that nothing has changed, the former prisoners of war are not satisfied, their victors are not satisfied, Josef is not allowed to speak to either, he having to tread carefully between each, it being the least of his worries that they should only laugh at him, but instead they will threaten him and be hostile should he tell of his memories and thoughts, and thus he will remain silent. But if he can no longer remain silent, what will become of him?

Josef looks at the sea before him, the fog beginning to rise over the coastline, the wind still, the fog climbing ever closer, encasing everything in white, Launceston already blanketed, all sounds muffled as well, every noise silenced, everything recognizable now hidden, no way to distinguish what's far and near. The fog is comforting and pleasant to the observer who can fathom what stands before his eyes. Josef sees the sea, a quiet sea, a still and softly swaying sea in which pain and pleasure are brothers, where forgetting is united with remembrance, a sea that celebrates remote memories. Josef floats upon the sea, wanting to be borne and cradled by it, the fallen castle tower of Launceston the last island in the endless sea, only a single sound rising within the sea, a swaying gong that sounds continuously, its constant call more lonesome than any silence, Josef himself the gong that sounds in the distant sea, the fish swimming about Josef in surprise at his submersion, he perhaps having sunk into the pool of the world, perhaps everything is finished and gone. Any attempts to find him will fail should anyone seek to, for vainly his name and number are called out at sea, because he floats, and no one is ready to climb the tower, people are too tired to do so, they tarry in the depths, water sprites, fish people, and fountain mermaids slowly crawling along the ocean floor, all of them magical and therefore unable to sense that they live in water and are sunk below, and since they can breathe without gills they are at home in this element, shedding their fate as easily as their clothes in order to feel at home, bringing with them what they need for the everyday—dented tin tools, mallets and funnels, round-bellied pipes with ties and scissors and coffee cups from the windowsill, beaten-up washbowls and cracked plates, diaries and books of poetry. The fish easily ready themselves for a *bal paré* in the castle pool, not noticing the electrified fence, the current circulating throughout, through the macrocosm and the microcosm, the fish looking through microscopes and telescopes, though they don't see that the Conqueror is already standing in the fish trap and hurrying all the fish to the transports, the next train now leaving for Pitchipoi, though the fish don't realize it and count their yearly earnings as they flounder in the cinema sea at the gala lecture about the great minds and get their VIP seats without a ticket, the Red Cross gratis to the red fish, lost bathers scraping off the scales of the fish, blood trickling out from under the fins, then it's off to the baths, breathing not allowed here, though the fish don't know that they will be killed, as they turn into people again, reining in their sorrows, earning their money, tidying their rooms, preparing their meals and their tidbits, Josef thinking about people and for once feeling indebted to them, he owing them everything, for it is they who make the world turn that he is able to observe, and that is without end.

Thus Josef is conscious that nothing has ended for him, no decisive change has come about, nor is there even a pause. It's a passage, because even during the quiet and abidance he is carried forward unawares, he at times seeing what he confronts, then as he dives in he finds that any of the questions he faces again return him to an ongoing confusion, as he is still somewhat asleep, a dreamy expression in his eyes, but quickly the first wind of the day blows it away, Josef able to talk reasonably, his demeanor no different from that of others, his nature taking hold of him and admonishing him that he is acting cocky, he's not so special, only little more than nothing has anything to do with you, even though most individuals are inclined to overestimate their own importance, though rightfully his surroundings rein in the scope of his influence. Each is granted his lot, which in turn makes demands upon him, the only exception allowed being his right to look after his little pastimes, should they be granted him, after which he again must fulfill his duty, while whoever smiles at this or even tries to ignore it is foolish and upsets the balance of the world. But is any of this satisfactory? Can one finally say that something has been attained? The panorama offers Josef no answer to this. Much can be demonstrated, but not everything. The wish dissolves when no longer repressed, but nonetheless it persists. At one time it's a thorn that is pressed into the world around us, at another time it bores into its own realm. Man is a creature who wishes, who desires matter, but who wants to transform matter into essence, but regardless of how hard man tries to do so he never succeeds. Matter is indeed pliable, but nonetheless it remains unconquerable, refusing to give up its hold until the sweet end. Matter is the victor over essence, which in turn likes to be immortalized as the unvanquished.

Josef's thoughts spin in circles, the ancient questions not letting go of him and never letting go of him, even if he wants them to. If only he could finally silence them! For what would it be like if things never changed, if they just continued on this way forever? When Josef was a child in the panorama he never thought about things in this way, he lived continually in the present, day-to-day life structured in such a way that he never had to worry about anything, just as he never had to worry about buying tickets for the panorama, he remaining free of any such worry as much at the conclusion of the show as at the start, the experience having swallowed up the boy, whisking him away and not yet declaring the need for him to account for himself. Instead he was regularly overwhelmed, and in no way attained any consciousness, even if he could begin to perceive the formulation of this consciousness within himself, something continuing to grow inside him which saturated his every fiber and was continual. Josef had only to go along with it all, nothing more or nothing less demanded of him or even possible, and everything was understood, the gift of an irrepressible vitality, Josef found it inexhaustible, he feeling the same even during the most extreme solitude, while even in the grip of seeming doom, his ability to contemplate what he observed spread beyond the searing pain of the sharpest despair, such fulfillment the result of all the reflections taken in of the various views and linkages arising on their own.

Not a pause, but a passage, a panoramic view that allows the eyes to take account, and now Josef is posed or positioned, he readies himself or is readied, he turns himself or is turned, he is answerable to himself and that, indeed, means answerable to fate as well, and when he stands his ground he is no longer tied to certain limited experiences but instead is separate from them, and as a result there arises some apparent progress in relation to how things have been, in reality an exit, whereby nothing more than the question "What now?" is faced by Josef. He has gone too far, he should say goodbye to all his journeying for good and head home . . . right, but home to where? This question is hard to answer, but it is also idle, since for Josef no return home is possible, that would also mean a step backward and the presumption of a home that doesn't exist for him, there being no way to feel at home, but instead something else, a kind of order that allows oneself to find oneself, even if it doesn't involve finding one's way back but instead involves indeed finding something, a location, and that is a state of being that presumes habit and habitation, and so it happens, and this stands for what other people call returning home, and is what Josef accepts. In order to get this, Josef needs only to wake up, get up, walk down the few steps below in the park, then out the gate and along the streets into the town, across the square to The Red Bull, then request the bill, ask after the next train to London, then on and on and away, no more tarrying, the return occurring quickly after a couple of days when the current situation is left behind for good.

Yet Josef thinks this is a lie, for he does not believe in the possibility of such a return, even though he knows that he can't abandon it, but a gulf remains between him and the images of the panorama, he no longer able to press his eyes so tight against the peepholes, since too often he has to peek over at his neighbor. He will indeed not attempt to look behind where the images are placed in their frames and then are sent along, but he grasps intuitively that this has already occurred, and that's why he has come to Launceston, but nonetheless the sober, dissembling gaze into what's behind the images is not allowed, as that would break the last law that keeps him attached to his surroundings. He considers a peek behind the images to be an incursion known as death, or no, it's not the onrush of death, it's suicide, and Josef has not survived until this day to do that. Josef instead will remain in front of the images, and force himself to, though indeed as a result he will also be behind the images, he only waiting for certain images that present themselves without his having wanted them to, though he promises as well to persist without wavering. He will not close his eyes in front of certain images or turn away from them, he only wants to ready himself for the arrival of certain images that he believes belong to him, knowing that he is attached to the panorama once again.

Josef decides to be grateful for this, for indeed he is generally disposed toward feeling capacious gratitude. He thinks of it as the only response available to humankind in light of our awareness of our own consciousness. Gratitude is likely a result of grace, and then one can say that gratitude is a transmutation of freedom that is granted to essence, a transmutation that shuns arrogance, for man's freedom is a limited good. As a result, Josef is able to come to terms with himself, since through this he can think of his freedom as limited by the lack of freedom common to man. Gratitude, at the same time, inverts the freedom of man, it puts sacrifice in the place of pleasure, and most likely the sacrifice is better than the pleasure, particularly since enjoyment is limited in life, as it encounters antagonism and resistance, and ends up admonished for its selfishness, which in turn causes even grace to turn away. Though there is something found in gratitude that never has to wait for grace to be granted, as gratitude is indeed a human answer to grace, but this answer must not look to be expressed in a specific manner, it needs no special blessings or prayers, it being much better that it is felt silently and practiced continually, nor need it worry about the condition of the world as a whole, nor is it tied to the situation from which it arises. For gratitude is pervasive and is not solely attached to the two principles of creation, nor to that which stands outside of creation, there being no border or measure set upon it, as it also cannot be diminished by anything. There is nothing like it, and—for whoever grasps it—it has no opposite, for it is always free and at the same time an entity unto itself. Thus it is the only thing that man can keep hold of in all circumstances, if he wants to do more than only accept things as they are and persist in readying himself for the worst, because gratitude is an activity by which man doesn't lose anything, by which he doesn't err and isn't confused, from which he must not allow himself to be distracted, and which does not impede any other activity. It can accompany everything, exist beside everything, nothing able to influence it, nor does it exhaust human beings like other states or activities of the mind. At the same time, it grants a certain measure of certainty and constancy, and although it is best employed for the sake of everything and for nothing at once—this being neither a play on words nor an audacious comparison—nevertheless it bestows a happiness that is never selfish or fleeting, since it remains free of all vanity.

Thus Josef's sleep is realized, since he has arrived at this certainty, he is now genuinely at ease and finds in this awareness a solution or a mediation between governing conditions and the unattainable goal. Josef knows that everything is the way it has always been, but in the figure of gratitude he can be free. This is not a random event, nor does it mean that anything has changed or changed for certain, for neither Josef nor the world has changed, as everything has remained exactly as it always was, though the loss felt in the heart appears to be assuaged. Nor does it only appear so, it's for certain. Something exists which no longer has to look back at the things of the world, although this backward look remains from here on out, for it has in fact not changed, though there has been a liberation from despair, from hopelessness, arrived at through resignation, in future the heart not needing to be caught up in warnings and fears, action and acceptance taking control of bitterness and confusion. Then what dawns on Josef is that within all anxieties that have been overcome there is much grace that can befall one, because simply to *be* is grace in itself, and he indeed has *been* as often as he has been, he has felt things and lived, and there can be no difference between the value placed on that by him and by another. Good, Josef has lived it all, he is present within himself, he has always stood in the present, and wherever he stood he could only accept it. Therefore he experienced grace, because it was without merit, if not indeed contrary to all merit, and so it is also easy to be thankful. That's why gratitude is no merit, far from it, but it is also not a duty, unless one chooses to put oneself under the obligation of feeling it.

Gratitude is without compare, but the question of man demands more, it is not the case that now certain kinds of experience will be overcome, nothing in the world having changed in the past hour, such an assumption appearing foolish to Josef, for it would only cloud the view, and therefore Josef is no different. Instead he will simply try to continue to do what he has done thus far, and indeed it is an attempt that he will continue to make. Nonetheless it remains true that he is as dependent on and subject to conditions as he formerly was, whether soon consciously or unconsciously, or soon willing or unwilling. Then Josef decides that after this sleep there will be no escaping this panorama, and as he considers this the fog slowly begins to lift and the view is restored once more, it by now familiar to Josef, an image that will last a good while, such that it cannot depart from him, as it abides and betokens so much. Josef indeed considers whether he has had enough of this view, but then he realizes that it's not up to him to decide, and so he waits and knows that his weariness will decide for him, he having remembered too much, his emotions not being able to recede so easily, slowly they will have to settle down, in the stillness they will have to die away. He cannot continue to agonize and wear himself out if he is to remain patient as the abandoned figures visit and ask, have you done enough for us? He has to answer, you brothers of love and hate, it's not enough, for I have considered you too lightly and profited from you, and therefore I stand too much in your debt to repudiate you. Josef now sees that the abandoned figures, as good or as bad as they were, have bestowed only good upon him through guilt and innocence. Thus he owes them his gratitude, in order that they remain real and not just empty words.

Josef no longer tries to repudiate the dualism at the heart of creation, but there really is no contradiction between dualism and freedom, because no dissociation can continue to exist in the face of freedom. If Josef wants to feel grateful, no dualism can stand in the face of gratitude, for it knows no real contradiction, even if the language has use for the word "ingratitude," which certainly makes sense and is true, but Josef feels nevertheless that gratitude and ingratitude cannot be set against each other as opposites, no matter how much logic may think they should be. The logical approach doesn't reveal that there's a spiritual contradiction between them, such that the spirit does not take its nature from matter, as the spirit is no less and no more a part of reality than is matter, they simply postulate each other through their mere existence. What isn't a part of the opposition is incomprehensible, and therefore also cannot be logical. If it's nonetheless put into words, then it appears above all to contradict itself, which is acceptable, though that doesn't bother Josef anymore. As soon as he recognizes the limits of philosophy that make such questions unanswerable, then he no longer wishes to philosophize about that which is insoluble. Josef finds that philosophy is often refuted by life, which is full of contradictions and cannot be separated from them by any approach, though it doesn't entirely rest in these contradictions, even if it cannot be freed from them.

Now that Josef has finally slept, there is nothing more for him to draw on for encouragement. He feels safe. He wakes up and looks around him with eyes wide open. Now he waits patiently, awakening takes time, a temporal activity, since it is steeped in memories. Consciousness tries to sense itself, checking to see if it is indeed there. It poses small and general questions in order to reassure itself, and in doing so turns to the past. Every awakening is a trip to a past that must be reviewed if it is to be completed.

436 / H. G. ADLER

Only then is a person awake, after which he attempts his first steps in the new day and turns this way and that, it being good if he goes about familiar activities in order to find his place more easily, all the while new impressions readying him and sending him on his way. Then memory dissolves, though it saturates the subsurface of the new day, which without refamiliarizing itself with this realm would be plunged into chaotic ruins. Now, at last, everything is in order, and many experiences begin to build up, everything renewed as it returns once again, though not at the person's insistence as he goes on his way, even though he is free and can believe that it is his own way. Then the person sees many potential outcomes as he moves on and is called onward, but he really doesn't feel like it, since the questions have gone silent in him, having been withdrawn the moment that he thinks he can answer them. Yet won't he still be pursued, won't worry continue to haunt him?

Josef doesn't dare decide, yet it seems to him that it has been decided anyway, since he has nothing more to say about it. He has remained calm and wants to fit in, for the inevitable will occur anyway. It's a cause for concern, Josef grants, but it also leads one on, as it's a doubtless certainty, a stream amid constancy that carries on, and in which also worry, also questions, and the insoluble are givens. Man is nothing if he has nothing to protect him, for even that Josef who was robbed by his brothers of his multicolored coat and thrown into a pit had to put on something before he was sold to Potiphar. Neither spiritual nor physical poverty releases human beings from the need to clothe themselves, and thus it was the nadir of inhumanity, a sign of the most shameless murder, that the most loyal of the conspirators stripped the lost ones of their garments and then shot them or slaughtered them, while other conspirators granted their victims a bit of time, though not out of kindness, as after their bath in the sauna they were handed rags, this being, without the conspirators knowing, a sign that man as a result of his having gained knowledge in Paradise had to wear clothes. Man may be humble and humbled, lost or forgotten, but he cannot be unclad, the heart also needing to be covered, about that he can do nothing, whether he is awake or asleep.

However man tests himself or is tested, he can always only give thanks, for thanks can accompany anything, gratitude being that which clothes shame and at the same time a kind of naked fervency, gratitude the victim who does not have to be afraid of anything or ever betray himself. Grief exists, but gratitude does as well. This arrangement goes on forever, and so does stopping and resting, there being no calamitous collapse that results, but instead a quiet joy arises, which grows and flows throughout. Is terror then banished? Are the horrible events over? Do my lambs graze in innocence? Does no one lift a sword against another? And is the sword melted down into a plowshare? Is there something that can at last console? Oh, if terror would not turn into new terror and would do away with grief! Josef wants nothing to do with empty equivocation leading to lame optimism or self-deception, wishing to avoid any kind of blindness. He follows because he is challenged to, he doesn't withdraw, he is called, but not into the green sweet-tasting grassland of the fools who are not lambs at all. He is called to a decision that manifests itself every day, which is why he cannot stand aloof. The viewer is also the participant, there being nothing arbitrary, everything is tightly intertwined, thus forming Josef's garments. Neither to extricate oneself nor to unite oneself is the first task, but rather to make something of it, no matter what it takes out of you. Sometimes it seems easier to judge the run of affairs than to take part in them, but nothing happens if one does, and sometimes that means entering the fray. It may be tempting to flee to one's tower, but to do so is to sleep as the world goes by, and we sleep enough as it is, and thus we are compelled to be awake and to function, the piety of the solitary person shattered by the functioning of the world.

Josef gets up. Once more he takes in the view, observing it closely in order to retain it forever, he not wishing to forget anything and to hold on to the legacy of Launceston Castle, he wanting to remember it all forever, what he thought here and dreamed, though he also feels that now it is finally enough. He cannot stay any longer, everything is closed, while what he will keep is what has been these rich hours, invaluable moments of contemplation never granted him before, he never having felt so fulfilled and perhaps also so empty of desire, though it's not something that can continue or be surpassed. Josef wants to stay a bit longer, he wants to consider what happened to him here, he wants to pass it on to himself, to lock it within, so that it exists within him, as long as he exists. He recalls the whining pleas of a child who always wants to do something fun again, again, again, and again, and then one last time, but Josef is not waiting for that moment, he wants only to extend one moment before the onset of another, always just a little more, just a little, then a little less, the taste of the end already a sweet and slightly bitter honey on the tongue, and then the finale, a last blow marking the end, an end, and the gong, and the Lord is in that blink of an eye a single Lord, and only for the blink of an eye, the little blink into the end before the final blink of an eye, for absolutely the last time, arriving at the end that has not yet occurred, the honey growing heavier, the bees already circling, an extension of the blink of an eye into the timelessness of the deepest perception, everything taken in with the highest intensity. Remain human, don't keel over, don't fall, quiet yourself within, so everything coalesces inside you, all that you possess and all that you do not possess, and now observe how the blink of an eye at the end opens and closes you.

Josef gets hold of himself, gathers in details and perceives a wholeness, as if he cannot believe that it's there, yet he ascertains that he indeed apprehends something, it proving true, and Launceston lies as it always has at the foot of the hill, its streets winding about, the hill rising gently at first, then more sharply upward, the outer walls that once circled the castle capable only of being surmised but not actually seen. Josef finds it important that he's not standing on a peak, that he's not even at the highest elevation, the crumbling tower preventing any feeling of rising above the landscape, nor does it even allow one to look off in any direction, while behind Josef are walls, so if he wants to take in the entire view he must slowly walk around and circle the castle, after which he wants to go round again, though he walks round only once while contemplating. Then Josef remains standing at the spot where he rested for so long, he wishing to demonstrate his gratitude, though he doesn't know how to do that, he quickly dismissing a sacrilegious idea of making a wreath out of some wild flowers and grass, for he feels it shouldn't be any visible memorial, and such a feeble link to the memorial for the steadfast Quaker is forbidden, the latter having much nicer flowers than what Josef could pick from the little flowers growing in the grass, his hand brushing the lawn lightly, its blades bending slightly beneath his strokes, each leaf, each stalk bowing as if in reconciliation, the commemoration silent within. Thus Josef's memory remains the only memorial, but this memory will leave with him, and the gratitude felt toward this place is contained within it. Because he thinks it all and ponders it all again, he's filled with a thousand voices and wondrous feathers and glittery dust, tenderness displacing departure, abidance continuing on.

Now it's enough, Josef cannot linger any longer, he must carry out his decision, the border has been reached. He turns around and once more walks the length of the tower wall to the other side, where the steps lead down. He'd like to head off on the path to the castle dungeon once more, and he wavers, but then decides not to and gazes off toward the prison, it still being there, large leafy plants unfurling under the protection of the cool walls, no one allowed to disturb these weeds, no wind threatens their growth as they grow over the long-cosseted horrific story of this place, just as the cheery stories of other sites are also overgrown and mercifully enshrouded, the plants not sharing how they thrive on the works and deeds of humankind as long as they are not planted or tended.

Josef turns away and hurries along at a quick pace to the park exit, ignoring the plaques that proclaim the history of Launceston. Josef doesn't look for a crowning moment to his experience here but is instead simply pleased by his waking steps, he being happy about everything that has awakened within him, and the fact that he is awake and so awake, though it's not a heightened sense of satisfaction, nor does he feel any triumph because his sorrow has poured forth, for it is still tucked into every hollow and cleft and it looms above in every gable and treetop. Josef is enmeshed in the general run of things, he sees the people around him who are going about their business, some cars driving by, or he hears the long drawn-out whistle of a locomotive from the train yard, the abandoned barracks of the prisoners of war that are quickly falling victim to the elements. And everything that he sees and hears is open to the day, and indeed is simply there, spewed forth by open mouths and cavities, a single effusion into the day, into his salvation. And so Josef does not withdraw, for everything is present and not tied to the history that Josef has been pleased to say goodbye to, but he no longer knows that it is goodbye, for he is aware of no break between yesterday and today, all the colored threads having run together, an immense gushing, an overflow and a rippling stream in which the view that bursts forth from life, being a genuine blink of an eye, discerns nothing. And so Josef is not a lost one nor is he one who has been forgotten, he no longer hangs caught in a web of fleeting dreams that separate him from the everyday world, because nothing is true anymore, each view continuing on to its no longer contested aims.

Josef no longer knows what he is saying goodbye to once the tower is behind him, he not having been disburdened through any kind of simplification but instead he is no longer trapped in such questions, they requiring nothing more of him, though he doesn't doubt that each forward step will raise challenges. It's idle to wonder what the next hours will bring, everything will come in its own time, Josef ready for it all, he feels it deep inside, though he is now in his own way without a past, it not forgotten but rather lost, he having to strain himself to see it through a veil. What he once thought a possession is now something alien and unrecognizable. Josef doesn't know whether what history has to say has anything to do with him, whether it be this or that, because the past is so transparent in its intrusion that it no longer relates to any so-called "I" or "you," nor is Josef sure any longer whether he is someone who has acted or is a witness or a victim, or whether he is all of these together in having been part of history or if he simply overheard a bunch of tales. The joy and sorrow back then were much the same thing, Josef almost ashamed and almost shocked that the distinction can seem so frivolous, but he is comfortable with the view that in the end it's all the same to whatever in history clings to a certain event, since everything that happens is the price paid for living in the present, if only the individual accepts it. Josef accepts it, otherwise he wouldn't be able to go on, for he can attest to his own existence as a person only to the degree that he is no longer reduced to the limits of his own personality, this being what he has learned on the hill in the castle park of Launceston, where to this day he has woken.

AFTERWORD

Peter Demetz

H. G. ADLER WAS ALWAYS RELUCTANT TO EASILY ATTACH HIMSELF TO ANY group, class, or nation, preferring instead to think of himself as a "single unique individual," in the radical spirit of the Enlightenment, who over time would slowly gain acceptance from a growing readership. Since the deaths of Paul Celan, Peter Szondi, and Jean Améry, all of whom took their own lives, there have not been many Jewish authors who write in German, above all in that generation of aging men and women who survived persecution and the death camps and maintained the capacity to bear witness to their experience in history's Hell. This, though not only this, defines Adler's particular situation. Amid the epoch of the Shoah, I see him as allied with with Primo Levi and Elie Wiesel, and yet at the same time as different. Levi, who was a partisan before his arrest, was able to continue writing in Italian without hesitation (Italy's Fascist society never set up an Auschwitz, and the notorius Riseria of Trieste was founded by the Nazi district leader), and Wiesel managed to complete his Wandering Jew–like journey from French into American English without ever being untrue to his first loyalty,

Yiddish, and the traditions of the shtetl. Adler was confronted with different alternatives. Like many of his background, at certain moments he may have doubted that German could still be used to write and speak, and yet he decided that what he wanted to say and write had to be done in German, which was also the language of the murderers, be it those at their writing desks or those at the barbed wire. As an exile in London, he belonged nowhere. "Jews should not feel at home anywhere," he observed in an interview, refusing (although he valued his Jewish heritage) to identify with the national interests of the state of Israel or to serve as a "parade Jew" or "alibi" for the cultural and political establishment of the new German Republic. His exile involved a serious act of conscience, even if for him it was not at all a pleasant way to live.

Following a useful fiction coined by Max Brod, literary history often speaks of the Prague Circle of German writers, but the life of Adler would argue that one has to combine the circle with many other geometric figures in order to better appreciate the tangle of Prague writers amid their cafés and on their walks, while Robert Musil once said ironically that the majority of Prague writers were those who brilliantly managed to write nothing at all. Adler's ancestors, for instance, were composed of religious teachers and businessmen. His father was a stationer and printer, and his mother, who was born in Berlin, wanted to become a doctor but, as we read in *Panorama*, was barred from doing so by tradition. Family life was unhappy and unpleasant, and the sensitive boy was sent to strange families and boarding schools beyond the borders of Bohemia, and placed in a school in Moravia before he was at last allowed to return home to his parents' house and complete the graduate exams as an external student. The young man next sought the comforts of camaraderie in a scouting troop organized by youths, which was somewhat belatedly modeled on those founded in Berlin, after which he took refuge in his literary work. At eighteen it was clear to him that he had not the slightest curiosity or capacity to join any mass political movement or mystical circle, which in the Prague of the 1920s had a late flowering. Since the last third of the nineteenth century, Jewish fathers in Prague had more or less been successful businessmen, while the sons, who were denied access to any kind of political career in Czech Prague, chose, in protest against their materialistic fathers, to become poets, intellectuals, and scholars. (The wise grandfather of Karl Kraus's magical operetta about Prague life admonishes his grandson in vain to align himself much more with businesslike *"Tachles"* than with literary *"Schmonzes,"* for instance.) Adler studied literature, philosophy, and musicology at university in Prague, writing his dissertation on *Klopstock und die Musik*, and finding himself in Berlin (while doing research in the national library) as the triumphant colonnades of the storm troopers moved through the streets.

In good times, a young person with his interests and inclinations would certainly have been placed on a path toward an academic career, but for a Prague Jew it was already too late for that. He wrote for himself alone and also worked as a scholar, as was done in the eighteenth century, by earning his living as a tutor while, in a slightly more modern manner, serving as the secretary of the Urania, the famous Prague adult-education center, where he became friends with Golo Mann and Elias Canetti when they lectured there. During this time he also worked for the Prague radio station that sought to counter the spread of Nazi propaganda with support for the republic through ideas on liberty disseminated in German. When Hitler's realm mobilized against the Czech Republic, Adler traveled to Milan in order to prepare to immigrate to Brazil (where most likely things would have gone the way they did for Stefan Zweig), but the "beloved mother of Prague" (as Kafka knew) had her "claws," both soft and sharp, and held fast to her writers no matter the peril they were in. Adler remained and worked in the book repository of the Jewish religious community in Prague before he and his wife, the Prague doctor Gertrud Klepetar, were deported to Theresienstadt in February of 1942, and in October 1944 to Auschwitz, where his wife and her parents were killed soon after their arrival. He was then transported for two weeks to Auschwitz-Birkenau, and then on to the Buchenwald-Niederorschel camp, where in underground chambers aircraft parts were assembled. The number of dead from exhaustion, hunger, and illness climbed daily. However, Adler never said much about his liberation from the camp. Having made the return sooner than Primo Levi, by the summer of 1945 he was home, where he taught Jewish orphans and worked on the reorganization of the Jewish Museum that had been set up by the Nazis. However, for German-speaking Jews who did not want to collaborate with the Communist Party there were no future prospects. Two weeks before the Communist coup, he managed to travel to London and, after his marriage with the Prague sculptor Bettina Gross, set up a life there in a gloomy apartment in a London suburb, whose window, if I remember correctly, looked out onto a giant gas meter. In London he began, as an unknown refugee, to write for publication—namely, his scholarly work, such as the monograph on Theresienstadt and *Administered Man*, his poems, which still revealed his Prague roots, and his prose works, which never entirely dissolved into the fictional. In 1948, he wrote the first draft of *Panorama* in less than two weeks, the third draft of which was published by Walter-Verlag in 1968, and is the version translated here.

Adler himself warned in many interviews against reading *Panorama* as an autobiography, recommending instead that we take the text as "a novel saturated with autobiography." Josef Kramer, the narrator, is not entirely the same as H. G. Adler, though he shares Adler's thoughts and experiences; nor have critics been tempted, whether rightly or wrongly, to emphasize the autobiographical aspects of the narrative and supply a real date and place for each chapter. Chronicles and autobiographical accounts have chapters, but Adler's novel does not, the brief opening chapter and the title indicating that on aesthetic and philosophical grounds the novel works like an old-fashioned panorama that presents individual scenes (taken from the everyday world) which follow one after another with nothing more than a brief click in between. The "daily world disappears and is gone" (both in the panorama and in each concentrated reading); each image "is presented on its own and is clearly separated from the next"; there is no whole, only "individual pieces without end." The narrator, or presenter, who thinks of the world as a panorama consisting of repeated depictions in various configurations, stresses that the images are "outside of time," as are all works of art that await new viewers or readers. One looks at them "hard and fixed and tense," from the outside and from a distance, and that person, as a viewer, cannot "enter them." This they share with images in one's memory; they "remain for a brief while, as a little bell rings, attention, a new image is on the way, or an old one, it's hard to tell, the overview is lost, nothing left but heightened momentary views." The images of the panorama and memory have their aesthetic distance, but at the same time they bear witness to the attitude of the narrator, which is reflective, if not radically introverted.

In moments of bitter torment, he observes himself, but he cannot engage with the world outside, while finally, after leaving behind his terrible experiences, he arrives at the essential notion that it is high time to turn the panorama around and, rather than take in images, to present himself to the world. From the book's conclusion then, in the idea of the world as a panorama lies "great danger," which eludes any attempt to write, communicate, or act; nor is it impossible that in the central and structural metaphor there exists more than a grain of self-irony or self-criticism.

The image of the panorama (which is sustained by the division of the narrative and the pauses that occur in between, and which serves in the end as both a philosophical and an ethical motif) cannot hide the degree to which the narration is fashioned from what is heard, spoken, and thought, all of which predominates in each scene, such that, theoretical arguments notwithstanding, these narratives function as images that are heard more than seen, while if there were such a thing as an acoustical panorama this would be it. Josef reports again and again what he says, observes, replies, and answers, and he is never too tired to also tell us just as often what others say, observe, reply, and answer. As readers of Adler, we are close to the realm of Gertrude Stein, who firmly believed that the world is made up of those who talk and those who listen. (She felt that the truly gifted are those who can do both at the same time.) Elaborate descriptions of the immediately tangible, which was once a cornerstone of the realistic novel, exist nowhere, and direct speech, in quotes or as if spoken from the stage, flows quickly and seamlessly into indirect speech, except perhaps in the chapter on the Cultural Center, which, nonetheless, with its cinematic Marx Brothers effect is distinct from the other sections in a striking and sudden fashion. But the text does not just consist of one speech after another, for scenes, adventures, and experiences are continually brought to life, as if Josef were telling us about them, or what others say about them, and how what they say, as if it were a part of his inner monologue, is articulated now in a continual present. Josef has no bodily presence that responds to the charms and challenges of the world, but instead the consciousness inherent to his thinking, which is virtually bursting with the fullness and consequences of successive thoughts. The entire text involves the unfolding of consciousness, which works in waves, each paragraph an extended wave that runs almost the length of a page, and within these waves of consciousness, which think, hear, and articulate words, there is a surging current of continual gliding and streaming that leans toward parataxis, the combining of simple sentences, and which prefers to use the comma to bind together rather than to separate. It is in its own way a stream-of-consciousness epic, but one that still wishes to maintain the programmatic and fundamental ability to speak in a clear and orderly manner in order not to overwhelm the reader with an avalanche of words.

The refined sensitivity toward spoken language, which Josef unfailingly preserves in his consciousness, transforms Adler's book into a Prague novel that once again, or perhaps for the last time, brings to the ear the local German that would have been spoken in the families of Kafka and Werfel. The city itself, in Josef's consciousness, possesses nothing of the lyrical magic of "violet ink" that struck the young René Rilke, nor of the glowing decadence of the bordello as set down by Paul Leppin. Josef speaks of the modernity of the teeming city center in the new metropolis, but also of the old and suffocating "stony sea of this godforsaken city." Like all children, Josef recalls the obligatory Sunday outings along the Moldau on a steamship headed for Königsaal (about which Werfel wrote one of his loveliest poems), and thus continually seeks to escape the stifling, cramped, and busy city. He takes long walks, not in the historic old city but instead, in the sparsely populated outlying towns, where the fields open up and the bricklayers work with the clay that reminds him of the golem. In old Prague, street talk is a mixture of Austrian German and Czech in idiomatic disarray. The heavy food, such as *Grieskasch* (gruel) or *Powidl, Schkubanken und Platzken* (plum jam, potato pancakes, and latkes) confirming the setting, while a pitiful man is a *Hascherl*, a little child is a *Mimi* (from the tender Czech word *Miminko*, or "baby"), scouts do not like using *Papiersackeln* (paper sacks), one goes to the *Bio* rather than the *Kino*, or cinema, and everywhere there is the Prague fondness for mixing *möge* (may) and *möchte* (would like), which used to make Karl Kraus see red, and which celebrates a return here, while common Bohemian concoctions serve to return an unspoken tremor to the diaphragm, such as *zum Pukken prasken*, meaning when something is so ridiculous that the cover of a jar (which in Czech is *poklice* or *puklice*) bursts (*praskati*, the Czech infinitive). Even the name of the mystical gong player Johannes

Tvrdil brings a local element into ironic play. Johannes is the prophet, but someone who is called Tvrdil (Czech for "to assert") implies someone who is pigheaded, didactic, and unwilling to consider counterarguments. His name is an ironic counterpart to the Pythagorian use of *autòs ephá*, "to cut off debate."

Adler's critics show at times a marked tendency, with some justification, to read *Panorama* as a coming-of-age novel, but also to treat the final chapter as a philosophical summation separate from the rest of the book, and therefore to underestimate the continuity of the thought process behind it. It's not true that the first nine sections are concerned with events and the tenth is concerned only with piercing thought, such that everything happens only within conscious reflection. Instead, it may not be so easy to separate one from the other. Josef's philosophical determinations are anticipated long before in the earlier scenes, while the motif of thought emerges, fades away, and returns in ever more emphatic guises. The young Wanderer, who camps with his friends in the woods surrounding Landstein Castle, for instance, is already full of the intellectual possibilities that the survivor turns into moral determinations in the shadow of Launceston Castle. Josef, the lonely youth, is attracted to the "pack" who want to start "another life" with one another, in pureness and above all "independence," while the eighteen-year-old, who desires a "spiritual life," takes part in a mass political demonstration only "out of curiosity," thus experiencing the "dense crowd" in which people were "rubbing up against one another," feeling disgusted by the streams of beer and dogmatic phrases at a people's day arranged by the Party. The same happens in the circle of the mystics. "The true person defines himself," while the group "forwards a herd mentality," he managing to almost effortlessly resist the shimmering magic of the deafening gamelan. The months spent in the forced-labor camp while working on the railroad are for Josef particularly educational. As head of his group, he holds true to the youthful ideals of the Wanderers and remains unsatisfied by both the Marxist explanation of the political process, which Eugene lectures about, and the tragic, apocalyptic ideology of Dr. Siegler, who has lost all hope and has convinced himself that one can have the courage to look on with open eyes only while plunging into the abyss. The doctor is not aware what tenets of Nietzsche he is preaching, and Josef is right to reply that, without a moral purpose and a reason beyond itself, the world would make no sense at all.

While speaking with the apocalyptic doctor, Josef already touches upon those ideas that lead him to radically separate what is from what happens. He admits to feeling a conflicted "readiness to accept" the present. As a follower of Parmenides, not Heraclitus, inside the forced-labor camp, he separates true Being from that which is fleeting, if not fictional Time, which "controverts reality" and remains "always" in counterpoint to Being, "which is hardly or only partially bound to Time." Notions of Time exist only inside human beings and can be found in our own projections, not in things themselves. Therefore it is foolish to want to live in the past, for "in the outer world it is not manifest," the same holding true in awaiting some future threat, which Josef calls "unacceptable," indeed "impure" and "unclean." All of this sounds like an inhuman ontology, and yet this thinking constitutes for Josef, the survivor, the basis for a newly workable, secular, and tentative morality that does not hark back to memories; nor will allow itself to be frozen by fear of the future. "Nothing is more destructive than fear, for, senselessly, it leads to the death of meaning and is itself meaningless, fear able to enslave and murder before a death sentence is even lowered upon a man." A readiness to accept—in Auschwitz and Buchenwald? Yes, even there, amid the stoic congruence of his powers of resistance, Josef distinguishes between mere passivity and fatalism, both of which appear "almost comical" to him, as they are only a "rebellion on the part of the uncertain."

Josef himself knows that such thinking, which would provoke and anger his contemporaries, approaches "the limits of what is permissible." But after being saved, he wants to finally breathe, to compose and test his thoughts, and not to make dogmatic proclamations. It is not possible to separate his idea of the "readiness to accept" from the enclosed horizon of his convictions, all of which are directed at sensibly defining man's purpose in the world. And when Josef is inclined to tap concepts that belong more to the sphere of traditional religion, it's important to understand how he does so. He is a late descendant of Nathan the Wise, who admired the nobility of all historical religions and yet eventually moved beyond them. The controversial "readiness to accept" binds Josef's thinking closely with the concept of grace, which is resolved to "flow forth into life" from the beyond. Man can do nothing more than conjecture that it functions as the principle of "perfection" amid the human realm, and yet for the appearance of this grace, which he has experienced so often in his own life, he can only be grateful. He is obligated, at least in the modest means allowed him, to realize the perfection that he has been shown. Indeed, this insight is what leads to the "reversal" of the panorama, because from now on Josef will present himself to the world and act on behalf of his fellow men. Meanwhile, in a very late philosophical study published in 1987, Adler articulated many of Josef's thoughts as his own in developing an "experimental theology" that respectfully sought to move beyond traditional religion.

A book that presents itself as a novel, however, does not stand or fall on the consequences of a philosophy, and the critical conversation that began to blossom in the 1960s, and which, unfortunately, later began to abate somewhat, arrived at its best moments in the question of *how* Adler writes, and by what ways and means he forwards or moves beyond the epic tradition. The tendency of some critics to stamp Adler as a latter-day Austrian writer in the imperial mode of those writing before World War I, or as a Jewish Kakanier, and thus see him as a Prague colleague of Heimito von Doderer or Robert Musil, is more convincing as nostalgia than as literary insight. Prague writers (when they didn't come from Moravia, like Ernst Weiss) were drawn more to Berlin than to Vienna, for a variety of historical reasons, and the so-called "total novel"—i.e., the big, thick book that presents an entire epoch—can be found as much in the Viennese work of Doderer as in the writings of the Berliner Döblin. Rather, I find the beginning of a productive literary debate over *Panorama* already in the original reviews written by Martin Gregor-Dellin and Walter Jens, who radically disagreed with each other. Gregor-Dellin complained about the glut of realistic details, which the author surprises us with, calling it a "classic misunderstanding of the epic," while Jens praised precisely the presentness of all the particulars that characterize Josef's life, and asserted that the way they link us to the memory of our own experience is a sign of epic mastery. Yet both miss the chance to see that the abundance and density of details is not presented in an impersonal manner, as in a nineteenth-century novel, but rather appear and live entirely within Josef's unremitting consciousness.

The consequence of this is that Adler spares us, and himself, the need to externalize the world and reinvent it once again (as if that could be done with an Auschwitz), and instead lifts the sensual and visible, which is the first characteristic that we believe we recognize in all realistic novels, into the rapid unfolding of consciousness itself, which continually presses toward rhythmic, pulsing annotation. What we read, then, is a thought score on the brink of music.

ABOUT THE TRANSLATOR

PETER FILKINS is a poet and a translator. He is the recipient of a 2007 Translation Award from the Austrian Ministry for Education, Art, and Culture, a 2005 Berlin Prize from the American Academy in Berlin, and a past recipient of an Outstanding Translation Award from the American Literary Translators Association. He teaches literature and writing at Bard College at Simon's Rock. His translation of Adler's novel *The Journey* was published by Random House in 2008.